WOMEN DETERMINED ... DOM AND THEIR DREAMS ... MEN READY TO FIGHT AND DIE FOR THOSE THEY LOVE

SALLY—Street smart, passionate, indomitable, she's given a second chance at life by an act of selfless courage, but she'll have to fight a society that calls her trash ... and a man who calls her temptation.

CHARLOTTE—Delicate, pretty, pampered, her longing for pleasure makes her a victim of a vicious crime and leaves her a bitter, vindictive wife married to a man another woman loves.

BEN—Tough, idealistic, massively built, he has a vision of a new and better world, but his determination to "do the right thing" leads to a wrong he'll spend the rest of his life paying for.

TOBY—An independent, plucky blond urchin, at six he is ready to fight to save his beloved Sally and steal to survive. But only a tragic future awaits such a child in the violent London slums.

HANNAH—Plain in looks but a fiery amazon in spirit, she faces clubs and fists as she fights for women's freedom, but her privileged life has not prepared her for the terror of a prison door swinging shut.

A DREAM
OF SPRING

Teresa Crane

A Dell Book

Published by
Dell Publishing
a division of
Bantam Doubleday Dell Publishing Group, Inc.
666 Fifth Avenue
New York, New York 10103

The trademark Dell® is registered in the U.S. Patent and Trademark Office.

ISBN: 0-440-21099-2

Reprinted by arrangement with William Collins Sons & Co., Ltd., London, England

Printed in the United States of America

Published simultaneously in Canada

October 1991

10 9 8 7 6 5 4 3 2 1

RAD

FOR MY MOTHER,
WITH MUCH LOVE

And did those feet in ancient time
Walk upon England's mountains green?
And was the Holy Lamb of God
On England's pleasant pastures seen?
And did the countenance divine
Shine forth upon our clouded hills?
And was Jerusalem builded here
Among those dark Satanic mills?

Bring me my bow of burning gold:
Bring me my arrows of desire:
Bring me my spear: o clouds unfold!
Bring me my chariot of fire.
I will not cease from mental fight,
Nor shall my sword sleep in my hand
Till we have built Jerusalem
In England's green and pleasant land.

PART ONE

1906

Chapter One

I

The young man with the insolent eyes had come to the soup kitchen almost every day for the past fortnight. At least so it seemed to Charlotte Bedford, for he had certainly and most noticeably been there each day that she had taken her turn behind the long, oil-cloth-covered table where she stood now ladling the watery concoction into battered tin bowls and passing them into eager, dirty hands that, despite herself, she tried to avoid touching. He was a too handsome young fellow who looked not in the least in need of a penn'orth of charity soup; he lounged, long legged, by the door, raffishly and ridiculously self-assured, openly watching her, as he always did, his cap pushed to the back of his blue-black head, his flamboyantly knotted canary yellow neckerchief a brilliant splash of colour in the crushingly drab surroundings. Absurdly aware of his eyes upon her – and somehow certain that he knew it – she resolutely kept her own eyes upon the tricky business in hand, ladling the soup more carefully than usual, though she could not for her life prevent the mortifying rise of colour in her cheeks beneath his amused and too knowing gaze. Disconcerted and angry with herself at her own discomfiture she bestowed an especially brilliant smile upon the old man who had just, with surly ill humour, slammed his penny on to the table and stood waiting for his soup. 'Good morning, Mr Bennett – how are you today?'

The dirty, lined, unshaven face did not alter. Pale and clouded eyes lifted to hers for a moment, totally expressionless. Then the old man, either in reply to the question or to the smile, hawked loudly and unpleasantly in his throat and after a bare moment's hesitation turned his head, preparing to spit on the floor.

She watched him helplessly and with a lift of anger that did nothing but tie her tongue and root her to the floor. Then, as he took breath, a small, bright-headed whirlwind swooped past Charlotte and planted herself before him, small arm extended, steady finger pointing at the door. 'Out!' Cissy Barnes snapped with high-tempered economy.

He hesitated.

'*Out!*'

Mouth clamped shut, pale eyes murderous, the man turned and shambled to the door. Cissy, hands planted on her hips, the fire in her face matching the carrot brightness of her hair, glared after him in undaunted and righteous anger. 'And you'll go to the end of the line and queue again!' she called after him.

Charlotte stood, the bowl of cooling soup in her hand and watched him go. Hearing his noisy expectoration beyond the door her stomach quivered a little, delicately nauseous. She could not handle these people, and they knew it. Even little Cissy, five foot nothing and built like a sparrow, could take command of a situation in a way that she, Charlotte, could not. Did not indeed want to. Why should she? The old intense and useless rebellion stirred, lifting in her mind and in her heart like a tide of tears. What was she doing here? Why did she not tell them, all of them, how much she hated it? For no matter how she tried, hate it she did. She knew very well that Doctor Will was absolutely right when he explained in his gentle, meticulous way that most of these people were not poor nor ignorant through their own fault but through the faults of a system that allowed the squalor of the East

End slums and the disease and exploitation they bred, that positively encouraged the cutting of wages to protect profits, that sent small children into sweatshops and their older brothers and sisters as like as not into crime and prostitution. She knew it. But she could not bring herself to care – not at any rate in the way that Doctor Will cared, and Ben, and Hannah, and even her own brother Ralph. The squalor appalled her, the seething, rapacious life of the East End streets frightened and repelled her. She could not find in these dirty, sometimes sullen, often ill-mannered people a cause for which to burn. She was young – barely eighteen, and two years now an orphan. She was pretty, indeed there were times when she knew that given the chance, given silks and satins, feathers and lace, given perfumed water to wash her fluffy, curling hair and perfumed lotions to soothe the small, well-shaped hands that lately were so often rough and sore, given even the minimum comforts and aids that a girl of her age and station might reasonably expect to enjoy, she could be beautiful. She did not belong here; no one in their right minds could believe that she did. Yet the impossible thought of hurting Doctor Will, of causing disappointment to Hannah and to Ben, who with no thought or misgiving had absorbed the two young Bedfords into the warm Patten family circle as if they were as much a natural part of it as their own much-loved and beguilingly light-minded younger brother Peter, held her here as firmly as padlocks and chains of steel. She sighed and straightened her aching back, lifting her head unwarily, looking straight into a pair of heartlessly brilliant blue eyes, one of which winked deliberately and gracelessly. Her face flamed again. Damn the boy! How dared he?

Cissy, dusting her hands decisively, came back around the table. As she did so a small boy of perhaps four or five years, dirty, honey-blond curls a tangle above a wicked, cherub's face danced behind her, mimicking her brisk, birdlike walk and the motions of her hands exactly, an act worthy of any music hall stage. As Charlotte watched him, happy to have something to distract her attention from the disturbing young man with the even more disturbing blue eyes, a narrow, grubby hand buried itself in the wealth of his greasy curls and pulled him up painfully short.

'Be still, Toby Jug, or you'll get your ear clipped!' It was an unexpectedly attractive voice, low pitched and with a throaty break in it, like that of an adolescent boy's. The tone, however, amused and indulgent, belied the words and the grinning child obviously knew it. Charlotte glanced at the girl who had spoken. She was tall, and thin to the point of gauntness. Her brown hair of which there seemed to be a remarkable amount, was stuffed untidily into a battered straw hat to which still clung the sorry looking remains of a bunch of silk daisies. Her skin had the unhealthy pallor brought about by inadequate nourishment and worse than inadequate living conditions. Her eyes were tired. Yet she returned the child's cheeky laughter with a flashing grin of her own that lit her face for a moment as lightning lights a storm-dark sky, imparting to it little of beauty but something of vivid life.

Charlotte looked with distaste at the cooling bowl of soup that she still held. A scum of grease had formed on top and small pieces of unrecognizable vegetables had sunk to an unpleasant lump at the bottom. The girl with the child laughed aloud as the boy swung himself like a monkey on her hand. How could they do it? How could these people laugh still, and love, when home was a filthy tenement in an alley that ran like a midden? When dinner was a bowl of tasteless charity soup and a chunk of bread, often the only meal of the day? She watched as the girl cuffed the still-laughing child and hauled him into her dirty skirts. Then she turned to say something to her companion, a big-built and stolid-looking young woman with breasts that perilously strained the threadbare bodice of her blouse. The large young woman shrugged. 'I doan' know why yer bother yerself,' she said, heaving her bulk a step closer to the table. 'It ain't even as if the kid's yours, is it?'

'If 'e's not mine we don't know whose 'e is, do we, Tobe?' The dirty hand ruffled the child's hair with infinite tenderness. The little boy leaned to her, the glint of his mischievous eyes blue as summer skies.

The big girl shifted her weight from one foot to another, and the blouse sagged open. 'What yer doin' 'ere anyway, Sal? I thought you was on at Bodger's?'

'Yeah, I was.' The other girl's tone was dry with a kind of self-derisive amusement.

Charlotte averted her eyes from the display offered by the open blouse. 'We're running out of soup,' she said to Cissy.

'There's more on the stove. I'll get it.'

Alone, the focus of all eyes, and particularly of a pair brilliant and challenging beneath a shining thatch of black hair Charlotte stood, her features composed into a small, vacantly pleasant smile, and determinedly looked nowhere.

'What 'appened then?'

'You bin at Bodger's?'

'Yeah. Worked there for a month or two last year.'

'Yer know Billy Simpson, the charge 'and?'

'Gawd, I should say.'

''E 'appened.'

The big girl giggled, or rather gurgled at terrible stress to her overburdened blouse. 'Go on!'

'Straight up. I told 'im to keep 'is bleedin' 'ands – ter say nothin' of other more private parts – to 'imself. An' 'e told me ter bugger off. So I did. An' 'ere we are again. Tobe's got to eat, 'aven't yer, Toby Jug?'

'Yer tried Levy's?'

'Yeah. An' Goldstein's, an' Jessop's – nothin' doin' just now.' For a moment the girl's narrow shoulders had slumped, but she lifted her head and smiled jauntily, 'Still, somethin'll turn up. It always does. P'raps I'll try up west. One o' those fancy shops or somethin'. An' anyway –' she jerked her head in the direction of the door and lifted her voice a little, a sharp, almost taunting edge to the husky tones, 'seems like I'm in good company, eh? Seems like all the best people are comin' ter the kitchen nowadays?' Her friend, following the direction of the unfriendly glance she had directed towards the doorway tried unsuccessfully to control another eruption of amusement.

The young man by the door had straightened to a considerable, lean, broad-shouldered height, and stood now with his hands in his pockets, rocking on his heels, his lips pursed to a soundless whistle, those remarkable eyes narrowed a little, their expression far from affable.

Charlotte shifted the congealing and odorous bowl of soup further down the table and smiled at the wizened woman next in line who waited with the infinite patience of the defeated and who could have been aged anything from twenty-five to fifty. 'There'll be some fresh in a moment.'

The woman nodded tiredly, unsmiling. Charlotte closed her eyes for the briefest of moments, blotting out the sights, if not the sounds, around her. It was no good; she would have to tell them. She would have to tell them, at least, that she did not want to come to the soup kitchen any more. The milk depot she did not mind so much; indeed, oddly, she quite liked the sweetish smell of the sterilized milk mixture, the neat little baskets packed along the shelves and filled with sealed and sterilized bottles. She liked the 'weighing days' and the gratitude of mothers who saw their babies growing and thriving where brothers and sisters had wasted and perished. But this? No. It added insult to injury that today should in fact have been her day at the depot and Hannah's at the kitchen. But Hannah – strong, plain, distressingly energetic Hannah – had had other more important fish to fry and had not for a moment considered Charlotte's needs or feelings – who in the busy Patten household did in matters such as this? – when she had crisply and efficiently reorganized the family rota to accord with her own plans.

'More soup.' Cissy, coping manfully with an urn almost as big as herself, thumped it upon the table before Charlotte then peered a little doubtfully into its depths. 'I think it's the same as the last lot. It's hard to tell.' She pulled a half-humorous, half-rueful face and the mouth of the drab woman next in line twitched in surprising sympathy.

Charlotte reached for a tin bowl. And with her vacant, pleasant smile still firmly in place, she retreated, as she so often did, with deliberate and self-defensive intent, into a recess of her mind, seductive and secretive, behind curtains of velvet and silk – never revealed to and so never defiled by any other living soul. Her salvation and her refuge.

A drawing room, prettily patterned and scented; a woman's room this, delicate, delightful, the very picture of elegant femininity. Beautifully furnished, exquisitely decorated. She could dream for hours of the velvet chairs and rosewood writing desk, the discreetly ornate mantel-piece, the elegant card tables. Mirrors, tall and gilded, reflected to infinity the lovely room and its equally lovely occupant.

An old woman snatched at the bowl Charlotte held, spilling some of the scalding soup on to her bare hand. She smiled on.

A calling card. Ah, of course, the young man she had met at the Cavendish ball last night. The naughty thing had been so smitten he would have danced every dance with her had he been allowed. Oh – show' him in, of course – though truly she could only spare a moment. And then, the Suitor. Often, though not always in uniform. Always, and without exception, young, handsome and ardent. Booted and elegant, but yet perhaps just a little awkward in this most feminine of rooms, and most devastating of company. His face – she could never quite see his face –

'What's going on?' Cissy asked, and as she spoke the words were drowned in a raucous screech of laughter. Charlotte blinked a little, brought back with an unpleasant jolt to the long, stuffy, ill-lit and ill-ventilated room, chipped brown paint, the acrid smells of a hot summer's day in the overcrowded slums of London. She glanced down at her hand, surprised. It was sore, an angry red patch had appeared on the pale skin. Automatically she handed out another bowl of soup. The line moved on. The crowd was thinning. Someone was singing, softly, a popular music hall song that Charlotte half recognized. The fat girl was rocking with laughter.

> *Of me you may have read, I'm Fashionable Fred.*
> *And no matter where I chance to show my face,*
> *I'm looked on as the cheese,*
> *And all the girls I please.*
> *I'm a model swell of elegance and grace.*

It was the brown-haired girl singing, softly but very clearly indeed, her face innocent as an angel's. Small Toby swung on her skirt, alive with mischief, and for some reason their overweight companion was all but apoplectic with laughter which she was trying to smother with a large and dirty handkerchief.

'*Yes, I'm just about the cut for Bel-gravia –*'

'Shut it, Sal.'

To Charlotte's surprise the sharp interruption had come from the young man at the door. He had stopped looking at Charlotte and the cornflower eyes were fixed in unfriendly fashion on the singing girl.

The girl ignored him.

> To keep the proper pace I know the plan.
> Wire in and go ahead, For Fashionable Fred.

She paused, lifted her hand in the manner of a conductor and Charlotte, remembering the last line of this cheeky chorus winced a little, glancing at the dangerous colour that was rising in the young man's face as the fat girl joined in gustily, 'I'm Fashionable Fred, the la-adies' man!'

'Will you shut it?'

She turned the innocent face, derisively, to meet the blaze of anger in the astounding blue eyes. 'What's the matter, Jackie?' Her voice was mildly injured, 'I know I'm not Vesta Tilly.'

'That you're bloody not.' The lilt in the voice bore out the flamboyant Irish good looks. Black haired, blue eyed, built like a barn, Jackie Pilgrim had inherited in full his mother's bright beauty and his navvy father's hard-hearted, hard-handed temper.

The girl lifted a bony shoulder in insolent scorn and turned her back on him, slanting a smile of pure wickedness at her friend as she did so. She hummed for a moment, as if to herself, then sang again.

> 'Though in the park I walk,
> And with the ladies talk,
> My tailor's bills do get me on the run.
> I canter in the Row,
> And when to balls I go –'

The other girl was obviously torn between a growing alarm and what seemed to Charlotte unjustifiably hysterical laughter. 'Sal – for Pete's sake!'

> 'I gallop with the charmin' girls like fun.
> I'm ready for a lark,
> No matter light or dark,
> Up to any game is Fashionable Fred.'

Along the queue a few faces had lightened. A woman glanced furtively at Jackie's face and grinned a little.

Jackie Pilgrim moved, lithe and full of venom.

'*I'm Fashionable Fred the la-adies man!*' The girl Sal stopped as a hard hand clamped on her shoulder. She looked up, apparently surprised, her pale, bony face innocent as dawn.

Charlotte watched, as did everyone else, unwillingly fascinated. It took no imagination to guess how painful that docker's grip on the narrow shoulder must be, but the girl grinned derision and showed no sign.

'I told you to shut it, Sal.'

'Why, so yer did,' she agreed tranquilly. 'Taken over the place, 'ave yer? Sellin' licences ter sing? I wouldn't put it past yer, Jackie lad. We all know yer'd sell anythin' else. Yer got any sisters left?'

His face was brilliant with rage. The grip on her shoulder tightened. The smile faded from the girl's face, and unable to keep up her show of nonchalance she lifted her chin, tightened her mouth and stared defiance.

'Thunder and lightning!' Cissy said. 'When will they learn to behave?' And with no hesitation all five feet of her stalked into the arena, ignoring the charged atmosphere of violence that had caused others, more wise in the ways of the streets, to shuffle backwards and to leave isolated the two young people in the centre of the room. 'Young man,' Cissy said very sharply, a governess, knowing her authority, speaking to a recalcitrant child, 'I think you had better leave. And as for you –' she swung upon the brown-haired girl, who ignored her, her eyes still bright and challenging on Jackie's angry face, 'if you wish food for yourself and for the child then I suggest you keep very quiet.'

The girl turned cool, unimpressed eyes upon her. Jackie's hand released the thin shoulder. The young man turned his head, looking first at Cissy and then across the room at Charlotte. Anger and pride flamed in the handsome face, lit the lucent eyes like fire upon water. Somewhere deep in Charlotte a small, wild flame lifted in answer and died, swiftly and furiously quenched.

'I'm sorry,' Cissy said firmly, 'but we really cannot tolerate such disruptive behaviour. You will have to leave. And without your soup.'

He turned fully to face her, towering above her. Jackie Pilgrim wasn't here for soup; two weeks earlier he had followed one pretty face into the kitchen and stayed to eye another. 'Sod your soup, little lady,' he said pleasantly enough, his anger dying as quickly as it had flared, a hard smile in the eyes that he lifted once more to look directly at Charlotte. 'Now what in the world makes you think I came for soup?'

Charlotte, embarrassed, her face on fire, tried to withdraw from the strange, powerful clash of their glances and could not. For a fraction of a second she stood quite still, transfixed by that blue fire, helpless. Then with a smile and a derisive flip of his fingers to the peak of his cap he was gone, striding tall and arrow-straight into the sultry warmth of the afternoon. His going left a small, tense silence. A low buzz of conversation broke out and Cissy turned and clipped briskly back behind the table, her skirts swishing. 'The impudence of that young man! Who is he, do you know?'

Charlotte ladled soup and shook her head.

'Too flash by half, that one. Heading for trouble as sure as eggs. I know the type. Mind you,' Cissy flashed a sly look at Charlotte,' he's a good-looking devil, isn't he? Quite a tom-cat amongst the pigeons – oh, Charlie, now look what you've done! There's more soup on the table than in the bowl! Here, let me. Why don't you be a darling and start to wipe over the tables? We're nearly finished and – it's so very hot – I'd really like to get away on time today.'

Half an hour later the two girls, dressed identically in what Charlotte termed privately their 'do-gooding uniform' of mannish, crisp white shirts and serviceable dark skirts, their small boaters decorously trimmed with plain ribbon, their black buttoned boots dusty from unswept pavements and their hands encased in the inevitable white kid gloves without which even in this sticky weather and even in the swarming – and uncaring – streets of Poplar no young lady would be seen, were walking through caverns of grimy buildings that trapped the heat of the June day like an oven without allowing any stray finger of sunlight to penetrate their depths. At ground level only the heat spoke of summer – that and the brilliance of the sky that sparkled above the grim, dirty windowed buildings and told of a lovely day that in country or park or well-tended garden would be scented and sweet and full of promise, whilst here the sultry heat simply shortened tempers and bred disease.

'You're very quiet?' Cissy, bouncing briskly along by Charlotte's side, turned brightly inquisitive eyes upon her friend. 'Penny for them?' Her voice was lifted against the ear-splitting rattle of the teeming traffic that rolled and bumped along the rutted road – hand-carts and donkey-carts, great wagons from the docks, the occasional hansom.

Charlotte smiled, vaguely and shook her head. 'They aren't worth a penny actually. I wasn't really thinking of anything in particular.' Which was a downright lie; she had been thinking of something very particular indeed. She had been thinking of the quite extraordinary, not to say disturbing, emotions that the recent scene between the young man called Jackie and the girl he had called Sal had aroused in her. Embarrassment she had identified immediately and easily; no gently reared young lady dutifully fulfilling her obligation to assist those less fortunate than herself should be subjected to such an outright and arrogant challenge as she sensed had been flung at her by the wantonly handsome Jackie Pilgrim before he had stalked off like an insulted young prince. Anger, too, rooted in much the same cause. But jealousy?

Yes, she had to admit it, jealousy. There had been something between those two, something that smouldered beneath the surface, something more than an impudently sung music-hall song and an almost casual insult. Offence had been taken far too quickly, and defiance had been too strong and only thinly disguised by the apparently feckless mischief making. Charlotte – and surely everyone else in the room? – had sensed the violence between them, the violence and – something else. Something the thought of which now, as she hurried with Cissy through the heavy summer air of the squalid East End streets, brought an uncomfortable flush of warmth to her face and an odd and not very pleasant creeping of the hairs on her skin; a strange, small frisson of danger and of excitement.

'Charlotte?' Cissy touched her arm.

'I'm sorry?'

Cissy laughed, good naturedly. 'For heaven's sake – where *are* you today?'

'I – I don't know. I have something of a headache. It's the heat I expect.'

'I asked you what you were doing at the kitchen today? It isn't your day, is it?'

'No. But Hannah had a meeting – or a rally – oh, something, I'm not sure what. So she asked me to come instead.'

'Good old Hannah. Still running the world, eh?'

Charlotte smiled, more than a little wryly. 'Something like that.'

'What is it this time? The Women Against Sweated Labour Committee? A trade union march? A suffragists' meeting?'

'Lord knows. Any or all of them in one afternoon perhaps. I'm sure she could manage it. She really can be quite exhausting at times.'

Cissy glanced sideways at her and then with an odd sympathy in the gesture she slid her hand into the crook of Charlotte's arm. 'You aren't altogether happy, are you?' she asked shrewdly. 'With the Pattens?'

For the space of half a dozen steps Charlotte did not answer. How could she honestly answer such a question when she was herself so hopelessly confused? Had anyone but Cissy asked it she would not have tried, would have brushed it aside with a swift denial and changed the subject. But Cissy was the closest to a best friend she had ever had and deserved better than that. 'I – I wouldn't exactly put it like that. Doctor Will's an absolute love, he's been as much a father as a godfather to Ralph and to me since Papa died, as you know. I don't know what we would have done without him. Ralph was, after all, only seventeen and I sixteen. I truly think he loves us as well as he does his own children. And Hannah is really very kind, and Peter is fun –'

Cissy cocked a ginger, inquisitive head in that characteristic, enquiring, birdlike way. 'And Ben?'

Charlotte shrugged. 'Ben's all right. Though sometimes he seems a hundred years old to me. You'd never think he wasn't thirty yet.'

They had turned a corner into a quieter street. Cissy glanced around her at the crowded tenements, at a group of children, half-clothed and filthy, who played, voices raised to shatter glass, in the dry and foul-smelling gutter, at a woman whose brood they must be, though she ignored the blood battle in which they appeared to be engaged, who sat upon a broken chair, her back against the wall watching the world dull-eyed whilst the child at her flat, grimy breast whimpered plaintively. 'It can't be easy being a doctor around here.'

Charlotte stopped so suddenly that Cissy had taken a couple of steps on alone before she realized it. 'But – that's the *point*, isn't it? They don't *have* to be doctors around here! They could do what my father did – what your father does! He doesn't turn away a poor man who can't pay his fees, does he? Of course not! He gives his services to the charity hospital. He sits on the Board of Guardians. He's as socialist as Doctor Will is – as Ben is – as Papa was! But he doesn't make you all live in Poplar, does he? There's nothing wrong in living and practising somewhere decent and giving your services when and how they're needed elsewhere, is there? The Pattens have got money – as we have – no fortune, but enough. They don't *have* to *live* here,' she repeated just a little wildly, the pent-up frustrations of months in the words, 'live in that ridiculous, rambling,' she paused, casting about for a word, '*uncouth* building – all nooks and crannies and spiders' webs! They don't *have* to take personal responsibility for every orphaned child, every sick man, every starving woman between Stepney and the Isle of Dogs!' She stopped, and drew a breath, shook her head ruefully. 'Oh, Lord, that's so unfair, isn't it? I know it. They're wonderful people. And they do truly believe in what they're doing.'

'And you don't?' Cissy's pale eyes were shrewd but not unkind.

Charlotte made a small, impatient gesture, 'But yes! You know I do. We were none of us brought up to ignore or condone the injustice around us, were we? We've all been taught from the cradle of the price our country has paid for commercial success and the blessed Empire!' She threw up her hands in half-comic emphasis. 'We were *weaned* on oppression, the rights of the common man, votes for all regardless of property, paid MPs. You and Wilfred, me and Ralph, the Pattens! The Three Musketeers they called our fathers in medical school, didn't they? All for one and one for all – up with the Charter and down with oppression. And of course I know they're right. Of course I agree that we must fight. Of course it's outrageous that a man – or a woman! – shouldn't be paid a fair day's wage for a fair day's work. Of course the children should be in the schools and not in the sweatshops. Of course decent food, fresh water, clean air should be there for all, not for the privileged few who can afford to pay their cost! But Cissy – for goodness' sake! – I can't be earnest about it all the time! I'm eighteen years old! I want to live somewhere nice, like you do! Have some pretty clothes, go to parties, like I used to. I'm not Hannah! I *won't* grow old attending meetings and organizing committees!'

'She must be all of twenty-one?' the nearly twenty-year-old Cissy said, mildly.

Charlotte shook her head impatiently, 'Oh, Cissy don't be so tiresome! You know what I mean. She could be forty! Look at the way she dresses – the same old skirts and blouses, the same old hats! She never goes anywhere nor does anything that isn't in a good cause. And they all expect me to be the same. No,' she corrected herself, 'even that isn't true. Expect is too strong a word. It never *occurs* to them – not even to my own brother – that I might want something else. I mean, Hannah will never get married, will she? How will she ever *meet* anyone!'

Cissy slanted a quick look at her, grinning.

Charlotte almost stamped her foot. 'Don't laugh at me Cissy Barnes! I'm serious!'

Cissy tucked her hand back into the crook of Charlotte's arm and more slowly they resumed walking. 'I know you are, darling. I'm just not sure it's *Hannah* that you're so concerned about "not meeting anyone". And – oh, Charlotte you're as blind as a bat sometimes – I don't think that it bothers your Ralph one little bit the way Hannah dresses.'

'Oh, Ralph! He's as bad as Doctor Will and Ben. Worse! Living with the Pattens this past two years has made him more one of them than they are themselves! Why, he's talking about –' Charlotte stopped, thunderstruck, incredulity on her pretty face as the underlying meaning of Cissy's words belatedly caught up with her. 'Cissy! What can you mean?'

Cissy was laughing outright now. 'Charlie, you *must* have seen the way he looks at her? Everyone's noticed it,' she giggled again, 'except possibly Hannah herself. Ralph's been tagging along behind her for a full year now –'

'But – he's known her all his life!'

'So? What's wrong with that?'

'I – don't know. Nothing I suppose.' Charlotte walked on in a very thoughtful silence for a moment or two, then made a small, disbelieving sound, half-laughter. 'Oh, Cissy – are you sure?'

'Certain. And so is Mother. She thinks it a very suitable match.'

As she had made no bones about showing that she would think a match between her own son and dear dead Gwendoline's pretty daughter Charlotte – Charlotte hastily steered the conversation away from Mrs Barnes's matchmaking plans, which had plagued her quite enough over the past months, especially as she had good reason to believe that Wilfred did not find them quite as absurd as she did.

'Well. It's their business I suppose. What a thing! Hannah and Ralph!' The preposterous thought was so diverting that with a characteristic butterfly swing of mood she had all but forgotten her ill-temper of a moment ago. She laughed genuinely, a clear peal of girlish amusement. 'Hannah and Ralph! Oh, no – I can't believe it! Oh, Cissy – imagine – do you think they kiss?'

'Charlotte!'

'Well, people do, you know!'

'And other people – well-brought-up people – don't talk about it!' Despite herself, Cissy was laughing too.

'Well, I can't think why not. Tell me – tell me truly – have you ever been kissed?'

The silence that greeted the question opened her clear, forget-me-not eyes very wide indeed. 'Cissy Barnes! You have! Who? Oh – you must tell me who!'

Cissy's face, the fine pale skin already flushed with the heat had suddenly under the small brim of her boater turned a shade to rival her hair.

Charlotte, face alight with childish mischief, affected to think, then raised a small gloved finger. 'I know! David Batty! At the musicale – you took a turn around the garden –'

Cissy shook her head.

Charlotte frowned a little. 'Oh? Who then? Oh, Cissy, not that awful brother of his, surely? What's his name? Robert?'

'No.'

'Then who?'

'It really isn't your business, Charlie.' But the protest was weak, and Charlotte pounced on it like a kitten upon a ball.

'You're dying to tell me! You know you are! Come on. I shall pester until you do!'

'Well –' Cissy chewed her lip for a moment, her face still painfully fiery, 'you wouldn't tell? You promise?'

'Oh, of course not!'

'As a matter of fact it was Peter. Last Christmas. When we went carol singing.'

There was a small, startled silence. Then 'Peter?' Charlotte said, in astonishment that could not have been assumed. '*Our* Peter?'

'Yes.' Cissy was defensive. 'Why not?'

'But – *Peter*? He's – he's younger than you – he's only a year older than me –'

'He's fourteen months older than you and that makes him just eight months younger than me. Lord, Charlotte – you make me sound like Methuselah!'

'Oh, no, I didn't mean that – of course I didn't.' Charlotte was all but choking with graceless laughter. 'But – oh, Cissy – *Peter*? Ouch!' She rubbed her arm in injured surprise. 'You pinched me!'

'I'll do worse than that.'

Charlotte giggled again. Composed herself. 'I'm sorry.'

'So I should think.'

And they both within seconds were in such unladylike gales of laughter that they clung to each other for support.

'What was it like?' Charlotte asked when some degree of breath and sobriety had returned. 'Do tell me. Was it nice?'

Cissy swung her small embroidered hand bag carelessly and lifted her chin. 'As a matter of fact it was. Very nice indeed.'

'Cissy Barnes! You're positively swaggering!'

Cissy grinned.

'Would you – want to do it again?' Charlotte's curiosity, once aroused, was relentless.

The other girl nodded. 'Certainly.'

'With Peter?'

A narrow shoulder lifted, a mite too casually, 'I might. Why not?'

Charlotte really had stopped laughing now, her fair, pointed face was imprinted with an expression of pure puzzlement. Peter Patten, graceless young gadabout that he was, had for as long as she could remember been as much a brother to her as had Ralph. The idea that a sensible girl like Cissy might find him kissable – which she quite demonstrably did – astounded her.

Cissy at that point considered it politic to change the subject. Not for the world would she answer the questions she saw dawning in her friend's inquisitive little face. 'Did you know the Gipsy Fair's coming this weekend?'

Charlotte was distracted at once as Cissy knew she would be. 'No? Where?'

'On the waste ground behind Fulton's Hardware, by Villa Street Chapel. There's a notice up.'

'Oh, Cissy – do let's go! It was such fun last year! Do you remember the acrobats? And the girl in the red dress who danced?'

Cissy nodded. 'Why don't we all go? Ask Hannah, and Ralph and – oh anyone who'd like to. You could all come back to supper or something afterwards. Mother would love to see you, I know.'

So engrossed in her own excitement was Charlotte that she completely missed the significance of the name so carefully not mentioned. 'Will the fire-eater be there, do you think?'

'Oh, I should think so. He usually is. And – I tell you what – let's have our fortunes told this year.'

'You said that last year. And then you lost your nerve and wouldn't go!'

'I did not.' Cissy was indignant. 'Wilfred wouldn't let me – he said it wasn't ladylike. Well he shan't stop me this year, so there! Did you know Susan Batty was told that a golden future would be hers very soon and – presto! – a month or so later some old aunt or other died and left her all her jewellery! Pretty awful stuff, actually but – well, it just shows, doesn't it? And Elizabeth Harvey –'

'Oh, Cissy, you don't really believe in all that, do you?'

The carroty curls tossed. 'Oh, of course not. It's only a bit of fun. But I shall try it just the same. So – what do you think? Shall we all go? And would you like to come back for supper afterwards?'

They were approaching the corner where stood the eccentric abode of Doctor William Patten, his family, his dependants and what seemed to Charlotte sometimes to be half the waifs and strays of east London. 'That would be nice. I'll ask them. Though I seem to remember that Ben and Hannah are organizing some meeting or other on Saturday night.'

'That's not to stop you and – well anyone else who wants to come, is it?' Cissy was brightly nonchalant. Wild horses would not have dragged Peter Patten's name from her again.

'All right. I'll see what I can do. Will you come here

first? Say – four o'clock? Nothing really gets started before then, does it?'

They had reached the corner. Cissy reached up to peck a quick kiss upon Charlotte's cheek. 'Lovely. I'm quite sure Wilfred will want to come. And perhaps the Battys. I'll see, shall I?' She smiled, a sudden, gentle smile, 'And who knows – perhaps Prince Charming will tire of his ivory tower and drop in to see the fun? And to discover his beautiful Princess Charlotte –'

Charlotte wrinkled her nose. 'On the wasteland behind Fulton's Hardware? Hardly!' She lifted a hand in farewell, then stood and watched the other girl as she hurried down the street to catch the omnibus in the Commercial Road that would take her back to the neat, well-tended little road in a not-too-fashionable part of the West End where her father had his practice. Where her neat, well-kept, not-too-fashionable mother would be awaiting her with smiles and cups of tea and feminine gossip. Where a bath would have been readied for the young mistress – Cissy, these two years past, having had a maid of her very own – and a light and pretty summer dress laid out upon her bed. There would be tea in the garden with yet another maid, neat in black and white, to serve it. Charlotte sighed a little. The Barnes's residence might not be the tall and elegant house furnished with taste and finesse and overlooking Hyde Park of which she so often – and she knew so absurdly – dreamed; but at least it was better than the lathe and plaster maze that had once in Tudor times been the famous Inn of the Dancing Bear and was now, with its jumble of dark rooms, its three staircases, its courtyard at the back that was the arena more often than not for tooth-and-nail battles between the urchins that Doctor Will – and Ben – seemed to collect as other people collected stamps or cigarette cards, her home.

Sighing again, her high spirits fled, she pushed open the door.

II

Hannah Patten surveyed with a rue that was still too coloured with the excitement of the day to be termed real regret, the broken brim and crushed roses of the object that had been her favourite dark straw hat, and the fraying rip in the sleeve of her best silk blouse. She'd had the hat for years, and had been rather fond of it, as hats went; an old friend which, anchored with a pin long enough to skewer the Sunday joint, sat upon her ridiculous hair with at least some semblance of – well, if not elegance, at least what might be termed style. She touched the broken rim with her finger and a few more strands crackled and snapped. Never again. Ah well. It had been worth it, and more than worth it. If she lived to be a hundred she'd never forget this day; never forget the feeling as she and her comrades had marched into Cavendish Square, white flags and banners brave in the sunshine, a small group of soldiers, the vanguard, pray God, of an army, come to demand justice and freedom – to demand! – no longer to beg. Now they would see – the Campbell-Bannermans and the Lloyd Georges with their sanctimonious, lip-service promises and the Gladstones and the Asquiths with their venomous but at least more honest opposition – now they would see that the women meant business. They would have the vote and they would have it now! And if it came to a fight, well then, so be it. One of the time-worn, arid arguments so often used against women's suffrage was that since women were precluded by their gentle natures, tender sensibilities and lack of physical strength from fighting for their country then of course they must necessarily be debarred from taking any part in its government. So perhaps it was time to demonstrate to the tedious gentlemen who so conveniently believed it that gentle natures could be stubborn, tender sensibilities toughened, and physical strength reinforced by intelligence, guile and courage. There had been no obvious lack of muscle or determination in the East End working women who had marched side by side with her behind the deputation that had visited Mr Asquith's house this afternoon! The gentlemen had had their chance – and look what a damned mess they'd made of it! Now let them look to their precious privileges; the women, and the workers, were snapping at their heels –

'Hannah! What on earth – ?'

Hannah turned to the open door, where stood Charlotte, staring, her wide eyes taking in Hannah's dishevelled appearance, the torn blouse, the fast-purpling bruise on her cheekbone. Charlotte came into the room, hands fluttering like pretty, helpless little doves. 'Has there been an accident? Are you badly hurt? Oh – let me call Doctor Will – or Ben!'

'No, no, no. It's nothing. I'm perfectly well.' Hannah tossed the ruined hat upon the table. Excitement still sang in her blood, bringing colour to her usually sallow cheeks and putting something close to a sparkle into her unremarkable brown eyes. 'Oh, Charlotte, you should have been there, my dear! What a day! What a splendid day!'

'Hannah, what are you talking about? You stand there with your blouse in shreds, your hat ruined, your face looking as if you might have had an argument with a prizefighter and you talk about "a splendid day"? Have you gone mad?'

Hannah chuckled.

'How did you hurt your face?'

'A policeman hit me.' The words were perfectly collected.

Charlotte stared at her for a very long time, then gave her head a sharp, perplexed shake. 'Now I know you're mad. I'm going for Doctor Will.'

Hannah laughed outright, detained her with a hand

upon her arm. 'No, really Charlotte. I truly am perfectly all right – there are no bones broken, and I do assure you that I am absolutely sane. Mrs Briggs is bringing me a cup of tea and that, I promise you, is all the attention I need.'

'Then will you for heaven's sake explain? For truly I can't believe what I see!'

Hannah paced across the room, turned and paced back again, the always abundant energy that so characterized her, driving her to movement when any other woman – any normal woman, Charlotte found herself thinking a little tiredly – might be expected to collapse in an exhausted heap on the nearest sofa. 'We went to Mr Asquith's house to deliver a letter –'

'But I thought you'd done that two days ago?'

'We tried, but he avoided us, the coward. So today we went back to Cavendish Square determined to see him.'

'And?'

'And the police were waiting. The *police*! Can you believe it? We were not to be allowed to see Mr Asquith – were not even to be allowed near his house to post our letter through the letter box –'

'What did you do?'

'We marched in orderly fashion around the Square, at least that's what we tried to do. But the police apparently were under orders not to allow us to do that either.'

Charlotte smiled faintly, irresistibly diverted by the thought of a gawky young police constable faced with the sight of Hannah in full, righteously energetic advance. 'But you did it anyway?'

'Of course. And in the ensuing –' she hesitated, '– flurry my hat was spoiled and a young constable's knuckles somehow caught my face.'

Charlotte had unpinned and removed her straw boater and dropped it upon the table beside Hannah's larger, old-fashioned, ruined creation. She was shaking her head, very slowly, her expression an entertaining and entertained mixture of incredulity, amusement and downright shock. 'You *fought*? With the *police*?'

'I – don't think I'd put it that strongly.'

'You'd put it that strongly if Peter came home from an alehouse with a face like that!'

'Really, Charlotte, that's hardly a fitting comparison.' The words were injured and faintly acid.

'Hannah –!' Charlotte lifted small hands, and let them fall in a gesture that conveyed exactly her inability to credit the bizarre story she had just heard. Well-brought-up young ladies – and however eccentric her background Hannah Patten was certainly that – simply did not brawl with policemen in the fashionable squares of London, whatever the cause. It was inconceivable. An aberration.

As if reading her mind Hannah swung upon her, excitement shining in her face. 'This is the beginning, Charlotte! The beginning of a crusade! We will have the vote; we will not be denied! Whatever it takes to achieve our freedom, our full citizenship of our own country – whatever sacrifice – we are ready for it.'

Charlotte, hot, tired, but never less than graceful, sank prettily on to the sofa. 'Hannah, you are crazed. You'll stand alone, you and your handful of friends, don't you see that? Most women – if they ever think of it at all – don't want the vote. They don't care! The poor ones are too busy wondering where the next penny's coming from, scraping a living, feeding too many children and watching them die, even to think about such things. The rich ones that can be bothered have long since discovered other paths to influence. And most of the ones in the middle are far more concerned about the health of their children, their husbands' dinners, the colour of a new hat –'

Hannah shook her head vigorously. 'You're wrong, Charlotte. Half the women who came to Cavendish Square this afternoon were working women from Stepney, Bow and Poplar.'

'Dragged along there by that Pankhurst woman I suppose? What does she know of the East End? She comes from Manchester, doesn't she? And she's an art student, or some such thing –? Honestly, Hannah, can't you see the trouble she'll cause?'

'Sylvia Pankhurst is a very fine young woman,' Hannah said, stiffly, a dangerous gleam in the phlegmatic brown eyes.

'I'm sure she is.' Charlotte, in her turn, was conciliatory, but yet sharp impatience edged her tone like frost on a winter's leaf. The thought had come to her that afternoon, as she had spoken to Cissy that perhaps she might talk to Hannah – try to explain her frustrations and feelings to someone who at the very least surely must understand her budding womanhood, her need for something other than causes and sacrifice and backbreaking labour. And as quickly as the thought had been born, so swiftly had it died. And this was why. Hannah inhabited such a different world from Charlotte that they might have lived in different hemispheres, spoken different tongues. Not in a thousand years would either one ever understand the other's needs, views and aspirations, and no amount of affection, no amount of effort would ever change that. Yet still, with good will, they tried. 'Hannah,' Charlotte said now as patiently as she could manage, 'working *men* don't have the vote – who knows if they ever will, despite the promises? How will you ever hope to rally enough support for the *women*?'

'We already have support. We have support in the country and support in Parliament.'

'But you can't get your Bills through, can you? Even though the Prime Minister himself says he's on your side. Time and again they talk them out. Just last year it happened all over again.'

'Next time we'll win.'

'How?'

'In the same way the men did.' Hannah, still pacing, lifted a prophetic finger. 'Did men achieve the widening of the franchise by sitting on their hands and asking nicely? Of course they didn't. They fought for it. They marched and they fought –'

'They rioted and committed arson and were hanged and deported for it as I remember it,' Charlotte said drily.

Hannah ignored her. 'They heckled and they protested. They fought the politicians to a standstill. They refused to take "no" for an answer. They were in the right, and they knew it, and right prevailed, as it always must. And when you speak of the women who don't support us – they will, Charlotte, they will. When they realize what we are doing and why, then they will support us. We live in a society that enslaves its women. You know it. At beck and bidding of husband or father, fortunate only if the yoke is a light one, held to be incapable of managing their own affairs. A mother doesn't even have the legal right to the guardianship of her own children, no matter how much of a blackguard the father might be.' She raised an arm, pointing through the tiny, multi-paned window to the shabby, sweltering streets beyond. 'You know as well as I do what goes on out there! Women beaten and misused, with no redress, women – and children too – worked to blindness or to death in the sweatshops, women dying in childbed, children dying of neglect and disease – and these things are preventable! But they will only be prevented when women have a hand in framing the laws of the country. If now we protest we have no voice, for those that govern us tell us that – although, of course, they deplore these things and although, yes, they see the urgent need for reform, there are more pressing things to be dealt with. They are responsible not to women – not to the people – but to the men who voted them to power, and who, God help us, keep them there, playing their vicious games of wealth and war. And so there is no time for the reforms that women need. First

37

the vote, Charlotte, and then see what we shall do for this country!'

Impressed despite herself, Charlotte said nothing. It was hot. So very hot. Suddenly self-conscious Hannah moved to the mantel mirror and tried without success to repin the hanks of shining hair that had fallen about her face. Charlotte watched her. Hannah's only real physical beauty, her only claim to the attention of a casual observer, was her hair. It had the sheen of new-peeled chestnuts, and the colour, and was abundant and shining and straight as rain. And what did she do with it? She dragged it back from her plain, sallow face and stuffed it in ugly, old-fashioned nets. Or she filled it so hopelessly and inefficiently full of ill-placed pins that the things constantly slid out, and her only alternative to looking like a demented pincushion was an ineffective, constant and habitual search for them, a vague patting and pushing as she spoke or as she listened that could drive one to distraction on a bad day. Hannah leaned now closer to the mirror, looking at the dark smudge on her cheekbone. 'Oh dear. That really has become rather more noticeable than I had thought.' Her voice was vaguely surprised, had lost the fierceness and fervour of a moment before. 'Perhaps I should pop along to the surgery and put something on it?' She laughed a little, that sudden, mischievous chuckle that always came with such warmth and was such a surprise, 'I can hardly walk around veiled for a week, can I? Charlotte darling – when Mrs Briggs brings the tea, ask her to be a love and bring me a cup in my room, would you? I really am very tired.'

'Of course. Oh, and Hannah –?'

Hannah, on her way to the door, stopped.

'– the fair comes on Saturday. Shall we go, do you think?'

'Why of course dear. If you'd like to. We usually do.'

'Cissy asked if we might like to go back to them for supper?'

Hannah thought for a moment. 'You and Peter may certainly go, I should think. Ben, Ralph and I are expected at the Labour Committee Rooms at six, so it's probably best if we come back here. But yes, do go, dear. I daresay there'll be music. You'll enjoy that – you've such a pretty voice.' Hannah stopped, surveyed for a moment the pale, pointed, lovely little face that was upturned to her beneath its halo of softly curling hair. The child – for so she thought of Charlotte despite the mere three years that separated them in age – disturbed her sometimes. Delightful, obliging, soft as a flower and as sweet, loving as a child, yet sometimes, when she had time to consider it, she found herself wondering if Charlotte were truly happy. Like a flower she sometimes wilted. Like a child she sometimes sulked. And her apparently placid obedience to the will of anyone who cared to impose on her more often than not gave the impression that was negative rather than positive: she simply could not think for herself of anything better to do. 'I'm sorry I lectured,' she said a little clumsily.

Charlotte smiled. 'You didn't. Well –' she tilted her head prettily to the side and spread her hands, 'only a little.'

Hannah looked at her with real affection, real pleasure in her loveliness. 'We'll go to the fair,' she said, 'you and Ralph, Peter and I. I don't suppose for a moment we'll be able to persuade Ben or Father along. But we'll go. Perhaps the fire-eater will be there?'

Charlotte smiled a little and nodded.

'Well,' Hannah, big-boned and untidy, the bruise on her cheek darkening by the moment to a splendid purple, stood for one more oddly awkward moment, 'if you wouldn't mind about the tea?'

'Of course not. I'll bring it myself.'

Charlotte sat for a long, quiet time after Hannah had gone, her eyes fixed upon her folded hands, her thoughts not particularly good companions. Then she lifted her head and surveyed the room about her. It was, as always, gloomy, and untidy to the point of chaos. Doctor Will's glasses lay discarded upon the table. He had, no doubt, she thought with fond exasperation, been searching high and low for them for hours. Several newspapers had been dropped on the seat of the fireside chair. A bright red waistcoat, Peter's undoubtedly, lay upon a footstool, brilliant and abandoned. Untidy. The chairs which usually stood evenly about the table had been dragged and clustered in companionship at one end of the room and left where they stood. Poor Mrs Briggs. She would bustle in with her tea and click her tongue and set again about the helpless task of tidying a room – a family – a residence – so peculiar that it defied description, and that resolutely refused to be tidied.

Charlotte stood up and walked to the mirror above the fireplace. Her face, she noted with disapproval, was lightly sheened with perspiration, tendrils of fair curling hair clung to her neck. She felt sticky and uncomfortable, her dark skirt flaring from padded hips too hot, the neck of her severe shirt too high for comfort. She stood for a long time looking into the mirror, taking stock as she did so often of the fair face, the pretty hair, the cupid's bow of mouth, the wide, palely gleaming eyes. Pensively she lifted the wilful, wispy curls from her neck. 'Well, Charlotte Bedford,' she said softly aloud, 'tell me. Do you want the vote? Would you – could you – fight policemen for it?' In the street outside the winkle man called, his chanting cry all but lost in the dull, persistent rumble of the traffic, 'Winkles a' cockles. Winkles a' cockles.' 'And if not,' Charlotte continued her conversation with herself, 'what do you want?' Knowing the answer. Seeing again, with no effort at all, superimposed upon her shadowed reflection in the mirror the elegant room, the long mirrors, the lovely, expensive, flattering clothes –

Outside the door crisp footsteps sounded in the long flagged corridor that connected this room, which once had been the main bar of the inn and now, as the parlour, was the general meeting room and sitting room of the house, to in one direction the courtyard in which stood the old stables, Doctor Will's 'unofficial orphanage', and in the other some parts of the rest of the house, the rest, absurdly being reached by an outside staircase in the courtyard. She heard the quiet murmur of Doctor Will's voice, and then, louder and more incisive, Ben's voice answering him. 'I know that, Pa. Of course I know it. But compulsory health inspections and free school meals are more important! If we're going to give the poor little devils more than half a chance to learn – even to *want* to learn – even, God help us, to get them to school in the first place, we have to start with the basics. The money, initially, needs to go on health – preventive medicine – food – a decent meal for every child every day. *Then* perhaps we can teach them to think.'

Their voices faded as they passed the open door and went on out into the courtyard. Charlotte closed her eyes against the spasm of sheer temper that overtook her. She was tired of it. *Tired* of it! Everyone was so concerned, so very concerned, about the unnamed, unfaced hordes of poverty. No one knew – no one cared – what *she* wanted. In their care for the whole damned world they could not see unhappiness right under their silly noses. With all the force of her romantic, eighteen-year-old self-centred soul she pitied herself. Her mouth set, miserably sulky. She tilted her head, took a long breath, with deliberation projected herself into her dream. Sunshine gleamed through ivory lace and lay in glowing, shadowed patterns across priceless, jewel-coloured rugs. A young man clicked his booted heels, bent a shining head reverently over her offered hand.

And when he straightened she realized with a shock that brought her quite hastily and blushingly to herself and to the sound of the ponderous advance of Mrs Briggs and her rattling tea-tray that the silly phantom, until now ever vague, had this time inexplicably acquired the disturbing cornflower eyes and the thatch of blue-black curls that in real life belonged to the faintly terrifying Jackie Pilgrim.

Chapter Two

I

'Kill 'im, Joey boy!'

'Knock 'is block off, lad!'

Poplar sweltered. The sky above the soot-blackened buildings was brazen with heat, the air heavy and suffocatingly still. Even in the long shadows of the tenements that surrounded the patch of waste ground where the fairground booths had been set up, the milling, shirt-sleeved crowd sweated, red-faced, their heavy, shuffling boots raising a dust to choke the devil himself.

'Come on, Joey! Stop arsin' about! Show the greasy little bugger what's what!'

Ralph Bedford stood on the fringes of the crowd, blinking behind his ill-fitting wire-rimmed spectacles against the acrid and unpleasant smell of perspiring humanity and the lifting dust. He was no expert on prize-fighting — far from it — but it seemed to him that the huge, fair young man at whom the crowd's advice was aimed, stripped to the waist, sheened with sweat, the thin, milk-pale Anglo-Saxon skin of his body marked savagely by the punishment he was receiving, had about as much chance of showing his viciously agile young opponent what was what as he had of sprouting wings and flying. The gipsy fighter flitted around him graceful as a dancer, on his dark, unmarked face the shadow of a purely malicious smile, his flashing, spiteful blows taking the bemused young docker where and when they pleased. The fair young man had long given up trying to duck – had indeed all but given up trying to land a telling blow of his own – and seemed, understandably thought Ralph, intent merely upon defending his already badly damaged face with glove and forearm, determined only to stay on the feet that were planted so flatly upon the wooden boards of the ring for one more round and collect his hard-earned guinea. Joey might be – and looking at him probably was – a good lad in a bare-knuckle bar-room brawl at the Prospect of Whitby or the Newcastle, but he was clearly no match for this ferociously elegant young professional, hard of body and harder of hand who was cutting him to ribbons with no apparent effort and even less apparent concern. Despite himself Ralph flinched as another well-placed blow landed, and big Joey's grunt of pain was clearly audible, even at this distance. His opponent danced away, still smiling, wolf-like in the shadows. The crowd muttered, shouted half-hearted, scathing encouragement to their almost fallen champion.

'Come on, Joey – what yer waitin' for, Christmas?'

'Give 'im what for, Joe boy.'

'No chance, I'd say.' Peter Patten, standing beside Ralph, a full head shorter than his lanky companion, dapper in well-fitting light grey suit, a straw boater at a dashing angle upon his fair young head, grinned a little, blithely unsympathetic. 'The gipsy lad could take him with one hand tied behind his back, for all his size.'

'The gipsy's a professional.' Ralph averted his eyes from the punishment being meted out in the ring. The crowd had fallen silent.

'He is that.' Peter, despite the heat, somehow contrived to appear cool as a cucumber. Ralph on the other hand was uncomfortably hot, and knew that he must look it, his shirt beneath the none-too-well-fitting jacket drenched with sweat, his thin dark hair plastered to his head.

'Where are the girls?'

'They were over at the skittle alley with Cissy and that twerp of a brother of hers. Ah – there they are –' Peter waved a hand, 'over here!'

Charlotte, dainty and cool beneath a fringed ivory silk parasol, waved back and in a moment she, Hannah and their companions had joined the two young men. 'Ralph – Peter! What on earth are you doing over here? We thought we had mislaid you entirely! You surely aren't *watching* this – this barbarity?' Charlotte's small straight nose wrinkled in undisguised distaste.

The young docker was reeling now upon the ropes as his slighter, faster, more venomous opponent launched a last attack. The crowd, mostly the foolhardy Joey's workmates who had until a moment before been offering raucous support, turned on him now in defeat, the low, animal growl of their displeasure rising to a ragged, wordless shout as the battered loser retreated and fell beneath a barrage of short, viciously jabbing blows a scant – and, Ralph wondered, calculated? – moment before he could have earned his guinea.

'Oh – really!' Twirling her parasol, Charlotte turned fastidiously away, then stopped, her eye resting upon a tall figure who, some short distance from her, leaned with negligent grace upon the high, painted wheel of a gipsy wagon, cap tipped to the back of his shining dark head as he watched the fight.

'Charlotte's right, Ralph – do come away.' Hannah surveyed Charlotte's brother, mild surprise upon her strong, plain face. 'You surely don't want to watch this?'

'Of course he didn't,' her own young brother answered for Ralph, grinning unrepentantly, 'I did.'

Hannah tutted exasperatedly. 'I might have known. But do come away now. You've surely seen enough?'

The young docker had disappeared from sight, man-handled half-conscious from the ring by his disappointed, and none-too-sympathetic mates. In the ring the barker was calling for new volunteers.

'Come on now, all you brave lads – roll up! Roll up! Oo'll 'ave a go? A guinea if yer stay three rounds, two if yer can knock 'im over. Oo'll 'ave a go, I say? You ain't a-scared o' Gipsy Mike, are yer?'

Peter nudged Wilfred, Cissy's slight, sandy haired brother. 'There you are, Wilf. There's a chance for you. A couple of guineas in your pocket and a chance to impress the girls,' he grinned gracelessly, his eyes flicking to Charlotte and back to Wilfred's reddening face. Charlotte herself ignored both of them; she stood with her back half turned to them smoothing, with great care and concentration, her immaculate white lace gloves to slim fingers, holding her long narrow hands before her to inspect the effect of her efforts, an apparently absorbed and, critical little frown upon her face, which was suddenly and prettily flushed.

'Don't be such a fool, Pete,' Wilfred muttered.

'Where are we going now?' Cissy asked briskly. 'I do declare I'm almost dying of thirst. Why don't we have some lemonade?'

'Ripping idea.' Peter was standing on tiptoe, looking about him, 'If you'll just give me a moment – ah!' His sharp and laughing eye had lit upon a villainous-looking man in dirty vest and a battered top hat that sported an unlikely bright green feather. 'I'll pick up the where-withal, and then it's my treat.'

Hannah watched blankly as the young man slid swiftly through the crowds like a minnow through waterweed. 'Now where's he going?' Her voice held that trace of affectionate exasperation that always in Hannah seemed to accompany speech to or about her scapegrace young brother.

'To pick up his winnings, I suspect,' Ralph said with a small smile.

'His – winnings? You mean he *gambled* on this awful business?'

'I do believe so.'

Hannah shook her head in disbelief. Cissy giggled. Charlotte had turned away, parasol tilted at a flirtatious angle over her shoulder, and was strolling very slowly and with elaborate composure a little way from her companions, turning her head, smiling dazzlingly at a hurdy-gurdy man's gaudily dressed monkey as it pattered and danced upon its master's shoulder.

'Charlotte?'

So engrossed had she been in her pretty show that the unexpected voice at her shoulder took her unawares. She caught her breath in irritation and surprise. 'Oh. Wilfred. It's you. You startled me.' Less than graciously, a small line of ill temper fretting her forehead, she shook free of the hand he had laid upon her arm.

'Will you let me buy you some lemonade?'

She lifted a delicate shoulder clad in pale muslin the same shade as the parasol and scattered with tiny light blue flowers that exactly matched her eyes. 'If you like. Where are the others?' She glanced around, apparently casually. Amused and knowing vivid blue eyes acknowledged her little display, a long-fingered dirty hand that clasped a pocket flask openly toasted her, then the dark curly head tilted as Jackie Pilgrim drank deeply, and for one astounding, almost frightening moment she found that she could not look away from the strong, exposed column of the young man's throat, the muscles moving as he drank. He straightened, pocketed the flask, wiped his mouth with the back of his wrist. His neckerchief today was scarlet as was the handkerchief tucked with gaudy style into his top pocket. He looked a young brigand; reckless, handsome, more than a little dangerous.

For her life, she could not take her eyes off him.

He smiled again, his own eyes veiled for a moment by the long dark lashes, then he flicked his fingers to his cap in that small and somehow mocking gesture and turned and strolled into the crowd, long-legged, swaggering, drawing her eyes after him like a magnet.

'There they are – waiting for us. Everyone's dying of thirst in this heat. Do come and have some lemonade?' Wilfred, in trying to tread the impossible line between a would-be lover's coaxing and a would-be husband's masterliness succeeded only in sounding peevish.

Pointedly, Charlotte moved her parasol to her left shoulder, thereby denying her unwanted swain access to her arm and strolled towards the refreshment booth where the others waited, wrinkling her nose a little at the smell as she passed the whelk and winkle stall.

Sally Smith, her fingers busy in a plateful of cockles, watched her go by with a grin that was perhaps not as kindly as it might have been. She had watched, entertained, the whole pretty charade. 'Better'n a peep-show,' she said with mischievous mockery to her companion, a handsome, dark-haired girl in neat and respectable blue cotton with a touch of white at neck and wrist and a gay cluster of forget-me-nots upon her white straw hat. Josie Dickson's eyes crinkled into laughter. She was Sally's best – indeed Sally thought of her as her only – friend; and by some, she knew, who perhaps regarded Sally Smith as being no better than she should be, the friendship was regarded as an odd one. Josie's father Bill and her older brother Dan were stevedores, working aristocrats of the docklands, her brother Walter a lighter-man saving penny by penny to own his own craft. As docking families went the Dicksons were well off and well respected – for even in the bad times there was almost always work for the skilled. It was the casual labourers, the unskilled workers – of whom there were so many – that suffered most from the traditional, cut-throat and corrupt system of 'calling on'. Even in times of high employment a large percentage of the mass of workers who clamoured at the dock gates at dawn and midday for work would likely be turned away empty-handed, destitute and sometimes dangerous victims of a system designed to keep labour cheap and plentiful and to line the owners' pockets at whatever cost to working families who were often left without bread. But for the Dicksons a day without work was hardly known and, hard working and respectable, taking pride in their skill and their strength, they gave good measure for their hire. They were a likeable and close-knit family, the only one of its kind that Sally Smith in her short life had encountered. Though red-hot irons might well have had to be employed to make her admit it in so many words, she admired them all enormously, envied them more than a little and greatly valued the affection and esteem that they, for reasons she had never been able to fathom, offered unstintingly to her.

Josie, who like Sally had watched with wry but not entirely unsympathetic amusement Charlotte's beguiling and naïve attempts to hold Jackie Pilgrim's fickle attention, laughed a little now softly. 'Oh, come on, Sal. Don't be so hard on her. She's a pretty little thing. And if she is a bit on the daft side – well, she'll come to no harm, will she? She's well protected. Which is just as well.' She lifted bright, dark eyes to the sky. 'The Lord only knows what Jackie'd do to her if he did get his hands on her!'

Sally, deftly and with some style, conveyed more vinegar-soaked cockles to her mouth. 'She wouldn't know what 'ad 'it 'er. An' I'm not jokin'.' There was a sudden, small, raw edge to her husky voice.

Josie pulled a face. 'He's not my cup of tea I must say. Never has been. And even if he was,' she giggled a little, 'can you imagine me dad's face if I turned up at Bolton Terrace with Jackie Pilgrim in tow?'

'Never mind about yer dad – can you imagine Dan's? 'E'd knock 'is block off. An' yours for good measure.'

Josie shook her head. 'Well believe me it's not something that'll ever get put to the test. He may be a pretty lad, and there's no denying that, but I wouldn't get near him with a bargepole. He's nothing but trouble.'

Sally, with efficient, grimy, square-tipped fingers, cleared her plate of the last moist scraps, relishing them, licking the salty vinegar from her skin. 'Jackie?' she said mildly. 'Oh, come on – that's a bit 'ard, Josie – Jackie's not so bad.' She smiled, drily, tilted her head so that the broken daisies upon her hat brim nodded drunkenly. 'Oh, 'e's vicious, an' 'e's stupid, an' I wouldn't trust 'im with 'is own mother after a few pints – but apart from that 'e's all right.'

Her companion laughed a little, but her bright eyes were shrewd. 'A little bird tells me that you didn't always feel like that?'

Sally shook her head. 'Don't never believe all them little birds tell yer, Jose. They're terrible liars. Didn't yer know?'

'Oh, come on, Sal. Isn't it true that you and Jackie were – well – a bit more than friends some little while back?'

Sally appeared to consider that seriously. 'Ter be a bit more than friends, Josie love, you 'ave ter be friends in the first place, right? An' I'd no more make friends with the likes of Jackie Pilgrim than I'd put me right 'and in a snake pit. Or me left fer that matter. Not now an' not then. But,' a flashing grin lit her face, gleamed in her narrow hazel eyes, '– like yer said, he's a pretty enough lad. An' – yes – there was a time when I thought it might be worth the try –'

'And was it?'

The other girl turned to put her plate on the stall, adjusted about her bony shoulders the brilliant, thread-bare, silky shawl that was her dearest possession and had been donned despite the weather for this festive afternoon. 'No. It wasn't,' she said shortly. 'I should 'ave 'ad me 'ead examined first. But there – yer live an' learn, or so they say – where's the Jug? Can yer see 'im? Toby? *Tobe*! Come 'ere yer little monster! Where is the little blighter? *Toby*! Get out from under there!'

Tousled blond curls topping a small, wicked face had appeared from beneath the counter.

'Little bleeder! Just wait till I get me 'ands on you! What the 'ell's that you've got? Tobe! Give it back!'

The child gleefully slipped between them avoiding both the swift hand that Sally extended to catch him and the bellowing stall holder, a short, burly man too large to follow the child under the counter and too short of arm to reach him over the top. Sally lunged at him again, took a swipe at his ear and missed again. 'Little bugger! Let it go!'

The eel the laughing child held wriggled and cracked like a small live whip in his hands. A woman shrieked. A man stepped hastily backwards on to his companion's foot. Chaos threatened.

'*Toby*!'

For a few more seconds Toby held on to the slippery, wriggling thing, then, unable to keep his grip he flicked it high into the air. Pandemonium broke out as the eel writhed in its flight and came to land across a man's shoulders before slithering to the ground. Plates of whelks and winkles were hastily dropped as people leapt out of its way. The onlookers scattered. Toby took one look at Sally's face and deciding that discretion for the moment was most certainly the better part of valour fled into the crowd.

Josie, despite herself, was giggling uncontrollably as the sweating, red-faced stall holder chased the eel across the trodden, dusty grass. 'Oh, Sal, he's a little devil and no mistake!'

'Yer can say that twice,' Sally said tersely. Grim-faced she was surveying the crowd, watching for the boy. 'Wait till I get my 'ands on 'im. 'E won't sit down without a cushion fer a week. Toby? *Toby*! Get back 'ere!'

'Leave him. He'll come.' The excitement had died down. People were back with their whelks, their winkles and their cockles. The stall holder had now recovered his eel and dropped it back into the basket from which mischievous fingers had released it. Sally eyed him a little cautiously, but he made no move towards her. Around them a hubbub of talk and no little laughter rose. 'There,' Josie said, 'no great harm done. Now – why don't we go and see the freaks?'

Sally shook her head.

'Oh, Sally, please! I don't want to go alone.'

Sally grinned. 'I'll wait for you at the door. Make sure they'll let you out.'

'But Sally –'

'Josie –' Sally was good humoured, but the note in her voice was absolutely final. 'No. Apart from the fact that I sometimes think I'm too much a freak meself to feel comfortable peering at those poor blighters, it's three-pence. And I 'aven't got threepence. No –' she held up both hands, palms out, 'I already owe you fer the cockles. I'm not takin' any more. I've got tuppence in me pocket. An' I promised that little monster a go on the roundabout and a penn'orth of sausage fer supper.'

'Sally, I wish you'd come to us – both of you – just until you –'

'No. I know yer dad wouldn't mind me – but Tobe'd drive 'im round the bend. And anyway, I don't scrounge off me friends. Yer know me better than that. 'Sides, we've got enough ter keep body an' soul tergether for a while yet – I earned a few bob from Patsy O'Reilly the other day lookin' after his stall. We'll be all right, Jose, don't you fret. It's just a bad patch, that's all. If the worst comes to the worst I might try up west – one o' those fancy shops – though what I'd do with the nipper then I don't know, what with livin' in an' all.' She stopped, her whole face changing, the lines tautening, the eyes narrowing warily. 'Well, well,' she said, pleasantly enough, 'look what the cat's let drop.'

Jackie Pilgrim, tall, lean but with shoulders as broad as any Covent Garden porter's lounged against the stall, his cap tilted forward to keep the sun from his face. Sally lifted her face to him, smiled derisively into the astonishing blue eyes. 'An' 'ow's God's gift to the ladies this fine day? Keepin' 'em all happy, are we?' The low-pitched voice was harsh.

Josie pulled her arm a little nervously. 'Sal!'

Jackie kept his own cocky smile in place. The smell of brandy was strong about him. 'Sure an' I've had no complaints.'

Her smile became sweeter, her narrow eyes more contemptuous. 'Well, o' course – yer wouldn't, would yer? Unless yer've actually found a girl that likes 'avin' 'er face smashed in? Are there girls like that? You'd know, o' course. You're the expert.'

Very precisely he spat at her feet. His smile had gone.

The air rang with her sudden husky laughter. 'Charmin' I'm sure! Never let it be said Jackie Pilgrim's not a blue-blooded gentleman. Perish the thought. Descended from the kings of Ireland 'e is, so 'tis said. Descended's the word –'

'Piss off,' he said. The swift-rising rage in him was palpable. It gleamed in his eyes, brought his lean, broad frame from its lounging stance to tower above the two girls.

'Sal – for God's sake –' Josie hissed, truly alarmed. She'd heard too many stories about Jackie Pilgrim not to be afraid of that wicked temper.

Sally ignored her. Recklessness born of remembered pain, of squalid humiliation, of the need to hurt, of the ache to revenge engulfed her as it always did when she saw him. The beatings she had sustained from those big, shapely, dirty hands had scarred her body; but the other and worse abuse that this flawed and arrogant boy inflicted upon his women had scoured her soul and left it raw still. For a short, unbearable time she had been as abject a slave as he could have wished. She had begged for his touch, for his brutal lovemaking, had crawled to him like a bitch on heat; had degraded herself for his gratification, offered herself a desperate, willing sacrifice to his vicious pleasures. And had one morning woken up detesting and despising him and – worse – detesting and despising herself. Now the mere sight of him stirred an emotion even deeper than the besotted infatuation that had smitten her as suddenly as a summer fever and had, thank God, as suddenly evaporated. In the back streets of Poplar self-respect was a prize hard won, and for those who achieved it it was a possession as precious as any miser's gold. Jackie Pilgrim had, for however short a time, deprived her of her pride and her dignity, and for that she could never forgive him. The fact that he had, too, physically dominated her with his overwhelming strength – as indeed any young man in his prime who is ready to abuse the gift of muscular power can physically dominate a woman – she found, perhaps oddly, more easy to live with; indeed she had discovered in that a mocking weapon to use against him. She knew well, of course, what her taunting did to him, understood better than most the risks she ran in challenging him, but it seemed that she could not stop. When, unable to believe her rejection of him he had used that strength of his to force her, she had lain helpless beneath him and laughed at him. She had spat her scorn, hissed her contempt of his manhood; and as he had thrashed her for it, defiantly mocking she had laughed still, flinging his pride in his face. 'You're a coward, Jackie Pilgrim! Half a man! And stupid! You're like a stupid, brutal kid that breaks the things he can't understand!' And now, still, many a long month later those words and the others she had spat through bloody lips lay between them, a fierce, necessary defiance and an ever-present danger. She turned her head a little now, addressing Josie, not giving an inch to the man who towered so threateningly above her. 'Aren't yer glad y'er a girl, Jose? I mean, all that brute force an' ignorance must be bloody 'ard ter live with, wouldn't yer say? I could almost feel sorry fer the brute.' She was aware of the strong, brandy smell of his breath, the darkening of his sunbrowned face in which the cornflower eyes were such a contrast and a strange beauty.

'Sally – please – come away –'

He reached for her. And as he did so a small tornado hit him, sending him staggering, sharp teeth burying themselves into his thigh as, like a terrier attacking a lion, Toby flung himself to the defence of the only person in his young life who had ever shown him kindness.

Jackie yelped, and tried to shake the child off. Toby clung tenaciously. The young man swept a huge hand down, fastened on to the boy's collar and twisted. Choking and coughing Toby held on. Then Jackie jerked hard, and the boy dangled helpless in the air, arms and legs flailing, small face scarlet and distorted with rage, fear and lack of air.

'Put 'im down,' Sally said. She stood tense as an animal about to attack, dangerous as a tigress whose young is endangered.

'I'll kill the little devil. Do everyone a favour.'

'*Put 'im down!*'

For a moment they stood so, glaring at each other, the boy dangling between them. Then the weight of the struggling child proved too much for the threadbare material of his jacket and with a sharp sound it gave way, leaving Jackie with a handful of all but rotten material and Toby a small, snivelling heap upon the ground. But in Toby, a child of the streets and back alleys of London's slumlands, self-preservation was paramount always and could be paralysed neither by fear nor by surprise. He moved like a small rodent; in a flash he was behind Sally, the big hand that snapped out to catch him missing by a hair's breadth.

'Kids now?' Sally asked, tartly scornful, one hand holding the child to her.

They were attracting attention; sidelong glances, the turn of interested heads.

Jackie took a deep breath, and the brandy fumes settled a little in his brain. How did she do it, this skin-and-bone know-nothing little cow? How did she manage to rile him so, to make him lose control – to make him, on occasion, he suspected look a fool? What he'd ever seen in her he'd never know; and what he'd ever done to earn the contempt and hostility he always saw in those odd, narrow, green-flecked eyes he'd never understand either. He hadn't treated her any differently than he'd treated any other woman; they liked it, didn't they? They certainly queued up for it. And whether she liked it or whether she didn't she'd been in there with the others, queuing too, by God. The thought made him feel better. In the distance he saw an ivory parasol, bobbing amongst the flowered hats, the flat caps, the boaters and the bonnets. That made him feel better too. A real lady that one. A fancy piece if ever there was one. And throwing herself at him like any tuppenny street girl. Sure – who said Jackie Pilgrim wasn't as good as the rest of them? He'd show them, he would – and Miss Sally bloody Smith along with them. He straightened his cap. Brushed his coat. Turned away without a word.

The two girls watched him go. Josie shook her head. 'You'll get your come uppance one day from that one if you aren't careful,' she said.

Sally was trembling a little, as if a chill wind had suddenly cooled her sunwarmed skin. Her grin was brash. 'No chance. Take more than 'is nibs ter get me. Come on, yer little tyke,' she hauled the child from behind her, cuffed him lightly, 'let's go an' find the bleedin' roundabout, shall we? Though what I'm doin' spendin' pennies on that when you've just ruined yer only coat I don't know.'

II

Charlotte watched the fire-eater, a paunchy, middle-aged man dressed in incongruous leopardskin, with wide eyes, impressed as a child. 'How does he do that? How doesn't he burn himself?'

Wilfred, standing beside her and agonizing as to whether to take the cool smooth arm that was so tantalizingly close, shook his head. 'I don't know.'

'It isn't real fire,' practical Cissy said. 'It can't be.'

'Well, it looks real enough.' Charlotte moved, irritably, 'Wilfred, for heaven's sake, either take my arm or don't – but don't tickle!'

'I'm sorry.'

'I thought everyone was thirsty?' Peter had long since lost interest in the fire-eater. The refreshment booth was close and his throat was parched. 'Who's for a glass of cider?'

'Lemonade will do nicely, thank you,' Hannah said in gently pleasant, sisterly warning.

'Oh come on – a glass of cider won't do anyone any harm.' Wrangling amiably they led the way, Cissy and Ralph behind them, towards the gaily striped booth. As Charlotte turned to follow them she was prevented by the pressure of Wilfred's hand on her arm.

'Charlotte?'

She smiled at him, vaguely. 'Yes?'

'Will you – shall you be coming home with us this evening? Peter's coming. And the Battys are invited. We thought perhaps – a musical evening? And – well – that wouldn't be the same without you, you know. You play the piano far better than Mary Batty, and you have such a very pretty singing voice.'

Torn between gratification at his flattery and a quite unjust but urgent desire to extricate her arm from his chill and slightly damp clasp, Charlotte simply looked elsewhere. 'Oh look, a juggler.' A lithe young man balancing spinning plates upon chin and forehead was tossing a dozen shining coloured balls into the air, his hands moving faster than the eye could follow. 'Oh – isn't that clever?'

'Will you?' Wilfred was being, for him, unusually persistent. Normally the mere suspicion of a frown, the tiniest hint of disinterest on her part shut him up for a good half hour. She sighed exasperatedly. In Wilfred his sister's vivid colouring had been toned from fire and cream to sand and milk, as her bright and practical personality had become in her younger brother an odd and excessively irritating mixture of assertiveness and self-conscious diffidence – each of these traits, it seemed to an unimpressed Charlotte, invariably showing themselves, as now, at precisely the wrong moment.

'I really don't know,' she said. 'It's awfully hot. And it's been a very long day.' Could she stand an evening of sheep's eyes from Wilfred, watched approvingly by his doting mother, of the noisy, competitive Battys, who would argue – with each other and with anyone else who cared to oblige – all night, of Cissy – dear Cissy, truly her best friend – so bright, so contented, so distressingly *certain* – so lacking in romance? On the other hand, could she stand the alternative? Ben, Hannah and Ralph at one of their interminable meetings. Doctor Will, bless him, puffing away at his pipe behind his open paper, or poring over some obscure medical journal – oh, Lord! what a choice! 'I really don't know,' she said again.

'Well, I wouldn't dream of trying to make you do something you didn't want to, of course,' poor Wilfred said very stiffly.

'Oh, Wilf, don't be so *stuffy*! I said I didn't know – '

'You said it as if you didn't want to come,' he said, his pale, sandy-fringed eyes obstinately hurt.

She pulled her arm away from his, flouncing a little.

'For heaven's sake don't be such an idiot. You make such an *issue* of everything. I tell you I'm tired, that's all, and it's really very hot.'

'So you don't want to come?'

'I didn't say that.'

'As good as, it seems to me.'

'Charlotte? Wilfred? Come along, do,' Cissy called. The others had seated themselves by the refreshment booth, where chairs and tables had been set in the meagre shade of the single very small tree the wasteland could boast.

In a difficult silence that neither would be the first to breach they joined their companions. Charlotte, fanning herself theatrically, sank with grace amidst a pretty drift of ivory and blue into a chair between Cissy and Peter, leaving Wilfred to stand awkwardly for a moment or two behind her, turning his narrow-brimmed bowler in his hands, before he took himself with bad grace to the other side of the table where a couple of chairs stood empty. In silence he sat, ramrod straight, his pale, abundantly freckled face gloomy.

'Right,' Peter spun a gleaming coin into the air and caught it deftly. 'My treat. Cider all round, right?'

'Lemonade, thank you,' Hannah said firmly.

He shrugged. 'Charlotte?'

Charlotte noted with exasperation the expression upon Wilfred's face, an awkward combination of injury and sanctimonious disapproval. She smiled brightly at Peter. 'Cider would be lovely, thank you.' As she spoke a fiddle began to play, wildly gay, an infectious call to dance. Charlotte turned her head, tapping her foot and swaying a little to the gipsy rhythms. A child, fair haired and dirty faced fled laughing through the crowds, tripping over feet, treading on trailing skirts. Behind him came the girl Charlotte had seen in the soup kitchen, the girl she remembered was called Sally. 'Come *back* 'ere, yer little devil! I'll 'ave yer guts fer garters, see if I don't!'

The child cast a mischief-filled glance over his shoulder and dived back into the crowds like a rabbit into a hole.

'Here we are – cider, cool as can be.'

Charlotte gulped the sparkling amber drink. It certainly was good; cool and tart and wonderfully refreshing. She drank again.

'That's the girl,' Peter was regarding her with benign surprise; behind him Wilfred scowled.

'Have another?' Peter asked, grinning.

Hannah lifted an eyebrow.

'Yes,' Charlotte said. 'I'd love one. Thank you.' It might not be champagne. It might not be the subtle brews of the east. But at least it wasn't boring lemonade. Her spirits lifted a little as the second glass of cider bubbled on her tongue. Wilfred was watching her moodily, his pale eyes unblinking, his lemonade untouched. She turned ostentatiously in her chair, putting her back to him. Really, he was like a child, a small boy refused a treat –

The fiddler came closer, drawing the crowds. A girl in a brilliant red dress was walking beside him, a tambourine in her hands which she tapped and shook as she moved, arrogantly lovely, along the path that opened before her. Every now and again she took a few, dancing steps. Not far from where Charlotte sat they stopped. The fiddler's bow flashed, the girl lifted long, graceful arms above her head, the tambourine rattling musically, enticingly. A few people clapped. The girl began to move, slowly at first and then faster, wheeling and dipping, spinning and turning to the wild music, slim legs flashing in the swirl of her flounced crimson skirts. Her skin was smooth and dark as amber silk, her hair raven black; her body, slim and strong-looking, curved voluptuously in the dress which fitted to her hips like a second skin. In the last rays of the sinking sun she whirled and stamped, arrogant, beautiful, exciting.

Free. Free as a bird lifting upon the summer air. As a jungle cat flitting through dangerous shadows.

Unexpectedly Charlotte felt a stab of an all-too-familiar feeling; the vague fretting of discontent, the yearning for something – anything! – to happen beyond the everyday humdrum safety of her life. Oh, Lord! Nothing exciting – but nothing! – was ever going to happen to her, she knew it. She would grow old if not with Wilfred then with someone like him – safe, secure, respectable. She would live in a safe, secure and respectable house with her safe, secure and respectable children and her safe, secure and respectable friends –

Behind her she could hear the others talking. Cissy and Peter were laughing. She could positively feel Wilfred's hurt eyes boring into her back. She tossed back the last of her cider, stood up – and staggered very slightly as for an alarming and rather amusing second the world tilted a little around her. She suppressed a sudden silly desire to giggle. 'I shan't be a moment.'

'Where are you going?' It was Hannah, surprised.

'I'm –' Where was she going? Anywhere. Just anywhere away from them all for a moment, '– just over to the ribbon stall. I need some lemon silk for my new hat. I shan't be long.'

Hannah set aside her lemonade. 'I'll come with you.'

'No! No – truly, there's no need. Finish your drink. It's only over there – look – just a little way. I shall be perfectly safe alone.' And that at least was true. It was well understood that, whilst daylight lasted at least, these young people associated with Doctor Will Patten need fear no harm in these rough and crowded streets. All were known, all were protected; though once night fell with the rats creeping from their sewers and the human vermin slinking from their holes it was a different story. Then, like all sensible people they remained within doors or walked protected and in pairs. Except Doctor Will and Ben. No one would hurt the one and not many cared to challenge the other.

Hannah sank back on to her chair. Her hair, inevitably,

had begun to slide untidily from its pins and clung uncomfortably to her neck; the sensible brown dress she wore seemed to trap the heat and intensify it. 'Well, all right. But don't be long, dear, for we shall have to be going soon.'

Charlotte strolled to the ribbon stall, revelling even in this small freedom. A young man watched her, open admiration written upon his face. Studiedly she ignored him. An older man, his wife upon his arm, both dressed in Sunday best despite the heat tipped a civil cap to her. 'Afternoon, Miss.' She smiled gracefully, nodding her head. At the stall, which was a tumble of brightly coloured silk and satin ribbons, she took her time in choosing, lifting the brilliant, shining streamers in her small, nicely shaped hands, holding them to the evening light, knowing well the pretty picture she presented to the passing world. Scarlet and blue, green and yellow, gleaming silver and soft cream –

'Buy a ribbon, pretty Miss – farthin' a yard the narrow, 'a'penny the broad. A ribbon for your pretty hair?'

She selected some wide lemon satin for her hat and a narrow crimson silk for her hair simply because it reminded her of the dress the dancing girl wore. She watched the old woman wind and wrap it with dark, gnarled hands that moved surprisingly deftly. 'Thank you.'

She took her time in making her way back to the others. The girl was still dancing, the crowd around her several deep. Charlotte paused for a moment to watch. The wild tempo had died, the tambourine had been laid aside. Clicking long fingers in a hypnotically complicated rhythm the girl moved slowly and with insolent grace around the circle of onlookers, flaunting her full, lovely body, her face disdainful. The notes of the fiddle hung on the hot evening air, haunting and beautiful, rousing again in Charlotte that strange, almost sensual feeling of restiveness, of nameless and disturbing longing. The tempo quickened. The girl stamped rhythmically, moving still about the circle. Then she stopped and, back arched, fingers clicking rapidly above her head, she turned slowly, displaying herself, knowing her own beauty, revelling in its attraction. The faintest glimmer of a smile lifted the corner of lips as red as the dress she wore – surely, Charlotte found herself wondering, not naturally so? – and an answering, appreciative grin lit the handsome face of the young man who was quite evidently the amused recipient of her wayward attentions, his sapphire eyes agleam. Despite all she could do to prevent herself, Charlotte found herself watching him with the same avidity with which those about her watched the dancing girl. How brown and smooth was his skin, how wide and strong his shoulders; and how those untidy blue-black curls absorbed the evening light, transmuting it to shining darkness – for a long moment she watched him openly, studying the quite unconscious grace of his body, the cocky and very conscious set of his handsome head. The light and colour around her blurred a little, leaving the young man framed, vivid and beautiful, unaware of her eyes, alone. She blinked a little, for the first time suspecting that perhaps she had drunk Peter's cider just a little too quickly. Truly her head felt a little less than clear. Reluctantly she gathered her wits and her attention about her and turned to where she could see lanky Ralph's head above the crowds, short-sighted bespectacled eyes peering into the lamplit dusk, obviously looking for her.

As she joined him and Hannah she glanced around, surprised. 'Where are the others?'

'Cissy insisted on a visit to the fortune teller. Then they're going on home to supper. Peter's gone with them.'

She stared at her brother. 'They've – gone without me?'

His mild eyes blinked surprise behind the wire-rimmed glasses. 'Why, yes. Wilfred said that you'd told him you were too tired and wanted to come home with us.'

Temper rose, not cooled by the knowledge that it was unjustified. Charlotte all but stamped her foot. 'Well of all the –! I said no such thing!'

'Well, I must say I was a little surprised.' Ralph glanced vaguely about him as if hoping to conjure the other young people magically from the thinning crowd. 'They've not been gone long. Perhaps we can find them?'

Charlotte hesitated. She did not want to go to the Barnes's. But neither did she want to spend a Saturday evening in gentle and exasperatingly improving conversation with Doctor Will.

'Look – isn't that them?' Ralph pointed.

By the gaily decked fortune teller's tent a bright red head bobbed, glinting in lantern-light.

Charlotte stood on tiptoe. 'Oh of course. I'll go and catch them up. Oh, it's all right –', she put a detaining hand on her brother's arm as he made to accompany her, 'you and Hannah go off to your meeting. I'll be perfectly all right. I'll come home with Peter.'

'It is getting a little late.' Hannah consulted the watch that was pinned to her sensible brown lapel.

Charlotte pecked an affectionate kiss at Ralph's pale cheek, dropped another on Hannah's smooth one, 'I'll see you later. I'll have to run, or I'll miss them.'

She slipped through the crowds towards the fortune teller's tent. The sun had set. Mothers were gathering tired children. Little girls with babies fast asleep in arms that looked too frail to carry the weight and with younger brothers and sisters trailing wearily at their skirts were shepherding their charges home, whilst bands of brash and noisy young men in cloth caps and Saturday neckerchiefs and groups of brightly dressed giggling girls swaggered and promenaded for each other, the happy prospect of a long warm summer's evening lifting voices and lighting smiles. The hurdy-gurdy man crossed her path. She slipped around him, lost her sense of direction for a moment and then saw, a little way ahead, Cissy's fiery curls, free of the straw boater she usually wore. She pushed forward. 'Cissy!' then stopped, nonplussed, as an unknown girl turned enquiringly. 'Oh – I'm sorry – I thought you were someone else!'

The girl smiled, nodded her carrot head and turned back to her companions.

Blast it! Now what? Where on earth were they? Who would have thought there could have been two heads in the *world* that colour, let alone within a few yards of each other! She stood on tiptoe, looking around her. If she did not find them then it was back to the Bear to an evening with Doctor Will and his pipe, willy-nilly, for she had no money left to take her to the Barnes's by omnibus, and it was much too far to walk –

'Sure – is it me imagination, or is the lovely lady lookin' ever so slightly lost?'

The voice, the beguiling accent, the closeness of him so unexpectedly took her breath from her completely. She looked up. A dazzling smile and a sapphire gleam of eyes quickened her heart-beat absurdly. 'I – yes – as a matter of fact I seem to have lost my friends.'

He grinned engagingly. 'That was a mite careless, wasn't it?'

She laughed nervously. 'Yes. I suppose it was.' She lifted her chin, her pulse quickening. He was looking down at her with an appreciative, gracelessly speculative smile that was the most exciting thing she had ever encountered. There was neither respect nor a trace of proper deference in his manner. He smelled strongly of brandy and tobacco and of something else she could not identify, something male and frightening and utterly fascinating. He had no business talking to her. They both knew it. And she had no business listening. She should walk away. Now. This moment. She should, firmly and courteously, put him in his place and leave.

'I thought I saw them,' she said foolishly, the first thing that came into her head, 'but it was someone else.'

Obligingly he smiled. 'The redhead and the two young fellers, was it?'

'Yes.'

'Well, sure, I saw them meself just a minute or two ago. At this very spot.' He was still watching her with a warmth in those spectacular eyes that was doing purely dreadful things to the pit of her stomach. 'Will we look for them for you?'

Alarm bells rang loudly in her befuddled brain. This was impossible. She should not – she *should not*! – be seen here talking to this unknown and outrageously handsome young man like any shopgirl with her fancy lad. 'I – thank you, but – I think I must have missed them –'

'Nonsense. Come. We'll find them.' Smiling, he took her arm, and by his touch effortlessly and apparently unknowingly destroyed the last of her precarious hold upon herself and upon her wayward emotions. She allowed him to draw her back into the crowd, leaned to him as he steered her through, his hand warm and hard upon her arm, his spare, broad frame protecting her. There was no sign of Hannah or of Ralph; they had obviously assumed her to be safe with the others and had left for home. The thought sang suddenly in her heart like a freed bird; for a moment, just for a moment, she was free. For this short space of time she could do as she pleased. Not for long, of course – the mistake would be discovered, an anxious search launched. But for this little while it could surely do no harm to take pleasure in this small adventure, to accept and enjoy the excitement that the warmth and strength of his grip on her arm afforded her, to encourage, just a little, that flattering, frightening look in his wonderful eyes?

It somehow came as no surprise at all to find herself skilfully manoeuvred into a quiet, shadowed space between two gaily painted gipsy wagons, away from the now swelling evening crowds and with no sign whatsoever of the friends for whom – ostensibly – they had been looking. For whom, she knew, they had not been looking at all in these last five minutes.

He leaned, smiling, against the side of the wagon, long legs crossed in front of him, eyes bright and appreciative on her face. 'Seems you were right. You have lost them.'

It was growing darker by the moment. The bright blossom of lanterns glimmered in the shadows across the fairground. Where they stood the wagons offered a false and intimate shelter.

'I – should go.' She had to force the words out. The look in his eyes had stained her face to scarlet. But she could neither move nor look away from him.

Jackie Pilgrim smiled, reached into his pocket, pulled out his flask. 'Why? Surely there's not such a very great hurry, is there? You'll come to no harm, I promise you. I'll see you meself to your doorstep, an' that's a promise. No one'll hurt you while you're with Jackie Pilgrim.' He was pleasantly drunk, and he knew it. The brandy he had steadily consumed throughout the afternoon had brought, as it always did, a shining confidence, an utter, happy satisfaction with himself and with life and all its varied, recklessly taken pleasures. And now this silly, pretty girl with her fluffy hair and clean, smooth skin, her dainty sprigged cotton that showed neither patch nor stain, was standing looking at him as at her hope of heaven. Jesus, Mary and Joseph he'd have to be mad to pass up this chance. And wouldn't the lads at the Prospect give their eye teeth to be Jackie Pilgrim at this moment? Wouldn't they always? And God rot that stupid Smith bitch with her ugly face and scornful eyes. What did she know? Jealous – that was what it was – jealous as a green-eyed cat. And with good cause – perfectly steadily, his eyes still warm and intimate on Charlotte Bedford's pointed, kitten's face, he held out the flask. 'Will you take a wee drop? 'Tis good for the health. Good,' he smiled a little, 'for the heart, so they say.' His voice was softly persuasive.

She bit her lip. Shook her head.

The smile widened, wolfish as the gipsy fighter's as he had stepped in to Joey's destruction. 'Aw, come on now – it won't harm you, I promise.' He put the flask into her small hand, covered it with his large strong one, curling her fingers about the smooth, warm metal, guiding it gently to her lips, 'Just a wee drop. A wee drop of Jackie's brandy –'

III

Sally had had enough. Full darkness had fallen an hour ago, Josie had gone off to cook supper for her father and brothers, her plea to have Sally and Toby join them pleasantly but very firmly rejected. Sally Smith hadn't yet fallen so low that she could bring herself to cadge a favour from friends that she well knew she would not be able to return. She smiled a little grimly to herself. Not yet, anyway. She tousled Toby's dirty curls. 'Come on, Toby Jug – time for home.'

'O – oh!' He caught her hand, swinging on it like a monkey. 'Can't we stay? Oh Sal – go on! Just a little while?' The child's blue eyes were huge and shadowed with tiredness, yet still bright with the Godless mischief that was her bane and her joy. A year ago she had found him – caught him, rather, an urchin not above four or five with his small fingers in her purse whilst those merry eyes beguiled her. A changeling. An imp of mischief. A ray of sunshine in a life that had not lately seen too much of warmth or of light. Someone to care for – a small, dependent being whose devotion to her more than compensated for the need to work for two. She grinned now, catching his ear none too gently with her free hand. 'No. Home I said an' home it is. I thought you wanted a sausage?'

He cocked his head, his small face wicked. 'I'd rather have another go on the merry-go-round.'

'Aren't you hungry?' Sally's own stomach was rumbling, uncomfortably empty. He shrugged, suddenly avoiding her eyes. With a quick, unexpected movement Sally caught his chin and turned the small, dirty face to the light of a near-by lantern. He struggled for a moment, then subsided, his expression the embodiment of innocence. On one cheek and around his mouth were tell-tale smears. 'What you bin eatin'?' Sally's voice was suddenly, dangerously quiet, her grip on his chin fierce.

He said nothing. Smiled, treacherously trustful, artfully affectionate.

'Tobe!' The word rang with warning.

'Toffee apple,' he said.

With a sharp, exasperated exclamation she let go of him and straightened, half turning from him. He watched her warily, one small booted foot rubbing against the threadbare material of his trouser leg, his expression not quite as certain as it had been. Sally stood for a moment fighting a temper that was always touch-paper quick. 'You thieved it,' she said.

He shrugged.

She swung on him, caught him by the shoulders, shaking him roughly. 'You bloody thieved it! Didn't you?'

'Yes.'

'Tobe, 'ow many *times* must I tell you? What do I 'ave ter do ter stop you? You know what they'll do if they catch you? Do yer?'

'Yes,' he said again, subdued not, she knew in despair, by any regret at wrongdoing nor any understanding of the peril in which he put himself, but because he had been discovered and had brought her wrath upon his curly head. He tried a small, tentative smile, unable to believe that she could remain angry with him for long.

She hunkered down beside him on the pavement, holding his hands, careless of her skirts in the dust, her expression grave. 'Toby – listen to me. You won't get the things you want by thieving. Believe me, I've tried it. It isn't worth it. It'll bring nothin' but trouble – to you, an' to me. To me, Tobe. Is that what you want?'

He shook his head. Sudden, easy tears brimmed in the tired, forget-me-not eyes.

Sally tried for a moment longer, unsuccessfully, to hold on to her anger; then, with a quick, rough movement she pulled the child to her, hugging him fiercely. His thin arms wound about her neck and he clung like a limpet, his face buried in her bony shoulder. 'It'll be all right,' she said, 'I'll get work soon, you'll see. An' then, little old Toby Jug, you can 'ave as many toffee apples as you like. But – please! – stop pinchin' things. You worry me sick!'

'I'm sorry,' his voice was a whisper, 'I won't do it again.'

She put him from her, studying the small, woebegone face with clear doubt in her eyes. 'You promise?'

'I promise.' Anything. Anything to bring the warm smile back to those narrow eyes, to iron out the fierce lines of displeasure and anxiety that disfigured what to Toby was the loveliest and most loved face in the world.

She stood, and took his hand in her own narrow, hard one. 'Right. We'll forget about it then. Let's go an' get that sausage.'

His elfin smile was like sunshine after rain. He opened his mouth – and 'No,' she said severely and with her laughter firmly repressed, 'a sausage it is. No more merry-go-rounds for you old son! You'll bring that toffee apple straight back up – an' serve you right!'

They walked together from the bright and noisy fairground into the shadowed, quiet streets, the sounds of voices and of the hurdy-gurdy dying slowly behind them. A gas lamp glimmered in an alley that scuttled with scavenging life. Neither Sally nor Toby noticed – as they did not notice the foetid smells that hung heavily upon the warm air, the bundle of rags that stirred and stilled in a dark doorway as they passed, the echoes of domestic battle that rang suddenly from a window above their heads. This was warp and weft of their lives, a fabric threadbare and stained with which they were so familiar that they barely looked at it any more. This was home, and these things were an unremarkable part of it, as were the narrow, crowded houses, the scurrying rats, the stench of cheap gin, the filth of alleys too narrow to be cleaned, the summer spread of disease from hovel to hovel and the winter cold that could kill just as surely.

Toby's feet were starting to drag a little. Sally put an arm about the child's shoulders. 'Tired?'

He nodded.

'Right. 'Ere we go. Ups-a-daisy.' She leaned down and swung his light weight easily on to her hip. He smiled a little – that sweet smile that first had enslaved her – and laid his head upon her meagrely fleshed shoulder. She strode on, adjusting her long stride to the child's weight. They passed a public house, lamplight gleaming across the dirty pavement, raucous noise and a drifting cloud of foul-smelling smoke issuing from the open windows. A small knot of children played in the street outside; one of their number slept peacefully in the gutter, head pillowed upon a thin arm. An urchin stuck out a foot as she passed, trying to trip her up, then dodged laughing out of the way of her hand as she reached to clip his ear. She rounded a corner. ''Ere we are.'

The windows of the pie and mash shop, shut tight despite the weather, were steamed up, the shop itself brightly lit and crowded. The appetizing smell brought a sudden uncontrollable flood of water to her mouth. How long had it been since she had eaten properly?

'Evenin', Sal.'

'Evenin', Bert. Give the kid a penn'orth of sausage, would yer?'

The precious penny was passed across the counter. Toby took the sausage, dripping fat and almost too hot to hold. Sally grinned. 'Give us a bite, eh? I 'aven't 'ad no toffee apple!' He held it out to her and she bit into it, grease running down her chin and dripping on to the bodice of her dress. God, it was good! And, God, she was hungry! 'Get it down yer,' she said brusquely, lifting him back on to her hip, the luscious-smelling sausage inches from her face, 'it'll put some 'air on yer chest.'

Not far from the pie and mash shop they turned into a street, poor and ill lit, off the main thoroughfare. No lamps here – just the fitful light from a few uncurtained windows and opened doors that let straight out on to the cobbled lane. A cat yowled at her feet. Someone cursed harshly, and a woman's voice answered with shrill laughter. With the smell of Toby's sausage tantalizing her empty belly she turned into a narrow alley that ran between two high tenement buildings, stopping at an open doorway through which could be seen a dimly lit stairway. 'Right. I'm not carryin' yer up them stairs, I'll tell yer that fer nothin'. You'll 'ave ter walk.' She swung him neatly on to his feet. The sausage had gone. Savouring the very last taste, he licked dirty fingers. 'Come on,' she tucked his greasy hand into hers and began to climb the stairs. This was home – a room in the attic of a rotting house that held more than two score of souls in a lesser or greater degree of comfort depending on how far up this rickety staircase you climbed. The first two floors were not too bad – indeed to Sally they often seemed the height of luxury; the rooms were quite big and the water from the leaking roof did not reach so far. Even better the toilet, which had the luxury of a door, more often than not worked and was shared only by half a dozen rooms. The single lavatory that served the squalid and overcrowded upstairs floors neither flushed with any degree of regularity nor, since the winter before when someone had removed the door for firewood, did it offer any hope of privacy. Sally's attic room was freezing in the winter and a stifling oven in the summer. The draughty window had been nailed shut, and the chimney that served the tiny grate had been blocked up – which was just as well since she could rarely if ever afford coal. But neither she nor Toby complained. It was a roof, a refuge, and both knew well what it was to live without such luxury. That they could not, and would probably never be able to, afford a downstairs room of the kind in which Jackie Pilgrim lived in comparative affluence concerned them not at all. The strong in this world of theirs took the best, and a girl and a child alone took what was left and were grateful. Sally, slowing her steps to the child's weary legs, found herself suddenly thinking of Josie and her family: of the small, clean house in Bolton Terrace with its scoured doorstep and polished knocker; of the decent, well-darned clothes, the plain, wholesome, plentiful food. She was a fool for having refused the offer of a good meal. For what? Her pride? The corner of her mouth pulled ruefully down as the child stumbled and she caught him quickly. What a pity you couldn't eat pride – or wear it on your back. She stopped. They had reached the first landing and Toby was hanging back. Jackie Pilgrim's door stood a little ajar. And from behind it came the unmistakable sounds of violence.

'No!' It was a girl's voice, sobbing and distraught, '*Please*! No – not again!' There was a crash, and then another. The girl shrieked.

'Stupid little bitch. Come back here –' Jackie's voice was slurred with temper and with drink.

Sally gripped Toby's hand, her mouth tight. Irish savage! She hauled the frightened child towards the stairs, intent upon getting clear of danger as quickly as possible.

'*No*! Let *go* of me! Let *go*!'

Sally and Toby were level with the door when it flew open, sending light across the landing, catching them in its beam like rabbits in a trap. Jackie's huge, threatening, naked frame loomed in the doorway. Behind him, her small face ugly with tears and terror, her pretty clothes in ribbons, her fair hair cascading wildly about her shoulders was the girl that Sally had seen at the fair, the girl from the soup kitchen, the girl from another world whose appearance here and in such a condition was so utterly shocking, so totally unbelievable that Sally, instead of running for the stairs as she had intended, stopped, staring, eyes and mouth open. And in that moment Charlotte saw her. 'Oh – please! help me!' She was crying uncontrollably.

Sally's eyes moved from the girl to the swaying Jackie. 'Bleedin' 'ell,' she said, absurdly calmly, 'you gone ravin' mad?'

He moved threateningly. 'Bugger off. This is none of your business.'

'Too true it's not.' Every line of Sally's face had tightened. Somewhere inside her a bright and terrible flame flickered, flared and then burned steadily, consuming fear.

Charlotte, sobbing like a distraught child, had backed away, her hands to her mouth. Blood smeared her torn skirt.

Very carefully Sally drew Toby behind her, reaching for him behind her back, transferring him from hand to hand so that, guarded and protected by her body he passed the open door and stood at the foot of the next flight of stairs. She could feel the trembling of his small frame through his clutching fingers. Toby had felt the brunt of Jackie's temper too often before. Sally did not look at him. 'Get upstairs, Tobe,' she said quietly, 'an' shove the big chest up against the door. Don't open it till you 'ear me come. Go.'

The child's hand clung for a moment longer to hers. She shook it free, saw from the corner of her eye the flash of his movement as he fled up the stairs.

Jackie leaned, clearly and dangerously drunk, supporting himself on the door frame with an arm like the branch of a small oak. 'Piss off, Sally.' His bright, beautiful eyes were infinitely hard, infinitely menacing, his handsome face flushed with unsightly colour. 'Like I said. This is none of your business.'

Charlotte's sobs had quieted a little. She stood now, her brimming eyes fixed upon Sally as if upon an avenging guardian angel, pleading and desperate. Every sensible fibre of Sally's being told her to get out of this while she had a whole skin. She knew — who better? — the depths of violence to which Jackie could sink if his will were thwarted, his authority challenged. But still the flame burned, steady, bright and all-consuming.

'Your problem', she said softly and very clearly, directly into that suffused face, 'is you got balls instead of brains.' Her eyes flicked to Charlotte and away, a swift, barely readable message.

He pushed himself away from the door, lowering his head like a bull preparing to charge. Charlotte, behind him, moved a little, her eyes fixed fearfully upon Jackie's long, naked back.

'What kind of trouble do yer think you've landed yerself in this time?' She had to keep him occupied, to keep his attention away from the moving girl. She fought the blaze of hatred and temper, that once allowed to flame unchecked would bring her down to his level and defeat her in violence. Her voice was acid, edged lightly with scorn. 'If you *ave* got any brains – which I doubt – why don't yer try usin' them for a change?' She allowed her eyes to flick towards Charlotte, who was still moving very slowly towards the open doorway. 'You've picked the wrong one there, Jackie lad. The brandy finally addled yer lovely Irish wits, yer realize that? This isn't any Commercial Road street-walker. This is a young lady. With friends. An' money. An' influence. All the things the likes of you an' me some'ow manage ter live without. Think about it, Jackie –'

He blinked. Charlotte moved again, closer to the door, closer to freedom, but afraid to make that final dash that would bring her within reach of his brutal hands. A small white breast, viciously scratched, was all but exposed by a rent in her dress, a bruise showed in purple violence upon her cheekbone. She was still crying, though almost silently, a helpless, heedless flow of tears that seemed as if it might never stop.

75

'God 'elp a lad 'oo asn't the sense ter stick to 'is own,' Sally said softly. 'They'll bloody crucify yer, Jackie – think, man.'

He swayed again, the vast quantity of alcohol he had consumed that day finally taking its toll. The atmosphere was stifling. Charlotte stared at the taut, tough girl on the other side of the door. If she could just get to her –

'She asked for it,' he said sullenly, 'begged for it. Be God – yer must ha' seen it for yerself?'

Sally lifted a shoulder, summoning up a small, derisive smile. ''Oo's goin' ter believe that? The examinin' magistrate? I should cocoa.' Her eyes still firm on Jackie's, she moved a little to the side, extending a courageous, encouraging hand to the girl who trembled a few yards from comparative safety. 'Yer want ter tell 'em that at Bow Street while she grizzles into 'er lace 'ankie?' She looked then at last directly at Charlotte, jerked her head fiercely and impatiently. With a sob Charlotte flung herself past Jackie and through the door. Jackie's half-hearted attempt to stop her was no more than a gesture. He was watching Sally, frowning ferociously.

Charlotte flung herself upon Sally, clinging, crying noisily. Sally staggered under the onslaught, righted herself, put a protective arm about the slim, shaking, firm-fleshed shoulders. Oddly, even at such extremes, she was aware of the fresh cleanliness of the other girl, the clear, sweet fragrance. The passage was narrow, the drunken, violent young giant a step away. She lifted her chin. 'Well?' she challenged. 'What yer goin' ter do about it? Take both of us?'

'I'll break your back,' he said with clear, pure hatred.

'P'raps. P'raps not. I'm takin' 'er 'ome.'

He was breathing heavily, the sculptured muscles of his broad chest lifting rhythmically.

''Ave a grain o' sense, Jackie,' she said softly. 'You do more 'arm an' you'll swing for it this time. Yer backed the wrong filly. Cut yer losses while yer can.'

Charlotte was fighting for breath and composure. 'I won't say anything. I swear it!' The words fell over each other, 'Just let me go. *Please* – let me go. I won't tell anyone. I promise I won't –'

There was a long moment of aggressive silence. Then, with no further word but with a final savage glance at Sally that boded ill for their next encounter, Jackie stepped back and slammed the door in their faces. Both girls stood for a moment, each in her own way coping with a hammering heart, a sweat of fear.

'Right,' Sally said at last calmly, 'we'd best get you 'ome.'

Charlotte began to stammer thanks, but in the face of the other girl's apparent indifference fell to miserable silence.

'Yer live at Doctor Will's place, don't yer? The old Bear?'

'Y-yes.'

They stepped out into the narrow alley. Sally peered at the other girl in the darkness, 'Can yer get yerself 'ome?'

Charlotte stood, beaten, bruised, brimful of tears and shook her head. 'I – I don't know where I am.'

'It's only up the street –' Sally stopped. In the darkest recess of her mind Jackie Pilgrim heaved aside a rickety door, a worm-ridden, empty chest-of-drawers and confronted a small, terrified child. 'Oh, come on, then,' she said brusquely, 'I'll get yer back. But yer'll 'ave ter 'urry.'

Charlotte stumbled along beside this unlikely saviour, whose pace took account neither of distress nor of the dragging pain and soreness that was a dreadful reminder of what had happened to her. Rape. She had heard the word whispered, read it in forbidden writings beneath the sheets in dangerous candlelight. But this? This was filth. This was disgrace. This was the end of a life. The end of a dream. Who would take her now? Who would smile a dazzling, tender smile and lead her to a flower-decked altar knowing of this? Her body ached. The fiery pain between her legs made walking an agony. She wanted to die. Quite simply to crumple into the gutter and to die –

''Ere we are.' The long-legged girl beside her stopped. The building that once had been the Inn of the Dancing Bear rambled for half a street, a long, low, two-storeyed building with overhanging eaves, its fabric rotten as moth-eaten wool, its face that of an ancient crone, versed in the ways of the world and by no means beguiled by them.

Sally turned to face her. 'What you goin' ter do?'

Defeated, Charlotte sucked her lip.

Sally took her by the shoulders, a blaze of impatience and exasperation. 'What?'

'I –' Some semblance of reality was returning to her in the shade of the familiar building. The shock of what had happened had cleared her brain of the effects of the unaccustomed alcohol she had so recklessly drunk, but it had curdled in her stomach, bringing nausea. She looked up at the big, ramshackle house. Here was home. Here was safety; and in equal proportion, danger. She stood for a moment. A light burned in the surgery. Doctor Will, working late. Every other window was dark. Peter had not returned from the Barnes's. Ben, Hannah and Ralph were still setting the world to rights at their meeting. Incredibly, no one had apparently yet missed her. The faintest and most feeble gleam of hope entered her harrowed soul. 'I might be able to sneak in,' she said, suddenly and astoundingly composed. 'No one's back yet. And my room is at the back. It has its own staircase. This is a rather peculiar building you see.'

Sally's narrow, green-gleaming eyes flickered astonishment. The last thing she had expected to hear from this stupid little girl was anything remotely like sense. Trouble in the back streets of Poplar was always a word spelled in the tallest of letters. She had, against her nature and against her inclination, breached a code of behaviour tonight that one way or the other could only bring her to

grief, and she was heartily regretting it already. But still –
if kept private the grief would be short and painful at the
hands of a man whose brutality she knew and, with luck,
could cope with. Brought into the open the chancy
opinion of the close-knit community in which she lived
could come down heavily against her. In many minds if
Jackie should be brought to book by the law for tonight's
little episode the word to brand Sally Smith would be
'traitor'. And she had a life to live. She put out a hand.
Charlotte had begun to tremble violently, her teeth chattering, her body jerking convulsively. 'You all right?'

'If you could – just help me up the stairs?'

They walked into the darkness of the archway that led
to the old yard, where once stage coaches had come and
gone in a flurry of noisy and colourful activity. An
uncertain flight of steps led up to a gallery on the first
floor. 'Here.' Sally all but carried the slight, exhausted girl
through the door she indicated. Beyond it was a large,
pleasant room in which a lamp had been lit to await her
peaceful return. The light gleamed on rose silk and pale
satin. Comfortable chairs were set about a now empty
grate that was filled with fresh flowers in a great copper
pot. At one end of the room stood a testered bed that
seemed to Sally's dazzled and caustic eyes, remembering
the pallet that she shared with Toby, big enough to sleep
six. She stood for an awkward moment as the other girl
with a small sob of thankfulness sank into a deep
armchair, bowed her head into her hands. Gradually, very
gradually, the trembling eased. Charlotte lifted her head,
wrapping her arms about her body as if holding herself
against pain, against remembered fear, against brutal
invasion. She looked very frail and very frightened.

'I'd best be off,' Sally said shortly.

Charlotte, with some difficulty, focused her eyes upon
her. 'I – won't tell anyone,' she said, her voice soft and
stark with desperation, 'Please. Believe me. I won't cause
trouble. No one will know. I couldn't bear it. I'll tell them

– I missed Cissy – couldn't find the others – so I came home here alone. Ben and Hannah had left.. Doctor Will was working. I – fell.' She lifted a hand to her bruised face, 'I fell – in the darkness – down the stairs outside –'

'What about your dress? It's ruined. Won't someone notice?'

Charlotte shook her head, vaguely. 'Oh, no. I've plenty more. I'll hide it – throw it away – no one around here ever notices what anyone's wearing.'

A small, caustic smile lit Sally's face for a moment. 'That a fact?' She turned to the door.

Charlotte's head lifted sharply. Her face, already pale, drained to the shade of skimmed milk. 'You – you aren't going back there? To that – that dreadful man?'

Sally lifted an eloquent shoulder, her face expressionless.

'But – if you go back – what will he do to you?'

'What will 'e do to the kid if I don't?' The words were terse, the husky voice flat and hard.

Tears brimmed helplessly in Charlotte's eyes, ran with no check down her marked cheeks.

With no word and no gesture of farewell Sally left her, closing the door firmly behind her.

Chapter Three

I

More than once in the sultry month that followed that exhilarating, if in many eyes outrageous, demonstration in Cavendish Square against the detested Mr Asquith, Chancellor of the Exchequer in His Majesty's Government and avowed opponent of woman's suffrage, Hannah Patten, with the fervour of a zealot, wished herself in gaol. The crusade was on, and martyrs there already were, suffering bravely and defiantly for the cause, but to her regret she was not of their number. Quite obviously she had been too restrained; apparently the forcible removal of a bemused young policeman's helmet had not proved protest enough. She would do better next time. In the meantime, with the country's alarmed eyes focused at last upon them, with fervent protests in Parliament both for and against the women, with a debate in the press that raged from John O'Groats to Land's End, that aroused passion and prejudice, support and condemnation – in short that was making people *think* – there was plenty of work on hand for those still free to do it. In the House of Commons Mr Keir Hardie, respected leader of the infant Independent Labour Party which had had its own first political success earlier that year when in the General Election that had brought a Liberal landslide no less than twenty-nine Labour Candidates had been elected, was a champion indeed. Why, he demanded, in a free country such as Britain claimed to be, was it considered necessary to apply the letter of the law so severely that it became an offence for a deputation to approach a private house? Why too, if offence it were, should it be considered a crime heinous enough to warrant a two-month prison sentence? The women in Holloway were suffering for nothing but their desire to take advantage of what should be every citizen's right, to protest to the Government about injustice. And on street corners, in market squares, outside railway stations and in shopping arcades women stood on their chairs or on their soapboxes echoing him fiercely – and were in many cases as fiercely heckled by their audience. Battles raged in the correspondence columns of the newspapers, one man's – or woman's – heroine was another's 'female hooligan'. But at least, and at last, no one in their senses could any longer ignore the lifting of these women's voices, who had been protesting – and had been ignored – for so long.

'The vote is not, or should not be, about property, about profit and loss!' Hannah proclaimed sturdily from a rickety chair on the corner of Angel Street. 'It is, or it should be, about education for our children, health for our families, support for our aged and unemployed.'

'Get back to your kitchen sink, woman!'

'I can vote as well from there as can you from the dockside!'

'Ah!' the man pounced, eyes sharp, work-hardened finger jabbing the air. 'But I can't, can I, by God? Why in 'ell's name should women get the vote when most workin' men can't? Answer me that!'

'Universal suffrage will follow! It's bound to! But first we have to have equality under the system as it stands.'

'Equality to vote the bloody Tories back an' keep Labour out!'

'Don't throw me that old chestnut!' She turned, appealing to the crowd, her plain face lit with laughter. 'Wouldn't you think a good Poplar lad would have more sense than Henry Asquith?' And then, as they chuckled, she targeted a face in the crowd, a woman in her twenties, who had been listening intently, unsmiling, a shawl over her head, a baby in her arms. 'What do they think women are? Foolish dolls to vote as they are told by father or husband? Brainless idiots who can't make up their own minds about what's important and what isn't? Children whose *sons* are thought to know more than they do? What nonsense! We live in their world, we obey their laws, we pay their taxes, it is *our* world, they are *our* laws, *our* taxes. Why should we have no voice in the running of it, the framing of the laws, the spending of the revenue?' The young woman nodded vigorously.

'Why don't you try wearin' the trousers while you're about it?' called a young wit from the back of the crowd.

She found him, regarded him with interest. 'You mean the wearing of trousers improves the working of one's mind? Strange – I hadn't noticed it to be so.'

Hannah always came away from these small battles stimulated. A young woman of sense and courage, she was rarely intimidated, a warm and loyal personality she found the comradeship of the votes for women movement very much to her liking. And – passionately and with no reservations – she believed in her cause, and counted herself lucky to be in the position to fight for it. That her own menfolk were ready to support her was a happy bonus, and one, she knew, not enjoyed by all her comrades in arms. Her father, remarkable man that he was, had from the start treated her as the equal of her brothers; she had been educated as they had, had been encouraged to form and argue her own opinions, had never been shackled by the chains of convention with which so many nineteenth-century fathers still attempted to curb their twentieth-century daughters. Her older brother Ben, fierce champion of socialism, was himself a strong advocate of universal suffrage – and if he were not so certain as she that extending to privileged women the ability to vote now enjoyed by equally privileged men would automatically lead to the democratic, and for some still fearsomely revolutionary, ideal of one man one vote, he did not make it any great cause for conflict. Peter, of course, did not pretend to care one way or another, though he would always blithely and readily admit that his sister would use the vote to which he would one day be entitled far more knowledgeably than he ever would himself. And Ralph, who though no actual blood relation was, she felt, as much a brother to her as either of the others, supported the fight for woman's suffrage as fervently as she did herself. That he did it as much to please her as from his own undoubtedly sincere convictions – something that anyone else in the household could have told her – never so much as crossed her mind.

It was in Charlotte, who like Ralph had been accepted on their father's death two years before openheartedly into the Patten family circle, the sister for whom Hannah had always openly longed, that she was sometimes secretly disappointed. How wonderful it would have been to find a true comrade in arms there. But try as she might she could detect no likelihood of it. It seemed to Hannah sometimes that pretty, fragile Charlotte had no convictions at all. Like an obedient child she would agree eagerly with anything she was told, anxious not to offend, anxious always to be liked, and never, that Hannah could see, using her brain for any exercise more testing than a decision about the colour of a ribbon on a new hat or the dedicated and absorbed perusal of the latest romantic novel. Informed by Hannah that in being born an unenfranchised woman she had been born to be exploited, underrated and enslaved she would placidly agree – and as placidly, Hannah suspected, subscribe to a luncheon partner's opinion that the suffragists were immoral, unwomanly fiends out to shred the very fabric of society, who deserved nothing so much as a sound flogging from husband or father. Sometimes, it was true, some small spark of interest would surface – but, especially lately, those moments had been very few and far between. In fact, during this last month of even more than usually strenuous activity, in between the soapboxes on street corners, the meetings of the Working Woman's Suffrage Society, the Clean Water Committee, the Worker's Educational Association and the small network of dedicated women who had joined her as health visitors to her father's deprived and ever-fertile flock, some small nagging anxiety had lately made itself felt with regard to Charlotte. She had become listless, her pretty face pale, pinched even. Taxed with concerned questions she had murmured convincingly about the weather – and certainly it had been extraordinarily hot – a summer cold, a loss of energy. But if the weather and a summer cold might account for her unusual lethargy, her quite obvious and uncharacteristic preference for her own company, a less than enthusiastic application to tasks and duties she would normally have undertaken with biddable good humour, they could hardly explain the odd and obvious sharpening of her nerves and her temper, the frequent lift of tears in those wide blue eyes. Several times Hannah had started the day determined that she should have a quiet word with Ben, or with her father, about the change in Charlotte; but each time a thousand things had occurred to distract her and the word had not yet been spoken. And perhaps, indeed, it never should be. Hannah truly detested interference in her own life, and so would certainly think twice about interfering in another's. The notion had occurred to her – based she would be the first to admit upon hearsay rather than personal experience – that the symptoms Charlotte was displaying might well be those of nothing more desperate than the agonies of a first love affair gone awry; young Wilfred Barnes had noticeably not been much in evidence lately. And if that were the case then understandably and justifiably Charlotte would thank no one for drawing Ben's eagle eye in her direction. For all his apparent commitment to equality her estimable brother still retained a downright primitive, occasionally welcome but much more often irritating protective instinct that could, as Hannah knew only too well, lead him confidently and exasperatingly to meddle with affairs not in the least his business. And so, with some degree of relief, she did nothing.

Meanwhile, as Charlotte drooped through the end of June and into a blazing, suffocatingly hot July, fever flickered like fire in the squalid back streets of Poplar, Bow and Limehouse, flaring here and there into a conflagration, smothered in places by the carbolic, the hot water, the limewash, the scoldings and the good practical advice administered by Hannah and her fellow health visitors in those places where such commodities were welcomed and accepted. And in Holloway gently born women learned to live without light and without freedom, to scrub their own floors and empty their own foetid slop buckets, to exist in many cases in a degradation beyond anything they had ever imagined.

And Sally Smith – unenfranchised, unemployed, unprotected and on the whole uncaring about any of these things since, to her, they were the norm – watched her pitiful savings diminish terrifyingly and knew, grimly, that the open door of the workhouse beckoned; a door to be avoided at any cost. Before she saw Toby separated from her, cowed and brutalized, savagely and publicly thrashed for the slightest misdemeanour, she would turn him loose again in the streets. Before she herself became one of that army of defeated, despairing women, isolated, imprisoned and punished by the Poor Laws for the crime of being destitute she would have sold herself and – if she had had one – her sister. But in her current state of health finding work was beyond her. She had to regain her strength. She had to!

The inevitable confrontation with Jackie Pilgrim had been as dire, if not as immediate, as she had known with certainty it would be. For a week and more that downstairs door had remained shut, a threat to be scuttled past, to be laughed at in bravado, to terrify in night shadows as she lay listening to the steady breathing of the child beside her. A thousand, thousand times she had castigated herself for her foolishness in coming to Charlotte's aid that night – and no recollection of the other girl's tear-stained, terrified face and frail, innocent, battered body had persuaded her that she had not been utterly mad to challenge Jackie so. What had possessed her? Who, in similar circumstances had ever held – or would ever hold – a helping hand to her? Why had she not left well alone, left the silly little beggar to the consequences of her own actions? Inevitably word had got round – exaggerated as it flitted, in whispers and chuckles, from ear to ear. Jackie was not by a long chalk the most popular lad in the area, certainly not amongst those young rivals who did not possess the physical attractions and insolent Irish dash that he used to such devastating effect. Had the law been invoked to punish him, Jackie it was who would have been the hero, Sally the villain. But given that – apparently – no such retribution was to fall, the story spread and grew happily in the telling. Everyone knew Sally Smith for a shrew with a tongue as friendly as a stinging nettle and a temper to match, and the younger half of the street population of Poplar was more than ready to credit her with the nerve to march in and steal Jackie's prize from under his very nose or, as the more extreme tales would have it, from under an even larger and more famous piece of his anatomy. That the girl – whose name thankfully remained unknown whilst her social status advanced with each telling – had already been raped God, Jackie and she only knew how many times often escaped the story altogether. The myth grew, Jackie's fuse grew shorter with every gibe, and, one night almost two weeks after the incident he came after Sally not with his fists and his feet as she had expected and as she had survived before but – sodden with several days' steady intake of cheap brandy – with a knife.

She had given him fair exchange, meeting him with desperate and angry courage, fighting like a demon with tooth and nail and booted foot, leaving him at last sprawled upon her attic floor, dazed for an instant by a well-aimed blow with her cracked chamber pot. Then she had fled into the street, a terrified Toby at her skirts, blood pouring from a horribly deep wound in her upper arm. They had spent two nights in the open, afraid to return, and in the close and unhealthy atmosphere as they slept huddled in rat-infested corners the brutal wound, inflicted by a filthy knife, had festered. On the third day they had crept back to that oven of an attic, and in the wrecked room Sally had fallen on to the pallet weak and feverish and in intolerable pain, Toby beside her, his worried eyes fixed fearfully upon her burning face.

She remembered little of the following days. Toby it was, child of the streets, who had fed them by means known only to himself and which Sally had been too drained and too sickly to question. He had begged, borrowed or she suspected more often stolen bread, milk and cheese that had all but choked her as she forced it down her dry and swollen throat. He had gone to the Dicksons once, but finding the neat little house empty, its occupants at work – Josie at the laundry, the menfolk at the West India Docks – had been afraid to wait, afraid to leave Sally alone for too long and so had returned empty handed. The fever had subsided a little at last; the wound, though still savagely inflamed and very painful had begun to knit. Angry at her own weakness she had forced herself from her bed to look for work: but if employment had been hard to find before it was impossible now, thin and weak-looking as she had become and with the flush of fever more often than not on her cheeks. The wound had closed, but even to her unpractised eye it looked less than healthy, and it still gave her a great deal of pain. With the stoicism of her kind she endured and as far as possible ignored it; such things happened – they got better, or they did not. For now she simply existed from day to day, their only hope of sustenance the soup kitchen or the scraps that Toby so dubiously acquired, her small, precious store of savings diminishing at a terrifying rate as the rent man called, and the tally man from whom Toby's threadbare and now ruined jacket had been purchased in better times.

Jackie had left them alone. Once they had seen him, lounging in his doorway as they went downstairs. Toby's hand had tightened convulsively in Sally's. Sally had ignored the watching figure, head up, thin, flushed face stony, and he had neither moved nor spoken as they had passed.

For a while then the pain had eased – or perhaps she had simply got used to it? She wasn't sure – and the puckered flesh around the wound had come to look a little less baleful, though it was still an unhealthy colour and almost unbearably painful to touch. She slept a little better, ate with a little more appetite. It had seemed that the worst was over and that she was mending.

Until this morning.

She had known during the night, awakening to a suffocating, airless darkness and a fiery stab in her arm more agonizing than had been that first, vicious blow, that all was far from well. She had lain, teeth gritted against the pain and the renewed lift of fever, trying not to move, not to disturb the child who slept beside her, his dirty, cherub's face peaceful. She had battled with a will stubborn as ever but weakened by nearly two debilitating weeks of misery and ill health against the tearing agony of the infected wound, the rise of delirium as the poison pulsed through her body with her blood, bringing crashing pain to her head and lightning flashes of lurid brilliance behind her closed lids. Dawn had found her burning with fever again. Grimly aware that this time she could not hope to cope alone she set herself to rest a while, gathering her strength. The time for pride was long past: simple survival was now the question. She would do what she knew she should have done in the first place; she would go to the Dicksons, accept the help she knew – had known all along – they would freely offer. But since the journey must be made on foot and the Isle of Dogs was no mean step away for a fevered girl and a small child, she must wait until she felt ready to tackle it – and, too, the soup kitchen in Angel Street was on their way and would be open at twelve, a place to stop and rest and for the child at least to eat.

Late in the morning she struggled from her bed. Her skin was dry and blazing hot, as sore to touch as if she had been flayed. The throbbing agony of her arm seemed to swell with each movement, invading her body, bringing back those shattering anvil clashes of light and pain to her head. She said little, teeth clenched against the torment until her rigid jaw became just another, smaller pain in the sea through which she moved and which threatened any minute to drown her. Toby held her other hand, unusually subdued, his face paler and thinner than usual, his eyes desperate with worry as he cast swift glances at her from beneath long lashes. She walked very carefully, avoiding any possibility of contact with the world about her, almost oblivious to her surroundings except inasmuch as they threatened her.

As they turned the corner into Angel Street they found themselves confronted with a small, noisy crowd gathered about a speaker, a woman who stood upon a chair, and another who, with the muffin man's bell she had used to attract the crowds tucked under one arm, was distributing leaflets to any hand willing to take them.

'We are not slaves! We are not toys to be bought and sold – children to be seen and not heard! We are adults with a right to have an equal say in the running of our lives and the running of the country in which we live!' The speaker was a young woman, rather shabbily dressed, soft brown hair parted in the middle and piled untidily upon her head, her smooth-skinned, wide-mouthed face passionate as she spoke. Sally gritted her teeth as a woman jostled her excitedly, sidestepped into the road to avoid more painful contact. Toby drew protectively close to her. A tall, spare young woman, with a strong, square face that Sally vaguely recognized, smiled and offered a leaflet. Intent only on getting to the comparative peace and safety of the soup kitchen – where at least for a blessed few minutes she would be able to stop moving – Sally shook her head jerkily and stumbled on.

'We must make this Government give us the vote. We must force it from them! Now! This very session! Then we'll see the changes that will be wrought upon this country of ours!' As the girl's impassioned voice was lost behind her in the sound of the traffic, Sally, her bemused brain still functioning despite the siege of pain and discomfort, found herself all but smiling her derision. Changes? And what changes, she wondered, would the fine young lady make that might affect Sally Smith and her kind? Would she stop the likes of Jackie Pilgrim from preying on his women? Would she stop death in childbed or the outrage of sweated labour? Would she find for women the solution to the problems of their own fertility and of the grinding treadmill of poverty-stricken hand-to-mouth living which that fertility inevitably brought? She doubted it.

She tripped up the curb and stumbled, catching her breath at the pain. At the door of the soup kitchen she leaned for a moment, rallying her strength, allowing her reddened eyes to adjust to the gloom. The place was half-empty. A lethargic queue of about half a dozen waited patiently. There were plenty of seats at the long scrubbed table at the end of the room. Thankfully she ushered Toby towards the counter.

The light touch on her arm was a hammer-stroke of

pain. She stopped. Toby took his bowl of soup and hunk of dark bread and set off towards the table.

'Please. I have to talk to you. I have to!'

Wearily Sally turned, knowing from the voice, from the light, pleasant smell of wholesome cleanliness who had accosted her. She had not seen Charlotte Bedford since that night a month or so ago when she had left her in the safety of a rose-pink room to return to the tenement and the threat of Jackie Pilgrim. How many times since had she wished that she had never seen her – that she had ignored that cry for help that she had known then, too well, could only lead to trouble?

'Please!' Charlotte said again. In the month that had passed she had changed, even Sally could see it. Her pretty face had sharpened, her small, well-shaped mouth was pinched, and the pale eyes were blurred with tiredness and a constant threat of tears. 'I must talk to you!'

Sally shook her head, turned away.

Charlotte caught at her arm again, then snatched her hand away as the other girl threw back her head in a convulsion of pain. 'What's the matter?'

'Nothing.' Sally wanted nothing from her. Nor was she ready to give more than she already had.

'Please,' Charlotte was whispering, her face truly desperate, the words intense and very fast, 'oh, please help me. I know I have no right. I'm sure I must have brought you to trouble but – please understand! – I've no one else to turn to. Give me a moment. Just a moment. Some advice, that's all.'

The girl behind the counter, small, red-headed, sharp-eyed, was watching them in open surprise and curiosity. One or two people in the queue turned.

'Please?'

Toby was watching them, his eyes hostile upon Charlotte, worried upon Sally. He had not touched his soup.

'Eat yer soup, Tobe, there's a good lad. I won't be a minute.'

Charlotte clenched herself against the awful, easy tears that threatened again. Since she had come to her terrible decision she had looked for this girl as the only contact she had with the world in which such things could happen. She could not fail now. She must not. 'Outside,' she said, 'there's a storeroom – we won't be interrupted – I won't keep you a moment, I promise.'

Sally hesitated for an instant longer then, touched despite herself by the pathetic, frightened intensity of this pale, pretty, pampered girl she nodded, 'All right.'

She followed Charlotte into a dark corridor and through an open door. The small room, lined from floor to ceiling with shelves that were filled with neatly stacked tins, jars and packets, was airless, its tiny window, against which buzzed a great, bloated bluebottle, tight shut. The air was dry and dusty and tickled the throat unpleasantly. Sally walked past Charlotte to lean against a large butler's sink. Blood thudded in her ears and pain throbbed as rhythmically in her arm. She felt very ill indeed. 'Well?'

Charlotte stared at her helplessly, seeing not a girl in pain and near to the end of her strength but a pair of narrow, suspicious eyes and a mouth as straight and uncompromising in its dislike as a drawn line. 'I –', having come so far, having planned this, rehearsed it, all but learned her lines word for word she could not go on. 'I need your help – your advice –'

Sally raised impatient brows. 'So yer said.'

'I need – please – I need to know – the name of someone – someone who can help me.' Charlotte's face was contorted with effort, her hands clasped white-knuckled before her, her breath coming in small, sharp gasps like that of a child who has run too far.

Sally passed a bemused hand over her burning face.

'I need an abortion.' The words came out very suddenly and on a hysterical lift of voice that echoed too loudly. Tears spilled over from the blue eyes, ran down the hollows of the small, haunted face. 'Oh please! I can't have it! I can't! And I don't know what to do – where to go – I'll die if they find out – Doctor Will – Ben – Hannah – the others. You have to help me! *Please!*' She was openly sobbing.

Sally stared at her.

Charlotte fought for control of her voice, but still it lifted wildly. 'Don't you hear me? I'm expecting his child! I'll die! You hear me? I mean it! I'll die if I have to have it – if they find out – oh, you must know someone? Somewhere I can go?'

'No.' The word was harsh.

'You *must*! Or – I swear – I'll kill myself! If you don't help me – won't help me – I'll kill myself! *Please!*'

Sally stared at her. In the fevered recesses of her mind she relived the one dark occasion she had stepped across the threshold of the woman the tenements called Ma Spencer, a terrified, abandoned child of thirteen. She remembered the squalor, the pain. She remembered the dirty, bloody knitting needle. 'You don't now what you're talkin' about.'

'I mean it! I do! I won't go through with it! I won't have them know! I couldn't stand it – I'll kill myself first!'

'You go to Ma Spencer and she'll as likely kill yer anyway,' Sally said grimly.

'Spencer?' Charlotte was on the name like a cat on a mouse. 'Is that her name? Then you *do* know? Oh tell me, please tell me, where can I find her?'

'No.'

'Please!'

'*No!*'

With a sudden movement Charlotte stepped forward, reached for Sally's shoulders, shaking her. '*Tell me!*'

The world spun, a whirlpool of pain. As Charlotte stepped quickly back, white-faced and suddenly frightened at what she saw in the other girl's face, there was a movement in the darkness behind her. Sally, her eyes unfocused, could see nothing of the man who loomed in the doorway but his immense size, could do nothing through the haze of agony that all but blinded her to warn the girl who stood before her, sobbing with terror, frustration and rage. 'Please tell me – I'll pay you anything – I'll pay her anything – I have to get rid of it – quickly – before they find out.' Suddenly aware of that other presence behind her, she froze, her shrill voice cut off as if by a knife, her already pale face ashen. Very, very slowly she turned. Sally swayed, clinging to the sink, fighting nausea and the mortifying buckling of her knees.

'What in God's name is going on in here?'

He was a huge man, with docker's shoulders and a craggy docker's face; square and pugnacious, a nose like a blade, an untidy shock of reddish brown hair, a straight and at the moment harsh mouth, a jaw like a granite block. A face that scowled easily, as it was scowling now; a cool and incisive voice at odds with his appearance.

Charlotte was trembling visibly. She took a step backwards, shaking her head. 'Ben –'

A wave of sickness rose in Sally, her head was splintering with pain. She clutched at the sink, fighting to stay upright. Through the wicked pounding in her head she heard their voices, through her own fever-glazed eyes saw Charlotte's abandoned tears. The world throbbed about her; the figure of the man grew to manic proportions, the jutting brow and fierce nose, the hard mouth and deepset slate-dark eyes magnifying horribly and then as horribly shrinking, receding, a mannikin figure like the painted figures in the toy theatre in Boswell's toy shop that Toby had so coveted. She saw that face turn suddenly and sharply to her, put up an unthinking hand to ward it off and in doing so released her grip upon the sink and collapsed with no sound and no hope of saving herself, striking her head upon the heavy porcelain for good measure as she fell. Ben Patten was quick, but not quick enough to catch her. He knelt swiftly by her side, took her wrist in cool, hard fingers.

She felt the fingers and the racing pulse they counted. She lay for a moment, eyes closed, gathering herself, the star-split darkness behind her lids a momentary refuge from a world of pain and explanations.

'Get her a glass of water,' Ben said. 'Quickly.'

Charlotte was still sobbing uncontrollably. She stumbled to the sink. 'There's no glass.'

'Then damned well get one!'

'I –'

He turned his head and looked at her. She fled, returned a moment later with a small glass which she filled at the sink. Gently but very firmly, cradling Sally's head expertly so that she could do nothing but allow it, he lifted her and put the glass to her lips. 'Drink this, just a little.'

She sipped at it. Her stomach settled a little. The pain in her arm gnawed like a rat.

He waited a moment. 'Feeling better?'

She nodded, her eyes still closed. She could hear Charlotte still crying, quietly now, like a helpless child.

'Charlotte, for God's sake stop snivelling.' It was said perfectly levelly. 'It does no good. Think about someone other than yourself for a minute, will you? Who is she?'

'I – don't know.' Charlotte hiccoughed, swallowed a sob, 'That is – her name's Sally. That's all – I know.'

'Sally,' he said, and then she felt a firm hand on her chin. 'Sally?' His voice had taken on some small warmth, an almost imperceptible edge of gentleness. 'What's wrong? Where are you hurt?'

She opened her eyes. 'My arm.' The husky voice cracked a little, exhausted.

'Come and hold her.' Ben did not look at Charlotte, his voice was peremptory. And, 'Be careful!' he snapped as she knelt behind Sally, taking her head upon her lap.

Sally lay like a doll. Firm fingers tore the material of her sleeve, unwrapped the dirty scrap of bandage. She flinched, closed her eyes again.

'Mother of God,' he said. And Sally felt Charlotte's involuntary sharp movement as she turned her head away.

'When did this happen?'

'About two weeks ago.'

'Why the devil did you let it go so far? Why didn't you come to us?'

She opened her eyes and looked at him. Saw the tightening of the muscles about his long mouth, suspected that under different circumstances she would have heard a rougher edge to his tongue. She glanced down at the wound and, like Charlotte, looked hastily away from its puffy ugliness, the seeping of filth that stained the torn sleeve.

He touched it gently, face absorbed, a faint, vertical line between his brows. 'Can you sit up?'

She nodded and struggled to a sitting position.

'Good, good. Easy now. Don't overdo it.' He held her steady. 'Now then,' he frowned a little, obviously a habitual expression, 'we have to get you to the surgery. My father's there. He'll patch you up. Can you walk?'

'I bin walkin' fer the last nineteen years or so.'

His mouth twitched very slightly. 'I'd take you myself, but I do have an urgent case waiting.'

'Don't bother.' She knew how brusque that had sounded, but the effort of talking at all was great enough without the added strain of pleasantries.

'Charlotte will go with you.' He threw the other girl a sharp, impersonal glance that was tantamount to an order and brooked no argument. 'Now – let's get you on your feet.'

As effortlessly as if she had been a child he almost lifted her to her feet. She swayed a little. 'Toby,' she said.

'What?'

'Toby,' Charlotte supplied. 'It's the child – her child, I think – anyway, he's always with her. He's outside with his soup.'

'Take him with you.'

For one rocky moment Sally felt her knees buckling again. Firm hands held her. She steadied herself, drew away. 'I'm all right.'

'You will be, I think. But in another day –' he let the sentence hang in the air. Why were some of these people so idiotically stubborn about accepting help? Why couldn't they see that they hurt no one but themselves with their distrust and their useless, obstinate pride? 'I'd come myself,' he said again, 'but I have a confinement. A bad one. The mother needs me.'

'It's all right,' she said, and resolutely fought the temptation simply to let go, to surrender to the almost welcome darkness that hovered, waiting to claim her, 'I can manage.'

He watched her for a moment, eyes keen. Then he nodded. 'Yes. Well, take it easy. It isn't far.'

She nodded, too exhausted to speak.

'Ben,' Charlotte said, tentatively.

He shook his head brusquely, his eyes still on Sally. 'Later, Charlotte.'

'But –'

'Later, I said. Take her and the child to the surgery. Father's there. She'll need a bed. Arrange it.'

Numbly Charlotte nodded. Turned away. Stopped. Turned a face to him that was stripped to the bone with anguish. 'Ben? What – what am I going to do?'

'Later,' he said again, his voice more gentle. 'We'll talk of it later, Charlotte.'

That walk to the surgery was not an experience that Sally ever had any wish to repeat. At every step she was convinced she could go no further, every contact of foot with ground sending shock waves of pain through her body and into her head. Yet somehow she stumbled on, small Charlotte on one side, even smaller Toby on the other, the child now openly crying, his expression and attitude a contradictory mixture of abject terror and heartbreaking fierce protectiveness.

'It's all right, Tobe.' The words were slurred a little. She could not precisely control her tongue. 'We're – goin' to a doctor. A proper one.'

'I'm comin' too,' he said, sniffing. 'I can look after you, Sal. I can!'

By the time they reached the Bear she was at the end of her strength and had someone offered to cut off her arm with an axe she would have submitted with no argument. Charlotte led her through a door and down a narrow corridor into a room that gleamed with cleanliness. Through a disorientating haze of pain she was aware of blessed coolness and the heartless yet not unpleasant smell of antiseptic. She eyed with uncertainty a forbiddingly tall, sharp-featured woman in crisp apron and even crisper cap, whose skirts rustled officiously as she moved and whose voice was as cool and fresh-laundered as the apron and cap. She heard Charlotte's voice, murmuring some explanation, felt Toby's small, hot hand almost prised from hers.

'It's all right, Tobe. Do as y'er told now, there's a good boy.'

She closed her eyes as they undressed her, clad her in a loose nightgown so starched that it might have been made of white cardboard. She heard the nurse tut fussily at sight of her arm, felt a noticeable gentling of her brisk hands. Then they laid her upon a high, hard bed and left her in the cool, bright room, alone with the pain, too exhausted to be afraid or even to be curious. She was still at last, and that for the moment was enough, any need for thought, any need for action thankfully suspended, her precarious hold on reality slipping from her into feverish dreams, the strength to hold it gone.

'Well, young lady, here's a thing.' The voice came to her from what seemed an immense distance. Like his son he was huge, but his face was kinder. The searing pain brought by his touch on her arm opened her eyes and caught her breath in her throat. He gentled her with a strong and kindly hand. Picked up something that glinted steel in the light, gleaming wickedly. She fastened her teeth firmly into her lip.

'There's a brave lass. Hold on now. This won't take a moment.'

But she could not. This time, blessedly, the darkness was swift, sudden and absolute.

II

She woke up in a room that she knew vaguely to be familiar, a room she had seen before – in a dream, perhaps, or a nightmare. It took some considerable time and an immense amount of concentration for the realization to come to her that the dream had been reality, that her drifting in and out of this room, her recollection of the faces and the voices that went with it were no nightmare, no matter of a feverish imagination. She had lain in this bed for days. She had been held down in her delirium by firm hands, had been bathed and fed and tended by strangers. Their hands had cooled her burning forehead, their voices had spoken above her head, distant and unintelligible. She lay very still for a long time, taking in the surroundings that were so strange and yet so oddly familiar. A narrow room, painted white. A tall window, curtains drawn, beyond it sunlight, the muted sound of traffic. A table and a chair of scrubbed, bare wood, upon the table a bowl and a selection of jugs and shallow dishes. A functional room, clean and cool, yet made more personal by the sprigged material of the curtains, the matching cushion on the chair, the bright flower print upon the wall. She lay quite still, movement and thought suspended. There was no need to move. No need to think. Not now. Not yet. Where there had been agony there was now a small, throbbing soreness. Where there had been bitter, bone-deep exhaustion there was now a pleasant lassitude. It was enough. She closed her eyes and slept again.

'Well, now – and how are we feeling today? Better, I think?' The voice and the figure were those she remembered best from these past, all but lost days; gruff but not unkindly tone, big, bulky body and a sweetly humorous face beneath a thatch of greying hair as untidy as any she had ever seen. Doctor Will. That was the name she had heard. She smiled, astonished that such a small and usually unthinking action should require such effort.

'Right. Let's take a look at this arm, shall we?'

Helpless and weak as a newborn child, she lay as he gently pushed up the wide sleeve of her nightdress, exposing her upper arm. Vaguely and with the beginnings of discomfiture she recalled that more personal liberties than this had been necessary over the past few days.

'Yes – yes – very good. It's coming along nicely. A fresh dressing, I think, Miss Reid, and then perhaps our young patient might find herself able to partake of something a little more solid than the beef tea you've been pouring down her these past days?'

Sally smiled again into the dark, twinkling eyes.

'Good – good. Now, if you feel up to it we have a small visitor for you. Well, rather more like a guard really. If we had allowed it I do believe that he would have slept across your threshold and bitten any ankle he suspected of being less than friendly – you have a devoted slave, Miss Smith.'

'Toby,' she said, her usually vibrant voice a grating whisper.

'The very same.' He raised his voice a little, 'Come on, then, lad. See for yourself. The corner is turned, as I told you it would be.'

There was a small eruption by the door, and then a stillness. 'Sal?' The young voice was doubtful, the clean and shining face only half hopeful.

'Good Gawd,' she said faintly caustic, 'I thought they said it was young Toby?'

'It is.' He fidgeted with the neat, plain but clean clothes, ducked a shining head. 'Go on, Sal! You know it is.'

She smiled infinitely gently, lifted her good hand in invitation. He flew to her, skidded to a halt by the bedside, took her hand with beguiling care.

'It's all right. I won't break.'

He said nothing, seemed content for the moment simply to cling to the hand he had held so often – and that had clipped his ear almost as frequently – that now was so unaccustomedly soft and acquiescent in his.

The nurse finished tying the fresh bandage with deftly impersonal fingers. 'There.' She stood up, 'Rest, I think now, Doctor Will? Don't you agree?' She held out a commanding hand. 'Come along, young man.'

Toby's hand clutched tighter at Sally's. He scowled murderously. Miss Reid tutted, her lips pursed. Sally got the distinct impression that these were not the opening hostilities between these two.

'Oh – we can leave him for a while I think, Miss Reid.' Doctor Will leaned over and ruffled the gleaming gold curls, winking conspiratorially at Sally. 'He's waited long enough for this moment. He'll do no harm.'

Toby cast sly, triumphant eyes in the starched direction of his enemy.

She sniffed. 'If you say so, Doctor.'

They left, a taut, offended back and a large tolerant one. The door closed.

'You all right?' Toby asked after a long moment, his voice a whisper, overawed despite himself.

'Course. Look at me. Good as new. Almost.'

He grinned at that.

She turned her head on the pillow to look at him. In the faint light from the curtained windows he fairly glowed with cleanliness and good health. She lifted the small paw that was still clasped in hers. It was clean as a babe's, the nails trimmed, no trace of grime anywhere about it. 'Yer lookin' pretty dandy yerself.'

He laughed, the characteristic mischievous gurgle that she found so infectious.

'I'd lay odds they didn't find it easy?'

He shook his head, still grinning. 'I bit 'er. Twice.'

'Little beast.'

There was a long moment's quiet.

'Tobe?'

'Mm?'

'What's it like 'ere? I mean,' her eyes slid to the door and back, 'what they really like?'

He thought about it. 'Not bad, most of 'em. She's a pain – the nurse woman – but the rest – they're all right. Grub's good. An' there's tons of it. There's bacon for breakfast almost every day, an' supper every single night.'

'Where you bin sleepin'?'

'With the other kids.'

'What other kids?'

He waved a vague hand. 'Oh – there's lots of 'em. They live 'ere.'

She nodded her head, not exactly in understanding.

'One of 'em's ever so nice.'

'What – one of the kids?'

'Nah!' The negative was threaded with pure disgust at such a silly assumption. 'One o' them.' He jerked his head towards the door. ''E's a teacher or somethin'. 'E's a real gent. Makes yer laugh. Tells yer stories.'

'Oh?'

The bright head snapped round. 'Not as good as yours. Course not. But they aren't bad.'

'Well – if 'e's a teacher –'

'Tha'ss right.' The child, more confident now, dropped her hand and clambered on to the narrow bed, sat swinging his legs, his clean young profile bright and beautiful against the sunlit curtains. 'Name o' Mr Ralph.' He turned his head to look at her, his face unwontedly solemn. ''E teaches the other kids to read. Says 'e could me, if I wanted.'

'Does 'e now?' Sally's voice, stronger now, carried an edge of the old, tart cynicism.

The boy, hearing it, grinned his pleasure.

She reached a hand, poked his knee with a long, bony finger. 'Take a pretty clever teacher ter teach the likes o' *you* ter read!'

He chuckled.

She left her hand resting upon his leg. A sudden wave of tiredness engulfed her. Her eyelids drooped.

'Young man – off that bed at once!' The door had opened. A long, thin, starched silhouette pointed an outraged finger. '*At once!*'

Toby slid from the bed and fled. The door closed. Sally slept.

The Mr Ralph that Toby had spoken of, to Sally's surprise, came to visit her a couple of days later. She was propped up in bed, still surprisingly weak, but greatly improved in health, her arm healing cleanly now, her tough constitution fighting the ill effects of the fever. In those days that she had lost July had moved into August. The curtains of the tall window were drawn open now, and the windows themselves thrown up to let what little air there was enter the narrow room. Outside the window the leaves of the tree which stood in the old stable yard hung in summer stillness, dusty and scorched a little by the drought, but a haven nevertheless for busy sparrows and greedy, squawking starlings. The traffic noise was muted. Ralph stood a little hesitantly in the doorway, a small bunch of flowers in his hand, a diffident expression on his good-natured face. 'Hello. I'm Ralph Bedford. May I come in?'

She was astounded that he should ask. 'Course.'

He ambled across the room, proffered the flowers. 'I – I thought you might like these?'

'Well – thanks.' Entirely nonplussed she took them. No one in her entire life had ever offered her flowers before. They were daisies; very few, and rather wilted, but she laid them as carefully upon the white counterpane as if they had been orchids and carnations.

'May I sit down?'

She nodded, watched him curiously as he arranged his long body and lanky legs into some semblance of order and perched upon the only chair. She saw a tall, untidy young man, pale of face, dark of hair and eye, unremarkable in appearance. His straight hair was a little lank, the wire-rimmed spectacles he wore gave him somehow an air of vagueness, his big hands were very bony, his Adam's apple prominent. Yet there was an ungainly gentleness about him that was immediately endearing, even attractive, an air of unassumed and tranquil kindness that put her immediately at her ease. So this was Ralph, who told her Toby stories and suggested that he might be taught to read?

'How are you feeling?'

'I'm very well, thank you. I'm being so very well looked after.'

He smiled his gentle smile. 'So I should think. And especially since Ben appears to have taken you under his wing. That warrants even more special treatment.'

It was said lightly, but she said nothing and her silence was wary. She had no idea how much anyone knew of the circumstances that had brought her here. Her well-developed instinct for self-preservation warned her to be very careful. The whole affair was nothing but trouble and the least said the better: her main aim in life at the moment was to get better, regain her strength and get out of here – with Toby – just as fast as she could.

The silence lengthened, a little awkwardly. Ralph sat, elbows on knees, big hands clasped before him. Sally, whose life until now had contained little of the social niceties and nothing at all of small talk, waited.

'I – wanted to talk to you about young Toby.'

'Ah.' The narrow eyes narrowed further, defensively.

'He's your son?'

She hesitated, every instinct, every nerve telling her to lie. Her general experience, both first and second hand of those helpful souls who so earnestly desired to aid the lame and the destitute was not good. If she admitted that Toby was not her son – was not in fact any blood relative at all – how much easier would it be for this well-meaning and earnest young man to take him from her?

'Please.' For all the world as if he had read the thought in her mind he held up a quick hand. 'Don't worry. It really doesn't matter. You don't have to tell me. I just wondered. You seem so very young.'

She shrugged. 'I found 'im. Year or so ago. Roamin' the streets, 'e was – beggin', pickin' pockets, thievin' what 'e could from the stalls in Petticoat Lane. 'Alf starved 'e was, poor little beggar.'

'And you took him in?'

'I s'pose so, yes.'

He smiled. 'It's no wonder he thinks so very much of you. Does he have a family?'

She shook her head. 'Not that we know of. All 'e remembers is a woman who must 'a' bin his mother. When she died there was no one else.'

'I see. And that was when you found him?'

'Yes. 'E 'ad 'is thievin' little fingers in my purse.' She grinned at the recollection.

There was a small, careful silence. 'He's a very bright little boy.'

She looked at him, hard-eyed and suspicious. 'Yes. I daresay 'e is.'

'And you know of course that by law he should be in school?'

Just as she had expected! Stupid! Why hadn't she kept her stupid mouth shut? Her whole face tightened.

He shook his head gently. 'Please – don't be alarmed.

We all know there are many children who for one reason or the other fall through that net. There's not a lot anyone will do about it if I don't tell them. You can walk away from here with him with no worry.'

She stared at him, suspiciously.

'But – would that be fair?'

You can bet your life it would. What would you do for him that I can't apart from fill his head with rubbish, give him hopes and dreams that can never come to anything, knowledge he can never use? She said nothing, watching him narrowly.

'It's a shame to waste such intelligence, don't you think?' The words were quiet. 'He should learn to read, and to write –'

'Why?' she asked bluntly.

He opened his mouth. Shut it again. Stood up awkwardly. 'I'm sorry. It's too early. I'm tiring you when you should be resting. Please don't worry about what I've said. No one – no one! – is going to take Toby away from you.'

'You think anyone could?' she asked, a little harshly.

'No. I'm quite sure that they couldn't. But – please – just think about what I've said. We both know what happens to bright, intelligent, under-educated children in these back streets of ours. They have to use their talents somehow, and left to themselves I'm sure you know better than I what grief they can come to.'

She knew. Too well she knew. She said nothing.

'So – I'll leave you to rest. But please don't worry. Just think about what I've said.' He smiled then and, despite herself, she found herself half-smiling back, half-trusting him, half-believing him. Lord, her stay in this place must have softened her head –

She watched him to the door, heard his exclamation of surprise. 'Why, Ben – hello.'

'Morning, Ralph.' Ben Patten's voice was cool and sharp. Had he asked 'What the devil are you doing here?' he could not have been much more explicit.

'I came to see how Miss Smith was progressing – and to have a word about Toby.'

'I don't think she's ready to be bothered about such things just yet.'

'No. I think you're right. I'm sorry. I'll come back in a day or so. Oh – are you coming with us to Miss Pankhurst's tonight?'

The rough, reddish head shook. 'No. I'm on at the hospital.'

'Ah. Well, I'm taking Hannah, of course. It should be a very entertaining evening.'

Ben grunted.

Ralph threw a swift smile at Sally and left, leaving her to face the craggy scowl of a busy man not in the best of tempers.

He crossed the room in three brusque strides. 'How are you feeling?'

'Much better.' She hesitated, 'Thank you.'

He took her wrist in cool and competent fingers, laid a hand to her forehead. 'Yes. It seems so.'

She watched him as he straightened, filling the room with his height and bulk. Never had she seen anyone who looked more like a prize-fighter or less like a doctor. He ran a hand through already wildly tangled hair. On sure instinct and with a sudden spurt of amusement it came to Sally that Ralph Bedford was not the only member of this rather odd household to have come in search of favours from insignificant Sally Smith this morning. He cleared his throat a little with what she knew with certainty to be unaccustomed awkwardness. 'Miss Smith –'

She grinned, a little wryly. What a bunch they were for the proper addressing of a waif and stray in a charity nightdress. 'Yes?'

'I – have a favour to ask.'

Surprising herself, she took sudden pity on him. 'You don't 'ave to.'

He looked at her, sharply.

'You're goin' ter ask me ter keep it ter meself — what 'appened with Jackie Pilgrim an' the young lady —'

'Yes.'

She shrugged. 'What yer take me for? I would 'a done anyway.'

He had a habit of stillness that was arresting in so big a man. He stood now, unsmiling, his hands in his pockets, looking down at her, studying her, weighing her, it seemed, on some very private mental scale. Then quite suddenly, he smiled and the effect was astounding, lighting the rather forbidding face like sunshine upon a rugged granite cliff. 'I do believe you mean that.'

'Course I do. I'm no trouble-maker, Doctor Patten. Trouble 'as a nasty 'abit of bitin' the 'and that feeds it, so to speak. I don't usually meddle with other people's affairs.'

'In this case I have to thank God that you did — from what Charlotte has told me heaven only knows what might have happened if you hadn't helped her.'

'Well, that's as might be. But you've no call to worry. Me an' Tobe'll be on our way just as soon as we can. No one'll 'ear nothin' from me, I promise.'

'Thank you.'

'No thanks needed. If you owed me, you paid me.' She lifted her chin, looked directly at him, 'I reckon you saved me life — an' for that I thank you.'

'It's my job,' but he was smiling again.

She nodded.

'So — now —', he was the doctor again, brisk and impersonal, 'I think you should rest.' He moved with those long strides to the window and closed the curtains. 'We'll soon have you up and about again — though believe me, Miss Smith, you have been very ill indeed and it may take you a little longer than you expect to regain your strength. But — get plenty of rest and you'll be right as ninepence, I promise you.'

She snuggled into her pillows, weary again, thankful

enough for the promise of peace, happy enough to do as she was bid. He picked up the flowers that Ralph had left and dropped them with no ceremony into the sink, splashing water from the jug upon them, then continued on to the door. Once there he stopped, turning, looming in the shadows, a bulk of darkness. 'Perhaps you may be interested to know that Charlotte – Miss Bedford – has agreed to marry me.' His voice was completely cool again, completely lacking in any emotion. 'It seemed to be best.' The door closed very quietly behind him.

Sally, startled awake, listened to his measured footsteps as they receded into that mysterious, unknown world that lay beyond her closed door. And as she lay trying to give a name to the emotion that his words had surprised in her she frowned a little, astounded to discover it to be sympathy. For whom she would have been hard put to say, but sympathy nevertheless. A dangerous emotion, and one it could not be said that Sally Smith was much given to.

She was not too surprised when Charlotte paid her a visit later that afternoon. She had slept well and felt rested. She had submitted to Miss Reid's brusque blanket bath, and felt the better for it, had swallowed her medicine, eaten the meal that she thought of as dinner though Miss Reid would insist upon calling it luncheon, had passed a friendly word with Bron, the nicer of the two girls who cleaned her room, whose unusual name was explained the moment she opened her mouth and the musical sing-song of Wales lilted forth, and was now contentedly watching the sparrows that squabbled in the tree outside her window and awaiting a promised visit by Toby. When the door opened, expecting the child, she turned her head upon the propped pillows, smiling.

Charlotte, pale and withdrawn, hesitated on the threshold. She was wearing a pretty shade of pink, pearl-sheened as her soft skin. Her fair hair was piled becomingly upon her small head. 'May I come in?'

Sally struggled to a sitting position. 'Of course.'

The other girl entered the room, moving very quietly, closing the door very carefully behind her; in fact it struck the watching Sally forcibly that she did everything very carefully – she moved, sat, folded her hands as if the air about her were fragile as spun glass and might splinter and wound at a sharp or thoughtless movement. She sat for a moment, apparently composed, looking down at her small clasped hands that lay perfectly still upon her neat lap. Then she lifted her head in a slow movement, as if that fine, pile of hair were too heavy a load for the slim neck.

'Ben says I am to apologize to you', she said very calmly, entirely without spirit or expression, 'for making the assumption that you would know where I might – might –' she swallowed, 'where I might find someone to perform an abortion.' Her face was drained with the effort of that. She took a breath.

Sally took refuge in a disbelieving bark of laughter that she later realized might have been misconstrued as unkind. 'Don't be daft. I did know.'

The fair head lifted, Charlotte's baby blue eyes were steady; steady and empty. 'Yes. But you see – Ben's right – it was wrong of me to assume so just the same, wasn't it? And I do apologize – for that and for everything else.'

'There's no need. What's done is done.'

For another disconcerting moment wide, blank, blue eyes held narrow, alert hazel ones. 'Yes. That's true, isn't it?'

There was a long and not too comfortable moment of silence. Then Charlotte stood and walked to the window, stood looking out, her slim silhouette sharp in the light and straight as an arrow. 'I am to marry Doctor Patten. I think he told you?'

'Yes. He did.'

'No one knows what happened of course. No one knows – Ben says no one ever will – how criminally stupid I've been. Isn't he clever? And kind – for I'm quite sure of course that he doesn't truly want to marry me.' The unnerving evenness of her tone did not falter. 'Everyone's very surprised of course. But pleased too, I think. Except Wilfred. But then –' she drew a small, shallow breath '– I couldn't have married Wilfred anyway. I simply couldn't.' She was talking now almost as if to herself. She moved and spoke, Sally thought, as if every vestige of life, every last drop of the spirit that had been Charlotte Bedford had been drained from her, leaving a pretty, obliging, empty shell. Appalled at such damage so wantonly inflicted, on a sudden and violent lift of rage she cursed the mother that had given birth to Jackie Pilgrim.

Charlotte turned. 'I do hope I won't let Ben down. I'm not sure that I can be the kind of wife he needs – the kind he deserves. He has such ideals, you see. Such dreams.' She walked aimlessly to the table, trailed her fingers along its scrubbed edge, 'Not the sort of dreams that other people have – of love, and comfort, and riches perhaps, or children. He dreams for others. He wants to build Jerusalem. In England's green and pleasant land. You know, like in the hymn? Oh, not today, perhaps. But tomorrow. Or at the very latest the day after. He'll wait no longer than that for his social justice, his health care for all, his working man's Parliament.' She turned, leaned against the table, the lucent, remote eyes on Sally again. 'It's a very laudable ambition, isn't it?'

Caustic words rose, but stopped, very sensibly, before they reached Sally's tongue.

'But not one – I suspect – in which I will be able – or perhaps even expected – to assist.' She moved to the end of the bed, stood like a chastened, demure little girl who has broken a teacup, still and submissive, hands linked quietly in front of her. 'I am truly sorry for what happened. Can you forgive me?'

The desire to break something – preferably Jackie Pilgrim's neck – stirred in Sally again. 'There's nothin' to be sorry for.'

Charlotte smiled, neither in thanks nor in friendship but in simple, empty acceptance. 'Thank you.'

She left as quietly as she had come, leaving behind her a mist of cool unhappiness on the warm summer air. Sally thought of Ben Patten, of the drive in the man, the granite power, of the sheer overwhelming size of him. For all his good and no doubt noble intentions, how could he do anything but crush the girl? She sighed and laid back against the pillows, her eyes on the sparrows that still squabbled like small ferocious schoolboys outside the window. 'Jerusalem?' she said aloud, her voice purely disbelieving, 'in – what did she say? – England's bloody green and pleasant land?' She shook her head in pure mystification. Beyond the tree the roofs and chimneys of Poplar stood, soot-blackened and filthy against the smoky August sky.

There was no doubt about it. None at all. The sooner she and Toby could get away from here the better she would like it.

Chapter Four

I

Sally heard a great deal about the forthcoming marriage in the days that followed – mostly from the irrepressible Bron who, characteristically, was ready to see the whole unexpected affair as a romance of quite fairy-tale proportions and from Kate, the Patten's other servant girl, who most definitely was not.

'Whoever would have believed it?' marvelled Bron in her pretty, sing-song voice. 'If it had been Mr Peter, now, I wouldn't have been near so surprised – I always rather thought that he and Miss Charlotte would make a pretty enough pair – but Doctor Ben! There's a dark horse! I never thought he'd ever marry again, let alone pick Miss Charlotte!'

'Again?' Sally was faintly surprised. 'He's been married before?'

'Oh, yes.' Bron settled herself companionably upon the bed, her duster idle in her hands, her soft brown eyes misted with ready emotion, her voice dropping to the level of confidences, 'Oh, tragic it was. Truly tragic. Years ago, mind. Childhood sweethearts they were.'

'What happened?'

Bron leaned close. 'She died, see. In childbirth. And the boy with her. Less than a year they were married and there she was gone. Inconsolable he was, so they say. Nearly went out of his mind. So they say. And now – Miss Charlotte! Who ever would have thought it?'

Not Kate Buckley, certainly. 'Well — so little Miss Charlotte decided to land the biggest fish available from the looks of it.' She was a handsome girl, strong and well made with clear, pale skin and a mass of dark hair of which she was inordinately proud. Sally had, to her own mild surprise, disliked the girl the instant she had opened her mouth. She was openly unkind to poor Bron, who went in fear of her and her harsh tongue, blandly deferential to her employers' faces whilst rarely missing an opportunity for scornful — sometimes scurrilous — disrespect behind their backs. The only one she apparently had any time for at all was Ben Patten — and he, quite evidently, had now forfeited that privileged position by his decision to marry a girl whom Kate had decided was empty-headed, flighty and no match for him at all. Privately — very privately — Sally thought she was probably right, but in this as in most other things she held her tongue firmly and would not be drawn either to opinion or to any conversation that required anything more constructive than idle curiosity on her part. But, like Bron, Kate needed no active participation from her audience to keep her tongue wagging. 'Just shows you. He's as bad as the rest of 'em when it gets down to it,' she pronounced, polishing the spotless window as if she intended to rub it clean away. 'Show him a pretty face and a neat ankle and he's off. Well — she's bitten off more than she can chew there, I can tell you.'

'You think so?'

'Think? I bloody know it! Little Miss Pretty's going to find that life as Mrs Ben isn't as easy as I daresay she imagines. She'll have to do a bit more about runnin' the house than she does now for a start — what with Miss Hannah forever chasing round with them daft friends of hers and Doctor Will with his nose never out of a book, the damn' place could fall down and I doubt they'd know it! How poor Mrs Briggs puts up with it I don't know. It's time someone took the lot of them in hand if you ask me

– and if Doctor Ben had been considering matrimony strikes me he'd have done better finding himself someone with more than half an ounce of brains in her silly head that might have done it for him. But no. She bats those baby eyes and off he goes. I really thought he'd 'ave had more sense!'

That, even given Kate's habitual ill humour, seemed to contain an unnecessarily strong thread of bitterness to Sally's ears, and Bron, later, confirmed it. 'She's always been the same. Can't bear anyone to get near Doctor Ben, can't Kate. Got a very soft spot for him she has, like. It's understandable, mind. He rescued her, see.' Her voice dropped to an awed whisper. 'A fallen woman she was. You know?'

'Oh?'

'Oh yes. Came to Doctor Ben with – well, you know –' the girl blushed furiously. 'Always says Doctor Ben was the first man ever treated her like a real person. Oh very kind he can be, you know. If you're in trouble, like.'

Sally smiled.

'Well of course you know. But sharp too, mind, if he doesn't get his own way. Very hard on a person he can be. I shouldn't like to cross him, I don't mind telling you that. In fact if truth be told the man scares me stiff. I keep out of his way if I can. Very chancy that temper of his, see? An' I'm not the only one thinks so, either.'

'But – Kate – she surely didn't expect – I mean she must have known he'd marry some day? They all do, don't they – broken 'earts an' all?'

Bron grinned acknowledgement of this small piece of feminine cynicism. 'Oh I'm not saying she'd ever expect him to look at *her*. No, no. She wouldn't expect that. It's just – she's never cared much for Miss Charlotte, see? An' she thinks she isn't good enough for him.'

Sally yawned tiredly, settled comfortably upon her pillows. 'Well – I don't s'pose what Kate – or you an' me – think about it all 'll worry either of 'em a lot!'

Bron was a natural fount of information: she loved nothing so much as a good gossip. Flitting about the room with duster or mop she would chatter like a small Welsh sparrow, the words tumbling over themselves, interspersed with her lilting, infectious giggle, and never a shade of malice or spite to cloud the bright sunlight of her. Only the uncharitable Kate – of whom she was truly terrified – could cow her to silence.

During those first few long days of convalescence Sally found herself listening with a growing degree of interest. She learned of 'poor' Mr Ralph's unrequited passion for Miss Hannah, of Miss Hannah's own blindness in that respect, to say nothing of her disregard for convention and the natural proprieties. 'Fills the house she does with such funny people! Some friends of hers are in prison! Imagine! "Oh Bron," she says to me the other day, "How I wish I could be there with them!" – Lord, me Da'd have *killed* me if I'd got mixed up with such goings on! But no – Doctor Will sees nothing wrong in it, or so it seems. It's all this silly voting business, see.' Bron straightened from her task, planted small hands on all but non-existent hips, 'Do you know, she asked Kate and me to go to one of those meetings of hers? You know, the votes for women nonsense?'

'Did you go?'

Bron was shocked. 'The very idea! Of course not! What d'you take me for? What's it got to do with me?'

'Did Kate?' Sally asked shrewdly.

Bron's small, generous face tightened a little into the expression that only the mention of Kate could bring. 'Course she did. Once or twice. Not that she thinks more of it all than I do – but it was Miss Hannah'd asked, see?'

Sally saw. 'And?'

Bron shrugged. 'She said it was all just a lot of talk. The young lady Miss Hannah thinks so much of – oh, I can't remember the name, got a terrible memory for names I have – anyway Kate said she talked an' talked about the rights of working women and how we'd all be free and happy if we could vote – well, something like that anyway. An' Miss Hannah made a speech – even Kate said it was a pretty good one, mind, so it can't have been bad, can it? – an' there was lots of girls like us there, so it seems, but Kate didn't care much for any of them.'

'Who does Kate care for?'

Bron smiled swiftly. 'No one I know. So then they started talkin' about marching to Parliament with banners an' things.'

'And Kate lost interest?' Sally asked, a little slyly.

'Oh yes.' Bron was tranquil and entirely ingenuous. 'I mean – that's how Miss Hannah's friends got put in prison, isn't it? With their marching, and their banners and all. It's against the law.'

'Is it?'

'Why of course. Stands to reason.'

'Not for everyone it isn't. Wally and Dan Dickson were up there with banners in the strike last year. No one tried to arrest them.'

Bron was scandalized. 'The strike? But Sally – that was the docks. That was men.'

'Why, so it was,' Sally said.

It did not take any great perception to realize that if Kate's favourite in the family was Ben Patten, Bron's was, unequivocally, Ben's younger brother Peter. Any mention of 'Mr Peter' always brought a breathless giggle and a shine to the soft brown eyes. 'Oh, a right ha'porth he is! Always has been, see. But a good lad, mind. Not an unkind bone in his body that one. And laugh – he'd make the devil himself laugh if he set his mind to it. A lovely boy, really. Breaks a heart a week, or so his Da' always says.' Ralph Bedford too got more than his fair share of warmth. 'Oh, he's ever so kind. Quiet like, but nothing's ever too much trouble for Mr Ralph – cares about people, if you know what I mean. Taught me and Kate to read he did, an' to write too. He's got a lovely way with him has

Mr Ralph. Gentle, you know? The youngsters all love him.'

'Yes. I 'ad noticed.'

Bron ignored or perhaps did not notice the faintly waspish tone. 'He lives and dies for those youngsters.'

'Where do they come from? The kids, I mean?'

'Oh,' Bron waved a small, airy hand, 'all over. Street children Doctor Ben calls them, and that's about it. Orphans, see? Roamin' the streets, homeless until here. Well – you know – you must have seen them? Now they're fed and clothed and taught their letters. Cared for, like.'

'So – what is this place? An orphanage?'

'A bit like, I suppose, yes. But don't you let them hear you call it that, mind. A home's what they call it. A children's home. An' that's what it is too. More of a home than any of these little devils have had before. It's a shame some don't appreciate it!'

''Ow many of them are there?'

'Oh – I'm not sure. It varies, see? There are ten, I think, at the moment. And your Toby, of course. Now there's a lovely lad. I like your Toby. And Mr Ralph was saying just yesterday what a bright little mite he was.'

'Was 'e indeed?' There was no mistaking this time the sharp edge to Sally's tone. Twice in two days Toby had come to see her and twice in two days she had had to listen to him chattering for the whole of the time he was with her about Ralph Bedford. He had been like a cat on hot coals within five minutes of arriving, dying to be off again and unable to hide it.

'You got an appointment or somethin'?' Sally had asked caustically.

'It's just – Mr Ralph's got the tin soldiers out. 'E's goin' to tell us about a famous battle.'

'Ah. Well – don't let me keep you, General.'

She was more disturbed than she cared to admit even to herself about Toby's obvious liking and admiration for a man whose ideas about what was or was not good for him were likely to be very different from Sally Smith's. Lying alone, the nagging worry would not leave her. What kind of influences were working on Toby while she lay helpless here? What kind of harm might these well-meaning people wreak? What could she give him in face of what might be offered here? Ralph himself had not come to see her again – neither indeed had anyone else apart from Doctor Will, who had checked on her progress with that twinkling smile and pronounced it, with some trace of caution, satisfactory.

'But only satisfactory,' he had added, lifting a warning finger, 'you aren't out of the woods entirely, my dear. Rest and quiet is what you're going to need for a good few days yet.'

And rest and quiet were indeed what she got, with only Bron and sometimes Kate to talk to and Toby's looked-for visits becoming rarer and rarer. In the end she was reduced to asking Bron to find him for her; and even then it was a good half hour before the small blond head peered around the door.

'Well, well –' she lifted dark, quarrelsome brows, 'took yer long enough ter get 'ere, didn't it? Come by Bow, did yer?'

The smile died on his face. He lifted a shoulder.

'Cat got yer tongue?' She knew how badly she was handling him, but was powerless to stop herself. At sight of his face, at sight of the wide, clear eyes, the soft, still-babyish curve of his cheeks, an ache worse than the pain in her arm had ever been seemed to have taken root within her. The ache of anticipated loss.

'I was havin' a lesson.' He was sullen.

'What sort o' lesson?' Even his speech, she realized, was changing.

'Times tables.' He flashed a blue glance from beneath long lashes. 'I can say my times two right the way through.'

'That right?'

The glimmer of an eager smile broke through. He nodded. 'Mr Ralph says he's never known anyone learn it so fast. D'you want to hear it?'

She held out for an injured moment longer, then grinned and patted the bed beside her.

He ran to her, laughing, anxious as a puppy to be friends, uncertain as a puppy as to how he might have offended. He scrambled on to the bed. 'Once two is two,' he chanted rapidly, 'two twos are four –'

She watched him, watched the handsome tilt of his head, the play of light on the shining wheat-coloured curls. And, absurdly, she felt the sudden weakness of rising tears. Over a year now they had been together, through thick and thin, a year of constant companionship, of shared hardship, of sometimes desperate struggle and of high, comradely humour. Had he been flesh of her flesh, child of her body, she could not have cared more for him. She could not – would not! – lose him.

Not even to someone who could give him all the things that she could not?

'Eleven twos are twenty-two. Twelve twos are twenty-four.'

'Are they indeed? I never knew that,' she said straight-faced. 'So – what yer bin doin' with yerself while I've bin layin' 'ere like Lady Muck?'

He swung his legs. 'Oh, messing about.'

'Who with?'

'Alice and Sophie. An' Charlie. An' Siddie –'

'Sounds like quite a gang?'

He grinned. 'Mr Ralph calls us the Terrors.'

'An' what are they like, this Alice an' Sophie, an' Charlie an' Siddie?'

He glanced at the door, one foot kicking restlessly at the other. 'They're all right. Alice an' Sophie are sisters. Sophie's pretty, but Alice is nicer.' He slid from the bed, stood leaning, standing on one leg, fidgeting with the toe of the other foot on the leg of the bed. 'Charlie's all right. Siddie an' me fight a lot.'

'That right?' She bit down words of quick irritation as the bed shook.

He looked at the door again.

'Tell you what,' she said, 'it's bin a long time since we've 'eard from Jack Spratt an' Able Cable, 'asn't it?'

He turned back to her, smiling, but his eyes were vague. 'Mm.'

'Think they're back from their treasure island yet?' These two mythical sailor lads, products of Sally's fertile imagination, had seen them through many a long and sometimes hungry night as, giggling together on their narrow pallet, she had embroidered upon their more and more fantastic adventures. 'Think they got away from them cannibals?'

'Don't know.'

She lay quite still, watching him. 'An' maybe don't care a lot either?' she asked quietly and evenly.

'Aw, Sal – it isn't that.'

'Looks like it from 'ere.' She turned her head on the pillow tiredly. 'Go on, yer little tyke. Off yer go. Anyone'd think I'd got yer 'andcuffed.'

He hesitated, banging the leg of the bed again. 'You sure?'

'Course. But, Tobe –?'

He stopped in mid-flight, turned.

'Come an' see me a bit more often, eh? I miss you.'

He nodded, threw her a sparkling smile and was off, scampering to freedom. And to the wonderful Mr Ralph.

She closed her eyes miserably. Her face was hot and her arm ached. Unhappy, stupid tears rose behind her lids. She clenched herself fiercely against them, refusing to let them fall. If the damned child found this damned Bedford man so damned interesting then just at the moment there was nothing she could do about it and she might as well stop fretting. But just wait till she was up and about again. He'd come back to her then. Oh yes. Of course he would.

He came, as it happened, later that afternoon, dragging with him two little girls of perhaps five and seven years old, their close relationship clearly printed upon their faces although one, as Toby had said, was rather prettier than the other. Their reluctance to enter the sickroom was very obvious. Toby however was having none of it. 'Come *on*!' He hauled the smaller and prettier of the two girls unceremoniously behind him. 'Sal – this is Sophie. That's Alice.'

The girls hung back, ducking their brown heads.

''Ow d'yer do,' Sally said gravely.

Toby gave her a brilliant smile, pleased with himself, certain that this gesture would heal the breach that had begun to open between them. He was by no means a stupid or an insensitive child, especially where Sally was concerned. He had seen in the thin, sickly looking face that afternoon how much he had hurt her by his unthinking neglect. This was his apology and his gift, and he knew she would know it. 'I told 'em that you were the best story teller in the world,' he said with total confidence.

'Is that all?'

'Alice likes stories best of all. She told me. It's probably because she can't do her times tables,' he added, more than a little ungenerously but with another shining smile that somehow took the bite from the words.

Sally smiled at the taller of the two children. 'What's your favourite?'

'Snow White and Rose Red.' It was a whisper. The girl lifted shy eyes to Sally's for a moment then looked away.

Sally frowned thoughtfully. 'Snow White an' Rose Red. Yes – I remember – the one about the two little sisters and the bear –'

'Yes.'

'And the 'orrible little dwarf –'

The child nodded, a little more confidently, 'And the handsome prince,' she whispered still shyly.

'Oh, I should say! Mustn't forget the 'andsome prince.'

'Can you tell it to them?' Toby asked, carefully disassociating himself from any such ghastly girlish rubbish. 'I don't s'pose Mr Ralph knows that one.'

Sally smiled at him, knowing well what he offered her, loving him for it, her earlier disappointment and unhappiness melting as he had known it would. 'I 'spect I can, yes. 'Ere – come an' sit on the bed. But you'll 'ave ter scarper if we 'ear the dragon lady comin', all right?'

The two little girls, giggling at Sally's irreverent description of Miss Reid, scrambled on to the bed.

'It's all right. I'll keep watch.' Gallantly self-important, Toby stationed himself beside the door.

'Now – let's see –' Sally thought for a moment, 'once upon a time there was this poor widder-woman who lived alone in a cottage in a deep dark wood, with only 'er two dear little girls for company –'

The smaller of the two girls, Sophie, snuggled a little closer and put her thumb into her mouth.

'– but she was all right because these two little sisters were the nicest, kindest, sweetest little 'uns you're ever likely to come across.'

The words, as always, came effortlessly to her tongue. Always there had been the stories, the magic shield between her and a childhood world even harsher than the one in which she now lived. Her mother's had been the lap upon which she had learned these tales that had never left her, never lost their enchantment, her mother's the melodic young voice that had woven a glittering spell about a cold and hungry little girl. Her mother. Lucy Smith. A soft and once-pretty young woman who had died before her twenty-fifth birthday of despair and malnutrition when the effort of keeping body and soul together had finally proved too much despite her ten-year-old daughter's desperate pleas. Lucy Smith. Had that been her true name? Sally doubted it. A country parson's daughter so far fallen from grace and with a bastard child in her belly when she was turned from her father's house would hardly be likely to keep that father's name. She had drifted to London, survived Sally's birth, somehow laboured to keep herself and her child alive; and when that labour had seemed no longer necessary she had given up the fight and died, leaving her daughter as legacy a crown of shining brown hair, a store of fairy stories and a memory that grew fainter with each passing year of a tired, careworn face, gentle hands and a soft, well-modulated voice. As a child Sally had spoken as her mother spoke, and had suffered for it. Now she knew better.

'— "Stupid thing!" shouted the dwarf. "Don't stand there gawpin'! 'Elp me out of 'ere!"'

The heritage had certainly been better than none at all. The magic of the stories had never left her, nor had the recollection of those precious moments of comparative safety in a cruelly dangerous world, curled into her mother's lap, her thumb in her mouth just as Sophie's now was. When Toby had come she had presented the treasure to him, and he too had known its value, curled against her in that chill attic, the hard narrow bed a magic carpet to fly Sinbad to his princess or Aladdin from his cave.

'"Spare me, my great Lord Bear!" cried the wicked old dwarf, "an' I'll give you all my treasures!"'

Footsteps sounded in the corridor outside, and Alice looked up, alarmed. But these were not the unmistakably brisk, efficient footsteps of Miss Reid. They were slower and quieter.

'It's Mr Ralph,' Toby said, his whole face split in two by his smile.

'Mr Ralph!' Sophie slid from the bed and flew to the door to clasp the hand of the man who stood ruffling Toby's hair, smiling pleasantly at Sally.

Sally did not smile back.

'Please — I've interrupted — you were telling a story. Do go on. I only came to check that the Terrors weren't bothering you. Doctor Will says you still need to rest.'

'They aren't bothering me.'

If he noticed the slight, dry emphasis on the first word of the sentence he gave no sign. His smile widened. Gently he disengaged his hand from Sophie's and gave her a small push towards the bed. 'Please — do go on.' He walked to the chair and folded himself, ungainly, into it.

She couldn't. She could not. The magic words had flown, her brain was like lead. She heard the harshness of her own voice, the ugliness of the ill-pronounced words. Sophie fidgeted. Toby had given up his guard and was leaning against Ralph Bedford's knee, playing with his watch chain.

'— An' so the bear turned into a handsome prince and 'e married Snow White an' Rose Red married 'is brother,' Sally finished curtly.

'— An' they all lived happily ever after,' Alice prompted.

'Course they did.'

The silence was awkward, and quite deliberately Sally let it remain so.

'Can we come again?' Alice asked unexpectedly.

'If yer like.'

'Do you know any more stories?'

'Tons.'

'Thousands,' Toby said, still playing with the gold watch chain, 'millions.'

'Bet she doesn't,' pragmatic Sophie said. 'Not *millions*.'

'Bet she does!'

Ralph held up his hands, laughing. 'All right, all right, enough's enough. Off you go. It's teatime. And Miss Smith is supposed to be resting.'

The children tumbled to the door. Toby stopped, looked back expectantly, grinning.

'Thanks, Tobe.'

His smile widened, and then he was gone. Ralph

remained sitting, as always awkwardly, upon the chair, elbows on knees, large hands clasped loosely together. 'He's a very special young man, your Toby.'

'I'd noticed.' She made no effort to hide her sullen hostility. She would not look at him.

'Miss Smith,' Ralph said gently, 'I really feel that we should talk.'

She lifted her head, her thin face harsh, the narrow eyes perilous. 'What about?'

He ploughed on. 'About Toby. Please – you have to believe that we aren't trying to take him away from you.'

She glared at him for a moment, but the effort of defiance in her weakened state was simply too much. Abruptly she laid back on to the pillows and closed her eyes. 'Yer could 'a fooled me,' she said very quietly.

'No. Please – listen.' Ralph's voice was suddenly determined. He had outfaced such stubborn and he sometimes suspected deliberate misconstruction of his intentions and motives before: and where the welfare of a child was concerned he knew that he could be every bit as tenacious as this tough, tired girl who lay now, eyes and face closed against him, her long bony hands clenched upon the counterpane, her skin as white as the bleached linen in which she lay. 'Yes, I make no bones about it, I'd like to keep Toby here. Miss Smith, the lad's safe here. He's happy. He's learning – I've never known a child with a quicker or more receptive brain. And he's removed from temptation.'

They both knew what he meant. Sally would not ask how he had come to know the child so quickly and so well. ''E's all right with me.'

'Of course he is.' Ralph smiled a little. 'And that's why I'm asking you to consider staying too.' He held up his hand as her eyes flew open and she opened her mouth. 'Wait – please wait. For a long time we've needed another pair of hands here at the home. Kate isn't very good with the children and they run rings around Bron. You could be the very one we're looking for.'

She was shaking her head. 'No.'

He spread big, exasperated hands, 'But —'

'No!'

He straightened, stood awkwardly. 'Miss Smith —'

'Mr Bedford —!' she interrupted, harshly, the distinctive voice very low and very dangerous, 'From where you stand, with your ordered life, your wonderful convictions an' your full belly I might not look much. But let me tell you you're wrong. I just got to get better, that's all. Then we'll get out of your way an' won't bother you no more. Just a few more days an' we'll be off. With many thanks, of course. An' I mean that. Don't think I don't know what you've done for me, an' for Toby. I'm not stupid, an' whatever it seems I'm not ungrateful. But we don't need your charity, Mr Bedford. We've got an 'ome, an' we've got a life of our own. An' I'll thank you, as soon as I'm strong enough, to let us get on an' live it. I won't lose 'im, Mr Bedford — you 'ear me?' — I won't. Not to you. Not to no one. 'E's all I've got. An' I'm all 'e's got. An' that's enough for us. Like I said — we don't need your charity.'

'Please! You misunderstand entirely!'

'No,' she said flatly, 'I don't. I understand that you think you're actin' for the best. What you 'ave to understand, Mr Bedford, is that whatever you might believe you an' your like don't necessarily *know* what's best for me an' mine. Leave us alone, Mr Bedford. Just leave us alone.' She closed her eyes again, suddenly exhausted. There were two bright, angry-looking patches upon her cheeks.

There was a long, careful silence. Then she heard him move quietly towards the door. She heard him take breath once, as if he were about to speak and she steeled herself wearily against argument. But, 'Toby put us in touch with a Miss Josie Dickson,' he said quietly. 'She's coming to visit you this evening. Do you feel strong enough?'

Her eyes snapped open. 'Josie?'

He nodded.

Weak and infuriating tears rose again. She blinked them furiously away. 'Yes. I'd like to see Josie.'

Toby, beaming, brought Josie to her as the long warm August evening began, with the air of a conjurer producing a particularly spectacular rabbit out of a hat. Sally, her spirits lifted at the prospect of the visit, had convinced herself that she felt better. When Miss Reid had bustled brusquely in to tidy the room and supervise the patient's supper she had not mentioned that she still felt too warm for comfort and that her arm throbbed with a faint but regular pulse of pain that had not been evident that morning.

'Sally – oh, Sally – it's so lovely to *see* you!' Josie flew across the room, stopped just short of flinging herself upon her friend and bent to kiss her cheek instead. 'We've been frantic with worry, Sal! You just disappeared!'

'I was comin' to you. But – I was taken sick at the soup kitchen. Doctor Ben was there. 'E sent me 'ere.'

'And a jolly good job he did! What *happened*? What's wrong? And how are you feeling now?'

With economy Sally told the story, inventing nothing, simply leaving out those things that might bring questions awkward for the Pattens, to whom for all her present resentments she suspected she owed her life. She and Jackie had quarrelled. Jackie had got drunk and come after her with a knife. The wound had festered. Here she was.

'But why didn't you come to *us*?'

'I told you – I was comin'.'

'Two weeks after it happened!'

Sally shrugged and grinned a little, apologetically. 'Can't rush these things.'

'Sally Smith, you're impossible!'

'There's more than you around to think that. Now – tell me what's bin 'appenin' in the wide world. The old dragon said you couldn't stay too long, so don't let's waste time. 'Ow's the family?'

'They're well. Dad's back's playing him up a bit again – oh, and Wally broke a finger, but it's healing. Dan sends his love. He wants to know can he come to visit you?'

'No.' The word was far too hasty. Sally flushed a little. 'Er – no. They don't like too many people traipsing in an' out. Yer can't blame them really.'

'No. Of course not. He'll understand. Anyway – he'll see plenty of you when you come home.'

Sally looked at her blankly. 'Home?'

'To us. Of course. Where else were you thinking of going? You said yourself you were coming to us.'

'That was when I was sick. When I get out of 'ere I'll be better. Tobe an' I can go on 'ome an' I'll get a job.' She stopped. 'What the 'ell's the matter with you two?' she asked suspiciously.

Josie and Toby had cast a quick and unmistakably worried glance at each other, too meaningful to be missed.

'Well?'

Josie perched on the edge of the bed and took her hand. 'Your room's gone, Sal. The landlord's let it.'

'E's *what*?'

'You missed your rent. He thought you'd scarpered.'

It hit her harder than she would have believed possible. That attic room might not have been the Savoy, but it had been hers, hers and Toby's. It had come to be home. 'What about me things?'

'Betty downstairs 'as got them,' Toby volunteered. 'I went back, a couple of days ago, to see what was 'appening.'

'There's a family of five living in your room,' Josie put in. 'God knows where they sleep.'

'Soddin' bloody landlord,' Sally said with faint but blistering rancour. 'I'll wring 'is bleedin' neck.' But the threat was without substance. Her voice was tired.

'So,' Josie said tentatively, 'you do see? You'll have to come to us. For a while at any rate. Until you get on your feet.'

'An' what does your dad think of that idea?' Sally asked, softly, shaking her head a little.

Josie ignored the question. 'You can come in with me. And I'm sure we can fit a truckle into the kitchen for Toby.'

Sally chose not to notice the look of desperation Toby cast her. She was still struggling to contain this latest blow. She took a long breath that somehow turned into a sigh of defeated exhaustion. Bloody landlords. Bloody world. 'Give us – give us a day or so to think about it, eh?'

Toby nibbled his lip.

'Of course. Just as soon as you're strong enough, come to tea. You'll see. Everything's going to be fine.'

Sally nodded.

Josie stood. 'I should go now, I think. I mustn't tire you. I'll come again soon. And just as soon as you're well Dan and I will come over to get you and you must come to tea so we can make some plans. All right?'

Sally nodded, too tired to argue.

Josie kissed her, swiftly and fiercely. 'Lord, I've been so worried!'

'I'm sorry.' With her good hand Sally gripped the slim, strong wrist, 'You'd no call ter worry, though. Yer know me. Always the bad penny. Yer won't get rid o' me that easy!'

'I'm sorry – really sorry – about the room.'

'Yes,' Sally said a little grimly, 'so'm I.'

The other girl dropped a quick kiss on Toby's head, lifted a hand to Sally, smiled her farewell. 'I'll see you very soon.'

In the quiet of the sunlit room after her departure the boy and the young woman listened as the sound of her footsteps faded. Austerely Sally held the blue, bright eyes with her own. 'We bin 'omeless before, Toby Jug,' she said at last, flatly, but with the faintest thread of question in her voice.

Toby said nothing.

'Tobe?'

He looked up, his small face suddenly fierce, and shook his head.

She closed her eyes, and through the sun-spangled darkness behind the lids, heard him leave with no word.

II

The proposed visit to the Dicksons could not, as events turned out, be undertaken until a full ten days later. During the night that followed Josie's visit Sally's temperature rose alarmingly. The next twenty-four hours passed in a fog of fever, a fog that lifted occasionally to reveal a small, fair, anxious face, a craggy, almost angry one, a pale, narrow visage bespectacled and topped with lank dark hair that hovered always at a distance and which brought on her worst nightmares, despite its obvious concern. The awful dreams besieged her. She was running, running for her life down narrow alleys in darkness and intolerable heat, the menacing shadow that flitted behind her wearing sometimes Jackie Pilgrim's face, sometimes that of a stranger, sometimes – the worst times – no face at all. She drifted on a fierce red sea of darkness, lost and alone, Toby's voice somewhere, calling, his face unseen, his hand never meeting the desperate one she stretched to him. Exhausting and terrifying, the nightmares gave her no rest. Time ceased to exist. Toby was gone, and she could find him nowhere.

At last, worn out, she drifted into true sleep; and awoke to find another sultry August evening and twenty-four hours lost to her entirely.

'Well, young lady, what was all that about?' Even

frowning Doctor Will's face never seemed to lose its twinkle.

She gave a precarious and weakly smile.

'Right. This time you'll do exactly as you're told. Or I'll tie you down and lock the door! *Rest*, young lady! *Rest!*'

This time she did. She could not, she knew, afford to do anything else. She had lost twenty-four hours – twenty-four hours of progress, twenty-four hours of Toby to Ralph Bedford, twenty-four hours of her future to the busily planning Dicksons. She had to get well. With a savage effort of will she rested. She ate everything that was put in front of her. She stayed calm, she had few visitors, obviously on the express orders of Doctor Will. In three days she had regained the ground she had lost, and more. By the end of the week she was sitting in the chair by the window and a reluctant Miss Reid gave permission for Toby and his friends to visit her. At first it was just the girls, and the stories were Cinderella and Snow White, but a couple of days later the two boys, Charlie and Siddie – with whom, as he had said, Toby showed a constant and regrettable urge to fight – had joined them, intrigued, ready to scoff, and she had searched in her treasure chest for more bloodthirsty and rousing dramas. Wolves and soldiers, dragons and magicians. And, of course, the wonderful, entirely original and absolutely impossible adventures of those intrepid sailor lads Able Cable and Jack Spratt.

'Just ring the bell if those children are bothering you.' Miss Reid pursed disapproving lips.

'They're not.' On the contrary she looked forward to their coming, listened for their voices, watched particularly for one fair, curly head, a pair of blue eyes, mischievous and confident. If the truth be known all the stories were for him. Every unsparing effort she made, from swallowing the sweet milky tea she abominated to rousing herself to ever greater flights of fancy in her storytelling was for him. She would not lose him. When she left — and she still had every intention of leaving as soon as possible — he would come with her.

Her iron resolve to leave the Bear was strengthened on the day that the children turned up, twittering excitedly, trailing behind Toby, who carried a large book. It was a week after her relapse. Clothed in decent, sober skirt and blouse a good size too large for her Sally sat in the chair by the window. Alice helped Toby to heave the book on to the bed. 'Mr Ralph said we could bring it,' she said shyly, leafing through the bright pages. 'He thought you might like to see it. It's a fairy-story book, see? It isn't half nice. It's got lots of pictures — look — of all the stories you've told us. There's Cinderella — d'you see? — in her ballgown. And this — is —' She hesitated.

Toby leaned forward, ferociously concentrating. 'S-L-E-E-P — Sleeping Beauty!' he snapped, his quick mind leaping ahead to supply the answer before all the individual letters could be recognized and assimilated.

'Is it now?' Sally asked.

Toby glanced at her warily, recognizing too well the tone.

Sally looked at the book with its bright, intricately beautiful pictures, its mass of stupid, meaningless marks that marched, precise and defeating, across the pages and resisted with some difficulty the urge to rip it to shreds.

'What's this one?' small Sophie demanded. 'It's a witch, look — and she's got a cat. What's the cat's name? Toby — what's the cat's name?'

'I'll tell you later,' Toby muttered, eyes flicking back to the storm building on Sally's face. He shut the book with a snap.

'O — oh!' the girls chorused together.

But Toby knew well when he had backed a loser. 'Come on,' he said, 'it's probably better if we leave Sal to rest for a bit. We can look at this downstairs.' And with a back as straight as an arrow and fairly bristling with resentment and injury he marched from the room, his flock of small acolytes following.

Sally scowled after them.

'I've come to meet Scheherezade. May I come in?' The amused voice from the open doorway startled her. A tall, angular young woman stood there, heavy chestnut hair wildly astray from an untidy chignon, laughter on her plain, pleasant face, a tea tray in her hands. 'I just bumped into young Toby and his henchmen. Are you exhausted? Should I come back later?'

Sally shook her head. 'No. No, it's all right. They didn't stay for long.' She smiled the small, wry smile that tilted one corner of her mouth, 'They've got other fish to fry this afternoon.'

'So you're abandoned?'

'Somethin' like that.'

'Tea, then,' the other girl said briskly and pleasantly, 'if you'd like?'

'Yes. Thank you.'

Hannah put the tray down, extended a strong hand. 'I'm Hannah Patten.'

'Yes, I know. I've seen you.' Sally hesitated for a brief moment, then lifted her head proudly, 'At the soup kitchen.'

Hannah nodded, entirely casually, unimpressed by such prickles. 'Oh yes, of course. Well I'm sorry I haven't been before but it seemed to me that you were rather over-burdened with Pattens and Bedfords without my adding to their number. Sugar?'

'Yes please. Two.'

'I know all about you, of course. Ever since my brother Ben came charging back from Maisie Wilmott's confinement demanding to know where you were and what had been done for you the household has followed your progress with enormous interest.'

'Oh?' The single syllable was tense, as wary as the lifting of a wild thing's head to a hostile scent.

Hannah smiled, her long, bony face utterly open. 'Oh, don't worry. I'll tell you at once that I'm not going to ask how you were hurt. Ben has impressed upon us all that it isn't something you care to speak of. Though from the way he spoke I gather you did something rather splendid – I think he believes you should be awarded the Victoria Cross at least!'

Sally felt colour lift in her face, shook her head.

Hannah, apparently as unaware of embarrassment as she was of tender pride, handed her a cup of tea, talking easily and inconsequentially. 'I must say I've sometimes wondered how I'd cope in a real emergency – a dangerous one, I mean, that required real physical courage.' She turned back to the tray, picked up her own cup and saucer, hoisted herself in none too ladylike fashion on to the bed, 'I'd like to think I'd be splendid of course – a Victorian heroine standing fearless against the natives, Florence Nightingale ordering all those awful generals about.' She broke off into a sudden, utterly disarming gurgle of laughter, 'I'm sure I should do no such thing. I'd probably scream and run.'

Sally found herself laughing with her. 'I've seen you, though,' she said, 'in the streets. Makin' them speeches. An' people shouting at you.'

Hannah dismissed that poppycock with a brisk shake of the head. 'Oh no, that's not the same at all. It's not brave – not *heroine* brave. I don't suppose I'll ever get the chance to discover if I'm that.'

They drank their tea in a moment of remarkably companionable silence. Sally found herself relaxing. Instinctively she liked this young woman. Liked the straightness of her, the lack of airs and graces. Liked the humour that crinkled the unremarkable brown eyes and quirked the long mouth to a natural smile.

Hannah drained her cup, lifted her head. Smiled her disarmingly frank smile. 'I believe', she said, 'that you sent our Ralph away with a flea in his ear?'

Sally nearly choked.

Matter of factly Hannah patted her back, relieved her of her cup. 'I do understand, believe me. Ralph can be a positive curse when he gets a bee in his bonnet. More tea?'

'Yes. Please.' Sally took a firm grip of her shaken nerves. Another attack, then, from a different quarter. Let them try. She wouldn't be caught off guard again.

The tea was duly poured, stirred, handed to her. Hannah perched on the bed, watching her, saying nothing, smiling pleasantly.

Sally, despite resistance, found herself forced into speech. 'He – Mr Bedford – wants Toby to stay here.' She found she was making an effort to enunciate clearly, to recover that way of speech taught by her mother and so despised by her peers. Obscurely the thought made her angry again.

'He wants you both to stay,' Hannah said calmly.

Sally shook a stubborn head.

'But yes – I promise you. It isn't just Toby he wants. He truly does need someone to help in the home. I'm useless – I'm hardly ever here – and Charlotte –' she made a vague gesture with her hand. 'Neither Kate nor Bron are interested in the children. They find the tougher ones impossible to handle. Ralph seems to think you wouldn't.'

'What gave 'im that idea?' The words bordered on the truculent.

Hannah shook her head unruffled. 'I really don't know. He's spent a lot of time with Toby. Perhaps he's said something?'

Damn' kid should know by now when to keep his mouth shut. I'll skin him alive. She did not say the words, but something of their import was perceived by Hannah in her face.

'Oh, don't be angry with poor Toby. He talks about you all the time, you know. He thinks you're the most wonderful person in the whole world. He loves you dearly. You're very lucky.'

137

It was beyond Sally to argue with that novel idea. 'I can't stay,' she said. 'I don't want to.'

'That's fair enough, I suppose. But — won't you think about it?'

In her most ungracious gesture to date — and she was uncomfortably aware that grace had not been her hallmark over the past few minutes — Sally lifted a dismissive shoulder.

Hannah quietly and neatly collected the cups and set them on the tray. 'May I say something?'

Sally had retreated entirely into panic. If Ralph had everyone in the family working on Toby what chance did she — Sally — stand against them? 'Suit yourself,' she said expressionlessly.

'I believe that you may think that we're trying to trick you. You don't know us, after all. Why should you trust us? I believe that you think that we want to take Toby from you and want you to stay just long enough for him to get settled here — to make it impossible for you to take him away — and then — presto — out you go. Am I right?'

She could not have expressed it better herself. She said nothing.

'You're wrong,' Hannah said simply. 'Truly you are. Think of this. Legally we probably could take Toby from you. How would you fight us? He isn't your child, is he?' She did not wait for an answer, 'He's living with you virtually in the streets. He should be in school. Ralph says he's one of the brightest children he's ever come across. Miss Smith — surely you can see that he should be educated? Would you deny him that? Would you deny him his chance to prepare for a brighter future? A better tomorrow?'

Tomorrow. Unexpectedly Charlotte's voice came to her, desolate and empty. Her eyes narrowed. 'So 'e can live in this Jerusalem of yours?' she asked bitterly.

'Yes,' Hannah said thoughtfully, but with no hesitation. 'Exactly. But Miss Smith — it's your future too, don't you see that? And – please don't misunderstand – I'm only pointing out that we *could* take him from you if we were determined. But I promise you we'd never do that. We want you *both* to stay. For a while at least. Won't you try it? Think about it? Ralph thinks that Toby is a quite remarkable child. We all know, don't we, what can happen to such a child? Miss Smith – please believe me – we want to *help* you both.'

Sally, carefully, for she was still very shaky on her legs, stood up, lifted her chin. 'I told Mr Bedford –'

'Yes,' ruefully Hannah interrupted, for the first time her manner a fraction less than confident, 'I know what you told him. It shook him quite badly. You said that people like us don't necessary know what's best for –' she hesitated.

'For people like me.' Sally finished for her, her voice oddly gentle. 'Miss Hannah, I'm sorry if I'm upsettin' you all – but don't you think you'd be better off helpin' them as wants to be helped an' leavin' them as doesn't ter themselves?'

Hannah stood for what seemed a long time, thoughtful, an honest and pensive frown upon her wide forehead. 'I hope not,' she said at last, 'I really do. But then – I can see that you may be right.' She smiled again, her attractive, easy smile, 'It's difficult, isn't it, in this difficult world, really to know what's best and what isn't?' She turned, picked up the tray, smiled back at Sally. 'Perhaps we've each given the other something to think about? Would you mind if I popped in to see you again?'

'Course not.'

'Thank you. I shall look forward to it. I can't stay longer now – it's a great day today – I'm going to meet some friends who are coming out of prison.'

Sally raised half-amused eyebrows. 'Throwin' a party, are yer?'

Hannah laughed. 'Oh yes. Of course.'

Sally nodded. 'Nothin' like a party when yer mates get out of nick. 'Olloway, was it?'

'Yes.' Unlike Sally Hannah seemed to find nothing remarkable in the bizarre conversation.

Sally's mouth twitched into a faint smile. 'Ask 'em about Big Beryl. They'll 'ave some tales to tell about 'er I'll be bound. You ask 'em.'

Hannah laughed aloud. 'I shall. I shall indeed.' The echo of her laughter hung on the air full moments after she had left the room.

Sally, very thoughtfully, listened to her departing footsteps and found herself hoping fervently that the forthright and likeable Hannah Patten did not come to see her too often.

III

Once started, Sally's recovery this time was swift. Though weakened by the fever that had so nearly killed her, her tough constitution, nurtured by good food and rest, asserted itself, and within a couple of days she was well and truly back on her feet. Accompanied by Toby and those of his friends who were not at school she walked a little in the courtyard in the afternoons; cooped up in her room she took to pacing back and forth from window to door, restless now and eager to be away, though in her gratitude to Doctor Will she had found herself agreeing to stay until he decreed her well enough to leave. Of one thing she was certain, and became more so with each passing day, each added ounce of strength; she must get out of here, under her own steam and to her own destination. With or without Toby. Her independence was all she had – she would surrender it neither to the well-meaning Pattens nor, much as she loved them, to the equally freedom-threatening Dicksons.

As to the last, Toby too had strong feelings, and for his own reasons single-mindedly set about making certain that this particular threat would not materialize. Tea at the Dicksons', a few days after Hannah Patten's visit to Sally, was a near-complete disaster.

Toby misbehaved from the start, deliberately Sally was certain, despite his later fervent denials. Josie's father, Bill, a big man like both of his sons, with the massive shoulders and square, heavy face of the docklands held his tongue before the pleading eyes of his daughter, but no one could miss the clear itch in him to clip the recalcitrant child's ear, and hard.

'Tobe, fer God's sake be'ave yerself!' Sally said in desperation. 'Put that thing down an' come over 'ere.'

With great delicacy, Toby replaced the china cat he had been holding not quite squarely upon the narrow mantelpiece. Before anyone could move to save it, it teetered and fell with a splintering crash on to the tiled hearth.

Thunderous, Bill Dickson half-rose in his chair. No boy of his had ever been allowed to behave so, he'd made certain of that, and while the heavy belt that had knocked his two into order was still to hand he saw no reason why this too-clever-by-half young whippersnapper should be allowed to run rings around his elders and betters –

Josie slipped between them. 'Oh dear! Never mind. I never did much like that cat.' She dropped to her knees, picking up the shattered pieces. Sally looked pure murder into a pair of raised, defiantly innocent blue eyes. 'Come 'ere!' she ordered, perilously quiet.

Face mutinous, he obeyed. Wally cuffed him lightly as he passed. 'Clumsy little beggar!' but his tone was tolerant and his hand light. Dan, quiet in his corner, watched not Toby but – as she was too well aware – Sally as she caught the lad's wrist in a rough grip and pulled him to her side. 'Be'ave!' she hissed furiously into his reddened young ear, 'or I swear I'll skin yer!'

The child sat through tea scowling, managing to drop his buttered crumpet upon the floor, splash his tea upon

Josie's snow-white tablecloth and apply a good deal more jam to his face and fingers than he did to his scone. The conversation, despite all Josie's and Wally's best efforts was stilted, with Sally like a cat on hot bricks each time Toby moved or opened his mouth. When at last Josie broached the subject of their moving in temporarily with the Dicksons she shook her head sharply, 'No – really. We couldn't. You 'aven't got the room.'

Bill Dickson, his eyes on Toby, did not disagree.

'There's plenty of space in Josie's room for an extra bed.' Slow-spoken Dan crumbled a piece of cake in a huge hand, 'An' we can easily stick a truckle in the kitchen for the lad. It's only for a bit. Until you get on your feet.'

She cast an almost despairing look at him. His broad, good-natured face was as close to pleading as it could possibly come. On the tram that had brought them from Poplar he had spoken, quietly stubborn, of their staying at Bolton Terrace, had phlegmatically refuted every argument she had mustered against the plan. He sat now, steadfastly refusing to look at his father, an obstinate refusal to be budged written all over his face. He wanted Sally Smith here, under his eyes and within his reach. Then, surely, he could convince her how much she needed a good steady man, a strong arm, a decent home of her own, a couple of her own kids at her skirt.

'It's puttin' you to too much trouble.' When it came to stubbornness Sally was in there with the best of them. 'I'll find work soon – we can easily find a room then. P'raps round 'ere somewhere,' she added weakly, a sop to the open disappointment and hurt she read in his broad, uncomplicated face.

'It wouldn't be any trouble,' he said doggedly. 'Josie says you've been really sick. You mustn't try to work yet.'

She flashed him a glance of wry amusement at that. ''Oo d'yer think you're talkin' to, Dan? Lady Muck?

Since when did the likes of you an' me take to our beds an' stay there?'

He grinned at that, as did the others. The atmosphere eased a little.

Toby knocked his cup and the tea slurped on to the now well-stained cloth.

'There's another meal in that cloth, Josie,' her father said, eyeing the child repressively, 'if yer put it through the mangle.'

Sally glanced around the tiny, neat room, cluttered now with so many in it, and shook her head. 'It's kind of you – but no – there isn't the room, Jose. Yer dad's got the right to come 'ome to a tidy 'ouse after a day's work. 'E don't want us fillin' the place. Do yer, Mr Dickson?'

Caught, as she had intended, unawares by the direct question, Bill Dickson frowned ferociously. 'I – er –' he cleared his throat, his ruddy face suddenly afire.

'Dad!' Josie said.

Dan's face dropped.

Sally covered Josie's hand with hers. 'I'll find us a room somewhere close. I promise. But we got to be on our own, Jose. You do see that?'

The battle well and truly lost, Josie nodded with good grace. 'All right. I suppose so.' She would not look at her much-loved older brother's tongue-tied disappointment. With wry exasperation she dumped the last large piece of fruit cake on Toby's plate. 'Here, Toby. Make a pig of yourself with that.'

'Thanks fer your 'elp,' Sally said drily to Toby later as they walked through the busy streets to the tram stop, Sally having adamantly refused Dan's eager offer of escort, 'but I could ha' done very well without it. I don't want to live there either.'

Toby glanced unrepentantly at her face, gauging her mood. 'Where we going ter live, then?' he asked tentatively.

'Like I said. We'll find a room.'

His face dropped.

She slanted a narrow glance at him. 'Yer don't like the idea?'

He was silent.

'Tobe?' Her voice was very quiet. 'We've always bin all right on our own before. 'Aven't we?'

'Course.'

'So – what's changed?'

He shrugged.

She stopped walking, turned him to face her, oblivious of the hurrying crowds about them, the noisy, slow-moving traffic. 'Toby? Tell me. You want ter stay with them instead of comin' with me?' There was no need to be more specific she knew.

His head shot up like a startled young animal's. 'No! No, Sal! Course not!' He hesitated then, his young face troubled, 'At least –'

'What?'

'Oh, Sal – can't we both stay? Mr Ralph says we can.'

She shook her head. 'No.'

'But why not?'

'Fer the same reason we're not goin' ter the Dicksons. You 'ave ter stand alone in this life, Toby lad. If yer don't – if yer trust too much – if yer let people take yer over – you've got nothin' left. Believe me. I know.'

'But – you an' me – we trust each other.'

'Yes. Well – we're different, aren't we?' Her voice was crisp. 'You an' me against the rest, eh? That's the way it's bin. Why change it?'

The child sighed.

She took his hand again. 'Right then. That's settled. But before we find a new 'ome,' they dodged across the road, skipping behind a clanking tram, ignoring the bad-tempered whip-flourishing of the driver of a cart stacked with strong-smelling fish boxes, 'we're goin' ter get our things back from the old one.'

*

The girl Betty, slovenly in a stained robe that gaped to show drooping, naked breasts, gawped at her visitors. 'Gawd! It's Sally, isn't it? 'Eard tell you were dead!'

'Just goes ter show yer shouldn't believe all you 'ear. You goin' ter let us in?'

The girl glanced uncomfortably over her shoulder and drew the door to behind her. 'Well – it's awkward yer see –'

'What the 'ell yer doin', Bet?' A man's voice, hoarse, irritated.

Betty shrugged, half-apologetically. 'See what I mean?' Her voice was low. 'Sorry, Sal – you'll 'ave ter go –'

'Not without me things.'

'Things?' The girl looked vague. Her hair was like a bird's nest and she smelled of stale perspiration and cheap gin.

Sally put a purposeful foot in the door. 'Yes, Bet,' she said pleasantly, 'things. The things yer took from the room upstairs when the poxy landlord threw them out. Ter keep for me, so I was told.'

Betty shot a murderous look at Toby. 'Oh, yeah. Them things.' She hesitated a moment longer. 'Wait a mo. I'll get them.'

She closed the door. Sally and Toby stood in silence. The door opposite – Jackie Pilgrim's door – stood shut. Toby pressed a little closer to Sally. His eyes were huge in the semi-darkness of the landing. Sally wondered how in so short a time she could have forgotten the vileness of smell spewed up by the tenements.

''Ere you are. All I could salvage.' Betty's door opened and unceremoniously she dumped a small bundle into Sally's arms.

'This all?'

'Yes. I swear, Sal. The bleedin' landlord kept the rest. In lieu of rent. I swear. You're lucky I saved anythin'.' Her voice was injured.

Sally watched her pugnaciously for a moment, then shrugged. 'All right. Thanks.' She turned to go.

'Hey – Sal?'

Sally waited.

''Oo was the 'eavy that saw ter Jackie?' Betty jerked her frowsty head at the closed door opposite.

Sally frowned. 'Saw to 'im?'

Betty grinned, revealing wide-gapped, incredibly dirty teeth. 'I should say. Not the toff 'e was, our Jackie. Ruined 'is pretty face 'e did –'

''Oo did?'

'The lad that came after 'im. Big feller. Built like a barn. Reddish 'air. Everyone reckoned 'e must be a mate o' yours. You don't know 'im?'

Very positively Sally shook her head. 'What 'appened?'

'Like I said – 'e wiped the floor with Jackie an' threw 'im out. Told 'im in no uncertain terms what'd 'appen if 'e tried ter crawl back. Our Jackie ain't bin seen since. Can't say I blame 'im.' She grinned again, indicating with a long-nailed thumb over her shoulder the occupant of the room behind her, 'The new lad's moved in. Not half bad.'

Right on cue the hoarse voice called, 'Bet!'

'I'm comin'! Keep yer 'air on!' She turned back to Sally. 'So – this bloke – the one that saw ter Jackie – 'e wasn't a pal o' yours?'

'No.'

'Ah. Thought 'e might be. But then again, might 'a bin somethin' ter do with that other business – the girl, yer know? 'Cos 'e might 'ave looked like a prizefighter, but 'e surely didn't talk like one. Talked real posh 'e did. Didn't come from round 'ere.'

'*Betty*!'

She raised eyes to heaven, lifted a hand. 'See you sometime, p'raps?'

Sally nodded. Watched as the door closed.

Big. Built like a barn. Reddish hair. Talked posh. The description so fitted Doctor Ben Patten that she almost laughed aloud. It couldn't be. Not possibly. But funny to think that somewhere loose in the East End of London was someone like enough to him who was capable of roughing up Jackie Pilgrim –

Laughing still she hitched her meagre bundle under her arm, took Toby's hand and marched down the stairs.

She laid her plans firmly. She wanted no arguments, no recriminations. She would leave the Bear, and no one would stop her. Needless to say the last precious pennies of her savings had gone from the bundle she had collected from Betty, but still there was one good dress and a spare pair of shoes, and she had too the clothes that the Pattens had given her. Abie Mendleshon the pawnbroker would see her through on those with enough for a room and a couple of meals. Then she'd find work – any work. There was always a way to turn a penny if you were really desperate. She wouldn't die of it. They'd be all right.

'No,' Toby said.

Sally stared at him, her heart suddenly slowing in a strange, sickly way. 'What?'

Miserably the child stood, tears sliding down his fair, rounded cheeks. 'Sal – please! – I don't want to go! I want to stay here!'

She swallowed. 'We can't always 'ave what we want, Tobe.'

'But we can have this! They *want* us to stay!'

'No!' The word was fierce. 'They want *you* ter stay, yer little fool! Can't yer see that? They don't want me! Why would they? It's *you* they want. They want ter put yer in school. They want ter take you away from me, Tobe. I'm what they'd call a bad influence on a kid like you.' Her voice was bitter.

'No,' he said desperately, pleading. 'No, Sal.'

She straightened, her face bleak. With difficulty and an

enormous exercise of will she suppressed the churning of her stomach and the sudden, defeated urge to give in, to bring a smile back to Toby's face, to keep what little she could of him for as long as she could. 'Well,' she said tonelessly, 'looks like they've done it, doesn't it? It 'ad ter 'appen, I suppose, some time.'

'You're still going? Without me?' He could not believe it.

'Yes. Like I said. Tomorrow morning. First thing. With you or without. It's up ter you. Five o'clock, Tobe. Not a minute later. If you don't come, I'll go alone.' She bent, suddenly and swiftly, to kiss him. Sobbing he clung to her. Through her own tears, 'Stop snivelling,' she said, 'this is me only decent blouse.' She propelled him, stumbling, towards the door. 'Five o'clock,' she said, sniffing hard. 'If yer want ter come. Don't forget. And Tobe –'

He turned a tear-stained face to her.

'– not a word. You hear? Not a single, solitary word. To anyone. Or I'll wring yer neck. All right?'

He nodded. She jerked her head roughly. He turned and ran from the room.

She walked to the window, face clenched against a storm of tears that once broken would defeat her entirely. She'd be better off without the little blighter. On her own and fancy free. One mouth was a damn sight easier to feed than two –

He did not come. She waited as the light strengthened and noise began to seep from the streets. He had, perhaps, overslept. But no. Her own night's sleep had been troubled; she doubted if the child's had been much better.

Ten minutes. Twenty minutes.

She was then, on her own again. Mouth set she picked up her bundle, glanced around the room, suddenly and alarmingly reluctant to leave. Then she slipped through the door, down the corridor and out into the chill morning air of the courtyard.

She was half-way down the street before he caught up with her, sniffing ostentatiously, wiping his cuff across his nose. He was carrying a small bundle and a spare pair of boots were slung around his neck, the laces tied together.

She swallowed hard.

He neither spoke nor looked at her. Nor, as he usually so naturally did, would he take the hand she offered. His narrow shoulders were hunched, his head bowed. In his right hand he held his bundle. The left was shoved firmly in his pocket. They walked several paces. Obstinately he kept his face averted.

'So. Yer decided ter come after all?'

He nodded.

'Cat got yer tongue?'

He plodded on, refusing to answer, refusing to lift his head and look at her.

She stopped. The street was empty apart from a skin and bone cat that scavenged the gutter with single-minded patience and an ancient horse and cart that ambled by piled high with sacks, its driver, swathed in a moth-eaten blanket fast asleep at the reins. 'Toby?'

He lifted his face at last. It was the very picture of misery. The bright eyes, reddened and drowned in tears, were sunk dark into shadows, the small and usually rosy face pinched and fragile looking. His soft lips quivered uncontrollably.

She stood for a long moment looking down at him, her face expressionless, her eyes narrowed, until the green and amber gleam of them all but disappeared behind the dark lashes. Then, with a sigh half exasperation half resignation she leaned and twitched the bundle from his unresisting hand. 'All right, Toby Jug. You win. But listen – we stay fer just as long as it takes fer you to find out you've made a bad mistake, right? Then we're bloody off. You 'ear me?'

He nodded, the woebegone little face suddenly utterly transformed.

She took his hand, turned around. 'Yes,' she said very firmly and quite evidently as much to herself as to him. 'Only till then. Then we're bloody off.'

PART TWO

❧❀❧

1907

Chapter Five

I

Rachel Patten was born on a chill and overcast April day in 1907, and was, grudgingly to be sure, admitted by the midwife to be quite the prettiest newborn babe she had ever seen. Exhausted and not attempting to fight the waves of black depression that already threatened to swamp her, Charlotte Patten took one look at her daughter's damp black curls and deep, brilliant eyes and turned away. She would never have believed she could endure such agony. The labour had been long and difficult: the memory of the last days and nights appalled her, the thought of its ever happening again was a nightmare she could not bear to contemplate. And for what? To produce this scrap for whom she felt nothing and in whom she knew with certainty she would never see anything but a reminder of humiliation, of shame and the waste of a life. Her life.

'Come along, Mother. Don't you want to hold the little one?'

'No.'

The midwife, one of Hannah's stalwarts, tutted, handed the child to Hannah who stood near by, and busied herself about Charlotte's battered, uncaring body.

Hannah, in some awe, laid the child very carefully in the crib beside the bed. 'I'll fetch Ben.' The words had a faint questioning intonation. She eyed Charlotte, waiting for some answer, some reaction even, and received none. Charlotte's thin face was utterly withdrawn, her eyes remote. She lay like a doll beneath the brisk, ministering hands, distancing herself from the brutal realities of pain and blood and an unwanted child as she had to the best of her ability distanced herself over the past months from the knowledge that her marriage was a disaster, her life, in her own eyes, a ruin. Once, in the days before she had enclosed herself in this merciful, docile shell she had shrieked at Ben, using a street language she would not have credited herself with knowing, saying the most dreadful, the most unforgivable things in an attempt to break through her husband's relentless good manners, his merciless and meticulous care of her to the man beneath. The man who had saved her. The man who, surely, must despise her. The man of whom she had discovered she knew nothing. The man who had married her to protect her and his family from scandal and his father from pain, who had given her the shelter of his name and absolutely nothing else. And who did not understand to what despairing depths such well-meaning imprisonment could condemn a tender soul. 'Don't worry,' she had screamed, 'with any bloody luck at all I'll die like Henrietta did and save you all no end of trouble!', the words a final and fatal blow to a marriage that had been a disaster for them both from the beginning.

'Lively enough little thing,' the midwife said now, busying herself with the child, 'and pretty as a picture. I must say — small she may be, but she certainly looks healthy enough. Especially for a premature child —' She glanced slyly at Charlotte.

Charlotte, with very little effort, ignored her. From outside the door came the murmur of voices. She shut her eyes. Go away. Please. All of you. Go away. Leave me alone.

'Charlotte?' Ben's voice was quiet.

She tried to keep her eyes closed, tried to retreat into darkness.

'Charlotte.'

Very reluctantly she opened her eyes. He loomed above her, enormous, craggy, unsmiling. He laid professional fingers to her wrist. 'How are you feeling?'

'Sore.'

He nodded. 'It will pass. It was a hard birth. You were very brave.'

She said nothing.

Hannah stood beside him, the swathed bundle of the child in her arms. 'Your daughter,' she smiled. 'Charlotte, she's truly lovely. Just look at those eyes –'

Ben took the baby. Charlotte looked away. The room was hot and stuffy. Airless. Charlotte thought – hoped – that the struggle to breathe might at any minute defeat her.

Hannah was making absurdly aunt-like clucking noises, her long skinny finger playing with the tiny curled hands. 'Oh, Ben – isn't she lovely?'

'Yes. She is.'

That brought Charlotte's head round. She looked at her husband. He was watching the child, his dark, slate-grey eyes intent upon the small face. 'Yes. She is,' he said again, very softly.

'Let Mother have the baby now, Doctor Patten,' the midwife was brisk. It wasn't often she had the opportunity to order Ben Patten around, and she was making the most of the chance. 'We must get the little mite feeding.'

Charlotte clenched her teeth. She couldn't. She could not.

Ben leaned to her with the child. With rigid care she accepted the small, warm bundle. But as the midwife began to fumble with the buttons and ribbons of her nightdress she pulled away with a sudden snap of surprising strength. 'No! I'll do it myself. In a moment.'

Ben's smile faded. He straightened. 'Best if we go, perhaps. Father would like to visit with you later, and Ralph. Will that be all right?'

'Of course.'

'After you've slept.'

She nodded. They might have been strangers exchanging pleasantries on a railway station. The baby coughed a little, mewed faintly. Charlotte, despite her every effort felt her mouth tighten in distaste; and knew that, before he turned away, Ben had seen it.

'Now, Mother,' the midwife said, ominously crisp, 'let's give baby her first feed, shall we?'

Charlotte fumbled with the buttons of her nightdress. She wanted nothing so much as to sleep; to turn her back on the world, on this monstrous thing that had happened to her, on this child she did not want, and sleep. The child nuzzled her breast. Charlotte stiffened, jaw rigid with revulsion. The small mouth opened. Charlotte shrank back into the pillows.

'No, no –!' The nurse leaned forward, taking the small head in her remorselessly capable hand, forcing the little, wet mouth to the nipple. 'There. That's better.'

Blinded by tears, her lower lip clamped painfully between her teeth Charlotte endured the suckling, hating it. Like a limpet the child clung. Like a leech. 'I can't!' Charlotte said suddenly, 'I *can't*!' She jerked the nipple from the greedy mouth, gasping at the pain of it. Tears ran down her thin face. 'Please – I can't –'

The midwife, unmarried and childless, had faced – and outfaced – such tantrums before in young mothers. 'Don't be a silly girl now. Of course you can. You'll get used to it. Here. Try again.'

Charlotte was crying uncontrollably. In two days of labour she had not shed a tear, had in fact even at the worst times barely made a sound at all. But now the dam had burst, and she could not stop herself. The child, deprived of the nipple and sensing her mother's distress screamed shrilly, repetitively, wailing on each short, newly taken breath. Charlotte was trembling, near hysteria. 'Take her away! I can't! I won't! Take her away!'

'Oh, come now – what a fuss!' Very firmly and with no feeling whatsoever the other woman thrust the baby's face back to the breast. The small mouth fastened again upon the dug. A thin, hot wire of intolerable pain skewered the most private depths of Charlotte's body, defiling her. Her womb contracted agonizingly as she tensed against it. The rhythmic suckling of the child disgusted her. Milky liquid ran down the child's chin, drenching Charlotte's night-dress. The midwife's hand was still firmly upon the baby's head, forcing it to the breast. Charlotte clenched her eyes tight shut, wanting to struggle, to scream, to break free from this nightmare; instead she sobbed brokenly, like a child herself, overwrought, overtired, desperately un-happy.

'There you are, you see? Of course you can do it. Now — try the other side — just for a moment or two.'

The room was dark when Charlotte woke. Her body felt bruised; she ached as if she had been beaten. A small fire glowed in the hearth and a lamp burned low beside the bed. In the dark well of the cradle the child slept, sniffling. Charlotte's head ached and so, intolerably, did her engorged breasts. Her eyes were swollen and sore. She lay for a moment, apathetic and disorientated, until a faint movement in the quiet told her that she was not, as she had thought, alone. 'Who's that?'

There was the slightest moment of hesitation. 'It's me, ma'am.' The voice was cool, neutral and instantly recog-nizable.

'Sally?'

'Yes, ma'am.'

With an effort, Charlotte turned her head tiredly upon the pillow. She could see now the outline of the other girl's head, limned by fireglow, the mass of brown hair piled and coiled neatly, the long slender neck and sharp profile very still. Through all the months of Charlotte's pregnancy these two in unspoken and reluctant conspiracy had avoided each other, each made uncomfortable, and worse

157

than uncomfortable, by a bitter shared memory, an unwanted knowledge, an irredeemable debt that bound each to the other in a strange, unwelcome but unavoidable sisterhood. 'What time is it?' Charlotte asked.

'Nearly eight. Miss Brown's gone down to supper. She wanted someone to sit with you.' Over the past months Sally's speech, under the tutelage of Hannah and Ralph had become clearer and more carefully enunciated. 'She said you wouldn't wake for hours yet.'

Some small, wry spark of humour stirred. Charlotte smiled wearily. 'Otherwise you wouldn't have offered?'

She saw in the darkness the faint glimmer of a smile. 'Oh, I didn't offer. I was told. Our Miss Brown doesn't take kindly to "no" for an answer. Can I get you anything?'

'Thank you. I'm very thirsty. Perhaps a glass of water?'

Sally turned up the lamp, poured the water, helped Charlotte to struggle to a sitting position, propping her with pillows. She had, despite herself, been shocked at the sight of the thin, haggard face on the pillow. Even with the ordeal of childbirth safely over Charlotte looked ill, her skin sickly pale, her eyes sunk deep into shadows. She gave Charlotte the glass, then turned to look at the sleeping child. 'The little one's lovely,' she found herself saying, 'everyone's saying what a beauty she'll be.'

There was a long, stony silence. 'I don't care.' Charlotte's voice was flat, entirely without expression. And then, 'It would have been better if she'd died. And me with her.'

Sally's head moved sharply round at that. In the world she still thought of as hers death came too often and too easily to speak so. 'That's a wicked thing to say,' she said very quietly.

'I suppose it is. But I don't care. It's true. You and I know it.' A small, pale hand played restlessly with the fringe of the bedspread. 'You, I and my husband.' The words were barely audible.

Sally shook her head sharply. 'That isn't so. It's funny –' she hesitated for a moment.

'What?'

'It – well – it seems to me he's pleased as punch. He can't leave her be.'

Charlotte did not reply, but her head moved on the pillow, a tired negative.

Sally moved away from the bed, sat, straight backed and a little awkward, in the low nursing chair by the fire.

'Sally?' The word broke an openly difficult silence.

Sally turned a wary head. Ever since that day that she and Toby had slipped back into the Bear unchallenged and apparently unnoticed, her position in the house had been an odd one. She was servant certainly – she willingly fetched and carried, scrubbed and polished, took care of the children in the home, and she was paid for it. But Ralph, simply and undisguisedly delighted at her change of heart, was teaching her, with Toby, to read and to write and Hannah, sensing a deep-seated if wary interest in those things about which she herself felt so passionately, had sought her out in growing and enthusiastic friendship, had spent painstaking and rewarding hours in discussion and explanation. And always Ben Patten's unspoken, somewhat distant but none the less quite open patronage had set her apart from the other serving-girls – a fact that she knew had in no way endeared her to the spiteful Kate. But yet, with all but Hannah and Doctor Will she was uncomfortable. Ralph for all his kindness she still eyed with some distrust when Toby's bright head was between them. Of Charlotte's and Ben's marriage, knowing its roots, she guessed too much, and was uncomfortable with them both. Peter's cavalier friendliness baffled her entirely. Like a young animal set loose in a jungle not its own she watched always for threat or danger despite the apparent good will that undoubtedly surrounded her. Even Doctor Will's unfailingly good-tempered benevolence and Hannah's friendship she sometimes eyed with caustic caution. They were not her people. And to Ben and Charlotte she must, knowing what she knew, constitute a threat. Why should they offer her the hand of friendship? How long before gratitude wore thin and she found herself jobless and back in the tenements? And – worm of a thought, hardly ever leaving her – without Toby? It was in self defence that she had avoided Charlotte for all these past months; indeed had she not been assured that she slept and should continue to sleep, not even Miss Brown's forceful ways would have persuaded her into the room this evening. The last thing she wanted or was prepared for was a personal conversation.

'Sally?' Charlotte asked again, unable to see the other girl's expression in the gloom.

'Yes?'

'Tell me – are you happy here?' Exactly what prompted the question even Charlotte was not certain. Each glimpse of Sally's face over these past months, each sight of the sharp features and the long-lashed narrow eyes, each sound of that distinctive voice had, just as Sally had suspected, brought back with brutal force the memory of fear, of pain and of shameful humiliation. Ben's apparently heartless determination to keep the girl with them had been a constant cause of conflict in a marriage that had been unstable from the start. She had begged him to settle Sally elsewhere, to give her money, offer her a ticket to America – anything – but to put her where Charlotte would not be subject to the constant reminder of her presence. She flinched still when she remembered the chill anger that her pleading had aroused. 'Are you so completely self-centred?' Ben had asked with ill-concealed distaste. 'Do you have no thought for anyone but yourself? The girl risked her life to save you – she knew that if you didn't. She nearly died for it. And you'd turn her and the child who's probably the only thing in the world she's ever loved into the streets with a few pounds and a promise? Charlotte, for God's sake, do you know what you're suggesting? Do you know what would inevitably happen to her, to the child, if we abandon them now? And for what? For your comfort?'

She had watched him, cowed to silence by his anger, only the voice in her head arguing – pleading – but Ben, what of me? What of us? What of the child she knows is a bastard? What if she's spiteful? Think of the harm she could do. Why do you take her part against me, your wife?

Yet waiting now for the answer to her question she had to admit that Ben had been right in his estimate of the girl's character. It could not be said that by word or by deed Sally had ever given her cause for worry. On the contrary it was quite obvious that the girl was as awkward in her company as was Charlotte in hers. She sat now, a small straight line of thought between her eyes, considering the question she had been asked.

'Yes,' she said at last slowly. 'Happier than I expected. Everyone's very kind. An' Toby loves it.'

'Ralph says he's very clever?'

Sally's face tightened almost imperceptibly. 'Seems so, yes. He's jumped a class in school, so they tell me.'

'He'll be going in for the scholarship in a couple of years' time I daresay?'

Sally said nothing.

Some compulsion of curiosity pushed Charlotte to probe further despite the other girl's obvious reluctance. At least talking took her mind from the child who snuffled and murmured in the crib between them. 'And you? Hannah told me you'd been going to some meetings with her?'

Sally nodded, a faint movement in the darkness. The baby stirred in the cot. Charlotte turned her head away. 'I could never see the point of it all,' she admitted. 'I went a couple of times – to meetings with that friend of Hannah's – what's her name? Sylvia something?'

'Pankhurst. Sylvia Pankhurst.' Nothing in Sally's quiet voice revealed the intensity of feeling the name evoked. When Sylvia Pankhurst spoke, she spoke directly to the hearts and minds not of the educated middle-class women so dear to her campaigning mother and sister, founders and leaders of the militant Women's Social and Political Union, but of the women who knew what it was to work a shift as long as their menfolk's and then to come home to the soulbreaking battle of running a home in a crumbling tenement, of feeding too many mouths on too little income, of fighting dirt and the disease and death that so often struck at the children. She spoke to the likes of Sally Smith. And her words made a compelling sense.

'Oh, yes. That's right. Pankhurst.'

The baby moved again, caught her breath a little as if preparing to cry. Charlotte discovered that her hands were tensely clenched upon the counterpane, clenched so tightly that they ached with the effort. With infinite care she forced them to relax, uncurling her fingers and flexing them gently. 'Did you go with them to any of the demonstrations at the Houses of Parliament last year?'

'No. But I went on the march in February.' The demonstrations at the House of Commons had been during the previous year; Sally had resisted all Hannah's blandishments until Christmas, had indeed with the rest of the servant household been mildly amused at Miss Hannah's antics with her disreputable friends. Not until, with wary misgiving, she had at last allowed herself to be persuaded one winter's night to accompany Hannah to a small meeting in a local church hall – a meeting at which Sylvia Pankhurst had spoken with her passionate, simple and flawless conviction of the righting of wrongs, the lighting of darkness, of the radical transformation of an imbalanced society – had she even begun to understand Hannah's commitment to her cause: but the conversion, once brought about, had been of the order of that of Paul on the road to Damascus. That there might be any possibility of creating a world where women ceased to be the chattels of their menfolk, had rights and freedoms of their own, had never so much as crossed Sally's mind before. To hear Sylvia's level yet passionate logic, to understand that she,

Sally Smith, was being called to make some contribution of her own, would be valued as an ally and a friend by those who were working to this astounding end had amazed and excited her. She had attended more meetings, asked more questions, and had discovered that the answers and ideas she heard made a wonderful sense. With Hannah she had marched proudly behind the banners through dreadful February weather – that had given the parade the nickname of the Mud March – from Hyde Park to Exeter Hall in the Strand. There she had listened enthralled to Mr Keir Hardie – already a hero of hers through the devotion of the not easily-impressed Dickson men. This dedicated Labour leader had made history fifteen years before when he had proudly, in cloth cap and tweed jacket, taken his place as the first representative of the working man in the people's Parliament at Westminster. The more fiery Mr Israel Zangwill had also spoken and with his unashamed exhortations to militancy had brought the women to their feet in a rapturous storm of applause. 'A majority in Parliament have promised to vote for women's suffrage. But *whom* have they promised? Women! And women have no votes. Therefore the MPs do not take them seriously. You see the vicious circle? In order for women to get votes they must have votes already. And so the men will bemock and befool them from session to session., Who can wonder if, tired of these gay deceivers, they begin to take the law into their own hands? And public opinion – I warn the Government – public opinion is with the women.' Sally had cheered with the rest, grinning at her nearest neighbour, waving her home-made white flag with blithe vigour. The talk of tactics, of by-elections, of constituencies being the arena of battle had passed her by, but Zangwill's oratory had to her own surprise brought an emotional burning to her eyes when he had touched on matters closer to her own experience. 'And so to these myriads of tired women who rise in the raw dawn and troop to their cheerless factories and who, when twilight falls, return not to rest but to the labours of a squalid household, to these the thought of women's suffrage, which comes as a sneer to the man about town, comes as a hope and as a prayer.' Hannah's grip on Sally's arm had been unconsciously fierce with excitement, her plain face had been lit with dedicated enthusiasm, 'Today's woman cries "I *fight* for justice! – And I *shall* have it!"'

Sally and Hannah had not been the only ones to come to their feet at that: and three days later, again at Hannah's side, Sally had been in the crowds that had attended the first 'Women's Parliament' at Caxton Hall and who, on hearing that yet again the King's Speech made no reference to votes for women had promptly passed a resolution of their own and marched with it to the House of Commons. In the ensuing fracas Sally had not only acquitted herself with commendable – not to say, perhaps regrettably, practised – competence, but had succeeded by dint of quick thinking and a sharpish turn of speed in preventing both herself and her mentor from being taken into custody by an over-enthusiastic and beefy young constable, a favour for which Hannah had thanked her ruefully but half regretfully.

'Strike a light!' Sally had laughed, panting, exhilarated by the battle, gathering handsful of the hair that had slithered about her shoulders and stuffing them into her hat, 'Next time I'll leave you to the Rozzers!' and then had stopped, struck to silence by the echo of her own easy insolence to a woman who was, after all, her employer's daughter. But Hannah had laughed, unaware, and slipped an arm through hers. 'Come on – let's go to Brown's for a pot of tea. We deserve it.'

'Wasn't Sylvia Pankhurst one of those who were arrested that day?' Charlotte asked now, idly curious, breaking into the silence.

'Yes, she was. Miss Hannah went to visit her.' And had come away from the forbidding pile of Holloway, Sally remembered, more than a little subdued.

The child in the cot whimpered a little and then suddenly set up a hungry bawling that set Charlotte's teeth on edge and strung her nerves to breaking point. Her breasts ached and her nipples were sore. She hated the sound that the baby made; thin, desperate, demanding.

'Well, well, and what's happening here, might I ask? Why no lights when baby's ready for supper? Come along – Sally, isn't it? – jump to it. Lamps, please. And hot water for baby's bath.' The officious Miss Brown swept into the room on a cloud of starch and carbolic. Charlotte lay back and closed her eyes, fighting panic and a stirring of physical sickness.

'Now, Mother –' Relentlessly brisk, Miss Brown picked up the screaming child and dumped her into Charlotte's stiffly unwilling arms. 'Off we go. Supper time.'

II

Sally, escaping the too-warm sickly-smelling room as soon as was decently possible, fled to the sanctuary of her own small bedroom. The Pattens did not, as did so many others, work their people from dawn to dusk and sleep them in attic dormitories that were airless ovens in summer and ice-boxes in winter. Each girl's hours were strictly and fairly laid down and each had a tiny room to herself in the huge old stable block, now the ever-expanding children's home. Sally's room, though hat-box small, looked down over the little walled garden where Mrs Briggs did her gallant best to nurture a few herbs and vegetables – heritage, she often said a little wistfully, of a country childhood – and it was far enough from the road to be relatively quiet. It was simply decorated with pale, stippled walls and a whitewashed ceiling, and even more simply furnished. It held a narrow bed, a wash stand, a chest of drawers and a chair, all sturdy scrubbed wood that shone with beeswax. The fireplace was minute, but the little box of coal and wood that sat beside it was well stocked at all times of the year. On one wall was an ancient, fly-specked mirror, on another a faded embroidered text, much embellished with ill-executed violets and roses. She knew the words by heart, knew every stitch of their construction. 'Blessed Are The Pure In Heart, For They Shall See God.' In those months that Sally had struggled to master her letters, those words, together and separately, so tantalizingly hung above her head as she lay in bed, had been a spur of the kind that could never have been imagined by their original creator, for she had refused to ask their meaning, had waited for the triumphant day when she could painstakingly spell them out for herself. Beside the bed was a small set of shelves upon which lay a battered bible – which for the present was still way beyond her reading skills – a book of Aesop's fables lent to her by Ralph and printed in clear strong letters, and the big book of fairy tales with which Toby, to her astonishment, had presented her on the afternoon of that day nearly eight months before when they had crept back into the awakening house like thieves in reverse, hastily hiding their bundles, covering the traces of their attempted flight. 'Mr Ralph says you can keep it,' he had said of the book, nonchalantly.

'Why? What would he give me something like that for?'

He had lifted a small shoulder. 'I dunno. But 'e says we – you – can have it. Come on, Sal – open it – find the one about the three little pigs.'

It was lying open now, on the bed where she had left it, the ruler she still used to follow the words ready on the counterpane beside it. Not to anyone had she admitted how much sheer pleasure she got from this hard-won achievement of reading and writing. From the frustration of the first weeks, when Toby's quick mind had appeared to absorb everything and anything it encountered as surely as hers had rejected it, she had moved slowly and stubbornly through the first faint glimmerings of understanding to a breakthrough that had been like the sun rising upon a night's darkness. She would never, she suspected, read with the easy facility that Toby already seemed to have acquired – but if not swift her progress had been sure, and the words and the shades of their meaning were a joy and a delight to her. She settled now beside the small fire that had been lit against the unseasonal spring chill, a thin finger marking the words as she read, a frown of concentration on her face. She had not, however, managed more than a couple of lines when a noise by the doorway, the slight creaking of a hinge snapped her head up irritably. Not Bron again, surely? Did the girl never want to spend a moment on her own?

'Who's that?'

There was a small scuffling sound, a smothered giggle.

Not Bron.

Lips twitching to laughter despite herself, she laid the book down quietly and crept to the door, flinging it open to reveal two small children and a fiercely struggling bundle of black fur. The little girl shrieked as the door flew open and collapsed into helpless giggles. The boy, who was clutching the almost demented kitten apparently totally unaware both of the small animal's struggles and of the damage the tiny, razor sharp claws were inflicting, grinned broadly. 'We brought Fluff to see you.'

She eyed the angry animal doubtfully. 'Did you indeed? He doesn't seem very pleased about it.'

'Yes 'e is. 'Course 'e is. 'E wanted ter come.'

'Really?'

The urchin nodded.

Sally eyed the cheeky face, trying not to laugh. 'Any particular reason for that?'

'I 'spec' 'e wanted to 'ear a story,' the child said, straight faced. His sister burst into embarrassed giggles again, hiding her face in her pinafore.

'I see. Well – you'd best come in, hadn't you?'

The two children scuttled into the room, stood together

waiting, expectancy in their identical pale blue eyes. The kitten struggled with manic determination.

'I think perhaps you'd better let Fluff go, don't you?'

'All right.' Unceremoniously the child dropped the little cat, which landed on its feet and streaked under the bed.

'A story, you said?' Sally asked pensively.

Two small heads nodded in unison.

'Any particular story?'

'One of yours,' the little girl said, 'not out of a book. A twin story.' Then, overcome at her own temerity she buried her scarlet face again in her apron.

Sally surveyed them. Two months before she had been in the room known as the nursery when Ben Patten had brought these two in, having found them scavenging, half-starved, in the hospital rubbish dump. Sullen and savagely defiant the boy had been filthy, his skin covered in sores and scabs, his small frame skeletal from undernourishment. The girl, obviously his twin, had been as bad, her long hair matted and evil smelling, eyes and nose running with mucus. The boy had snarled like a small animal. The girl had said nothing.

'Well, well,' Hannah had said collectedly, 'here's a handful and no mistake.'

She had been right. The boy, Bertie, who now watched Sally with sharp, hopeful, healthily cheeky eyes, had bitten Ben, Ralph and Hannah and scratched Sally's arms to ribbons as they had bathed him. For a fortnight he had spoken nothing but obscenities; his sister – Annie – had spoken not at all. Even Ralph had begun to despair of them. They had wolfed the food they were given, had refused to use the lavatories provided for the children but slunk into the yard at night, had screamed and fought like wild animals if any attempt was made to part them even for a moment. They had refused utterly to respond to a friendly overture.

Until the day that Sally, sitting with four or five of the younger children who did not yet attend school, had begun to tell a story.

It had been an uneasy movement amongst her small audience that had first alerted her: heads had turned, one or two of the youngsters had squeezed a little closer to her. Bertie and Annie had not at that time been the home's most popular inmates. Sally had looked up. The two children were standing sullenly by the open door, neither in nor out of the room, Annie as always a step behind her brother, who stood truculently, four-square on his skinny, scabbed legs, his thin face warily hostile as eyes turned towards him. They had looked like two abandoned and savage wild creatures, and Sally's heart had ached for them. But instinctively she had ignored them, turning back to her young audience, inviting their attention with a small, dramatic gesture.

'– so – along comes this little lad and says, "Oi! That's *my* green bean you got there –!"'

'What was 'is name, Miss?'

Sally looked up in comical surprise. 'What – the bean?'

The child who had interrupted squealed with laughter. '*No!* The little boy!'

'Ah.' Sally put a thoughtful finger to her lip. 'I think – yes I think it was something like – Albert. No. Posher than that it was, now I stop to think about it. Bertram. That's it. Bertram. Of course everyone called him Bertie. He'd almost forgotten his real name. He had a sister –' she had stopped again, as if thinking. The two at the door were watching her, faces expressionless. Sally kept her eyes upon the upturned, eager faces in front of her. 'Rose-Anne her name was. Pretty name. But everyone called her Annie, of course.'

By the time Ralph had come to join them an hour or so later the twins had been sitting some distance from the group, their backs firmly and defensively to the wall, but none the less listening intently to the improvised story of their namesakes and the rest of the children, equally enthralled by the unlikely adventures of the two Sally had dubbed the Terrible Twins were happily ignoring them. It had been the least disruptive hour the two had spent since being brought to the Bear.

'Well done!' With quiet warmth Ralph had put an arm about Sally's shoulders and hugged her. 'I truly was beginning to feel that we were never going to break through to those two.'

'They didn't say much.'

'They didn't have to. You'll see. They'll come round now.'

And they had. The breach once made, Sally had watched, impressed despite herself, Ben Patten's gentle but determined conquering of the twins' fear and hostility, Ralph's cheerful and steady refusal to accept continued illbehaviour. Bron – surprisingly – had mothered them, Kate – not surprisingly – would have nothing to do with them. But their steady favourite since that day had been Sally; and to her own surprise she had been pleased and touched by their fierce devotion. They laughed now with an ease she would have thought impossible a month or so ago, vying with each other with outrageous ideas for new stories. They had, she knew, been saved in the true and basic sense of the word. And in admitting that she knew that she herself was beginning to lose her distrust of the Pattens and their motives. No one could have watched the change in these two unmoved. If the home never did anything else, here was justification for the Pattens and their crusade; and she had been a part of it. Ralph and Hannah had both been openly delighted. Ben had gone out of his way to thank her for her help and even to ask her advice. 'Can we separate them, do you think? Perhaps at least get them to do things rather more individually? If they are eventually to go to school they'll have to get used to being apart sometimes.'

Sally had shaken her head firmly. Too well she knew the world from which these children had come. 'No. Not yet. Not for a long time, I should think. Wait till they're ready. They've no one but each other. Try to split them and you'll lose them.'

Her advice had been taken, in this case and in others. Realizing that her knowledge and understanding of these children was grounded in a harsh experience that he himself lacked, Ralph in particular had often come to her with a difficult child, and even though her own doubts of him with regard to Toby were never far from the surface she enjoyed working with him and with the children.

'Well now,' she said now, the Terrible Twins extricated once more from a tricky situation and ready to do battle another day, 'enough's enough, I'd say. Time for supper.'

'O-oh!' The protest, as everything else with these two, was in perfect unison.

She clapped her hands. 'No argument! Off you go. Or Mrs Briggs'll have my guts for garters!'

Grinning at that, they turned as a tap sounded at the door and Hannah popped her head around it. 'Sorry – are you busy?'

'No. They're just leaving. Come on, you kids – off you go –'

'Can we come agen termorrer?'

She grinned and ruffled a bright head. 'Only if you eat every scrap of your supper, *including* your cabbage, and then spend a whole hour learning your letters.'

'An *hour*?' Bertie was aghast.

'An hour,' Sally said repressively.

Annie grabbed her brother's arm. 'All right,' she said valiantly, 'we'll do it. If we can come back termorrer.'

Hannah smiled as they tumbled past her. 'What a difference in those two! I've still got the scars where that little devil bit me – yet look at him – you've got him eating out of your hand!'

Sally smiled. 'We understand each other, him an' me.'

'I came to bring you this.' Hannah dropped a dark-printed sheet of paper on to the chest-of-drawers. 'It's the pamphlet Sylvia was talking about the other day. You said you wanted to read it.'

'Yes. Thank you.'

Hannah turned back to the door. Stopped. Stood for a moment pushing distractedly at a cascade of loosened hairpins. 'Sally?'

Sally looked enquiringly.

'You – you're sure you want to come with me tomorrow? To the meeting?'

'Of course.'

Uncharacteristically hesitant, and still fiddling with the hairpins, Hannah said, 'You do know – you do realize – that there could be real trouble?'

Staunchly Sally grinned. 'Can't be worse than a bad Saturday night down the Commercial Road.'

Hannah laughed a little but sobered quickly. Faint lines of tension around her eyes made her look older than her twenty-two years. With sudden insight Sally saw a nervousness that verged on fear in the plain, likeable face. On the following day Mr Sydney Buxton, MP was to speak in Poplar. Hannah Patten was one of the small brave band pledged to question him on the Liberal Government's so far empty promises concerning the enfranchisement of women. Up and down the country at such meetings women – and men too – were exercising their constitutional right to ask such questions. And up and down the country reaction had been brutal. Questioners had been evicted violently from meetings while the police looked on and did nothing. Dragged by the hair, punched and kicked by the stewards, the women and their allies were sometimes badly injured. Only last week a young woman's arm had been broken as she was forcibly ejected from a Cabinet Minister's public meeting.

'Ralph's coming,' Hannah said, 'but Ben can't, though he wanted to, of course. He's absolutely got to go to the Health Committee meeting – after fighting all these years for compulsory medical examinations in schools he can't miss the meeting where they're discussing how to implement the new law. Given half a chance quite a few would ignore it if they could, as he well knows.'

'What time's the Buxton meeting?'

'Six thirty. We plan to be there by six. We need good seats.'

'I'll be ready.'

Hannah still hesitated, a warrior more than ready to risk her own neck but not so ready to be responsible for another's. 'You are sure?'

Sally laughed, picked up a wide white sash that hung over the wash stand. 'Of course I'm sure. I wouldn't miss it for anything. Bin a long time since I've bin in a rough house!' she smiled mischievously at Hannah's doubtful expression. 'Look – I've even done a bit of needlework for the occasion.' She held out the sash. Hannah took it, laughed softly at the tiny words embroidered repeatedly around it. 'Votes for Women.' She shook her head, laughing still. 'We aren't supposed to give away who we are until we ask our question. We don't want to be thrown out before we open our mouths.'

Sally took the sash back, held it about her waist. 'There. You'd never know what it says.' The needlework, in dark green to match the dress Sally intended to wear, looked simply like a decorative edging.

Hannah eyed her in surprised amusement. 'I do believe you're looking forward to it!'

Sally took a moment to consider that. 'Yes. I do believe I am.'

When Hannah had left, still patting distractedly at her tumbling hair, Sally walked to the window, the sash still dangling from her fingers. Josie, a frequent and welcome visitor to this cheery little room had called the day before and had voiced much the same doubts. 'There's been real trouble at these meetings, Sal. All over the place. It's been in the papers. Are you sure you should go?'

Sally had cocked a jaunty eyebrow, inviting laughter. 'Sure? Of course I am. Blimey, girl, never let it be said that Sally Smith left a mate in the lurch. Perish the thought!'

A mate? She smiled a little at the unlikely thought, stood looking down into the tiny, neat patch of garden below. The black kitten, seeing the coast was clear had crawled from beneath the bed and fawned about her ankles, purring anxiously. Absentmindedly she bent to pick it up, soothing the ruffled fur. Thoughts of Josie had brought thoughts of her brother Dan; with whom the last time she had seen him, despite all her efforts and to Josie's clear distress, she had quarrelled bitterly. For days she had been trying not to think of it, but the words that had been spoken so angrily still rang in her head, and try as she might she could not dismiss them. Dan – solid, dependable, obstinate and unimaginative Dan – had asked her to marry him. And she, inevitably, had said no. His disappointment and hurt, his incomprehension, had been painful to see. 'But why, Sal? I've got a steady job – I'd care for you well. An' Toby too. I've savings. We could buy a little house –'

'Dan!'

'I'd be good to you, Sal, you know I would.'

'Oh, of course I know it!'

'Well then? What is it? Is it that – you don't care for me?'

She had looked at him in despair. If she could not entirely explain to herself why she knew so surely that she should not marry him then how, without hurt, could she possibly explain it to him? 'Of course I care for you, Dan. You know it. As a friend. A dear and trusted friend. But – oh, Dan, I'm not ready to marry. Not you. Not anyone.'

Stubbornly he had held his ground. 'Strikes me you don't know what you do want. Give yourself a bit of time – time to think about it.'

'*No*.' He had flinched at the sharpness of the word. She had tried to force her voice to quiet, to reason. 'No, Dan. It would do no good. I'm not a kid. I could think till kingdom come, and it still wouldn't be right. I know it.'

He had turned from her then, a painful bitterness in his eyes. 'What then? Too good for us now, are you? Is that it?'

'Dan, no, of course that isn't it.'

He had been too hurt, too humiliated to listen. High colour had risen in the blunt-featured face. 'Dan Dickson's not good enough for you I suppose? With all this readin' and writin' and speechifyin', set your sights on somethin' higher, have you?'

Quick and justifiable anger had stirred. 'That's a stupid thing to say.'

'You think so? Well, seems to me Sal Smith that it's not just the way you talk's changed over the past few months –'

'What do you mean? What the *hell* do you mean?'

He was too far gone in misery to curb his tongue, anger and mortification had fed his disappointment and turned it into uncharacteristic and irrational fury. 'Gadding about with them votes for women females who're old enough and ugly enough to know better! Making a spectacle of yourself – marching through the streets banging a bloody drum! I tell you straight I think you must have taken clean leave of your senses – you an' them hoity toity new pals of yours.'

Sally's own uncertain temper had slipped its leash. She winced now to remember the things she had said. Josie, hearing raised voices, had come in to try to calm them, but too late. The damage, as so often when tongues ran ahead of hearts and brains, was done. She sighed now. She had not, she knew, handled the situation well. She had not wanted to quarrel with Dan. Yet still his attitude to her suffragette friends stirred anger in her many days later. All the old, mindless arguments had been flung at her – the women who were ready to fight for political strength as a way to freedom were nothing but frustrated spinsters who couldn't catch a husband, or man-haters who wouldn't know what to do with one if they found him. Dry, unwomanly creatures. An outrage to the natural scheme of things, their aims nothing short of anarchic. They deserved nothing so much as a good thrashing from husband, or father, or any other good, strong – male – arm within reach. She had heard it all before, of course, to her amazement from some women as well as from men, but never in such a personal way and never from someone whose opinion she had until now always respected. Dan had, she learned later from Josie, regretted the hasty words almost as soon as they had been spoken, but spoken they had been and the damage could not be undone; the damage, that was, to her relationship with Dan, for if anything the incident had strengthened her feelings for the cause and for those who fought for it. 'We fight', Sylvia Pankhurst had said at the last meeting she had attended above the baker's shop in Bow, 'against ignorance, against cynicism and against wanton prejudice – and we shall win!'

She lifted the sash she still held and surveyed it pensively. Never in her life before had she felt herself to be anything but a lone individual, pitted against a hostile world. This simple and slightly absurd piece of embroidered material symbolized something that even now, as she contemplated it, astounded her.

III

Hannah woke after a restless night to mixed feelings of excitement and dread. This was The Day. Her turn had come at last.

It was very early, the strengthening grey light of a spring dawn seeped gently through the closed curtains. The house was still. In the distance Charlotte's baby cried, a thin, tentative wail that was swiftly hushed. Hannah threw back the bedclothes and padded on bare feet to the window, drawing the curtains on a morning fresh and breezy and – even in these dingy London streets – bright as a new pin. The narrow road below was empty apart from a stalking cat. She watched as the animal picked its delicate way from doorway to doorway. Then, restless and unsettled, she moved about the room, touched her hairbrush, aimlessly rearranged the dressing table with its assortment of all but unused bottles and jars, its red velvet pin cushion into which, untidily, were stuck haphazardly half a dozen hatpins. She stood for a moment, brush in hand, tidying the jars, rearranging the pins. Then she slowly lifted her head to study with strange care her reflection in the mirror. Her face was pale and her eyes looked tired after a night of shallow and disturbed sleep. The shining cloak of her heavy hair hung about her shoulders, dark against the rumpled frills of her high-necked white nightgown. She did not, she decided wryly, look at this moment like any kind of crusader, let alone one preparing to martyr herself for her cause. Behind her, upon the wardrobe door, she could see the neat dark suit she had chosen to wear for the meeting this evening. She lifted her chin, composing her features to a severe and undaunted expression. 'Mr Buxton,' she asked her reflection softly, 'will the Government – no, will this Liberal Government – give votes to women?' Her voice sounded odd in the quiet of the room. She tried the question again, with a different inflection. Tried to imagine a crowded hall. A possibly hostile audience. 'I will do it,' she said suddenly. 'I will!' and with an odd lightening of her heart she began to brush her hair with long, sure strokes.

She was dressed and ready long before it was time to leave for the meeting. All day as she had gone about her normal tasks – dispensing the neatly packed baskets of milk to the mothers at the depot, visiting a woman in Angel Street whose new baby, the youngest child of eight and not by a long chalk the strongest was the latest to fall victim to the epidemic of measles that was spreading like fire through the crowded tenements, drinking afternoon tea with a Charlotte whose silence and tense, peaky looks disturbed even Hannah's already over-preoccupied mind – there had been a constant, small, nervous stirring at the pit of her stomach that had made eating difficult and sitting still impossible.

'Will this Liberal Government give votes to women?'

She would ask her question, and she would stand her ground until it was answered, or until they tired of her and threw her out.

She knew too well which of those two alternatives was most likely.

Promptly at six she, Ralph and Sally set out for the hall where the meeting was to be held, quietly finding themselves seats just a few rows back from the front and in the centre of the row where it would be difficult for anyone to reach her from the aisles. Flanked by the other two she sat, straight-backed and calm, as the hall filled around her. Upon the bunting-draped platform were a long table and half a dozen chairs. Jugs of water and tall glasses were set ready. The back of the stage was adorned by large pictures of Sir Henry Campbell-Bannerman, the Liberal Prime Minister, a man who whilst openly and personally supporting the principle of the franchise for women refused adamantly to take the political risk of committing his Government to bringing in the necessary legislation. Sally fidgeted a little beside her. Hannah glanced at her and the other girl flashed a quick and mischievous smile, the warmth of conspiracy in her eyes. Hannah found herself smiling back. The hall was almost full now. Self-important-looking stewards with large yellow rosettes in their lapels were ushering people to the few empty seats. The buzz of talk died, and a hush fell as the platform party filed on to the stage.

Hannah heard nothing of the introductory speech. She sat very still, trying to control the oddly irregular beating of a heart that rarely behaved in any way but calmly. She focused her eyes upon a half-empty jug of water upon the table and concentrated fiercely on marshalling her nerves and her dignity. Her hands were very cold but perfectly steady upon her lap. She saw Sydney Buxton rise, floridly prosperous-looking and completely at his ease, heard his thanks to the constituency for inviting him, for organizing the meeting so splendidly, for supporting it so well. For half an hour, then, he spoke eloquently and well, answering questions as they arose from the hall, talking of the Liberal Government's record as a power for radical change, of its honest desire to see the working man's lot improved –

Hannah stood.

'Will this Liberal Government give votes to women?'

Her voice was very clear and very steady in the quiet.

The speaker looked at her, tight-lipped for the briefest of moments then, ignoring her completely, took up his theme again. 'We plan the introduction of a national insurance scheme that –'

'Mr Buxton, will this Liberal Government give votes to women?'

'Sit down!'

'Be quiet!'

'Shut yer bloody silly mouth, woman!'

'Let the lady speak –'

The sudden pandemonium of shouts drowned the speaker's words as, his face determinedly turned from Hannah, with ferocious determination he attempted to plough through the interruptions. From the corner of her eye Hannah saw a large man with a rosette in his lapel hurrying from the back of the hall. Another had moved from the side door to the end of the aisle.

'I ask again. Will the Liberal Government give women the vote?'

Someone behind her caught the jacket of her suit, pulling at it, trying to force her to sit down. Beside her Sally turned, umbrella at the ready, and the tugging stopped abruptly.

'Throw 'er out!'

'Shut 'er up!'

'Shut up yerself! Why shouldn't she ask a question, same as everyone else?'

There was confusion now on the platform. The organizer was on his feet, Buxton held his hands, palms out, trying to calm the rising crescendo of noise, of shout and counter-shout, of fierce argument from row to row. 'Ladies and gentlemen –'

'Answer the question!' someone shouted from the back of the hall.

'Votes for women!' Sally was on her feet, umbrella brandished like a banner in the air. 'Votes for women!'

'Throw them out!'

'Let them be! Answer the question!'

In the pandemonium Hannah stood her ground, head thrown back, her eyes fixed on her target who, she noticed, face blotched with anger, looked anywhere but at her. 'Will this Liberal Government give women the vote?' Her voice and the reiterated question were all but lost in the hubbub. Sydney Buxton with a gesture of irritation sat down. The Party Organizer, on his feet, waved his arms angrily. 'Order! Order!'

'Votes for women!' Sally's hoarse and cheerful voice rose gleefully above the din. 'Votes for women!'

A burly steward was fighting his way along the row towards them. Ralph with a mildly apologetic smile and a shaken head blocked his passage. Other stewards were converging on them.

'Votes for women!' Sally shouted again grinning blithely, the light of battle in her eyes.

'Get out of my way!' The big steward pushed Ralph hard and unceremoniously in the chest, almost tipping the slighter man over into the row behind. The chairs, linked together like a metal chain tilted and then swung, catching Sally behind the knees almost knocking her from her feet. With the agility of a cat she regained her balance and jumped on to the chair. 'Votes for women!'

'Sling 'em out!'

'Let 'em be!'

'Shut yer mouth, yer stupid female!'

'Good beltin's what you need!'

The steward had doubled Ralph up with an elbow harshly and effectively in the midriff and was reaching for Hannah. An elderly woman in the row behind clipped him smartly over the head with her umbrella. Sally grinned. 'That's the ticket!' In the brief respite Hannah opened her mouth once more. 'Will this Liberal Gov –' A rough hand was clamped over her mouth and she was lifted bodily over Ralph's gasping form and dragged to the end of the row. She made no attempt to resist – struggling, she knew could simply encourage more violence.

'Oh no you don't!' Sally launched herself after them, the shattered umbrella wielded two-handed. The surprised steward's grip on Hannah slackened. She struggled free. Other hands reached for her as stewards from all over the hall converged. Sally swung her umbrella. There was laughter as one of the stewards yelped and clutched his ear.

'Votes for women! Votes for women!' Sally started the chant. Hannah's was not the only voice in the hall to take it up. 'Votes for women! Votes for women!'

The heavy hand closed upon Hannah's mouth again, rough and hard, painfully crushing her lips against her teeth, suffocating. It reeked revoltingly of tobacco. Tasted of it. A steward had taken Sally from behind, an arm like an iron band about her narrow waist, lifting her with ease a foot or so from the floor.

'Shame!'

'Leave them be!'

'Throw them out!'

The hall was bedlam.

'Votes for wom–!' Sally's strong, hoarse voice was cut off too by a brutally rough hand. Kicking and scratching she was being dragged towards the back of the hall. The hand slipped. Blood streaked her chin. 'Votes for women!'

The hand that covered Hannah's mouth covered her nose too. Panic stricken she threw her head back, desperately trying to breathe. Her captor grunted, grabbed her arm, twisting it viciously behind her back. Both the crack of bone and her sharp shriek of pain were lost in the general uproar. Sally was fighting every inch of the way. Her hair was down, her blouse torn, an ugly bruise stained her cheekbone and one eye was all but shut. Blood from her broken lip ran down her chin.

'Shame!' a man's voice shouted. 'Give 'em a chance to speak!'

'Votes for women!' Sally shrieked, the power of her voice almost gone.

'Votes for monkeys!' someone else shouted.

'Votes for cats! Votes for dogs! Votes for donkeys!'

Hannah's shoulder was a ball of fiery pain. She could not breathe. She twisted, burying her teeth in a horny finger. Her captor swore, released her mouth, twisted his hand instead into her thick, loosened hair dragging her head savagely back. Tears of pain filled her eyes. Ralph was nowhere to be seen.

'The coppers,' someone said. ''Ere come the coppers. They'll take care of the little bleeders!'

They were dragged to the back of the hall and out on to the steps beyond the doors. With huge and entirely unnecessary force the steward who held Hannah thrust her forward, all but throwing her down the flight of steps and into the arms of an obviously bemused young policeman. A moment later the bundle of flailing arms and legs that was Sally Smith followed, if anything even more forcibly, it having taken three men to subdue her, two of whom would certainly bear the scars home to their wives. Sally landed on hands and knees, her hair wild about her shoulders. The stewards who had manhandled her from the hall stood above her, dusting their hands and grinning. She sat back on her heels, almost on the enormous shining boot of a portly, fatherly looking moustachioed policeman, lifted her head to look at them. And in tones as pleasant and clear as a bell in the silence that had fallen she told them in a few most picturesque and imaginative phrases garnered directly from her early life exactly what she thought of them, their mothers, their brothers and their sisters, and what they could do with themselves now that they had finished defending their masters from two frail women.

Hannah thought she had never seen anyone look so

utterly thunderstruck. The pain in her shoulder notwith-standing she found herself spluttering with a laughter that was dangerously close to hysteria. She bit her lip, still giggling.

The portly policeman bent down and helped Sally to her feet. Sally rose with ridiculous grace, thanked him politely and demurely, a wicked sparkle in her one good eye. The younger of the two policemen grinned at her, obviously much entertained. 'Well, ladies,' he said cheerfully, 'any chance that if we pat you on the head and send you home you'll go, like good little girls?'

Sally and Hannah exchanged glances. 'None,' they said in unison.

He nodded equably. 'That's what I thought. In that case I'm very much afraid that you'll have to come along with us –'

'Hannah!' It was Ralph, at the top of the steps, bruised and dishevelled, his glasses gone, eyes squinting myopic-ally in the gathering dusk.

Hannah, her hand still clutching her shoulder, smiled at her policeman. 'Would you give me a moment?'

'Of course.'

She mounted the steps carefully, easing her shoulder.

'Hannah – what's happening?'

'It would appear', she said composedly, 'that we've been arrested. Tell Pa, would you, and Ben? And tell Mrs Briggs we won't be back for supper.'

Ralph blinked bemusedly. In that moment, her hair like Sally's, wild about her face and shoulders, the colour of action and excitement in her face, the strong, blunt features alight and determined, she looked to his short-sighted eyes positively beautiful. He hesitated, took breath to tell her so.

'It's all right,' she said, forestalling him. 'It's only my shoulder, nothing too desperate. Don't worry. It'll only be for a week or two. We'll be home plaguing you all again in no time.'

Chapter Six

I

The long-bodied, springless and all but windowless van popularly – or perhaps unpopularly – known as the Black Maria lumbered and bumped over the uneven surface of the road. The fat wardress who sat at the end of the aisle separating the two rows of tiny barred cells inside the vehicle, swayed with the movement, her head nodding. Sally had noticed about her as she had ushered them into their cramped quarters a strong smell of gin. She snored gently. The only other inhabitant of the cells apart from Sally and Hannah – a small, rat-faced child of thirteen or so, convicted of prostitution and robbery – hummed quietly to herself, looking at no one.

'Why didn't you *tell* us?' Hannah hissed, one wary eye on the dozing wardress, finding a moment at last for a question she had been trying to ask from the moment the sentences had been handed down.

Sally lifted innocent brows. 'What?'

'Oh, Sal! You know very well what! That you'd – that you'd been –' embarrassed Hannah could find no diplomatic way to express herself, '– that you weren't a first-time offender,' she hissed at last, fiercely.

Sally turned level eyes upon her. 'Why should I have told you? What difference would it have made?' There was a certain cool challenge in the words.

The exasperated Hannah missed the inference entirely. She shook her head angrily. 'Of *course* it would have made a difference! You know it would! First offenders get a couple of weeks in the second division. But – Sally! A month! And in the third division!' She stopped, flinching, her hand going to her shoulder as the van lurched around a corner.

Sally did not notice the gesture. Her own shoulders lifted in a shrug. She was still defensive, still not entirely sure that Hannah's concern was for her and not for the good name of the cause, besmirched by the support of a convicted criminal. The judge had sanctimoniously, and she supposed predictably, made much of a childhood conviction for thieving from a market stall. He had not of course, as he much enjoyed pointing out, been surprised. What else could one expect from an ill-educated, working-class female hooligan? She turned her head to look out of the tiny window in the door of the Maria. An urchin was capering along behind the slow-moving van, poking his tongue out, showing off to his mates. She shifted a little, trying to find a more comfortable position. To call the narrow ledge on which the prisoners were forced to perch a seat – the ceiling being too low to allow them to stand – would have been to overdignify it. To prevent herself from being thrown off it entirely Sally's legs were braced uncomfortably in front of her against the opposite wall of the tiny compartment.

'I'd *never* have let you risk coming with me if I'd known!' Hannah's voice was miserable.

Sally turned her head, and suddenly a quick smile flashed in the gloom. 'Right. And *that's* why I didn't tell you.'

The vehicle bumped and swayed again. Hannah bit her lip.

Sally frowned, watching her through the bars. 'You all right?'

'I'm fine. It's just – my shoulder. It's rather badly bruised I think.'

'Has anyone looked at it?'

Hannah shook her head. Her face was very pale, and there were dark shadows beneath the brown, tired-looking eyes. The night they had spent in the cold and uncomfortable police cells – harbinger as she knew of many such nights to come – and the ordeal in the court that morning with her family sitting not six feet from her as the judge with vitriolic ill temper had lectured her on her pre-ordained place in a society whose affairs were patently too complicated and important to be understood by women had been, despite her determination, a strain. Her badly swollen shoulder throbbed with every movement, and every so often an agonizing pain stabbed beneath her ribs. And now, the excitement was done and the price must be paid; two weeks shut away in an alien world, deprived of the sunshine and the fresh air, of any kind of absorbing occupation and of the company of those she loved. And for Sally – a month, and in the third and lowest division of prisoners, amongst the most hardened criminals, where the regime was harsher and even the few privileges accorded to second division prisoners were denied. 'You should have told me!' she whispered again.

The wardress stirred. 'Quiet, you!' she said threateningly.

Sally pulled a ferocious face. The child in the other cell sang softly, ignoring them all.

It was a long half hour in those stuffy, ill-smelling and uncomfortable conditions before the Black Maria pulled up at the great, menacing gates of Holloway Prison.

The fat woman stood. 'Right, you lot. Out. An' not a word – you 'ear me? Not a single soddin' word exceptin' when you're spoken to.'

In single file they passed through the massive gates to find themselves in a long corridor divided into cubicles on either side. A woman officer in the same dark blue uniform as the fat woman, a dark blue bonnet upon her head and a huge bunch of keys jangling at her waist awaited them, a list in her hand.

'Polly Dingle. Six months. Third division.'

The child smiled biddably.

'In here.' Impatiently the woman pushed her into a cubicle, slammed and locked the door.

'Hannah Patten. Two weeks. Second division.'

'Yes.'

'In here.'

Hannah avoided the woman's thrusting hand, stepped into the cubicle. It was perhaps four feet square and very dark. The metal walls were about six feet high beneath the vaulted space of the roof. The floor was stone, the whole place was cold as death. A narrow bench ran along one wall, and there was a bucket in the corner. Hannah almost gagged at the stench. The pain stabbed beneath her ribs again.

'Sally Smith. One month. Third division.'

Hannah heard the door of the next door cubicle slam behind Sally. The wardress's footsteps passed.

'Dingle. Can you read?'

'No, m'um.'

'Write?'

'No, m'um.'

'You can sew, I take it?' The voice was heavily sarcastic.

'Yes, m'um.'

'Religion?'

'Don't know, m'um.'

The spy hole in Hannah's door opened with a click. 'Patten. Can you read?'

'Yes.'

There was a small, somehow ominous silence. 'Yes – ma'am,' the woman said, very precisely.

'Yes, ma'am,' Hannah agreed, stiff-lipped.

'Write?'

'Yes – ma'am.'

'Sew?'

Hannah nodded.

'Patten, I asked you a question.'

'Yes – ma'am.'

'Religion?'

'Church of England, ma'am.'

The spy hole clicked shut and the woman moved on.

'Smith. You read?'

'Yes, ma'am.' Sally's voice was a caricature of servility. Hannah found herself suddenly having to suppress the rise of a small almost hysterical giggle.

'Write?'

'Oh yes, ma'am.' Again the simpering, mocking show of deference.

The wardress peered suspiciously through the peep-hole. 'Can you sew?'

'Like the Virgin Mary herself, so I've been told, ma'am.' Sally said, straight-faced, pure subversion in every word.

'Smith,' the wardress said with more restraint than Hannah had expected, 'don't come it. Or you'll find yourself on bread and water in the punishment cells before you can say "knife". Understood?'

'Yes, ma'am.' There was a grin in Sally's low voice.

The woman's sharp footsteps echoed along the stone corridor and were gone. In the cold and empty silence her going left, Hannah groped her way gingerly to the narrow bench and sat down, holding her breath against pain. Her feet felt like blocks of ice on the stone floor.

'You all right?' Sally's quiet voice reached her over the open top of the partition.

Hannah laughed a little shakily. 'Yes, I think so.'

'It'll get worse before it gets better.' There was a grim humour in the words that was absurdly reassuring.

'Yes, I'm sure you're right.'

They sat in silence for a while. Hannah hugged herself against the cold. Then, suddenly and surprisingly in the quiet she heard Sally's voice lifted softly in song.

> 'Arise, though pain or loss betide,
> Grudge naught of Freedom's toll –'

Delighted, quietly Hannah joined in this favourite marching song.

> 'For what they loved the martyrs died,
> Are we of meaner soul?'

Verse after verse they sang, their voices lifting carelessly louder, Sally beating time on the metal partition.

'Quiet you two! Quiet I say!'

They ignored the angry order. The last verse rang to the gloomy roof.

> 'To Freedom's Cause to death
> We swear our fealty.
> March on! March on! Face to the dawn,
> The dawn of Liberty!'

'By God, I'll –'

'What's going on here, Adams?' A new voice, crisp and impatient.

'Two of them there suffragettes, ma'am. Singing.'

'Are they indeed? Well – I doubt they'll find much to sing about here. The other van is arriving. Get them checked in as fast as you can, then get the lot of them up to the baths.'

'Yes, ma'am.'

'Yes, ma'am,' Sally echoed mockingly, very very quietly, 'No, ma'am. Three bags full, ma'am.'

The great outer door swung open again. Hannah heard the shuffle of footsteps and hushed voices. A woman laughed harshly and was quickly hushed.

'May Harris. Six months. Third division. In here.'

On it went as a dozen or so more prisoners were locked in the reception cubicles. Hannah had begun to shiver with cold and her shoulder hurt abominably. But the thought of Sally so close, the recollection of the quick, subversive grin, of the small defiance of their song warmed and cheered her. The new prisoners, locked into their tiny cubicles were calling to each other, shouting and laughing apparently oblivious of the angry protests of the wardresses, many of them obviously old acquaintances.

'What-oh, Elsie – back in the old 'otel again, eh? What yer bin up to this time? Stole the crown jewels?'

'I'll swing fer that effin' judge, I swear I will. A month 'e's given me! A bloody month!'

'Seen that feller of yours last week, Vi. Large as life an' twice as 'ansome. With that little tart Bessie Shilton 'e was!'

'Piss orf.'

The door to Hannah's cubicle swung open. A wardress in the blue holland uniform, the strings of her bonnet dangling untidily, jerked her head. 'Out.'

Stiffly Hannah came to her feet. In the corridor outside she found herself beside Sally at the head of a crocodile of women, two by two. 'What's happening?'

'Doctor,' Sally whispered.

'Shut it, you two. Smith, Patten – by the left – follow me!'

They were marched at the head of the procession of women along a short corridor, then lined up against the wall outside a heavy metal door.

'Get yerselves undone.'

Hannah, puzzled, glanced at Sally for enlightenment. Sally grinned encouragingly. 'Buttons,' she said, unbuttoning her own shirt.

'Right – Smith – in you go.'

Sally stepped through the door. Hannah fumbled with frozen and not quite steady fingers with the small buttons of her blouse.

'Patten.'

She looked up, surprised. Sally had reappeared, buttoning her shirt: it could hardly have been a full minute since she had left the line.

'Patten! Jump to it!'

She hurried through the door. Every step she took jolted through her damaged shoulder and ribs like fire. A tired-looking man with the bloodshot eyes and too-bright complexion of the heavy drinker half leaned, half sat upon a heavy desk. A stethoscope dangled from its leads about his neck. Beside him two strapping wardresses in the already familiar uniform stood, arms crossed, observing the proceedings.

'Are you all right?' the doctor asked, flatly and with not the slightest sign of interest.

'I – beg your pardon?'

Irritation flitted across the bad-tempered looking face. 'I said, are you all right?'

'I – yes – that is – I've hurt my shoulder, and –'

The mouth of the larger of the wardresses tightened. 'Enough of your lip,' the other one snapped.

The doctor jerked his head for her to approach, lifting the stethoscope. When she reached him he barely touched her chest with the instrument, dropped it, nodded. 'She's all right.'

The wardress nearest the door jerked her head. 'Out.'

Bemusedly buttoning her blouse, Hannah obeyed. As she joined Sally in the line the other girl winked. 'Next stop Harley Street, eh?'

In less than ten minutes the ludicrous medical examination was over and they were formed into their crocodile once more. 'Where now?' Hannah whispered as they set off down the dark corridor.

'Bath,' Sally said, succinctly and threw a small, slanting, oddly commiserative look at the other girl. 'I hate to tell you this, but it's not quite like home.'

Hannah never in her life forgot the hour that followed. Marched into the depths of the vast building, the prisoners found themselves in a great chill cavern of a room lined with shelves. A couple of wardresses patrolled the room and another three stood, faces forbidding, arms folded, behind a table upon which was piled what looked like nothing so much as a heap of grey dishcloths.

Sally nudged Hannah with the shadow of a grin. 'Faith,

Hope and Charity,' she murmured, her eyes flickering to the three enormous, grim-faced women behind the table.

'Quiet, there!' roared Faith. Charity scowled. Hannah's attempt to prevent nervous laughter hurt abominably.

'Get these on an' look lively.'

The old hands, knowing what was expected of them, shuffled to the table, took the bedraggled grey garments that were handed to them and then began, unconcernedly and in full view, to undress.

Hannah discovered that suddenly she had begun to shake, not violently but with a slight, relentless trembling that seemed rooted at the chill core of her body and was impossible to control. She gritted her teeth, tensing herself against it. 'What's happening?'

Sally had collected a short, rough-textured chemise from the table. 'We have to strip off and put on one of these.' The slight brusqueness of the tone was utterly belied by the acute sympathy in her eyes.

'I –' Hannah shook her head, bit her lip.

Sally put a firm hand on her arm. 'Just do it, love. Take a deep breath and do it. Or they'll do it for you. An' that's not funny.'

On shaking legs Hannah approached the table. The wardress barely glanced at her as she thrust the chemise into her hand. 'Get a move on. We 'aven't got all day to wait for you, you know.'

Clutching the chemise Hannah retreated to where Sally was calmly unpinning her hat, kicking off boots, stripping off shirt, skirt, petticoats, chemise, stockings and – to Hannah's horror – drawers, all of which she folded neatly on the floor beside her before slipping her arms into the short chemise and pulling it over her head. Her slim, strong body was pale as milk and lean as a boy's. The nipples of her small breasts stood erect and dark in the bitterly cold air. The ugly scar on her upper arm was still a raw red. 'Hurry up!' she hissed.

'I can't,' Hannah said flatly.

'You've got to!'

'What's goin' on over 'ere?' The wardress Sally had christened Faith approached, frowning suspiciously. 'Patten, isn't it? What the 'ell d'you think you're up to? Look lively!'

Sally cast Hannah a fierce glance.

Without a word Hannah unpinned her hat and let it drop to the floor beside her. Then she ducked her head and, scarlet-faced and almost blinded with humiliation, she began to undress. In her whole adolescent and adult life she had never taken off so much as a shoe before the eyes of others. Whilst the extreme prudery that had undoubtedly been a part of the age had never found favour or expression in the Patten household, modesty and propriety certainly had. To stand thus in the open and to strip herself naked before the eyes of strangers was a torture it had never even occurred to her to contemplate. To her horror she felt the rise and sting of tears. Awkwardly she fumbled with buttons and tapes.

'Here, let me.' Sally's cold, efficient hands busied themselves.

'Lady Muck can't undress herself?' asked one of the wardresses, not too ill-naturedly.

'There.' Sally contrived as best she could to come between Hannah and the amused, derisive eyes that were being turned upon her as she tugged the rough grey chemise over her head. 'You'll have to let your hair down too.'

All the women were shaking their hair out. Hannah started her usual hunt for the host of hairpins that were needed to secure her heavy hair. With an angry and enormous effort of will she tried to stop the shaking that was making her teeth chatter and her fingers thumbs, but to no avail; the combined onslaught of cold and nerves defeated her and she trembled like a leaf in the wind.

'Come on.' Sally picked up Hannah's pile of clothes and dumped them in her arms, topping them with her hat. 'Follow me.'

Hannah did as she was bidden, taking her clothes to the table, watching as a wardress bundled them up and put them on the shelf, answering like an automaton the questions she was asked. Name? Age? Offence? Sentence? Married? Next of kin? – Laboriously the woman entered the particulars in a huge book. Hannah's bare feet had lost all feeling on the stone floor. The rough cloth of the chemise rubbed the tender skin of her injured shoulder and her ribs ached. Like an emotionless doll she submitted to the further humiliation of being searched, her arms held above her head whilst hard hands ran over her body, probing and squeezing, unnecessarily and salaciously rough. The wardress gave her a push. 'Line up.'

She rejoined Sally, eyes cast down, not looking at the other girl. Sally slipped a hand in hers, her grip strong. 'Nearly over.'

Touched by the attempt at encouragement, she forced a smile.

Sally grinned back. 'That's the ticket. Don't let them get you down. That's what they want.'

'Stop nattering you two. By the left. Follow me.' They followed Charity's broad blue back through a door into a huge room in which stood twenty or so ancient iron baths, each in a small cubicle separated from its neighbour by a low partition.

'Smith. Patten. Dingle. Peabody.' The women were assigned each to a bath. Hannah pushed through the low, swinging door, stood staring, horror finally shaking her from the shocked stupor into which she had fallen. She shook her head. 'No,' she said very firmly.

Sally's head popped furtively over the partition. 'What's the matter?'

Hannah lifted a pointing finger that trembled noticeably. 'Look at it! It's filthy!'

The black iron bath had been given at some time a thin coating of white paint, most of which had worn off. The bath was half full of fresh and fairly warm water, through which could be seen the layers and rings of grime that were ground into what was left of the paint.

'Get in!' Sally hissed.

Hannah's stomach stirred queasily, her face wrinkled in disgust. 'I can't.' She looked at the other girl in true desperation. 'Sally, I *can't*!'

'What can't you do?' The voice that came from behind her was dangerously conversational, the eyes beneath the dark blue bonnet hard. Sally's head disappeared.

'The bath's dirty,' Hannah said stiff-lipped.

'Get in.'

Hannah shook her head.

The wardress very calmly unclipped a whistle that hung from her waist by a chain and put it to her lips. 'I count to ten,' she said equably, 'then I blow this. You want to bath yourself – or you want half a dozen of us to do it for you? Please yourself. One – two – three –'

Hannah stared at her for one long, rebellious moment.

'– four – five – six –'

Hannah closed her eyes. 'All right.'

The woman stopped counting, lowered the whistle. But she did not move.

Hannah bit her lip.

'In,' her tormentor said simply. 'I'm here to see it.'

Hannah turned her back, struggled the chemise over her head, stepped into the water with closed eyes.

'You want me to scrub your back?' The heavy-handed humour was entirely malicious. The woman, Hannah realized, was actually enjoying herself.

'No, thank you.'

The vast blue bulk loomed above her. 'No, thank you, ma'am.'

Hannah sighed. 'No, thank you, ma'am.'

Alone she sat hunched in the water, avoiding the filthy sides. Though barely lukewarm the water was surprisingly comforting to her cold, tense body. She scrubbed quickly at arms and legs with the rough, strong-smelling soap. At least, slowly, the trembling was easing.

'You all right?' The whisper came from the top of the partition. Hannah turned her head. Sally's concerned face peeped at her, broke into a small, droll smile at sight of her. 'There, you see? I said it wouldn't be so –' she broke off. 'Jesus, Hannah!'

'What?'

'Your shoulder! I didn't realize how bad it was. What a bloody mess!'

Hannah hastily shook her hair back about her shoulders, reached for the rough towel that hung by the bath. 'It's nothing.'

'Nothing! It's all the colours of the rainbow! And swollen to twice its size!'

'Smith! You got time fer a nice little chat? Good – then yer can come out 'ere an' chat with me. An' earn yer bloody keep while you're about it!'

'Get something *done* about that!' Sally hissed fiercely. Then, 'Coming, ma'am,' she sang out sweetly, her face ferocious, and disappeared.

Hannah clambered gingerly from the bath, dried herself as best as she could on the harsh towel, put on the skimpy chemise. An oppressive weariness had suddenly overcome her. Her eyelids drooped, her limbs were like lead. Listlessly she left the cubicle, joined the inevitable queue at the table, where Sally was helping a wardress dole out the clothes that would be the women's uniform for the length of their sentences: rough and ill-made calico underclothing, thick stockings of heavy black wool with red stripes going around the legs and no means that Hannah could see of holding them up, and ill-fitting brown serge skirt and bodice, all marked with the conspicuous broad arrow that was the insignia of their imprisonment. But at least they were decent covering and it was with some relief that Hannah struggled into hers, battling with the manic arrangement of tapes and strings that held the shapeless garments together. With hasty hands she stuffed her hair into a too-small bonnet and tied the strings beneath her chin, then slipped her feet into awkward and badly fitting shoes that were at least three sizes too big for her narrow feet. Someone threw her a huge blue and white checked apron, which she tied about her waist.

'Right. By the left. Follow me.'

They were led through more corridors to the strangest building Hannah had ever seen; a skeleton building, its metal bones raw in the cold light. Tier upon tier of landings rose above them. Weary and subdued they trod the metal stairs.

'Second division prisoners fall out.'

Four women stepped from the line.

'Peabody, four. McCann, seven. Patten, eleven. Ashe, twenty-three.'

Sally let go of Hannah's hand with a last squeeze of the fingers and a quick, reassuring smile before she was marched off. Hannah with the other three followed the wardress along a landing that was lined with grim iron-studded doors. At the designated doors they stopped, the door was unlocked, the prisoner stepped inside and the door was locked behind her.

Cell eleven was Hannah's.

The wardress jerked her head. 'In you go, Eleven.'

Hannah stepped through the door that clanged shut behind her like the very knell of doom. Number Eleven. She was no longer Hannah Patten. No longer, even, Patten. She was Number Eleven, Landing C.

She stumbled to the wooden shelf that ran the length of the narrow, whitewashed, almost bare cell, sank down on it and buried her face in her hands. She was trembling again, violently now, and the pain in her shoulder and ribs was all but unbearable. Dry-eyed and utterly miserable she sat, unable to think, unable to lift her head. Two weeks. Two long, awful weeks.

In that moment of near despair it might have been a lifetime.

II

To a young woman reared as gently as Hannah Patten had been, prison life was bound to come as a shock to test the fortitude of even her strong character. There was no indulgence and little compassion behind these bleak walls. A prisoner was a criminal and was treated as such. The regime was harsh in the extreme, the days unvarying and soul-crushing in their deadly, mindless boredom. She awoke each morning at dawn, in a cell roughly twelve feet long and perhaps seven wide, to the heavy tramp of feet and the strident ringing of bells. The floor was of stone, the tiny window, high up near the ceiling, small-paned and heavily barred, allowing the passage of neither light nor air and the sight only of a tiny square of grim brick wall. Beside the cell door, guarded by thick opaque glass, a gas jet flickered. Beneath that a small shelf and a tiny stool were the closest the cell could boast to a chair and table. Upon the shelf lay a bible, a hymn book and a bound copy of the prison rules. In the corner beneath the high window were two more shelves, the lower to accommodate her thin mattress and meagre bedding during the day, the upper containing the bare essentials of living – a wooden spoon, a tin mug, a piece of soap, a handleless hairbrush – all of which, on pain of punishment, must be kept in pre-ordained and never varying positions. On the floor beneath the shelves were a few simple utensils – a plate, a slop pail, a shallow basin and a small water-tin containing two or three pints of water. A tiny towel and a tinier tablecloth – more the size of a napkin – both much faded and worn, hung upon a nail. The plank bed would be folded up against the wall by day and pulled down each evening.

In the chill darkness of dawn in the unheated cell ablutions were speedy and – given at the most three pints of water – necessarily sketchy. In the distance the rattling and slamming of doors coming ever closer forced haste too into the chore of dressing in the heavy, awkward clothing, until the door flew open, crashing against the wall. 'Empty your slops, Eleven.' This unpleasant chore completed, there was the bedding to pack away for the day, each item to be folded precisely to formula and piled in unvarying order on an unvarying spot on the shelf. Then the tins used for meals must be cleaned with bath-brick and rags until they shone like silver. A pail of water delivered to the cell must then be used to scrub everything – floor, bed, stool and shelves – before breakfast consisting of a pint of thin gruel and a few ounces of bread could be eaten. After that, with fingers stiff and sore from cold water, she would start upon her day's quota of sewing – sheets, at least fifteen a week, to be hemmed top and bottom, a seam in the centre that must be sewn with neatness and precision or the inspecting wardress, with no regard for protests or tears, would rip it open and throw it back to be sewn again.

At eight thirty she would join one of the long columns of women who were trudging down the staircases to the Chapel, this at least a small, welcome break, a chance to exchange a smile, perhaps even a few forbidden words, to see something approaching a friendly face; but all the time under a running fire of orders and criticisms, 'Hold your head up, Twenty-Five!' 'Quiet, Number Two!' 'Pick up your feet, Fourteen! Don't slouch!' 'Silence there!'

Back in the cell, sewing her sheets, the silence was the silence of utter loneliness, disorientating and depressing. And, steadily the pain in her shoulder and ribs worsened.

Dinner was at twelve – oatmeal porridge and bread, or perhaps suet pudding; two days a week potatoes and bread. From then onwards the only thing to break the mind-numbing monotony of lonely imprisonment was a trip to fetch some water some time between two and three in the afternoon, or, three days out of the seven, a precious exercise period spent shuffling in silent single file about the prison yard beneath a high square of sky where birds wheeled and called in a freedom that was almost too painful to watch. Supper, at five, was, like breakfast, gruel and bread. That finished there was the bed to make up before the gas jet died and the cell was given over to the silent shadows of twilight, the prisoner, locked in till morning, left to face the worst battle of the day: to try to sleep.

From the first awful night Hannah was utterly unable to sleep for two consecutive hours at a time. The bed was like rock, the pillow stone, the air foul. The meagre sheet and blanket was barely of a size to cover her, and certainly did nothing to protect her from the cold that crept from the white, sweating walls and the grey stone floor. Her damaged shoulder and ribs, bad enough during the day, at night became torture. Three mornings she lay, and then a fourth, watching a dawn that had taken agonizing hours to break smudge her tiny window with light. On the fifth morning, as she struggled to dress before the door was flung open, she wrenched the shoulder again. Gasping and grey-faced she leaned against the cold wall as the world tilted sickeningly about her. She heard, but her eyes unfocused by the unbearable pain did not see, the opening of the door.

'Empty your slops, Eleven.'

Cold sweat trickled down her face and her back, crept at her armpits.

'Your slops, Eleven! What's the matter with you?'

She pushed herself away from the wall, noted with an almost comical amazement the way in which her knees buckled as with a painful and ungainly thump she collapsed upon the floor and lay as still as death.

On the sixth day of her confinement Sally, to her utter astonishment, received a visitor. Her cell, in the third division, was slightly smaller than Hannah's, every bit as cold, damper and even worse lit. She was perched upon her stool, hunched over the detested sewing when the door opened.

'Out yer come, Twenty-Three.'

Sally lifted a wary head, eyed the wardress she still thought of as Hope with suspicion. 'Why?'

The woman grinned, showing a picturesque row of broken and blackened teeth. 'You'll find out. Just come along of me.'

'But –'

'Stop arguing, Twenty-Three, an' jump to it!'

Resignedly Sally dumped her sheet on the shelf and stood up. Whatever this was about it was bound to be bad. Her mind scanned the last twenty-four hours anxiously. They surely couldn't have discovered about the extra piece of bread she had filched whilst scrubbing the floor of the kitchen the day before yesterday? The deed was long done and the evidence gulped in a mouthful. She'd been reprimanded two days running for using the prisoners' dumb alphabet to communicate with other inmates in the Chapel, but she'd paid a price for that already in losing her potato ration yesterday lunchtime. What else?

'Where are we going?'

'You'll see, Twenty-Three. Just shut yer mouth an' do as yer told.'

She followed the woman along the corridor to a barred door with a grille in it. The woman knocked smartly. A face appeared.

'Yes?'

'Number Twenty-Three.'

The door opened. 'Ten minutes,' Hope said repressively, 'then I come back for you.'

Puzzled Sally entered the room. It was bare but for a single wooden table. The inevitable tiny, barred, dirty window high up in the wall blocked out more light than it let in, and a gas jet flared by the door. A heavy-boned wardress – she whom Sally had christened Charity – stood guard. As Sally entered the room the tall, broad-shouldered figure who stood by the table turned.

Sally gaped.

'Hello, Sally.' Ben Patten's craggy face was in shadow. 'How are you?'

After a heartbeat's stunned silence Sally to her horror found herself laughing, a small, nervous, embarrassing cough of laughter that sounded over-loud in the confines of the room. 'Er – as well as can be expected is probably the best way to put it.'

He smiled a little, and stepped closer to her, to where the dim yellow gas light shone upon his square-jawed face. Though the long, straight mouth was still tilted in the small smile the dark grey eyes were sombre. Sally's heart lurched. This was no social call.

'What's the matter,' she asked bluntly, 'what's wrong?'

Ben readily took his cue from her and did not prevaricate. 'It's Hannah. I've paid her fine. I'm taking her home.'

Genuine relief lifted Sally's heart. 'That's good. This is no place for her.'

'It isn't that. In fact she's furious. I doubt if she'll ever talk to me again.' The wry smile flickered again and was gone. 'It's her injuries. I suspect she has a couple of cracked ribs. And in my honest opinion if she doesn't get proper medical attention for her shoulder it could be permanently damaged. Principles or no principles she can't stay here in that condition.'

Sally nodded. 'Good for you. I bet she kicked up a stink, though?'

'You could say that.'

Charity sniffed loudly, hawked, spat into a bucket in the corner. A shadow of distaste flickered in Ben's face. There was a small, slightly awkward silence.

Then, 'I want you to let me take you home too,' Ben said flatly and quietly.

She was ready for him. 'No.' Her tone matched his exactly.

'Sally – please. You've made your point. What good are you doing in here? A month in the third division is too much to ask of anyone. Everyone wants you out.'

'No.'

'For Hannah's sake if not your own. It will break her heart to leave you in here.'

'Hannah's hurt.' Sally's lips twitched into a little, dry smile. 'I'm not.'

Ben leaned upon the table, palms flat, head down for a moment so that she could not see his face. One of her ugly woollen stockings was sliding inexorably down her leg, gathering in lax wrinkles at her ankle. She contemplated the inelegance of lifting her skirts to pull it up, settled for trying to prevent its total collapse by trying to hitch it up with her other leg. Surprisingly the silence lengthened. With a sudden intuition she looked at his bowed head. The stocking settled in graceless discomfort around her ankle. 'What else?' she asked, quietly.

He lifted his head. 'There's been an accident,' he said baldly.

'Accident? What sort of accident?' Considering the cold panic that had suddenly stopped her heart and dried her throat the words were remarkably composed. Toby! Something terrible had happened to Toby!

'Your friend, Miss Dickson –'

It took a moment to sink in, a moment to fight the swift and terrible feeling of relief. Not Toby then, at least. 'Josie? What's happened to her?'

'She was brought to the hospital the day before yesterday.' He was still not looking at her, but his voice was cool, clinical. The voice of a doctor. 'There was an accident at the laundry a week or so ago.' He lifted his head then, and in his eyes that belied the cool voice was pure pain at what she must be told. 'She caught her hand – her right hand – between the rollers of the steam mangle.'

'Oh, no!' Sally's hand had gone to her mouth, her eyes were appalled.

'She was taken to St Mary's, and the hand was dressed,' he continued quietly. 'Four or five days later she went to her own doctor. She was in terrible pain. The hand was poisoned. He sent her to us.'

She was staring at him, very pale, her hand still to her mouth. 'What –?' She could not go on.

'We couldn't save the hand.' His voice was very quiet, the words very clear.

She turned from him, took a distracted step towards a blank, damp-marked wall. Searing images flickered like fire in her brain. She pressed her hands to her eyes for a moment, trying to blot them out. 'Poor Josie! Oh, poor Josie!'

Charity phlegmatically consulted the watch that was pinned to her massive bosom, folded her arms, sniffed again, loudly and unpleasantly.

Ben came around the table, caught Sally by the shoulders, turning her towards him. 'Sally, come home. You've done enough. Miss Dickson needs you.' He hesitated. 'Everyone needs you. The children are asking for you. And young Toby – he has a calendar – he marks off every day –'

'No!' She pulled roughly away from him. Her cheeks were shining with tears. 'No! I've done it and I'll stick with it. Toby'll have to wait. And Josie – there's nothing I can do for her, is there? I can't–', she swallowed, 'I can't give her her hand back, can I?' The thought was too much for her. In a sudden, violent movement she buried her face in her hands and sobbed wildly. Josie, of all people. Kind, generous, loving Josie. What harm had she ever done that she should suffer this?

She felt his supporting arm go about her, but he made no other attempt to soothe or comfort her, nor did he try to stem the flood of tears. He simply held her shaking body, cupped the head that was buried in his chest with a big hand, holding her. At last the tears eased. The shock was ebbing. She steadied herself, drew away from him, took the handkerchief he wordlessly offered. 'I'm sorry.'

'There's no need. It's perfectly natural. You've had an awful shock.' His voice was very calm, almost impersonal. She slipped away from his still-supporting arm, stood for a moment with her back to him, fighting for control, mopping at her streaming eyes. Then she turned, head up, still sniffing a little, held out the handkerchief. 'Thank you.'

'Keep it.'

She shook her head. 'They won't let me.'

A spasm of something she could not identify – irritation? exasperation? – flickered across his face. He opened his mouth.

She held up a swift, absolutely intransigent hand. 'No, Doctor Patten. Thank you, but no. I don't want you to pay my fine. I'll serve my sentence.' She could not put into words the complexities of how and why it was so important to her that she should see her sentence through. She did not try. Somehow, strangely, she was certain that he knew.

He surveyed her in an odd, searching silence for a moment. 'You do know', he leaned back on the table and folded his arms, 'that I don't in fact need your permission? I could pay your fine willy-nilly and out you'd go, bag and baggage.'

'Yes, I know. But you won't.'

'How do you know that? I've paid Hannah's against her wishes.'

She shrugged. 'I just know you won't. Hannah's different.'

He pushed himself away from the table, his square, ruddy face inscrutable. 'No, Sally Smith,' he said, 'I think perhaps you're the one who's different. You are certainly the most stubborn young woman I've ever come across in my life. Not to say the most wilful.'

She grinned a watery grin, not her usual style but a creditable attempt. 'Thanks.'

His eyes crinkled. 'I'm not sure it was meant as a compliment.'

'That's not to stop me taking it as one if I feel like it.' The jauntiness was a little ragged at the edges, but like the smile it was a good try. The tears that somehow refused to stop still streamed down her face. She ignored them.

He held out his hand. 'If you're sure?'

She took it. It was hard and strong and very warm. Her own felt very rough and very dirty. She shook his hand quickly and stepped back. 'Absolutely. It isn't a life sentence, you know. In three weeks, one day and about three hours I'll be back to plague you all.'

He nodded, but a shadow had passed over his face. Again, intuitively, she sensed something beyond the simple words that had been spoken between them. 'Doctor Patten?' The ragged edge of grief and panic made her husky voice sharper than she had meant. 'Josie – she will be all right, won't she? I mean,' she swallowed, 'apart from the hand?'

He hesitated for too long, confirming the sudden rise of her fears. 'I'm sorry. I can't say. She's very sick. Very sick indeed.'

'But – you can make her well? Can't you? You – you're a doctor – she's in hospital. That's what you're for, isn't it?' Miserably aggressive she caught his arm, 'To make people well?'

He nodded. 'Yes. That's what we're for.'

'I mean – she hasn't got the plague, has she? People can live with only one hand. Can't they? She'll be all right. Won't she?'

'I hope so.'

'Time's up,' Charity said tonelessly, heaving herself away from the door.

Sally's shoulders slumped a little. She stepped back from Ben, her arms crossed in front of her, holding herself as if against the cold. Her face was set.

For a brief moment he stood indecisively.

'Time's up, sir,' Charity was brusque.

He nodded, turned to the door, stopped, threw Sally one more questioning glance.

She shook her head.

'Back you go, Twenty-Three.' The wardress who had escorted her from her cell had entered the room. Not unkindly she took Sally's arm. 'Time's up.'

'Yes.' Numbly Sally allowed herself to be ushered out into the corridor. Ben Patten's firm footsteps sounded upon the stone floor as he walked very fast away from her, his back ramrod straight, his head held at an angle that somehow hinted at anger.

'Doctor Patten!' Her voice was urgent.

He turned.

'Give her – Josie – my love?'

He nodded unsmiling. 'Of course.' And then he turned and walked briskly away from her; and if he knew that she stood for a long moment watching after him, yet he did not turn again to look back before he disappeared around the corner of the passage.

III

For all her determination, Sally did not in the end, serve out her sentence. For when Ben Patten came to the prison again, just twelve days after that first visit, one look at the austere face and troubled eyes told her that this time no choice was being offered. This time he would not take 'no' for an answer. In those twelve intervening days the thought of Josie's tragedy had haunted her, in the true sense of the word, always at her shoulder, trailing in her footsteps, hounding her dreams. Her already broken nights had been punctuated with nightmares, the long, mind-numbing days full of miserable worry. The tension in the end had betrayed her into a loss of temper and control that

207

had landed her in the punishment cells on bread and water for three days, her only consolation the recollection of the satisfying crack her heavy shoe had made as it had connected unerringly and violently with Charity's shin.

On the nineteenth day of her confinement, back in her own cell which after the punishment cell she noted with grim amusement felt almost like home, as she woke to the bells and the tramping feet there was nothing to indicate that the day would be any different from any other. Not until mid-morning when, as she sat huddled over her sewing, the door crashed open to reveal Charity, grim-faced as always, was the monotony broken.

'On yer feet, Twenty-Three.'

Sally stood.

Charity jerked a dirty thumb. 'With me.'

'Where to?'

The rough grey head turned. 'Ter the Guv'nor's office, no less.'

Defensive alarm stiffened Sally's spine. 'What for?'

The woman slouched against the door, her fleshy mouth turned down in a parody of an unpleasant smile. 'Seems you got friends in 'igh places. 'Oity-Toity.'

Puzzled, Sally followed her through the maze of passages and staircases to the Prison Governor's office. And there, standing by the window, was Ben. Sally's eyes were riveted to him from the moment she entered the room.

'You're being released, Smith.' The Governor, a tall, thin woman, sallow-faced and severe, was peremptory. 'Your things are in the ante-room. Sign for them and change, please.'

Sally was still looking at Ben. 'I asked you', she said quietly and stubbornly, 'not to pay my fine.'

'I haven't.' Not by a flicker did Ben betray the shock that the sight of her had dealt him. Pasty-faced, thin to gauntness, her bones stood through skin that looked paper-thin and the usually clear hazel eyes were dull and strained.

The Governor looked up from the papers she had been studying. 'You are being released into Doctor Patten's custody on compassionate grounds.'

'Compassionate?' Sally stopped. Her anxious eyes scanned Ben's sombre face. 'Compassionate grounds?' she asked very softly, a thread of painful question in the words.

'Get your things, Smith.' The Governor was impatient. 'And for God's sake have the sense to stay out of trouble. I don't want to see you here again. God above, haven't we got problems enough without you people?'

'Get changed, Sally,' Ben said very quietly. 'I'm taking you home.'

It was half an hour later, when they were sitting in the hansom that was taking them back to Poplar that Sally finally asked the question which had hammered in her head ever since the first sight of Ben Patten's face. In all her prison dreams of freedom she had never – could never have – foreseen such an unjoyful release. 'It's Josie?' she asked.

'Yes.'

'She's not – ?' She stopped.

He shook his head. For the first time she noticed how tired he looked. He turned a compassionate face to her. 'No. She isn't dead. But there's very little hope.'

She had known it – somehow she had known it – but nevertheless the shock was awful. 'But, how can that be? She can't die! Not like this! She can't!'

Ben said nothing. The hansom swayed and rattled on cobblestones.

Sally shook her head. 'She can't!' she said again doggedly.

Ben reached out and took her thin, dirty, hardened hand in his. 'I'm sorry,' he said.

And Sally, staring at him in misery, thought she had never heard anything so horrifyingly final as those two simple words.

She stared at him defiantly. 'No,' she said. 'I don't – I won't – believe it.'

Ben said nothing.

The hansom rattled steadily through the summer streets to Poplar.

Chapter Seven

I

Josie Dickson was dying; worse, she knew she was dying, though she did her calm and gallant best to keep that knowledge from those she loved.

'Oh, I'm miles better, love,' she said smiling, sweet and dismissive, at Sally. 'I'll be out of here in no time. I've been asking and asking to go home, and I'm sure Doctor Patten would let me. Even Dad agrees I'd be better off at home. It's just silly Dan that's making me stay. But Sally! Just look at you! You're thin as a rail! What on earth have they done to you?'

'Well, Holloway isn't exactly the Savoy.' Sally was still struggling to master the shock of her first sight of Josie, warned though she had been – warm, clear-skinned, bright-eyed Josie, who had become skeletal in her brief illness, her skin like thin and bloodless silk stretched too tightly over fragile bone, an unhealthy flush in her cheeks, her brown eyes sunken and burned out with recurrent fever. Her left hand lay as if already lifeless upon the starched white counterpane. The right arm of her nightdress was pinned in awkward emptiness across her breast. Two days before, in a final attempt to stop the spread of the poison that was slowly but certainly killing her, the surgeon had amputated to the elbow. Sally, weak still from her own recent ordeal and less in charge of her emotions than she cared to admit even to herself had been shaken almost to tears at first sight of her friend; but Dan, before ever allowing her to the bedside, had been fierce. 'I tell you flat, Sal — I don't want any tears. Whatever you do, don't cry. Don't let her see that the sight of her upsets you. I won't have it. She needs help. She needs strength. She needs to see a smiling face. She needs normality. The last thing she needs is anyone weeping over her. If you can't manage it, then you'll have to stay away from her. We won't save her by collapsing all over her in tears. She needs hope. If you can't give her that then I tell you straight I won't let you see her.'

And Sally, understanding, had promised and had fought the horror that had gripped her at the sight of that gaunt, pain-filled face. Yet still she had to clear her throat awkwardly before continuing. 'You don't get fat on prison gruel.'

The thin left hand moved a little. Sally took it and squeezed it gently, afraid even in her own weakened state of crushing the brittle-feeling bones, of tearing that hot, fine-drawn skin. 'I think you were ever so brave.' Josie smiled again, the old, sweet smile, 'I was ever so proud of you. I couldn't have done it. Not for anything. It must have been awful.'

Sally grinned lopsidedly. 'You forget — I'm an old lag. I knew what to expect.'

'That makes you more brave, not less.' Josie's voice was positive. 'Miss Patten said so too. When she came with Doctor Patten to see me. She said everyone was proud of you.'

Sally shrugged and shook her head. 'And what about you, then? Lord — I can't leave you for a minute, can I? Look at the state you get yourself into the moment I take my eye off you!'

Josie moved her head on the pillow and laughed a little. Her eyes were heavy-lidded. As Sally watched they drooped with sickly weariness.

'You're tired,' she said anxiously. 'Should I go?'

The hand that lay in hers moved spasmodically. 'No. Don't go. Stay a while. I'll be all right in a tick.'

They sat in silence. Josie propped against her mountain of pillows with her eyes shut, apparently dozing, Sally tense as a leashed animal upon the chair beside her watching her, willing strength into that terrifying frail body, resolution into the failing will. Around them the bustle of visiting time washed like a sea of movement about the still island of the high, narrow bed. Nurses in their long dark skirts, high collars, frilled caps and vast pinafores swished past, rustling with inevitable, starchy indifference. Other visitors murmured to their bedridden friends and relatives, or sat in difficult silence too distressed or perhaps simply too awkward to speak. Beyond the narrow window, behind Josie's still, gaunt face, warm June sunshine flooded the sky and turned the air, even in the dust of the overcrowded city to summer gold.

'Sally?' Josie's eyes flickered open suddenly.

'Yes?'

'You – you have made it up with Dan, haven't you?'

Sally nodded, faint colour in her cheeks. 'Course.'

'I can't bear you to be bad friends.'

'We're not. Course we're not.'

'He can be pig-headed I know –'

Sally grinned at that. 'You can say that again.'

'– but he loves you.'

Sally ducked her head, looked at their two hands linked upon the counterpane, her own thin, hard, full of strength, Josie's with pale, oddly blotched skin and fingers that could barely curl about the narrow hand that held them.

'Sally –' the low voice was insistent.

Sally lifted her head.

'Did you hear what I said?'

'I heard.'

'He does love you.' The lax fingers twitched a little. 'Please – don't hurt him.'

'I won't.' The words were guarded. 'You know I won't.'

The reassurance seemed to satisfy the sick girl for all its ambivalence. She sighed a little. Closed her eyes again.

Sally waited until the even rhythm of her breathing spoke of true sleep then gently disentangled her fingers from the limp hand and stood up. At the door of the long ward Dan stood waiting. For a brief, silent moment her eyes met his stubborn, unflinching gaze. Before she could speak a brisk nurse paused by her side. 'Miss Smith?'

'Yes.'

'Doctor Patten asked that you spare him a moment.'

'Yes. Of course.'

'Will you follow me, please?'

Before following the nurse Sally stopped for the space of a heart-beat by Josie's silent brother, put up a hand gently to touch his cheek as she passed. His slow smile was difficult, edged with the misery he doggedly refused to acknowledge. She followed the nurse down a dreary, seemingly endless corridor, their footsteps echoing sharply from the impersonal tiled walls. In the brown-painted, cluttered office into which Sally was shown were a desk and chair, a huge wooden filing cabinet, a screen folded haphazardly against the wall and a high couch covered with a brown blanket. There was paper everywhere. A glass-fronted cupboard in the corner was filled with neat rows of jars and bottles. There was no sign of Ben Patten.

The nurse tutted. 'He was here just a moment or so ago. He must have been called away. Will you wait?'

'Yes.' Sally stood looking round as the door closed behind her, shutting out the sharp clip of footsteps, the rattle of a trolley. She walked to the window. A huge plane tree stood between the window and the noisy road, mottled trunk gleaming, big dusty leaves bathed in sunshine, quivering at the movement of the squabbling sparrows that flitted busily amongst the branches. Sally laid her forehead tiredly against the smudged glass. She had been out of prison for two days, and still she felt oddly disorientated. Her stomach was unready to digest the quantities of food she was offered, however simple the fare. She found the constant company of people strangely

214

stressful after those long solitary days of confinement. Even Toby's happy chatter could tire her after a while. But to see the sky, to watch these silly, quarrelling birds, to know that she was free to sit, to stand, to come, go, speak or be still as she liked was a joy to be savoured as she had never savoured any other; or had been until she had seen Josie's thin face against the pillows, understood that if her own incarceration were over Josie's – harder, more terrifying, infinitely more unjust – was not and very possibly in this life never would be. For Josie the only release from her imprisonment in that failing body was likely to come through death. She sucked her bottom lip, hard, biting it, stopping tears. She would not believe it! Superstitiously she crossed her fingers – who knew but that believing things might make them happen?

She closed her eyes against the sunshine, against the noisy, careless birds, against the bright summer light and the sheer exuberant noise of the city streets that reached her through the shield of the window. How could the world go about its business so cruelly indifferent when Josie lay dying inch by inch for the sake of a careless moment, an inefficient guard upon a simple machine, a split-second mistake?

She did not hear the door open behind her, nor the slight click of its shutting.

'Sally?'

She turned. Ben Patten dumped his battered bag on top of the papers on his desk. Balanced in his other hand was a tray upon which stood two steaming mugs. 'Tea,' he said.

She accepted a mug, thanking him. He looked gauntly tired. 'Sorry I wasn't here. I got called away. An emergency in the fever ward. There's something of an epidemic on.' He sat down behind the desk, gulped a mouthful of tea, rested his bowed head for a moment on the fingertips of his free hand. 'It's so damned overcrowded down there,' he muttered quietly, almost to himself, 'no wonder we can't stop them dying like flies.'

Sally watched him in silence, sipping her tea, leashing her sympathy. The affairs of the fever ward were not at that moment her priority. There was one thing she wanted to know and one thing only. Yet something kept her still, allowing him a moment to emerge from whatever pain it was she sensed was gripping him, clenching his face and his big, capable hand, making the straight line of his mouth grim. And as she stood in silence and watched him she found herself to her own intense astonishment suppressing an absurd rise of compassion, a ridiculous urge to lay a hand upon the tensely hunched shoulder, to smooth the rough, untidy hair, to offer comfort, however slight, respite from the battle he fought normally so coolly and so well. Behind his back her mouth pursed in wry self-derision. The day that Doctor Ben Patten needed – or even noticed – Sally Smith's sympathy would be a day indeed.

'You wanted to talk to me?' Her husky voice was cool.

'Yes.' He lifted his head, almost shaking it, like a dog emerging from water, freeing himself from the weight of his thoughts. He looked at the girl who stood with her back to the light watching him dispassionately. As always her sharp-featured face beneath its untidy crown of light brown hair was unnervingly collected, the slanting greenish eyes a little wary, giving away nothing.

'About Josie?'

He paused for the briefest of moments. 'Yes. And about her brother.'

She waited.

He stood up restlessly, prowled the room for a moment. Then with a sweep of his hand he cleared a spot on the desk and perched upon it, one leg dangling. He sipped his tea, eyed the mug pensively for a second, lifted his head. 'Miss Dickson wants to go home. Her brother won't allow it.'

Sally was staring at him. 'Go *home*?' she interrupted incredulously. 'In that state? Of course she can't go home!'

He looked back down at the mug in his hand. 'It's her wish,' he said quietly.

She stood very, very still for what seemed a very long time. 'To go home', she said at last flatly, disbelievingly, accusingly, 'to die?'

In the silence a clock ticked. 'Yes.'

'You've given up? You aren't even going to *try* to save her?'

His glance was quick and edged with anger at that. 'We have tried.'

'And now you're giving up?' The words were bitter, more statement than question.

He moved a weary head. 'Sally – believe me – there's nothing we can do. Nothing. It's gone too far. Her whole body is poisoned. We have nothing with which to fight it.' He waited for a moment, studying her face. Then he spread his hands eloquently. 'She hates it here. She's unhappy. Sally – I'm sorry, but don't you see – she doesn't want to die here amongst strangers. She wants to go home. Her father understands. Her brother won't listen. And she won't go against him.'

She turned away from him, back to the window. 'And that's why you got me out of Holloway? To persuade Dan to let his sister go home to die? To release one of your precious beds?' The tone was unforgivable; cruelly bitter. She did not care. The birds still fought their silly battles in the tree before her blurred eyes.

He came behind her quietly; she was taken entirely by surprise by the hand on her shoulder that swung her forcibly to face him, equally taken aback by the flaring anger in his eyes. For an odd, suspended moment they glared at each other, each wrapped in self-righteous fury. Then she saw the blaze in his face die. His hand dropped from her shoulder. 'Is that truly what you think?' he asked quietly.

She had spoken in haste and judged too harshly, and she knew it; but she would not answer.

Abruptly he turned from her, went back to the desk, stood for a moment, rock still and controlled, his back to her.

She watched him in silence. Then, 'Is there truly no hope?' she asked at last, bleakly and quietly.

He shook his head. 'None.'

'How long?'

'A day. Perhaps two or three. She's very weak.'

'I see.'

He turned to face her, and he was calm again. 'Sally, believe me. If a miracle is to occur it will as well occur at home as it will here. At least she'll be happy. She truly hates it here.' He shrugged, 'And who can blame her? It's a drear enough place, God knows. Will you speak to her brother?' The square, strong face was intent.

She held him eye to eye for a moment, then, 'Yes,' she said.

He nodded. 'Thank you. Hannah will find a nurse for her. She'll be as well cared for there as here. And more comfortable.'

Sally said nothing.

He watched her for a long moment with flint-dark eyes. 'Sally – have you any idea what we're up against here?' he asked suddenly, gesturing, the wave of his hand taking in not only the cluttered office but the hospital beyond. 'Do you know how many people we treat and under what disadvantage? The ratio of doctors to patients in the better-off parts of London is one to less than five hundred. Do you know what it is here? One to more than five thousand. We haven't the facilities, we haven't the staff, and we haven't the money to cope. Most of us work for next to nothing. We care about what we do. But we aren't miracle workers! With that kind of injury Miss Dickson should never have been treated as an outpatient in the first place. And then, once the hand became septic she should never have left it as long as she did before coming to us. We could only do too little and too late. But we did our best.' He ran a huge hand through his untidy hair. 'We did our best,' he repeated quietly, but with force.

Sally was regarding him with narrowed, guarded eyes.

She wanted to be angry. She did not want to feel sorry for him. She did not want to be moved by his words, nor by the tired lines in his face, the uncharacteristic note of weariness in his voice. She did not above all want to experience the strange pang of almost tender sympathy that unexpectedly struck her as he bent his head and absentmindedly and tiredly rubbed the back of his neck; an odd and painful emotion of the kind she sometimes felt for Toby when he was hurt or disappointed.

'I'll go talk to Dan,' she said brusquely, 'though that isn't to say he'll listen.'

He smiled a little at that, drily. 'Miss Dickson seemed to think that you're the only one likely to influence him. She has every faith that he'll listen to you.'

For some reason she found herself flushing. She shook her head. She felt quite ridiculously and inexplicably confused, just as ridiculously and even more inexplicably reluctant to leave him with the atmosphere between them still several shades less than friendly. Face set she marched to the door.

'Sally – I'm sorry. Truly sorry.'

'Yes,' she said ungraciously, 'so are we all, aren't we? I don't suppose that's much consolation to Josie,' and shut the door with a sharp click very firmly upon his silence.

Josie was taken home that afternoon. Two days later, her brothers and her father by her side, she died. Sally, arriving at the house half an hour later knew the moment she turned the corner of the street and saw the drawn curtains that the worst had happened. Dan opened the door to her and, with no word spoken she stepped straight and simply into his open arms and wept as if her heart were breaking, shedding the tears that in these last few awful days had built into a dam of grief behind the smiles that had made Josie's last days bearable. As they stood so, Walter came to them, hugging an arm about each of them, tears coursing unashamedly down his weather-darkened face. Bill Dickson sat by his daughter's bedside, unmoving and unspeaking, nodding to Sally as she entered the darkened room, his face drained and wooden with grief.

Silently Sally took his hand, stood beside him looking down at the lifeless shell that had been Josie. Memory flickered: Josie laughing, Josie talking, Josie smiling in pleasure at the gathering of those she loved about her. A simple, happy soul, the light of life snuffed out by the venom that had spread its wicked fingers through her blood. Unnecessarily? She could not bear to think so.

Dan had come to stand on the opposite side of the bed, his eyes not on his dead sister but upon Sally's tear-drenched face.

A snippet of conversation from the day before drifted into Sally's numbed brain; Hannah saying, 'I truly think my brother must be taking leave of his senses altogether. He tells me he intends to make a particular study of the causes and treatment of septicaemia – not instead of everything else, of course, but as well as – whenever does the silly man think he'll find time to sleep?' So Ben Patten had been truly moved by the tragedy of Josie, and by her courage in facing it. Perhaps one day, because of her, a life would be saved that might have been lost. Not for nothing then, but poor consolation.

Sally became suddenly and uncomfortably aware of Dan's fixed gaze upon her. Gently she disentangled her hand from the bereaved father's, 'Someone should go for the doctor.'

The funeral service was an ordeal. Josie had been a happy and popular girl, she had died in her twentieth year, full of joy and promise. There were many tears shed, many muffled sobs as the simple coffin was lowered. Afterwards at the Dickson home Sally helped with the obligatory funeral feast, and was astonished at the bizarre lift of spirits in the little house once the tea was brewed, the beer keg broached, the sandwiches and cakes spread upon the table. From a subdued and tearful beginning in half an hour voices were raised in a buzz of talk, there was the occasional lift of laughter as friends and relations, many of whom had not crossed each other's path since the last wedding, christening or funeral exchanged gossip. Josie's picture stood upon the mantelpiece, black-draped.

'Oh, she was a lovely girl,' with maudlin sentimentality an elderly woman in vast purple nodded her head to her companion, 'a lovely girl. Like they say – the Lord takes them as 'e loves young.'

Sally passed through the throng, offering sandwiches, smiling and nodding, dexterously and determinedly avoiding conversation. In the narrow, well-trimmed garden Bill Dickson stood with his sons, a tot of sustaining rum in his hand, accepting stoically the murmured sympathy of friends and neighbours, 'Such a lovely girl, our Josie.' 'Never 'eard a cross word from 'er, that I swear.' 'You'll miss 'er, Bill lad. We all will.'

Sally turned to slip away; found her way blocked apologetically but firmly by a stretched arm the muscles of which showed clearly and strongly through the shirt-sleeve. Dan's broad, good-natured face was calm, his still reddened eyes steady. He had for her a small smile, affectionate and warm. 'Thank you for your help.'

She smiled acknowledgement.

'I – wondered –' he hesitated.

'Yes?'

'Do they – do they let you have visitors at that children's place of yours?'

Her hesitation was minimal. 'Course they do. It isn't a prison.'

'I just thought – p'raps I could pop over and see you one day?'

She nibbled her lip. 'Dan –'

'Oh, don't worry. I won't push you, I promise. It's just – with Josie gone – I'd hate us to lose touch.'

'Yes. Me too.'

'I can then? Come and see you?'

'Of course you can.' Her smile was genuine, but her heart was heavy. 'Please don't hurt him,' Josie had said, and she had promised. But which hurt might be greater? To refuse him her friendship now, or to refuse him her love – as she knew she would have to – later? Whatever he might hope, Josie's death had changed nothing. She smiled and excused herself, slipped with relief into the relative quiet of the kitchen. 'Hello, Mrs Dobson – need a hand with the washing up?'

Hannah, nursing the small pleasure of a cheering secret, was waiting in the parlour for Sally to return when she heard the other girl's footsteps in the yard and saw her light go on. Moving a little stiffly still because of her strapped ribs and shoulder she slipped quietly up the stairs, past the doors of the children's dormitories, and tapped on the door. Sally opened it, surprise on her tired face. 'Miss Hannah!'

'Oh, for goodness' sake – I thought we'd dropped all that?' Hannah smiled. 'At least when we're off duty. May I come in? I know you must be exhausted, but I promise I won't stay. I just wanted a word with you.'

Sally opened the door wider, stepping back. The shapeless black hat she had borrowed from Hannah for the funeral lay upon the bed where she had tossed it a moment before. Her eyes were dark-shadowed.

'Was it awful?' Hannah asked with quick sympathy.

'A bit, yes.'

'I hate funerals. But then I suppose everyone does.'

Sally shook her head with the shadow of her wry smile. 'Wrong. Everyone doesn't. Some people can manage positively to enjoy them.'

'Oh dear. Bad as that? Would you like a cup of tea?'

'No thanks. I'm swimming in the stuff already.' Politely Sally waited. She was dog tired and needed her bed.

Hannah took her cue. 'Right. I just came to tell you that there's a meeting tomorrow at the Caxton Hall, and we've been specially invited.'

'I'm on duty tomorrow evening.'

Hannah shook her head briskly. 'No you aren't. I've arranged for Bron to swap with you. I'll come for you at six. You will be ready?'

'I –' Sally moved her head a little helplessly. She could not think. The last thing she wanted to do was to organize tomorrow.

'Of course you will. I won't take "no" for an answer. It will do you good.'

Sally gleamed a small smile. 'If you say so, doctor.'

'I do.' With absent efficiency Hannah caught a capricious hairpin as it slid from the coils of her hair, pushed it firmly back. 'I'll see you tomorrow.'

Sally walked to the window, watched the brisk figure cross the courtyard. She rubbed her eyes tiredly. Strange. Death was such a momentous thing. Such a very terrible thing when it came to someone as young, as full of promise as Josie had been. And yet nothing really changed. Life went on, with just a small rent in its fabric to show where death had claimed his due, a rent that she knew, however miserably one might want to deny it at the time, would gradually heal, making the fabric whole again.

Sighing she threw off her clothes, leaving them in a scrambled heap on the floor as she turned down the lamp and crawled, bone-tired and aching, into bed.

Ben Patten, standing with his pipe in the deepest shadows of the yard saw the light flicker and dim. Sally was up later than usual this evening. Then he remembered. Of course. It had been the Dickson girl's funeral today. He drew deeply on his pipe, determinedly ignoring the faint trembling of the hand that held it. Bloody shame that. Bloody waste. Interesting paper he'd found though, whilst studying the case – there had to be an answer, an antidote to the poisoning of the blood.

The obstinately logical workings of his mind jammed somewhere on the thought. Charlotte's face, unhealthily plump and pale and fraught with tears and terror – as it had been moments before when he left her – hung accusingly in the darkness before him.

'No!' she had said, trembling and cowering from him, 'I can't! Don't touch me! I won't! It's – it's too soon – I can't – please – don't touch me!' She had reeled away from him, her nightgown clutched across full breasts.

He had recognized hysteria, seen too her fear of him, her fear of his body, etched into the distorted lines of her face. It had shaken him to the soul. The desire that had prompted him to reach for her had fled. Coldly he had drawn away from her. In silence had left her to her desperate sobbing.

And now he stood alone in the darkness as the lights of the Dancing Bear went out one by one around him.

II

Caxton Hall was packed; and not just with women, Sally was quick to notice as she and Hannah took their seats, but with a fair sprinkling of men as well. They were late – the hall was full and the platform party already seated. Sally's spirits, still low after the events of the week, lifted a little at the sight of the handsome figure of Emmeline Pankhurst flanked by her two daughters. With all the Pankhursts here it would certainly be, as Hannah had promised with a confident smile, a special meeting. With them on the platform were the well-known and well-loved figures of Emmeline Pethick-Lawrence, the treasurer of the WSPU and her husband, a staunch supporter, and beside them the slight, fair figure of Annie Kenney, the Manchester working girl who had just the year before arrived from the north with nothing but courage and two pounds in her pocket, her brief to 'rouse London'. Her passionate dedication to the Pankhursts and their cause had already cost her her freedom twice and was more than likely to do so again. Sally studied her. Here was a girl very like herself, a girl disadvantaged, ill-educated, who still wore proudly the clogs and shawl she had worn as she trudged morning and evening to the mill where she had scraped a living. She was also a girl who had been accepted into the most inner circles of the Union, whose praises were sung by everyone who knew her; a girl who had won an enviable and admired place for herself by her own efforts, her own courage.

When Christabel Pankhurst, trim, attractive and shining with fervour rose to speak, she was cheered to the echo before she could open her mouth. Darling of the movement, this eloquent, passionate and intelligent girl personified for many the spirit of their cause. Witty and independent – in defiance of convention she had studied law in Manchester, as her sister Sylvia had studied art – she could hold an audience in the palm of her small, capable hand. She spoke now of the necessary drive for funds, of the hundreds of meetings being organized up and down the country to win support for the fight for women's suffrage. 'Twenty thousand people came to cheer and to contribute in Manchester – twenty thousand! Let the Liberal Government beware! In Hyde Park thousands come each Sunday to support us! Let the Liberal Government beware! The women want the vote! The women will have the vote! Let the Liberal Government beware!' The last, fierce words were lost in a storm of cheering. Smiling she waited until the noise died a little. Then, dropping her voice she asked, looking keenly around the hall, 'And what is this vote?'

Silence fell.

She let it build for a moment before continuing. 'What is this vote for which women are ready to fight, ready to shed their blood and sacrifice their freedom?'

Sally, with most of the rest of the audience was still and

tense as a drawn bow in her chair, leaning forward a little, eyes and ears intent upon that small, charismatic figure, enthralled.

'I'll tell you what it is. It is a key. It is a very small key to a very large door. It is a symbol. A symbol of citizenship. A symbol of freedom. It is not an end, but a beginning!' She stopped, let the words sink in to the hearts and minds of her audience, knowing she had them. 'Let the Liberal Government beware,' she said very quietly, very finally.

The roof nearly lifted. Sally and Hannah were on their feet with the rest, clapping and shouting, grinning at each other like children, exhilarated. It was full minutes before a smiling Emmeline Pankhurst could, with lifted hands, quieten the meeting. 'Friends –'

The uproar continued.

She waited. 'Friends –' This time quiet slowly fell. Seats clattered as people sat down. Mrs Pankhurst, tall and dignified, waited until full silence had taken the hall. 'Friends,' she said again, 'thank you. Thank you for your support and for your donations. Thank you for your efforts. Thank you for coming to listen to us tonight.' She paused for a moment, looking round, including everyone in the hall in that warm glance. 'As my daughter Christabel has just said, we are fighting for a cause. As she also pointed out that cause already has its martyrs, brave women who risk injury – yes perhaps even death – to stand up for – to demand! – their rights as citizens of this great country. Who go to prison rather than forswear their beliefs. With such courage – such sheer valiance – behind us, how can we help but win?' She lifted her head proudly. Like her daughter she held them, breath bated, by the sheer force of her personality. 'And does not such bravery deserve recognition? We have with us tonight two young women who have suffered so. I ask you now to thank them. To show your gratitude for their gallantry in your cause. Ladies and gentlemen, I ask you to clap the prisoners to the platform.'

Sally had been listening in growing, glowing confusion.

Smiling glances had been thrown her way as Mrs Pankhurst spoke. Hannah sat, head proudly high, eyes shining, beside her. At the last words she rose and taking Sally by the hand drew her to her feet with her. A thunderous, rhythmic clapping and stamping filled the hall. In a daze Sally allowed herself to be ushered along the row to the aisle that led to the stage. Eager hands reached, taking hers, patting her shoulders. Face aflame she walked with Hannah in time to the joyous clapping towards the brightly lit stage. They climbed the steps, walked along the line of the platform party shaking hands.

'Well done, my dears!' Mrs Pethick-Lawrence was beaming. 'A blow for freedom!'

'Splendid!' Christabel's hand was strong and warm, the slanting green eyes asparkle.

'Hannah! Sally!' Sylvia, a familiar and friendly face, kissed them both warmly, 'Oh, I'm so proud of you both!'

Annie Kenney grinned, pumping their hands with a vigour that entirely belied her frail appearance.

'A small token.' Emmeline Pankhurst, graceful and commanding, pinned small enamelled brooches on to their lapels – a white dove in flight with the words 'Votes for Women' emblazoned beneath it. 'We'll show them what brave soldiers we have in our ranks!'

Sally had never been so taken aback, never in her life felt so proud. As the din of the applause echoed to the roof, she smiled dazedly at Hannah. So. It was true then. Sally Smith was no longer alone and pitched solitarily against a hostile world. She was one of a team. Part of an army. She had friends.

In sheer exuberance at the edge of the stage she stopped, lifted a small clenched fist. 'Votes for women!'

And 'Votes for women!' roared back the audience, delighted, and clapped them with enthusiasm back to their seats.

*

The months that followed that meeting, through the summer and autumn of 1907, saw an upsurge in militancy: they also saw a split in the movement. Perhaps inevitably the constitutionalists, who had been fighting for the vote for so long through constitutional means, were uncomfortable and on occasion in outright and outraged disagreement with the more direct action favoured by the Pankhursts and their followers. As throughout the summer political meetings were broken up and more women arrested and imprisoned, the breach between the two sides grew: both were passionately dedicated to the same end, but as to the means they differed, and in some cases differed bitterly. There were also some discontented and uneasy mutterings about the high-handed behaviour of both Emmeline Pankhurst and her daughter Christabel, with whose crusading fervour and disregard for convention it must be said not everyone was comfortable. At the beginning of October the differences came to a head and the movement split, the more moderate constitutionalists finally taking the name of the Women's Freedom League, whilst the militants lined proudly behind the Pankhursts and their Women's Social and Political Union banner. There was never any question but that Hannah and Sally would stay with the militant Union. To Sally particularly, talk of petitions and by-elections, of constitutional rights and of Private Member's Bills meant nothing. It was the way of life, so far as she had ever known it, that nothing came easily. If you wanted something, you fought for it.

On 12 October Mr Sydney Buxton held yet another meeting in Poplar. On the 13th, Sally Smith, Hannah Patten and half a dozen others were sentenced by a not unsympathetic but mildly exasperated judge to two weeks in the second division; and this time they served their time.

Charlotte Patten watched it all with puzzled and disinterested eyes. What possessed Hannah, or the girl Sally or any other madwoman engaged in this lunatic battle for a vote that no one so far as she could see wanted she could not imagine. Life was surely complicated enough without wilfully making it more so? Was it not bad enough that her brother Ralph talked with such sober concern of growing dissatisfaction amongst the labouring classes, the need for drastic social reform, even, with in Charlotte's eyes absurd earnestness, of the possible stirrings of revolution? Or that Doctor Will and Ben had little apparent concern with anything but the setting up of a panel to monitor the health of schoolchildren, the provision of school meals for the needy, the insistence upon registration of births and vaccination for every Tom, Dick or Harry of a baby? Who in all of this cared about her? Who cared that she had neither the will nor the energy sometimes to get out of bed in the morning? Who cared that when she looked in her mirror – which nowadays was seldom – she barely recognized the pale, plump face set in downward, ageing lines, that looked back at her? Who was in the least concerned that on occasion the mere sight of her child was enough to bring on a sick headache that could confine her to a darkened room for hours?

No one.

Whilst Hannah cavorted in this ridiculous and – yes, it had to be said, demeaning – way with her social inferiors, whilst Ralph split his time almost equally between his beastly deprived children and their even beastlier and apparently even more deprived elders, and Peter, blithe as always, pursued – as always – his own capricious affairs she, Charlotte, was left alone in this teeming madhouse of a household. Alone to face Mrs Winterbottom, the widowed nurse Ben had at last agreed should be hired to help with the child; to cope with a Mrs Briggs whose phlegmatic and unsettling refusal to take the reins of the chaotic household entirely back into her own hands now that there was a 'Mrs Ben' to take the responsibility was driving Charlotte to distraction; and worse and, last and most fearful, to watch in resentful and helpless self-pity as her relationship with her husband – for what it had ever been worth – distintegrated entirely. He was polite. He was correct in every way. He was as distant as a well-mannered stranger on an omnibus. Almost she longed for those days when at least she had been able to rouse him to anger with her outbursts. Now he treated her, firmly but not unkindly, like a child: no – like a slightly ill-behaved and unwanted child with whom he had been saddled and of whom, in all good faith, he could not be rid. That this was as much her own fault as his did not make it easier to accept or bear. She was not now certain that she had intended him to take her seriously when she had petulantly demanded that she be allowed to return to the sanctuary of her own pink and white bedroom until her health improved: but he did. Nor when she had brushed off a calmly professional enquiry as to how she did with a brusquely peevish demand that he leave her alone had she actually meant him to take her literally at her word: but he had. She saw him rarely – he was up and off long before she rose in the morning, on call all day and half the night either at the hospital or with his local patients. He was, it seemed to her, on every committee that God or man had seen fit to constitute in Poplar and the surrounding area and what spare time he did miraculously manage to squeeze from his days was spent either with the children in the home, pursuing this new passion of his about cures for poison in the blood or some such thing or – most galling of all – with the child he called his daughter in the little room under the eaves that the whole household had dubbed the nursery. Charlotte rarely went up there herself; but the occasion that she had, and had found Ben tossing a small, squealing bundle into the air whilst Mrs Winterbottom watched in quite fatuous approval, had brought on a headache that had lasted for days.

Confused and unhappy she spent most of her time in her bedroom, her only companions a romantic novel and a box of chocolates for which since Rachel's birth she had conceived a passion she seemed utterly unable in her misery to deny. It was the only escape she could manage. Even Peter, in her eyes the only lively and normal member of the household, who once had delighted in teasing and entertaining his pretty young sister-in-law had lost interest and abandoned her. Her only other interest was letter writing. Lacking a confidante – Cissy had never recovered, unfairly Charlotte considered, from Charlotte's treatment of her brother – she took to writing letters to the few, far-flung female relatives whose addresses she found in an old notebook of her mother's. Cousin Annabel, married to a dashing young lieutenant in the Indian Army. Cousin Adèle, who lived with her parson husband and a vast brood of children outside Brighton. Aunt Alice, her father's somewhat eccentric sister, who had married – of all things – a Belgian and settled in Bruges where they ran, true to family form, a children's home much like the Pattens' own; indeed it had been, Charlotte remembered as she had sealed the letter, through the Patten family that Aunt Alice had actually met her Belgian groom, who had been a close friend of Doctor Will's. Not much hope of sympathy there, then. Her letter writing in any case was no great success. Cousin Annabel's letter disappeared without trace, and neither did Aunt Alice at first reply. Only Adèle apparently welcomed the correspondence – and that more to air her own grievances and disappointments than to lend an ear to Charlotte's. Charlotte very soon lost interest. Adèle's letters lay, half-read, abandoned, unanswered upon the dressing table, whilst Charlotte curled in her chair, a box of sweetmeats by her side, the exploits of the latest of Mrs Henry Bidding's fair heroines more real to her than the exhausting, pointless activity that filled the world beyond her door.

It was on the day that things came to a head with Kate that Aunt Alice's reply to Charlotte's letter finally arrived from Belgium.

Any brush with Kate had come to be something that Charlotte dreaded; her problems with the girl had been, if not the worst of her worries, a niggling thorn in the side, another small unpleasantness to stretch nerves already fraught to breaking point. That Kate had never either liked or respected her she did not know – mere months ago it would not have occurred to her to care. But that Kate of all the household seemed best aware of the situation between Charlotte and her husband had been made very clear on the day of the move back into the pink bedroom.

Kate it had been who had aired the room and made up the bed; Kate's keen and insolent eyes had watched with the unpleasant hint of a smile as Charlotte had moved her few personal possessions back on to the little kidney-shaped dressing table.

'Not feelin' too good, Miss?' No one could have missed the faint thread of scorn in the words, nor the pointed lack of respect in the title.

'I – no.' Charlotte had neither the strength nor the energy to defend herself against the other girl's half-recognized wholly incomprehensible malice.

'Well,' Kate had paused at the door, smiling, 'you'll find it nice an' quiet here. No one ter bother you. An' I expect Doctor Ben'll find things a good deal easier too.' And on that neat piece of insolence she had shut the door.

The incident had opened Charlotte's eyes to the way that the girl seemed bent upon flouting her: the orders either ignored or executed in a slipshod manner; the way the bold eyes held hers with no attempt to disguise a disrespect that sometimes bordered on contempt; the way in which, if another member of the household were present in the room Kate would contrive to ignore Charlotte and take her orders from elsewhere. And on occasion, with no other ears to hear her, downright insolence.

'I'd like you to polish the silver in the dining room please, Kate. It's looking very dull.'

'Mr Ralph's asked me to black the fire in the school-room, miss.' Never would the girl use the more appropriate and respectful 'ma'am'.

'You can do that later.'

'I'd rather not, miss. I don't like to upset Mr Ralph.'

And somehow, as Kate appeared to know, Charlotte could never stand up to her, but would blush and stammer and let the matter drop. Amidst her other miseries she simply could not summon the energy necessary to defend herself against the other girl's inexplicable yet wounding hostility.

On the morning in October when Aunt Alice's letter arrived Charlotte was breakfasting alone in the dining room. Kate, sent to the kitchen for fresh toast, performed the errand with her usual bad grace. She banged the plate on the table.

Charlotte, deep in her letter, reached for a piece of toast. Not until the butter was poised on the knife did she glance at it. 'Kate?'

Kate, at the side table collecting empty dishes, did not turn. 'Yes?'

'What's happened to this? It's dirty.' With a fastidious shudder Charlotte held up the toast between two finger-tips.

Kate still did not turn. 'I dunno.'

It was too much, even for Charlotte. 'Kate! I'll thank you to face me when I speak to you!'

The girl took her time to stack the silver dishes, turned very slowly, leaning against the side table.

'I asked you what happened to this? See – it's dirty. Kate – did you drop it?'

The infinitesimal hesitation was damning. 'No.'

Charlotte stared at her in rising anger. 'I think you did.'

The girl all but shrugged. Sighed a little.

'Kate!' Charlotte's voice was rising.

'Well, you can think all you like, can't you? I say I didn't.'

Charlotte jumped to her feet. She could feel the burning rise of humiliating tears behind her eyes, knew surely that the other girl sensed it. 'Don't be impertinent!'

'I'm not bein' impertinent. I'm tellin' you –'

'And that, I think, is quite enough.' The quiet voice stopped them both in their tracks. 'Kate, I think you'll agree you've gone too far. You have until this evening to pack your bags. I will, of course, make up your wages and I can give you at least a fair reference. See me in the surgery at five.'

Kate stared at the figure that loomed in the doorway. 'Doctor Ben! Oh, no – that isn't fair!'

He regarded her levelly. 'On the contrary. I think it very fair indeed. Give me credit for some sense, Kate. I'm neither blind nor deaf. You're lucky to get a reference and I think you know it.'

It was total defeat. Kate scowled first at Ben, then at Charlotte, and slammed from the room.

Charlotte sank back into her seat, biting her lip. 'Thank you.'

'You shouldn't have let it go so far.' His voice was cool. 'You let her get away with too much.'

'Yes, I know. I couldn't seem to help it.'

He looked at her for a long moment in silence then turned to the door.

'Ben!'

The sharp word stopped him. He waited.

She was turning the letter over and over in her hands. She had not had time to think about it – knew instinctively that if she had she would never have found the courage to ask what she was about to ask. 'This – this letter – it's from Aunt Alice.' She glanced at him. His face was politely puzzled.

'You know – my father's sister. She married a friend of your father's – Anselm van Damme – they live in Belgium. In Bruges.'

'Ah. Yes, of course.'

'Ben – she's invited me to visit her. Just for a couple of weeks – well,' she blushed a little, 'both of us actually – you and me – but you wouldn't want to go, would you? You couldn't leave your work. But oh Ben, please! May I go? I do so want to. I've been – I've been so very wretched lately –' again the helpless, infuriating rise of tears. She ducked her head, the strong, black writing on the envelope blurred.

The silence this time was a long one. She felt him move from the door and sit down at the table opposite her. He held out his hand. 'May I see the letter?'

Her hesitation was telling. Her aunt was an articulate and efficient woman; she had answered or commented upon Charlotte's outpourings meticulously and with care, obviously sensing the need. With obvious reluctance Charlotte handed over the letter. As Ben read it she watched him, tensed as an overwound spring.

Ben took a long time. Then he raised his eyes to hers. 'I see,' he said quietly.

She flushed but did not drop her gaze. 'Ben, please,' she said again, desperation giving her courage. Her aunt's kindly suggestion had come like a ray of light into a darkened room. To get away from here, to see new places, meet new people, and above all to be with a woman of sense and sympathy who might be able to help, to advise, to console – the idea had taken hold of the motherless Charlotte and would not relinquish its grip.

'You couldn't possibly go alone. And what of the child?' The words were in no way forbidding. Charlotte's heart lifted.

'Well of course I'd take Rachel with me. But Nurse Winterbottom could come. There'd be no difficulty in that.'

He sucked his lip doubtfully.

'You or Ralph could see me to Harwich,' she rushed on, 'and Aunt Alice says that Cousin Philippe will meet me at the other side. Bruges is only a very little way from the coast. Oh, Ben, please do say yes. I do so want to go.'

He looked at the letter again. Far from insensitive, he was well able to read between the lines. He lifted his eyes to Charlotte's eager face. He had not seen her so animated in months. Not since the birth of the child. 'Very well,' he said decisively, and tried unsuccessfully to suppress a lift of his own spirits at the thought of being free, for however short a time, from the look in those pale, somehow accusing eyes, the petulant voice, the trying, childish behaviour. 'I don't see why not. If as you say I escort you to Harwich and your cousin meets you from the ship I don't suppose the journey will be too arduous –'

She could not believe it. 'You mean – I can go?'

'Of course.' He stood, folded the letter, handed it back to her. 'It will do you good.'

It would, he thought with relief, do them both good.

Chapter Eight

I

When Hannah and Sally emerged from their second incarceration in Holloway, tired and pale but triumphantly pleased with themselves and their fellow suffragette prisoners, who between them and under the most adverse of circumstances had managed to defy the system and produce a sense of solidarity and camaraderie that might have shamed the Scots Guards, it was to find the adult complement of the Bear unexpectedly depleted, a circumstance of which the younger members of the small community were taking full and understandable advantage. Kate had left, fiercely and resentfully silent, leaving poor Bron to cope almost single-handedly with the marauding urchins when they were not directly under Ralph's indulgent eye. The Welsh girl was almost tearfully glad to see Sally.

'Oh, *terrible* it's been without you! Young Annie almost bit the finger off little Betty – and your Toby's been runnin' that wild – winds them up, he does, like little clockwork toys, then sits back an' watches the devilment.'

Sally, sighing in relief to be stretched out upon her own bed at last, reflected in passing that Bron was perhaps more astute than most would give credit for. 'So where is everyone?'

'Well! Such upheaval there's bin!' Bron settled herself comfortably on her chair for a little earnest gossiping. 'Kate was sacked, she was! By Doctor Ben, of all people. Bye – I thought she'd explode with rage, mind! No –' she added at the climbing of Sally's brows, '– no, I don't know what happened exactly. Kate wasn't saying, an' I wasn't pushing her, mind. An' now Doctor Ben's gone off to put Miss Charlotte on a boat.'

'A boat?' Sally looked blank.

'To Belgium, see?'

'Belgium?'

In full flow Bron hardly even stopped for breath. 'Yes, Belgium. Somewhere near France it is, I think. She had a letter, see? Seems she's got an aunt out there an' she asked her to visit. Well – off she was like a shot from a gun, I don't mind telling you. Taken the baby and that Nurse Winterbottom with her. An' what with you an' Miss Hannah being –', the torrent of words faltered delicately, '– away, like – well, it's bin a madhouse here, I don't mind tellin' you!'

Bron's overly excitably Celtic nature had in fact this time, as Sally very quickly discovered, led her to exaggerate less than might have been imagined. The children, sensing the lack of a firm hand, were indeed in that excitable and anarchic state that invariably leads to trouble, and their leader, inevitably and as Bron had guessed, was the graceless and subversive Toby, who perfectly obviously had not enjoyed himself so much for years. On her first night back Sally broke up two far from friendly dormitory pillow fights and intercepted a raiding party on its way to the kitchen.

'Hey, you!' She caught with ungentle fingers a tangle of fair curls. 'I want a word. The rest of you – hop it, and quick. Back to bed. Another word – another deep breath! – an' you'll have me to answer to. Now scarper!'

Back in her room she faced him, sighing. The beguiling blue eyes were innocent as ever and clear as summer skies. 'Tobe – for heaven's sake! I'm tired! I haven't had a decent night's sleep in a fortnight! I can do without you leadin' a bloody revolution around here!'

'I'm not,' he assured her with ready earnestness, and then in the same breath, eagerly, 'what was it like in Holloway?'

'Tough. And you are. You think I don't see your sticky little fingers in what's going on around here?'

He shrugged a little, tried tentatively his sweetest smile.

'Less of that. Answer me.'

He fiddled with the fringe of the counterpane.

She reached for him, drew him forward until he stood at her knees. With their eyes on a level she took his shoulders in firm hands, forcing him to look at her. 'Toby Jug, listen.' she said, her eyes intent upon his. 'This was your idea, remember? You wanted to stay. Well –', she hesitated for a moment, 'well – you were right. We're both better off here. And we'd both bloody miss it if we lost it. But Tobe – you can't have your cake and eat it too. You've got to learn to behave. Is Mr Ralph still talking about that scholarship?'

He nodded.

'Well – think on this. If you're going to some posh school you're going to have a pretty rough time of it if you don't know how to behave, if you can't tell the difference between fun and real mischief, if you get yourself a reputation as a trouble-maker. You got no rich dad to back you, remember. You'll be out on your ear and with no feather bed to land on.'

He watched her in a silence she deliberately lengthened. Then she smiled.

'All right – I know a lad needs a bit of spirit, and you've certainly got that.' The look that flashed between them contained all of the old affectionate conspiracy, but Sally's strong fingers had not relaxed their grip. 'But you're going to need something besides. You're clever, and you're a lot tougher than you look. But that won't be enough in a fancy school where the other kids have got what you've never had. Money. Manners.' He was looking at her now with sudden rapt interest. She made a fist and, grinning, grazed it against his smooth jaw, 'Sense.'

He smiled a little too, but his eyes were attentive.

'Now's the time to learn. Don't fight us – join us. You can handle those kids better than anyone. Keep them in order – oh, I don't mean never a laugh, never a bit of mischief – but know when to stop. It might be fun to wreck things, Tobe, but believe me you've got to learn that it's a bloody sight harder to put things back together than it is to take them apart.' She waited then, her narrowed eyes studying his face, and was rewarded after a moment by a brilliant, unflawed smile of understanding.

'Right?' she asked.

'Right,' he said.

By the time Ben arrived back from seeing Charlotte safely on her way, the home was once again running like clockwork.

'It's young Sally Smith,' his father tamped down a pipeful of tobacco, took a long and leisurely moment to light it. 'She's magic with those youngsters. Straightened them out in twenty-four hours. You did a good day's work the day you found her.'

'Uncle Will's right.' Ralph, sitting on the opposite side of the fireplace, looked up from his book, peering short-sightedly over the wire rims of his glasses. 'Since she's been back we haven't had half the trouble. Mind you, we're still very short-handed. We'll have to take on at least another girl to replace Kate. We've more children, and less people. Hannah's more and more involved with her suffragette work, as well as the health visiting and the baby clinic. Charlotte – well, Charlotte's never been terribly interested, has she? I'm on hand some of the time, of course – but I have the school too – they need more than that. A matron, perhaps? Someone to take on the day-to-day running of the place, to be there for the children if she's needed. It really is all getting terribly disorganized.'

Ben shook his head. 'We can't afford a trained matron.'

Will puffed his pipe thoughtfully.

'Well, we're going to have to do something,' Ralph persisted. 'We can't take the children off the streets and then let them run wild here – it simply doesn't work. We need someone in charge who can control the kids, look after them, gain their trust.'

'Weren't we just telling Ben', Will said tranquilly between puffs, 'what a find he'd made in Sally Smith?'

The other two looked at him. 'Sally?' Ben asked doubtfully. 'But Pa – she has no training – no experience.'

Will raised mild eyebrows. 'Oh? I'd have said experience is just what she has had. She knows those children – who better? They trust her. She's one of them. That's why she can handle them so well. Damn' sight better than some prissy Miss with a diploma, I'd have thought.' The pipe went back between his teeth and he settled deeper into the armchair.

'Sally,' Ben said again. And then after a long and thoughtful moment, 'Do you really think she could do it?'

His father surveyed the battered pipe, tapped it, lifted shrewd, twinkling eyes. 'Only one way to find out.'

'What do you mean, "in charge"?' Sally asked warily.

'Just that. A kind of – house mother. Running the place – well like a proper home. Making sure the youngsters behave, making sure they're happy. Keeping them occupied and out of mischief, watching their progress. Liaising with Ralph, of course, and with me. Ralph and Hannah both think it a splendid idea.'

She cocked a narrow, repressive eye.

Realizing what he had said, Ben grinned, a sudden boyish smile that took years from him, 'And so do I.'

She shook her head, thoughtfully, determinedly tamping down a rising excitement. 'I don't know – Bron's been here longer than I have.'

'Hannah's spoken to Bron. She doesn't mind a bit. She

thinks it's a good idea. She'd throw a fit if we asked her to take it on. No, Bron's very happy as she is, so long as we get another couple of girls in to help, which of course we will. Please – will you give it a try? With Hannah so busy and Ralph involved in the Schools' Committee with me we desperately need help here. It's very important to all of us.'

Sally would not allow her pleasure to show in eye or voice. She shrugged. 'All right, then. If you really mean it. I'll give it a go,' and then spoiled the effect entirely by answering his smile with a wide grin of her own that lit her face like sunshine.

Nothing had ever given her so much pleasure, so much satisfaction. Within a month, with the verve and enthusiasm of any convert she had immersed herself in the reorganization of the children's home. She pestered Ralph, she pestered Hannah, she pestered anyone who would listen, who would advise, who would discuss the changes she wanted to make. At first, lacking in confidence, she always took the smallest innovation to one of the family before she implemented it. She split the children into small groups of a similar age, each group with its own timetable and its own tasks. She organized rotas, encouraging the children themselves to participate in the day-to-day running of their home – a venture in which Toby was her willing lieutenant. She reorganized the dormitories to give each child more privacy, a small patch to call his own upon which no one trespassed except at invitation. The younger children and those not yet skilled enough to go to school she supervised in the tasks that Ralph set them, and each afternoon there was a story session in the schoolroom to which all were invited, and to which most came. Most importantly she got to know each child individually, gaining their confidence, guarding the weak where she could and curbing the strong; no hand was heavier than hers on a bully's shoulder. Two new girls were hired to help – Maude, a fifteen-year-old orphan from Bow with a quick tongue and an unruly mass of black curls who could hold her own with the most intransigent of the children, and Betsy, a little mouse of a thing whose origins were uncertain and who within a week had become Toby's willing slave, thus unknowingly assuring herself of a privileged place in the children's hierarchy. As the autumn moved into what promised to be an especially miserable winter even Sally's suffragette activities came second to her new responsibilities. She was up at dawn and the last in bed at night; and often even then as much time would be spent worrying away like a terrier at a problem as sleeping. Her confidence grew. Gradually she came to rely less on the advice and opinions of others.

'Well, well.' Ben Patten, after one of his routine health inspections of the children, one November day paid a visit to the cubbyhole Sally had requisitioned as an office, 'How's it going?'

'I'm enjoying it.'

'You're doing a very good job indeed. I've never seen everything so shipshape.'

'Thank you.' Sally nodded to the teapot that stood on a side table. 'Cup of tea? It's a bit stewed, but drinkable.'

He nodded. 'Please.'

She eyed him as she poured. There could be no doubt about it – something had changed Ben Patten in the past month. His step was lighter, his smile more ready, the straight mouth in repose did not look so grim. 'Well, don't be daft!' Bron had said a few days before when she had mentioned it, 'Of course he's different! Miss Charlotte's away, isn't she, then?'

'Bron!'

'Well, everyone knows it, don't they? Not made in heaven, that one, as it's turned out – mind, not many are that I can see. All I hope is it lasts after she comes back – why I went down to the schoolroom the other day and there he was on the floor with the children all over him! Having the time of their lives they all were!'

She handed him his cup. It always astounded her that he never by so much as a word or a glance gave the slightest indication that he remembered – as he so surely must remember – the circumstances of their first meeting. And, oddly, as time slipped by even for her the memory was dimming. She sometimes found it difficult to believe that the Sally Smith who could sit here sipping tea with Doctor Ben Patten could possibly be the same fierce and ragged girl who had defied Jackie Pilgrim and so nearly died for it.

'Penny for them?'

She laughed, faintly embarrassed. 'I'm sorry. I was daydreaming.'

'Never a bad thing. The odd daydream doesn't do any of us any harm.'

Did she detect a certain rue in his voice? She watched him over the rim of her cup. He was an interesting man, this doctor with the prizefighter's jaw and hands that she knew could be gentle as a woman's; a man of contrasts, paradoxes even. Harsh, self-centred she suspected, often too certain of himself and his opinions, yet she had seen him intuitively gentle with a sick child, knew from experience how deeply – sometimes uncomfortably – perceptive he could be. And the humour that lurked so often in those dark eyes seemed as natural to him as the fierce temper and perilous moods that impatience could prompt. A complex and intriguing man at best, provoking and difficult at worst; and the man that pretty, silly Charlotte Bedford had married, to save herself from disgrace.

I would not have done that, she found herself thinking with certainty. Not in a million years. And then the sheer absurdity of the thought hit her and her lips twitched almost to laughter. Very likely, that Ben Patten would have offered his name to save Sally Smith from disgrace.

'Is little Bessie's skin complaint clearing up?' she asked soberly.

'Oh yes. She'll be fine.' He had perched himself easily on the desk, his leg swinging. 'And young Tom's coming on well too. He'll be up and about in a day or so. Let's see – how many children do we have that Ralph's still schooling here?'

'Seven. A couple of them are too young yet, the others will be at school next term. There are a couple he's giving some extra tuition to, and of course he's coaching Toby.'

'For the scholarship?'

'Yes.'

'Ralph tells me he has a good chance.'

'I hope so.'

Ben stood, leaving his mug on the desk. 'Right – no rest for the wicked – keep up the good work.'

'I will.'

The door closed behind him. Sally reached for the pencil and the column of figures she had laboriously been working on. Though she would never have admitted it figurework was still far from her strong point. Beyond the door she heard a child's piping voice and Ben Patten's cheerful greeting. The child squealed, laughing as he was obviously swept into strong arms.

She was smiling as she set to work.

A moment later she was interrupted again as Hannah's head popped around the door. 'Sally – can't stop – just to remind you that we're meeting at Clement's Inn tonight before – oh, Sally! You *can't* have forgotten?'

Sally hastily rearranged her startled expression. 'Why no. Of course not.'

'You are coming? It won't be the biggest meeting in the world, nor the most exciting I don't suppose – but Christabel's going to be there, so you never know – and you promised you'd sell *Votes for Women* with me.'

'Yes. Yes, of course. I'll be there.'

The door closed again. Sally sighed. Damn! She had in

fact forgotten the meeting and her promise to sell the Union's new magazine with Hannah. She would have to put off talking to Maude about the little ones' revised timetable. She leaned back for a moment, thoughtfully, in her chair. If Christabel Pankhurst were to be at the meeting there might after all be fireworks. Well, one thing she'd be damned sure not to do. She would not let them arrest her. Not this time. There was altogether too much to do.

Ben Patten was in the parlour by a dying fire when he heard the noise. Outside the wind blew like a fury, rattling the panes in the ancient windows and sending scurrying draughts about the old building. Rain hammered on the glass, teemed from the gutters.

He lifted his head, listening again. A small and stealthy sound had come from the room across the corridor that was his and his father's surgery. Very quietly he opened the parlour door. A lamp burned dimly in the surgery where none should be. Again there was quiet movement.

He stepped to the door, pushed it open. 'What the devil – good God! Sally! What on earth are you doing?'

Sally stood frozen in the act of opening a cupboard door. She turned her head.

'Sit down.' He was brisk. 'At once. And here – take this – you're bleeding all over everything.'

She did as she was bid, holding the clean towel he had handed her to her lower lip which gaped from the gash opened in it by a thug's brass-ringed knuckles. She was trembling with cold, with shock and with an almost uncontainable rage. Her clothes were drenched in blood from her lip and she was soaked through from the storm. One eye was closing painfully.

'Damned if I'm not beginning to feel there's a war on!' Ben growled, clattering at the sink. 'Who the hell did that to you? Here – hold this –'

She took the dish, held it beneath her chin, clenching her teeth against their chattering. 'Di-n't wann – get – 'rested –' she said, the words slurred, the gashed lip hanging and flopping obscenely.

'What?' He was cleaning the wound swiftly and efficiently.

'I – didn't – want – get – arrested –' she enunciated a little more clearly.

'I'm going to have to put a couple of stitches in it. Hold on. This is going to hurt, I'm afraid.'

It did. Despite all her efforts tears of pain started to her eyes. He worked quickly, his face intent. Then, stepping back he eyed the lip with professional satisfaction. 'There you are. You'll have a bit of a scar, but not too much. Anything else?'

'Only the eye.'

He shook his head. 'Nothing I can do about that, I'm afraid. You'll have a shiner and a half by morning.'

'Sods!' she muttered savagely under her breath, unable to contain herself. 'Vicious sods! Bloody spoiling for trouble.' She was still trembling like a leaf.

He could not prevent a small smile at the heartfelt, unladylike language. 'Doctor Patten prescribes a fair to middling shot of good brandy. Follow me. Where's Hannah?'

'She's all right.' She was talking gingerly, touching her sore lip with her fingertips. 'Ralph got her away. They've probably gone back to Clement's Inn. That was the plan.' The headquarters of the WSPU were situated at Clement's Inn and all operations were co-ordinated from there. Very shakily Sally followed Ben into the darkened parlour.

'God – you're dripping all over Pa's best carpet! Wait a minute –' He disappeared for a moment, came back carrying two blankets. 'Get out of those wet clothes. No point in giving yourself pneumonia.'

She clutched the blankets to her, but did not move.

He grinned lopsidedly. 'I'll wait outside. Two minutes.'

She scrambled from her uncomfortable, sopping wet clothes and with enormous relief swathed herself in the warm blankets. The fire glowed comfortingly. Her lip throbbed and stung, but at least it felt better than it had as she had hurried through the winter streets holding the gash together with her fingers, her hand slick with blood. She tucked herself comfortably into the big old armchair that was normally Doctor Will's. She could smell the pipe tobacco in the fabric of the upholstery.

'Are you decent?'

'Yes.'

He came into the shadowed room, went immediately to the fire, fed it with kindling until it flared brightly then tucked a small log and a few pieces of coal on top of the dancing flames. 'There. Soon be warm.'

To Sally, chilled to the bone, the room was already warm as the womb. She snuggled further into the chair.

With movements remarkably quiet and contained for a man of his bulk, Ben went to the sideboard. She heard the clink of glass, the splashing of the brandy.

'Here.' He towered above her, his face in shadow, 'Drink this.'

With hands that still shook she took the heavy, wide-bowled glass. Tilted her head. Choked. Her lip screamed.

He laughed a little. 'Steady on. You don't drink it like medicine, you know!'

But like medicine it was doing her good. The pain in her lip was bludgeoned to numbness, her trembling had eased. He leaned forward, watching her. 'Slowly now. What happened?'

She sipped the brandy. Held it up between her eyes and the firelight. It glowed like dark molten gold. 'We had a meeting. In Marylebone. Nothing special, just a meeting. Organized by the local branch; it was no big affair. There should have been no trouble.'

'But – there was?'

'Yes. There certainly was.' With a swift movement she tossed back her brandy.

Ben thoughtfully swilled his around the glass, then he too tilted his head and took the last of his drink at a mouthful, savouring it. 'Go on.'

'There were trouble makers in the audience – young men – planted I think –' She twirled the empty glass in her hands. 'They heckled the speakers – I mean really heckled – they didn't ask questions, they didn't want to listen to answers. They shouted. Abuse, mostly.' Her mouth was tight with anger.

'I can imagine,' he said.

She turned an impassioned face to him. 'It's impossible when they do that! In men's meetings, the political meetings that we attend to ask questions, they have stewards – men, strong men – who can stop people – haul them out – and they damned well do!' She was almost inarticulate with fury and with the pain of her lip. 'But what can we do against such –', she tried to stop herself but could not contain the words '– bloody-minded hooligans?' she finished, fiercely. '*Our* stewards, if that's what you can call them – what are they? What would you expect them to be? – Nice, well-brought-up young ladies who've never said "boo" to a goose until now – what can we expect them to do about a hulking great brute who's just out to make trouble? Ask him politely to leave? The police won't help us, and alone we don't have the force –' The tone of her voice suggested clearly to her listener that on this occasion at any rate Sally Smith would have been happy to provide the force single handed. She did not, perhaps fortunately, catch the sudden faint gleam of amusement in his eyes.

'What happened?'

She shrugged, a muffled movement in the enveloping blankets. 'The meeting broke up – as I s'pose our visitors had intended. When we got outside the police were there. They'd obviously been warned. Tipped off. They were hustling the women – pushing them – saying things – they were arresting *us*! Not them – not the trouble makers.' She stopped, gritting her teeth against anger. The fire flared. Ben threw another log to the flames, gently relieved Sally of her glass, moved to the sideboard, came back with the brandy bottle in his hand. She watched as he splashed the clear amber liquid into the glasses. Remembering what had happened earlier this evening, the quiet suddenly seemed extraordinarily quiet, the warmth and comfort extraordinarily warm and comfortable. She blinked a little, took the glass he held out to her in smiling silence. The quiet settled easily about them.

'Then what?' he asked at last.

'Oh – well, Hannah and me – we'd been selling the magazine – you know, *Votes for Women*. I suppose it made us targets in a way. Like I said, the coppers weren't arresting them.' She tilted her glass and sipped, holding the burning liquid on her tongue before letting it slip like mellow fire down her throat, 'They were arresting us. Or trying to.' Her smile was quiet, a swift flash of wanton mischief, a movement of the eyes as much as of the damaged mouth. Ben stirred in his chair, and was still. 'I'd decided I wasn't ready for another stretch. Too much going on here. So – I dodged out. Mr Ralph had already got Miss Hannah away. I saw them go.'

'And?'

She shrugged again. 'Some fancy lad decided he didn't want to see me get away.'

'So – he blacked your eye and split your lip?' Anger smouldered, seething beneath the light tone.

'That's right,' she said, placidly enough.

In the silence they drank.

He watched her. Some small gleam in her face tilted his head in question. 'And what did you do to him?'

She grinned her damaged, abrasive grin, 'I doubt he'll be pleasing his girlfriend too much for the next few weeks.'

His chuckle was warm. 'Another brandy?'

They were sitting there still an hour later, the soaked

heap of Sally's discarded clothes steaming in the warmth of the now-roaring fire. The bottle was all but empty. For the last few minutes an easy silence had fallen. A little hazily Sally found herself wondering what on earth they could have found to talk about for that long. Or had she been talking and he listening? She could not be sure. She eyed him from beneath lowered lashes. He looked like a rock in the shadows, strong and still and utterly sure. Mischief stirred in her. 'They tell me', she said, looking at him through her raised and almost empty glass, 'that you want to build Jerusalem?'

He laughed a little. 'Is that what they say?'

She nodded slowly and pensively.

With sudden attention, the ease of the indolent moment gone, he looked at her, interest in his eyes. 'You don't approve?' he asked.

The acute perception took her aback. Her question had been light, anything but disapproving. Her mouth twitched to a small, sore smile; who in the world cared if Sally Smith approved of anything or not?

'Please. Tell me.'

She regretted having opened her mouth. ''Tisn't for me to say, is it?'

He leaned forward, his face intent. 'But yes. Of course it is.'

Cornered, she shrugged. 'Well – all right then –' she paused for a second, knowing her thoughts, suddenly painfully aware of her limitations in expressing them. 'I can see what you're after. Better now than before because – well, because I know you, I s'pose. And yes, I think you're probably right. But what I wonder is –' she stopped.

He gave her no help, no escape. He watched her, waiting.

'What I wonder is what Joe down the road thinks of your Jerusalem. Your –' she hesitated, glancing at him beneath lowered lashes, smiling self-consciously '– your tomorrow Jerusalem. I mean – you can see, can't you? – if you spend the best part of your life keeping body and soul together, hanging on like grim death to the roof over your head, fighting for work, not getting it more often than not, nagged by the wife, your kids going shoeless and hungry, no decent bed to sleep on, the workhouse threatening – well –'

'Yes?'

'Then p'raps you'd swop Jerusalem tomorrow for bread today. For coal in the bucket, tuppence in your pocket for a trip to the boozer. It's hard for a bloke like Joe down the road to see that – well, that a dream's worth fighting for.' She stopped, oddly embarrassed at the emotive words.

He picked up the brandy bottle, eyed it against the flames, proffered it across the space between them. 'And does that mean that no one should? Fight for the dream – the principle – I mean? That comes a bit oddly, doesn't it, from a girl that's been to Holloway twice and just taken two stitches in her lip for – a principle?'

She had never met anyone who argued so, sharply and thoughtfully. For the moment it was beyond her. She thought about it as she held out her glass, watched as he splashed the two last measures out. 'I suppose –' she said at last, '– I suppose that that's what you know and I don't. And neither does Joe. And', she added with a touch of mild asperity, 'I'm not saying that makes Joe and me wrong.'

With a small, guarded and appreciative smile he leaned back. 'I should say not. Now, tell me, Sally Smith. How long did it take for you to decide not to tell us all to piss off?'

She hesitated for just a moment. Decided upon honesty.

'So tell me,' Ben said, ten minutes later, lifting his head, the granite-sharp features softened by firelight, 'you aren't sorry that you came back that day?'

Sally shook her head. Her lip was swollen now, and the stitches pulled. 'Like I said – it was the Jug that did it. But for him I'd have gone. But – I've told him – I would have been wrong.'

'It would have been our loss as much as yours.'

She smiled. Winced.

He leaned forward. 'Your lip. It's painful?'

'Yes.'

He went on his knees in front of her, his hands upon either side of her face, lifting and turning her head to the light of the fire. 'It'll get worse overnight, I'm afraid. But it's clean. It'll get better.'

She laughed softly, holding her mouth still in his protective hands. 'As I remember, that's what I told Hannah about Holloway. Well – more or less.'

He smiled, still holding her narrow face in his hands. Then, very abruptly he released her and sat back in his chair. For a long moment they both watched the fire. The silence that had been so easy was suddenly oddly and subtly charged. Sally's none-too-clear mind danced like a butterfly, settled capriciously, fired by the brandy. 'Can I ask you something?'

He turned his head. 'Of course.'

All at once, clearly aware of possible affront, she hesitated.

'Well?'

'I – just wondered – someone saw off Jackie Pilgrim. Made a damn' good job of him by all accounts. Someone who – sounded a lot like you.'

He rubbed his jaw.

She had gone too far to retreat. 'Well? Was it?' she asked bluntly.

And as bluntly. 'Yes,' he said.

There was a moment's silence then she gurgled with laughter. 'Oh, good for you!' she said. 'Good for you!'

He slanted a glance at her. 'No one else knows. No one.'

She toasted him with her empty glass, blood trickling in a thread from her sewn lip. 'And no one shall.'

He made her a small bow in his chair. 'Thank you.'

Suddenly intolerably, overwhelmingly tired she leaned her head against the back of her chair. 'I think I need my bed.'

'I'll take you.'

He was beside her. It seemed the most natural thing in the world that he should bend to her, lift her in those strong arms as if she had been no more weight than a child. She laid her head contentedly on his shoulder.

In silence he walked the darkened house, the light, tough burden in his arms. In her small room, bare as a cell it seemed to him, he laid her gently upon the bed. Blood still seeped on to her chin. He wiped it with his handkerchief. Rain hammered upon the windows. The wind tossed the branches of the tree in the courtyard.

'You're sure you're all right? I could bring you a sleeping draught.'

'I'm fine.' The strange, slanting eyes opened suddenly, for a moment no longer narrowed in their usual defensive way, but wide and clear as a child's. 'Thank you.'

For the space of a heart-beat the back of his hand rested against her cheek, then without a word he left her.

His face shuttered he went back down to the parlour, picked up the brandy bottle that stood by the hearth. It was empty. A full one stood on the sideboard. He picked it up, looked at it for a moment before, very precisely, replacing it unopened. Then, with his usual contained and efficient movements he gathered up Sally's damp, discarded clothes, delivered them to the laundry room and took himself to bed.

II

Charlotte did not want to go home. She did not want to go back to England, let alone to the squalor of Poplar and the teeming activity of the Bear.

She had fallen in love.

She had fallen in love with Bruges. She had fallen in love with the van Damme family, and with their lovely, tall gabled house overlooking the canal on the Groenerei, which was like something from a fairy tale with its stepped gables and diamond-paned windows, its steeply sloping tiled roofs and tall chimneys. The orphanage – smaller and very much better organized than the Bear – was run with care and kindness by Aunt Alice, her husband Anselm, their son Philippe, who was about Charlotte's own age, and their daughter Annette and her husband. Two younger children had been lost in an epidemic of typhoid three years before. They were the happiest of families, united in their dedication to each other and to the children in their care. Aunt Alice was a plump, motherly, warm-natured person, an ordinary-looking little woman of wisdom and perception whom, it seemed to Charlotte, no one could fail to love. Within days their relationship had blossomed to the confidences of mother and daughter, and within days Charlotte was too under the spell of the lovely old city in which Aunt Alice had chosen to live. She felt as if she had known the van Dammes all of her life. Rachel, of course, was made much of – particularly by Annette, who was herself carrying her first child, and by the lively Philippe, who delighted in Rachel's gurgles of laughter as he bounced her on his knee or tossed her boisterously in the air, at risk to limb if not to life. He delighted too in showing off the beautiful little city that was his home. As the cobbled streets basked in the soft sunshine of a balmy late autumn he escorted Charlotte, Nurse Winterbottom and the bouncing perambulator containing a happily cooing Rachel upon walks along the banks of the picturesque canals that were lined so prettily with Hansel and Gretel houses and delicately spired churches. Ancient bridges spanned the waterways and willows bowed with grace, autumnal fronds drifting, like long-haired girls admiring their reflection in the still sunlit mirror of the water. They took coffee and cakes in the Market Square, to the mellow and lovely sound of the carillon housed in the Halles tower, the forty-seven bells pealing joyously across the spires of the city in the still and golden autumn air. Bruges was a city of bells, a city of quiet cobbled streets, of markets gay with flowers, of shimmering, peaceful water that reflected the lovely façades of the medieval buildings like an illustration from an ancient romance. A city from the dreams of childhood, enclosed by its ancient walls and embankments, watched over by its windmills. And Charlotte was enchanted. She regained her spirits and her looks. The exercise she took brought the bloom back to her cheeks and brightened her eyes. Her figure grew trim again. She laughed with a wholehearted delight she had not felt in years, joined in the games and the musicales of which the van Dammes, were so fond, flirted light-heartedly with Philippe – a game of their own in which he joined in with enthusiasm.

She did not want to go home.

She spent long hours in the big old kitchen with Aunt Alice, who herself cooked for the whole household, and within the first week had confided most of her troubles, although never did the secret of Rachel's parentage escape her, for the thought of risking losing Aunt Alice's good opinion was too awful to be contemplated. However, simply to have a sympathetic ear into which to pour her miseries was a balm beyond price.

'Ben always could be a solemn little chap,' Aunt Alice volunteered a little unexpectedly one day. 'Very – intense – even as a small boy.' She smiled fondly. 'But such a mischief!'

'Really?' Charlotte was surprised.

Up to her elbows in flour, cheeks pink from her exertions and from the warmth of the huge stove, Alice laughed. 'Oh, yes! The scrapes he got into! He used to drive his poor mother mad! She always used to say he could make a living in the circus!'

Charlotte pulled a mildly bemused face. She had never

thought to imagine Ben as a child, let alone a mischievous one with a mother who thought he belonged in the circus.

'It was when Henrietta died that he really changed, of course.' Alice's eyes were placid upon the dough she kneaded so expertly upon the board. 'Poor lad. He was in an awful state. He blamed himself. They'd known each other – loved each other – for years. They were true childhood sweethearts. He adored her,' she glanced at Charlotte. The full lower lip was out, prettily sullen. Charlotte picked with impatient fingers at the lace trimming of her skirt. Alice shook her head gently. 'Don't begrudge it to her, my dear. It lasted for such a little time, and ended so very tragically. She was dead within the year and his child with her. Can you wonder that he nearly went out of his mind? Or that, when he recovered, he was never quite the same young man he'd been?'

'I remember a little,' Charlotte conceded, trying hard not to sound grumpy. 'I was about ten years old at the time, I think. Ben was so much older. I never really knew him.'

The kindly eyes met hers in silence: and she flushed very slightly at their gentle message.

The weeks slipped by. The weather chilled and broke. Four weeks. Five.

She did not want to go home.

'Is that from Charlotte?' Hannah asked Ben at the breakfast table. 'Is she coming home?'

Ben shook his head, folding the letter. 'No. She wants to stay for another week or so.'

Hannah looked doubtful. 'It's November already. If they leave it much longer the weather could be very bad for the crossing.'

He shrugged. 'She's enjoying the break. She sounds happier than she's been for months. There's no reason for her to hurry back.' He applied himself to his toast and marmalade.

Hannah shot a small, doubtful glance at him, but said nothing.

Peter reached for his hat. 'Good for her. Wouldn't mind a few weeks off in foreign climes myself. But hey-ho for the daily grind – Hodges and Son, here I come.' He perched the hat at a jaunty angle, grinned like an irrepressible child, 'Only one thing keeps me going. There's always the hope that this is the day I can persuade old Hodges to sack me – eh?'

Hannah tried unsuccessfully not to laugh at him. 'Mrs Briggs was asking if you'd be in to dinner tonight?'

He breezed to the door, turned. 'No. I've got –' he tapped the side of his well-shaped nose secretively, eyes bright, '– a little business to attend to. 'Bye.'

Hannah shook her head ruefully as, humming cheerfully, he clipped off down the corridor. 'Mother always swore he was a changeling,' she said, 'I sometimes think she might have been right!'

Ben smiled and stood up, folding the newspaper.

'Ben?'

He looked at her.

'How much longer do you think Charlotte will stay away?' In her sisterly concern she could be every bit as stubborn as he was.

'I don't know. All I know is that the trip seems to be doing her some good. Another couple of weeks won't hurt.'

'But –'

'Hannah –' Very firmly he opened the paper and spread it in front of her. 'Read the paper –'

'And mind my own business?'

'I didn't say that. It's just – Charlotte is my wife – you have to let me decide what's best.'

Hannah nodded. 'Sorry.' She glanced at the paper, raised her brows at headlines an inch high. 'What's all this?'

He shrugged. 'Whitehall paranoia I'd say, most of it. A disease Fleet Street is always very quick to catch.'

Hannah scanned the article quickly. 'You don't think the build up of the German Fleet is a threat?'

'Who knows? Possibly. Possibly not. What I do suspect is that it makes a very convenient red herring.'

'Oh?' She looked up at him, interested. 'In what way?'

He reached to take the last of the toast, munching it absently. 'If there's trouble brewing – and there is – I don't think it's coming from Germany. Not yet, anyway.'

'Where then?'

'Here. Right under our noses.' He finished the toast, walked to the door. 'Ask Ralph. There are men working the wharves who haven't had a rise in wages since they won their "docker's tanner" upwards of ten or twelve years ago. Have you seen the price of bread lately? Some employers are making noises about actually cutting wages – not just here in the docks, but in Wales in the mines, in the north in the mills. There's a good few beginning to ask why they should spend their strength making money for the owners when their own children go shoeless and hungry.' A memory flickered elusively. Where had he heard that phrase?

'What can they do about it?'

He shrugged. 'They can sit down under it or they can fight it. And there are plenty to encourage them to fight.'

'Fight?' Hannah looked at him in true amazement. 'You mean – really fight? Physically fight?'

'If it comes to it, yes. You know as well as I that the syndicalists in the docks have been advocating firm action for years. So have some of the more militant miners. What do you think will happen if they get together? Do you think the Government would allow working men to cripple the country with industrial action? Of course not. No – if things keep drifting the way they seem to be, then British soldiers are as likely to be used on the streets of England and Wales as they are against Germany, fleet or no fleet. What happened a couple of years ago in Russia could just as easily happen here.'

'Oh, surely not! I can't believe that! Why – that was almost full-blown revolution! And repressed so bloodily! Oh, no, Ben! That could never happen here!'

He shrugged. 'Let's hope you're right.' He stopped at the door an expression of deep and earnest thought on his face, 'I don't think it would be absolutely the first time, though I'm damned if I can actually remember the last time it happened.'

'Pig!' she said mildly, smiling her affection. 'When brothers were handed out, didn't I get a pair?'

The heavy November sky seemed to rest upon the pointed roofs of the fairy-tale houses. The wind cut across the flatlands of Flanders, scouring the countryside. Rain drove in gusts along the swollen canals, drenched the cobblestones, ran in small rivers in the gutters. In the warmth of the kitchen on the Groenerei Charlotte sat at the table, slicing cabbage. Stew bubbled on the hob and the savoury smell filled the room. Charlotte's face was downcast, her mouth set miserably.

'I'm sorry, my dear – we don't want to lose you, you know we don't – so far as we're concerned you could stay forever. But it's barely three weeks to Christmas. Your family –'

Charlotte nodded. 'Yes. I know. I'll make the arrangements. I'll telegraph Ben today.'

'But no!' Philippe stood at the door, hands spread in a characteristic, laughing gesture. 'Not today! It cannot possibly be permitted before Monday! For we have our musicale on Saturday night – and who will sing so sweetly for us if you go? We won't hear of it! Next week, eh, Mama? Stay till next week!'

'So Miss Charlotte's coming home at last, eh?' Bron tucked bedclothes and plumped pillows with the unthinking efficiency of habit. ''Bout time too if you ask me! It's weeks and weeks she's bin gone – and with Christmas just round the corner, mind! A pair of extra hands might have come in handy round here. It's all very well to go off gallivanting, isn't it – but at such a time of the year?'

Sally let her chatter. For herself she had come to admit, not without some difficulty, that if Charlotte never came home at all it would be too soon for Sally Smith. The house was so much easier without her moods and tantrums, her dull, resentful silences. There was more than enough work with the children without having a self-pitying semi-invalid taking up everyone's time and energy.

She straightened, sighing, rubbing her back. That wasn't it. Why pretend it was? How many times had she impressed on Toby – lying to others was one thing; lying to oneself was a fool's game. She did not want Charlotte Patten back at the Bear because, quite simply, she did not want her near Ben. She did not want to see those lines of tension back in his face, the grim, unsmiling set of his mouth. And – to carry honesty to its cruellest extent – neither would she welcome back a changed Charlotte. If the break had truly helped her – if she came back the pretty, laughing girl she had been before Rachel's birth, ready to make amends, ready to share her husband's bed and board like any devoted young wife –

'Bron, for heaven's sake! What are you doing with that? It looks like a haystack!' Ill-temperedly Sally pulled the sheets from the bed Bron had been making. 'Here – take the other side. If you'd talk a bit less and concentrate a bit more on what you're doing –'

Bron fell to injured silence. They made the bed. Sally pulled a rueful face, reached a hand to the other girl. 'I'm sorry. I'm tired, that's all.'

Bron could not have held a grudge for more than a moment if she had tried. She beamed. 'That's all right. We all have our off days, mind.'

Back in her cubbyhole Sally sat, elbows on her desk, face resting in her spread hands. An off day? Was that what you called it, she wondered with a twist of wry humour? An off day? When you could not get a man's face from your mind? When you spent your days ridiculously listening for the sound of his voice, the rare peal of his laughter? When a smile could light a room like a lamp and a sharp word cut like a knife? Jesus, Mary and Joseph – had she taken leave of her senses? Or was it true – could it possibly be true? – that since the night Ben Patten had stitched her damaged lip there had been something between them? Something so nebulous, so fragile that to try to name it – almost to think of it – would be to destroy it, to dispel it like mist in the sun? Like a half-caught image at the corner of the eye that vanished at the turn of a head. Had she imagined over these past weeks the especial gleam in his eyes when he looked at her? The lightening of that craggy face when she walked into a room? Had she wanted so much to see it that she had created it in her own heart; a mirage, a lie? Certainly their rapport when they worked together was not in doubt – each seemed to understand the other's view or idea before more than half a dozen words had been spoken. And a shared dry humour, an often hidden amusement at the perversities of life, acknowledged by a flicker of the eyes, a lift of the head, often created an odd bond, as if the two of them were alone together in a world that teemed with people.

An off day.

She lifted her head, stretched her neck tiredly, resolutely kept her mind from the absurd, all but lunatic longings that had kept her from sleep the night before.

No. Sally Smith did not want Miss Charlotte to come home.

Chapter Nine

I

Christmas time for the Pattens and their charges was a special time indeed. Everyone was part of it, a part of the hints and secrets, the preparations and anticipation. Sally had been planning it for a month. After church in the morning the children were to sit down to a special meal – goose followed by plum pudding – cooked by Mrs Briggs and served in the gaily decorated schoolroom. After that there were to be games and then, treat of the day, tea in the parlour with Doctor Will and his family, where presents from the tree that sparkled like a small, colourful miracle in the corner of the room would be handed out. Under Sally's guidance the children were making little gifts for the family. The 'babies' were painting bright pictures for Doctor Will and Miss Charlotte, the 'seconds' – a group of half a dozen six and seven year olds – were making cardboard bookmarks for Mr Ralph and an ingenious cardboard tiepin holder for Mr Peter, and the others – eight children ranging between the ages of eight and twelve – were producing a desk tidy for Doctor Ben and a neat sewing box for Miss Hannah. They worked like little demons in the week leading up to Christmas, every room in the home littered with seashells, beads, cardboard and multi-coloured scraps of cloth, all to be hastily hidden away amidst much shoving and giggling if the intended recipient of the gift should come near.

'Well, at least it keeps them occupied,' an all-but

exhausted Sally said to Hannah two days before Christmas Eve, 'even if not entirely out of mischief. The things they get up to, even right under our noses!' She laughed a little wryly. 'That young Tom for instance – he's got the makings of a market trader if ever I saw one! He'd sell a grindstone to a knife sharpener that one. You know what he did the other day? He swopped a piece of red sticky paper for Billy's last two bull's eyes. God! The one thing we've got more of than trouble is red sticky paper! When Billy found out he was ready to tear Master Tom limb from limb. Tom took off like a jack rabbit all over the house and it took us a good hour to get the place back to normal again!'

Hannah laughed. 'You're making such a wonderful job of the children, Sally. Ralph's delighted.'

Sally smiled her swift, slightly crooked smile. 'Thanks.'

'I came to say that Pa wants you to come to dinner with us on Christmas night – you, Bron and Mrs Briggs. After the children are settled. Would you like to?'

The day before, Dan had asked her, 'Christmas Night, Sal – Surely they'll let you off for that?'

And, 'P'raps Boxing Day,' she had said to him gently, 'I'll come to tea on Boxing Day.' Because she had not wanted to be away from the Bear on Christmas Day; perverse it may be to force herself through torment, but she did not want to be away from the Bear on any day.

'Thank you,' she said again, firmly suppressing the memory of a blunt, square, baffled face, 'that would be nice.'

Nice? To sit at the same table as Ben Patten? To watch his meticulous attentions to his newly returned, pretty young wife who alternately glittered like a chandelier or sat in a strangely provocative, childlike silence, her eyes lit with secret dreams. *Nice*?

'Good. Pa's arranged for help in the kitchen so that Mrs Briggs can eat with us. A couple of friends of Peter's are coming, too. It should be fun.'

Sally nodded. 'I'll look forward to it.'

And – blimey, she thought with deliberate wryness as Hannah turned to leave, I'm sounding more like one of them every day!

But not enough. Never enough.

Christmas Day went well. After the dreary weather that had preceded it, the day was clear and cold and bright. The children, apart from a couple of scuffles, behaved themselves well enough in church – at least until the last five minutes when the tooth and nail affair that broke out between Tom, Toby's first lieutenant, and Billy Turner, his only real rival for the leadership of the children, was smartly broken up by Ralph and Ben. Toby himself knelt, hands joined in innocence before him, eyes fixed upon the candlelit altar, the very picture of cherubic boyhood, ignoring Sally's furious glare. Dinner was suitably and predictably exhausting and thoroughly enjoyed by its young participants. Roast goose and roast potatoes, stuffing and sauce, cabbage and Brussels sprouts, all disappeared at lightning speed down young throats that still had time and breath to roar out Christmas carols or squabble with automatic rancour with a neighbour. The plum pudding and custard, Sally noted, kept them quiet for a full three minutes. Then it was blind man's buff, hunt the thimble, musical chairs and yet another set-to between Tom and Billy.

'Enough, you two!' Sally hauled them apart and cuffed them with indiscriminate force. 'One more squeak – just one! – and you're in bed for the rest of the day! Now – upstairs, and quick about it. I want you all smartened up and clean as a whistle in fifteen minutes!'

Twenty minutes later they filed two by two, bright, shiny, brushed and for the moment overawed to silence, into the parlour. The small, communal gasp of pleasure and amazement when they saw the Christmas tree with its candles and its gleaming decorations brought smiles to the faces of those already assembled.

'Is it magic?' little Betsy whispered, and blushed scarlet as the words dropped loudly into the silence.

'Yes, little one – that's exactly what it is – magic!' Peter Patten swept her into his arms, his fair, bright face alight with laughter and sudden tenderness. 'Come on, play Saint Nicholas with me. Help me give out the presents.'

Hannah, with Sally's help, had done her job well. Dolls and books, trains and puzzles, all were grasped by small eager hands that had held few enough such things before. For a short while even the roughest of the youngsters was subdued by the munificence. With awkward grace the gifts they themselves had made were handed out, and Sally was touched almost to tears by the ungainly picture of her that the babies had painstakingly painted, the shell box the older children had constructed and above all the small string of beads that Toby nonchalantly proffered. 'I pinched them,' he volunteered with an angelic smile, 'from the ones the girls were sewing on to Miss Hannah's box.'

She hugged him, blinking. 'Thanks, Tobe. Here. I bought something for you, too.' She fished in her pocket.

He stood with bowed head, looking at the shiny, brand new fountain pen that lay in his slim, pale fingers.

'It's – to help you with the scholarship. For – for good luck.' She was taken aback by this stillness, the lack of reaction. Did he not, after all her thought, like her gift?

'Thanks.' He cleared his throat. 'Thanks,' he said again, and lifted his face for her kiss, the arms that he flung about her neck all but strangling her, saying the things his young tongue could not master.

'You like it?'

'It's the best present I've ever had,' he said simply. 'And the best I ever will have.'

Tea was taken in a well-mannered calm that astounded even Sally, who was, it must be said, the source of the imaginative threats that had brought it about. The girls smiled and dimpled their 'pleases' and 'thank yous' and the boys did their level best to come up to such perfection.

'Splendid!' Doctor Will said beaming. 'You've all been absolutely splendid! And as a reward — tomorrow you shall all go to the zoo! What do you think of that?'

Toby, ever a man for the moment, sprang to his feet. 'Hurrah! Hurrah for Doctor Will! Hurrah for the zoo!'

The children cheered themselves hoarse.

'Hurrah for everyone! Hurrah for Christmas!'

The adults, laughing, joined in that one.

'Hurrah for a quick story and hurrah for bed,' Sally said crisply, sensing the moment with a sure instinct. Little Bessie, having eaten more in one day than she would usually manage in a week, was looking decidedly pale.

'O-oh!' The chorus, disappointed though it was, could not disguise a certain weariness. It had been a very long day.

Sally clapped her hands. 'Zoo tomorrow, so a good night's sleep tonight. But before you go — what do you say?' She was suddenly, uncomfortably aware of Ben's eyes upon her, his face relaxed and laughing.

Toby, still standing, raised his small hands elegantly, like the conductor of a symphony orchestra. 'Thank you, Doctor Will,' the children chanted obediently, grinning. 'Thank you, Miss Hannah. Thank you, Mr Ralph. God bless you, and a merry Christmas.' And then, forgetting at this last moment the hard-drilled lessons of the week before, in a tangle of arms and legs, pushing and tumbling like unruly puppies, they left the table and fled through the door, the bounty of their presents clutched in sticky fingers, the prospect of tomorrow's outing lighting their eyes like beacons.

Sally, about to follow them found herself stopped by a hand on her arm. 'Wonderful work, Miss Smith,' Doctor Will said. 'You've got the little barbarians eating out of your hand.'

She laughed. 'Not quite. But thanks anyway.'

'Your speciality, is it? Taming barbarians?' It was Ben, the rugged face creased into laughter. She lifted her head and for a moment their eyes met. The communication between them was instant and warm and totally unexpected for them both. Some flash of laughter, an instinctive rapport, flickered between them. She had not imagined it; she knew she had not. A sudden, irrational and blinding happiness rose. She felt the warmth of colour creep into her face.

'Why?' She tilted her head in smiling challenge, 'Do you know any that need it?'

For the strangest moment they might have been the only people in the full and chattering room. The quality of his smile changed as she watched, the long sweep of his dark lashes veiled his eyes. Her heart all but stopped, laughter fled. 'I think', she said, carefully composed, 'that Betsy might be going to be sick. I'd better go.'

'You are coming to dine this evening?' Doctor Will asked genially.

She tore her eyes from a strangely questing, even more strangely uncertain face of his son, who stood looking at her she thought as if he had never seen her before. 'Yes, I'm coming,' she smiled a swift smile, directed at anyone and everyone but Ben, 'after I've seen the barbarians tucked safely into bed.'

Sally spent more time before her mirror that night than she ever had in her life, though that, to be truthful, was not saying much in an age when a lady of leisure might contrive to spend the best part of her day so. She had no special dress to wear; her two good, serviceable white blouses and dark skirt were her only decent clothes, but she had washed and neatly pressed the prettier of the two blouses and had accepted gratefully from Bron the offer of a small brooch to pin at the neck. The sleeves were puffed at the shoulder and were full and soft to the wrist, disguising, she hoped, the lack of plump, soft flesh that no amount of Mrs Briggs's wholesome cooking seemed to remedy. She was still thin and angular, her face narrow, the bones prominent. Piling the weight of her brown hair inexpertly upon her head she admitted a little ruefully that even in the softening candlelight no one would ever call her a beauty. But her skin at least was now clean, clear and smooth, her hair shone and her long-lashed, slanting eyes beneath their dark, tilted brows were bright. She leaned closer to the mirror inspecting the white scar that flawed her lower lip. Ben Patten had done a good job – her always slightly lopsided smile was perhaps a little more crooked, but the scar did not disfigure. She sat back. So; it might not be a pretty face that looked steadily back at her – but it was hers, and it was like no other face she knew. That would have to do.

She stuck the last pin firmly into her hair, gave her reflection one last, long and far from enchanted inspection and prepared to take herself downstairs.

Dinner was a far more rowdy affair than she had expected, thanks mainly to Peter Patten and his two sidekicks who, flushed with wine and the glory of the season made sure that not one dull moment was allowed to intrude upon the fun. A constant stream of jokes and anecdotes kept the company laughing, whilst the young men indulged with some gusto in fulsome compliments and outrageous flirtation with every female at the table, from the plump, flustered and flattered Mrs Briggs and the blushing Bron to the over-gay, exquisitely pretty Charlotte. Every now and again, by way of a change Peter would demand a Christmas carol, and the loved old words would echo heartily around the ancient room that must have heard them so many times before. The meal was splendid and passed in a tempest of conversation and laughter. Sally, seated between Peter and a friend he had introduced as Crispin, found herself the target of her fair share of attention. Crispin, who had obviously enjoyed a tot or two before arriving at the Bear, spent a good deal of time with his hand upon her knee; she spent an equal amount of time laughingly but firmly removing it. The candles in their silver candlesticks upon the table gleamed and flickered upon the happy faces, shone in the glasses, glowed in the wine.

'A toast!' Peter jumped to his feet as the last of the great plum pudding was carried away and the glasses were charged yet again.

A silence fell, in which Bron giggled loudly and then, blushing furiously fell to silence as smiling eyes turned to her. Crispin, sitting opposite her, discreetly removed his foot from hers and attempted once more an exploration of Sally's upper leg. Very firmly, as she might have with an errant puppy or kitten, she picked up his hand and placed it back on the table. He smiled winningly.

'To Mrs Briggs, her helpers and her splendid dinner! The King himself can't have partaken of a better feast!'

'Hear, hear!' The toast was drunk.

'And to us all.' Peter looked affectionately from face to face. 'As a more literary brain than mine has put it: God bless us, every one!'

Again glasses were lifted amidst a smiling murmur.

'And now –' he waved his arm, a general commanding his troops, '– to the parlour. And bring your glasses. There's champagne for everyone.'

The parlour was bright with lamps and candles, the tree glowed in its corner. Beneath it a new pile of presents had been laid. Amidst squeals and cries of delight they were handed out.

'Oh, Peter, how lovely! Do, please, help me to put it on!' Obligingly Peter clasped a small locket about his pretty sister-in-law's neck.

'My goodness, how splendid.' Will eyed his new pipe a little doubtfully.

Hannah kissed him. 'I just hope it smells a little better than the old one!'

'Well, I do declare!' Mrs Briggs held up a pair of soft slippers, 'Just look at that! And quite the right size, too!'

Ralph leafed through a book, lost to the world for a moment, oblivious of them all. Ben and Hannah exchanged amused and affectionate glances.

Hannah came to Sally, smiling. 'For you. From us all.'

Startled, Sally took the small, soft package. 'But –' she stopped, embarrassed. Although now earning her keep her salary was no fortune and every spare penny she had saved had gone on the pen for Toby.

Hannah beamed. 'Open it, then.'

She tore the paper, looked in absolute silence at the pretty tumble of soft green silk in her lap.

'Do you like it?' Hannah asked, a little anxiously.

'I've never seen anything so pretty,' Sally said simply. 'Never.' She lifted the blouse, with its drift of lace at collar and cuffs, held the soft material to her face.

'The colour will suit you very well. It matches your eyes.'

'But – I haven't got anything to give –'

'Oh, nonsense.' Hannah interrupted her briskly, 'No one would expect it. Happy Christmas, my dear fellow prisoner!' and she dropped a laughing kiss on Sally's cheek which, even more than the present had a rather alarming effect on Sally's emotions. She blinked rapidly. Entirely unable to speak, she smiled her thanks.

'And now,' Peter again had assumed the role of master of ceremonies, 'ladies and gentlemen, for your delight and delectation,' he paused, grinning, savouring the puzzled expectancy on the faces about him 'the *pièce de résistance!*' He walked to the table, upon which lay a solid, rectangular shape hidden beneath a fringed shawl. 'Ladies and gentlemen, girls and boys – here it is! – my present to the household.' With a dramatic gesture he whipped the shawl away to reveal a long, beautifully inlaid box that shone with a mellow loveliness in the light, its elaborately decorated brass hinges and lock shining like gold. The company pressed forward, murmuring at the sheer beauty of the thing.

'But – what is it?' Charlotte ran a small finger in wonder over the shining wood and then, in sudden understanding, delightedly answered her own question. 'Oh, Peter! It isn't –? It is! A musical box!'

Pleased with the effect of his gift Peter leaned forward and lifted the heavy lid, revealing to gasps of admiration an extraordinary arrangement of brass cylinders and bells, the whole thing polished and gleaming like precious metal.

'Oh, look! Butterflies!' Charlotte clapped her hands. 'Oh, Peter – quickly! – how do you play it?'

He leaned forward and flicked a switch. There was a whirr and a click, loud in the expectant silence, and then the cylinder began to turn and the music played, clear and precisely beautiful, intricate and charming as the pattern of sunshine on water. The bells chimed, struck prettily by the metal butterflies that, on their slender metal rods, swooped about the box in time to the lilting music.

'Oh, *Danube so blue* –' Peter had seized the giggling Bron and was waltzing her about the room, 'la-la, la-la.'

In moments Crispin had caught Charlotte about the waist and Ralph had taken Hannah's hand. The musical box played on, weaving an enchantment of sound such as Sally had never in her life imagined could exist.

She of all of them had made no sound, no exclamation. She stared at the lovely thing like a child, in wonder, watching the magic intricacies of its movement, enthralled by the chiming music. The harps of the angels could not have sounded lovelier to her ears.

She heard Charlotte, 'Peter! What extravagance! It must have cost a *fortune!*'

Peter leaned to her ear, a wary eye on his father. 'Had a bit of luck on the gee-gees, actually.'

'Wicked!' She pushed him playfully.

Fascinated, Sally watched the slowly turning cylinder,

with its bright brass pins. She had never seen anything so amazing in her whole life.

'Let's push the chairs back – make a bit more room. Then we can all dance.'

'Why aren't you dancing?' Peter's other friend, whose name she had not caught, slid an arm about her waist. 'Come on, join the fun. "After the ball was over, After the night was through".'

It was undoubtedly the loveliest evening she had ever experienced. She danced with Peter, she danced – rather less exuberantly – with Doctor Will. She shared a glass of champagne with Crispin and drank another all to herself. She laughed a lot and talked more about nothing than she would ever have believed possible. And then she turned to find Ben beside her, that dear, warm smile lighting his square face, a hand held out in invitation. She stepped into his arms as if it were the most natural thing in the world to do. The room was crowded. Crispin and Hannah bumped into them, careered away. Ben's arms tightened about her protectively. She could feel the warmth of him, the incredible, unlikely strength of the man, smell the indefinably male smell of him. She closed her eyes. They danced in absolute silence, a small bubble of intimacy in that noisy room. The musical box was slowing down. Peter disengaged himself from Bron's eager arms. 'Wait, everyone. It just needs rewinding –'

They stood very close, Ben's arm about her waist, hers resting lightly upon his shoulder, their other hands clasped, waiting for the music. Then Sally lifted her head to look at him; and caught her breath at what she saw. If at any time over these past, confused weeks she had convinced herself that the intense attraction she felt for Ben Patten was not returned, in that moment such doubts were dispelled. Before he could veil it she saw the deep hunger in his eyes as he looked at her. They stood for a moment in still silence amidst the talk and the laughter.

'There we are – *Oh, Danube so blue* –' Peter waltzed

back into Bron's waiting arms. The couples about them started to move. For an odd, suspended second Sally and Ben stood, still and alone, looking at each other. And then the spell was broken. They moved with the music, a little stiffly, awkward with each other. He steered her to the table where the champagne and glasses stood.

'A little refreshment. It's really remarkably warm in here.' He poured two glasses of champagne, handed her one, drank his own much too quickly.

'So there you are, Benjamin Patten – do you know you haven't danced with your only sister yet?' Hannah claimed him, laughing. Sally sipped her champagne, holding the sparkling, heady liquid upon her tongue, savouring it, savouring that moment, that look she had surprised upon Ben Patten's face. She had not imagined it. She knew she had not. Her eyes went to where he danced with Hannah. As if drawn he glanced at her, and then quickly away.

She drained the narrow glass.

'Lordy, Miss Sally,' an extremely tipsy Crispin bowed before her, 'what are you doing standing alone? Pray d-do me the honour?'

It was almost midnight when Hannah slipped up to her, leaning to her ear confidentially, 'Sal, it's Bron – I don't think she feels terribly well. I don't want to embarrass her – she'll die if I go over there. I'm sorry to ask – but do you think you could get her to bed? A little too much champagne I suspect.'

Sally, her own head swimming a little, looked to where Bron stood by the table, an empty glass in her hand and a slightly bemused expression on her face. She was very pale. The party was breaking up; Doctor Will and Mrs Briggs had long ago departed for their beds, Peter's friends were wrapped in greatcoats and preparing to brave the winter's cold.

Sally moved to Bron, slipped an arm about her waist. 'Time for bed, I think?'

Bron turned startled eyes to her. 'I feel that queer!' she whispered. 'I'm not sure I can move!'

Sally suppressed a grin, took the glass from the girl's unresisting fingers. 'Take a couple of deep breaths. That's right. Now – hold on to me. We'll go round and say good night to everyone together.' She steered the girl around the room bidding the remaining guests good night. Hannah and Ralph were collecting the glasses together, Charlotte, her slippers off, curled into one of the big armchairs, was playing a silly word game with Peter. Of Ben there was no sign. Bron tripped over her own feet once or twice but managed, creditably, to remain upright and more or less under her own steam until they left the room. Once through the door, however, she slumped against the wall, moaning.

'Oh, Sal! I feel that bad! Truly I do!'

'Come on, my love. Bed's what you need.' Encouragingly Sally caught her arm and hauled her upright, guiding her towards the courtyard door. 'Once you're lying down you'll feel right as rain,' she said with more faith than conviction.

When the cold night air hit the girl, she reeled. 'It's no good. I'm going to be sick –' and she was, very sick indeed. Twice.

Sally waited. It was a clear, cold windy night. Stars as chill as chips of ice studded the dark sky. 'Feeling better?' she asked the shivering Bron at last sympathetically. 'Come on, now. One more effort. Up the stairs, then you can lie down.'

Half-way up the rickety stairs poor Bron began to cry miserably. 'Such a fool I've made of myself!'

'Oh, rubbish! No one noticed a thing,' Sally lied cheerfully. 'Don't spoil it, now. It's been such a lovely evening.' She put a supportive arm about the other girl's shoulders, her own eyes distant with her own thoughts. It had indeed been a lovely evening. An evening of magic. She would at that moment readily have sacrificed five years of her lifespan to live through those few hours again.

She guided Bron to her room, helped her to undress and loaded her unceremoniously into her bed where, after a couple of heartfelt groans, she fell immediately to snoring. Grinning, Sally tucked her in and tiptoed from the room. If she knew anything at all of such things poor Bron was going to have a head like a haystack in the morning.

She went to her own room, humming. '*Oh, Danube so blue* –' She turned up the lamp, let down her hair, brushed it with long, lazy strokes in time to the tune she sang softly, beneath her breath. In the mirror her eyes glowed and sparkled. She leaned forward, watching herself intently. What had he seen when he had looked at her that had lit his eyes so? Her eyes gleamed green in the candlelight, bright and soft as the silk of the blouse Hannah had given her. She smiled at the thought. It was a lovely present – quite the prettiest thing she had ever owned. And Hannah was right, it would suit her. She would wear it tomorrow – the thought brought her up short.

So busy had she been getting Bron to bed she had left her present in the parlour.

'Damn it,' she said aloud mildly. Could she be bothered? The wind rattled the window. But yes – she really did want to wear the blouse tomorrow. Impulsively she reached for a warm shawl, threw it about her shoulders and sped to the door.

The parlour was deserted and dark apart from one low-burning lamp and the light from the fire. The house was silent. She slipped through the open door, saw the blouse at once, where she had left it on the arm of the sofa. She picked it up and as she turned her eye was caught by the shape of the musical box on the table. She moved to it, running her fingers over the fine inlay that shone in the firelight. Greatly daring she lifted the lid, to peep at the bells and butterflies that glimmered beneath it.

Very close, someone cleared his throat.

She almost jumped from her skin. She dropped the lid

of the box with a crash that rang the metal of the bells.

'I'm sorry,' Ben said. 'I didn't mean to startle you.'

She laughed shakily. 'Startle me,' she said, her husky voice cracking a little, 'you nearly frightened me to death!'

He laughed with her, softly and apologetically. 'I came to turn out the lamp.'

She held up the shirt. 'I came for this. I left it behind.'

Their eyes held for a moment. Then he moved past her to the table.

'Splendid thing, isn't it? Trust Peter to outdo us all.'

'It's the most wonderful thing I've ever seen or heard,' she said with an earnest simplicity that brought the smallest twitch of a smile to his lips.

He lifted the lid, flicked the brass switch with his finger. *'Oh, Danube so blue –'* the pretty, tinkling notes filled the air about them. Smiling, eyes half closed, she swayed to the music, humming to the music.

He turned to watch her, the smile suddenly gone from his face. She had never been so aware of anything as she was of his eyes upon her. She tilted her head, lifting her face to the soft light. Her long hair hung like a heavy brown curtain down her back, swaying to her movements. 'La-la, la-la-la –' She wanted him to touch her. She wanted it with an urgency that she had never experienced in her life before. She wanted it with every pore of her skin, every ounce of her energy. Her breasts tingled and ached at the thought of his hands upon them, the muscles of her belly contracted.

He moved abruptly. Checked himself.

She smiled. Lifted her arms. Danced the few steps to him, swaying gently and gracefully.

He held her as if she had been a butterfly, a fragile flower. As if he were afraid of his own strength, his own towering need. They danced in the half light, drifting in a dream, isolated from the world by the enchantment of the tinkling music.

In perfect contentment she rested her cheek against the

roughness of his jacket, closing her eyes, loving the feel of it, loving him, revelling in the strength of the arms that held her, aware of every movement of his body. She hardly noticed the moment when they stopped dancing and stood, still and trembling, close as lovers yet barely, lightly touching each other, suspending the moment, stretching the ecstasy of expectancy that held them both. She lifted her head at the precise time that he bowed his. Their lips brushed gently, brushed again and then, blindly and in a sudden fury of passion her arms had lifted about his neck and his had tightened about her, his hard mouth hurting hers, his strength crushing the breath from her body. She clung to him with hands and lips and thighs. She felt his hand upon her breast, the long, strong fingers manipulating the rigid nipple. She arched her back fiercely. His hand was tangled painfully in her hair, pulling her head back. His lips moved savagely to her throat, her shoulder, her breast. Only his huge strength held her upright, her own was spent in the demented wave of emotion that surged through her body at his touch.

His sudden, fierce rejection of her took her so much by surprise that she nearly fell. He released her with such violence that she stumbled against the table. He backed away from her, the back of one hand to his mouth as if he would wipe away the imprint of hers upon it. 'You little fool! What the *hell* do you think you're playing at? Get away from me!'

She flinched as if he had slapped her. 'Ben!' It was the first and only time she had called him by name.

He scrubbed harshly at his mouth. 'Get out!'

She stared at him, her hands clutched at her breast where her shirt gaped open. The musical box played on heartlessly, mockingly gay.

He turned his massive back upon her, stood hands clenched as if in uncontainable anger by his side, his head thrown back.

Dazed and frightened, she backed away from him. At the

door she tried one more plea. 'Ben – please,' her low voice was an abject whisper. '*Please!*'

He flung around to face her, his expression terrifying. '*Get out I say!*'

Sick with hurt and humiliation, blinded by tears, she fled.

Behind her the sweet, terrible, chiming music stopped abruptly.

PART THREE

❧✕❧

1911—14

Chapter Ten

I

The first year of which Rachel Patten had any clear recollection was the year of her fourth birthday – the year that handsome, funny Uncle Peter first came home on leave in his officer's uniform, the year that wonderful Cousin Philippe came to stay. 1911 was, too, the year when she finally got Toby Smith to admit that she was no longer a baby, the year that Mama pestered Papa into buying a motor car. It was a year that built to a long, hot, blazing summer during which she, Mama and Nurse Winterbottom spent three blissful weeks in a small house by the sea, Nurse Winterbottom muttering darkly about something called 'anarchy' which was happening in London, whilst Mama – pretty as a picture in her wide hats and drifting pastel dresses – strolled along the front beneath a frilled parasol or took tea on the small verandah with her friends the Westons, and Rachel in her sailor-suit dress built and demolished sand castles, paddled in the sea, collected shells and generally had the best time of her short life. The only cloud on the summer horizon for the child had been the absence of her big, beloved Papa, though to be sure he had explained very carefully to her, for all the world as if she had been grown up, why he had not been able to stay at Brightsea with them. Even Mama, in those three happy weeks, had smiled at her, if rather absently, more often than usual. Oh yes, for little Rachel Patten 1911 was a very good year indeed.

But not so for everyone. In a country where real wages had fallen steadily for three years whilst unemployment had as steadily risen, where a constitutional crisis the year before – brought about by the House of Lords' arrogant refusal to accept the elected Liberal Government's so-called People's Budget – had precipitated two General Elections and reduced the political life of the country to chaos and confrontation, where a king had died sincerely mourned by his people and another had come to the throne amidst seething industrial unrest and discontent, not everyone was going to remember Rachel's fifth year with such pleasure.

For Hannah it was the year of her fourth term of imprisonment and of her first hunger strike. It was also her first experience of the savage and inhumane practice of forcible feeding. In the preceding three years the women had time and again been promised reform and time and again they had been betrayed. Their leaders had been gaoled, the treatment meted out by police to demonstrators had been markedly more brutal. In November 1910 there had been a confrontation outside the Houses of Parliament between the Pankhursts and their supporters, who had been trying to deliver a petition to the Government and a police force who, under the new Home Secretary Winston Churchill, had been instructed to stop them at all costs, to make as few arrests as possible and to discourage them from ever trying again. The resulting pitched battle had lasted for six hours and, predictably and many said deliberately, very many women had been injured. Hannah had found herself nursing a fractured arm and Sally had received nasty bruises when she had been trampled by a police horse. But such tactics worked no better against the women than they did against the brave and stubborn miners of the Rhondda. Under their WSPU banners of purple, white and green the suffragettes marched, obstinately heckled Cabinet Ministers at public meetings, drew up, signed and tried to deliver petitions. The fight went on.

For Sally Smith, who would ever afterwards remember this as a year that changed her life, it began quietly enough with Dan Dickson's third proposal of marriage and her own third, still apparently firm, refusal. But she knew, and thought he might suspect, that faced with this endearing, stubborn devotion she was weakening. He was kind, he was strong, he was steady and he loved her: what more might she expect from anyone? They were good friends, and he respected her: what better basis than that for marriage? As she guessed, he sensed her wavering, and though he said nothing as the year moved on to that stifling summer in which the docklands of London were as much a tinderbox of near-revolution as were the mining valleys of Wales and the dark mill towns of the north, he watched her, and patiently he waited.

As did Ralph for a Hannah whose passions were so totally committed elsewhere that she did not notice.

Of passion between Charlotte and Ben Patten there was none. Their physical relationship had all but ceased; Charlotte had moved back into her own room and rare – and for her disagreeable – were the nights he sought her out. On those occasions that he did she would lie rigid beneath him, hatefully overwhelmed by the bulk and the strength of him, untouched and unmoved by the need that brought him to her; terrified of the possibility of pregnancy. Beyond the bedroom, however, the marriage was a fairly civilized affair, not too far removed from many others of the day, of polite and shallow friendship. It could not be said they cared nothing for each other: frivolous, discontented and self-centred she might be, but yet Charlotte in her prettiest mood, like a spoiled but appealing child, could be difficult entirely to resist. And Ben, whilst utterly lacking that handsome, easy and attentive charm that was almost the only quality that Charlotte looked for in a man was – at his best – neither unkind nor ungenerous. Mismatched they undoubtedly were, but each in their way was guardedly ready to make the best of it – Charlotte because now, in honesty, even the possibility that she might do anything but what the world expected of her never entered her head and Ben because his rocklike conception of his duty would not allow him to do anything else.

It was in early June with the London docks in seething unrest that threatened, like fire or fever, to spread uncontrolled through the other service industries of the capital, and with the distant rumblings of yet another war scare beginning to make themselves heard above the domestic din that Charlotte was more than happy to climb with Rachel, an openly nervous Nurse Winterbottom and enough luggage to accompany a royal progress to India into the new motor car and to be driven by Ben to the small house that he had after much persuasion rented for them on the Sussex coast.

'I declare I intend not to read a single newspaper!' she announced lightly. 'Not one. If the tiresome Germans come, then they come – though it all sounds a most unlikely storm in a teacup to me. Why should we be concerned with a silly and probably smelly place in Africa? And as for unions, strikes and – picket-lines or whatever you call them – I'm tired to death of all of them. Why they can't just take their wages and give a good day's work as they used to do is completely beyond me. I intend to read, to stroll a little by the sea, to take tea in that darling little tea shop. I expect I shall make a friend or two. Rachel, pull your bonnet forward, for goodness' sake. The sun's in your face. You'll end up looking like a little gipsy if you aren't careful.'

Ben eyed her with some amusement. She looked undeniably fetching in her neat motoring outfit, a froth of pale silk at neck and wrist, her huge, veiled, flower-decked hat tied becomingly beneath her chin with a gauzy scarf.

'I want to be back by the twenty-first, of course. I wouldn't miss the Coronation for anything.' She sounded for all the world as if she had been invited by King George in person to occupy the front pew at the Abbey.

'Either Ralph or I will be down to fetch you on the eighteenth or nineteenth.'

She slanted a glance at him from beneath her veil. Really, sometimes he could look quite presentable. In his brown tweed motoring suit and cap he cut so much more of a dash than in his usual, rusty doctor's black – 'Is there any chance you'll come to join us, for a day or so perhaps? A weekend?'

Rachel cocked sharp ears, fixed her father's back with a fierce and longing eye.

'Possibly. I'll have to see what happens.'

'You mean you'll have to see if those stupid dockers cause trouble they can't handle and need you to mend their heads,' she said with unusual asperity and even more unusual perception.

He smiled.

The car bumped along the uneven road, clouds of dust billowing behind it. In the villages children ran beside them, shouting. Charlotte smiled graciously and waved at them. Rachel, a wary weather eye upon her mother's back, poked her tongue out. Nurse Winterbottom was at that moment too openly terrified of the unnatural speed at which they were travelling to pose any kind of threat.

'Really,' Charlotte said lightly, obviously pleased, 'one would think they had never seen a motor car before.'

Ben negotiated a bend designed – if that were the word – for nothing faster than a pony and trap. 'That won't take long to change. In America a chap named Ford's building them quicker than he can sell them. Cars for everyone. Built cheap and fast on what they call an assembly line.'

'Oh?'

Rachel hid a smile at the faintly offended tone of her mother's voice. She shifted in her seat a little and lifted her teddy bear so that he too could see the green countryside as it swooped past them. She liked riding in the motor car. One day she would drive, like Aunt Hannah; but she would have a motor of her very own. She watched as her mother with a dainty gesture adjusted her hat against the wind. She could not imagine her mother ever taking the wheel of the car. The only thing, it seemed to Rachel, that Mama knew about this marvellous machine was that it was a lowly Rover and not the Lanchester she had wanted. About that for a short while she had talked endlessly. The child's mind wandered pleasantly. When Uncle Peter had come home a few weeks before – wearing a most smart and splendid uniform of khaki and shining brown leather that Rachel had thought far more striking and handsome than the scarlet and gold of Toby's silly toys, for all Mama's disappointed complaints – he had talked to her about aeroplanes. Uncle Peter – wonderful, *lucky* Uncle Peter – had been in one, and had told her about it, spreading his arms like wings and zooming around the room until she had got hiccoughs from excitement and laughter.

'They've flown the Channel, little one – it'll be the Atlantic next, you'll see. America next stop!'

She liked Uncle Peter. Sometimes she still wondered with interest about the fuss that had attended his typically capricious and sudden decision to join the army, and the family upset it had caused. Something had happened that neither Grandfather nor Mama or Papa had much cared for, though no one had ever got round to explaining the problem to the intrigued child. She well remembered the strange day when a man had called at the Bear and shouted about Uncle Peter. And a silly lady had cried. Rachel remembered that quite clearly too, because she had been so fascinated to see a grown-up woman sobbing in public – a thing Rachel herself would never be allowed to do – that she had quite forgotten her manners and stared. For which Nurse Winterbottom had slapped her soundly. She directed a small, triumphant glance at her companion in the back seat of the car. Nurse Winterbottom was not in a fit state to slap anyone at the moment. She was clinging to her seat in terror, her eyes shut. She was scared. Scared as a pussy cat. Scared as stupid little Bessie Harper had been when Toby had chased her with a spider – Rachel grinned at the thought.

'Sit up straight, Rachel. Young ladies don't slouch,' Charlotte called over her shoulder, above the noise of the wind and the engine, and without turning her head.

Automatically Rachel straightened her back, sighing. She truly sometimes believed that Mama had eyes in the back of her head.

Ben's thoughts, like Rachel's, had turned to his scapegrace young brother. 'Peter seems settled at last. Army life seems to suit him.'

'I should think anything would suit him better than marriage to that milk and water miss who'd set her cap at him,' she said a little waspishly.

He smiled a little. 'You're probably right. Not the marrying kind, our Peter. He certainly makes a dashing young lieutenant.'

'Second lieutenant,' she corrected him, still tart. 'And, oh, Ben, do slow down a little! I declare I shall be quite sick if you don't!'

Brightsea was a pleasant little place, as much a large village as a town, which straggled up low, chalky cliffs from a small sandy beach. Over the past few years several fair-sized and substantial houses had been built for those with fortune and time at their disposal to enjoy summer by the sea. There were too several very respectable boarding houses and a few villas and cottages to let. The main street contained perhaps a half dozen small shops and the tea shop, run by a genteel widow and her daughter, which had caught Charlotte's eye when they had visited the place earlier in the year. It was, she thought, an agreeable enough place to spend a couple of weeks. Anywhere was better than Poplar, from where, for all her scheming and pleading, she could not persuade her stubborn husband to move.

The house they had rented looked out over the sea and was a mere five-minute stroll from the beach. A cook and housemaid came with the let, the rooms were large and comfortably furnished. She stood on the balcony and looked across the glittering space of the seascape. In the road below a handsome young couple glanced up, paused, then acknowledged her with smiles and slight bows. Graciously she nodded. Oh yes, Brightsea might really prove quite an entertaining break in a life that lately had been quite provokingly tedious.

Ben, knowing with neither surprise nor resentment that he would not be missed at least by his wife, motored back to a London where half the population strolled in the sunshine of the parks, rowed on the peaceful river or attended the summer race meetings in their new motor cars whilst the other half looked on with growing anger and discontent.

'Real trouble coming if I'm any judge,' Will commented that evening. He had aged in the past couple of years. His hair had thinned and his eyes, though still bright and sharp were tired.

'You think so?'

He nodded, tamping down his pipe. 'Been building for months. And the damned weather doesn't help.' He stopped as the parlour door opened and a harassed Sally popped her head around it.

'Ah, there you are – could one of you come, please? The new little boy – Harry Potts – has fallen off the stable roof. I think his arm might be broken.'

Ben grabbed the bag that was never far from his hand, 'I'll come.'

She led him, hurrying, across the courtyard to the home, to where Bron sat in the schoolroom nursing a sobbing little boy. Ben dropped to his knees beside them, gently took the child's arm. 'Well, now, what's all this?'

Dispassionately Sally watched him. There had been a time when she would have gone to almost any lengths to avoid this close a contact, but no more. How she had ever found courage to face him at all after that Christmas night three years before she had never known. The temptation to run away, to hide, never to come near nor by the Bear again had been so overwhelming that at first there had been no resisting it. She could not stay. She would not! But there had been Toby to consider – what would she tell him? How explain a decision to leave, to ruin all the plans they had laid for his future? And to a lesser degree there had been Hannah, who had extended the open and generous hand of friendship – how could she betray her trust by simply running away? She had lain the next day alone in her darkened room after a bitter and sleepless night, by turns savagely, defensively angry and filled with an intolerable humiliation. She had thrown herself at Ben Patten like any street walker: and like any street walker she had been roughly rejected. It served her right, she supposed, though it was a bleak and bitter thought. For twenty-four hours she had neither eaten nor slept. And when she emerged from her room it was with the decision made that, Toby or no Toby, Hannah or no Hannah, she would have to leave.

The first person she had met had been Ben Patten. Whether by design or accident she had never known, but his was the face she saw as she crossed the courtyard, his the voice that said calmly, 'Ah – Sally – Bron was looking for you. There's a crisis in the Seconds' dormitory that seems quite beyond her.'

She had stared at him. Opened her mouth.

Very quickly he had held up his hand to prevent the words. Slowly and firmly he had shaken his head. 'Don't say it. Don't say anything. There is no need.' The granite face had been completely expressionless.

And so, after a moment's hesitation, wordlessly she had pushed past him and taken up her responsibilities again, and though in the months that had followed she had avoided him as much as was humanly possible – as, she was certain, he had her – in a surprisingly short while she had mastered her emotions, though even now the sight of him could sometimes bring an unexpected twinge, a small, almost nauseous twist of humiliation and hurt that would quickly transmute itself into a welcome edge of resentment, almost of dislike, which she made little effort to hide. And, with the passing of time the wound had healed, as most wounds did: it was, after all, as she had told herself constantly during those first hard months, only her pride that had been hurt.

'Not broken,' Ben said now, straightening. 'A bad sprain is all. Cold water compresses should sort it out – oh, and –' he rummaged in his bag, '– a jelly baby. That should do the trick.'

The industrial unrest both in London and in the rest of the country did indeed, as Will had predicted, become steadily worse as the month progressed towards the Coronation of George the Fifth. By the time Ben arrived at Brightsea to pick up Charlotte and Rachel two days before the event, the ports of London, Hull and Southampton were crippled by strikes; a piece of information that did not impress Charlotte a jot compared to the other news Ben carried. 'But *Ben*! Why didn't someone let me know? When did he arrive?'

Ben piled the last piece of luggage into the boot of the car. 'Only the day before yesterday. And we had no time to tell anyone. He telegraphed on Monday and arrived the next day. It's partly a business trip – Aunt Alice has financial affairs in London that he keeps an eye on – and partly pleasure. He decided he wanted to be here for the Coronation.'

Charlotte clapped her hands like a child. 'But that's *wonderful*! Oh, what fun it will be showing him London!'

Rachel, eyeing her mother's unusual excitement a little warily, tugged at her father's sleeve. 'Who's come?'

He bent and scooped her into his arms. 'Your Cousin Philippe from Belgium. Well – strictly speaking, your second cousin.'

'Why is he only second? Who came first?' the child

asked, interested in an apparent pecking order she had never before come across.

He laughed. 'No – Philippe is your mother's and Uncle Ralph's cousin. So that makes him your second cousin.'

'Ben – do come!' Charlotte was waiting impatiently to be handed into the car. 'Or we'll never get away!'

Ben deposited Rachel upon the back seat next to the already pale-faced Nurse Winterbottom and extended a hand to his wife. 'So – you've enjoyed your holiday?'

'Oh yes. Well enough, thank you.' The words were light. 'You weren't lonely?'

'No, not at all. We met a charming young woman. A Miss Weston. Holidaying with her mother. She made a most pleasant companion.'

Rachel cocked her head to one side. Odd that Mama had made no mention of Miss Weston's brother who had, it seemed to Rachel, spent even more time with them than had Miss Weston or her mother. He had made the most splendid sand castles and had not seemed to mind a bit when she had jumped on them and knocked them down. In fact – astonishingly – even Mama had laughed. She had laughed quite a lot when young Mr Weston was with them.

Ben wound the handle and the engine jumped to life. Charlotte settled happily into her seat, delicately adjusting the brim of her hat. 'Cousin Philippe! How marvellous. What a lovely surprise!'

They arrived in London, hot and tired, a little after tea time. Rachel, heavy-eyed and crumpled, held up her arms to her father. Charlotte, however, stepped brightly down, shaking out her skirts and untying the scarf that fastened her hat, looking round expectantly. 'Where is everybody?'

'Taken some of the youngsters to the park for a picnic. They'll be back soon.' Will stood at the door, leaning on a stick. 'Welcome home, my dear.' His old eyes sparkled as they always did at sight of her pretty face. 'We've missed you.'

'Thank you.' She dropped a quick and slightly absent kiss upon his cheek. 'And Cousin Philippe? Is he here?'

He shook his head. 'No. He's gone off with the others to Regent's Park. In fact it was his idea. But they won't be long now.'

'Oh.' Disappointment pulled down the corners of Charlotte's mouth a little. Then she brightened. All the better, it gave her a chance to make herself especially pretty. 'Ben – I really feel a terrible fright. I'll bathe, I think, and change my clothes before we eat. Nurse – take Rachel to the nursery, please, for tea. And then straight to bed, if you please. She's had a very tiring day.'

'But Mama!' Rachel was outraged. The only thing that had kept her cheerful during the long, hot journey back had been the thought of meeting her intriguing-sounding second cousin from Belgium, wherever that was. A sharp-eyed and quick-witted child, she had not missed her mother's interest.

Charlotte quelled her with an irritated glance. 'Bed,' she said.

It was more than two hours later in the long June twilight that the picnic party returned.

Charlotte heard the singing before, looking out of her bedroom window, she saw a wide cart drawn by an ancient, shambling horse pull into the courtyard. Ralph held the reins, Hannah, laughing and dishevelled, beside him. The flat body of the cart was a tumble of children, in the midst of whom Sally Smith stood, swaying to the movement, hatless and breathless with laughter. '*Today's the day the teddy bears have their picnic!*' Seated upon a bale of hay in the corner of the vehicle sat a figure in straw hat and shirtsleeves, his jacket flung carelessly over one shoulder, the long, dark, amused face Charlotte remembered so well lifted to the singer. As she watched he unfolded his tall, oddly elegant frame, vaulted lightly over the shallow side of the cart and lifted a courteous hand to help Sally down.

Smiling, Charlotte turned back to her mirror. Outside Sally's distinctive, husky, slightly off-key voice was threaded with tiredness and laughter. 'Down you get – *Picnic time for teddy bears – the little teddy bears have had a lovely time today*. Whoops!' There came the sound of a tumble, a long, childishly aggrieved wail. The song broke off. 'Ups-a-daisy,' Sally said easily, 'nothing broken.'

What very tiresome beings children were. Charlotte applied herself to her reflection. She did hope that her sojourn by the sea – enjoyable as it had been – had not put too much colour into her delicate complexion, which Philippe, in those weeks in Bruges, had so often commented upon.

II

London, despite her troubles, put on a brave face and gala dress for the Coronation of George the Fifth. The city was decked with flags and with flowers, the streets thronged with people dressed in their Sunday best, out in the sunshine to enjoy the pageantry of the occasion, the fairy-tale procession with its handsome coaches, prancing horses and brilliantly uniformed soldiers. It was a day for rejoicing, and many were ready to put aside their grievances for a while and enjoy it. Tomorrow they might be facing these very soldiers across a picket line or at a dock gate, but for today they were ready to cheer themselves hoarse as the trim and picturesque columns rode proudly by escorting their monarch to his crowning.

In common with the rest of the city the party from the Bear were up and about early. They took an omnibus through the gaily decorated streets to the Mall, the great thoroughfare that led to Buckingham Palace, where they staked their claim to a section of pavement in front of the park, spread their rugs and settled down to a picnic breakfast. Everyone was there with the exception of the very smallest children, the timid Maud who had stayed willingly behind to care for them, Mrs Briggs who had flatly refused – even for her sovereign – to brave crowded streets that she insisted were alive with thieves and vagabonds, and Doctor Will, who had insisted good naturedly that if someone had to stay behind and hold the fort it might as well be him. Rachel, sitting in triumphant elevation upon her father's wide shoulders as they walked down the Mall, had a splendid view all the way down the grand, sweeping avenue to the palace at the end. Soldiers in bright red jackets glittering with brass that gleamed like gold, and with tall bearskins on their heads ceremoniously guarded the way. Rachel waved her Union Jack with enthusiasm. 'When's the King coming?'

'Not for hours yet.' A little peevishly Charlotte, before settling herself upon the rug, smoothed the skirt of the pretty white dress she had chosen for the day: high-waisted, slender-skirted, it showed off her figure to perfection. Red and blue flowers decorated her wide-brimmed hat and ribbons of the same colours fluttered from her narrow waist. She looked lovely and she knew it; but yet the set of her mouth was not happy. The day that had started in such hope and excitement was already, for Charlotte, turning sour. Around her were laughter and exhilaration, children shrieked and played under the indulgent eyes of their elders. A Punch and Judy man had set up in the park behind them and the squawks and squeals of the puppets and of their young audience added to the excited commotion. A flower seller with a basket of red, white and blue flowers sang her wares in a sweet and piercing voice. Somewhere not far away a barrel organ played. Charlotte twitched her skirt away from the sticky fingers of one of the orphanage children. Toby was organizing them into ranks, small ones at the front. 'There. Now you'll all be able to see. And don't forget to wave your flags.' The boy was resplendent in the smart school uniform that Ralph had, over Charlotte's protests, bought for him in celebration of his gaining his scholarship to a school in the City.

A little way away Sally Smith stood with Hannah. She was dressed in cool pale green and white, a pretty hat that Charlotte had never seen before perched upon the piled soft brown hair, the wide brim shading her laughing face. As Charlotte watched, Philippe van Damme joined them, tall and striking in his elegantly casual slacks and striped blazer, his long, engagingly mobile face vivid with laughter and interest.

Charlotte turned away.

'Mama – may I go to see the Punch and Judy?'

'No,' Charlotte said ill-temperedly, 'stay here with us, or you'll get lost. And I've no intention of spending my day looking for you.' She could hear Philippe's voice, and then Sally's, husky and distinctive. Hannah let out a shout of unladylike laughter.

Upon her lap, folded in apparent calm, Charlotte's laced fingers tightened to a painful grip upon each other. How could he? How could he prefer the company of – of that girl – to hers? For there could no longer be any denying it, he certainly did. From the first, light, cousinly kiss of greeting he had made it perfectly clear that she, Charlotte, had no special claim upon his time. He had, of course, in those moments he had spared her been charming and pleasant, the very soul of courtesy – he was Philippe, he could not be otherwise. But the warmth she so well remembered, the special, flattering interest – that, she had seen to her disbelief and mortification, had been bestowed elsewhere.

She glanced at the laughing group again. She had not been wrong. Philippe was watching the animated Sally in a way that tightened the line of Charlotte's mouth still further. Sally, apparently unaware, was talking to Hannah. Eyes narrowed, Charlotte stared at her: the girl could never be described as pretty. Her face was all bone, her skin dark as a gipsy's in the sun, and those odd eyes and slanting brows made her look like nothing in Charlotte's opinion so much as a skinny stray cat.

So why was Philippe, who had hardly spoken a word to Charlotte all morning, watching Sally with such open delight? Why had he spent so much time in her company these past few days? Why had he sought her out so openly — as now — whilst she, Charlotte, was ignored and neglected?

'Rachel — will you stop fidgeting, or I'll slap you!'

Rachel looked aggrieved. Ben looked at Charlotte, surprised. Charlotte looked away.

The morning was a long one.

When the Coronation procession at last wound its way out of the palace gates, however, and down the wide boulevard of the Mall, even Charlotte had to admit it was the most magnificent sight she had ever seen. The children cheered themselves into a frenzy as, harness jangling musically, the cavalry troops rode by, breastplates gleaming bravely in the sunshine.

Of the serious-faced King sitting in his coach of gold, the handsome palace servants and outriders accompanying him, Rachel asked her father, 'Why isn't he smiling?'

'Because it's a very solemn thing to be crowned a king. And I believe he's a man to take his duties to heart. It's no picnic to be King of England nowadays.'

The procession jingled into the distance. Rachel, fingers buried in her father's mop of hair, squirmed to get down. 'May we have lunch now? Mrs Briggs has made pork pie.'

They ate their lunch upon the pavement, not wanting to give up their favoured position by moving on to the grass in the park. The hurdy-gurdy man had moved nearer to them and the children capered to the music. Irritably Charlotte rubbed her forehead. 'Do tell him to move on, Ben. The noise is quite making my head split.'

'Ah, but Charlotte — see — the children are enjoying it so very much.' Philippe folded his long legs and settled upon the rug beside her like a light and elegant crane-fly. 'Let them dance – hmm?' He cocked his head in a characteristic gesture, his eyes warm and smiling.

Pleased, she smiled sweetly and bravely. 'Of course. My head really isn't too dreadful. And you're right – the children are enjoying it.'

He looked at her in unassumed concern. 'A walk perhaps? Ben – Charlotte needs a walk – in the park perhaps, to clear her poor head?'

'No, no.' Charlotte said hastily as Ben glanced at her enquiringly. The last thing she wanted, having got Philippe by her side at last, was to be squired about the park by her husband. 'I shall be perfectly all right, I promise you. I should have brought a parasol – but with so much to think about –' she gestured with pretty diffidence at the group gathered about them as if only her own efforts had planned the campaign that had brought them here, 'I quite forgot.'

'But Sally has one. She'll lend it to you, I'm sure.' The young man leapt obligingly to his feet and within moments was back carrying a small, frilled parasol. 'There.' He opened it, shook out the frills and handed it to her.

She thanked him prettily, set the parasol at a becoming angle upon her shoulder, thus effectively blocking out the rest of the party, and patted the rug beside her invitingly. 'Do please come and tell me all about your lovely Bruges. I declare that since we came back from the sea I've been so very busy I've had simply no time at all to talk to you. I feel positively guilty for neglecting you so! You must let me make it up to you.'

And so the time until the anointed King returned to his palace and the plaudits of his people passed pleasantly after all, in shared reminiscences, gentle, entertaining banter and – balm to Charlotte's sore heart – compliments upon her appearance, upon the glow of health that Philippe perceived about her and, a little less pleasing, upon the grace and good behaviour of her beautiful daughter. And when Sally and Hannah declared their intention of going off to find the gingerbread lady as a treat for the children,

Philippe did not move and it was Ralph, Charlotte saw with satisfaction, who jumped to his feet to accompany them.

'Oh, I should so love to see Bruges again – and your dear Mama – and Annette – why, her little boy must be nearly three years old and I've never met him!'

'Ah, yes. You must come. Mama speaks of you often. You are a great favourite of hers.'

And so it was a better-tempered Charlotte who made her way with the others to the omnibus stop later that afternoon and boarded the vehicle to return to Poplar. The streets were full of revellers and the journey was slow. Charlotte had contrived to sit next to Philippe, leaving Ben with Rachel. Sally, as was only fit, was somewhere in the midst of the children. When they arrived in the East India Dock Road the tired youngsters were ushered into crocodile file with Toby at the head and a brisk Sally bringing up the rear.

Hannah joined her. 'They've been so very good. We should take them out more. Most of the poor little devils have never seen anything but their own back yard.'

Sally, who had not seen much more herself, grinned and nodded.

'I've been thinking –' as always when she became animated Hannah's plain face lit with enthusiasm, '– what about an excursion? A day at the seaside?'

Sally glanced at her, interested but rather more than a little doubtful. 'You mean it? Could we?'

'I don't see why not. We could go to Southend – or Clacton. That's it – Clacton – the beach is better for the children. They run daily excursion trains from Liverpool Street – oh, Sal it would be such fun for them.'

And not just for them. Sally sucked her lower lip, trying to keep her own excitement down. She had never seen the sea. 'You sure we could manage it? With all of them?'

Hannah's enthusiasm roused was no easy thing to quench. 'Why of course we could. With Toby there are fifteen children. Rachel makes it sixteen. There are –' she counted, '– two – four – six adults. And Bron and the other two girls would probably want to come as well. Good Lord, that's less than two children apiece. We'll take a picnic, and bats and balls and we'll buy buckets and spades – ' She turned. 'Listen everyone – I've had the most splendid idea!'

Charlotte, suspecting rightly that she would be expected to help like everyone else, was not so sure it was so splendid; but she was overruled. 'Philippe doesn't want to be dragged to the seaside with a lot of children!'

'Oh, but yes! At home we do it often.' Philippe was delighted by the idea.

Even Ben was amused by the notion. 'It might be fun, yes. And the fresh air would most certainly do the children good.'

'It's settled then. Tomorrow I shall make enquiries. Clacton. We'll all go to Clacton.' Beaming happily at her own inspiration, Hannah deftly caught a hairpin as it tried to escape from beneath the brim of her hat, 'I really can't think why we haven't done it before!'

With Hannah, as usual, it was a case of no sooner the word than the deed. Quickly and efficiently she made the arrangements, whilst Sally cajoled and bullied Mrs Briggs into producing and packing the biggest picnic any of them had ever seen.

They were going to the seaside.

Most of the party that boarded the early morning excursion train at Liverpool Street the following Wednesday were excited to the point of explosion. True to form little Bessie had been thoroughly sick. Rachel, the only one of the children to have had first-hand experience of the seaside, had lorded it over them all until someone had surreptitiously but firmly pinched her and caused floods of tears and a reading of the Riot Act by Hannah. Yet still the journey was a gay one, and trouble-free – the children on the whole being so absorbed in the wonders of the countryside that flew past the windows that even the most graceless had no time for mischief. The party being so big, they were split between two separate compartments which they had to themselves. Sally, her own intense excitement, she hoped, severely controlled, found herself with Hannah, Philippe and Bron. As she organized rotas of children to sit by the window, checked the baskets and bags upon the netted racks above their heads, separated the quarrelsome from the timid, put the tongue-tied amongst the talkers, Philippe watched her, smiling.

He smiled, too, when he held out a hand to help her from the train when they reached their destination. And as they tumbled on to the already crowded beach, squabbling and shrieking, fetching deck chairs, spreading rugs. They settled themselves between the pier and the small stage – empty at the moment – where a notice proclaimed that later in the day Popplewell and Pullan's Yorkshire pierrots would perform. Though even in these relatively calm Essex waters there could be no question of the inexperienced children bathing, shoes and stockings flew as they were unceremoniously pulled off and dumped in a heap. Then the youngsters, who had gazed in amazement at the great, moving mass of water that lapped the sand and shingle beach, rushed to the water's edge to paddle.

Rachel, shrieking with the best of them and clinging to Toby's hand, was pulled up painfully short by her mother's fierce grip on her arm.

'And where do you think you're going, young lady?'

Wise beyond her years, and for good reason, she swallowed childish temper. 'To paddle, please, Mama.'

'I think it best not.'

'Oh, let the child go, Charlotte,' Ben said easily. 'You can't keep her here with the rest up to their knees in the sea. Let her go.'

Charlotte released her grip. Toby and Rachel flew after the others. 'She plays too much with that boy,' Charlotte said coolly. 'He's too old for her. And besides –' she stopped. Suddenly Sally's eyes were on her, narrowed and sharp.

Ben had not caught her words. 'I'm sorry, Charlotte? What did you say?'

She shook her head. 'Nothing.'

Sally sat back, relaxing. The sun sparkled on the sea like light on gemstones. From a row of huts further up the beach a group of young men and women emerged dressed in bathing costumes, the men in body-hugging, knee-length suits, the girls in bloomers or calf-length skirts, short puffed sleeves, bodices ruched and ribboned, many of them with their hair stuffed into frilled mob caps. Sally stared, taken aback. Giggled a little, beneath her breath.

'Do you swim?'

The young man was beside her again, as he so often had been in these past few days, his dark eyes with that warm, confusing light glinting humorously in their depths fixed upon hers.

She shook her head. 'Not me. I've never even seen the sea before.'

The young people splashed into the waves, squealing as the cold water washed upon their sun-warmed skin. She watched them, her face turned from him: but yet she was acutely, almost painfully aware of the regard of those dark, steady eyes.

A slim, fair girl in a navy and white costume gave a small scream as a wave lifted her from her feet and deposited her, neatly and with grace, into the waiting arms of the young man beside her.

'You should try it. It's a lot of fun.' Philippe's voice too held that undertone of humour, as if there were nothing in this life that he could bring himself to take entirely seriously. She stole a glance at him. When first she had seen him she had been disconcerted to find herself thinking that she had never seen a more attractive young man. She still thought so. Not that he had the startling, almost beautiful good looks of Jackie Pilgrim, which were steadily making themselves so embarrassingly apparent in Rachel, nor yet the fair handsomeness of Peter Patten. To some eyes, she supposed, he might appear a perfectly ordinary young man. He was tall and very slim. Everything about him was long; the sensitive face, the mobile hands, the lean body, the lanky legs. Yet there was an unflawed grace about the way he moved; and there was the humour, gentle, mocking, never far beneath the surface. These things were Philippe van Damme – and Sally, to her consternation, had discovered that they added up to a quite ridiculously disturbing whole.

'Sally –' he said. And, absolutely on cue, a shriek echoed from the waterside.

'Oh, Lord.' To her own amazement her voice sounded perfectly and placidly composed, 'It looks as if Tommy's trying to drown young Beggar. I really should try to stop him.'

They built sandcastles – supervised by Rachel – they played a game of cricket, though with some difficulty on the crowded beach, during which Toby managed to lose two balls by hitting them with such lofty power that no one saw where they went. After a picnic lunch those that wished paid their pennies to sit on the benches with Hannah and watch the pierrots. Bessie was lost and found, Toby disappeared for an hour or more and came back with a suspiciously angelic look on his face. Both the absence and the look – which no one else had noticed – Sally chose to ignore. It was three o'clock and an hour or so before they were due to pack up and leave that Philippe took her arm and said, 'Mrs Briggs's sausage rolls are wonderful, but so filling! Come for a stroll with me to – ah, what do you say in English? – to walk them off. I hear music. Shall we go to listen to the band?'

'Oh, but –' In some confusion Sally gestured to the chaos of children, rumpled rugs, buckets and spades and discarded shoes and stockings about them. 'I don't think –'

'Nonsense. There are enough and more than enough to take care of the children. Bron?' The girl looked at him, smiling shyly. 'I shall take Sally to hear the band. You can manage without her for a moment, can't you?'

Bron's eyes flicked to Sally and the girl giggled a little. 'Oh yes, sir. Of course.'

He pulled Sally to her feet. Her face was flushed with sunshine, her skirt sandy. Smiling, he offered his arm. Suddenly laughing she took it with a small flourish, and with an equally light-hearted show of perfectly silly gallantry he escorted her across the hot beach to the promenade.

Neither of them noticed the tightening of Charlotte's mouth as they left. And not even Charlotte noticed the cool light in her husband's eyes as he watched them stroll, laughing, across the sand.

The ornate bandstand where the band was playing was on the greensward beyond the beach. They stood for a moment listening, humming the pompous Sousa march. When Sally had tried to disengage her arm when the walking had become easier he had gently but very firmly resisted, so she stood with her arm linked in happy harmony in his, her head barely coming to his narrow shoulder. A soft breeze blew now, welcome and cool, ruffling the hair that had drifted from beneath the brim of her hat. The music changed. Philippe smiled, swayed a little to the music. '*Oh, Danube so blue —*'

Sally stood absolutely still. She hated that tune. Oh, how she hated it. Suddenly all the joy of the afternoon evaporated as if it had never been. 'We should be getting back.'

He glanced at her in surprise, but with that sure instinct that was so much a part of him he gauged her sudden change of mood, shrugged and surrendered gracefully. 'If you wish. But see —' Across the road a brightly coloured barrow stood, festooned with balloons. 'Ice cream. It is my passion. I insist — before we go back — that you let me treat you to one.'

They bought ice cream from the voluble Italian vendor, perched upon a bench to eat it. In the distance the band played again, oom-pa-pa, oom-pa-pa — Sally relaxed suddenly. How very silly. A tune, that was all. A stupid tune.

She turned to find his eyes full on her, and an expression in them that brought a sudden and uncontrollable flush to her face. For a long and disarming moment they looked at one another before, oddly enough, it was Philippe who turned his eyes away. 'Shall we ask the ice-cream man to move a little down the beach? I should like to treat the children.'

They travelled home, sunflushed and tired, Hannah with her head unexpectedly on Ralph's shoulders, sound asleep, Ben and Charlotte bolt upright each in their own corner, Rachel dead to the world upon her father's lap. In the other carriage Sally sat, head back, eyes half closed, a tousled sleepy head in her lap, Toby leaning heavily upon her shoulder, and upon her lips a small, almost unconsciously happy smile.

Chapter Eleven

I

'Sally.'

The voice came from beneath the tree in the courtyard. Sally, hurrying from schoolroom to dormitory, stopped. Philippe unfolded his spare frame from the dusty ground where he had been waiting. The weather was sultry, the still air too hot to breathe. The children were fractious, the news nothing but bad. The strikes of seamen and 'coalies' at Britain's ports seemed certain to spread to the docks and there was talk of army camps being set up in the parks of London. Britain and Germany snarled at each other's throats over a far-flung unknown place whose name – Agadir – was suddenly on everyone's lips.

Yet she smiled as he came to her, her narrow eyes warm. Since the outing to Clacton they had not seen each other alone; she had made very sure of that, knowing danger surely when she met it, almost certainly knowing better than him the gulf that lay between them.

'You have a day off tomorrow,' he said, with no preamble.

She was astonished. 'Yes. How did you know?'

He did not bother to reply. Even he in this heat was a little rumpled. Sweat beaded his forehead, his white shirt was damp. 'Ben has kindly agreed that I might take the motor car. I have some business in Kent – an associate of my father's – I promised I would see him.'

She waited. Her heart was beating in an absurdly suffocating way.

'Please. Would you come with me?' His voice with its faint, attractive accent was soft. 'I will take you to the country for the day, where it is cool, and green.' He made that characteristic, lifting gesture with his long hands. 'Please? You haven't other arrangements?'

She had half agreed to see Dan. With the trouble that was brewing in the docks they had not had much chance to see each other lately. 'No,' she said faintly. 'I haven't.'

'Then you'll come?'

'I –'

'Please.'

'Yes, I'll come.'

Why had she agreed? She stood the next morning staring nonplussed at her image in the mirror. Why? A day in the country with Philippe van Damme, cousin to Charlotte and Ralph Bedford, respectable son of a respectable family? What a harebrained notion! No possible good could come of it.

But – he had asked her, and so pleasantly. And – she had never been in a motor car before, never seen the green fields of Kent. The woman who had used to live downstairs in the tenement had gone every year into the country to pick hops. For six or eight weeks each autumn she would pick up her household – children, cooking utensils, bedclothes and all – and take them on the 'Hopper's Special' off to Kent. To hear her speak the place was paradise; though Sally, of course, had always listened with the cynical ear of the town dweller. She leaned forward anxiously, fiddling with her hair that was freshly washed and absolutely refused to behave sensibly. She'd never keep her hat on. Except – she had seen Charlotte with her wide-brimmed hats fastened by a scarf – perhaps that was it? Hastily she rummaged about the room, came up at last with a long, crumpled scarf that she had borrowed some time ago from Hannah and never got around to giving back. She perched her hat upon the soft and ridiculously springy mass of her hair and tied the scarf about it, fastening it under her chin. She smiled a little. There. That really looked quite presentable. She smoothed down the folds of her green and white dress – it was the same she had worn to watch the Coronation procession, but there was nothing she could do about that since it was the only walking-out dress she had – and stepped back from the mirror. Once again her stomach churned. Why had he asked her? Why? And – stranger still – why had she accepted? What would she say to him? What would people think of her, spending all day alone in his company?

The thought brought her up short. What kind of nonsense was that? Sally Smith had never been in a motor car, had never seen this Kent that was supposed to be so special. Now here was her chance. And she was going to take it, the world and her own good sense notwithstanding.

With a final glance in the mirror she straightened the scarf and her shoulders, turned quickly and almost ran from the room before she could change her mind.

The green fields and orchards of the Garden of England lay tranquil and tinged with gold beneath the summer sun. Huge trees – chestnut, elm, oak, – cast shade across the greens of the picturesque villages or gave shelter in the pastures to the plump, contented livestock. In the shade of the apple, plum and cherry orchards the grass was particularly lush, the shadows deep and cool. The day was radiant with sunshine.

Sally could hardly believe the evidence of her eyes.

She sat beside Philippe enthralled. She had never believed the world could possibly be so beautiful. As they chugged along the narrow lanes between hedges gay with wild flowers and alive with birdsong she drank in greedily every detail of the lovely countryside: grand houses nestling in rolling, ancient parkland; tiny cottages, thatched or tiled, their gardens a riot of summer colour; the orchards with their precise, military rows of trees; the occasional glimpse of a river gleaming between green banks, sparkling in dappled shade and sunshine.

'It's very beautiful,' Philippe had said some few minutes before, and she had nodded, unable to speak. There simply were not the words to describe it. A scant few miles and an entire world divided this lush, rolling, utterly peaceful countryside from the swarming, dirty, squalid streets that Sally had always called home. It had never occurred to her that anything could be so enchanting. She sat like a delighted child, dazed with the beauty of it.

The car chugged neatly to a halt.

Surprised, she turned to look at Philippe.

'I have a confession to make,' he said, his face as serious as it seemed possible for him to make it, his dark eyes dancing with laughter.

'Oh?' She was a little wary.

'I told –' he spread his hands engagingly, '– an untruth.'

'Who to?'

'To Ben.' He wrinkled his nose like a small boy. 'And to you.'

She waited, trying to keep her face severe.

He pulled a funny, rueful face. 'There is no friend of my father. No business to transact. I made it up.'

Her mouth twitched.

'I made it up because I wanted to take you in the car to a beautiful place.'

'But, Philippe,' absurdly it was the first time she had used his name, and she savoured it, '– that's *wicked*!'

He eyed her uncertainly. 'Yes, I know. Very wicked.'

She stifled laughter. 'What will you tell them? What will you say when they ask you?'

He shrugged Gallicly, waved his hands, 'I shall say – we got lost. Look at your English lanes! How does anyone ever find their way?'

'And the business?'

'I shall say – I send a letter.'

She could contain her laughter no longer. More relieved than he was ready to admit he watched her, smiling broadly, until her infectious giggles started him off too. Together they laughed themselves almost to tears. 'Oh, honestly,' she spluttered at last, 'it really was wicked of you.'

'Yes, I know. But you forgive me?'

She turned to look at him, the laughter dying a little. 'Oh yes, I forgive you.' They looked at each other for a long, warmly happy moment. 'So tell me,' she said at last, 'what diabolical plans have you laid for the day?'

'None,' he said promptly. 'Except that I have a picnic in the boot, and we shall find a field by a river and eat it.'

She nodded. 'I couldn't have come up with anything better myself.'

She watched him as he drove, listened to the fluent, laughing words, savouring the perilous joy of the moment. That the day and its joyousness were utter madness she could not doubt; but neither could she ever remember being so easy in a man's company. No one had ever offered her such warmth and laughter, such carefree happiness. Certainly not poor Dan, with his quiet, slow ways and sober attitudes. Singing as they went, they clattered through the quiet lanes until, with the sun high in the sky they came, as if by magic, to the spot for which Philippe insisted he had been looking. A wide, slow-moving river swirled beneath an ancient stone bridge. Beside the bridge a stile led into a green pasture dappled by the shade of the great trees that grew by the river bank.

'There –' he waved his hand. 'Perfect, no?'

Town-bred Sally was not so sure. 'Are we allowed? I mean – isn't that someone's land?'

'But yes. Of course.'

'Then –'

He laughed, pointing. 'There is a footpath. Where there is a footpath one may walk. Where one may walk one may certainly sit. And where one sits –' he turned his palms

311

outward in comical parody of the gesture he made so often, '– one eats!' Gracefully he vaulted from the car and came to hand her down to the road. His hand was warm and strong and held hers firmly. From the boot he produced a basket. Then, as naturally as if they had been children, he took her hand again and led her to the stile.

Sally eyed it, laughingly doubtful. 'I think,' she said, 'that you had better look the other way.'

Smiling he looked down at her. Shook his head, his eyes full of laughter, and of something else, something that lifted her heart and her spirits to a height from which the world and its opinions were so distanced that they might not have existed at all. With a gurgle of laughter she lifted her skirts and clambered with his help over the rickety wooden structure, showing a quite disgraceful length of leg as she did so. As he lifted her down into the field the other side he held her for a moment, and she let him. His long, bony body was light against hers, his shirt crisp and clean and sweetsmelling against her cheek. Her skirts swirled in the lush grass that was golden with buttercups. She tilted her head, grinned provocatively. 'When do we eat? I'm starving.'

They picnicked on the river bank in the green filtered light of the sunshine beneath a great stand of trees. On the bank opposite plump cattle grazed, cropping the moist grass, munching placidly. Sleepy birds called in the high heat of the day. No breath of air disturbed the stillness, and the dark and secret waters of the river slid by in silky silence. Over pork pie and cider he told her of Bruges, of its canals and its flowers, its steeples and its bells. He told her of the great Procession of the Holy Blood that took place on each Ascension Day, of the flower market and the fish market, of the windmills that turned upon the fields and dykes of Flanders. He told her of his family, of his English mother and his kindly Flemish father, of his sister Annette, her husband, her child. He told her of the orphanage on the Groenerei. She listened, smiling, and said little. She did not tell him of the seduction of a country parson's daughter, of her death in the back streets of London, of the child who had been left to fend for herself in brutal squalor. She did not tell him how she came to be with the Pattens, nor why her affinity with the deprived children that they rescued was so great. His soft voice, his dark, ardent eyes were for the moment a barrier between her and such things. The time to face them again would come tomorrow. Meanwhile she sat in dappled sunshine by the moving waters and let herself believe that the moment could last for ever.

He stretched out, long legs crossed, arms behind his head. She had picked a bunch of daisies and was making a chain, as he had shown her. Silence fell easily between them, broken only by the murmuring sounds of the sleepy countryside. She glanced at him. His eyes were closed and he was breathing evenly. Her busy fingers stilled. The dark hair was soft above a high brow, his lashes curled against the sunbrowned skin. His mouth was wide and mobile, and even in repose seemed about to smile. The column of his throat was long and strong. She could have sat so, simply looking at him, for ever.

The lashes fluttered. His eyes opened, looking straight into hers: she knew with certainty that he had been aware all along of her intense regard. She did not look away. Neither of them spoke. He reached a hand to her. She took it, allowed him to pull her gently towards him. She leaned above him, watching him. His face was as still and as serious as she had ever seen it, his eyes intent. Slowly she bent to him, gentle as the brush of wings she kissed him. He lay quite still, his mouth opening a little beneath hers. She drew back slightly, their faces bare inches apart. Neither had closed their eyes.

'Loosen your hair,' he said.

She sat up, lifted her arms, unpinning her hair, perfectly aware of the provocative, lifting curve of her breasts beneath the fine, light cotton of her gown, revelling in his eyes upon her, in the quick movement of his chest as his breath quickened. She shook her head a little and the soft waves of her brown hair drifted about her shoulders. She leaned to him again, brushed her mouth upon his and then, suddenly and with a small, wordless sound she kissed him, softly but with a kind of savage tenderness, a wild, gentle longing that could not have startled him more than it did her. She felt his reaction beneath her, was ready for the hand that dragged her to him, crushing her mouth upon his. For the slightness of his build he was remarkably strong. She let him, as he kissed her, lift her and lay her upon the grass beside him, his weight heavy upon her. It was long, long moments before he lifted his head. She looked up at him. His face was flushed, his intense dark eyes gleamed in the dappled sunshine. His hand was upon her breast, and not gentle. He kissed her again, small, sharp, biting kisses, ran the tip of his tongue down her throat. Her nipples throbbed; she felt their hardening.

And then he stilled.

She felt the change in him. He lay for a moment absolutely unmoving, his face buried in her throat, his long hand cupped about her breast. Then he sat up. His face was flaming. 'I'm sorry.'

Sorry? She looked at him in disbelief.

'It must seem –' he stopped. 'Please. Believe me – I didn't mean this to happen. I did not –' In abject confusion he stopped.

In sudden, loving understanding she smiled. She reached a finger to his face, ran it down his cheek. 'You didn't lie to Ben – and to me –' she said softly, '– in order to bring me into your field by a river and seduce me.'

'No! I did not!'

'I know.' She saw his trembling, felt the intensity with which he wanted her. 'I know.'

He turned from her, sat hunched, his arms about his knees. His face was beaded lightly with perspiration, his hair ruffled. She came to her knees beside him, smiling, loving his need and the intensity with which he restrained it. 'It was I who kissed you,' she said softly and simply.

He turned, slanted a look at her.

She smiled.

And with a small sound, of laughter and of pure happiness, he threw his arms about her, hugging her, burying his face in her hair, kissing her eyes, her nose, her lips.

Laughing like a child she returned his embrace, her hands upon his face, his shoulders, his long, slim back, playing with his ears, her fingers tracing the line of his lips. He caught her finger between his teeth and bit it, sharply enough to make her catch her breath, to make her throw her head back in laughing provocation, narrow cat's eyes gleaming.

'You're beautiful,' he said.

That did make her laugh. 'Me? Never!'

'There is a saying, is there not?' he paused, the laughter gone. 'Beauty is in the eye of the beholder.'

She looked at him for a long, suddenly sober moment. Blinked. 'Philippe – is there any of that lovely cider left? I'm dry as a bone.'

They did not touch each other again, nor, oddly, did the interlude obviously intrude upon their easy companion-ship. As Philippe packed up the remnants of the picnic, Sally deftly recoiled her hair and pinned her hat upon it. Then, easily, hand in hand, they made their way back to the car, pored over the primitive map with which Ben had provided them.

But inevitably the relationship was changed. Like the river beside which they had picnicked the surface was calm, but beneath it deep currents surged. The touch of a hand, the catching of an eye, could charge the air between them. Excitement hovered, an edge of tension sang be-tween them. They drove through the summer's afternoon past cherry orchards where the pickers called and sang towards the clouded walls of London in virtual silence.

315

And that night, after whispered laughter at the lies Philippe had so easily told, after thanks and half-promises, after a swift and oddly awkward kiss, Sally went to bed. And in her bed, briefly, she cried.

II

At the beginning of August, ironically at the very time when the miners in Wales had been finally starved back to work the expected storm that had been simmering for so many weeks over London's docklands broke, and an all-out strike was called. Others around the country followed, and London's carmen too came out. The capital, still in the grip of a sultry heatwave, ground almost to a halt. Troops were used for essential services, resentment seethed. In the North Sea the German Fleet steamed within striking distance of the British coast, the two nations at daggers drawn over the dreams and the rewards of Empire.

No one asked the inhabitants of the little but strategic port of Agadir how they felt at being the bone of contention between two mighty powers.

Talk of open hostilities between Britain and Germany was the only thing Sally saw bring a real, grim shadow to Philippe's face.

'God forbid. If Britain and Germany go to war – if France should be involved – where would poor little Belgium be?' He rubbed his hands together graphically. 'A nut within the crackers.'

'But Belgium is neutral, isn't it?' Hannah asked. 'Everyone has guaranteed that, haven't they?'

The long face was unwontedly cynical. 'You think that will count for anything when the day comes? No. Pray for my country's sake if not for your own that it is never put to the test.'

He had put off time and time again his return home. Since their day in the country he and Sally had been alone together only two or three times; a stroll through one of London's parks, a trip to the Embankment to watch the busy river. But even these innocent outings had aroused overt antagonism on two fronts. Dan Dickson, having possessed heart and soul in patience for three years, was not about to stand by and watch his advantage taken effortlessly from him. He was, Sally knew, under great strain. He was out on strike and a member of the Strike Committee. But then life had not been too easy on her lately either. The intense heat made the Bear like a cauldron, the dock strike had left them short of food and other essentials. Toby was playing her up as only Toby could. She tried to hold her tongue and her temper over Dan's resentment at the time she spent with Philippe – which to her seemed little enough, God knew – but after a particularly peevish outbreak when he accused her of 'gallivanting about with a Frenchy' whilst he, Dan, undertook a man's job in organizing the strike, her fury broke loose.

'He's *not* a "Frenchy"! And he has a name – as you well know! I'm ashamed of you, Dan Dickson. You hear me? Ashamed! Do you think you own me or something? What's it to you who I see or who I don't? My God! To think I was actually considering *marrying* you!'

'Sally –'

She turned on her heel, old habits dying hard. 'Sod off,' she said crisply and with feeling, and left.

Toby was another kettle of fish.

He was happy with Ralph, charming with Hannah, his manners when Philippe was around were flawless. He deferred to Doctor Ben, kept his nature and his charm within bounds when Charlotte was about. He kept Bron enslaved and the children in duly adoring order.

Sally he ignored.

It took a day or so for her to see it. Since he had taken his place at the new school, understandably he had changed. The first year had been tough, though he had never said a word. She had seen it, and her heart had bled for him, but she had known not to interfere. Had he come to her, had he asked for help, she would have been there, defending him like a tigress her young. But he did not, and fret as she might yet still she had loved the valiant courage of the child. He had obdurately refused to explain the bruise on his cheek, the odd black eye, the grazed knuckles that to someone of Sally's experience spoke louder than any words. His laughter, his graceless charm had for a while been replaced by a grim and defensive quiet. He had worked harder than she had ever seen anyone work, harder even than he had worked in those days when he had been studying for the all-important scholarship. The pale light of his small lamp in the little room he now had to himself had burned to the early hours of the morning day after day, and still she had not interfered. She knew him too well. He never came to her with his troubles, whatever they might have been. She gleaned what little she could, and guessed the rest. No one had ever thought it would be easy for him.

Then had come the first Speech Day. She, Ralph and Hannah had attended, all of them outwardly easy, privately concerned. Nothing had prepared them for the day.

Top first year student: Toby Smith.

Top lower school mathematics student: Toby Smith.

Winner of the Bassett Award for literature: Toby Smith.

And so it had gone on. Established, he had the next year taken the lower school captaincy of the cricket team and played for the school's under-fourteen rugby fifteen. The old Toby had blossomed again, sheened by success and by a rapidly expanding awareness of the world and its pleasures. He and Sally had grown closer than ever, a small conspiracy, humorous and supportive, in a world they were both coming to know but which would never entirely know them.

And now – he had stopped talking to her.

She cornered him on a hot August evening as he crossed the courtyard heading towards the schoolroom.

'Toby!'

He stopped. In the past couple of years he had grown at an incredible pace. At eleven, perhaps twelve—his true age had always been a matter for conjecture—he was only an inch or so shorter than she was. The rounded, cherubic lines of his face had hardened and sharpened, but with no loss of beauty. The wide forget-me-not eyes were as lucent and as clear as ever. They gave nothing away.

He waited, saying nothing, his face closed.

'Tobe – is something wrong?'

He shook his head.

'Well, you could fool me. Haven't seen a lot of you lately?'

'I've been busy.' His clipped and tutored accent matched that of the Patten family and was far from Sally's own still unconsciously defiant London speech.

'So have we all, my love.' She cocked her head, looked him in the eye, daring him to pretend to misunderstand her.

He did not. A sudden painful flush of colour lifted in his young face. He ducked his head.

'What's up?'

He struggled for a moment. She waited, refusing to help him.

He lifted his head, oddly calm. 'You aren't interested in me any more.'

He might have hit her. She gasped as if he had. 'That isn't true!'

He shrugged.

'Toby – that isn't true! What ever makes you think –' She stopped, facing the truth he had shown her. The past weeks had been lived in the strangest fashion; the times when Philippe had been close had been real, the times when he had not she had carried on the business of life as if the blood had run out of it.

What foolishness.

They looked at each other in silence, eye to eye.

'He's going home,' Toby said with breathtaking cruelty. 'Ralph told me. He's going home to his stupid Belgium. Next week.' And he left her, standing alone and hurt, facing a world she had known that one day she must face; a world without Philippe, a world where she would not meet him unexpectedly crossing the yard or playing with the children; a world where she would never again encounter that quick smile, the warmth of his laughter.

He had not told her.

Despite London's problems the suffragette marches and meetings went on.

'Hyde Park,' Hannah had said to them all, 'on Sunday. And I want you all there. No excuses!'

Ben took them in the motor car; Ralph, a protesting Charlotte – 'Truly, Hannah, if my head splits – and it will – I shall blame you' – Philippe and Sally. The crowds had gathered. Sally wore a white dress with a broad green sash and a bright bunch of velvet violets in her lapel. Her widebrimmed white hat was trimmed with violet and green ribbons. She had agreed, with Hannah, to sell copies of *Votes for Women* before the meeting. All went well. The stage was set, the Pankhursts had arrived. Sally, gratifyingly sold out of her penny magazine, rejoined the others.

Philippe, utterly unabashed by onlookers, took her hand. 'Walk with me.'

She shook her head. 'Don't be silly, Philippe. The meeting is about to start. The speeches –'

'I have a speech of my own.' He was utterly calm, apparently oblivious of other ears. 'Please, Sally. Come with me.'

Beneath the astonished gaze of his cousins she allowed him to lead her away from the benches that had been set before the makeshift stage. Firmly he tucked her arm into his, walked her away from the meeting and into the park.

'Philippe! – The meeting!' Sally tried to pull away. She had not spoken to him since Toby had told her that Philippe intended to return to Bruges.

He shook his head. They walked in silence for a few

minutes until they came to an empty bench, quiet beneath a tree. Far in the distance voices could be heard, and the background roar of the city's traffic. He brushed the bench with his handkerchief, gestured for her to sit. She perched uncomfortably on the edge of the slatted seat. He settled beside her.

'I want you to marry me.' The words were softly blunt, there was no trace of humour in his eyes.

She stared at him.

He waited equably, his dark eyes veiled.

'Are you – have you taken leave of your senses?' she asked when she had gathered enough breath.

'No. On the contrary. I've never been so sane. You surely aren't surprised?'

'I –' She stopped. 'Yes. I'm surprised.'

His face softened. Suddenly and terribly she wanted to touch him, to hold him, to tell him, over and over, how very much she loved him. She turned away from him. 'Philippe – you know it isn't possible.'

'But why not?' His puzzlement was genuine.

She stood up, walked straight-backed a few paces from him. 'It isn't possible,' she repeated.

'Why not?' He was behind her, with a hand upon her shoulder had swung her towards him. His young, suddenly vulnerable face was a blaze of emotion. It struck her to silence. 'Why not?' he asked more quietly.

She made a small, helpless gesture. 'Because –' she stopped.

He frowned. 'You don't love me?' The words were incredulous and under other circumstances would have warranted laughter by their almost childish disbelief.

She closed her eyes.

He caught her by the shoulders. 'Sally? You don't love me?'

She stood for a moment longer, containing pain, before she opened her eyes to meet his dark gaze. 'Love you? You fool. I love you more than I love my life,' she said simply.

He smiled. 'And I you. So – we marry –'

'Philippe, don't be ridiculous! – We *can't!*' She stared at him in helpless anger, turned from the bafflement in his eyes. 'Life isn't that simple.'

'But yes. It's simple. I love you. You love me.' He laughed a little, tentatively. 'We marry and – as you say in your stories – we live happily ever after –'

'No!'

His jaw tightened a little. 'But why not?'

She lifted her head. 'Because you don't know me.' Quiet anguish threaded her voice, 'Philippe, you don't *know* me. You don't know what I am –' she swallowed, '– what I have been –'

'Oh, yes. Of course I do.'

She stared at him, the slanting brows drawing together.

'Hannah has told me, and Ralph, because I asked.' His mouth drew down a little wryly, 'And Charlotte also, though I did not ask.' He lifted a shoulder in a shrug. 'What difference?'

'But –'

He stepped to her, caught her by the shoulders, pulled her quickly to him and before she could avoid it kissed her, with lingering and thorough strength. Somewhere in another world a woman's voice echoed through a loud hailer, and voices lifted in a cheer. She pulled away from him, breathless. He was smiling again, the loved and loving humour back in his eyes. 'My beautiful Sally – what you were ten years ago – five years ago – the day before yesterday – counts for nothing. It's what you are today that matters.'

'And what's that?' The husky break in her voice made the words all but inaudible, but he heard them, surely.

'You are the woman who – no matter what the world might say – no matter what my family or my cousins might say –' he laughed softly, '– no matter what you might say – I intend to marry.'

Chapter Twelve

I

'Sally – please –' Ben Patten turned at last from the window. He had conducted most of this openly difficult conversation with his back to her, despite which – creditably she felt – Sally had kept a tight rein on tongue and on temper, and said very little. 'I don't want you to misunderstand what I'm saying. I'm simply asking you to consider very carefully before you take such a –' he paused, still not looking at her, 'such a very serious decision.'

Once he had called her a fool, and she had not forgiven nor forgotten it. She lifted her chin. 'I'm neither stupid nor a child, Doctor Patten,' she said very evenly, and her use of the professional title was both deliberate and chill. 'Of course I've considered. Very carefully indeed. For several months, as a matter of fact.'

In a brusque movement that might have been impatience he lifted his head sharply and looked at last directly into her face. 'But –'

'Are you sure that you aren't trying to tell me –' she interrupted him, her voice very calm and very cool, her eyes direct, '– that – because of what you know of me – you don't consider me good enough to marry your wife's cousin?'

'Good God, no!' The words were shocked from him, the tone angry.

'What, then, exactly is it that you are trying to say?'

He made a small, oddly awkward gesture with his big

hands. 'I'm simply pointing out to you that you could be putting yourself in a very difficult situation – you hardly know Philippe, for heaven's sake – you don't know his family – his country – his language.'

'I can learn.'

She had waited, resisting her own needs and Philippe's pleadings, for six months. She had told herself – and Philippe – over and over again, all the things that Ben Patten was trying to tell her now. Why, then, did it anger her so to hear it from him? Patiently and with laughter Philippe had wooed her, had convinced her. She had faced and withstood Dan Dickson's hurt and anger, Toby's furious and flaring resentment, his bitter accusations – astonishing, unexpected and horribly hurtful – of selfishness and betrayal. Why then should she give a toss what Ben Patten thought? Why this seething resentment, this temptation to scream at him like a fishwife, to fly at his throat like any street urchin? She took a breath. 'Doctor Patten, there's something that I think you misunderstand.'

He lifted his brows a little in question.

'The truth is – Philippe, who loves me, has shown me – that there is no "difficult situation". The difficulties – if there ever were difficulties – are solved. Philippe asked me months ago to marry him. I said no. For all the reasons that you can think of.' She paused, 'And more, believe me.' Her distinctive voice was still low and controlled, but in the silence of the winter-darkened room it rang very clear and sure. She kept her eyes very steadily upon him. 'Philippe never believed in these – difficulties. And I have no doubt now that he has been right all along. My only regret is that I have wasted these past months. Philippe has spoken to his family. He has persuaded me. He has shown me there is no problem. Not for me. And most certainly not for you. In fact, if you'll forgive me,' the evenness of her tone quite flatly indicated, as she had intended, that his forgiveness or lack of it was of no moment whatsoever, 'it's none of your business. Please understand. I'm not asking for your permission to marry Philippe. I'm telling you. To give you time to get a replacement. I want neither advice nor warnings. You cannot tell me anything that I've not already told myself. But I love Philippe. He loves me. We are to be married in May. That's an end to it.'

The silence was absolute.

'I see.'

The naked antagonism between them was palpable; it glistened in the air like frost on a winter's morning, sharp and cold. They watched each other for a long, hostile moment.

'The children will miss you,' he said.

'And I them.'

'And Toby?'

Was it deliberate, she wondered, the needle probe of that name, the sure touching of the most tender spot? 'He's staying here. He's settled at school – more than settled. It would be too disruptive to take him to Belgium. He'll come for holidays, of course.'

– 'Sod your holidays,' the boy had said shaking, the angel's face white as death. 'Who wants your bloody holidays?' –

Ben nodded, then said, his voice all but expressionless. 'So – may I wish you both luck?'

She waited for a long moment before, calculated and cruel, in direct retaliation for the mention of Toby, she said, 'Philippe and I don't need luck, Doctor Patten. We have each other,' said it knowing instinctively the emptiness of this man's dedicated and duty-filled life.

He watched her as she walked, straight-backed and quiet to the door, stood for a long while after it had closed behind her, unmoving, his face disciplined to stillness. Then he moved to the sideboard, picked up the brandy bottle, poured a small quantity into a glass and with a swift, controlled movement tilted his head to drink. He hesitated, splashed some more into the glass, stood staring at it before, suddenly and explosively he slammed it onto the table and threw his head back, jaw clenched. 'Damn!' he said, harshly and very quietly. 'Damn and blast it!'

The few weeks which followed that provoking interview with Ben and led up to her marriage were far from calm. Within the suffragette movement the split between constitutionalists and militants widened and grew more bitter, coming to a head when the Pankhursts' followers took to the streets of London's fashionable West End in an orgy of stone-throwing and window-breaking that resulted in the arrest and imprisonment of more than two hundred women. In March, in a vain attempt to suppress the militant side of the movement the Government, which faced both a Home Rule crisis in Ireland that threatened to become civil war and more serious industrial unrest at home, had the active leadership arrested. Only Christabel Pankhurst by accidental good fortune escaped the net and, urged by her followers who did not want to see the militants entirely leaderless, fled to France. Amidst heated discussion both in and out of Parliament as to the right of the imprisoned women to be treated as political prisoners and not as common criminals, the Conciliation Bill, aimed at widening the franchise, came up once again in the House. When it became obvious, to the women's outrage, that the Bill, despite vague and veiled promises, still did not contain a clause on votes for women, the campaign, the arrests, the hunger strikes escalated. Hannah and Sally, avoiding arrest by the skin of their teeth and the good offices of a sympathetic young constable – of whom there were surprisingly many – continued in those weeks to organize and attend meetings and marches and to sell the now weekly *Votes for Women* despite the fact that often the magazine was so heavily censored that only the headlines remained to be read for a penny.

Dissatisfaction and worse simmered too on the industrial front. Early in the spring a wave of strikes by workers demanding a minimum national wage brought the machinery of British industry almost to a standstill again. By March the coalfields were crippled, and a month later the docks were out.

Sally, with an obstinate burst of courage that surprised herself, found herself knocking on the once more strikebound Dicksons' door on the first day of May, just two weeks before her wedding. With dogged determination she outfaced the cool hostility of her welcome. This was Josie's family; she could not – would not! – leave with their friendship spoiled after so long. Alone with Dan she came straight to the point. 'I've come to say sorry. Not for loving Philippe. I could never apologize for that, not even to you. But for hurting you. For not being strong enough to make you see long ago that – you and me – it could never have been right. I always said so.'

'Yes,' he said quietly. 'That you did.'

She eyed him, ready, despite her errand and her resolutions, to be defensive. 'You never listened.'

'No.' Dan Dickson was not – could never be – an unreasonable man. The first understandable disappointment and anger had long since eased enough to allow justice and good sense to have their say. But yet he was human enough not to make it too easy for her.

She struggled for a long moment, unable to find words. Then, 'I'm sorry, Dan,' she said simply, 'truly sorry. I wouldn't have hurt you for the world if I could have avoided it. But – I couldn't.'

He did not smile, but the broad, good-natured face relaxed a little. 'I know, girl. I know.'

'I couldn't bear to leave bad friends. We – we aren't, are we?'

He did not answer directly. He watched her for a moment, undisguised affection in his eyes. Then he laid a huge, gentle hand upon her narrow shoulder. 'Dad's got the kettle on. Stop for a cuppa before you go?'

So it was that they spent an hour so like old times that

Sally slipped into the discussion as if she had never been away, hearing the names she had grown up with in the back streets of these docklands – Keir Hardie, Tom Mann, Ben Tillet – and the arguments, and the injustices, were the same as well and it seemed to her, sadly, never likely to change for all the strikes and the endless talk of political change and revolution. They were good men, these three; but whoever, in this world of profit and loss, of employers and employed, of a political system geared for centuries to wealth and to ownership, would listen to them? She was pleased and touched when they agreed to attend the wedding. 'Josie would have wanted it,' Dan said calmly; and to that there was no answer.

And so the Dicksons were in the small, smoke-darkened stone church of St Mary-le-Grey to see Sally Smith wed Philippe van Damme: the bride – over her own half-hearted protests – gowned in ivory silk and cream lace; plain, beaming Hannah, endearingly homely in sprigged lavender her chief bridesmaid; and every little girl from the home – six of them no less – in pale pinks and blues, shining and garlanded, the best behaved train of brides-maids ever to grace a wedding. There too were all of the Pattens and the Bedfords and several of Philippe's relations including his mother and his sister, to both of whom, to Sally's delight, she had taken on the instant of meeting, a compliment they seemed to have little trouble in return-ing.

'But of course, my love!' Philippe had said, laughing as always. 'They are my family. You love me – of course you will love them! And I adore you – so of course they will too!'

'Philippe, Philippe! If only life could really be so simple!'

'But yes. It is.' He spread expressive, comical hands. 'Did you not know?'

He awaited her now, calmly and with a smile as, with nerves jumping like marionettes, she walked down the short aisle on Doctor Will's arm, every face in the small congregation turned to her. She had spent the day in an absolute and ridiculous daze, joking with Bron, laughing with Hannah, letting them dress her in her absurd finery, the cost of which might in the old days have kept her and Toby for several weeks, letting them deck her with ribbons and lace and fresh, lovely flowers: and all with the odd distraction of a pleasant dream. It could not, of course, be real. This could not be Sally Smith – was that even her name? – dressed like a princess, perfumed and coiffed, walking in May sunshine to be married in a flower-filled church to a man whose home she had never seen and whose native language she could not speak. Such things simply did not happen, except in the stories she so loved to tell.

Yet at the moment that she stepped to his side, at the moment he turned to look at her, took her hand in his, all feelings of unreality fell away. This was reality. The only reality. And she had never known such happiness in all of her life.

II

She often thought, after the world had gone mad and such happiness seemed indeed the stuff of fairy tales, that for the duration of her marriage that feeling never left her: that in those thirty happy months of life with Philippe and his family she experienced more happiness, more content-ment, more pure joy than do most people in a lifetime. And in that at least they were blessed. Until the time that the dreadful storm clouds of war that had been inexorably gathering on Europe's horizon for so long finally rolled across their lives and engulfed them, they were simply, utterly and blissfully happy. The arrival of their daughter on a blustery February night in 1913 only served to complete the charmed circle.

'She's just the prettiest little thing you've ever seen,'

Sally wrote in one of her frequent and regular letters to Hannah. 'And I'm not in the least bit biased, I promise you – Philippe and all the family think the same!'

Her correspondence with Hannah, and rather more sporadically with Toby, kept her well in touch with all that was happening in England and within the family. In the months before and after the birth of little Philippa – always and immediately known as Flip – Hannah wrote with blithe fervour of the escalation of militancy in the fight for the vote. To Sally, perhaps now distanced by rather more than the mere miles that lay between them, the resort to fire-raising and personal violence seemed rather more questionable than Hannah ever gave signs of thinking. Certainly she found herself wondering if such tactics might not prove counter-productive, losing rather more sympathy than they gained and simply supplying more ammunition to those who so loved to depict those women who were fighting for the right to vote as graceless and unnatural female hooligans; though she chuckled with real and appreciative amusement to hear how the flags on the royal Balmoral golf course had overnight mysteriously changed to white, purple and green, and had nothing but wholehearted admiration for the women who marched from Edinburgh to London to publicize the intolerable conditions suffered by women and children in the sweated industries of Britain's great cities. Hannah herself was still active and twice in those months was arrested and sent to prison, each time using the perilous weapon of the hunger strike to secure an early release. She never in her letters to Sally dwelt upon the painful terrorization of forcible feeding and its equally intolerable painful aftermath; but Sally knew enough of the barbaric practice to wonder at Hannah's courage in facing it not once but twice and in being ready in her obstinate dedication to her cause and her leaders, who themselves had suffered even more, to face it again. It was from an English newspaper and not from Hannah that she learned that a suffragette in the very week that Flip was born had nearly died from the savage treatment meted out to her whilst being forcibly fed, though in fact it was not until June of that year that in Emily Davison, who threw herself beneath the hooves of the King's horse at Epsom, the cause found itself mourning its first martyr.

Toby's letters were both less frequent and less intense. To Sally's inestimable relief he seemed to have overcome his antagonism towards her marriage, though she could not help noticing that he rarely mentioned or asked about Philippe or the baby. He had so far declined to visit them, but always with grace and never without a good excuse. He was studying for examinations. He had 'nabbed the lead' in the school play. He was captaining the middle school eleven, leading his house rugby team. His letters were short, entertaining, often flippant and, Sally was not slow to realize, gave away very little. But they came, and they made her smile, and that was enough. She herself wrote as often as she thought he would want – not, in fact, nearly often enough for her – and, taking her lead from him, kept her own letters short and light-hearted. His absence was the only flaw in a life that was happier than she could have believed possible. In Philippe she had found a lover in every sense of the word, their life together full of laughter, their love-making rich and fulfilling for them both. There were times when a glance, the mischievous flicker of an eye, the smallest, provocative movement of a head could bring them, laughing like children, to their lovely, spacious, pine-panelled room in the attics of the tall house in the Groenerei. Often, half dressed and impatient for each other they would make love fiercely and at once, brought in moments by the almost unbearable excitement of their loving to a climax that would leave them sprawled, exhausted, limbs entangled upon the wide bed. But there were other, quieter times, times of gentle questing, of tender, wanton teasing, of sheer erotic enjoyment, long, long, languorous moments when for them time seemed to stand still and life stretched before them for ever.

They knew, of course, that in all likelihood, at least in its present undisturbed and delightful form, it did not. They knew, too well, the perilous world in which they lived; knew it as in 1913 in the Balkans Serbia, Greece, Rumania and an all but exhausted Turkey united against Bulgaria, and armies marched; knew it as relations between Britain and Germany deteriorated further, each eyeing the other's possessions and claims with avid, grudging eyes, each watching the build up of the other's seagoing forces with distrust. But they were young and they were happy and it was hard to take such things too seriously. For Sally those years were doubly precious – for in her marriage she had found not only a much-loved husband and an adored daughter, but the mother she had never really known and a sister for good measure. Alice, calm, loving, warm-natured would have found it difficult to resist any girl her Philippe loved so wholeheartedly; to discover beneath Sally's self-sufficiency and composure a girl more than ready to be loved and mothered, almost heartbreakingly eager to become part of the family, was an unlooked-for pleasure. Annette too, as beguilingly uncomplicated as her brother, took to the newcomer as the sister she had never had. Flip's birth put the seal on a warm family circle that Sally had never in her wildest dreams thought to be a part of; only Toby's absence, the recollection of his bitterness at what he had plainly seen as her desertion of him, sometimes brought a shadow to the sunshine of her days.

Philippe, unerringly, knew it.

'It is time,' he said in the autumn of 1913, with Flip a little over six months old, 'for a visit to London, I think.' He picked up the plump, laughing baby and tossed her in the air, grinning at her shrieks of excited pleasure. 'We should show my English cousins something of the monster they unleashed into this world when they introduced us,

Sally my love. We should show them our so terrible daughter!'

Sally contemplated the visit with open and happy anticipation and more than a few private misgivings. She wanted very much to see Hannah, and Ralph, and Doctor Will and Bron, the children at the home. She wanted more than she could admit to herself to see and to talk to Toby, to explain as she had not been able to explain the year before why she had done what she had done, why she had been unable for this first and most important time to put him before all other things, as she had come to realize he had expected.

But she did not want to see or speak to Ben Patten. Perhaps surprisingly she did not want to flaunt her happiness, to prove how wrong he had been. She did not want to see him; and she did not want to analyse why she felt so strongly about it. She did not, in her happiness, want to face the nervy hostility his presence always wrought in her, the desire, almost, to hurt.

She did not have to. Almost the first information that was forthcoming upon their arrival at the Bear was that Ben Patten was not there. The visit had coincided with a conference in Brighton – ' blood poisoning, or something equally gruesome', Charlotte said casually, and Sally flinched – and he had felt himself unable to break the commitment.

Toby was as tall as she was.

She laughed delightedly to see him – tall, slender, fecklessly handsome, poised as a young prince, mischief and charm emanating from him in about equal measures. He responded to her hug with laughter, all strain apparently gone. It took all five days of the visit for her to realize that she had lost him. As, she reassured herself, she had been bound to lose him as he grew up, as she had virtually and knowingly assured herself of losing him when she had agreed to stay at the Bear, to let him follow a road down which she could not possibly follow. It had nothing to do with her marriage, nothing to do with her leaving him; he was altogether too intelligent, too flexible for that. He was growing into a young man anyone would delight in, and she was proud of him. That his mischief was perhaps a little harsher, his quick wit occasionally a little more sharply edged and hurtful, the wide blue eyes cooler and more calculating, was perfectly understandable under the circumstances. No one understood better than Sally Smith what it was to be an outsider.

It was the sight of Hannah that brought the real shock. Always raw-boned, now she was gaunt, her face like putty, her mouth sunken, the sockets of her eyes cavernous. Her clothes hung upon her like rags. There were sores about her nose and mouth, running and livid, brought about by the brutal application of forcible feeding tubes. Like other victims of the savage 'Cat and Mouse' Act, her nerves, no matter how she tried to control them, were raw.

'Cat and Mouse?' Sally asked faintly, hardly crediting what she saw.

Hannah smiled a little. 'You have to hand it to them. It's damn' clever. They got tired of having to let us go, you see. Of seeing us make fools of them. So – now if we go on hunger strike they wait until our health is seriously at risk and then they let us go. On humanitarian grounds.' She smiled again mirthlessly. 'And then they watch us, and as soon as we show signs of improvement they re-arrest us to finish our sentence. Then, of course, we go on hunger strike again. Three months could take a year to serve. Perhaps more –'

'But – that's *torture*!'

'Yes. That's exactly what it is.'

Ralph sat and watched her, his anguished heart in his painfully short-sighted eyes; and Hannah, the exasperated Sally noted, still did not see it.

She visited the Dicksons, taking Flip with her, and her welcome, perhaps because of the child, was remarkably warm. They were in good heart and greatly encouraged by

334

an Act of Parliament, recently passed, that restored the political rights of Unions, that had been taken from them in 1908.

'Now we'll see something,' Walter declared. 'With the Unions able to back Labour, now we'll see some change at last!'

Sally smiled and sipped her tea, and did not comment.

'You're looking lovely, girl,' Dan said as he bid her goodbye on the doorstep when Philippe came to pick her up in a motor car that had every urchin in the street gathered about it the moment it stopped. 'No need to ask if you're happy.'

'No. No need.' She lifted her face and kissed him gently, the baby's warm, fuzzy head between them.

She remembered, long, long after that day, the warmth of his smile and the pressure of his big, hard hand.

She was not sorry to get back to Bruges; to lovely Bruges with its bell towers and its flowers, its canals and parks, its pretty step-gabled houses and steep, sloping roofs. In the short time she had lived there she had become enchanted by the place. It was her home, and nothing bad could happen there.

'Shall we buy a phonograph like the one the Pattens have?' Philippe asked her, smiling – for the whole of the length of their visit Charlotte had played, upon the machine that had taken the place of the music box, the ragtime records that Peter had brought home on his last leave until every tinny note had seemed etched into Sally's eardrums.

She shook her head, pulled him to her so that he fell on to the bed on top of her. 'When would we ever have time to play it?'

It was a few short months later, in the following June, that Archduke Franz Ferdinand of Bosnia and his wife were assassinated at Sarajevo, and the witches' brew of Europe,

335

simmering for so long, began to come to the boil. In England few people believed that an event so insignificant, so ridiculously *foreign*, could possibly concern them. In Belgium, knowing better the intricacies of European ambitions, alliances and ententes, knowing but perhaps not wanting to acknowledge the terrible vulnerability of a tiny, undefended state caught between two hostile powers, the citizens were not so sure; although certainly the more sanguine were loud in their opinion that war on a large scale in Europe had become an impossibility, that any conflict between the great powers would be so mutually destructive, would cost so much in terms of human and material assets, that the very thought was inconceivable.

Meanwhile Austria–Hungary attacked Serbia in retaliation for the killings in Sarajevo; Russia – the third partner in the Triple Entente with France and Britain – mobilized her forces to come to Serbia's aid; whereupon, at the beginning of August Germany – in support of her own ally, Austria–Hungary – declared war on Russia, and as a matter of course on Russia's ally France; and in doing so served her own long-held intentions of gaining dominance in Europe.

And standing between France and the might of the German armies was tiny Belgium, her fragile neutrality guaranteed by the Treaty of London which had been signed in 1839; a treaty that, by the beginning of August 1914, it had become obvious the Central Powers had no intention of honouring.

III

'You don't have to go. Philippe – you don't have to go! You're a married man with a family. Please!' Sally's voice shook in her efforts to contain her fear, to prevent the rise of almost hysterical tears.

Philippe faced her, his long, dark face painfully set, no laughter now about that mobile mouth. 'Sally, I have to. You know it.'

'I know no such thing! But I'll tell you what I do know – I know a hopeless situation when I see one! I know that a handful of ill-trained men with next to no weapons isn't going to hold back the Germans!'

'Liège is holding out –'

'How long for? And then what? Philippe – the Belgian army can't stand up against hundreds of thousands of well-armed, well-trained men! You must know it.'

'We have to try. If we can hold them for long enough then Britain and France will come to our rescue. We can't just sit on our hands and wait. We have to fight. We have to defend Antwerp and Brussels. We have to hold on until help arrives.'

She shook her head helplessly. 'It's not possible. The French have their own battles to fight – the Germans have already invaded French territory!'

'But Britain is in the war now. Troops are landing, coming to help us.' Gently he took her by the shoulders and drew her to him, laying his cheek upon her hair. She clenched her eyes against tears, clinging to him. 'Sally, my love, I have to go. Belgium needs her men.'

'*We* need you!' She lifted her head fiercely, 'Philippe, we need you! Supposing the Germans come? Supposing they come and you aren't here? Oh –' she saw him flinch from that, and hated herself for it, '– oh, I'm sorry. I didn't mean to say that. It's just – oh, Philippe, I can't bear it. I can't. If you were hurt – killed!'

He rocked her gently, his eyes sombre, saying nothing. Three days before, the German Minister to Brussels had formally asked for free passage of German troops through Belgium to the French borders. Grimly, knowing well what would follow, the Belgian King and his Government had firmly refused. Within two days the German army had marched upon Liège, where now, stubbornly, bravely,

337

helplessly, the defenders still held out, though the end was in no doubt. The tiny Belgian army, ill-equipped, hopelessly outnumbered was falling back to the River Gette, in the hope of saving Antwerp and Brussels. Philippe van Damme was going to join them.

They stood in silence for a long time. Peaceful August sunshine streamed through the window, patterned the polished wooden floor. Far off a bell tolled musically. Through the open window came the sounds of children playing, a woman's voice called. Eyes closed, Sally held her husband to her, every fibre of her concentrated upon him; the feel of the light, long body against hers, the roughness of his jacket against her skin, the fresh, male smell of him, the steady beat of his heart beneath her cheek.

'I have to go, my love.'

'Yes.' She stood back, calm with the miserable calm of near despair. How could it have come to this? How could it? How could things so far away, so outside their control possibly be tearing them apart? How could it be that Philippe, lovely, laughing Philippe who had never to her knowledge been able to harm a fly, was leaving her, to maim or to be maimed, to kill or to be killed? 'It's madness,' she said quietly, 'utter madness.'

By the middle of the month Liège had fallen, and within a couple of days both Louvain and Brussels had been overrun, whilst King Albert and his Government retired to the entrenched position of Antwerp. Thanks to the brave and stubborn defence put up by the Belgians however, the French had managed to reach the Sambre river, and the British Expeditionary Force under Sir John French was at Mons.

There was no word from Philippe.

The household on the Groenerei lived in fear: fear of the day that German boots would march across the bridges and into their streets, fear for Philippe, fear for themselves. Protesting, but seeing the sense of it, Annette and her husband at the outbreak of hostilities had fled to cousins in France with some of the children, leaving Sally and Philippe's parents with perhaps half a dozen children and Flip. Philippe's father over the past months had been far from well; he had lost weight and his breath was short. Alice, through the other anxieties, watched him with worried eyes.

'You should go to England, my dear,' Anselm said to Sally. 'Now. Whilst it's still possible.'

'Not till Philippe gets back. I'm not going anywhere without him.'

'But Sally – the child.'

'I don't care! I won't go! Not without Philippe!'

Doggedly she refused to believe that anything could happen to him. She would know – surely, surely she would know? – if he had been hurt.

The tide of war swept on. The British after initial success were falling back from Mons, terribly mauled. The French had been unable to hold the German advance. Rumours of atrocities committed by German troops in Brussels began to seep through.

The way to the coast was still open.

'Father's right, Sally. You should leave while you still can,' Alice said gently, an arm about Flip, who leaned unaware at her knee, playing with the brightly coloured tapes of her pinafore.

'I can't. I can't! How could I leave you both? How could I go without Philippe? When he comes we'll all go – when he comes –'

But he did not come. Nor since he had left had they heard a single word from him. Yet still she clung to hope.

The streets of Bruges were thronged with refugees coming, going, simply sitting on their bundles on street corners staring into space with puzzled, unfocused eyes. With them came the stories – of women raped and children

339

murdered, of babies spitted upon bayonets, of burnings and beatings and unspeakable horrors.

The terrible month moved on, and the news was bad. French troops, still fighting in the brilliant uniforms of the Napoleonic era, their white-gloved officers and gallant, sabre-waving cavalry as vulnerable to the chattering machine-gun fire and the vicious bombardment of the German big guns as the bright lines of infantry, suffered terrible defeats and were everywhere in retreat. The British, in retreat from Mons, were forced as much by fatigue as anything to stand and fight at Le Cateau, an indecisive battle with heavy losses on both sides. All along the Western Front the allies were being pushed back, towards the sea and towards Paris.

In the last week of August the remnants of the Belgian army, still stubbornly holding on in Antwerp, attacked the enemy from the rear, a brave terrier snapping at the heels of a wolf.

A few days later, on the first day of September, Philippe came home to Bruges.

Sally recognized the ragged, blood-soaked, skeletal figure that leaned against the kitchen door more by instinct than by anything else. Certainly there was nothing here of the Philippe who had left just a little less than a month before. A bloody bandage encircled his head and obscured most of the left side of his face. Through the great ragged holes in his uniform more filthy bandages could be seen; his left arm was strapped awkwardly across his chest, the hand a shapeless lump of stained and dirty dressings. His skin was yellow, dry as old parchment, his dark eyes blazed with fever. How he had ever made his way to her she would never know.

'Philippe!' She was across the floor in a moment, stopped an arm's length from him, afraid to touch him, afraid of hurting him.

He held out his good hand, the long mouth moved in a shadow of the old smile. 'Sally.' His breathing was quick and shallow, and she could see the painful movement of it in his bandaged chest.

There was one moment of terrible silence. Then she caught his good hand in both of hers. 'Come and sit down. Careful – oh, my love be careful!'

Perfectly obviously every movement was agony. Fresh blood was seeping through the old dark stains.

'Alice!' She shrieked the name, not letting go of his hand, not letting her eyes stray from his poor, damaged face. 'Alice, quickly! Quickly!'

He sat at the kitchen table, gingerly upright, holding himself rigidly against the agony of the gaping hole in his side, his long fingers clamped painfully about Sally's hand.

'Dear God.' Alice paused for a split second by the door, her quiet words a shocked prayer, and at the same time a small thanks. She hurried forward. Like Sally she knew she could not embrace him. 'Sally – run for Doctor Brabant! Quickly!' Her voice was calm and crisp.

Sally hovered. 'But –'

'Hurry! Greta and I will get him to bed. Go and fetch the doctor. He'll come quicker for you than for one of the maids.' For though she had every faith in the soundness of her daughter-in-law's nerves Alice instinctively knew it would be best to have the girl out of the house for the next few minutes. Philippe's uniform, what was left of it, and the bandages beneath it were fused to his body by the blood that had seeped, and dried and seeped again. To get him to bed and prepare him for the doctor would be a harrowing task.

For a week Sally hardly slept, and when she did it was on a pallet on the floor next to Philippe in case he woke and needed her. For a week she watched him, nursed him, willed him to live, willed him to fight the infection that

341

rose in his body like fire and sapped the last of his strength, bled the last of his reserves. She did not know and did not care what was happening in the outside world, hardly listened to the news that the retreat of the Allies had been stopped at last as a French victory at Guise turned the German Front and, for the moment at least, ensured the safety of threatened Paris, nor to the reports that Zeppelins had bombed the civilian citizens of Antwerp. Her every thought, her every energy, was spent upon Philippe. He could not die – not after having made this effort to get back to her – it was unthinkable. She held his good hand as he slept, willing her own good health into his battered, failing body. She made frantic bargains with God. She talked lovingly and softly when he was awake – of Flip, of their life together, of the future they would make, somehow, somewhere, away from this madness, when he was better. She refused to see the signs of death upon him.

'She's killing herself,' Alice said, her own exhausted anguish tamped down, a damped furnace to burn slowly and deeply beneath a calm, still surface. 'She won't leave him. She won't let anyone else nurse him.'

'It's natural.' Her husband sat by the kitchen range, his kindly face drawn and grey. He reached for her hand, and she was shocked at the lack of strength in his grasp. He coughed a great deal now, and for the past two nights had passed the restless, sleepless hours sitting upright in the bedroom chair. 'And it's best for both of them. If anyone can save him it's Sally.'

Sadly, slowly, Alice shook her head.

Philippe lay in a cocoon of pain, his jaw smashed, his left hand mangled, his ribcage cracked and broken, a fist-sized hole in his left side from which pieces of shrapnel still worked themselves in a mess of blood and pus. He drifted sometimes in a welcome haze of delirium, more efficacious than any of the puny drugs that Doctor Brabant had to hand to tame the pain.

Until the morning, very early, when he woke and felt nothing.

The first faint light of the day crept through the shutters. The bells of the city tolled the hour. Sally slept in a chair beside him, her hair tumbled about her drawn face. His body was light, and still and totally painless. He tried to move the hand that lay near Sally's and could not. Faintly surprised but in no way alarmed, he closed his eyes for a moment, exhausted by so small an effort. When he opened them again she was watching him. As his eyes met hers she smiled, a smile of exhaustion, of indomitable love. The first rays of September sunshine danced upon the pine-panelled walls, lit her tousled hair to a halo about her face.

'Philippe?' Her voice seemed to come from very far away, a sweet whisper, calling him from the still, painless peace in which he lay. He smiled, or thought he did, once more tried to reach for her hand.

Correctly interpreting the faint movement of the long, pale, bony fingers that lay so helpless upon the bedspread, she reached a hand to cover his, and was shocked at its chill. 'Philippe?' she said again very steadily, very quietly, doggedly ignoring the sudden, fleet flash of fear that stopped her breath and twisted in her empty stomach like the claws of an animal. 'Philippe, my love?'

She leaned to him, clinging to his hand, her face close to his. The flesh of him had fallen away, the bones of his skull stood clear. He opened his eyes, remote, unfocused.

'No,' she said, the word a whisper in the silence. 'No, Philippe! Don't leave me. You can't leave me!' Fiercely she lifted the all but lifeless hand to her lips. The fingers uncurled, lifted to her face, then lost all strength. 'No,' she said again, 'You can't. *You can't.* Try Philippe, for Christ's sake, *try*. Don't give in! Think of Flip – think of me – of us – think of rowing on the canal – think of summer picnics – think of feeding the swans and the ducks on a Sunday morning – think of the son we don't yet have – *Philippe!*'

When Alice came half an hour later she was still sitting,

343

rigid and cold to the bone, holding the dead hand, her dry eyes empty. Even Alice's own tears could not, it seemed break through the icy shell of her grief and shock. For the two days until the hastily arranged funeral – not the first to be held lately in such circumstances in the stricken city – she barely spoke, cried not at all. Nor, despite her exhaustion, did she sleep. The light in the attic bedroom burned bright and steady all night. Even Flip, bemused and unhappy, though barely understanding what had happened, could not reach her.

'Sally, my love,' the grieving Alice, worried half to death at the effect Philippe's death had had upon his ailing father, yet still had time to watch and worry over her daughter-in-law, 'you must try to eat. For our sakes as well as your own. And – please – why won't you let Doctor Brabant prescribe something to make you sleep a little?'

'No.' Flatly Sally shook her head and then, more softly added, 'No, thank you. I – don't want to sleep.' Her eyes, as always now, were distant, as if they looked upon something she alone could see. Nothing roused her. In France the Government had left the still-threatened city of Paris for Bordeaux while the French armies stubbornly held out on the Marne. The British too were pushing cautiously forward. The battle lines that were to last for so long and to cost so dear were being drawn. Antwerp was being battered. Sally ignored it all. It was as if the living, breathing girl who had loved Philippe van Damme had been buried in his grave beside him, leaving to the world – to her daughter and to the family who loved her – an empty shell.

The shell cracked at last one sunny Sunday afternoon, a week after Philippe's death. Alice had persuaded Sally to accompany her and some of the children on a walk beside the canal. Sally, holding Flip's hand, walked in silence, the children tumbling and laughing about her like puppies. They fed the swans with the stale bread they had

344

brought for the purpose, and then turned back to cross the bridge. Lifting her head, looking into the setting sun, Sally stopped as if thunderstruck, her face alight.

Alice followed the direction of her gaze.

Standing upon the bridge, silhouetted against the sun, was a tall, limber young man in army uniform, his kit-bag resting upon the parapet of the bridge, his dark head bent to consult a piece of paper held in long, steady hands. For a moment Alice's own heart lurched, and then in sudden horror she said, 'No, Sally! Oh, no!'

Too late. Sally had dropped Flip's hand and was running, feet flying over the ground towards the young man. Alice saw him lift his head, watching the running girl with a pleasant, enquiring, slightly puzzled expression. Yards from him Sally stopped as if she had run into a brick wall. Alice too had picked up her skirts and started to run, hampered by the children, who tumbled and laughed beside her, loving this new game. 'Sally!'

The sound the girl made stopped her in her tracks. The young man, concerned now, stepped forward, hands outstretched. Sally backed away from him, warding him off, flinching from him, hiding her face. A couple passing across the bridge turned to look, puzzled. Sally cried out again, a terrible sound full of savage, almost animal misery. As Alice reached her, her knees buckled. Tears streamed down her face, tears that had been pent for too long, that would no longer be denied, tears that flowed now as if they would never stop. She raised hands that were crooked like fierce claws to her face, her whole body shuddering to the anguished, ugly sobs. The young man hovered, worried, confused – had he done something? – could he do something? Alice, her arms fast about the trembling, crying girl shook her head. 'She mistook you for someone.'

A flash of understanding darkened the pleasant face, and suddenly he looked older. 'I'm sorry.'

'Come, my love.' Gently Alice cradled the distraught

girl. 'Come along home.' And in her heart she thanked God for the healing tears.

Sally slept like the dead for twenty-four hours, woke up to a plate of broth and some thick, dark bread, then slept again. When she woke she was quiet, melancholy, but rational. Her first action was to seek out her daughter and to hug her, hard, her face pressed against the dark curls. When someone spoke she heard and she answered, her interest in the children was as it had always been. She took her turn in helping to nurse Philippe's father, who was now all but bedridden, talked with him of the news of the war. On the Marne the trenches had been dug, the big guns bedded in and the first hint of stalemate was in the air, the first signs of the terrible pattern of modern warfare as men died in their hundreds and then in their thousands taking a few square yards of land that in days, or even hours, would be lost again. In Belgium itself the pressure upon Antwerp was growing; it was becoming obvious that the gallant and beleaguered young King even with help from his French Allies could not hold out for much longer. Then the defensive dam would burst and the muddy, destructive waters of war would be upon them. But for now the way to the coast was still clear and a steady stream of refugees was using it, fleeing towards Holland, France, England.

'Go while you can, Sally – you and Flip – please!'

But Sally's loyalties were divided, her mind and her will still not recovered from the virtual breakdown caused by Philippe's death. She did not want to leave Philippe's parents, who had become like a mother and father to her. She did not want to embark on such a perilous journey alone, with the child – who knew what might happen, or what they might be called upon to face? Yet as steadily as the flood of refugees grew, so grew the brutal stories of atrocities committed by an army determined to terrify the population into submission, of barbarities that caused

346

the adults' eyes to meet above the heads of the innocent children in horror. If the enemy came to Bruges – and who could doubt that they would – then such things could happen here. And Sally was English.

'But – so are you!' she said in fierce concern to Alice.

Alice shook her head, oddly tranquil. 'I'm old. What would they want with me? But you – you should go. While you can.'

On 25 September the Germans launched a massive bombardment upon Antwerp, apparently intent upon reducing the rebel city to rubble, obviously the forerunner to the final attack that would lay the way open to the coast. And still, as the roads clogged with people fleeing from the vicious fighting, Sally vacillated.

On the day that she opened the kitchen door to a peremptory knock and saw a uniformed man standing upon Alice's scrubbed white doorstep she nearly fainted with fright. Too late, then, they had come. It was several full, speechless seconds before her wits informed her that the uniform was not of the dreaded field grey but the more familiar and friendly British khaki. And – most astonishing of all – the square, craggy face beneath the neat peaked cap was no stranger's.

She could not believe her eyes. 'Ben,' she said faintly, 'Ben Patten. It can't be! Wh – what in the world are you doing here?'

The shock he had felt at the sight of her was well if not easily concealed. He half-smiled, sketched a very vaguely military salute. 'Lord only knows how it happened but I seem to find myself – at least temporarily IC Refugees, Bruges,' he said, neatly removing his cap, tucking it under his arm, stepping past her into the warm, clean kitchen. 'While it lasts, I don't suppose you know anyone who could do with a lift back to Blighty?'

Chapter Thirteen

I

The way to the North Sea – and to freedom – was still open, though how long it would remain so, as Ben Patten soberly pointed out, God alone knew. Sooner or later – and of the two any realist would say that sooner was the more probable – Antwerp was bound to fall, and the tide of war would flood to the coast, cutting off all hope of escape.

'It's difficult enough now. The roads are jammed with refugees and with troops. Your only chance is to leave at once. It'll soon be impossible.' Ben sat at the kitchen table sipping weak coffee, his eyes on Sally's gaunt face.

Alice watched them both. 'Could you take the children?' she asked Ben quietly.

'How many?'

'Ten. Aged between five and twelve. And there's Philippa, of course.'

He nodded. 'I can get hold of a motor truck. As a matter of fact I've already arranged it, more or less. I'm stopping over at Zeebrugge for a couple of days. Troop ships are unloading there every day. I can get you all berths on the return trip.'

Alice shook her head, gently. 'Sally and the children, yes. But – Anselm and I will stay.' She held up a swift hand as both Sally and Ben opened their mouths to protest. 'I'm sorry, but no – it's no use to argue. It would kill him, I think, the journey. And anyway – this is our home. All we have is here. How can we leave it to – to them? If they come, they come. We are old. Why should they harm us?'

Ben pushed his chair away from the table. 'Anselm's unwell?'

Alice nodded.

Ben stood up. 'You'll let me take a look at him?'

'Of course. I had hoped that you would.'

Sally sat alone in the big, quiet kitchen. Somewhere in the tall house a child's voice called. And in the distance something rumbled in the air, like the faintest, menacing echo of thunder. She tilted her head, listening, but it had died; or perhaps she had imagined it?

She got to her feet and walked, wearily restless, to the shining black kitchen range upon which bubbled a large pot of vegetable stew. It had been a full week since they had been able to buy meat. She lifted the lid, stirred the savoury liquid, sat down again at the table, her chin resting on her hands.

Ben had come.

She could not believe it.

She closed her eyes for a moment. She was tired; desperately, painfully, defeatedly tired. Her body and her brain ached with deadly fatigue – as they ached with desolation and grief at the brutal loss of Philippe. If he had been alive she would not be sitting here like a spineless doll waiting to be told what to do. She would, she knew, have been up and active, grasping with both hands the chance for them all to escape – organizing, scolding, urging them all to haste.

If Philippe had been here.

She opened her hands and, bowing her head, covered her face. Not for the first time the shattering sense of loss washed over her. She would never see him again. Never hear his voice. Never wake to the touch of his hands, the feel of his long, limber body lying against hers. Yet it was a terrible hurt that in her head and in her heart, in the deepest recesses of her body, he still lived. She could see him, hear him, feel him. She could see the long, mobile, kindly face, hear his laughter – oh yes, she would always hear that – feel the subtle pleasures wrought by his hands and body upon hers.

She threw back her head, teeth gritted, glaring determinedly at the whitewashed ceiling, battling tired, despairing tears. If she started to cry again she truly feared she might never stop.

At least Ben had come. Somehow he would get them all back to England, where Flip would be safe. For of course they must all go – she could not leave Alice and her ailing husband to fend for themselves in this uncertain and dangerous world at war. Ben would arrange it. He'd get them all home. That was what he had come for – he had already admitted under Alice's shrewd questioning that this convenient stopover at Zeebrugge had been contrived with it in mind. He had not of course known about Philippe.

Philippe.

When Ben and Alice returned ten minutes later Sally was asleep, her head pillowed on her arms, tears streaking her face.

Alice tiptoed past her to the stove to check on the stew. 'It's nearly the children's dinner time, but it won't hurt them to wait a while longer. Don't wake her, Ben. She's had little enough sleep since –'

But quiet as her voice had been it penetrated the girl's shallow slumber. She lifted her head jerkily. She looked truly dreadful; was, Ben thought, almost unrecognizable as the girl he had known. The flesh had fallen from her always thin face, her eyes were sunken into bruised hollows that were like caverns. The small, neat scar on her mouth, the gash that he himself had stitched in another time – another life – stood white against her sallow skin. She shook her head a little like a tired, confused child. And Ben flinched to see the naked pain in her eyes as, waking, she remembered again.

He sat down very briskly at the table. 'Alice is right, I'm afraid,' he said, brusque and capable, not looking at Sally, 'Anselm's health won't withstand the journey to England. So –' he lifted opaque eyes to Sally's shadowed, impassive face, '– it's just you and the children. You have twenty-four hours. I'm going back to Zeebrugge now, to arrange the transport. I'll be back with a truck sometime early tomorrow afternoon.'

Sally was staring at him. Then she turned to look at the woman who had been so much a mother to her – who had been truly mother to the man she had loved. 'Alice?'

Alice faced her with tranquil strength, shook her head. 'It's no good, my dear. I have quite made up my mind. To move Anselm would probably be to kill him. This is our home: Here we will stay.'

'Then I'll stay too.'

'No!' It was Ben; faint, almost angry colour creeping into the taut skin about his cheekbones. 'I'm sorry, Sally, but that isn't an option. You have to come – you and little Philippa and the other children.'

'Why?' Sally's mouth had set in the familiar, stubborn line.

'Why? Sally, for the love of God, are you mad? Have you heard just half the stories that have come out of Liège, of Brussels?'

'Of course I have. But –'

'But nothing!' He was, inexplicably she thought, as fiercely angry as she had ever seen him, 'You and the children are getting out now, while you can. Who the hell knows what might happen? Do you want to find yourself in the middle of a battlefield, for Christ's sake? Supposing the Belgian army decided to make a stand in Bruges? God, girl, have you taken leave of your senses? Stay? You're coming home. If I have to tie you hand and foot and put you in a sack to get you there!' In his glowering belligerence he looked capable of carrying out the threat.

Sally glared back.

Alice moved quietly to the girl, put a hand on her shoulder. 'Sally, my dear – for me, please, and for Philippe – do as Ben says. If Philippe were here he would say the same. You know it.'

Sally covered the hand that rested upon her shoulder with her own and bowed her head.

Ben's chair scraped loudly on the tiled floor as he stood up, reaching for his hat and cane that lay upon the table. 'That's settled then. Early tomorrow afternoon.' His voice was clipped and clear. 'A small bag each is all, I'm afraid – each child will have to carry his own, so don't overload them.' He lifted his head, as did the two women, listening to the distant, thunderous rumble that had shifted the china upon the big old dresser.

'Guns,' he said.

In the distance they growled, infinitely menacing.

He turned to Sally. 'You'll be ready?'

'Yes. I'll be ready.'

It was like trying to organize a barrowload of monkeys. For most of the youngsters the whole thing was a game, and they saw no reason not to play it to the full. Each was allowed to take a favourite toy – Alice's idea – and a change of clothes. The dithering of a little girl who could not make up her mind between her baby doll and her teddy bear, the boisterous hooliganism of the older boys who tore about the house taking full advantage of the fascinating disorderly state of affairs that prevailed, the tears of a child who could not bear to leave a much-thumbed sleeping blanket almost drove Sally to distraction. As often as she organized half a dozen of her charges into some semblance of order so the other four or five confounded her, disappearing, fighting over the ownership of some cherished toy, snatching each other's bags, tossing them about like so many footballs. By the time the army truck that Ben had requisitioned turned the corner of the street she was at her wits' end; but at least the children were fed, packed and ready – more than ready most of them – for the adventure.

Thankfully she let Ben and the driver, a cheerful Cockney with a grin as cheeky as any of the children's, take charge of the task of loading the youngsters and their belongings and the provisions for the journey, whilst she and Philippa took five quiet minutes in the kitchen to say goodbye to Alice and Anselm, who, face and body gaunt and thin, an unhealthily bright flush upon his sharp cheekbones, was tucked into an armchair beside the stove. Alice and Sally clung to each other for a long, quiet time, Sally's head bowed upon the older woman's shoulder. A mildly tearful Philippa, affected by the adults' emotions, had climbed on to her grandfather's lap, where she sat sucking her thumb.

'Take great care of yourselves – both of you –' Sally looked from one to the other. Nothing could keep the harsh note of fear and grief from her husky voice. She stopped. What in God's name was there to say? She felt as if she were abandoning them; who knew when – or even if – they would see each other again? 'Alice –'

With the instinct of a mother Alice divined what she was about to say and interrupted. 'No! You must go, Sally. We've been through it all – you know it as well as I. For us. For Philippe. For Flip. For yourself. Take this chance of safety. We'll be together again, one day. I promise you.' Nothing in her steady voice betrayed her own uncertainty, her deadly fear, her conviction that in fact she would never see Sally or the children again. She moved to Anselm's side, took his hand in hers, smiling calmly. 'We'll be all right. Even if the Germans do come – why should they harm us?' She put her hand in the pocket of her apron, pulled out a long white envelope. 'Take this, my dear –'

'What is it?'

'A letter. To our solicitor in London. The address is on the envelope. The letter releases an income – a small one, but adequate, I hope – from our London funds to you.' She held up a hand as Sally opened her mouth to protest. 'We insist. You are our dear daughter, Philippa our grand-daughter. What else should we do?'

'Sally?' Ben appeared at the door, cap in hand, 'We're ready.'

Sally hesitated for one more brief moment, then she took the envelope, stooped quickly to kiss Anselm and to swing Philippa from his lap to her accustomed place astride her hip, smiled blindly through her tears at Alice and without a word followed Ben out into the street.

The children, remarkably docile, were sitting as if at a Sunday School treat upon two benches that ran down the sides of the open truck. A space had been left for Sally and Philippa on the end nearest to the open window that let on to the driver's cabin. Ben handed her aboard, lifting her as if she had been a child herself, handing Philippa up to her. One of the older boys fidgeted a little, pushing his neighbour. Ben's big hand fastened into the lad's thick curly hair, the gesture casual and nowhere near as rough as it looked. Ben shook his head warningly, his eyes crinkling into a smile. The boy grinned back. Sally, watching, seeing too the smiles on the faces of the other children, the way in which even the most excitable of them seemed to have calmed to good behaviour, was struck as she had been before by the man's immediate rapport with children, even youngsters such as these whose language he did not speak. 'Behave yourself, Willi,' she said to the boy in Flemish. 'See – Mother Alice has come to say goodbye. Wave to her, children.'

Alice had appeared, smiling dauntlessly, at the door of the house. The little girl sitting next to Sally sniffed loudly. Sally, smiling as brightly and as stubbornly as Alice herself, waved vigorously. Ben had swung himself into the driver's cabin beside Private Benson, the cheerful driver. The engine grumbled noisily into life. The truck moved slowly, bumping on the cobbled street. Alice's hand was still lifted. Sally smiled until her face ached. 'Wave children – wave to Mother Alice.' And then the truck turned a corner, and the tall, handsome house on the Groenerei was gone. Neatly and carefully, her face frozen into a mask of a smile, Sally settled herself upon the bench, fussed with Philippa on her lap. The truck rolled on to a bridge, bumping and swaying. The children swayed with it, exaggerating the movement, shrieking rowdily. The little girl next to Sally was in tears. Unable for the moment to speak, Sally tucked a comforting arm about her.

Ten minutes later the truck rolled out of the city and on to the coast road. Despite all that Ben had said it was only then, with a force that jolted her, that Sally was struck by the reality of the situation. The road was bedlam. A great river of refugees flooded it, heading for the coast: men, women, children, their belongings in bags and bundles, cases, prams and carts. Women dragged tired children, men carried them upon their shoulders. Everyone, down to the smallest toddling child carried some kind of bundle or pushed some wheeled contraption piled high with household goods. Dogs barked and snapped at heels, families sat wearily by the wayside, resting feet that were as often as not wrapped in rags. The truck in which Sally and the children travelled could not itself move at much more than walking pace. People lifted their heads as they passed, watching with lacklustre, envious eyes. Women held out babies and small children towards Sally, pleading for a lift.

'Ben –' Sally said through the open window.

Ben turned, shaking his head. 'No, Sally. Absolutely not. If we take one we'll be overwhelmed.'

'But – we have room –'

'No.' The word was utterly uncompromising. Sally subsided, lifted her eyes to the wide, flat Flanders countryside, trying to ignore the desperation in the eyes that followed the truck's progress. One or two other motor vehicles were on the road but most of the wheeled traffic was horsedrawn – farm carts, pony traps, delivery wagons of varying kinds, all packed with people, all overflowing with the goods and chattels of their wrecked and abandoned homes.

A red October sun gleamed in a sky that was heavy with

autumn mist. The still, flat lands on either side of the road were wreathed too in wisps of vapour, the occasional clump of trees standing like an island from a misty sea. Canals and drainage channels gleamed in the low-slanting sunshine. The columns of people tramped on, bowed beneath their loads, hardly looking up as the truck rumbled past them. Sally watched a young couple, the girl obviously far gone in pregnancy, her young husband supporting her, his arm about her shoulders, their belongings in a bundle upon his other shoulder. As she watched the girl stumbled on the uneven cobblestones, almost falling, and in his effort to save her the young man dropped the bundle, spilling its meagre contents on to the road. People coming from behind stepped over and around or simply kicked their way through the pots, pans, blankets and broken teacups without pausing in their steps. No one stopped to offer help.

Sally looked away.

A slow hour went by, and the best part of another. Under normal circumstances they would have been at the port by now; as things stood it was anyone's guess how long it might take. She opened the basket Alice had packed, handed out bread and cheese, apples and biscuits. Even the most fractious of the children were subdued and tired of the bruising, bumping and swaying of the truck. At one stop Ben swung down out of the driving cab and came to join them in the body of the truck, a small gesture of moral support for which Sally was more grateful than she would have cared to admit. Philippa was asleep on her lap, lulled by the movement and the feel of her mother's firm arms about her. Sally's left arm was numb beneath the weight. The little girl beside her was sleeping too, hunched uncomfortably against Sally's side. She shifted a little, trying to ease her own cramped joints and aching back without disturbing the children.

'Not long now,' Ben said gently. 'We'll soon be there.'

There was army traffic on the road now, some of it ploughing with some considerable difficulty in the opposite direction to the seemingly endless stream of refugees. Convoys of trucks, horse-drawn carts and guns, the occasional column of infantry, even a small band of cavalry, harness jingling, the young officer at its head jauntily saluting Ben as they passed.

Ben watched them, his slate dark eyes unreadable, his head shaking imperceptibly.

'What?' Sally asked.

He turned, and she saw real pain in his eyes. 'Two months ago that lad was on the polo field – or training his father's favourite hunter for the winter –' He stopped suddenly alert, lifting his head, listening.

Sally had heard it too, over the buzz and racket of the road. Distantly an explosion, and then another.

'What is it?'

'Wait!' Ben was frowning ferociously, concentrating, trying to listen. Then, suddenly and urgently, he was at the open window that led into the driver's cabin, his hand on Private Benson's bulky shoulder. 'Stop!'

'What? Here? But sir –!'

'Stop, I say!'

Sally stared at him. She was aware of a stir of unease around them. People were stumbling to a halt, pointing. There was an odd noise in the air, a thin droning, some kind of engine – there came the crunch of another explosion, much nearer. 'What – what is it?'

'Stop, damn you!'

'I'm trying, sir – it's the people –' Private Benson was steering the truck on to the verge.

'Out!' Ben snapped, hauling the child closest to him to her feet and dumping her, shrieking, over the side on to the grass, 'Get in the ditch!'

'Ben, what on earth are you –?'

'*Out!*' he roared.

The buzzing was louder. Excitedly Willi stood up, pointing. 'Look – an aeroplane!'

Ben caught him by the waist, swung him over the side of the truck. 'Down!'

As if to add emphasis to his words there was the bone-shaking crump of another explosion. This time Sally saw it. Perhaps a mile along the crowded road the world erupted. Cobblestones, a cartwheel, something that looked for all the world like a broken doll, were hurled into the air. Dust drifted across the sun. Around them people were screaming, standing in petrified terror as the small plane swooped and banked and turned towards them.

'God Almighty!' Sally was out of the truck in a moment, the squalling Philippa under one arm. She dumped the child unceremoniously in the ditch next to Willi – 'Hold on to her!' – and then was back at the truck helping Ben with the others. 'Quickly, quickly! Into the ditch. Put your heads down! Cover them with your arms.' Several children were crying, terrified. The plane swooped. Sally, glancing up, could quite clearly see the figure of the pilot in the small cockpit. Even in the heat and horror of the moment she had time to register the wave of hatred that swept over her at the sight of him. 'Bastard!' she muttered viciously under her breath, 'murdering bastard!' and was abashed to catch the quick flash of Ben's teeth as he almost threw the last of the children into her waiting arms.

The plane was almost upon them. Still holding the child she leapt for the ditch, flinging herself down upon her face, her body curled about that of the squirming, crying child. A moment later Ben was beside her, his arm across her shoulders, forcing her face into the ground, the protective weight of him pressing the breath from her lungs. There was a strange, still moment of suspense and then reverberations of the explosion as the pilot tossed the last of his hand grenades on to the crowded road was all around them, rupturing the air, erupting through the ground upon which they lay. Men, women and children were screaming. A horse bellowed its agony. Dirt and stones rained down on them as they lay. Somewhere near a woman shrieked and shrieked again.

Sally felt Ben's weight lift from her. Dazed she sat up. 'Philippa?'

'Mama!' A small whirlwind hit her, filthy, sobbing, thoroughly frightened, but whole.

'Flippy! Oh – Flippy!' Sally buried her face in the child's dirty hair, her eyes clenched tight against tears, her arms crushing the child to her. The road was chaos. The grenade had fallen perhaps fifty yards from them, opening a small crater in the road beside which a disembowelled horse lay still screaming its agony. Men and women were wandering, dazed and bleeding, or sitting in shocked silence. Ben was on his feet and, having ascertained that his own party was unscathed, had grabbed his bag from the cabin of the truck and was in amongst the wounded, calling over his shoulder to Sally as he went.

'Leave the children with Private Benson. Come on – I need you to translate.'

She followed him numbly, having handed the clinging Philippa into the strong arms of Private Benson. Almost as mindless with shock as were the victims of the explosion she helped Ben organize the wounded, translating for him as he cleaned and bound wounds as best as he could, splinted arms and legs with anything to hand. Within minutes both he and she were as covered in blood as any of the casualties. The horse had stopped screaming. A strange stillness had fallen, broken only by the quiet murmur of voices, the stifled sobbing of a woman, the occasional wail of a child.

'Ben –' Sally touched his arm. He finished tying a bandage, looked up. She nodded towards the side of the road, very close to where, miraculously, all of their own party of youngsters were sitting, cowed and quiet but unhurt, with Private Benson. A young woman nursing a baby sat, white-faced, her arm about a little boy of perhaps four or five, a sturdy, well-built little fellow clothed warmly and well, a tumble of fair curls falling on to his still babyish forehead as his head lolled in his mother's lap.

Sally looked in anguish at Ben.

Ben stood up, his face a mask.

Together they walked towards the woman. With the composure of shock she watched them approach, a look of polite enquiry on her face.

'The child is dead,' Ben said quietly.

'Yes,' Sally's whisper was barely audible. They reached the woman. Sally knelt by her. 'May I take the baby?' she asked gently in Flemish. 'I'll hold her for you.'

The girl smiled sweetly. She was very fair, her face pointed as an elf's. 'Thank you, but no. I don't want to wake her.'

''Madam –' Ben began, then stopped helplessly. As the woman moved to look up at him the dead child's head shifted in terrible travesty of life. There was no sign of wound, no blood. The woman's small hand rested firmly upon his shoulder, as it would upon that of a sleeping child.

Very gently Ben reached for her hand. The baby cried a little. As Ben lifted the mother's hand the body of the little boy slithered forwards, falling into the ditch.

The girl sat rigid for a moment, staring at the crumpled body of her merry, handsome son, her face suddenly blank with horror and grief. Then she screamed. Again and again she screamed, wordless, mindless, terrible.

Sally, heart and mind raked raw by the awful sound, the look in the girl's eyes, put her arms about her, baby and all, and drew her close, the screams that convulsed the slim body muffled against her breast.

Ben picked up the dead child, laid him gently upon the ground. His body was whole, his face peaceful. He might indeed have been asleep.

Sally, tears running down her face, rocked the screaming girl in her arms, head thrown back. 'Jesus Christ,' she said to the livid, dust-filled, sun-reddened sky. 'Sweet Jesus Christ!' and was not herself sure if she prayed or cursed.

II

The modern seaport of Zeebrugge was a teeming ant heap of frantic activity. Uniforms were everywhere; British, Belgian, some French. By the boat-load the British arrived, by the truck and train-load, on foot and on horseback they left, moving forward into the flat, fertile farmlands of Flanders, across which the German armies and armaments were advancing. The town was thronged too with refugees, every transport office besieged by them, every inch of shelter taken, every pawnbroker and market stall doing brisk business in barter.

Sally, two precious loaves of bread and a large hunk of cheese clutched to her breast in a paper bag, fought her way through the crowded streets back towards the warehouse where Ben had managed to billet her and the children for the two days and nights they had been in the town. He had been irritated that she had refused to take the first berths for England he had found for them; but how could she have left Marie-Clare to face the terrible ordeal of burying her tiny son alone? With the same calm obstinacy with which she had insisted over Ben's – she suspected half-hearted – protests that the woman, her baby and her dead child should join them after the air attack she had adamantly refused to take the first empty troop-ship home and abandon them. Marie-Clare quite obviously had been in no fit state to cope. Sally it had been, with Ben's help, who had arranged the pathetic and hasty little funeral, she and Marie-Clare the only mourners at the brief and somehow heartless little ceremony. Small, innocent Charles Ven-nigen had not been the first child to be buried so in Zeebrugge since the flood of refugees began to pour into the town. Sally supposed, grimly, that he would not be the last.

She pushed her way through the crowds at the dockside, thankful that she had Ben to rely on in the matter of transport back to England. Queues of people jostled and pushed, faces drawn and pale with worry, lack of sleep, lack of food. There seemed to Sally to be an even greater urgency in the air, a frightened thread of panic no less infectious for being subdued. She hurried her steps. In the small warehouse where truckle beds had been set up for her and the children it was comparatively quiet. Marie-Clare, her baby as always tucked into the crook of one arm, had a group of the smaller children in one corner; packing cases their improvised tables and chairs, they were playing some kind of game, relaxed and amazingly cheerful. In the past twenty-four hours Marie-Clare's open, loving nature had won them over entirely. Sally threw her a grateful smile. The girl smiled back, her heart in her eyes. If Sally van Damme had asked her to walk through fire Marie-Clare Vennigen would have done it with that same smile.

'Sally —'

Sally turned. Ben was at the door, beckoning. His face was grim. She lay the bread and cheese upon the table, called to one of the bigger boys. 'Albert — you and Willi share this out. Equal portions for everyone, mind. Marie-Clare will be watching you!' She had long since discovered that the best way to harness the subversive instincts of these two was to give them responsibility. With a task to do they were two eager pairs of hands, two active and clever minds. Idle they were devils. She watched the job started before joining Ben. 'What is it?'

'Antwerp's fallen.'

They stood in silence for a moment.

'So. Poor Belgium is lost,' Sally said very quietly.

'Yes.' His voice was soft. She glanced at him and quickly away, almost afraid of the compassion she saw in his face. She had not expected him to understand how much Philippe's country — her country for such a little, happy while — meant to her, how hard a blow it was to think of what would happen to it now. She looked down at her hands, which were clasped tightly in front of her.

What of Alice? What of Anselm? What of dear, beautiful Bruges?

She blinked rapidly, raised her head.

'I've berths for you at dawn tomorrow,' he said, and then, with a small twitch of the lips that could hardly be called a smile, 'I do suppose you're ready to take them? There are no more lame ducks to be helped, no more matters more urgent than safety?'

She grinned a little and shook her head. 'Thank you.' Suddenly and overwhelmingly she longed to be gone, to be out of this peril, to be in a land unthreatened by invasion. To be home.

'Marie-Clare and the baby will be going with you,' he said, absurdly casually.

That came closer to reducing her to tears than anything else. 'Oh – Ben! Thank you. Thank you!' Without a moment's thought she threw her arms about him, hugging him hard, lifted her face to his and kissed his taut, rough cheek. Then stood back, face flaming. 'I'll –' the words stumbled on her tongue, 'I'll go and tell her –'

His answering grin was warm, quick, utterly unembarrassed, almost boyish. 'Dinner tonight,' he said briskly.

Half turned from him she stopped, staring blankly. 'What?'

He laughed, and she flushed again, poppy bright, mortified at her own unseemly brusqueness.

'Dinner,' he repeated. 'This evening. Well – hardly dinner, but a bite to eat and a glass of wine in a little café I know. The patron owes me a favour or two. I won't keep you up late, I promise.'

'But –'

'Marie-Clare and those devious lieutenants of yours will give an eye to the children. I'll pick you up at seven.' Not waiting for her reply, he touched his stick to his cap and turned on his heels.

She watched him go, watched the tall, broad-shouldered figure through the crowds until he disappeared. Stood for a long moment her hand still upon the open door, her eyes distant and thoughtful before she turned back to the children.

'What will happen, do you think? Will it be over by Christmas as everyone seems to think?' Sally twirled her wine glass a little, watching the play of light in the rich, dark depths, then lifted her eyes to Ben's face, openly studying the square, strong lines of it.

He shook his head, taking a breath that might have been a sigh. 'No. Not this Christmas – possibly not next.'

She nodded, unsurprised. 'It's all so stupid, isn't it?' she asked at last softly, her eyes roaming about the crowded, smoky room. Young men in uniform stood at the bar, sat on and about the oilcloth-covered tables, drinking, laughing, smoking. One or two girls clung to khaki-clad arms or draped themselves about khaki-clad shoulders. In the corner a piano played, off key, fighting a losing battle in the hubbub of noise. 'Look at them all.' She nibbled her lip, turned a suddenly despairing face to him, 'It's – it's as if they think it's some kind of game?'

He nodded.

'And somewhere', she jerked her head at the window, 'out there – just a few score miles away there are other women's sons – other women's husbands – doing the same thing.'

Following her line of thought exactly he nodded wryly. 'Except that their mothers, sisters, wives are in Berlin, or Frankfurt –'

'Yes. And for what? Ben – what's it all about?' She was truly puzzled.

He shrugged.

She picked up her glass and with a quick movement drained it. 'Sorry. I didn't mean to get maudlin.'

'You aren't.' Ben picked up the empty bottle, lifted it and, catching the eye of the portly man who was serving at the tables, indicated his desire for another.

'Ben!' Sally could not suppress sudden laughter. 'What are you doing? We've already drunk a whole bottle!'

'And we are now about to drink another. Hand over that glass.' He glanced at her as he poured the wine. Gaunt still, her mouth too ready to fall into the straight line of unhappiness, yet she looked better than the dispirited scarecrow the sight of whom had so shocked him in Bruges. Her eyes were alive again, less inward looking. Her smile was natural.

Almost as if picking the thought from his mind Sally, with the glass he had pushed over to her, toasted him half smiling, her eyes sad. 'To you, Ben. With – oh, so many! – thanks. I don't know what I would have done if you hadn't come. I wasn't –' she stopped for a moment, her gaze dropping to the richly glinting wine, 'wasn't myself,' she finished, steadily enough.

The small silence was deep and warm with sympathy. 'I'm sorry,' Ben said at last without embarrassment, 'very sorry. About Philippe.'

'Yes.' Her eyes clung a little longer to the glimmering, impersonal liquid, then she looked at him. 'You were wrong.' Her voice was quiet, her eyes deadly serious.

'Yes. I know.'

'But – you meant it for the best, I think.'

His lips twitched a little. 'Another small good intention to pave the road to hell. Yes. I did.'

She nodded. Sipped her wine. Wondered a little uneasily at the odd, not unpleasant sensation that came as the liquid slipped warm and smooth down her throat. 'Well –' she had somehow, inexplicably, lost the thread of the conversation. She concentrated hard. 'Thank you again. For rescuing me. Us, that is.' She leaned her elbows on the table, put her chin on her hands, studying him. 'As a matter of fact – I don't think you should be here at all, should you?'

He grinned. His face, more relaxed than she had seen it

in years, was unnervingly attentive, glinting with mischief. 'That's very perceptive of you. No. I shouldn't be.'

'Where should you be?'

'Somewhere in France.'

'Ah.' She nodded sagely.

'Where I shall turn up tomorrow with some reasonably plausible story, having seen you on your way. The way this war is being run, believe me, no one will have missed me. Meanwhile,' he leaned forward, bottle in hand, 'this really is excellent claret.'

They talked for an hour or so longer, talked of home and of the people who waited there – of Hannah who, having with the rest of the sisterhood abandoned for the moment her political battle in order to give her wholehearted support to her country in time of war, was nursing in a London hospital determined to be posted to France; of Ralph, whose conscientious objections to fighting in a war he considered to be morally, humanly and politically indefensible were, to his mortification, all but nullified by eyesight that was so bad that no army would take him if he had begged them; of Peter, already in the thick of it fighting alongside the French on the Aisne in defence of Paris.

Neither of them, perhaps oddly, mentioned Charlotte.

They spoke of the Bear that was now, Ben told her, as full of Belgian refugees as of London's orphans, they spoke of Bron's adamant and indignant refusal to join most of her contemporaries in Silvertown, earning a small fortune in the armament factories.

Sally smiled. 'Good old Bron. She's worth a guinea a box that girl.'

Ben nodded. The noise around them had abated a little. At the table next to theirs a young lieutenant snored, his head on his arms.

'And Doctor Will?' Sally asked.

Ben tinkered with his glass. 'He's – older. But bearing up. He spends a lot of time at the hospital, of course. A lot of wounded were shipped back after Mons. That can only get

worse I should think. Pa will have as much to do as I have.'
He offered the bottle. She shook her head, smiling but
positive. He emptied the wine into his own glass, filling it
to the brim.

'And you?' she asked softly. 'What are you doing here?'

'Doctoring. What else?'

'But – in uniform?'

'You're surprised?'

She hesitated. 'Yes.'

'Why?'

'I don't know. I just am somehow.'

He watched her for a long moment, the old cool, wry
gleam in his eyes. Then he lifted the glass, savoured a
mouthful, put it down, the long mouth twitching to a self-
derisive smile. 'You aren't the only one, Sally Smith. I'm
pretty surprised myself.'

She did not correct the name, though she was tempted.
They sat for a long, companionably quiet moment. Outside, in the distance, the guns had started again, a sound
she had become used to in the last couple of days. She
looked at him, a quick gleam in her eyes. 'This little lot's
made a bit of a mess of your plans, hasn't it, Doctor
Patten?' she asked, only half humorously.

He tilted his head, watching her.

She was suddenly, inexplicably sorry for the impulse
that had translated thought into speech without considera-
tion. 'Your – "Jerusalem" –' She hesitated. 'If the Zeppelins bomb London, as they did Antwerp, if the German
armies smash Paris, if we retaliate in Berlin – what will be
left?'

He considered for a moment, his face serious. Only when
he lifted his head did she catch the ironic and affectionate
glint of laughter in his eyes. 'Don't worry about it, Sally,'
he said, 'it's a long-term plan.' He paused for a moment. 'It
always was, I suppose. A dream. And when reality catches
up with a dream –' he tilted his head, drained the last of his
wine, '– you shelve it. Put it into a pocket. Carry it about

with you. But you don't forget it. Now – come on, my lass. Off we go. You've an early start tomorrow.'

He walked her back through a dockland that was as busy now as it had been at eleven in the morning. Beneath huge lights the ships still berthed, the tired, singing, swearing Tommies still staggered down the gangplanks, boots clattering, kit-bags bouncing on weary shoulders. Cigarette smoke drifted on the air, a snatch of song rose, ragged in the night. Displaced, homeless families huddled under tarpaulins, behind packing cases, or just slept, exhausted, in the open, waiting for a place on the journey to freedom. At the tall door of the warehouse they stopped. The cool air had cleared Sally's head. She tilted her head to look at him. 'Thank you, Ben,' she said simply, 'for everything. Without you –' She stopped. Already the will-less, grief-stricken, despairing girl of those last weeks in Bruges seemed like a stranger. The grief was still there. It always would be, she knew, however deeply she managed to bury it. But she was alive again, bruised, confused and in pain – but alive. She lifted her head and smiled at him.

He stood looking down at her, hunched into his greatcoat against the autumn chill. Then, in an odd, tender gesture that took her completely by surprise he lifted his big hand and laid it softly against her cheek. Still smiling she tilted her head a little, resting her face against the warm strength of the hand that cupped it. They stood so, unmoving for the space of a dozen heart-beats. Then he let his hand drop to his side, grinned lopsidedly and left her, striding into the lit night, not looking back.

The last she saw of him was in the chill light of dawn the following day when, as the troop-ship slid into the grey, choppy swell of the North Sea he stood at the dockside, a solitary, bulky figure, greatcoat collar turned up about his ears, hands in pockets, watching her go. It was an image she carried with her for a long time.

It came as a shock to remember, inconsequentially, as she gingerly descended the steep ladders to join Marie-

Clare and the children that the war was only two months old. Already, she realized a little grimly, it seemed a way of life.

III

Charlotte Patten – she would not have denied it – was enjoying her war. Despite the constant scares about the possibility of German airships bombing British cities – there had been near-panic in London after the well-publicized raid on Antwerp – and despite the ever-lengthening casualty lists that were published in the papers each day, for her the world had come alive again. No one had been more surprised than she when Ben had announced his intention of volunteering at the outbreak of war; and hers had been just about the only voice not raised to dissuade him. After he had gone she had resisted firmly Hannah's attempts to organize her into hospital work or to busy herself with the floods of refugees that were arriving in London. It was Peter, home for his first and so far only leave – embarkation leave before his posting to France – who had made the suggestion at which she had jumped. A small and not very fashionable club in the West End had turned itself, with War Office approval, into a staging post for young officers passing through London on their way to or from France. It so happened that the proprietor was a friend of Peter's – and it so happened that Peter knew that he was looking for young ladies of impeccable background to serve tea, biscuits and sisterly care to these brave young men far from home and the support of their families. So it was that three times a week, and sometimes more often, she took her turn behind the tea urn in the small club room, where young men, self-conscious in their neatly pressed, well-tailored new uniforms and often looking no older than the schoolboys they had actually been a few months before, could relax for a few hours, read the papers, play billiards or the piano, write letters, do anything to distract their minds from the uneasy thought that in weeks, perhaps days, they would be leading men as inexperienced as themselves into battle.

She was very good at her job, and she knew it. She always took especial care with her appearance, never missed the chance of a personal word, a sparkling, special smile. She would listen, endlessly patient, to any tale of woe, admire any photograph, boost any failing morale, ease, so far as she could, the pangs of homesickness. It pleased her that for a lot of these young men hers was the last womanly smile, the last soft and gentle voice, the last pretty face that they would encounter before finding themselves in the harsh male world of war. It pleased her too that none of them ever stayed for more than two days; most of them only for one; an endless stream of young, eager and mostly admiring faces, here today and gone tomorrow. It was better that way, she assured herself quite frequently; how foolish it would be in such troubled times to commit oneself to real friendship.

She hurried towards the Bear on this October evening, her steps quick and neat; she prided herself on being one of the few women she knew who managed to walk elegantly in the hobble skirts that were still fashionable. One of the most dreary things about the war was that clothes were already beginning to disappear from the shops – indeed it was coming to be seen as positively unpatriotic to be seen in a new outfit – and those that were available were truly ugly, mimicking uniform, all unsightly straight lines and deadly dull colours. Ah well, perhaps tomorrow she would go through her wardrobe. Bron was good with her needle – the odd remodelling here and there would make new out of old, and really she owed it to herself and to her young men. It was, after all, as much a part of the war effort to – she stopped short. She had reached the courtyard of the Bear, hoping to slip quietly up the rickety staircase to her own warm, feminine little room without being seen – Hannah had developed the most awful habit of buttonholing her to talk of advances and retreats, front lines and battles, for all the world as if she found such things truly comprehensible. The yard, however, was full of children; running, shrieking, laughing – though at least one was crying loudly and irritatingly – pushing, shoving. Charlotte stood watching them in horror, her hands to her ears to block the cacophony. She recognized none of them. They were foreign and they were rowdy. God in heaven, where had such an unruly crew come from?

The door to the schoolroom opened. A voice was lifted sharply; a voice so immediately recognizable that Charlotte blinked in disbelief. At the brisk command the chaos died. The children, as if by magic, ordered themselves into a single file and trooped obediently to the door.

'Sally,' Charlotte said a little faintly.

Sally looked over at her with a brief, distracted smile. She looked, Charlotte thought, worse than she had ever seen her, even in those far-off days of the soup kitchen. Her clothes were worn and dirty, her face haggard and sallow, her hair a bird's nest.

'When – when did you arrive?'

Sally smoothed the wild hair from her forehead, cuffed with rough affection at a child who muttered something as he passed her. She was deadly tired. The journey had exhausted her. 'An hour or so ago. I'm just getting the children settled –'

'And – Philippe? – He's with you?'

For a moment Sally's movements stilled. She took a tired breath. 'Philippe's dead,' she said, unable to be anything but brutally brief.

'D-dead?'

The war, so far, had not touched Charlotte. The dead, the mutilated, had belonged to others.

Sally nodded. Behind her in the schoolroom noise was rising again. 'I'm sorry – I'll have to go. I'll see you later.' She turned, stopped, turned back again, 'Oh – I'm sorry – I should have told you – I saw Ben – yesterday – he's fine.'

'Ben?'

'Yes. He's very well and – he sends his love.' Ben had done no such thing she realized suddenly. 'Charlotte – I really can't talk at the moment – they'll tear the place apart if I don't get them settled and fed. Ben's fine – he came to get us in Bruges. It was very brave of him, I think. I'll tell you later.' She went into the room, shutting the door behind her. Through the window Charlotte saw her hold up her hands firmly, suppressing near riot.

Very slowly Charlotte climbed the stairs to her room. She closed the door behind her, stood for a moment absolutely still, looking about her. The pretty room was warm and smelled of rose-water. Her cut-glass bottles and jars were neatly arranged upon the dressing table, their facets reflecting the flickering gas light, frilled pillows – pink, white, cream and gold – were banked upon the bed in apparently artless profusion. She slipped her cape from her shoulders, walked to the mirror, fussed for a moment with hair that needed no fussing. Then she turned, an oddly uncertain little figure, her hands clasped before her.

Philippe? Dead?

She had hardly thought of him for years. But – dead?

Her eye fell upon the wardrobe. Briskly she walked to it and flung open the door. It was packed with clothes, hung neatly; silks, satins, velvets in a rainbow of colour. She began pulling them out, examining each one, tossing it on the bed. Oh, yes; Bron and her clever needle were all that was needed here.

A week after Sally and the children reached London the first battle of Ypres began, the first of the bitter, bloody clashes that were to be fought around this small, pleasant and until now peaceful Flemish city. The slaughter was savage as the British unsuccessfully tried to wrest the high ground – such as it was in this flat, almost featureless land – from the defending Germans. Within a week the merciless bombardment had churned the fertile farmlands – the water table a mere eighteen inches from the surface – into mud. In another week the complex and ancient drainage system had been completely destroyed and the fields were a quagmire in which men marched, fought, advanced, retreated, ate, slept and died up to their knees in mud. Towards the end of October, with no sign of any lull in the fierce fighting, the Belgian army, still in retreat after the fall of Antwerp, saved their lines and kept a foothold in the country for which they had fought so gallantly by flooding the lowlands around Nieuwport and taking refuge in the strip of coast thus protected.

There was no news of Bruges, now behind enemy lines.

On the last day of the month, at Neuve-Chapelle, the shrapnel shells that rained upon the Allied front line had been treated with an irritant; it was the first time a chemical weapon had been used in warfare.

At home the casualty lists grew, and the streets were darkened for fear of the air raids that everyone was certain would come sooner or later. But morale was by no means low. The war could not possibly last – no one could stand for long against the might of the British Empire. The lion might be slow to wake – but once fangs and claws were bared, who could withstand them? Not the Hun, that was for sure. The lads were out there, weren't they, rescuing the damn' Frenchies who couldn't look after themselves? They'd all be home – well, if not by Christmas, then certainly by the spring.

At the Bear Sally's arrival with her small refugees had filled every corner, every nook and every cranny of the ramshackle building. There were small pallets in the schoolroom and in the dining room, the beds in the dormitories were packed like sardines. The Pattens had already, predictably, taken in far more than their share of displaced people, most of them Belgian. Sally's group joined an already established refugee centre, run – to Sally's surprise and delight – as much by a newly confident

Bron as by any of the family, all of whom had their own war concerns. She was ably assisted by two or three young Belgian mothers, who had fled with their children; Sally was delighted to see Marie-Clare and her little Louise accepted with immediate sympathy and understanding into the group. A shared exile, like a shared grief, she thought, must surely be easier to bear than a lonely one? For herself she was for now happy enough to be run off her feet helping Bron. While she worked herself to a standstill each day, fell dog tired into her bed at night she had no time for thought, no time for grieving. She and Philippa had been given Ben and Charlotte's old room – a large, dark, wood-panelled room in the main building with a huge fourposter bed that she shared with her daughter. It had always been Ben's room, and though Bron had done her best, the simple and austere masculinity of it defied all efforts to change it. Sally did not mind. The big old leather armchair that stood by the fireplace – empty now in these days of growing shortages – was comfortable, the colours of the worn rug glowed softly in the light from the small window; and in those moments when she needed to be alone it was a haven.

Toby's room was next door, a tiny room that had once served as a dressing room, but big enough to take a narrow bed, a table and chair and a wash stand. And though Toby was casual about it Sally knew how much it must mean to him to have a room of his own. He was still at school, still blazing his way through with a ruthless combination of charm and acute intelligence that was dangerously difficult to resist. His greeting to Sally had been affectionate and natural, he was never less than faultlessly polite; but still the barrier was there between them, and probably now would always be. She had long ago understood – though was far from accepting – that in winning Philippe she had lost Toby. One day, she consoled herself, when he was older, he would understand. For now she would have to be content with what he was ready to give.

Just once, for the briefest of moments, the old relationship had glimmered through. On an afternoon of late autumn sunshine soon after her arrival at the Bear she had been unpacking the few belongings she had managed to salvage, among them a photograph of Philippe in a wooden frame that at some point in that difficult journey had split. Sitting on the bed, she had carefully extracted the precious picture, and had sat for a moment that was too long for her self control, looking at it. Inevitably the bleak tears had risen. Despite her efforts to block the memories she saw it all – that day in Kent when it had all started, the laughter in his eyes when he had proposed to her in the park, the steady love in his face as she had joined him at the altar, his joy in their child and in their life together. And the bloodstained, shattered wreck that the war had sent back to her to die. Raw grief rose again, and with it had come the helpless tears. She had bowed her head, burying her face in her hands, shoulders shaking, the sobs desperately muffled. Oddly, when she had felt the arm about her shoulders she had known it was Toby. Without looking up she had leaned to him, sobbing hopelessly. His arms had been fierce about her, his strong, young man's hand had stroked her hair. For a moment he had rocked her gently in that age-old gesture of soothing and solace, as she so often had rocked him in his childhood terrors. 'Don't cry. I can't bear to see you cry.'

Had he really said it? Afterwards, in the confusion of her emotions and her tears she was never sure. The moment had passed. She had drawn away from him. And, picking up the photograph that she had dropped to the floor and setting it carefully upon the table, he had left her as quietly as he had come. Neither had ever mentioned the incident again; certainly it had made no difference to his attitude to her. He was bright, courteous, offhandedly affectionate even; and there was a wall as high as ever between them. She knew nothing of what he thought, or of what he wanted. He brought her neither his triumphs nor his sorrows, if he had any. She no longer knew what he truly felt or what he planned.

He was, she was pleased to see, still a great favourite in the household; indeed he had succeeded in making himself as much a part of the family as she now was. Ralph took a personal pride in his protegé's progress at school and was often to be found with him at the dining-room table, an arm about the boy's shoulders as he helped him with his homework. And as often as not where Toby was there young Rachel would be. He teased and tormented her, reduced her to fury and occasionally even to tears, lorded it over her in the patronizing, half-affectionate fashion of an older brother; she in her turn was always ready to hold her own against him. But like a small shadow she dogged his heels, and for a kind word or a casual, affectionate gesture she would forgive him anything. She was a strikingly pretty child, with a pale, flawless skin, a mass of glossy dark curls and brilliant blue eyes. Her nature was open and sunny and she had a temper like a firecracker; something of which Toby often took graceless advantage.

She sat one day with Sally in the parlour, head bent over a pair of long knitting needles, her tongue held between her teeth as she concentrated furiously on her task, a tangle of khaki wool untidy about her feet.

Sally laughed. 'You'll knit your tongue into that, young Rachel, if you aren't careful! What are you making?'

Rachel giggled. 'A bala – whatsit. For a soldier.'

Sally grinned. 'Balaclava.'

Toby looked up from the book he was studying. 'Pity the poor soldier that has to wear that!'

Rachel stuck her tongue out at him as far as it would go.

'Rachel!' The icy voice came from the door. Rachel jumped and deep colour rose in her face. 'You've the manners of a tinker!' Charlotte stepped into the room, her face rigid with anger and something very close to dislike. One of the needles slipped from the child's fingers, sliding out of the stitches. The huge, brilliant eyes gleamed with

376

sudden tears. Toby ducked his head and kept his eyes on the book. He had seen Charlotte's temper let loose upon Rachel before. 'Get upstairs to bed!' Charlotte snapped. 'At once.'

'But – Mama –'

'Don't argue with me! If you want to act like a naughty baby you must be treated like one. Go!'

Trembling Rachel stood up, the knitting dropping to the floor at her feet. With a small, sympathetic glance at the child's mortified face Sally stooped to pick it up. 'Please, Mama –'

'Upstairs I say!'

'It really wasn't her fault, Charlotte,' Sally said mildly. 'Toby was teasing her.'

Charlotte's mouth tightened. 'Rachel!'

Rachel, eyes and mouth mutinous, crept past her mother, not looking at her, and slunk up the stairs.

Sally rethreaded the slipped stitches and wrapped the wool neatly around the needles, then lifted her head to look at Charlotte. Charlotte flushed a little. Sally stood up. 'I'd better go and help Bron, I think.'

Wordlessly Charlotte stepped to one side, her expression daring anyone to criticize her treatment of her daughter.

Sally was still seething when she reached the kitchen. Really, Charlotte had been most unjust to the child – and not for the first time. It hardly seemed fair to hold the circumstances of Rachel's birth against her – for Sally had no doubt at all that that was the basis of Charlotte's obvious dislike of her daughter. It was a damned pity that the poor child in looks so took after her feckless father –

'Postman's been,' Bron said cheerily from the kitchen table. 'There's a letter on the mantelpiece for you. And guess who's just dropped by to show off her fancy clothes – our Kate no less! Working in munitions she is, an' money to burn she's getting! Thinks herself everybody now she's got a penny or two in her pocket. Well she can keep it, and her fancy clothes too – getting altogether too big for her boots is Kate.'

Sally grinned, picked up the letter. 'Funny. Who'd be writing to me?'

'Terrible gossip she is an' all, mind. Worse than ever – can't keep her tongue from anyone – Sally? Is something wrong?'

Sally, the letter in her hand, lifted her head, her face stricken. 'Dear God. Surely not.'

'What? What is it?'

'It's from old Mr Dickson. Here –' She held out the letter to the other girl, 'Read it.'

Bron read the letter, her cheerful face saddening. 'Dreadful! Both of them gone?'

'Both of them.' Dan and Walter Dickson, killed together in the muddy fields of Flanders. For what? Sally shook her head. 'Both of them,' she said again, and closed her eyes wearily. 'Oh, Bron – where is all this going to end?'

It promised to be a strange Christmas, that first Christmas of the war, with the young men away and the streets darkened for fear of the raiders who had that month struck at several towns along the east coast of England and must now surely be making preparations to bomb London. In the club room Charlotte and her friends hung garlands and holly, and a small tree was set in the corner, yet despite their efforts the atmosphere was muted, the celebrations, such as they were, strained.

'Do you think this party's a good idea?' Polly Andrews, a pretty, brown-haired girl with wide dark eyes and a snub nose, helped Charlotte to move the piano into the corner of the room. It was Christmas Eve afternoon, and Charlotte's last duty of the week.

'Hardly a party.' Charlotte opened the piano lid and tinkled a few notes. 'Just a bit of a get together for the lads who haven't been able to get home, that's all. God, this piano's dreadfully out of tune!'

'I don't suppose they'll notice. Here we go – get the urn on, Charlie – here comes our first customer.'

It was an hour or so later, with the smoky room crowded and the subdued buzz of conversation all but overwhelming the quiet notes of the piano where someone played a Christmas carol, one-fingered, that Charlotte, handing round ham sandwiches, found herself caught and held from behind, two firm hands laid across her eyes. 'Guess who?'

She giggled. 'I've no idea.'

'Try!'

'It's –' she twisted round, found herself looking into a fair, laughing face, '– it's *Peter!* What are you doing here? We thought you were in France!'

'And so I was. But here I am – forty-eight-hours leave! Haven't you got a kiss for your brother-in-law? It's a million years since I kissed a pretty girl!'

'Oh, Peter!' She threw her arms about him, hugging him hard. 'How lovely to see you! What a wonderful surprise!' She stood back, looking at him. 'You're handsomer than ever!' That was no exaggeration. His face was leaner, a little harder than she remembered it, his uniform, usually so meticulously smart was shabby. He looked jauntily attractive, vaguely – she hesitated over the word – vaguely dangerous.

'I should jolly well hope so,' he grinned engagingly. 'You going to be here much longer?'

'Another hour or so.' She grimaced a little. 'It's supposed to be a party, but – well – no one seems to feel much like partying.'

'Well –' he winked, face full of mischief; Polly, Charlotte noticed with some gratification, was gawping like a schoolgirl, '– let's see what we can do about that, eh? Come on, lads,' he lifted his voice, pushing his way through the grinning crowd to the piano, 'what is this, a party or a wake?' He stood by the piano, took a small flask from his pocket, tilted his head and drank, then crashed a melodic chord, 'Right – here we go – *Pack up your troubles in your old kit-bag and smile, smile, smile!'*

One by one the others joined in, drifting towards the piano. Peter pushed his cap to the back of his head, tossed his greatcoat onto a chair. The mudstained uniform stood out like battle colours from the rest. '*It's a long way to Tipperary –*'

Charlotte watched him, laughing as he caught her eye above the heads of the crowd around the piano. His vivid presence lit the room, the reckless, infectious gaiety warming the most solemn face to a smile.

Polly slid to Charlotte's side. 'And who exactly', she asked, big eyes bigger than ever, 'is that?'

Charlotte smiled. 'My brother-in-law.'

Polly mulled that over. 'I see.' She slanted a small, mischievous glance at Charlotte, 'And does that mean that he's – available?'

Charlotte laughed outright, and did not answer. Peter grinned, took another swig from the battered flask. 'Roll up, roll up – who'll give us a turn?'

'You certainly woke them up!' Charlotte, hurrying by his side through the driving rain, laughed delightedly. 'Fancy that young captain knowing all those music hall songs! It was as good as a night at the Palais!'

He grinned, tucked her hand into the warmth of his greatcoat pocket. 'It's my officer qualities coming out, you see – bringing out the best in people!'

They had turned into the courtyard of the Bear. In the light from one of the windows she tipped her head to look up at him. Slight, neatly built, his fair hair curling from beneath his rakishly angled cap, it struck her suddenly and quite astonishingly that he had become by far the most attractive young man she had ever seen. They had stopped walking at the same second, and for an odd, surprised moment their eyes held, each studying the other intently as if, although they had known each other for almost all of their lives, they each unexpectedly found themselves looking at an intriguing stranger. Charlotte felt a sudden flood of colour rise to her face, and somewhere very deep inside her a tiny shaft of excitement stabbed. Then, laughing she turned and the strange moment was gone. She pulled him inside, excited and impatient as a child, watched as he divested himself of dripping cap and coat. 'Come on, oh do come on! I'm dying to tell everyone you're here!' She led him to the parlour, flung the door open to an array of astounded faces, 'Surprise, surprise! Just look what I've found! I've brought you all a Christmas present!'

In some stretches of the trenches that Christmastide the guns fell silent for a few short hours, and enemies met, warily at first, in the wasteland over which they had fought for three endless months. They shared their cigarettes and their Christmas tots, played football like street urchins with makeshift goalposts. They exchanged names, admired photographs, talked longingly of London and of Berlin, of the green valleys of Wales and of the lovely mountains of Bavaria.

The next day normality returned; and the killing began again.

PART FOUR

1916–19

Chapter Fourteen

I

'Have the bloody Boches all gone to sleep out there?' The Honourable Fiona MacAdam clicked sharp fingernails impatiently upon the deep windowsill, scowling into the peaceful garden that lay in the dormancy of late winter beneath a drifting cloud of rain. Beyond the high wall at the bottom of the garden a stretch of green, unspoilt countryside lifted, a verdant, wooded hillside veiled by the misting rain. 'D'you think he's given up and gone home and our fellows haven't noticed?'

Hannah Patten, sitting at a desk in the corner of the large, cheerfully comfortable room, pen poised over the letter she was writing, lifted her head, smiling a little. She was dressed to go on duty, starched white collar, cuffs and apron gleaming against the severe dark blue of her uniform dress, a crisp white head-dress sitting neatly upon the dark cap of her short hair. 'Honestly, Fiona,' her voice was mild and held an edge of exasperated affection, 'to listen to you anyone would think you'd actually rather they were blowing us all to blazes.'

'Oh, don't be daft.' Fiona was unrepentantly brusque, 'It's just – you can't deny it – these lulls are so bloody unsettling.' She turned restlessly from the window, strode to stand with her back to the fire. She was dressed in the mannish and elegant riding habit that had accompanied her somehow unscathed from England to a dressing hut in Flanders and thence to this casualty clearing station in a

385

village just outside Albert, a few miles behind the almost static line that the war, now in its nineteenth month, had drawn across Europe in barbed wire, mud- and blood-sodden trenches and blasted villages and towns. 'This time three days ago we were run off our feet – now here we are suddenly twiddling our thumbs and playing nursemaid to a couple of heads and an abdominal, none of whom are going to do if you ask me – oh,' she cast a wickedly sharp look at Hannah, 'and our perfect pet of an artist boy of course.' She chuckled a little as colour rose, very faintly, in the other girl's face. 'It's really very unsporting of Fritz if you ask me – why can't he manage to keep them coming in a nice, steady stream – and where in the devil's name is this idiot that's supposed to be taking me riding? I can't even chase him up – I've forgotten his name. They really do all look alike, don't they? I can hardly stroll across to the cavalry lines asking for "What's-his-name with the blue eyes", can I?'

Hannah watched her as she marched to the window again. 'You're going out?'

'Well I'm not dressed like this to have tea with Matron. Yes, I'm going out. If the infant cavalry lieutenant who promised me a mount ever turns up, that is –' She broke off as the door opened, then turned away with a barely concealed expression of impatience.

Mercy Meredith, dressed, like Hannah, in her Sister's uniform, hovered in the doorway with the timid uncertainty that away from the wards so characterized her and which any contact with Fiona seemed to exacerbate to a barely controlled nervous panic. In her hand she held a bundle of letters. 'I – was just coming off duty – I met – Corporal Denton – with the post.' She had a light, little girl's voice that matched exactly her mouse-coloured, wispy hair and wide blue eyes. 'There are five for you, Hannah – so many people write to you, don't they? – and one each for Fiona and me.' She extended a large, cream-coloured envelope with an embossed crest upon the flap nervously towards the girl who stood by the window. Fiona took it without thanks, glanced at it, tossed it on the table unopened. Mercy sorted out a small and rather crumpled white envelope for herself and held out the rest to Hannah.

Hannah smiled her thanks as she took the letters, riffling quickly through them. 'How's the boy with the hole in his head? Captain Beaumont, isn't it?'

Mercy nodded. 'No different, I'm afraid. He – he was singing again when I left just now. I really do find it very unnerving. He sings and he smiles all day.'

'P'raps that's what it takes for some people,' Fiona said, without bothering to turn from her vantage point by the window, an edge of sardonic humour in her voice.

Mercy, as always, rose to the bait. 'I'm sorry?'

Hannah shot an exasperated look at Fiona's back.

'Singing and smiling all day,' Fiona said, elaborate patience in her cool voice. 'A hole in the head. Perhaps that's what it takes for some people?'

There was a small, injured silence, broken suddenly by the rumble of a gun, a distant explosion. Fiona lifted her head sharply, listening.

'Really, Fiona.' Mercy's frail voice was unsteady with indignation, 'You do have the most peculiar sense of humour sometimes.'

Fiona turned from the window, her elegant, high-boned face weary. 'Mercy! Mercy – look around you. Strikes me that even a fool could see that it's God that's got the peculiar sense of humour these days.'

Mercy stared at her for a moment, her small mouth tight. Fiona smiled sweetly.

Hannah turned to her letters, smiling to see Sally's all but unintelligible scribble. She tore the envelope open, ran her eye quickly over the single page it contained, full of exclamation marks and scrawled capitals. Sally was no classic letter writer. '– all well here – the zepps haven't got us yet – the Bear getting more like Brussels on a market day every day – so many able-bodied *sensible* people about they really don't need me – seems to me even Flip doesn't notice if I'm there or not – and who's to blame her? – still driving my daft old colonel around London (no – you're right –he's a love really!) but am *dying* to get out there with you – you're all doing such Patten-like and *useful* things –' Hannah smiled at that, almost hearing Sally's husky, laughing voice,' at least at last I'm doing something a *bit* more valiant than stirring porridge and changing nappies. Keep your fingers crossed for me –'

'Good news?' Fiona was watching her, lounging elegantly upon the windowsill, one booted foot swinging.

Mercy, also engrossed in her letter, sniffed.

Hannah grinned. 'Not really. Just someone who makes me laugh.' She sorted through the other envelopes. One from Ben, two from old friends from the suffragette days – how very long ago all of that seemed now – and one from – she lifted the envelope, looked at the neat, precise handwriting, sighed a little. Ralph.

'No bad thing to do.' Fiona slanted an undisguisedly pointed look at Mercy, 'More than can be said for some.'

Mercy's small nose had turned very red. Her large, rather pretty eyes were blurred with tears. She sucked her lower lip between her teeth as she read. Hannah and Fiona's glances met, Hannah's vexedly sympathetic, Fiona's openly and unkindly amused. Any letter from home was guaranteed to reduce poor Mercy to a state of miserable homesickness that could last anything from an hour to two days and which she found impossible to hide. Hannah, knowing herself uncharitable but unable to repress the thought, wished she would read her letters and shed her tears in the privacy of her own billet.

Mercy looked up. A large tear trembled upon her long, mousy lashes.

'Bad news?' Hannah asked, gently.

Mercy shook her head sniffing, trying to smile and failing miserably. 'No. It's – from my mother – the – the snowdrops are out – she's – pressed one for me.'

Fiona threw her head back in an explosion of scarcely muffled amusement. The guns rumbled again. Somewhere near the reedy sound of an aeroplane engine droned, insectlike.

With an attempt at dignity that Hannah found absurdly touching Mercy folded her precious letter carefully, put it back into its envelope and lifted her head to face Fiona's derisive gaze. 'You shouldn't be such a pig, Fiona.' She was trembling on the point of tears, 'You really shouldn't. It isn't kind to laugh at people the way you do.' She swallowed, unable to go on, and, turning, fled the room a small, hiccoughing sob echoing behind her before the door into the dining room across the hall banged loudly.

Fiona sighed exaggeratedly. 'Mercy Meredith! What a damned name!'

Hannah shook her head. 'You shouldn't torment her so, Fiona. It really isn't fair. She's a good nurse. And brave.'

'She's a little Daddy's girl who should never have left Brighton, or Winklesea or whatever the bloody place is, in the first place,' Fiona said shortly, shrugging. 'All right – you're right – she's fine on the wards – but I wouldn't want her with me if Jerry broke through and we had to fend for ourselves. If she wants to play Florence Nightingale she'd be better off doing it in some nice little Home Counties' convalescent home, and you know it.'

Hannah said nothing, watching her.

Fiona grinned, the expression in her long, pale eyes suddenly warm. 'Oh, go on, Mother Duck – go and pick up the pieces if you must. Aha – at last,' she leaned to the window at the sound of horses' hooves on the cobblestones, 'Sir Galahad, complete with charger – two, I hope. I'm off.'

She swung with an impudent grin past Hannah, pulled a small, barely sympathetic face at the closed dining-room door and was gone. 'Rolly, old lad – where on earth have you been? I thought p'raps Jerry had flushed you down the pan.' The crisp, uppercrust tones pealed into laughter.

Hannah eyed her unread letters a little regretfully, then with a sigh crossed the hall and pushed open the dining-room door. 'Come on out, Mercy. She's gone.'

There was a moment's silence, then, sniffing, Mercy emerged, as Hannah had known she would; she found herself thinking ruefully that almost as unfairly aggravating as the girl's total inability to stand up for herself was her pathetic eagerness at the slightest sign of kindness. 'Come on in,' Hannah shooed her across the hall like a mother hen with a chick. 'You really shouldn't take any notice of her you know – it's just her way. She doesn't mean to be unkind.'

Mercy shot her a glance of such utter disbelief at that that she had to laugh.

'No, really. She – well, she doesn't understand, I suppose. Doesn't realize how much she can hurt.'

'She laughs at everything. It's awful.'

'It's her way of coping. And not a bad way when you come to think of it. If you'd only try not to rise to her bait every single time – if she didn't get any reaction she'd stop doing it.' Echoes of a past Hannah in a past time – finger raised in admonition, one or other of the Bear's small inhabitants weeping at her knee – she straightened. 'Now – I'm on in half an hour. Anything new?'

The outer door banged. Sharp footsteps sounded in the hall.

'There's been a new intake. Not many – a couple of legs, another bad head wound and an abdominal that's being operated on now. Casualties from this morning's Hate.' Though this part of the line had been unusually quiet for a couple of days the ritual shelling, morning and evening, still went on. As always, the moment Mercy talked of the business of the Station it was as if her whole being changed, the small, helpless girl banished, the composed and efficient Sister taking her place. She barely looked up as Fiona strode, muttering, into the room, crossed to the windowsill and snatched up the forgotten riding crop that

390

lay there. 'Oh, and there's a new chest wound in Officers'. Matron seemed a little worried about it, though it seemed quite straightforward to me.'

'In Officers'? Perhaps I'd better keep a special eye. Which bed is he?'

'The one by the window. A Captain Angleton –'

Fiona, half-way back to the door, turned, her face suddenly still. 'Angleton?'

'Yes.'

'Are you sure?'

'Oh yes. I copied his label on to his card. You know I've a good memory for –'

'Of the Suffolks?'

'Yes. That's right. Do you know him?'

Elaborately casual Fiona tapped the crop against her boots. 'Could be. Derry? Or Michael?'

'The initial is "D".'

Fiona nodded. 'Ah. Well, Rolly of the Mounted Middlesex calls. I'll see you later.'

Hannah got ten precious minutes alone in her billet in a small house in the lane leading to the main square to read her letters before she went on duty. Ben's letter, short, affectionate and to the point informed her, in spare form and with much less pride and pleasure than the news actually warranted, that he had been taken on to the staff of Sir Brian Bix-Arnold, a respected specialist in the field of gas gangrene, the scourge that claimed so many victims from the Field Hospitals. Sir Brian, it seemed, had sought him out, his name known from some papers he had written before the war on the causes and treatment of gangrene. 'I swear we could cut our casualties by twenty per cent if we could contain it. If only this damned war were not being fought in such filthy conditions! Perhaps I should put a docket in to the Almighty – in triplicate of course – to make sure the next one is fought in conditions of complete asepsis?' The small, dry joke, so like Ben, made her smile. The two letters from her suffragette friends she tucked into her pocket for later reading, knowing if not their contents at least their style; newsy, amusing, encouraging – the very stuff of friendship.

The last envelope she sat and looked at, turning it in her fingers for a full minute before opening.

Ralph.

He had come to see her three weeks ago, on a twenty-four-hour pass. Thin and unsmiling, a shadow of the man she had known, his appearance had shocked her. For twenty of his twenty-four hours he had parried her concern with shrugs and dismissively self-deprecating words. Then, in the stuffy darkness of a dugout on the edge of the hospital compound, as high explosive shells whistled overhead and the ground around them shook, he had told her.

She tore open the envelope. The first words were hopes for her own well-being. Then, '– The friend we spoke of is getting better off by the day. There are jackals everywhere, he tells me, growing fat – and why should he not be one? Our Tom is in no better state than he was, I fear. Question is – and it haunts him – should he keep mum or should he split? Problem is that there's no doubt that the Head Boy knows what's going on – and no lowly first year is going to get the Housemaster to listen to him, is he? The roastings go on. Poor Tom. I don't know how much longer he can stand it.'

Hannah lifted her head. Outside, the rain had stopped. A sharp French voice called, scolding. Poor Tom. Poor Ralph. She saw him now, in the half-light of the bunker, his face anguished. 'They rob the dead, Hannah! And – not just the dead! Men they're supposed to be saving! God help an officer with a fine watch, wounded and left by his men if Bully Foster gets to him first!' He had buried his head in his cupped hands, his voice muffled, 'I saw him – saw him with his foot on a man's head – a *boy's* head – a boy subaltern – drowning him in mud – oh God –!'

She had sat, sickened by what she was hearing, wanting to deny that it happened, that it could happen. Knowing that she could not. There were always whispers. The greater percentage of the men who risked their own lives to save the wounded in this war that was already proving itself a slaughterhouse were as brave, often braver, than those who fought, and as dedicated as any. Their heroism under fire, their tough determination to get the battered wrecks they dug out of the mud or cut from the wire to help and safety were a byword. Very many died themselves helping their comrades. But, inevitably, there were other stories. Stories of corpse-stripping and worse. Stories of ruthlessness and self-interest. Stories of horror. Stories such as Ralph was telling.

Hannah sighed now, folding the letter. What in God's name had ever possessed Ralph, who had always abhorred the very thought of this war, who had argued passionately and unpopularly in the early days against it, suddenly to volunteer for the Medical Corps was a puzzle totally unfathomable to her. And now – the awful luck to find himself in a unit dominated by a brute of a man, bullied and intimidated into keeping a secret that was driving him, she feared to the edge of collapse. 'Tell someone!' she had said. 'In God's name – report them!'

His despair had been written on his face. 'Hannah, you don't understand. No one would listen to me. I'm already branded a Conshie –' his voice was bitter, 'an intellectual Conshie at that. A murderer would have been better received. A good kick up the arse is what the sergeant-major thinks I need. And that's what Bully Foster administers, quite frequently. *Tom Brown's Schooldays*, remember?'

'I should think I do. Brute of a book.'

'Well, I wouldn't accuse Bully of having read it,' his voice was wry. 'I wouldn't accuse him of having read anything beyond the King's Regulations – he's a barrack-room lawyer of the sharpest sort, wouldn't you know it? – but somewhere along the line he's picked up Flashman's methods.'

Poor Tom. Poor Ralph. She wondered what the censor had made of the references. Certain it was, as Ralph had well known, that had he spoken more openly the letter would never have reached her.

She picked up her cape, swung it about her shoulders. There was nothing — absolutely nothing — that she could do. It had to come from Ralph. Meanwhile, she had her own problems — a sudden vision of a pale, freckled, smiling face lifted in her mind — and her own small joys. Perhaps later she would have a word with Matron; Matron, it was becoming clear, was connected to some very big Brass hats — perhaps a word in the right ear?

The Clearing Station was quiet, very calm, very warm. As she toured the almost empty wards, she noticed with pleasure that someone had put small vases of snowdrops on tables and windowsills. The few men propped comfortably upon their pillows smiled a greeting to her. Most were the survivors of the men who had been in too bad a way to be moved when the last evacuation train had left a couple of days before; in the last two days perhaps a dozen or so had come in from the trenches. But there had been no attack for four days now, and so the atmosphere was quiet, the men happy to be spoiled and petted, the staff happy to stop for a word, write letters, hand out cigarettes, read papers and magazines to those unable to do for themselves. Resuscitation Ward was empty — the beds were made up, the stoves lit just in case, but the blinds were open, the pillows smooth, the air smelled clean and antiseptic. She stood at the door for a moment. A week or so before, she and two juniors together with half a dozen orderlies, amidst the crash and blaze of a bombardment that had destroyed the church next door and all but flattened the railway station two streets away, had fought here to keep men alive, indeed in one or two cases to bring them back to life, in order that they might stand the slenderest of chances on the operating table. A fight as tough, as dirty, as exhausting as any that went on in the line. Men blasted, frozen, drowned into shock so deep that it slowed their blood and stopped their hearts before ever their wounds or the terrible complications of gangrene could kill them.

She moved on. Preparation Ward too was empty, and in the theatres the operating tables were bare, scrubbed and clean. Waiting. In Acute Ward the two abdominals lay, almost certainly dying. One, so Matron had told her, had admitted to being sixteen years old, 'Army Age, nineteen,' he had grinned painfully. In Evacuation, awaiting the next train, several men sat about the window, smoking and playing cards. As she joined them, one held up a fan of cards; two out of the five were of a different pack. 'Found any new packs yet, Sister? This lot are cheatin' me blind – they've all got better memories than I 'ave!' The bandage that covered one of his eyes and the missing part of his head was clean and white. His companions chuckled.

'Sorry, Seth. I've looked everywhere,' nothing but the plain truth, 'there isn't a pack of cards to be had in France! P'raps you'll send us some when you get back to Blighty?'

'Sure will, Sister.'

Medical Ward was quiet; again most of the beds were empty. She checked on a couple of charts, passed a few words with the Sister in charge. In Surgical, a bed she had expected to find occupied was empty.

'Went this morning.' Sister Drews rubbed her eyes with long fingers. 'Bloody shame. I was so sure he was going to do – he had the second amputation yesterday. Really thought we'd saved him.'

'Gas gangrene.' It was not a question.

Sister Drews nodded.

'Sister –' Hannah said gently, 'how long have you been on duty?'

The other girl flushed a little guiltily, shrugged. 'I didn't want to leave him. When – when we saw the signs – I thought –' she made a weary gesture with her hands, 'I don't know what I thought. But anyway, Sister Warren needed a few hours off, so I stayed.'

Hannah shook her head. 'Time enough when we have to do that,' she said as severely as she could manage. 'First rule out here, Sister – when you can sleep – sleep!'

'Yes, Sister.'

'Matron's Ass speaking,' Hannah said, her plain face twitching to a smile.

The other girl was surprised into an abrupt giggle, hastily stifled. Hannah glanced around the ward; two beds occupied, both stable, both sleeping. 'Off you go – I'll keep an eye here.'

'Thanks.'

Next door, in Officers', a captain and a young lieutenant – Hannah automatically classified them as an Arm and Legs – were sitting at a table, smoking and reading the newspapers.

'Sister Patten,' gallantly, the captain stood. The empty arm of his dressing gown was pinned neatly across his chest. He executed an almost graceful half-bow.

'Captain Brittain. Lieutenant,' Hannah smiled.

The other young man, having no legs to stand on, shifted his wheelchair a little in salute, grinning.

'Stop press,' Hannah said. 'There's a train due tomorrow.' She hesitated, pulled a funny, doubtful face. 'Or perhaps the day after.'

The two men smiled acknowledgement. Hannah passed the time of day with two bed cases, glancing swiftly at the notes on the end of the bed, smiling, satisfied at their content.

'He's a bit quiet today,' said one, jerking his head in the direction in which they all knew the front line lay. 'Think he's planning something? Any gossip come down the line?'

'None that I know of.'

Briskly and efficiently Hannah smoothed and tucked in the bedclothes, plumped the pillows. All the time aware of a smile, of a pale, broad-boned face dusted with faded freckles, a pair of warm, green-brown eyes.

'They've given up and gone home.' The boy in the next bed, eyes bandaged, one leg slung from a pulley in the ceiling grinned widely, 'And HQ haven't noticed. They were all at a garden party at the time.'

'That's what Sister MacAdam thinks,' Hannah agreed. 'And she's gone off riding to prove it.'

'Now there's a lady who knows what she's about,' said a small, approving voice amidst the general laughter.

Hannah had arrived at a bed in which lay a dark-haired young man whose wide, spare shoulders all but filled the narrow bed and whose brown eyes, set beneath flaring dark brows, were full of humour.

'Well –' She studied the charts at the foot of the bed, looked up with a smile, 'The new boy. Welcome.'

'Captain Angleton, ma'am.'

'Pleased to meet you, Captain Angleton. How are you feeling?'

'Oh, right as ninepence.'

With a hole in his chest the size of a child's football. Hannah smiled. 'Captain Derry Angleton?'

The eyes widened a little. 'That's right.'

She patted the bedclothes lightly, a gesture only, careful not to jog or pain. 'You have a friend here already –'

He smiled. 'I just heard it. MacAdam? Fiona MacAdam? She's here?'

'Yes.'

His face was warm and guileless, a face, Hannah found herself thinking suddenly, that she had seen a thousand times before in these last months. Open and gallant, the pain concealed, the questions buried under generations of unquestioning. The marked face of youth, still smiling. 'Fiona! I'd heard she was up here somewhere – what luck – good old Fiona!'

'She'll be in later on. You're comfortable?'

'As a bug in a rug. Thank you, Sister.'

She smiled, moved on. To the one she had left till last. Had she really done that? Done it deliberately?

Yes. She could not deny it. Did not want to deny it.

'Lieutenant Redfern. You're looking better.'

'Sister Patten.' He smiled, nodded on the pillows. 'Yes.'

He was propped up, half sitting. The broad face was still unnaturally pale, the freckles, normally warmly assimilated into the fine skin, stood out like scars. On his knees rested a sheet of paper upon a board, in his hand a pencil.

'You certainly gave us a bad few minutes.'

He smiled ruefully. 'Sorry about that.'

The look that passed between them was warm far beyond the cool, polite words. He had been here a week, brought in with a chest wound, badly shocked. At first he had been just another bloody wreck to be cut from his stretcher and from his clothes, just another drained and bloodless face upon a pillow, just another cold, shocked body to bring to life, just another wound to dress, another case to watch for the dreaded signs of gangrene. Two days after admittance he had smiled at her, thanked her for her care – many, oh so many of them did that – and something in the soft voice, something in the broad, bony face had caught her attention – caught her heart? – and she had stayed perhaps longer than she should. His progress apparently steady she had visited him often, dropping in on her way to duty, on her way to rest. As time went on, looking forward to it. He was a great favourite with everyone; what Matron would call 'a pet'. And he was an artist. With him into Resuscitation had come a battered leather folder, clutched to him, prised from resistant fingers long after he should have been dead. 'Keep it for me.' Those had been the only words he had said in those first critical hours, looking at her with eyes that already had had the glaze of unreality. But he had remembered that. 'Keep it for me.' And so she had. It lay beside him now, that precious, battered catalogue of death, destruction and – amazingly – laughter. He had, absurdly shyly, shown it to her as he lay recovering, watching for her visits. 'They're wonderful,' she had said simply.

He had shaken his head. 'No. Not good enough. But – I try –'

She never tired of leafing through those sketches – terrible, some of them, records of an insanity, a Dante's Inferno, but real this, not imagined; shattered buildings and shattered bodies, mud-filled trenches and the awful beauty of high explosive. A dance of death. And then again – laughter. A jaunty figure, a subversive grin; smoke from a cigarette drifting across a relaxed, battle-hardened face that anyone who had been at the front for more than a week would have recognized. The unbelievable perfection of a wild flower. Woodland reduced uniformly to two-foot-high stumps.

For five days he had progressed well. The train was coming; he would leave with the rest.

Two hours before he was due to be evacuated he had collapsed with pneumonia.

She moved now to look at what he had been drawing. His fellow patients lounged upon the paper; splints and eye patches, cards and newspapers, empty sleeves, crutches – all the paraphernalia of a casualty clearing station. The faces all real, almost more human than life. A fierce-faced orderly, readily recognizable. Matron, with her firm, schoolma'am's face. The wounded – smiling, sleeping, introspective.

'You sat with me last night. Was it last night?' His voice was very quiet, meant for no one but her.

She hesitated. 'The night before last.'

He nodded.

'You should be resting,' she said.

'I am resting. I promise you.' He smiled a little, lifting the pencil. 'Life's too short to do nothing.'

The crisis had come quickly. She had watched him

through it. Why? It was a question she had not dared to ask herself.

'I – I have something for you. I hope you don't mind?' He fumbled for a moment amongst the sheaf of papers, produced a couple, shuffled them awkwardly. 'There.'

She looked at the sketched portrait in utter silence. It was Hannah Patten, no doubt about that – the face too bony, the jaw too square, the hair untidy – even short as it was she still couldn't somehow manage smooth containment, knew that habitually she still absent-mindedly hunted for pins that were no longer there – and there was the hand, patting distractedly, oh, yes, it was Hannah Patten. But softer. More –

She looked at him. He was carefully sorting his pieces of paper, not looking at her.

More beautiful.

'It's lovely,' she said.

His eyes flicked to hers. 'You like it?'

'It's very flattering. Too flattering. But – yes – I like it.'

'I'd like you to keep it.' He smiled a little, held out another sheet; a small sketch of an enchanting child, a little girl, perhaps ten years old. 'My little sister.'

Hannah took the drawing. 'Oh – Giles – she's lovely!'

When, in these quieter moments, had they taken to calling each other by their given names? Neither of them could have said. Neither of them, now, noticed.

'It's as I remember her. She probably isn't like that at all.' He grinned a little. 'She probably never was. I haven't been home for a year.'

'You'll go home now.'

He turned his head on the pillow. 'For a little, yes. But not for good, eh?'

They both knew it; he was mending. Not a 'Blighty', this. Good for a few months' convalescence, and pray God as everyone did, perhaps the war would be over – but –

'No. Not for good. You can't be sorry?'

What madness for men to welcome a crippling wound, a

'Blighty', a burden to themselves and their families for the rest of their lives –

'No. I'm not sorry.' It was said positively. He meant it.

'What other family do you have?'

'A brother – he's fighting further up the line. A good soldier, not a dabbler like me. And a married sister. She lives in Southwold. In Suffolk.'

She nodded. She ought to go.

'And you?'

'I have an older brother, Ben –' She paused for a second, a small smile on her face. He was watching her intently. 'He's a doctor, like my father, and is working now with Sir Brian Bix-Arnold – you won't know of him, but he's very well thought of – he – they are working in the field of gas gangrene. And then I have another brother, Peter, a regular soldier.'

'A regular?'

'Yes. He's been in this lot since the beginning.' She stopped. She had been about to say, 'I think he actually enjoys it,' but stopped herself, not because it was not true but because she knew it would give this gentle, intelligent man entirely the wrong impression of Peter.

'Sister Patten?'

The voice, crisp and carrying, came from the door.

Their eyes held, for a rueful, reluctant moment. Hannah stood. 'Yes, Matron?'

'There's a convoy on the way. Not a big one, but enough. We'll be taking in in about fifteen minutes. Check that all's prepared, would you, please?'

'Yes, Matron.'

His hand reached for hers. She took it. The captain with one arm smiled, looked elsewhere. 'Comes of being Matron's Ass,' she said. The common abbreviation of Assistant Matron always amused her.

He nodded. Dropped his hand from hers.

Briskly she hurried to the door and headed for Reception and Resuscitation.

II

Sally van Damme leaned forward and cuffed a small patch of the gleaming bonnet of the Talbot to a brighter shine. She truly loved this machine and took a quite personal and jealous pride in its appearance. A lot of the other girls, she knew, hated being responsible for their vehicles – driving, they felt, was one thing; but for a girl brought up served by stable lads, coachmen and chauffeurs, tinkering with an engine or polishing a car was quite another. Sally had no such inhibitions. 'Better than any damned mechanic I've ever come across,' she had heard 'her' Colonel Foster say in the weeks since she had joined him. 'Magic with that engine she is. Blessed car's never been in such good nick!' It stood now, clean and shining as a new pin in the early darkness of the February afternoon. She leaned against it, turning up the collar of her greatcoat about her ears, ramming her cap down to meet it, stuffing frozen hands into her pockets. God! It was cold! She hunched her shoulders about her ears. Across the road the windows of the Lyons Corner House were steamed up. It looked invitingly warm. The colonel had in fact suggested that while she waited for him she might slip over for a quick cup of tea. The thought was more than tempting. She eyed the imposing door through which he had disappeared. These meetings could sometimes take ages –

'That's a fair old monster you've got there, lass.'

She turned, startled.

'Any shinier, you'd likely be fined for signalling to Jerry.'

She smiled a little at that, stiff-lipped in the cold. The speaker was a young man not much taller than she, dark skinned and dark eyed beneath his peaked khaki cap, one eyebrow crooked higher than the other at an engagingly sardonic angle. He stood jauntily, one hand in his greatcoat pocket, the other steadying the kit-bag that balanced easily upon one shoulder. His accent was not of London; broad-vowelled, its intonation was, she thought, from the north.

'Talbot, isn't it?'

'Yes. Six cylinder.'

He grinned suddenly, his teeth very white against the dark skin of his face. 'That so?'

Somehow, unexpectedly, she found herself smiling back. 'That's so, yes.'

'Well, now, since I wouldn't know the difference between a cylinder an' a cardboard box, doesn't mean much to me.' He was watching her intently, frank and open interest in his eyes. 'You drive this thing, do you?'

She nodded.

He patted the car, exaggerated admiration in his face, though whether for the big machine itself or for her prowess in driving such a thing she was not sure. Nor was she completely certain that there was not a glint of quiet mockery in the dark eyes.

'Know all about it, too, do you?'

'A fair bit.'

She watched him in some amusement, waiting for him to leave, somehow sure that he would not. Not making it easy for him to stay.

He seemed happily oblivious of the silence. He shifted his kit-bag on his shoulder, glanced up at the lowering sky. 'Look like snow, d'you think?'

'Could be.'

'Bloody cold, I know that.'

She said nothing.

He turned his head, and again the bright, jaunty smile flashed. 'Got five minutes? Fancy a cup of tea?' He jerked his head towards the café across the road.

She had to laugh at the cheek of it. Her eyes flicked to the stripes on his sleeve. 'No thank you, Sergeant.'

He held out a hand. 'Sergeant Browne – Eddie Browne –' He waited expectantly, then when she made no move to introduce herself added easily, 'Stranded in this Godforsaken hole they call London for twenty-four hours before bein' shipped over. Likely I'll finish up sleepin' on the station. Sure you don't fancy a cup of tea?'

The impudent play for sympathy was blatant, and she knew it; but yet something in the lean dark face held her attention. His tone was light, almost self-mocking, admitting to his ploy; but there was, she suddenly saw, a certain strain about the face, a tiredness about the eyes. His greatcoat was shabby. 'You're going back?' she asked quietly.

He shrugged assent.

'Been over there long?'

'Since the start. I was at Mons – then Ypres –'

'You know Belgium?'

He grinned lopsidedly. 'Know it? Happen so, happen not – depends what you mean by "know". Bin up to my knees in mud there – bin shot at an' shelled –' He stopped, studying her disconcertingly closely. 'You know it though, lass,' he said quietly and with certainty.

'Yes.' She shoved her clenched hands further into her pockets, hunched her shoulders higher against the cold. Against the memories.

This time it was he who waited.

'I – was living there when war broke out,' she found herself saying. 'My husband was Belgian. He was killed after Antwerp.'

'Sorry for that, lass.' The words were simple. Eddie Browne had accosted the solitary, uniformed, obviously female figure for two reasons: first because he was, as he had said, stranded in a city he neither knew nor much cared for, on his way back to a war that for the moment at least had lost all attraction for him; and second because he had wanted to test the theory so often bandied about in dugout, blockhouse and waterlogged trench that the young women who were clamouring to don a uniform, to drive a bus, to rush to the factory, to 'do their bit', were in fact clamouring for rather more than that. He still thought it an interesting theory, and one well worth exploring if an opportunity should occur. But, watching this young woman's thin, sharp-featured face, the steady eyes, he sensed that the opportunity was not now. A pity. He smiled a little, acknowledging it, somehow certain that she knew his thoughts and did not resent them. He touched his free hand to his cap casually, turned to leave.

'Wait.' Sally pushed herself away from the car. What had possessed her to stop him from leaving she did not know, except perhaps the sudden touchingly determined straightening of his narrow shoulders the implications of that shabby, mudstained coat. The mention of Belgium. 'As a matter of fact – I was thinking of going for a cup of tea –' she hesitated, grinned suddenly, all the street knowledge of her youth in the sharpness of it, surprising him, '– just a cup of tea.'

The café was warm, dimly lit and stuffy, crowded with uniformed men and women in the dark, simply cut clothes that wartime economies had made fashionable. Her unexpected escort's uniform, she noticed as he took off his coat, was even scruffier than his greatcoat, mudstained and worn. They sat at the smudged and running window, where she could keep watch on the doorway across the street. The tea was steaming, strong and sweet. They spoke of the war – in nineteen months he had fought from Flanders to the Somme; he had also, he admitted with no trace of self-consciousness been promoted through the ranks from private to sergeant and back again, twice. 'Like snakes and ladders,' he said solemnly. 'If you ever see me again happen you'll have to count the stripes – as fast as they give them to me I seem to lose them.'

Sally laughed. She liked this brash little Yorkshireman – which was what she had discovered he was – with his dry humour, his quick understanding, and the underlying toughness that had seen him through these months of war unscathed. 'That's a bit careless of you, isn't it?'

He shrugged, returning her grin. 'They like what I do for them when Fritz comes at us—happen they aren't so keen on what I say when the noise dies down.' He cocked the sardonic eyebrow higher. 'Can't somehow be doin' with idiots,' he said laconically. 'Happen one day I'll learn to keep a still tongue.'

She found herself telling him of Philippe, of her return to England, of her determination to do something to help with the fight – 'Something real, you know? Something useful. Driving seemed the best thing. I want to go to France you see. I want to help—really help—I learned to drive in Belgium – but, well I kept applying and no one wanted me.'

He jerked his head at the monster that stood gleaming at the kerb across the road. 'So – how did you do it?'

'I took a crash course in mechanics—I already knew a bit—Philippe was hopeless at such things –' The name slipped easily into the conversation, as it might have had she been talking to an old friend. '– And then started the rounds again. Still with no luck. God, I was mad!' How often, frustrated and furious, had she nearly given up? Oh, so many, many times! And then, 'Then I met an old friend,' she flicked a glance from beneath dark lashes, her face innocent, 'a friend I'd been in prison with.'

He took it remarkably well, she thought amusedly. He neither choked nor stared, just cocked his head, faintly enquiring, dark eyes alight with interest. 'Oh, not murder or anything—nothing interesting like that—just handing out a few bits of paper that Mr Lloyd George didn't approve of.'

His expression now was truly and undisguisedly interested. 'Votes for women?'

'Yes.'

'Oh, aye.' The odd little expression gave nothing away.

She looked at him sharply, ready for affront. 'You don't approve?'

He chuckled then, throwing back his head. 'Happen if I hadn't approved me mother would have thrown me out of the house. She was organizer in Bradford. Went to a few meetings meself. Turned into as good a fight as I've had anywhere.'

'Well – as I said – I met up with this old friend – Peggy Wilmott she was when we shared a cell in Holloway,' she lifted wry brows, 'Lady Marston now. She'd started up this corps – girls to drive for her husband's War Office chums – and – here I am. My colonel's a real duck.'

'But you still aren't in France?'

'No. But not through want of trying, bless him. He's as keen as I am – came out of retirement for this lot – fought in South Africa sixteen, seventeen years ago – he's absolutely raring to get out there, but – no luck yet. Still – he's promised if he gets there I'll go with him –' She saw the expression on his face, stopped, her eyes suddenly, dangerously cool. 'You think I shouldn't? You think the women should stay behind and keep the home fires burning?'

He played with his teaspoon, clinking it against his cup, shrugged narrow shoulderss. 'No business of mine, lass – Sal –' his glance was gracelessly mischievous,' – mind if I call you Sal –?'

But she had glanced beyond him through the window. In the dying light a figure stood upon the pavement, leaning heavily upon a stick. 'Whoops! The colonel!' She grabbed her coat, struggled into it, stuffed her cap upon her head, fighting with the disordered coils of hair beneath it. Oh, lord! – she'd have to get it cut, as Hannah had done – 'I'll have to go. 'Bye – thanks for the tea.'

'Hey – wait.' He had torn off a corner of the menu, was scribbling rapidly. As she turned to run to the door, he thrust it into her hand. 'I'd take it kindly if you'd write.'

She hesitated.

He stood, slight and cocky, dark as a gipsy, his crooked smile, the look in his eyes at once warm and perilously provoking. 'I'm off to t'war, lass,' he grinned, thickening his accent comically, 'it's thee bounden duty –'

She laughed, grabbed the piece of paper, stuffed it in her pocket and ran.

She arrived a little short of breath at the car a moment or so later. She was aware of the faint smudge of light behind her that was the windows of the café, a smudge that in a bare few minutes would be extinguished as the blackout blinds were drawn. 'I'm sorry, Colonel.'

'Not to worry, my dear, not to worry – I told you to get yourself a cuppa. Too cold by half to hang about out here.'

She ran around the car to open the door for him, knowing better than to attempt to help as he swung his stiffened, ungainly leg. As she returned to her own side she glanced across the road. The blinds were down. As the car's engine purred into life the doors of the café opened for a moment and a man's figure was silhouetted, small and slight, kit-bag on shoulder. He stood for a moment – she could not see his face – before he turned and marched, arm swinging cheerily, down the road. She could, she thought, all but hear his whistling.

'Well, van Damme –' The colonel leaned back in his seat. As she pulled away from the pavement she glanced at him, suddenly sensing his excitement. His high-coloured, neatly moustachioed face was serious, but the sharp blue eyes sparkled. 'Still interested in going to la belle France?'

Her heart almost stopped. 'I – yes, sir.'

'What about the child? You're sure about leaving her?'

In the weeks they had known each other they had become friends, these two.

'Yes, sir. The arrangements are made. There are so many to look after her.' She turned her head, looking at him. 'You mean it, sir? We're going?'

'So it seems, van Damme, so it seems. Not to the front line, of course – too old a war horse for that, so the silly buggers tell me – no, staff job – HQ near Amiens. You game, van Damme?'

Sally turned her shining eyes to the difficult task of negotiating the dusky roads under street lights the bulbs of which had been three-quarters blacked out. 'Yes, sir. Oh, yes, sir! I'm game.'

III

'Sister Patten! – Hannah! – Oh, thank God I've found you!'

Hannah, curled in front of the fire in her billet a book open on her lap, looked up as the door burst open and a distraught and dishevelled figure fell into the room. 'Mercy? Whatever's wrong?'

Mercy stood for a moment, biting her lip, wringing her hands in agitation.

'*Mercy!* What is it?' Hannah jumped to her feet, thoughts of catastrophe – fire, plague, invasion – tumbling through her head.

'It's – it's Sister MacAdam.'

Hannah stared at her. 'Oh, Mercy! For heaven's sake – I thought –'

'I – just didn't know what to do! If Matron should see her –'

Hannah picked up the book that had tumbled to the floor. 'What?' her voice, for all her effort, was irritated. 'Mercy, what are you talking about?'

'She's – oh, Hannah – she's *drunk*!'

Hannah stopped, turned, stared. 'She's – what?'

'Drunk! And still drinking. I – I tried to stop her – to reason with her – she – oh, Hannah, she *threatened* me!'

Hannah was reaching for her cape. 'Where is she?'

'In her billet, in the road next to the Place. She – borrowed one of my manuals – well,' Mercy was calming now, and her voice was injured, 'well, she took it actually – and I needed it back. So I went round there –' She hesitated, 'Do – do you want me to come with you?' she asked uncertainly.

Anything more likely to provoke more trouble from a Fiona drunk or sober Hannah could not imagine. 'No,' she said kindly, knowing what it had taken to offer. 'It's all right. I'm sure I can manage.'

Fiona's billet was in a small house beside the village's

main square, which she shared with two other Sisters and a couple of junior nurses, the main Mess being the bigger establishment by the Clearing Station itself. The front door was open, the house still. From somewhere upstairs came the quiet sound of a woman's voice singing. Hannah made her way quietly up the stairs, stood outside the door she knew to be Fiona's. From the other side the softly melodious singing continued – a song Hannah recognized; a soldier's song, filthily obscene, subversive, savagely funny. A song she, like Fiona, had heard more than once from the fevered throat of a dying Tommy, thinking himself back in the trenches with his mates. Fiona sang it, lovingly and softly, as she might a favourite hymn. Hannah tapped on the door. 'Fiona? Fiona, are you there? It's me, Hannah.'

The singing stopped abruptly. Faintly, through the door, she heard the chink of glass.

'Fiona! Come on, now – what are you playing at? You've frightened the life out of poor Mercy!'

'Poor Mercy. Poor, poor Mercy.' Fiona's voice, to Hannah's relief, sounded perfectly steady, its acid edge sharp as ever. There was a moment's silence. She waited. Then, 'Well, come in if you're coming, Sister Patten,' Fiona said.

Hannah pushed open the door. In the hearth a small fire had been lit against the cold. The room was neat and tidy; bed, chair, table, cupboard, wardrobe. At the table sat Fiona in uniform except for her white cap, which she had tossed upon the bed. In her hand was a glass. On the table before her was a bottle of whisky, half empty. One elbow on the table, she leaned her chin upon her hand and watched Hannah into the room, a small, derisive smile on her face. 'Mummy's girl ran to Mummy, then,' she said, her eyes unfriendly. 'Surprise, surprise.'

'Fiona?'

The other girl tilted her head, drained her glass, offered it to Hannah. 'Have a drink.'

Hannah shook her head. 'Fiona!'

'But I insist! A drink –' With a hand that shook very

410

slightly she poured a large measure of whisky, clinking the bottle against the glass, '– a toast –' She lifted the glass to Hannah, and for the first time Hannah noticed in her face the signs of recent tears. 'To Derry Angleton. And to his brother Michael. Silly buggers.'

Hannah stood quite still for a moment, watching the other girl. Then she turned and walked to the bed, sat down on it heavily. 'He's dead?'

'Yes. He's dead.'

'But – I thought – he was doing well?'

Fiona held the glass up to the light, studied it with bleak eyes. 'He was. Then he did badly. Rather suddenly.'

The room fell to silence. Fiona sipped her whisky. Hannah watched her helplessly.

The day after Captain Derry Angleton had been admitted she had come into Officers' attracted by gales of laughter. Fiona had been standing by Derry's bed, Derry himself had been gasping with laughter, as had in rather more well-mannered and smothered fashion, most of the other, openly eavesdropping, patients. 'You always were a little devil,' Derry was saying, 'but by God that one beat the lot – riding that damned horse straight up the stairs and into the dining room! – The old man's face! – And how old were you?'

Grinning from ear to ear, Fiona had shrugged. 'Nine – ten?'

'And that bloody great hound that followed you every-where – what was the beast's name?'

'Mogul. I was in my barbarian phase. And anyway – it worked, didn't it? Riding up into the old baronial hall? At least the old fart let me go hunting with the rest of you the next day, which was the object of the exercise – Ah –' spying Hannah she had turned, reaching a hand, her long, light eyes alive with laughter, 'Hannah, come and be properly introduced. Sister Patten – Derry Angleton. An old, old friend. I grew up with him and his brother Michael –' She had turned back to Derry. Stopped almost in mid-sentence at the expression on his face. There had been a moment's silence. Then, 'He's copped it?' she had asked calmly and quietly.

The young man had nodded. 'Yes. Six weeks ago. Just down the line from here. Mater was pretty cut up about it. He was always her favourite, as you know, though she'd deny it till death.'

Fiona had nodded, the laughter fled. In the look that passed between them, Hannah thought, the grief was palpable as were the memories; a shared, wild, privileged childhood, a host of easy expectations, a world that had suddenly and inexplicably changed. Then Fiona had grinned, 'Well – we'd better take special care of you then, hadn't we?' She had turned to Hannah, raising a finger like a school teacher. 'That makes our Derry the sole surviving heir to a name that goes right back to –' she turned back to the bed, mischief in her eyes, '– some sheep thief that came over with the beastly French the only time they actually managed it, wasn't it?'

'Sodding war,' Fiona said now, very quietly, and hummed again the song she had been singing when Hannah had come in.

'Fiona – I am so very sorry.'

Fiona lifted blind, smiling eyes, still humming. Nodded. The tears slid unnoticed from the corners of her eyes.

'Should I tell Matron that – that you'll write –'

'The break-the-news letter?' Suddenly brisk, Fiona tossed back the whisky. 'Oh, yes, I'll do that.' She turned the empty glass upside down on the table, pushed it with her finger making patterns. 'Poor Derry,' she said, 'poor Michael.' She lifted her head. 'Poor us. Oh, Hannah, what a poisonous, heartless, immoral affair this stinking war is.'

'Yes.'

'You sure you won't have a drink?'

'Sure. Thank you.'

'Please yourself.' Fiona picked up bottle and glass, surveyed them, put them back down again, dropped her forehead to her clenched fists. 'I think – perhaps – I'd better get some sleep.'

'Would you like me to –'

'No.' The word was brusque. 'Off you go, old girl. I don't need my hand held.' She lifted a tired, tear-stained face, 'Thanks anyway.'

Hannah stood up, swung her cape about her shoulders, walked to the door.

'One thing you can do for me.'

Hannah paused, hand on the latch. 'Of course.'

'Keep that mealy-mouthed Mercy away from me for a few hours. There's enough bloody murder going on around here without me adding to it.'

Hannah half-smiled, nodded.

Fiona's answering smile was faint, but genuine. 'Oh – and I forgot to ask – how's the artistic lieutenant? The Redfern boy?'

Hannah hesitated.

'It's all right. I'm not that far gone.' The smile glimmered again, 'I can take it.'

'He'll do. He'll be off on the next train. Back to Blighty – for a while anyway.'

'Good. That's good news. It's good, isn't it,' very precisely Fiona replaced the cap on the bottle, stood up and put it on the mantelpiece, 'to hear some good news occasionally?'

'Fiona –'

Fiona turned, shaking her head sharply. 'No, Hannah. I'm all right. It's over. Off you go, now,' she smiled, almost her normal, brilliant, quarrelsome smile. 'I'm sure somewhere there must be someone who *does* want you to hold their hand.'

Outside the weather had worsened. Still bitterly cold it had begun to rain again, great driving gusts that beat into her face like driven needles. With the sadness of the loss of Derry Angleton heavy within her she could not rid herself of the thought of the men those few miles to the east, ankle

413

deep, knee deep, sometimes waist deep in mud, sleeping wet, waking wet; English, German, Russian, French – Indian, African, Australian – black, white, young, old; killing in the rain, dying in the rain. What madness. Over the past few days the air had been thick with rumour and snippets of news of a surprise German offensive upon the French at Verdun. The casualties on both sides were said to be terrible. It was also strongly rumoured that in order to take the pressure from the French forces some action would have to be taken by the British along the Somme –

She pushed open the door of her room with a sigh of thankfulness, wiping the rain from her drenched face, shaking the wet from her skirts. It took a moment for her to realize that she was not alone. Startled, she caught her breath as a figure stepped into the shadowed room from the window where he had been standing. Then 'Ralph!' Her exclamation was half exasperation, half relief. 'Goodness, you made me jump – What on earth are you –?' She stopped.

He too was wet, his uniform soaked. He was hatless, his hair plastered to his head. He was pale, thin; haggard. He stood for a moment, unsmiling and silent. Then, 'I've left, Hannah,' he said. 'Deserted. And I'm not going back.'

Chapter Fifteen

I

Hannah faced him in disbelief and shock, 'You don't mean that. Ralph – you can't mean it.'

'I do.' He turned from her back to the window, his narrow shoulders hunched. 'I do.'

In the silence the rain blew against the window, a bleak and lonely sound. 'They'll shoot you,' she said.

He said nothing.

A sudden savage stab of fear for him brought a surge of anger that took her across the room in a couple of strides, and with surprising strength she swung him to face her. 'Ralph! *They'll shoot you!* It's desertion.'

'I know. But before they shoot me they'll have to try me, won't they? And at least I'll get to have my say.'

'No! *No!* You won't! Oh, Ralph – have you taken leave of your senses? You *know* how these things are done! No one will listen to you – they'll brand you a coward and they'll shoot you! Listen? No one will listen! They can't afford to listen!'

He stood in stubborn silence.

With an effort she calmed her rising voice. 'Ralph. Please. You can't do this. You can't. If you won't think of yourself, think of us – of Ben, of Peter, of me, of Pa. Think of your sister. Think of the Bear and the children – it's all there, Ralph, all waiting for you. It's what we're fighting for.'

'Hannah, you don't understand –'

'I understand very well. Believe me, I do. You've been under terrible pressure.' She stepped back from him, shaking her head despairingly, 'What I don't understand – what I'll never understand – is what on earth possessed you to join up in the first place. You didn't have to – your eyes –' She gestured helplessly, fell to silence.

He lifted his head, his eyes intent upon her face. 'You don't know why I did it?' He stopped.

Hannah rubbed her forehead with her fingertips, shook her head again. 'I suppose it doesn't really matter, does it? The question is what to do now.'

In the silence the door downstairs slammed and hurrying footsteps sounded upon the stairs.

'How long since you left your unit?' Hannah asked.

He shrugged. 'Four – perhaps five hours. I hitched a lift in an ambulance.'

Her practical, nurse's mind had taken over. 'Will they have missed you?'

'Sister Patten!' A sharp knock on the door came only just before the precipitate entrance of a young nurse, rosy cheeked and dripping wet, 'Sister Patten, the train's in.' The girl stopped in awkward mid-sentence as she caught sight of Ralph. 'Oh – I'm sorry –'

It took a moment for the significance of the girl's news to break through Hannah's preoccupation. 'The train? The evacuation train?'

'Yes.'

Hannah stared at her blankly. 'I'm off duty. Has Matron sent you to –?'

'No. Oh, no.' The young nurse, a pretty thing whose hero-worship of Hannah had at times raised caustic comment from Fiona, was plainly discomfited. She glanced at Ralph again, clearly uncertain as to who he might be, clearly afraid of embarrassing Hannah. 'It's just – someone – well, that is – someone was asking for you. I think – I think he wanted to say goodbye.' The last words were mumbled, red-faced.

Giles.

416

The girl, still standing irresolutely by the door, looked pleadingly at Hannah. 'I'm sorry. I didn't realize you were – busy. Shall I say you couldn't come?'

Hannah glanced at Ralph's taut back. 'Yes – that is no –' An agony of indecision sounded in her voice. She couldn't let Giles leave without saying goodbye, she simply could not. The world was too perilous a place in these uncertain days. But – if she left Ralph –

He turned from the window. With what light there was behind him his expression was indecipherable in the shadowed room. 'Someone – special?' he asked quietly.

She hesitated, lifted her head in an oddly defiant gesture. 'Yes.' She had never overtly admitted so much even to herself before.

'Then of course you must go. I won't –' he hesitated, she saw the glimmer of his bleak smile, 'I won't run away. Off you go. I'll wait.'

'You're – you're sure?'

'Yes.'

The girl by the door shifted uncomfortably, 'If that's all, ma'am?'

Hannah nodded abstractedly. 'Oh, yes, Nurse Wilson. Thank you. You run along. I'll be there in a minute.'

'Yes, ma'am.' The girl threw one curious and vaguely apologetic glance at Ralph and fled.

Hannah turned back to Ralph. 'You don't mind? You promise you'll wait?'

'Of course.'

She did not notice that he had not answered the first part of her question. She fiddled with her hair, still torn, 'We weren't expecting the train until tomorrow, you see.'

'Go, Hannah. Don't let him leave without saying goodbye.' His voice was calm, the tension apparently gone. 'I'll stay here and wait for you. It'll give me a chance to think.'

'You won't –?' Hannah was already reaching for a heavy army greatcoat that hung behind the door.

'– run away?' He smiled a little, shook his head. 'No. I'll be here.'

He stepped to help her as she struggled into the blanket-like coat that reached almost to her ankles. Aware of the picture she made she smiled a little, ruefully. 'It's the only thing that keeps me warm.' Turning to go, she gripped his hand in hers. 'Ralph – promise me you won't do anything silly. It isn't too late. Promise you'll wait till I come back and we can talk.'

'Don't worry, my dear. Go and say goodbye to your – friend.' The pause was infinitesimal, Hannah did not notice it. 'I'll be here when you get back.'

She watched him for a moment, her eyes fraught with worry. Then she flung her arms about his neck and kissed him on the cheek. 'I won't let you do it, Ralph. I believe that you knew that when you came here.' Her voice was quiet, very intense, 'I simply won't let you do it. You *must* have known that. If nothing else – just think about us. Think how we all love you. Think what it would do to us to lose you – and in such a way. Is it worth it? Is anything worth that?'

He stood for a long time watching the closed door after she had gone. He had so nearly told her – so nearly explained what she had never understood; that his only reason for coming to France, for volunteering for duty in a war that he had abominated from the start had been because France was where Hannah Patten was, because he could not bear to stand back and see her serve whilst he did nothing.

He turned and walked back to the window. The shock of the realization that Hannah's heart was engaged elsewhere – and remembering the look in her eyes he had no doubt that it was – was still with him. With sudden clarity he realized that through all the years of his devotion, hopeless though he had assured himself it was, he had never really in his soul believed that in the end she would not be his. Through all her enthusiasms, her campaigns, he had supported her, and waited. But now – he stared sightlessly into the dreary little cobbled street, slick with rain – now it seemed he had truly lost her. For – if not this one, then there would be another. Of course there would. How absurd of him ever to have believed she would in the end turn to him – to the man she so clearly still regarded as a brother – almost as a child. And, as Hannah had unerringly divined, even in this final foolish action, this childish gesture of desertion, he had failed. She was absolutely right, and he supposed he had known it from the start; he was not the man to defy the world and take the consequences knowing that those consequences would be as bad, if not worse, for his loved ones as for himself. He would go back. Probably he had not even been missed.

Sighing he turned, and his eye was caught by a piece of paper, a pencil sketch, that lay upon the chest-of-drawers. He picked it up.

Giles's picture of Hannah smiled up at him.

He stood looking at it for a long time before the lines blurred. Still holding it, he walked to the table and laid the picture carefully upon it, smoothing the creases gently before sitting down and settling to wait for Hannah's return.

The station was bedlam. The walking wounded, bandaged, on crutches, supported by their comrades, shuffled in untidy lines the length of the wet platform, shepherded, organized and occasionally bullied by harassed orderlies. Stretcher cases were loaded like so many carcasses. 'Mind yer backs, there!' The train, already packed, was being packed further. Cigarette smoke drifted on the chill, wet air.

She could not find him.

The officers' bunks were full. Several familiar faces smiled at her and, a little distractedly, she smiled back.

'Back to Blighty, eh, Sister?'

'Thanks, Sister – if it hadn't been for you –'

'Good luck, Sister. Keep up the good work.'

She picked her way through stretchers packed upon the truck floor like sardines. Pale faces. Bandaged heads. Blinded eyes.

'Sister Partridge –' she caught at a nurse's arm as she passed, 'Captain Redfern – he's on the train?'

'Sorry – haven't seen him.' The girl made to move on, then stopped. 'Oh – there were an extra couple of carriages added – other end of the train – p'raps he's there?'

She scrambled from the train, cursing the greatcoat that might keep her warm but which, together with her uniform, made any kind of swift movement all but impossible. She ran along the crowded platform, glancing in windows, acknowledging greetings. In doing so she all but fell over a little, cheerful orderly who stood with a list waving the diminishing queue of hobbling wounded into the benched carriages. 'Ah, Corporal Denton,' her voice was relieved; at last a familiar face, 'Captain Redfern. He's on the train?'

'Sure is.' The little man grinned broadly, waved his pencil. 'Last carriage. You've got about four minutes.'

She picked up her skirts and ran. The door of the last carriage stood open. She hesitated. In the gloom several pairs of eyes looked at her.

'Hannah!'

She almost fell into the carriage. Then stopped, absurdly abashed. He lay strapped into a bunk, the inevitable leather case clutched to his breast. Trying to control her thumping heart and disordered breathing, she moved to him. The man in the upper bunk grinned at her, ostentatiously started a conversation with the man opposite.

He reached a hand. 'I – thought you weren't going to make it.'

'I very nearly didn't. I couldn't find you.'

The engine shrieked, the train jerked, clattered metallically, stilled.

Their linked hands were cold. 'Take care,' she said. 'Do everything they tell you. Get well.'

'I shall.'

'Perhaps –'

'May I write?' They spoke together.

She nodded. 'Please. I'd like that.'

'And you – you'll write to me?'

Again she nodded.

On the platform voices were raised. Doors slammed. A whistle shrilled. She dropped to one knee beside him, her face on a level with his. Very gently he lifted her hand to his lips. For a long, still moment they stayed so, silent, eyes locked.

Another whistle. An orderly came to the carriage door, swung it, stopped. 'You with the train, Sister?'

She stood up. 'No.'

He grinned. 'Well, you will be if you aren't careful.'

'I'm coming.'

Still their hands clung.

Then she let go, gently withdrawing her hand from his clasp. She turned. At the door his voice stopped her. 'Hannah?'

'Yes?'

'Be careful. Be very careful.'

'I will.'

She stepped from the carriage, swung the heavy door closed. All along the train people were stepping back, turning, walking away. She lifted a hand in farewell, saw him smile, his own hand lifted in answer.

Then she turned and hurried through the rain, back along the platform. The train chuffed asthmatically then, puffing small, determined explosions of steam it began to move, slowly at first, but picking up speed, wheels humming smoothly on the rails. Men leaned from the windows waving. She felt the wind of its passing.

As the carriage in which Giles lay sped past her she was at the gate and hurrying, back to Ralph.

*

To her surprise he was calm, reasonable; even apologetic. All the arguments she had marshalled so frantically as she hurried back from the station remained unuttered. As she stepped through the door he stood up, facing her, and said, 'You're right, of course. I'll go back.'

The wind taken from her sails entirely she stared at him, the wet greatcoat dripping on to the worn carpet. Outside the sky was darkening and the evening barrage had started, its fire flickering like lightning.

She slipped the heavy coat from her shoulders, hung it dripping on the back of the door. Her hair, she suddenly realized, was drenched. It clung to her head in sodden rats' tails. He smiled a little at sight of her, walked to the wash stand, tossed her a small towel. She rubbed her hair vigorously. Stopped. Looked at him. Rubbed it again. The room was darkening by the moment, the flash of the gunfire threw dancing shadows on the walls. The sound was like distant thunder, disregarded.

She ran her fingers through still damp hair. 'You're going back?'

'Yes.'

She looked at him in helpless puzzlement.

He shrugged. 'You're right. I don't suppose I ever actually intended to go through with it. Everything —' he hesitated, '— everything just got on top of me, that's all. But of course you're right. I can't get myself shot as a deserter.' He smiled very faintly, 'Apart from anything else Charlotte would definitely never speak to me again.'

Her attempt at a smile was as weak as his attempt at humour, but it brought an answering glimmer to his face. 'Will you get away with it, do you think? I mean — will you have been missed?'

'Possibly. I don't know. Depends how fast I can get back.'

'You'll be in trouble?'

'No more than usual.'

The words fell flatly into the dusk. She flinched a little

from them and from the inference of his expressionless voice.

'You saw your – friend – off?'

She turned to the fire, rubbing her cold hands. 'Yes.'

He waited, inviting her to say more. When she did not he moved to her side. She saw the flash of white in the gloom as he held up the picture. 'He did this?'

'Yes.'

'It's very good.' His voice was quiet.

Giles was gone. She was glad – so very glad – that he was out of danger, at least for a while, that he would be with his loved ones, mending, regaining his strength – and she was unhappy, with a depth of unhappiness that chilled her soul as the rain and wind had chilled her body. How long before she saw him again? She said nothing. She could not speak of him. Not, she realized in sudden surprise, without tears.

'Well –' Very carefully Ralph laid the picture upon the table, came back to her side, put an arm lightly about her shoulder. 'If I'm to have half a chance of getting back unnoticed I'd better be off.'

'You should have something to eat – a cup of tea –' She glanced vaguely about her, as if such things could be conjured from thin air.

'No. Don't worry. I'll find something on the way. There'll be ambulances going up the line. I'll hitch a lift. It'll be all right.'

She lifted her face to his. 'You're doing the right thing, Ralph.'

He smiled. Said nothing.

'I'm sorry – I haven't been much help.'

'I'm going back. That's what you wanted, isn't it?'

'Of course. But –'

He shook his head. 'It's I who should apologize. I shouldn't have come.' He leant to her, dropped the lightest of kisses on her damp hair. 'But – I'm glad I did.'

She took his hand. 'Let me know what happens. If you need any help –'

'I will.' Gently he disengaged himself, quietly walked to the door, raised his hand, and with no goodbye left her, pulling the door softly to behind him.

She stood for a very long time, silent and cold, watching the flames of the small fire, listening to the rumbling concussion of the guns.

When the tired and miserable tears began to drip from her chin on to her crumpled apron she made no move to stop them or to wipe them away.

It was a long, long time before she dashed her hand across her face, moved to the window, drew the heavy blinds and with a hand that shook a little lit the small lamp. That done she stood for a moment, aimlessly, sniffing a little. God damn this vile war. And damn too the accident that had placed her in a different billet from Fiona MacAdam and her whisky bottle.

II

Major Peter Patten's first leave in eighteen months fell in May 1916. His battalion had been in and out of the line around Ypres for four months, though for the moment that part of the Front, with the pressure still being mercilessly exerted on the French forces at Verdun further south, was relatively quiet. For a while there had been rumours that they would all be shipped down in support but, somewhat to his disappointment, nothing had come of it. Then, stronger and more reliable, word filtered through the grapevine; an offensive, and soon, by the British to draw the enemy's attention away from the savagely mauled French armies and give them time to recover from the terrible hammering they had received in the last months. There would be no leave once that started, he knew; so when an unexpected opportunity arose, he took it. On his way to the coast he stopped near Amiens to see his brother Ben. He found him in a comfortable billet in the servants' quarters of the château that had been converted into a base hospital, sitting in the sunlight that streamed through the open window, his feet on the windowsill, his nose in a book. The room was like a library – stacks of books overflowed the shelves on to tables, chairs and the floor. Reams of written notes were scattered about the room. Peter pushed his peaked hat to the back of his head and surveyed the disarray with mocking astonishment. 'Good Lord! When did the bomb drop?'

Ben glanced up, his first expression irritation, his second, as he recognized his unexpected visitor, pure pleasure. He unfolded his vast frame from the solid wooden chair in which he had been lounging and knocked over a pile of books in his good-natured lunge towards his brother. 'Peter! Good to see you! When did you get in?' They gripped hands, grinning broadly.

Peter, releasing his hand gingerly from the iron grip, slapped his brother on the back and then with the air of a magician producing a rabbit from a hat held up an unopened bottle of whisky. '*Voila*, as they tend to say in this area. *Où est* the glasses?'

Laughing, Ben rummaged amongst books and papers, produced a couple of wine glasses. 'All I've got, I'm afraid.'

'That'll do. Beats drinking out of the bottle.'

Ben watched as he splashed out two generous measures. 'I've been meaning to look you up. We were not far from you the other day – at the CCS at Poperinghe – unfortunately Fritz had other ideas. Cheers.' He took the glass, sipped it. They grinned at each other again over the rims of the inappropriate glasses. 'Oh, and I forgot to say – congratulations, Major Patten.'

'Thanks. And to you, Major – hear you've been put on Bix-Arnold's team?'

Ben nodded.

Peter laughed. 'Even I've heard of him.' He threw himself down in a chair, not bothering to move the papers that were scattered on its seat. Ben opened his mouth, shut it again, sat down himself. They looked at each other for a second of smiling silence, caught in a warm moment of pleasure.

Ben sipped from his glass. 'How come you're here? How long do you have?'

'Me – I'm off to Blighty. Ten days. Thought I'd drop by on the way.' He grinned again. 'You can take me out to dinner tonight if you'd like?'

'A pleasure.'

They sipped their drinks again, in the silence of those who had so much to tell that a starting point was hard to find. Peter leaned forward, elbows on knees. 'Seen anything of Hannah?'

'Once or twice, yes. She's not far from here – near Albert – and we get out there once or twice a month. Sir Brian's an old mate of her Matron's.'

Peter laughed. 'What a character *that* is! Have you been invited to one of her At Homes?'

Ben nodded, smiling.

'I've never seen anything like it! Sunday afternoon tea with all the trimmings – cucumber sandwiches, cakes from Harrods, a choice of Indian or China – *The Mikado* churning out on the gramophone – no wonder the poor bloody Boches can't win the war! She'd probably hold her tea parties in No Man's Land if she had to!'

'She very nearly did. She used to run a dressing station up near you – and come hell, high water or high explosive, Matron's At Homes were held regular as clockwork. She thinks it's good for the "dear boys" to get out of the trenches and into some sort of civilized company every now and again – by which, of course, she means the company of the gentler, and in her opinion the superior sex. She's probably right. Dinner jacket in the jungle and all that – you can't scoff at it entirely.'

'Am I scoffing? I should say not. I had a ripping time. That friend of Hannah's – Fiona something – now there's someone really special.' Peter leaned forward and replenished the glasses. 'She had a Jock captain almost down on his kilted knees and proposing within five minutes of meeting her!'

Ben leaned back, turning the glass in his hand. 'They're doing a wonderful job, all of them. But both Hannah and her Matron – she's Lady Bennet, by the way, did you know? – are agitating to get the Station moved up closer to the line.'

'Well if Matron Lady Bennet is as good at agitating as our Hannah you might as well tell whoever needs to be told to give in now and save themselves a lot of trouble.' Peter grinned, and then, more seriously, 'How much closer?'

'Close.' Ben was not smiling.

'Dangerously close?'

'Yes. And for a very good reason. They aren't being foolish, in fact it's hard to fault their arguments. We're losing a lot of men we shouldn't be losing simply because it takes so long to get them to the Clearing Stations. Chest and abdominal wounds – heads – they all need quick if not instant surgery. They lie out for hours, sometimes days, before they're picked up – and then the journey kills them. Or gas gangrene gets them. There'd be nowhere near the incidence if we could get to them quicker than we do – and, Hannah and Lady Bennet are absolutely right – the closer the CCS is to the line the more chance the casualties have of recovery. But –'

'But you can't put women in the front line. It's utterly unacceptable.' Peter drained his glass.

Ben surveyed his a little quizzically, tilting it, watching the sunlight reflected in the amber liquid. 'Tell Hannah that,' he said. 'Or Lady Bennet. Or Fiona MacAdam. But duck when you say it –'

They dined in a small restaurant in the town, the room full of English uniforms, the food good, the wine better. They exchanged news and rumour, compared notes, tried to make some sense of the progress of the war.

'Stalemate,' Peter said, pensively gathering crumbs with his thumb. 'Something's got to break – or someone. Though God knows what – or who. The French are taking a hell of a hammering in the south – Fritz must have expected to break through by now – but still they hang on, and still they throw him back. Word is it's our turn next.'

Ben nodded.

Peter leaned back, nursing his brandy glass. 'Roll on, I say. Sooner the better. By the way – did you know our Sally's out here?'

Ben's head lifted sharply. 'Sally? Out here? What do you mean?'

'She's driving for some colonel or other according to Hannah. They've seen quite a bit of each other over the past few weeks. Hannah and Sally, that is. Apparently Sal's based at HQ here at Amiens – or her colonel is – I'm surprised you haven't run across each other?'

'What about the child?'

'Philippa?' Peter shrugged. 'Sal's left her back at the Bear with the faithful Marie-Clare. Seems Sally couldn't bring herself to sit twiddling her thumbs and playing with the children for the duration. Come on, Ben,' he added, eyeing Ben's forbidding face a little curiously, 'knowing our Sal – and knowing the circumstances – you can hardly blame her?'

Ben shrugged. 'It's none of my business what the girl does. You're going home tomorrow?'

'That's right. Got passage from Le Havre. Ought to be back at the dear old Bear by Wednesday. Any messages?'

'Of course.' He smiled, a little selfconsciously. 'Lots of love and kisses to Rachel. Tell her I've got her the present she wanted – she'll know what I mean. Pass on, if you will, to Pa the things I've been telling you – I don't get enough time to write as often as I should, and I know he's interested in what we're doing out here – and Charlotte –' he paused, 'well, just give her my love. These Zeppelin raids – she doesn't say too much in her letters, but what little she does – they frighten her a lot. She's not –' he stopped.

Peter drained his glass. 'Sodding things,' he said cheerfully. 'Who's to blame her for being a bit funky? I'm not sure I'd be too keen myself. There doesn't seem to be a way of bringing the buggers down. But we'll find it. No doubt about that. Filthy thing to do, this bombing civilians. Women and kids. I mean – it's one thing to get Fritz in your sights and pull the trigger – or for him to do it to you, if he's quicker – or to lob the odd grenade into a bunker – but bombing civilians? Bloody bad show I call it.' His fair, handsome face was shadowed for a moment by indignation, then the quick grin returned. 'I say – I don't suppose you'd have any idea of the whereabouts of the tiniest game of chance this evening, do you? I feel the beginnings of a lucky streak coming on.'

Ben, smiling, surveyed his younger brother. There could be no doubt about it – Peter was one of those who were having a good war. A regular soldier for more than eight years now, the army was his life, his natural environment – and war, logically, the activity for which he was trained and best fitted. He was neither insensitive nor stupid; he knew the horrors, perhaps better than anyone, recognized the risks and the brutal dangers of a modern warfare that had somehow overtaken man's puny attempts to control it. But he was at his best in the trenches with his men; first over the top, last back, there with them in the sodden, mud-filled shell holes and amongst the clawing wire, brewing tea in a ruined farmhouse, swilling rum in a foetid, rat-infested blockhouse. And they loved him for it. If you were going to get gassed, shot at, blasted or burned then the major was more than likely going to be right there with you, yelling his lungs out and swearing like a trooper. All but worshipped by his men, popular with his peers, highly regarded by his commanding officer, he was the very model of a professional soldier. And how often, Ben wondered with a small, strange stirring of tenderness, watching the fair, restless face, the bright, unshadowed eyes, was he ever afraid? How often – if ever? – did he want to scream in terror, throw himself down, run from the death, the disfigurement, the threat of crippling that howled in the air about him as he breasted the sandbags, crawled through the wire, led his exhausted men into retaking another square yard of useless, skeleton-strewn land? He could not ask. 'Behind the barn,' he said. 'Pontoon. But watch your back teeth. They're Aussies – they gamble the way they fight – no holds barred.'

III

Peter arrived at the Bear in the late afternoon of a warm May day. The courtyard was deserted. From an open window young voices chanted in obedient unison. 'Once three is three, two threes are six, three threes are nine –' He pushed open the door into the house. The long, shadowed corridor was empty, a beam of sunlight gleaming at its end.

He walked towards the light. 'Hello? Hello!'

There was a flicker of movement in the shadows. 'Hello, yes, who's that?' Bron's unmistakable, sing-song voice. Then, 'Why – Mr *Peter*! It's Mr Peter!' Bron's brown eyes widened to saucers at sight of the familiar, dapper figure in the shabby uniform. 'Oh, sir! How lovely to see you – we weren't expecting – oh, my goodness!'

'Bron, my darling!' He had deposited his battered case upon the floor and thrown his arms about her, sweeping her from her feet before she could move, 'And how's my best girl, eh? Pretty as ever I see.'

'Oh, Mr Peter!' Blushing to the roots of her hair the girl struggled free, patting her hair and straightening her cap, 'Really now!' And then her smile broke free again, and the Welsh lilted in her excited voice, 'But oh, a pleasure to see you it is, home safe and sound. And us not expecting you, mind. Doctor Will's at the hospital – spends too much time he does there, mind, not taking care of himself – but Miss Charlotte's somewhere around –'

'Uncle Peter! Uncle *Peter*!' A small form hurtled from the shadows, launching herself upon him, clinging like a limpet, 'When did you get here? Why didn't anyone tell me you were coming? How long can you stay? Look, Flippy, it's Uncle Peter! Uncle Peter!'

He hitched the light, lanky figure up so that her face was level with his. She clung with long, twining legs and skinny arms. 'As I live and breathe it's Rachel!' he said solemnly. 'Your Daddy sent a message – he has the present you asked for. And I have a question of my own – when did you grow so beautiful?'

She laughed a little, pleased.

He swung so that she faced the light, seeing in some surprise that his light-hearted comment had been no less than the truth. The child was beautiful. Her lit eyes gleamed, blue as sapphires, her mass of black hair, curling and glossy, set off a skin pale as pearl. 'A little princess!' he said. 'A gipsy princess!'

Oddly, she stiffened, and the laughter faded. With a quick wriggle she had slipped from his grasp, landing like a long-legged cat upon the floor. 'This is Flippy,' she said, extending a hand, without taking her suddenly unsmiling eyes from Peter's face, to the child that hovered behind her. 'Come on, Flip, don't be daft. He won't hurt you. It's Uncle Peter.'

The other child moved shyly forward. She was solemn, a little chubby, her dark, straight hair flopping forward into eyes that stared in level question up at the stranger. Hazel eyes beneath dark, well-marked eyebrows. Sally's eyes. Peter dropped to his haunches beside her, extending his hand. 'Hello, Flippy. Remember me?'

The child shook her head.

Rachel moved impatiently. 'I told you. It's Uncle Peter. Come on,' she grabbed the smaller child by the hand, 'let's tell Toby.'

'You be careful, Miss Rachel,' Bron scolded, 'tearin' around like a wild thing.'

But Rachel and her small acolyte had gone, clattering up the stairs, calling excitedly, 'Toby! *Toby!* – Guess what!'

'Bron – what on earth are those children up to?' Charlotte had appeared at the door of the parlour, poised and slender in pale green silk, the sun a halo in her fine, spun-gold hair. She stopped, narrowing her eyes against the light. 'Who's that?' And then, '– Peter! Oh, it's Peter!'

He turned to her, holding out both hands. She took them, her wide, pale, laughing eyes searching his face, running over the worn and shabby uniform. 'Oh, Peter, look at you! Handsomer than ever and looking as if you've been pulled through a bush backwards! Why ever didn't you tell us you were coming?'

He followed her into the parlour. 'I didn't know myself until the last minute. Then I just grabbed the chance and ran so to speak. I'm not in the way?'

'In the *way?*' She turned to face him, vivacious and pretty, eyes shining with excitement, 'Oh, for heaven's sake! You're the best thing that's happened in absolute *ages!* – In the way indeed!'

'Shall I bring some tea, ma'am?' Bron hovered in the doorway, torn between wanting to stay to feast her eyes on the returned hero – for there was no doubt whatsoever in her mind that that was what he was – and wanting to be the first into the kitchen with the news.

'Oh, yes please, Bron. For what it's worth.' She pulled a face for Peter's benefit, 'It will be very weak tea, I'm afraid. It's rather hard to come by these days.'

Peter patted his pocket. 'Weak tea will be fine. I've something here that will beef it up.' He grinned a little and winked. 'Trench milk.'

Charlotte nodded to Bron, who scurried on her errand. As she left they heard a clatter, and Bron's voice, indulgently scolding, 'Come on, Toby lad – slow down – no fire is there, that I can see? Nearly had me off my feet you did.'

'Sorry, Bron.' The voice was deep, a young man's, with an attractive timbre, a hint of laughter. A moment later the door was darkened by a tall, slim figure in blazer and slacks, shirt open at the throat. He hesitated at the doorway.

'Toby?' Peter could not believe his eyes, and his voice betrayed the fact. Eighteen months ago this had been a boy, fair and pretty, smooth faced and immature. The young man who stood with eager shyness in the doorway might, despite the same fair curly hair and blue eyes have been a different person altogether. He stood easily and elegantly with no trace of the stoop that so many tall boys of his age tended to develop. He was well-muscled and athletically built, his chin was firm and square and had very obviously felt the razor that morning. This was no child, but an attractive and composed young man. Peter held out his hand. 'Toby.'

The boy came to him with long, easy strides, laid a bony hand in his with a smile. 'Hello.' There was a warmth in his eyes that Peter, with an affectionate amusement, could not help but recognize. One or two youngsters, in and out of uniform, had looked like that at him before; it was easy, in wartime, to make an idol of a soldier.

'Are you home for long?' Toby asked.

'A week or so.'

'You've come – straight from the front?'

He nodded.

'What's happening out there? I mean – the papers are always saying the end's in sight?'

Peter shook his head. 'Not that I can see.'

'So –' Charlotte's voice was waspish, 'you can rest easily tonight, Toby.' She turned to Peter, ignoring the unfriendly look the boy shot at her, 'He's crazy keen to get into the army. I do believe he prays each night that it won't all be over before he can join in the fun and games.'

Toby ignored the interruption. 'I'm a captain in the corps at school. They say I'll get a commission – when I leave next year.'

Peter threw himself into a chair, stretched his legs in front of him, tilted his head to look into the eager young face. 'Yes. I should think there's every chance you will.' If for no other reason than that the gaping gaps in the ranks of the young officers who were mown down each time the attack whistle was blown were becoming almost impossible to fill. He did not say it.

'Haven't you homework to do, Toby?' Charlotte asked coolly. 'I'm sure Peter's tired. There'll be plenty of time to talk to him later.'

The boy held her eyes for a moment, his own devoid of any expression, then he nodded, threw a brief smile towards Peter and left the room.

Charlotte watched him go with eyes that could not be called friendly. 'That was remarkably restrained,' she said, an acid edge to her voice. 'He's a cocky little monkey usually – Ah, Bron – tea – thank you. Put it there, would you?'

Bron placed the tray carefully upon the table, stood smoothing her apron.

'That will do, Bron. Thank you.' Charlotte waited until the door had closed, then very gracefully she moved to the table and poured the tea, knowing his eyes were upon her. The excitement that had started to sing inside her at her first thrillingly unexpected sight of him whispered still in her veins, heightening her colour, brightening her eyes; making her, she knew, more beautiful. She had thought of him so often since that moment of strange, still communion, eighteen months ago in the chill Christmas streets. Had imagined him suffering hardship, danger, the terrors of battle – so much more romantic than Ben, stuck in that blessed hospital with his horrible, decaying stumps. She remembered every moment of that day – his valiant gaiety, the blithe way he had lifted and dominated the men in the club; the light in his eyes as he had looked at her – and now, here he was, his face a little harder, his smile just a little less ready, the air of danger that had both fascinated and repelled her rather more obvious –

'Do you mind?' He was holding up the same battered flask she remembered, his face charmingly rueful, 'Gets to be a bit of a habit, I'm afraid – but if you'd rather I didn't?'

'Of course not.' She held the delicate cup and saucer as he splashed whisky into it. Then, studiedly poised, she picked up her own cup and drifted gracefully to a chair by the window where she sat, straight-backed, the light gilding her hair.

Peter could not take his eyes from her. He had known her all his life, from shy, too intense child to his brother's pretty if unexpected bride. He had never until that last Christmas leave, ever really looked at her. And even that glimpse had faded very quickly. He took a gulp of whisky-laced tea that all but choked him.

She watched him in a capricious, self-contained silence.

He lifted his head. In the distance traffic rumbled, and children's voices called. His ears sang in the quiet.

'What is it?' She was studying him so minutely she had sensed rather than seen his change of expression.

He laughed a little. 'The quiet. No guns, you see. It's – strange. You get used to them.'

Her face changed infinitesimally; no affectation here. She shivered a little. 'I wouldn't. I never would. Not if they're like the bombs those beastly airships drop.' Her face, he noticed with quick concern, had actually paled at the thought.

'Ben said you didn't like them.'

She lifted her head sharply. 'You've seen him?'

'Yesterday –' He stopped. 'No – day before yesterday. I called in on him on the way home.'

'He's well?' If her voice did not betray quite the depth of interest that the question merited, he did not appear to notice.

'Oh, yes. Tip-top, actually. He's done awfully well to get on the hyphenated Sir Brian's staff, hasn't he?'

'I suppose so, yes.'

'I gather it was a special request – the old man recognized his name from some work he did before the war. Quite an honour.'

She nodded.

'He sends his love, of course.' He grinned. 'And suggested that I might do him a favour by taking his lovely wife out for an evening or two, to cheer her up and take her mind off the war.' He eyed her a little warily. 'How does the lovely wife feel about the suggestion?'

She smiled, folding her hands composedly in her lap. 'Oh, she thinks it's a very nice idea. Very nice indeed.'

'I'm not *altogether* sure,' Charlotte said, chuckling delightedly two evenings later, her fingers curled about the fragile stem of a champagne glass, 'that my not very extravagant husband would *altogether* approve.'

'You aren't enjoying yourself?' Peter asked innocently.

On the small stage a ragtime band, not one of the players a day under forty, swung and stomped with enthusiasm; on the dance floor squealing girls and their dashing escorts, mostly but not all in uniform, danced as if their only aim in life were to wear out their shoes. A young man – not above twenty, Charlotte thought – shimmied and twirled, perfectly and gracefully balanced, his empty sleeve tucked into the pocket of his dinner suit; another, still in uniform, held his partner's hand, bouncing as frenetically as anyone, his milky eyes blank.

'Enjoying myself?' Charlotte picked up her glass, twirling it in her fingers, studying it provocatively as if thinking. 'I suppose –' she let the words trail into mid-air, glancing at him mischievously out of the corner of her eye.

He leaned forward, tapping her arm smartly. 'Careful. They throw you out of the Savoy if you aren't enjoying yourself. Didn't you know that? And there are spies everywhere.'

She giggled. 'All right then. I'd better say yes.'

'Well done. Stiff upper lip at all times. Playing fields of Eton and all that. That's what wins wars.'

Rather to her disappointment he had refused point blank to wear the mudstained uniform that Bron had not, for all her loving and meticulous efforts, succeeded in cleaning completely. He was dressed in his pre-war evening clothes, which hung a little loosely on his war-tempered frame but otherwise, she had to admit, looked very well indeed on him. She herself had spent a frantic two days remodelling a shimmering pale blue silk dress, intricately beading the neckline, taking out the sleeves, shortening it once, and then again, contriving from the offcuts an elegant turban-like hat trimmed with a matching ostrich feather. Her strapped shoes, hastily dyed, were still damp upon her feet but looked, she knew, the very height of style, matching the dress exactly. The ivory pins in her hair matched the daringly wicked foot-long cigarette holder. Her mother's diamanté glimmered at throat and ears – hardly diamonds, but surely at this time of austerity more patriotic? She had drawn more than one appreciative glance as she had followed the elderly waiter through the dancing throng to the table, and the knowledge had put colour into her cheeks and lifted her chin an attractive fraction higher.

'What did you think of the show?'

'It wasn't at all bad.' Not for a moment would she admit to the total, almost childlike delight the performance had given her. She had not been to a theatre since her marriage. *Mr Tower of London*, the show that had taken the capital by storm, had seemed to her a glimpse of magic; oh, to be on that stage, to glitter and gleam beneath those lights, to carry the watchers on the magic carpet of song – to be wooed and won so romantically and publicly – and then, next night, to do it all again –

'What did you think of Gracie?'

'She has a very pretty voice. But –' she pouted a little, 'not so very beautiful, I thought?'

Peter tilted his head pensively. 'Perhaps not. But what a personality. We'll hear more about Miss Gracie Fields. Bet your boots on it.'

She made a small, faintly dismissive gesture with her shoulders. She had noticed with some pleasure that a girl on a neighbouring table, ignoring her own middle-aged escort, was eyeing Peter with an undisguised degree of interest. She picked up her glass, very carefully sipped her champagne – nice it might be but she had no intention whatsoever of allowing herself to be anything less than in complete control of the situation. Peter, she knew, from the excellent claret at lunch through the habitual whisky with his tea that afternoon and on to the disguised rissoles but excellent wine that the Savoy had served with such aplomb at dinner, was very relaxed indeed. To her lightly probing comment on his drinking habits earlier in the evening he had replied, with a casual enough air, but it seemed to her fairly seriously, that there were no teetotal VCs. She had filed that away for further thought. She leaned to him now, smiling. 'Aren't you going to ask me to dance?'

He drained his glass, stood with fluent grace, extended a hand that after five days' leave was still tough as leather and ingrained with dirt, though she knew the effort that had gone into cleaning it. 'Will you do me the honour, my lady?'

And, happily aware of the pensive regard of the girl on the next table, she stood. 'I'd be delighted.'

'Mr Peter's enjoying his leave, then?' Kate leaned against the mantelpiece of the schoolroom, cigarette in hand, watching Bron as she dragged the narrow beds that had been stacked against the wall for the day into lines, turning the room into a makeshift dormitory for the night. 'And not just Mr Peter, either.' Kate's eyes were sly. 'Seems Miss Charlotte's enjoying it too?'

Bron straightened, hands on hips in exasperation. 'Enough of that, Kate! If you must know Doctor Ben asked Mister Peter to take Miss Charlotte out.'

Kate blew smoke in a derisive stream at the ceiling. 'Oh yes?'

'Yes! And you can put that nasty thing out in here, if you please – the children have to sleep in here, mind! Come on – don't just stand there – give us a hand!'

Taking her time Kate stubbed out the cigarette, sauntered to where Bron was struggling with another bed. Her hair was cut short as was her skirt – indecently so in Bron's opinion. And she was wearing lipstick. She made no attempt to help but stood watching, her head on one side. 'Saw them, I did,' she said.

Bron, struggling with the bed, did not look up.

'In the Strand. Holding hands.' Kate saw the other girl's momentary stillness and grinned. 'Asked him to do that too, did he?'

'Now look, you –!' Bron was furious. She straightened, pointed a grimy finger, 'You've got a wicked tongue, Kate Buckley! A wicked tongue and a dirty mind!'

Kate spread wide, innocent hands. 'I was only saying –'

'Well you can stop saying, d'you hear? There's no one here wants to listen! Now – if you're not going to help then get out of the road, will you? I've more to do than to stand here listening to your gossip – it's Mrs Briggs's night off and I'm to get Doctor Will's supper – surgery's packed mind, and him single handed – working himself into the ground, he is.'

Kate stepped back, but made no move to go. 'And Mr Peter and Miss Charlotte?' she asked, smiling knowingly. 'Are they going to be here for supper? Or are they off gallivanting again? Making hay while the sun shines, eh?'

'Will you stop that talk! You should be ashamed of yourself, that's what! Gossiping like an old woman – coming round here trying to make trouble!'

Kate's face tightened; she lifted a shoulder. 'Please

yourself.' She moved towards the door. 'But I know what I saw, so there! Holding hands they were! An' not like brother and sister, either – oh, no – not by a long chalk.'

'Out!' said Bron.

'I'm going. Keep your hair on.' Kate flounced to the door and left with no further word, leaving the door open behind her.

Bron stood for a long moment, looking after her, sucking her lower lip thoughtfully, her brows drawn together in a faint, worried frown.

'So. Six down, one to go – where shall we go tonight?'

Charlotte looked up. 'Oh, Peter – I can't – I'm on duty at the Club tonight.'

'Then I shall come with you and persuade the charming Polly to cover for you. You can't leave me on my own on my last evening. There's no knowing what mischief I might get into!'

She laughed a little. 'We-ell –'

'*Vanity Fair*'s on at the Palace – fancy it? Or we could go to the Ritz –'

'*Peter*! You really mustn't be so extravagant!'

'Why ever not? Eat drink and be merry and all that – oh, come on – I'm joking –' he said gently, seeing the sudden shock of fear in her face, 'joking!'

She looked down at her clasped hands. 'Not a very funny joke.' The past week had been one of the happiest of her life. She could not remember when last she had laughed so much, enjoyed herself so well, felt so young, so utterly carefree. As the week had passed, she had pushed to the back of her mind the knowledge that he would have to go back – to danger, to the possibility of death. As the days had passed she had spent them like golden guineas, recklessly and with no thought of the future. They had dined and danced, been to the theatre; he had come to the Club on the two occasions she had been on duty. It had been a week of frivolity and laughter, of silly jokes and chattered non-sense; they had hardly said a serious word to each other. 'You're like a couple of children,' Doctor Will had said of them indulgently at breakfast that morning as they had dissolved into helpless giggles over Bron's lumpy porridge. And so they had been – children, playing, with no thought for tomorrow.

Or had they?

She lifted her head, to find his eyes upon her. There was a moment's oddly tense silence. Then the familiar grin gleamed upon his face. 'Well? What's it to be? The Palace or the Ritzy Ritz?'

She could not somehow bring herself to smile back. 'Whichever you prefer.'

'The Ritz it is, then. We'll dine and dance and drink damnation to the enemy. Meanwhile,' he flung his jacket about his shoulders, 'I promised to go and see young Toby's corps on parade. See you later.'

She sat for a long time after he had gone, hands folded in her lap, staring pensively into space. Her husband's brother. She couldn't love him. No – more than that – she mustn't love him.

But she did. She knew it with a certainty that left no room for doubt. She did.

And he?

She had no idea. He was affectionate, certainly – but then Peter was affectionate to everyone. He had spent a lot of time with her – but then, who else was there, with almost everyone away? He had held her hand – but then, after champagne, it had seemed a perfectly natural thing to do. And he was Ben's brother. She knew the bond between them, knew he would never break trust with his brother. If he felt anything for her he would surely never acknowledge it, for that in his mind would be to betray Ben, and that she was sure he would never do.

But yet – she loved him. For the first time in the twenty-eight years of her life, suddenly she understood the meaning of the word. She loved him. And tomorrow she would kiss him lightly and send him back to the Front. And, if they all survived and this poisonous war ever ended, Ben would come home and they would settle again to a marriage that was no marriage –

With a quick movement she stood up and strode to the window, stood looking bleakly out into the dirty street that was lit with May sunshine. 'Damn it!' she muttered ferociously under her breath, 'damn and blast it!'

They were in Piccadilly when the bomb dropped. They had, as Peter had promised, wined and dined at the Ritz. They had danced their feet off, and come out into a night of rising wind and scudding cloud. As they stepped through the doors into the darkened street the guns were sounding. Charlotte stiffened, lifted her head to the sky. A searchlight beam swept the swift-moving clouds. Somewhere close a whistle blasted. 'Zepp raid!' someone shouted. 'Get off the street!'

Charlotte's stomach churned in cold terror. 'Peter!' She clutched at Peter's arm. She was trembling.

'It's all right, love –' Soothingly he had put an arm about her. 'They won't –' He stopped. In the silence they heard it; the droning sound of an engine, high above them. The guns boomed again. Charlotte turned her face into Peter's chest, her hands over her ears, all but paralysed with fear. She was truly terrified of these monsters and their bombs; they haunted her dreams.

'Come on. The station –' Peter caught her hand, trying to make her move.

'I can't,' her teeth were chattering. 'I *can't*!'

'Come on, sweetheart – you'll be safe in the station –'

She began to move jerkily, her legs trembling so badly she could barely stand upright. Peter held her, talking, coaxing, drawing her towards the station and safety. The explosion nearly deafened them. Dirt and debris flew around them. '*Down!*' Peter threw her to the ground, his body on top of her, shielding her. She was sobbing uncontrollably. The guns roared. The street was lit with a livid flicker of flame. 'It's all right. It's all right, my little love. I'm here. I'll take care of you – don't be frightened.' Peter's voice in her ear was gentle, his hands held her, firm and strong. 'There – you see? It's over. All over. And you're all right – come on, my love. Sit up. Show me that pretty face.'

She struggled to a sitting position. The building that had been hit further down the street blazed, blossoms of flame curling around the upstairs windows. A bell jangled. Men shouted. She was sitting on the kerb, Peter beside her, his arm firm about her shoulders. Her stockings and her frock were torn and dirty. One of her shoes had come off. Tears still ran down her face. 'I'm s-sorry. I'm s-such a coward!'

She saw the shine of his smile in the firelight. 'Don't be silly. Of course you aren't.' She looked like a fragile, terrified child huddled beside him, her hair full of dirt, her face smeared with tears.

'It's just – I c-can't s-stand them – the airships – and the bombs – they frighten me so – I try to be brave but –' Pathetically the tears began to roll again. She was still trembling.

The fire had taken hold. People stood watching. She shuddered and turned away. With no words he gathered her into his arms and held her, held her as she wept, her head upon his shoulder, her slender body shaking as if with a fever. 'They frighten me so!' she said again between the sobs.

He laid his cheek against her dirty hair, letting her cry, waiting for the terror to subside. After a few minutes the sobbing eased, and though she still shuddered every now and again the awful trembling had stopped. She sighed a little, like a child, snuggled closer to him, her breath still catching in her throat. He tightened his arms about her.

443

She sniffed. Smiling a little he reached for his handker-chief, tucked it into her hand. Still sheltered by his arm she wiped her eyes, blew her nose. Lifted her head. His face, lit by the flicker of the flames, was inches from hers. 'I'm — sorry,' she whispered. 'You must think me such a coward. I just —' she stopped. For a long moment neither of them moved, a small island of silence in the chaos around them. Then he bent his head. Their lips touched, very gently. She pulled away a little, watching him, her eyes enormous. Then with a small gasp she leaned to him, lifting her lips to his, clinging, murmuring, her hand behind his head, drawing him to her.

He had wanted to kiss her ever since that moment a week ago when she had appeared at the parlour door, slender and womanly in her pale silk. Had wanted to and had resisted it. She was Ben's wife. She was not — could not be — for him. He had teased her and laughed with her, he had watched her, taken pleasure in her pretty ways, her lovely face, her graceful body. But he had known, oh yes, all along he had known that the fruit was forbidden; and perhaps the more tantalizingly desirable for that. He had not touched her, had resisted the tasting; until now. And now, as they kissed and clung, as his hands slipped from her supple waist to her small breasts, thumbs rubbing gently at the nipples, as he felt her mouth open in a gasp beneath his, a small grim voice somewhere in his mind spoke of betrayal and disaster. But louder, much louder, spoke the urgent need of his body, the joy of touching her, the wonder of her desire that so obviously matched his. She broke away from him, buried her head in his chest, would not look at him. He was whispering — whispering — small endearments, loving words — in God's name what was he doing? 'Darling Charlotte — darling, darling Charlotte — I love you —'

And then she pulled away from him, sharply; sat hunched upon the kerb, watching him with enormous eyes that were full of fear, her hands to her cheeks. 'No,' she

444

said, her voice very low. 'No – Peter – we can't – he'd – he'd kill us –'

She saw him flinch from that, saw the pain flicker in his eyes at mention of Ben. Stiffly he scrambled to his feet, extended a hand to help her up. Her lower lip was trembling. She looked like a lovely, dirty little girl, terrified that the grown ups would discover she had been naughty. He wanted to grab her, crush her, hold her; protect her. Jesus! He was out of his mind.

'Well –' He bent, picked up his cap from the pavement and fixed it at a jaunty angle on his head. 'Good old Fritz, eh? You can always trust him to whip up a bit of excitement when things get dull. Come on, old bean – time for home, I think?'

She did not, as they had originally planned, go with him to the station the next day. They said their goodbyes in full view of the gathered inmates of the Bear, Doctor Will gruff, Bron sniffing into her handkerchief. The lips that brushed his cheek were cool; the hands that held his trembled very slightly.

Sitting on the train, staring moodily from the window at the peaceful countryside that sped past, he decided that it was no bad thing after all to be going back to France; the war might be bloody, but at least you knew where you were with Fritz, and the basic business of staying alive was comparatively uncomplicated – he leaned his head to the back of the seat and closed his eyes, trying with more determination than success to erase from his mind the blue eyes and delicately pretty face, the sweetly curving body of his brother's wife.

Chapter Sixteen

I

'Got five minutes, Miss? Fancy a cup of tea?'

Sally jumped. Curled into the driving seat of the Talbot, the June sun streaming on to her face, she had propped her chin on the arm that rested along the open window and, taking advantage of a habit she had acquired very rapidly since coming to France, dozed off. The voice that had woken her was oddly and faintly familiar; it belonged to a dark silhouette that moved and turned as she squinted into the sunlight, and resolved itself into a dark-skinned, dark-eyed face with a quizzical lift to one eyebrow and a grin like a schoolboy's bent upon mischief. 'Remember me?'

For the moment she did not. Bemused by sleep, she stared blankly.

The grin widened. 'Eddie Browne. Bloody London in the fog, remember?'

She pushed herself upright embarrassed, straightening her cap which had slipped to the side of her head. 'Oh, of course, I'm sorry – I dozed off – we were up the line last night and Fritz decided it was party time. We spent best part of the night sitting it out in a shelter, and there wasn't much sleep to be had.' She rubbed her eyes. Her face felt uncomfortably warm in the sun.

'You made it, then?'

'I'm sorry?'

He smiled again at her sleep-induced confusion. 'You made it – to France.'

'Oh. Yes. Look, I'm sorry. I'm an absolute idiot when I first wake up. Can we start again?'

'Happen so. I said, "Got five minutes, Miss – fancy a cup of tea?"'

She laughed at that, remembering. 'There's no Lyons Corner House with a steamed up window here. No tea worth drinking either, that I've found!'

'That's true. But there's a bar across the road.'

She shook her head. 'I really can't this time, Sergeant. I'm on duty –' She stopped, seeing his grin, then her eyes flicked to his sleeve, and stifling laughter she corrected herself. 'I beg your pardon – I really can't this time, *Corporal*. I really am on duty. What did you do?'

He sketched a disinterested shrug. 'The usual sort of thing. Does being on duty mean you can't talk to me?'

'No. It means I can't nip off to the nearest bar.'

'Ah. Well that's all right then. Fag?' He took a battered pack of cigarettes from his pocket and offered her one.

She shook her head, said, 'Go ahead,' as he cocked an enquiring brow, watched him as he lit up and drew a deep, satisfied breath. She had carried his hastily scribbled address for weeks, honestly intending to write but somehow in the whirl of departure never getting round to it. She had remembered their brief meeting with affection and amusement; something about this brash young man had appealed to her then, and did again now as he rested a foot on the running board and leaned with relaxed and easy stance upon his lifted knee, the cigarette held between long, nicotine-stained fingers. 'What a coincidence', she said, 'to meet again like this. After all it isn't as if –' She hesitated, quick to see the flicker of amusement in the dark eyes, the faintest negative shake of the head. 'Not a coincidence?' she asked, just a little warily.

He shook his head. 'Happen I don't believe in coincidences, lass. Happen I think life's too short to wait for 'em.'

'But – how?'

He shrugged a little, smiled blandly. 'I've got a few contacts, here an' there. Got a few friends, like, who owe me a few favours – you know? Couldn't forget a name like van Damme, now, could I? And when it began to look as if you weren't going to write – well – as they say in some parts – I put a few enquiries in hand.'

She chuckled at that, amused despite herself at the beguiling cheek of the man. 'Supposing I'd registered under my maiden name?'

'What was that?'

'Smith.'

His grin was appreciative. 'Happen I'd have had to rely on coincidence after all.' He let the grin die, watched her narrowly, the dark eyes direct. 'Why didn't you write? I'd the feeling that you would?'

She flushed a little, abashed by the directness of the question. 'I was going to. Honestly, I was. But – well the posting came through, and there was so much to do.'

He nodded.

'So – how *did* you find me? Today I mean?'

'We're out of the line for four days. Rest camp a few miles away. Rumour from HQ mentioned your name.' He grinned a little, 'Whatever you like to say there aren't all that many "lady drivers" about – thought I'd come and see for myself.'

'Been in the thick of it all, I suppose?'

'You could say so. Armentières and Houplines mostly.'

'Tough?'

He made a small, deprecating gesture with the hand that held the cigarette. Nodded. 'Tough enough. You?'

She ran her fingers about the steering wheel pensively. 'The colonel tries to keep me out of it – away from the line – if he can. But we're up at the Front quite a bit and the bullets have flown once or twice. And of course there's always the barrage. And when I'm off duty I quite often help with the running of personnel and supplies to the clearing stations or the dressing huts. That can be a bit hairy at times. But it's not like being in the front line.'

He grinned. 'Not far off it, I reckon.' It occurred to her that, exactly as had happened before, they were within minutes of meeting talking like old friends. 'How did you lose your stripe?' she asked.

For a moment she thought he would not reply. He took his foot from the running board, straightened, squinting in the sun, took a long drag on his cigarette. Then the grin reappeared. 'Same way I lost the others – found meself outside of a couple of glasses of non-issue rum – told some short-arsed toffee-nosed captain what I thought of his imperialists' war – an' told him for good measure what the working classes would do to his kind once we'd fought his sodding battles for him and saved his upper-crust skin – told him I'd got a sight more in common with poor old exploited Private Fritz over there than I had with him.'

'Eddie! They don't take your stripes away for that sort of talk! They shoot you!'

He leaned back to the window, tapping the side of his lean nose knowingly, his dark eyes full of laughter. 'I told you, van Damme – I've got friends.'

She was laughing outright. 'But they still take your stripes away.'

'Only because they enjoy watching me get them back again. Bloody hell,' he added mildly, straightening again, 'I reckon I could have been a brigadier at least by now if I'd kept trying.'

'The Bolshie Brigadier –' she sketched a laughing salute, 'yes, sir!'

They surveyed each other for a long, smiling, somehow satisfying moment. He cocked his head in coolly and humorously impertinent enquiry. 'You wouldn't be free this evening, by any chance, would you, Sally Smith van Damme?'

'As a matter of fact, Brigadier – I do think I might be able to manage that.'

'Caviare and champagne at the Amiens Ritz, happen – a box at the opera? Or rissoles and plonk at the local? Whichever you like – sky's the limit when you're out with Eddie Browne, lass.'

She grinned, 'Rissoles sound good.'

'Right-oh. I'll pick you up at your billet at eight.' He saluted her breezily, turned and swung jauntily away – without she noticed, laughing to herself, knowing the small cheeky gesture to be deliberate, having to ask where her billet was.

'You'd like him. He really is a character. He's got the cheek of a barrowload of monkeys, but you have to laugh at him. And underneath – well –' Sally found herself frowning a little thoughtfully, as she watched Hannah's deft and practised fingers neatly rolling freshly washed bandages, 'I get the feeling he's really a very intelligent man. Almost entirely self-taught – he left school at twelve to go into the mills – he knows an enormous lot about an enormous number of things. Well,' she added with a grin, 'he can convince you that he does – do you want a hand with that?'

'I wouldn't say no.'

Sally washed her hands, joined Hannah at the table, reached for a length of bandage. 'He's convinced that after the war there's going to be a change in British politics. He says the Labour Party – sooner or later – will form a government.'

'I've heard Ralph say the same thing. I must say it sounds like a bit of happy wishful thinking to me.'

'Perhaps. But he's a hard-headed lad – not like Ralph at all.' Her eyes upon her task, Sally did not see the shadow that flickered upon Hannah's face at mention of Ralph's name; though he had escaped official punishment for his escapade, his few and sketchy letters hinted at ongoing recrimination from 'Tom Brown's chums' who had obviously not so easily been fooled by his excuses and explanations. 'Eddie honestly seems to believe that it has to happen,' Sally was saying. 'He's going to stand for Parliament, no less – at least that's what he says.'

'Is he indeed?' Hannah lifted her head to look at Sally, suddenly quizzical. 'Sounds as if this young man's made quite an impression?'

'What? Oh, no! Nothing like that.' Sally shook a casual head, not altogether convincingly Hannah thought, 'He's just a friend, that's all. Good fun.' Her eyes flicked to Hannah's and away, but not before what she had seen in them had set her giggling. 'Just a friend, Hannah! That's all!'

'Well – we'll see.' Hannah grinned back, took up the bandage again. 'You've seen Ben?'

Sally's quick fingers faltered a little, then resumed the smooth motion of folding and rolling. 'I – no – I haven't got round to it actually.'

'But Sally!' Hannah was astonished. 'For heaven's sake! You know he's just at the base hospital! – Goodness, you must have been there this morning to pick up the supplies you brought us?'

'Well – yes, I was – but I don't have that much time – and I wanted to see you. I've got this arrangement with Sergeant Brice at the depot that anything to come out here I'm the first driver on the list. I couldn't spend too much time hanging around.'

'Well, maybe not – but you will pop in to see him, won't you? He'll be hurt if you don't.'

As I've been hurt that he hasn't come to find me – she did not put the quick and unexpected thought into words. 'I'll look him up soon.'

'I wish you would. You know Ben – all work and no play – ah, but I've just remembered, you're coming to Matron's At Home on Sunday, aren't you? With your colonel?'

'Yes, that's right.'

451

'Ben will be here, he's promised faithfully. So you can get together then.'

'Always provided she can fight her way past mournful Mercy.' The amused voice came from the open doorway. 'Hello there, Sal. How's tricks?' Fiona ambled elegantly into the room, turned up her nose at the pile of bandages. 'Ugh! Before the war – there was a before the war, wasn't there? It isn't a figment of my imagination? – before the war this is the kind of thing the tweeniest of the upstairs maids would do.' She feigned a long, bored yawn, 'What *is* Fiona MacAdam of the Stirlingshire MacAdams doing here, can you tell me?' She reached for a bandage and began to roll, slanted a glance at Sally, 'Well?'

'Well how's tricks? Or well what is Fiona MacAdam doing rolling bandages with the likes of me?' Sally asked, grinning. Between these two, oddly, had blossomed an immediate rapport from the first moment of their meeting. They teased each other constantly and with inventive and merciless humour, poking derisive fun each at the other's background and accent – Sally making no more effort to disguise the flat vowels and idiosyncratic turns of phrase which for all Ralph's years of patient coaching would always declare her less than exalted background, than did Fiona the affected drawl of privilege. Indeed it amused Hannah to note that in each other's company each would deliberately exaggerate her own speech mannerisms, Sally all but burlesquing the chirpy Cockney, Fiona striking attitudes of grandeur that would suddenly have them both helpless with laughter. Poor Mercy, of course, was hopelessly confused by it all. Thought of Mercy reminded her of Fiona's opening comment, and she interrupted before the double act could wind itself up too far.

'What do you mean about Sally fighting her way past Mercy?'

Fiona bestowed upon her a patient, languid look. 'For Pete's sake, Hannah – you *must* have noticed? The maddening Mercy has conceived a passion for your rapidly becoming famous brother that – for the mewling Mercy – is quite uncontrollable. By which I mean she moons over him from a distance and blushes like an adolescent or runs a mile if he actually addresses her. But – who knows? – if another female should approach him?' She waved her bandage dramatically. 'The ghastly girl might emerge in her true colours.'

'Mad Mercy?' Sally suggested straight faced.

'Malicious Mercy –' Fiona wound a bandage around her hands in the fashion of a garrotte and graphically mimed a strangling.

'Merciless Mercy!' Sally had begun to giggle.

'Stop it, you two!' Hannah could not entirely hide her own laughter.

Fiona drew a finger across her own throat. 'Mutilating Mercy! Ouch!' She turned an injured look on Hannah, 'What did you do that for?'

Hannah withdrew the foot with which she had trodden in no gentle manner on the other girl's toe and smiled brightly towards the doorway. 'Hello, Mercy? Were you looking for me?'

Fiona turned a sharply droll look on Sally. 'Well she certainly wouldn't have been looking for me!'

Mercy stood in the doorway, her pink and white face uncertain and suspicious at the same time. 'I – wondered if you needed any help with the bandages?'

'We do have rather a lot of hands already, actually.'

'Oh no you don't.' Fiona, with an angelic smile dropped her bandage and held her hands at shoulder height, 'You just lost a pair. I only came in to say hello to Sal.' She turned to Sally, 'Hello, Sal,' she said brightly, then, 'there, now I'm going. Oh – you are coming on Sunday?'

'Yes.'

'Good. Pray to whichever God you pray to that the weather holds. Matron is determined to have music and the darling boys are determined to pander to her determi-

nation. We've got the band of the Irish Guards coming –
and if I know anything they'll play come hell or high
water. Just the thought of listening to all that oompapa
in a confined space really makes me quite faint. So if the
weather's bad make sure you have your sal volatile
handy, won't you? 'Bye –'

Sally grinned at her departing back. 'What a lad she is.'

Mercy pursed her lips, not sure quite how to take that.

Sally, relenting, winked at her. 'Figs to Fiona?' she offered, a gingerly humorous apology; and was rewarded
more by Hannah's quick grin and by Fiona's own
muffled laughter as she walked away than by Mercy's
uncertain smile.

II

Fortunately for Fiona's nerves the weather held for
Matron's Sunday afternoon At Home, which was held, as
planned, in the garden of the big old house which served
as a Mess for the hospital staff. The garden, surrounding
three sides of the house, had been more than a little
neglected during nearly two years of wartime use, but
was perhaps rather the more beautiful for that. The
lawns were shaded by picturesquely overgrown shrubs
and trees, the roses that had scrambled riotously up the
high brick walls enclosing the garden were a blaze of
colour. As Sally rolled the car to a halt outside the
wrought-iron gates, the instantly recognizable strains of
Gilbert and Sullivan lifted on the warm summer air. Her
passenger leaned forward eagerly, smiling broadly, 'Ah,
that's Caroline all right; no tea party's complete without
The Mikado! You'll be all right parking the car, my
dear?'

Sally smothered a grin; always he asked, and always
she said the same thing. 'Yes, sir. I'm sure I can manage.'
The colonel had never got around to learning to drive.

'Good, good. I'll see you later then. Come and be introduced to Caroline. Splendid woman in my opinion. Splendid.'

'Yes, sir.' She moved the big car into a side street, considered and then decided against having a peaceful cigarette before joining Hannah and the others. When she reached the ornate cast-iron gates the garden was already busy. A small band, resplendent and sweating in brilliant scarlet tunics and bearskins, instruments and buttons shining like gold, was stationed beneath a spreading tree playing a Chopin waltz with the verve and military precision due to a Sousa march. Tables and chairs had been spread beneath the trees and upon the small terrace; each table had its white tablecloth, its plates, cups and saucers, its gleaming cutlery and a small bunch of flowers. Over and around the sound of music rang talk and laughter. Sally stood for a long moment watching. Had it not been for the uniforms, and for the intermittent sound of gunfire in the distance this might have been the very picture of a village fête held in the garden of a country vicarage in the heart of England. To be sure the young men outnumbered the women by four or five to one, and many of them – recovering, walking wounded from Officers' Ward – walked with sticks or carried an arm in a sling, but yet the atmosphere of innocent pleasantries and genteel laughter was so incongruous that for an unnerving moment she thought she might laugh aloud. Or cry.

'Sally!' Hannah hurried to her. 'There you are – you're late.'

'The road up by Bresle was shelled last night. We had to come the long way round.' She allowed Hannah to usher her to a table beneath a deep-shading chestnut tree, where sat Fiona and several young men in uniform, all of whom leapt to their feet as Hannah and Sally approached.

'So – the fearless chauffeuse has arrived at last.' Fiona raised a cheery hand, then turned a guileless smile upon her companions. 'I'm sorry, chaps, I really can't remember who's who. This is Sally van Damme – perhaps you'd be so kind as to introduce yourselves?'

Sally found her hand taken and shaken, eyes blue, brown and shades between smiled into hers, fair heads and brown were bared as the young men removed their headgear and murmured their introductions.

'Captain Mellors, Suffolks – how do you do?'

'Lieutenant Reece – Third Middlesex – very pleased to meet you.'

'Derby. Lieutenant Derby. Royal Engineers. Hello.'

She smiled and murmured her own replies, allowed herself to be manoeuvred into a chair between Lieutenant Reece and a red-headed young man in tartan-trimmed kilt and khaki who introduced himself as Rory MacAllister of the Seaforth Highlanders. She accepted cake, 'From Harrods, d'you know – what a wonder!' and tea, 'Darjeeling, no less! Good old Lady Bennet,' and politely involved herself with her own affairs whilst one of her escorts topped up his brew with a snifter of whisky from a dented flask. She agreed that it was a marvellous day, that it must at this moment be truly wonderful in the English countryside, that surely, soon, the expected Big Push must come – and watched the figure who stood in the frame of the big cast-iron gate looking about him, a half-smile on his straight mouth, the shock of hair, the wide shoulders, square jaw and high, broad cheekbones unmistakable even at this distance. She glanced at Hannah, who was deep in conversation with the lieutenant from the Royal Engineers and obviously had not yet noticed her brother's arrival. The band had very sensibly returned to the safety of Gilbert and Sullivan and a selection from *HMS Pinafore*. Ben's eyes roamed the gathering for a moment, then settled upon their table. A fraction of a second before she knew he would find them, Sally turned to the Highlander. 'Have you been in France long, Captain MacAllister?'

Moments later she heard Hannah's cry of welcome. 'Ben! Here you are at last!' and looked up to see Ben Patten,

456

whom she had last seen standing on the docks at Zee-brugge watching her sail home, smiling and hugging his sister, greeting the others about the table with affable courtesy, grinning a friendly hello at Fiona and finally reaching two big hands to her, a smiling warmth in his eyes as he said, 'Sally?' She took the strong hands, allowed him to draw her to her feet, felt the brush of his lips on her cheek. 'Hello, Ben.'

He did not for the moment release her hands. Conversation around them had lifted again. 'How are you?'

She could not take her eyes from his. 'I'm fine. You?'

'As you see.' He was relaxed, casual, friendly. He was thinner, less bulky, and his face was leaner than she remembered. He gave his sudden, rare, boyish grin. 'Life has its ups and downs. How's Philippa?'

'She's fine. She wrote me a letter last week. Well – almost –'

He laughed. 'And our poor little Belgian mother?'

'Marie-Clare? She's doing very well indeed. Louise is a lovely child, and Marie-Clare's found a perfect niche at the Bear.'

'Good.'

'I hear you're doing well?' Stupid words. Stilted. Meaningless. Something ridiculously like anger stirred, though whether with herself or with him, and what was at its root, she could not for her life have said.

He shrugged a little. 'There's a lot to do.' He had sobered a little. 'Sally?'

She disentangled the hands he was still holding, 'Yes?'

'Why haven't you come to see me?'

The inexplicable anger centred itself into a small needle flame. She smiled very brightly. 'As you say, there's a lot to do,' she repeated his words crisply, then turned away, reseating herself neatly between the Third Middlesex and the Seaforths. 'Lieutenant Reece – would you mind cutting me another slice of that wicked cake?'

She felt Ben's suddenly sharply puzzled eyes upon her

and in turning from them caught a quizzically sly and disconcertingly acute glance that brought a sudden rush of colour to her face. Fiona raised humorously knowing eyebrows and grinned openly at Sally's discomfiture before returning to the combined adulation of half a dozen eager young men.

Sally was aware that Ben had seated himself across the table from her, amongst Fiona's bevy of admirers. He did not glance at her again. She tried to concentrate on Lieutenant Reece's paeons of praise for her work and for the work of the female nursing staff of the hospitals and dressing stations. 'You can't know how topping it is for us to talk to an English girl – to know you're here – jolly brave I call it – too brave for words, really – everyone says it – and the nurses – well, no one can know what it's like if you're wounded to wake and find one of our own girls holding your hand. They're spiffing, aren't they?'

He paused for an answer. She summoned a smile. He looked, she thought with sudden shock, about a year older than Toby. If that. 'They certainly are. You've been wounded?'

'Oh, once or twice. Nothing too bad, you know.'

'You've been in France long?' Suddenly she was truly looking at him – the bruised sockets of the young eyes, the odd, nervous tic that every few seconds flicked a non-existent lick of hair from his forehead.

'A year, actually.' He made a small, self-deprecating gesture, 'Left Oxford to join up. Mater was awfully miffed, you know? But she's come round now.' For a single, awful second he looked like a very small, uncertain boy. 'I'm an only child, you see,' his voice was soft, apologetic. 'And two cousins have gone west since this little lot started. You can't blame her for worrying.'

'I'm sure she's very proud of you.' Sally's heart, suddenly, was like lead.

He grinned, a swift, conspiratorial grin. 'You just have

to treat it like a bit of a lark, really, don't you? I mean –
otherwise –' He stopped, looking into his teacup vaguely,
as if he had forgotten what he had intended to say. 'Well,
none of them over there know what it's like – what it's
really like – do they? When I go home –' He lifted his
eyes, shrugged wryly, 'Well, you know?'

She nodded. 'I know.'

'I say, Hannah,' Fiona's clear, aristocratic tones could
be ice-sharp and clear as a bell when she wanted, as now,
to cut through the general conversation, 'is this an ex-
patient I see before me? And could he possibly be misgui-
ded enough to have come in search of his own particular
ministering angel? Oh Lord,' she rolled maliciously bright
eyes, 'how extraordinarily artistic of him!'

Sally glanced first at Hannah, and was astonished to see
that, her eyes fixed upon the gate, she had lost all colour,
her plain, strong face, usually so full of vivacity, drained
to stillness. With the rest of the company – as the
provocative Fiona had no doubt intended – Sally looked
towards the gates. A tall young man, pale faced and sandy
haired, his uniform a little rumpled, his cap pushed to an
unmilitary angle on the back of his head, stood looking
uncertainly about the busy garden. Under his arm he held
a battered leather folder. As he hesitated a girl in nurse's
uniform approached him and he ducked his head to speak
to her.

Hannah stood up.

Fiona grinned and winked at Sally.

'Excuse me.' The words were a breath. Hannah looked
at no one around the table. Lifting her skirts and with no
further apology she edged around the table and started to
hurry across the lawn. The young man nodded to the
nurse and turned. Seeing Hannah – and, Sally thought
with wry sympathy, being utterly unaware of an audience
– he stood for a moment watching her approach.

'And if ever it could be said that a man's heart was in
his eyes –' Fiona, somehow, had materialized beside

Sally, the words breathed into her ear, 'there it is. Lucky old Hannah, eh?'

'Who is he?'

'Artist chappie. Giles Redfern. Caught it – oh – must be four months or so ago. Now he's back.' Fiona smiled, and her eyes on Hannah were affectionate, 'And good luck to him.'

Hannah had stopped, hesitating. Giles snatched his hat from his sandy head and ran to her; held out both hands. Shyly, Hannah took them in hers.

'Right-o, chaps,' Fiona moved easily, elegantly nonchalant, to the centre of the stage, 'who's game to chance a dance? Bags I someone', a long, pointed finger swept the circle and rested, pointing at the kilted Rory MacAllister, 'suggests forcibly to the dear band that a garden party is not the same without a small tea dance?'

'What about Matron?' someone asked.

'Ask her yourself. Here she is.'

Sally scrambled to her feet. Colonel Foster, his hand firm upon Matron's small arm, beamed at her. 'Caroline – here she is – Sally van Damme – best driver – best damn' mechanic – I've ever had!'

The diminutive Lady Bennet extended a capable hand and flashed a warm smile. 'Well done, my dear. We'll show 'em, eh?'

'Er – yes – ma'am.' Sally, feeling an ungainly, inarticulate and untidy giant beside the tiny, neatly uniformed woman, heard Fiona's soft laughter and, flushed to the roots of her hair.

Caroline, Lady Bennet, Matron in Charge of Number Two Casualty Clearing Station, Béthune, indulged in a wicked wink, and nudged her elderly escort. 'Home and hearth eh, Reginald? Wasn't that what I've heard you say? And where was your vote on women's suffrage, eh? Feeling a bit different now, are we?'

The colonel cleared his throat. Sally avoided his eyes and kept, with some difficulty, a dignified straight face.

Matron reached up to pat her arm maternally. 'They're used to us patching up their cuts and bruises, my dear. Not so used to having our fingers in their engines, eh?' She laughed, a clear, infectious laugh, 'Keep up the good work, my dear. We're driving the trams at home. They won't keep us down now.'

Sally grinned. 'Yes, ma'am.'

Lady Bennet bestowed a general smile, turned to leave.

'Matron?' Fiona flashed her own most beguiling smile, 'would you mind if we asked the – band –' the subversively graphic lift of her brows upon the word brought a few hastily disguised chuckles, 'to play a waltz or two? One or two of us wondered if we might dance? It's such a lovely afternoon.'

In the distance the guns grumbled.

'By all means, my dear, by all means. Enjoy yourselves – have some more cake.'

Fiona led her chosen beau to the bandmaster, bent to his ear. A moment later, baton high, he launched his men into an enthusiastic rendering of *Die Fledermaus*.

'I say – would you mind?'

Smiling, Sally allowed Lieutenant Reece to lead her into the grassy space beneath the tree. Other couples, laughing excitedly, were taking up the challenge, the girls in their nursing uniforms, the young men in muddy khaki. No man got a full dance; every few steps came a good-humoured tap upon the shoulder, another pair of arms in which to waltz. Fiona, Sally noticed with hilarity, actually had a queue waiting patiently in line for her to pass. She lost count of the number of young faces she smiled into, all so very different, all so very much the same. And then, suddenly, a face she knew; knew all too well. A pair of arms that would not give way to a tap on the shoulder, a breadth of shoulder and a coolness of eye with which no one would argue. They danced in silence, she and Ben, he with his eyes fixed upon some point in the far distance; waiting, she refusing to lift her head,

461

obscurely unwilling to look him in the eye, to face the questions, her own as well as his.

Then, with a flourish, the music changed, and she stumbled, missing her footing on the grass, having to grip Ben's arm to prevent herself falling.

Next to them a young man broke into song. '*Oh Danube so blue* – la la, la la –'

She stopped dancing. Shook her head. Ben tucked a firm hand beneath her arm and guided her through the tables, round the side of the house and into a tangle of overgrown fruit bushes through which a path meandered towards a tiny orchard. As a background to the birdsong and the sound of the music the war rumbled its own almost unnoticed refrain, far off. They walked slowly and in silence under the trees that were heavy with slow-forming, unripened fruit until, as if drawn by the same thread, they stopped, turned to each other in the dappled sunshine.

Sally stood like a statue, staring fixedly at the shining button, the crossed Sam Browne that was on a level with her eyes.

His hand lifted her chin, forced her to look at him. 'Well, Sally Smith? What is it?'

'What's what?' Her voice lacked conviction.

'I thought we were friends again? I thought – after Belgium – we were friends?'

'Of course we're friends. How could we not be? You saved me – and Philippa.'

'That isn't what I meant. You know it.'

She said nothing. Could not look away from his narrowed dark eyes. She sighed, the breath trembling in her throat.

'You've been in Amiens for three months. Why didn't you come to see me?'

'Why didn't *you* come to see *me*?' Her voice was impassioned.

He waited a long time before saying quietly, 'It's a fair question I suppose – except – I would have thought the answer obvious?'

'So obvious I can't see it.' Her voice was caustic. She turned from him, walked a little way away, stood picking at a tree trunk, scratching viciously with her fingernail.

He did not move to follow her. There was a long, thoughtful silence. 'A long time ago,' he said, his voice steady and very quiet, 'I hurt you very badly, I think. I wasn't sure – didn't know –' For the first time, beneath his control, she sensed the strain, the uncertainty, 'if Belgium made up for that? I hoped so. I thought we were friends. But then – thinking about it – I wasn't so sure – it seemed –' he hesitated, 'best to leave it to you. I thought you'd let me know, somehow, if you'd –' the pause was longer this time, 'forgiven me. Is that the word?'

She had turned to stare at him. She said nothing.

'When you arrived in France – it seemed best for me to wait; to give you the choice, to contact me or not. When you didn't –' He stopped.

A surge of something that she identified as fury – certainly it was strong enough, hot enough to be so described made her low voice shake. 'And why should I?'

She saw an answering spark of temper rise in his eyes and was glad of it. 'No reason, I suppose. I just hoped –'

'Hoped?' She picked up the word sharply, stepped closer to him, head up, challenging. 'What did you hope, Ben?'

For a moment they stood, the fine-drawn thread of attraction that had been strung between them so strongly and for so long, that both had denied and tried so hard to break, holding them, even now unwilling. It was the sudden, almost infinitesimal dropping of his shoulders, the helpless turn of his head that broke her.

'Ben,' she said, 'oh, Ben!' and her voice, suddenly was a breath away from tears. 'And *you* called *me* a fool!'

He stood for a moment, and for the first time since she had known him she saw him bewildered, less that certain of himself. He shook his head. 'Sally – I didn't mean –'

'Yes you did.' Her husky voice was positive. 'Don't lie

to yourself, Ben. Don't lie to me. We both know what you meant. Why don't we admit it?'

He looked at her then, and his face was full of anguish. 'Because we can't. I can't. Because I'm not free – because I can't offer you the things you deserve. Oh Christ, Sally, you were right – right again – I should have stayed away from you.'

'But you didn't. In the end, you didn't.'

'No.'

The silence lengthened. Faintly a shell whistled and boomed. Ben half turned away from her. She watched him. 'Ben?'

'Yes?'

'Why did you do it? Why were you so – so very cruel that night? Did you know what you were doing to me?'

He nodded.

She waited. When he said nothing, 'For my own good,' she said flatly.

He turned on her. 'Yes! Bloody yes! And it worked, didn't it? If I hadn't – if I'd taken what you were offering – what we both wanted – oh, yes, I don't deny it – where would you have been? What would you have had to offer Philippe?' He grabbed her shoulders, shook her. 'Well?'

She was very still in his hands, offering no resistance to the unthinking violence of his strength. 'You wanted me?' she asked very quietly.

'Jesus Christ. Of course I did.' He became aware it seemed of the savagery of his grip on her shoulders. Very suddenly he let her go, stepping back from her, his face calming. Tiredly he rubbed the back of his hand across his jaw. 'I'm a married man, Sally. I was then, I am now. There's nothing I can offer you.'

'I know.' She was watching him, her eyes unfathomable.

'I should have left you alone.'

'Yes.'

'Is it too late?'

She shrugged. 'Who knows?'

He struggled for a moment with the words, a complex, arrogant man unused to bending, 'Too late to be friends?'

She smiled at that suddenly, held out her hand, the tension gone. 'It's never too late for that.' Somewhere, very deep within her, something small and warm was moving, growing – something that had been cold and lifeless as stone since Philippe's death. She smiled calmly, guarding it, unwilling for the moment even to think about it, to acknowledge it. 'We'd better get back.'

He nodded, took her arm to guide her back along the narrow path towards the lawns. As they emerged into the sunshine they stopped, listening to laughter, watching the couples – only a dozen or so due to the lack of partners, even Matron herself being waltzed breezily across the grass by a fresh-faced young Guards officer. Ben dropped her arm and gave her a gentle push. 'Off you go. Poor little devils – caught in this ghastly game – Matron's right – they do deserve some fun. And so do you.'

The band's repertoire of waltz tunes was obviously exhausted and they had begun a second round. As the so-familiar strains of the 'Blue Danube' struck up yet again Sally turned her head, caught the smile in Ben's eyes as he watched her.

'I say – would you care to dance?' A breathless young man appeared before her, his head neatly bandaged, one eye covered in a patch.

'Thank you. Yes, I would.'

'One of my favourite tunes this – just about the only one I can manage.'

She swung into his arms, humming. He grinned from ear to ear. 'La la la la la, la-la, la-la.'

III

Sally was kept very busy for the next few days; it was quite obvious that something important was afoot. She ferried

Colonel Foster and various high-ranking companions to and from meetings and conferences; the odd word, dropped here and there, confirmed her suspicions. Battalions were moving into the line all along the Somme. Something big was coming.

'Well, lass – we'll be going over soon, I reckon,' Eddie said during the course of one of their infrequent meetings as he strolled by her side through the darkened streets, the fireworks of the front lighting the skies above them. 'You going to give me a kiss for luck?'

She laughed – it was so very easy to laugh with Eddie – and did not answer.

He pulled a comic, affronted face. 'There's plenty more fish in the sea, thee knows!' He exaggerated his Yorkshire accent, 'Happen thee'll be sorry when I'm dead an' gone!'

She turned swiftly. 'Don't say that! Not even in fun.'

He slid an arm about her shoulder. 'Aha! Caught you!' And – surprisingly gently – he turned her face to his and kissed her lightly. 'There. That weren't so bad, were it?'

She smiled her affection, tucked her arm into his as they turned to stroll on. 'No, Eddie. That weren't so bad.'

'Happen you'd like to try it again sometime?'

She was aware that his eyes were rather more serious than his bantering voice. 'Happen,' she said very lightly.

When he left her at her door that evening, stepping back with the half-mocking salute he always gave her, it was she who stopped him. 'Eddie –'

He waited, the thin, gipsy-dark face in shadow.

'You will be careful?'

'I always am.'

'I doubt that. But – this time – if I don't see you before – well, whatever is going to happen happens –' she hesitated, 'be specially careful? Don't go trying to get that stripe back?'

She saw the glint of his teeth. 'Any particular reason?'

She posed her head in parody of deep thought, then shook it. 'No. Nothing I can think of. It's just I've grown quite fond of rissoles and plonk, and I don't know anyone else who knows where to find them.'

His chuckle was warm. 'Good night, van Damme.'

'Good night, Corporal.'

She had little spare time; no one did. As well as fulfilling her official capacity as driver to the colonel, she spent a lot of time ferrying hospital personnel and supplies to new dressing huts and clearing stations that were being set up close to the line. Oh yes, she thought, as she bumped for the third time in a day along the dusty, rutted, shell-pocked road that led forward, past the endless marching lines of men, the processions of horse-drawn gun carriages, the plodding mule supply trains, the field ambulances grinding their slow way to the Front, something was very much in the air. But in the few precious spare moments she did get in those last long June days, despite the genuine friendship that was growing between her and Eddie, and despite her pleasure in watching Hannah, in brave defiance of the circumstances, grow daily more happy in her love for her Giles, one person and one person only seemed to monopolize her thoughts, no matter how hard she tried to prevent it.

Ben.

She had gone over and over, word for word, that strange conversation in the garden at Albert. She had recalled every expression, every nuance of every phrase. She could not get it out of her head. It was, in a strange way, as if the conversation had not been finished; as if there had been so much more to be said. For the first couple of days she had looked for him; surely, after what had been said – after what he had at last all but admitted – he would come to find her? But he had not, and deep in her heart she had not been surprised. He had said nothing that afternoon to suggest that he had changed, and the intransigent pride, the steel-strong sense of duty was still there, a barrier between them that must surely be almost insurmountable. No, she was disappointed but not surprised when

467

she did not hear from him. She knew, as surely as she knew night from day, that he would make no further move towards her. She could leave things as they were and nothing more would ever be said. He was a principled and honourable man, a man she knew who saw the world in black and white, a man who would not take easily to deception and betrayal.

But – deception of whom? Betrayal of whom – or what?

He did not love Charlotte. She did not love him. Would Charlotte know – would she care? – if her husband stole a few precious months of happiness from this nightmare in which they all found themselves? Weren't so many people doing it? Didn't the war change things?

And she always stopped there. Because she knew what he would say if she put it to him. No. The war did not change things. He was still married. He still could not do what for him would be dishonourable. So he would do nothing.

He was, of course, almost certainly right.

She sat one still, late evening towards the end of the month at the small table in her bedroom, the smoke from her cigarette drifting through the open window into the street where, with steady tramp, yet another column of men in dusty khaki, hung about with helmets and gas masks, packs and entrenching tools, water bottles, pouches and rifles, marched past in ragged formation, led and escorted by their mounted officers – heading, she supposed, as everyone in the world in these past days had been heading, for the front line. She watched them pass. It seemed to her that the Allied bombardment had increased tonight, the sound rolling together in a thunder that echoed constantly in the summer skies. She wondered with an odd stirring of something like excitement if that were significant. There had been more activity in the air, too – enemy and Allied planes challenging each other above the long line of observation balloons that drifted in the sky over the front line. Eddie's battalion had moved into the line two days before. Jaunty as ever he had waylaid her the evening before they had left and they had managed a snatched couple of hours, with, inevitably, rissoles and plonk, in Eddie's favourite bar. There had been about him she had thought, a little worriedly, a high-strung, vivid tension that had disturbed her.

'You're looking forward to it!' she had said suddenly, in some amazement. 'You're positively excited!'

He had leaned to her, elbows on table, smoke spiralling into the already smoky air. 'And why not, lass?' he had asked very softly. 'It's something happening, isn't it? It isn't sitting on your arse in a hole with Gerry lobbing over Jack Johnsons or HE, with rats big as cats gnawing at your boots, with food like pig swill and sodding officers shouting the odds about your buttons being shiny? It's doing something. In a funny way, once it starts, it's you, on your own.' He had grinned, stubbed out his cigarette, lit another immediately. 'Trench raids. That's how I keep getting my stripes back, see lass? Trench raids. For most of the lads – they'll break a leg not to go. Me? I'm God's own volunteer. Out there, on your own, crawl through the wire, freeze when the flares go up – God, lass, you don't know what it's like! No one knows who hasn't been there.' The dark eyes, lit by candlelight, had smouldered with excitement. 'Then it's up an' at 'em. Him or you.' He had laughed suddenly at the expression on her face. 'Hey up, lass – don't look so took aback! Isn't it what life's all about? Takin' a chance?'

Very pensively she lifted her cigarette, watched the drifting smoke. Beyond the window the world moved with clinking, rhythmic step towards – what?

– Isn't it what life's all about? Taking a chance? –

She stood up, stubbed the cigarette out very carefully, reached for her light, khaki jacket, crammed the peaked cap on her head and left the room.

*

He might, of course, have been on duty. Or at the Mess. Or out with friends. If he were, she had decided, as she had followed the road that led from the village to the once-grand château that was now the Base Hospital, she would take it as a sign. Not my fault, but Thine, o Lord. If I am not to see him, then just make him be somewhere else –

He was there.

When she pushed open the door he was in his favourite position in a deep chair by the window, taking advantage of the last of the summer light, his feet on the windowsill, a book propped in front of him. He turned in surprise as the door opened.

She stood for a moment in the open doorway. 'Hello, Ben.'

'Sally!' He scrambled to his feet, unfolding his huge frame, towering almost to the low ceiling.

She turned, shut the door behind her, stood for a moment, her back against it, watching him.

'Please –' he said, 'come in.' The first surprise had been overcome, voice and face were perfectly and politely controlled.

She shook her head. 'You may not want me to.' She heard herself the odd edge to a voice that was always husky.

He said nothing.

She stood for a moment, marshalling words. 'I could say that I'd come to ask how you were.' There was a jaunty defiance in the words, and, as always when she was under stress, she heard the almost deliberate harshness of London's back streets in her voice, 'or to tell you that I saw Hannah yesterday for two minutes; they've evacuated, and they're moving up to the line tomorrow, did you know? To a place called Bray-sur-Somme. And she's head over heels in love, bless her; isn't it fun?' She paused, added brightly, 'I s'pose I could say I've got a splinter in me finger?' She shrugged like an urchin, added more

470

softly, 'I could say that the mountain has come to Mohammed, or whatever his name was.'

The silence was absolute. Beneath the level, austere gaze she felt the colour rise to her cheeks. But she would not look away. She had decided to come, and here she was. She would see it through. Somehow, for good or for ill, this thing had to be finished, 'I could say that I love you,' she said.

The look on his face could not be denied; it was pure pain. He half turned from her. 'Sally!'

No more than he did she raise her voice. 'Don't tell me!' she said, in a ridiculously reasonable voice. 'Don't tell me about Charlotte and Rachel, and your Dad and Hannah, and everyone else, and what a respected and respectable man you are – don't tell me! I know! Do you think I don't? Do you think I'm blind? Or an idiot? Do you think – God help us! – that I don't *know* you?'

Outside a bird had begun to sing, solitary and sweet. The last rays of the dying sun stained the sky to the hue of blood and glinted on the metallic underbellies of the great observation balloons hanging in the distance. The guns boomed monotonously.

'There's a bloody war on,' she said, suddenly tired. 'We might all be dead tomorrow. Doesn't that change *anything*?'

'Sally – stop it! Please! I can offer you nothing!'

'You said that before. I've been thinking about it. Tell me – what does it actually mean? That you can't offer me marriage? I know.' She grinned a little, faintly caustic, 'Have I asked? That you can't offer me permanency? I know. That you can't offer me respectability? Your name? I know. I *know*! Ben – try the thing that you can offer me. Go on,' she moved a little towards him, her eyes intent upon his, 'try it.'

He said nothing.

'Ben?'

The square, craggy face was set. Still he did not speak.

She stepped lightly to him, lifted her face to look into his. 'Coward!' she said gently, 'bloody coward!'

He made the slightest of movements. Stopped. 'Yes,' he said.

She turned a little from him, bitterness in her face. 'Coward!' she said again, more quietly but with infinitely more honest feeling.

He moved then, a swift step, his hand hard on her arm. 'Sally, be careful! Don't push me too far.'

She swung on him, tears gleaming suddenly in her eyes. 'Damn care for a lark, Doctor Patten! That's what I came for! To see you lose control, just once! To see you do something – just once! – that *you* want to do! Something your heart – your *guts* – tell you to do – not your stupid, duty-bound, bone-headed head! To see Doctor Ben God almighty Patten act like a common or garden human being, not like Jesus Christ on a monument!'

'*Sally!*' He swung her to face him.

Tears were running down her face, hateful tears that she could not control; defeating tears. She wanted nothing now so much as simply to get away. 'Let me go!' Futilely she tried to wrench herself from his grip.

'Sally – please! – don't you see? It's you I'm thinking about! What about you? I couldn't hurt you – *use* you as I'd have to use you –'

'Why not?' She glared at him through reddened, tear-drowned eyes. '*Why not*? Think about it, Ben! If I say it's all right, then *why not*?'

He was watching her now, as shaken as she, in a fury of frustration. Almost he shook her, and furiously again she struggled to release herself and could not. 'Because –' he said, and stopped.

'Because your pride won't let you. Because your – bloody – man's – pride – won't let you. Because you think I'm a child, with no will, no needs, no *bloody pride* of my own! Righteous Ben Patten. Living everyone's lives for them! Sacrificing himself for others. But you can't accept sacrifice, can you? You aren't big enough for that! Well, damn your pride, Ben, and damn your obstinacy. And damn whatever part of you it is that bleats about a woman's freedom and then treats her like a child! It's time someone told you that you aren't always right! You don't always know what's best for everyone! I came because I wanted to. Because –' she struggled for a moment, lifted her head fiercely, 'because, God help me, I love you! If you can't accept that it's both our loss.' She was all but incoherent, 'Try thinking about what it cost me to get here! I should have had more bloody sense.' She turned blindly towards the door.

He caught her with easy strength, pulled her to him. They stood, clinging in a fraught and desperate silence. She was grimly fighting open tears. He waited a long time for the tension to ease. When he felt her relax a little he opened his arms and she walked away from him, dashing the back of her hand across her wet face. 'I'm sorry,' she said very quietly. 'I had no right to say any of those things. No right to come here.' She raised a tired, tear-stained face, attempted a bleak half-smile. 'That'll teach you to take homeless orphans in off the street, Ben Patten. Breeding will out, as they say –'

'Shut up, Sally. For Christ's sake – shut up.'

They stood in a long silence. The sun had sunk below the horizon; the sky was a glory of gold and red. Sally sniffed. Ben stood like a statue, his face expressionless as granite. She could all but feel the violence of the battle he was fighting. When he moved at last, slowly towards her, she lifted her chin, concealing the faint stirrings of something very like fear. He hesitated for one moment, waiting for her to move, giving her, she knew, a last chance to draw back.

She waited.

He kissed her with a ferocity that spoke of the disintegration of long-held control. His mouth was hard, his strength overpowering. Painfully he crushed her body against his, enveloping her, hurting her. She could feel his anguish and his anger; the overwhelming desire that, against his nature, drove him. He kissed her as if he would imprint himself on her soul, crush the life from her body. The explosion of his excitement was like a shellburst; and she burned with it. Fire against fire, she fought him; not to be free, but to possess him at last – to be possessed. She felt his hands at the buttons of her tunic, slid her own beneath his shirt, scratching and clinging, tangling her fingers in the matted hair of his chest, rubbing her thumbs across his nipples. Her hair fell tangled across her shoulders, which were bare and marked with his kisses. He took her savagely, standing, half-clothed, panting and streaming with sweat. At his climax he shouted agonizedly, throwing his head back, face clenched in a kind of fury. In the silence that followed she saw the glint of his tears, felt the faint, uncontrollable trembling of his body. Gently she drew his head to her, cradling him, drawing him to the bed. He lay like death, hardly breathing, his face buried in the crook of her arm as, with light and loving fingers she stroked his hair, traced the contour of neck and massive shoulder. Excitement ebbed, but her body still throbbed and glowed with the aftermath.

'Christ on the cross,' he said at last, his voice muffled, 'What have I done?'

'What we both wanted to do. What – if we're honest – we've both wanted to do for a very long time.'

He turned from her, throwing himself naked upon his back, his arm shielding his eyes, his mouth harsh with self-condemnation.

She leaned upon one elbow, watching him, running a fingertip across the dark mass of his chest, tracing his chin, resting lightly upon that uncompromising mouth. 'Ben.'

He did not move.

'Ben! Look at me.'

Very slowly he lifted his arm. There were salt smudges upon his cheeks. Very slowly and very deliberately she leaned above him and kissed him, tenderly, deeply and with every ounce of courage and love she could muster. For a moment his mouth stayed hard and ungiving beneath hers. Then his lips parted and he moved his head a little, his hand creeping up, holding her; but gently, gently and with no sign of the brutality he had just shown.

For an odd moment the guns had fallen silent.

She lifted her head. Smiled at him. He opened his mouth. She laid a finger on his lips. 'Don't you dare!'

He raised questioning brows.

'Apologize. Don't you dare apologize. I'll bloody kill you.'

The corners of his mouth twitched to a smile.

She snuggled beside him, her head on his shoulder, her arm across his chest. She felt, quite suddenly, the tension drain from him. He closed his eyes. She waited a long time, until the uneven thumping of his heart had settled to a quiet rhythm, and the arm that held her had relaxed a little. Then she turned her mouth to his ear, breathing the words, tongue and lips teasing. 'Next time', she said softly, 'could we take it a little slower? I do like to have time to take me boots off –' and was rewarded by the glint of laughter in his face as he turned to kiss her.

In those last days of June the bombardment laid across the eighteen miles of front that were the Somme valley escalated to a non-stop violence of noise and destruction that crushed the eardrums and shredded the nerves. On the last night of the month at a small village called Bus-les-Artois the band of the Leeds Pals gave a concert. Corporal Eddie Browne chose not to go; instead he sat in evening sunlight, his back against the rough boarding of a trench that was familiar enough to be called home meti-

475

culously honing and sharpening his bayonet, lifting it and turning it in the sunset light, smiling at the perilous glint of it.

'Not at the concert, Corporal?'

He looked up, squinting into the sun, at the young officer. 'No, sir.'

The youngster, fresh from England, in the line just three days, rubbed a hand absently upon his trouser leg. 'So – over the bags tomorrow, eh?'

'Yes, sir. Seems so, sir.'

The boy regarded the older man with his battle-stained uniform and tranquil, gipsy face with some envy. He indicated the sharpened bayonet with a small, nervous jerk of his head and an uncertain smile. 'Ready, then, Corporal?'

'Ready, sir.'

Eddie watched the slim figure back along the trench, something close to sympathy in his eyes. Poor little sprig; it was a good bet he'd wet his trousers before he went too far tomorrow. He picked up the bayonet again, and as he surveyed it a sudden, fleeting memory of husky, infectious laughter, a sharp-featured face flicked incongruously into his head. He frowned a little. Strange, how difficult he sometimes found it to keep the van Damme girl out of his mind. Eddie Browne rarely had that trouble with a woman. 'Two of a kind, Sal,' he remembered he'd said to her last time they'd met, 'we're two of a kind.' Bloody fool thing to say if he'd ever heard one. Scowling a little he went back to his sharpening.

At the northern end of the line, on a hillside overlooking Gommecourt, Peter Patten sat upon a fallen tree, elbows on knees, looking out over the bleak landscape that was No Man's Land, beyond the trenches where his men prepared themselves for the push tomorrow. In his hand he held a well-worn piece of paper; a letter that had been folded and refolded, worn at the edges and stained with mud. As he read it again he heard her voice, light and pretty, saw the wide, innocent, childlike eyes. Charlotte, surely, was the ideal of the womanhood for whom they were fighting, the very image of the way of life they had to protect, and for which they were ready to die.

And she was his brother's wife.

He folded the letter, started to tuck it back into his pocket, then stopped. Who knew what might happen tomorrow? Who knew, if worse came to worst, what mischief a small slip of paper found in the wrong pocket could wreak? Reluctantly he tore the letter up, and dropped the pieces, watching as they drifted in the still air to the dry dusty ground.

Giles Redfern, pencil in hand, sketched the skeletal outline of the basilica of Notre Dame de Brébières, with its perilously leaning virgin, which had become a symbol of the shattered towns and villages of France. Tucked into the corner of his leather folder was a small photograph, at which, every now and again, he glanced smiling.

Hannah, caught in serene and happy pose, smiled back.

Giles sketched and dared to think of the future.

Ralph Patten, some six miles to the south-east, stretched his legs in the dust before him, leaned in unthinking discomfort against the wheel of the field ambulance and thought of the coming morning.

•

Chapter Seventeen

I

At seven thirty on the morning of the first day of July 1916 – a glorious summer's day, unusual for that year, of sunshine and birdsong – the long-awaited Push, the Big Show, the battle that was, so it was said, to mark the beginning of the end for Jerry, to open the way to Berlin and the heartland of Germany, began. Not a man nor boy of the British Expeditionary Force along the Somme front that day but knew the importance of the action; proud they were to be there, and optimistic. It wouldn't be easy – no-one believed that any more – but they'd have Fritz running like a rabbit, see if they wouldn't – and then, in next to no time, it would be back home to Blighty –

When the whistles blew on that glorious morning battalion after battalion scrambled over the parapets and into No Man's Land confident – for hadn't they been told so? – that the enemy lines had already been demoralized if not entirely shattered by the British bombardment.

Not so.

Warned by the premature explosion of mines, dug deeply and securely into their concrete bunkers, the enemy was waiting; and as the British battalions, the boys of Kitchener's Army, struggled forward, rank upon rank, into a barbarous storm of bullets and high explosive, so they died, falling in their thousands and in their tens of thousands, climbing over the heaped bodies of their comrades to be mown down in their turn. It was a slaughter the scale of which had never been known by a British force before, the staggering extent of which was so great as to take weeks if not months to be understood or accepted even by those who were most closely involved with it. The day was a shambles, a horror of death and destruction barely comprehensible even to those who took part in it; it was the day when flesh, blood and bone were pitted against the advanced and merciless tools of modern warfare and lost. Some infantry battalions lost up to ninety per cent of their strength; dead and dying men littered the smoky, sunlit battlefields, a sacrifice ill-planned and, some said, for nothing.

Number Three Casualty Clearing Station, close by the village of Bray-sur-Somme, was swamped almost as soon as the battle started. Convoy after convoy rolled in from the Front with its pathetic load of crippled humanity. Limbless and eyeless they were carried, half dead already from shock and injury, into the great canvas wards. In Resuscitation they were warmed and coaxed back to a chance of life on the operating table, or they died, giving up the fight on a whisper of breath, too shocked and exhausted to battle further. In Preparation they lay in patient queues, awaiting a table and the precious time of an overworked surgeon, often unaware of how badly injured they were, the lucky ones lulled by shock and morphia into peaceful near-euphoria. An endless stream of shattered, blood-soaked, helpless bodies flowed back from the battlefields to the clearing stations, their only chance of life lying in the steady, overstrained hands of the doctors and nurses who awaited them. Work in the operating theatres went on non-stop as shells howled above the canvas roof and landed in the compound outside. There was no rest to be had and, as that first night fell, no sleep. The battle here was every bit as desperate as that being waged just a few short miles away, the high courage and dedication as great as any shown in the heat of combat.

Hannah worked for eighteen hours, slept fitfully for four and then came back on duty. The wards were packed now and the stretchers had overflowed into the compound, the wounded patiently waiting their turn, the more able-bodied sharing their cigarettes and their cheerful irreverent camaraderie with their less fortunate comrades, the delirious babbling incoherently to the open sky, those beyond help or relief lying in the summer dust as the flicker of life died within them. For two days and then for three the terrible traffic continued; the evacuation trains took those well enough to be moved, making room for a new influx. Many of the men now being brought in had lain beneath the sun for a day, perhaps two, and the signs of gangrene were already there. Hannah worked herself – as they all did – to the edge of exhaustion, then returned to the task after a snatched meal and an hour or two's disturbed sleep. It was difficult to keep track of the days. She heard in a message from Ben through one of his colleagues that Peter's battalion was fighting in the north, had sustained heavy casualties but had now partially achieved its objective and had dug in. Peter had come unscathed through that first terrible day.

There was no news of Giles.

At first she managed to push the thought of him to the back of her mind; there was so much to do, so very little time to think of one's own personal worries; but yet the rat gnawed.

By the fifth day the battle had shifted a little away from them, two evacuation trains had pulled away with their load within the last twenty-four hours and the Clearing Station was a little less like a blood-stained madhouse, though still a steady stream of wounded was coming in. Weary to the bone, the staff of the Station managed a little more time to themselves, time to eat, to lift their heads and to see that the lovely weather had held, time above all to sleep.

And time to worry.

When Fiona came to tell her that Matron was looking for her, her thoughts flew immediately to Giles.

Fiona shook her head sympathetically. 'Sorry, old girl, I couldn't tell you – there was a phone call from your brother, I think – the doctor one that is – best you cut along and find out.'

She had never seen Matron so tired; the small, determined face was grey with fatigue, the eyes deeply shadowed; but she smiled as Hannah entered her small cubbyhole and Hannah's heart lightened a little.

'Hannah, my dear – there's news come through.'

'Giles?'

Lady Bennet shook her head. 'Ah – no – I'm afraid not.'

So disappointed was she – and so terribly relieved – that for a moment she lost all sense of what was being said. No news. That, surely, must be good news? And – if he had been dead – surely she would know? 'I'm sorry?' she asked, a little dazedly.

'Your brother-in-law,' Matron repeated gently. She glanced at a piece of paper on her desk. 'Bedford? Ralph Bedford?'

Hannah looked at her blankly. 'What about him?'

'Your brother rang – your brother-in-law's been wounded. Quite badly I'm afraid.'

Hannah looked at her in total incomprehension. 'Ralph?'

With infinite patience Lady Bennet nodded, waiting for the news to sink in.

'*Ralph's* been wounded?'

'Yes.' Matron sat back in her chair tiredly. Her desk was militarily neat, the piles of paper regimented and weighted down with empty shell cases. 'On the first day. But the news is good – he's on the mend and on his way home. Major Patten seemed to think he'll do. He's quite the hero it seems.'

Hannah stared at her, this time as if one of them had taken leave of her senses. 'Ralph? A hero?'

Lady Bennet nodded. 'He's been recommended for a medal – I don't know the details of course, but according to your brother he put up quite a show. Major Patten asked me to tell you.'

'Yes. Of course. Thank you.' Hannah, still bemused, stood up and turned to the door.

'Hannah? I gather there's no news of Captain Redfern?'

Hannah shook her head. 'No. No news.'

Matron nodded again, kindly. 'No news is probably good news, child. Try not to worry.'

'Yes, Matron.'

She thought often in the days that followed of Ralph, and of the apparent heroism that had so unexpectedly earned him a medal; but she shared her thoughts with no one, not even with Ben when he managed the briefest of calls *en route* to one of the other clearing stations. Ben had a little more information – Ralph had, it seemed, with total disregard for personal danger, single-handedly rescued several men who had been mown down by an enemy machine-gun as they tried to break through the wire to the German trenches. Time and again he had gone in alone under the hail of bullets and dragged them clear. In the end his luck had failed him and he himself had lain wounded until darkness before anyone could bring him back to the lines. Ben shook his head, his face bemused and affectionate. 'Ralph! Who'd have guessed it? It's amazing the courage someone can show under such circumstances. I have to admit I'd never have thought it of him.'

'No,' Hannah said.

'I spoke to one of the men he rescued. "Brave as a lion," he called him. "No concern for his own safety at all." Good old Ralph, eh? Not that we should be surprised that he's come up trumps.'

'No.' There was no doubt at all in Hannah's mind as to what had happened; Ralph Bedford had decided to die and had survived, an unlikely hero. She could imagine now the rue of his smile as he contemplated such unlooked-for outcome.

And Giles? – Giles, who had so wanted to live? Where was he?

The answer came in a letter from his mother, the words restrained and sympathetic, the writing graceful and determined. Hannah read it blindly, '– found your photograph and letters among his possessions – so terribly sorry to have to tell you – hope very much that perhaps some day we might meet – a terrible loss to us, and I think to the world – what a very dreadful and wasteful thing this war is.' The words blurred. She crumpled the paper in her hand, bent her head to rest her forehead upon it, '– what a very dreadful and wasteful thing this war is.' She closed her eyes. Outside the whistles shrieked, heralding a raid.

She did not move.

'Bloody war.' Sally leaned at the window of Ben's room, looking out into the peace of the château's park. Wounded men strolled or chatted in the August sunshine, wheelchairs were pushed along the paths by uniformed nurses. A row of beds had been pulled out into the sunshine and their occupants lay enjoying the warmth on skin that was pale and bloodless. Ben had been away for nearly four weeks, on active duty at the Front. His message that afternoon had ended a time of nagging worry; he might not have been out there in No Man's Land with a rifle in his hand, but she knew the man well enough to know that he would not shirk danger. She had walked into his arms and they had made love almost without speaking. They had lain afterwards, limbs entangled, for a very long while, warm flesh to warm flesh, steadily beating hearts, whole, healthy bodies; alive and together and, for the moment at least, safe. In common with a large proportion of the rest of the world they were finding it harder and harder to think of tomorrow. 'I swore I wouldn't let this happen again,' Ben had said into her hair, his big hand caressing the soft skin of her belly.

She had tugged at his hair, hard enough to hurt. 'Enough of that sort of talk, you,' she had said. 'You may have survived four weeks in close proximity to Jerry – but don't fancy your chances with me if you start that!' And they had made love again violently, his hunger fed by hers. She turned now to look at him. He lay, still naked, on the bed his arms behind his head, eyes closed. They flickered open now at her words.

She crossed to the bed, sat beside him, ran a hand across the thick hair of his chest. 'I was just thinking of poor Hannah.'

He trapped her hand in his, brought it to his lips.

'Rotten luck, Giles going like that.'

'Yes.'

More than a month after that fateful day on the Somme the battle still raged the length of the Front, a deadly stalemate of death from which neither side could withdraw.

He opened her hand, kissed the flattened palm. 'Your friend – what's his name? – Eddie? He's all right?' The question was very casual.

She eyed him. 'He's fine.' She grinned a little, 'He's got his stripe back. He'll make brigadier yet.'

'You've seen him?'

'He's written once or twice.' She had spoken to Ben about Eddie in the same vein as she had told him of her other friends; it had surprised her to detect a faint and to her amusing trace of jealousy in his references to the younger man. She had not, of course, told Eddie about Ben. She had not told anyone.

She stood up reluctantly. 'I ought to go. I'm on duty in half an hour.'

He swung his legs to the floor and stood, cupping her face in his hands and kissing her nose. 'You'll come again?'

'Of course.'

He wrapped long arms about her. 'I hate this hole and corner business. I wish —'

She pulled away from him, shaking her head. 'Don't. Don't wish. There are altogether too many things to wish for, and most of them aren't possible anyway. Don't even talk about it. Just take things as they come. It's all we can do.' She had noticed, without comment, the small pile of letters on the table that had obviously been awaiting his return, all of them inscribed with Charlotte's pretty, feminine writing. 'I can't come tomorrow — the colonel's got me booked all day. But — perhaps the next day?' She kissed him lightly on the cheek and not so lightly on the mouth, then pushed him away, laughing at the all too obvious signs of his arousal. 'You're a positive ruffian, Ben Patten — a greedy one at that! And I've got to go!' She checked in the afternoon silence of the building that the coast was clear and slipped through the door and down the stairs.

He watched her go from the window, swinging across the park with her long, almost masculine stride, stopping for a brief word with a man in a wheelchair, her head bent attentively to his. He picked up Charlotte's letters, which he had not yet opened, looked at them for a long moment, slammed them back down upon the table with a sudden sharp movement of savage frustration, and turned back to the window, his face grim.

Sally had gone.

II

The battle for the Somme, which had deteriorated to a bleak and exhausting war of attrition, went on — into its second month, its third, and then incredibly on into October, with the casualty lists mounting on both sides. In the British mind, through the medium of the newspapers and their stirring prose, place names and nationalities became linked, in heroism and in blood; Thiepval and the Ulstermen, Beaumont-Hamel and the Newfoundlanders and Highlanders, the Australians at Pozière, the South Africans in Delville Wood; and all along the line the county regiments and shattered pals battalions fought with dogged courage. Everyone in the area was involved in the desperate, bloody and apparently interminable struggle; by early October Sally was spending as much time ferrying supplies and medical teams to the forward dressing huts and casualty clearing stations as she was in her duties with the colonel. Whenever she could she made her destination the Number Three Station outside Albert, so as to catch a few precious moments with Hannah. Number Three was one of four clearing stations clustered along the road and the makeshift railway out of the town. The Station was a big one, with several wards and two operating tents, and it was well situated right beside the railway siding so that the movable wounded could be transferred to the trains with a minimum of effort. A ruined farmhouse and a huge barn stood by the side of the road. The compound was very close to the front line and often suffered shelling and aircraft attack; it never failed to amuse Sally to see Hannah and her fellow nursing personnel neatly garbed in uniform and tin hat. The wounded were 'taken in' in a steady flow.

On a day early in October Sally popped her head around Ben's door and was rewarded by the warmth of the smile that lit his face at sight of her. She kissed him swiftly and lightly. 'Can't stop – I've literally got two minutes. I'm taking some supplies for Number Three – any messages for Hannah?'

He hugged her, shook his head. 'Nothing special. Just my love. And Ralph's home – she probably knows – limping but whole. At least he's safe. He won't be back.'

She had no need to ask where he had the information

from; a letter in Charlotte's clear hand lay upon the table. 'Any other news?' She was elaborately casual, refusing to ignore it. She hated those letters. Each time they came she saw – almost felt – the change in him. Ben Patten's conscience had a razor's edge that nothing it seemed could dull and that a letter from Charlotte could hone painfully fine. Their most passionate arguments always materialized after the arrival of such a letter, though, infuriatingly, Ben would constantly deny it.

'They've had some more bad raids, but since we've started shooting the blighters down they aren't so keen, apparently.'

'I saw that in the paper the other day. They seemed to think that the zepps are too vulnerable now – that the raids will stop pretty soon.'

'I hope so. Charlotte gets pretty scared, I think.'

There was a very faintly awkward silence. I get pretty scared myself sometimes; the words were so mawkishly obvious that she absolutely could not bring herself to speak them. 'And Doctor Will?'

'Working himself into the ground, as you'd expect. Tea? I've just made a cup –'

She shook her head. 'I really don't have the time. I just popped in on my way to the stores.'

Ben reached for the battered tin teapot. 'What's all this about Toby registering for conscription?'

Half-way to the door she stopped and very slowly turned. 'I beg your pardon?'

He looked up, surprised at her tone. 'Toby. Hasn't he told you? He's registered to join up next spring.'

'He can't,' she said flatly. 'He isn't old enough.'

There was a small silence. Then, 'We don't actually know that, do we?' Ben asked gently.

She shrugged. 'He isn't eighteen. I'm certain of it. He couldn't have been more than three years old when I found him and that was in 1904. That makes him fifteen or sixteen.'

'According to Charlotte he swears he's older. He looks it, she says.'

'But the school?'

'They've agreed to let him go, apparently. He's registered, with their permission, claiming that he's eighteen next April – he's hoping to get a commission.'

'Is he indeed?' Sally's voice was tight with anger. 'Well, we'll see about that.'

'Sally –'

She turned on him. 'Keep out of it, Ben. It's none of your business.'

'But – there's nothing you can do.'

'Oh no? Watch me. I'll get leave – I'll shoot myself in the bloody foot if I have to – I'll get back there and I'll bang some bloody sense into his head if it's the last thing I do! Of all the harebrained, stupid bloody notions I ever heard!' Fuming, she had reached the door. She turned. 'I'll have to go or the quartermaster will give the run to someone else. I'll see you tomorrow?' She was brusque with worry and with hurt. But still she smiled at him.

He nodded. She blew him a brief kiss. As she left he turned back to his letter.

Sally could not get Toby out of her mind. As she jolted painfully slowly along the rutted road she brooded upon the news. She had received a letter from him just last week – brief, blandly cheerful, totally uncommunicative, as she had come to expect. He wrote at least once every two or three weeks in reply to her doggedly more frequent letters. Not once had he mentioned joining the army. 'Silly little bugger!' Thoroughly put out she cursed viciously as she was forced to bump off the road to avoid a shell hole. The traffic in the opposite direction was getting heavier; ambulances, trucks, converted gun carriages with planks resting upon them on which sat wounded men, horses and carts. Even the odd group of walking wounded, thumbs up, hoping for a lift as each successive vehicle passed. Vaguely she registered the unusual increase, but was too concerned with her mental argument with Toby to take much notice. If this stinking war went on for another two or three years then he would have to go; but to lie about his age – voluntarily to put himself in such danger – Christ alive, the little fool had no idea what he was getting into!

The volume of oncoming traffic had grown all at once to perilous proportions; rumbling and jolting amidst clouds of dust, spreading across the road in a flood. Once or twice she was forced to a stop in the face of it. The barrage too, a mile, perhaps two away, was heavier than usual and seemed to be getting more violent. Jolted at last from her preoccupation, and suddenly alert, she manoeuvred her careful way through the last half-mile of crowded road.

The Clearing Station when she reached it was a scene of organized chaos.

She left the car and ran into the huge compound. 'What's going on?' She grabbed the arm of a passing orderly.

'We're evacuating, miss. Jerry's broken through the line in two places. Give an 'and, would yer? There's a train in.'

'Of course. How can I help?'

'Walkin' wounded to the front of the train – we're mostly loaded, but there's a few could do with a bit of an 'and.' He indicated a shuffling line of men, some supported by their comrades, others limping upon crutches or, eyes bandaged, being led, each man with a hand on the shoulder of the man in front. Sally hurried to where a patient, his own arm in plaster was with his good arm supporting a limping boy.

'Here – let me help –' she hitched the lad's arm over her shoulder.

He grinned, the smile all but toothless, his scarred face cheerful. 'Thanks, miss.'

They struggled to the crowded train, and she helped hitch the wounded lad aboard. Shells screamed wickedly close, and their bursting concussed the ears. Sally rammed her tin hat squarely upon her head as she ran back down the line of walking wounded. A young man sat upon a packing case, head drooping, crutch propped by his side.

'Come on, my love – up we come.'

He shook his head, tried to smile. 'Can't.'

'Of course you can. Here – take this.' She thrust the crutch at him, then slid an arm about his waist and hauled him, wincing and pale as death, upright. 'Only a little way –' If she had been a man she believed he would have refused, preferring to stay to be blown to pieces or captured than sustain the ordeal of the agonizing hundred yards between him and the train. But ready to face anything rather than to give way to such cowardice in front of a woman, he allowed her to half-drag him to where an orderly took him from her and loaded him on to the train as unceremoniously as a sack of potatoes. Nurses were everywhere, ushering their charges like busy and competent sheepdogs, turning not a hair as shells landed around them and in the not too far distance machine-gun fire chattered menacingly. She could see no sign of Hannah.

She made several more trips with wounded men, the last gripping hands with two blinded soldiers who, having waited patiently for someone to come for them, walked through the emptying compound as serenely brave as if they had been strolling on a golf course in the peaceful parklands of the Home Counties.

'Sally! What the devil are you doing here?' As she turned from seeing her charges safe on to the train she all but walked into a tin-hatted Fiona, and behind her Mercy, her arms full of bags and boxes.

The train had begun to move. The last few trucks were moving into line behind the field ambulances. A motorcycle roared. 'I'll have to move the car –' Sally shouted above the noise.

Fiona grabbed her arm. 'Jolly good! You've got the car? Bring it over to the barn. Mercy had the one good idea of her life – why leave the supplies to the Boche? There are drugs over there – we can't afford to lose them – we can load most of them into the car –' And she was gone, disappearing into the dusty haze as a line of trucks rumbled out of the compound.

As Sally, heart thumping, manoeuvred her car out of the way and closer to the stone barn which, reroofed with corrugated iron, was used as a store, the barrage began in earnest. Debris sprayed in a fearsome fountain, its centre a bloom of blood-red flame as a shell landed just a hundred yards outside the compound. Every instinct told her to turn the car and get out on to the road, back – back from the advancing enemy, back from the rain of death that was splitting from the sky.

'Right, here we are.' Grinning all over her blackened face, Fiona appeared at her side, dumping an armful of small boxes into the capacious back seat of the car.

'Where's Hannah?'

'She's on the train – gone – it's all right, she's safe. There are just a few more of these – Mercy's bringing them.'

They both turned at the same time to watch the door of the barn; both saw the figure that appeared silhouetted against the sudden inferno flare of flame within it.

'Mercy!' Fiona was running almost before the explosion happened. Sally, throwing herself down, felt the blast rock the ground beneath her. When she lifted her head it was to see that Fiona was up again, and running; running like a madwoman towards the spot where the tangle of limbs and torn flesh that had been Mercy Meredith lay like a discarded toy. Sally staggered to her feet. The barn was a roaring furnace, the old timbers devoured by the curling petals of flame, the tin roof crashing in a towering cascade of sparks. Another shell landed, and another. In the distance men were shouting, and the guns cracked. The stone wall of the barn shivered and rocked. Fiona was on her knees beside Mercy's wrecked remains.

'Fiona! Look out!'

Fiona began to tug at the body.

Without thought Sally flew to her, running as she had never run before, the heat from the blaze scorching her face. 'Fiona!' She grabbed the other girl's arm, not looking at the horror that lay on the ground beside her. 'Come on! Get out! The wall's coming down!'

Fighting her, Fiona bent to the body again. 'We can't leave her here!'

'Fiona – she's dead! Leave her! The wall!' Dragging and pulling at the other girl, shrieking like a maniac, Sally hauled her away, had almost got her clear when, caught by the blast of another explosion, the great wall collapsed, the stone shrieking and splintering as it fell. Fiona sprawled forward, caught by the blast. Sally felt a sharp pain like the sting of a wasp on her face as a sliver of flying stone caught her and cut to the cheekbone.

'You all right, miss?' There were figures then, hurrying through the smoke, anxious hands to lift her to her feet.

'My friend – she's hurt I think –'

Fiona was sitting, white faced, teeth gritted against pain. Bright blood stained the arm and shoulder of her nurse's uniform. 'Bandages and a splint if you've got one about you,' she said perfectly coolly. 'The arm's broken, and the shoulder doesn't feel too good.'

'We're going to have to get out of here, miss – excuse me – if you don't mind?' Quickly and efficiently the orderly was tearing up Fiona's own apron. 'Johnny – go find something to splint the arm – and jump to it lad, Fritz is almost here.'

Sally put a hand to her face, stared in puzzlement at the blood that smeared it. 'I'll get the car.'

'You sure you're all right, miss? You look a bit gruesome.'

'No. I'm fine. See to Fiona. I'll get the car.' The strangest calm had descended upon her. Without hurrying she walked to where the car stood. The sounds of battle were very close. The last of the trucks was pulling out of the compound.

'Here we are, miss.' The orderly, a large man with a neat moustache and a cheerful smile supported the bandaged Fiona to the passenger door and helped her in. 'Will you be all right?'

'Yes, thanks. I'll follow the trucks.'

The man slammed the door, sketched a quick salute and stepped back. Sally moved the big car smoothly to the end of the procession. In silence they bumped across the shell-pocked surface of the road. The early October evening was darkening; the sky was a wonder of light and colour as the barrage boomed about them. Behind them the great empty tents stood, ripped and torn by the bombardment. Tracer bullets seared the air. An aeroplane buzzed in the shell-burst sky. Sally drove as carefully as she could, aware that Fiona's teeth were clamped into her lower lip and that every time they lurched across a rut or crater she caught her breath in pain.

It was a long time before either of them spoke.

'Well, old girl – it seems highly likely that you just saved my life,' Fiona said. Behind them the sounds of violence were fading a little.

Sally smiled a little, eyes straining into the gathering darkness at the rocking tail lights of the lorry ahead. 'You'd have done the same for me.' She glanced at the white-faced girl beside her. 'You'd have done the same for Mercy if she hadn't been killed in the blast.'

There was a small silence. Then, 'Poor bloody Mercy,' Fiona said, the feeling in her voice as telling as prayer. 'She's not going to see Eastbourne again, is she?'

They finished the journey in silence.

III

Sally got her leave. She was shamefaced about using the spectacularly nasty-looking wound on her face as a lever, but not, in her determination, shamefaced enough to resist the temptation. The avuncular Colonel Foster was a committed if unknowing ally. 'A week, my dear girl. I wish I could have made it longer – really, Commander Lady Marston is quite a tartar!'

'A week is fine, sir. Thank you.'

It took two precious days to get to London; but her arrival at the Bear was worth the waiting. Bron stared, taken so open-mouthed that Sally laughed outright.

'It's me, Bron – it's Sal!'

'Well, I never! Well I never did! An' whatever have they done to you – oh, your poor face!'

'It's nothing. A nasty scratch. Oh, Bron – aren't you going to say "Hello"?'

They fell into each other's arms, laughing and talking all at once. When Charlotte came across them, very cool and contained in grey silk, her newly bobbed hair crisp about her head, it was like a shower of rain in the sunshine, damping the flying dust of their chatter. 'Good Lord,' she said. 'Sally, isn't it?'

It had not occurred to Sally until that moment that the uniform in which she stood had seen better – or certainly cleaner – days. One of the two tunics she owned had been spoiled by blood the day of the evacuation of the Clearing Station; the one she wore now had been on her back every day for three weeks. 'Yes,' she said carefully, appalled at the antagonism that flared in her at the sight of this woman who was married to Ben, 'it's Sally.'

She saw the faint flinch of distaste in the other

woman's eyes at the scabbed wound on her cheek; noticed with caustic amusement that she did not refer to it. 'Well, for heaven's sake,' Charlotte said lightly, 'shouldn't you come in? You're causing something of a draught standing there with the door open.'

Her reunion with Philippa was something she had alternately avidly anticipated and dreaded according to her mood. She need not have worried. The little girl, dark-haired, soft-eyed, heartbreakingly like her father, hesitated for only a moment in the doorway, whilst Marie-Clare, her face alight with pleasure, whispered in her ear. Then, 'Mama! Mama!' the child cried, and launched herself across the room into Sally's arms.

Sally whirled the small, warm bundle into the air, eyes clenched against tears.

'Mama – tell me about France!' Incredibly, Philippa's words were attractively tinged with a very un-English accent. Sally laughed towards Marie-Clare, who spread wide, not too apologetic hands. 'We pray for you every night,' the child said, 'and Marie-Clare reads your letters. Oh, Mama!' The small arms clung, the small, smooth face pressed tightly against Sally's uninjured cheek.

'Thank you,' she said later to Marie-Clare, 'I was very afraid that – that she might have forgotten me. It would be my own fault if she had, I know.'

Marie-Clare, slender and composed, the two-year-old Louise slumbering in her lap, shook her head. 'Rest assured, Sal-lee.' Still, for all her command of her new language, she made two pronounced syllables of the name, 'My charge of Flippy is a charge of love; for her, oh, yes, most certainly and above all for her – but for you also.' The quiet eyes were warm. 'How could I let her forget you?'

Toby was another matter entirely. 'Well –' his smile was by no means unpleasant – but neither was it the mischievous, gleaming thing that had conspired so often with her in the past. Nor was she prepared for the size of him, the easy, handsome confidence, 'behold the conquering heroine –'

'Don't be daft.' She lifted her face to his, received the briefest of salutes. 'Very dashing,' he said, indicating the still-raw scar on her face. 'How did that happen?'

'I –' She stood helpless. To someone who had been there, or some fiery place like it, to one who had been on any part of that endless Western Front for the past two years a few brief words would have sufficed; but how to explain to one who did not – could not – know? Suddenly she understood with flawless and painful clarity the damaging predicament of which she had so often heard; the isolation of a man, home from the war, unable to share his experiences with those he loved, allowing them to fester sleepless within him – glad in the end to go back, back to the comrades who understood. 'It was a shell. A piece of stone caught me. It isn't as bad as it looks.'

The smile became markedly less warm. 'That wasn't the way Hannah told it.'

'Hannah?'

'She wrote. Told us all the gory details.'

'She probably exaggerated.' As she said it she knew how badly she was handling him.

He shrugged. 'Yes. She probably did.'

'Toby – I heard that you'd registered to join the army next spring?'

'Oh?' The cool, fair eyebrows were questioning.

She shrugged a little, cursing herself. She had not intended to confront him so. 'The Patten grapevine. It works, even in France.' Her laugh was nervy, false. She saw the look in his eyes and cursed herself further.

'Then – yes. I've registered. I'm hoping to get a commission.'

'You aren't old enough.' The words were sharp, authoritarian. They made him, she saw with more than a little disquiet, smile.

'We don't know that.'

She took a breath. 'I know – I know that we don't know exactly how old you are – but you aren't eighteen – I'd swear to it.'

'Swear away.' His voice was even, his eyes cool.

She fought temper and trepidation in about equal parts. 'Toby, please, listen to me. You don't know what you're doing – you don't know what it's *like* over there!'

'And I never will unless I go.'

She fought for control; how many times had they flared at each other, fought like tigers, forgotten it in minutes? But this was too important, and the boy she faced was not the dirty-faced urchin she had known. 'Do you know why you're so likely to get a 'commission?'

He waited.

'Because the young men that took their commissions so eagerly two years ago – a year ago – yesterday! – are dead. That's why.'

The silence lengthened.

She raised fingers to her damaged cheek, rubbed at it distractedly; saw his eyes follow the movement avidly and snatched her hand away. 'Toby – give yourself a chance – you aren't old enough yet.'

'And if I wait?' he asked very reasonably. 'It might all be over before I can get there?'

'And would that be such a bad thing?'

'Yes, it bloody would.' The words were still even, very reasonable, but the blue eyes sparked. 'You're all out there – Peter, Ben – even Ralph's come home with a medal, God help us all! – you – Hannah!'

'It isn't what you think. It isn't fun. It isn't heroics. It's bloody murder. It's fear, and it's killing, and it's muddy trenches and foul food and choking gas –' She stopped, jolted by the look on his face, realizing with sudden awful clarity that she was, so far as he was concerned, arguing not her own case but his.

497

'I'm going,' he said. 'And I don't think you can stop me. I don't actually know why you want to.'

She opened her mouth, but he would not let her speak.

'You left me for Philippe – and now you've left me for the war – what right do you have to tell me what to do?' For the first time he let open antagonism show, not the hot resentment of childhood, she noticed with sinking heart, but the cool and considered judgement of a young mind matured in intolerance and misunderstanding.

'That isn't fair,' she said.

'Life isn't fair.' The small, taunting smile dared her to remember how often she had used those words to a hot-tempered child.

They looked at each other for a long, silent moment. Then 'Would you like some tea?' Toby asked lightly and very politely. 'You've probably heard that Mrs Briggs has left us – gone back to the country to nurse a crippled nephew I believe – but Bron really makes an excellent cup of char –'

'I'm sorry to say it, Sal,' Bron said a couple of days later, eyes and voice sympathetic as she busied herself at the big black range, 'but I doubt if you'll get the better of young master Toby once he's made his mind up. Not even Doctor Will or Miss Charlotte can do that. Never known such a one for his own way –'

'He won't even talk about it now,' Sally admitted gloomily. 'We had a bit of a row yesterday. And now he's avoiding me. Oh, Bron,' her voice was soft, 'we used to be so close.'

Bron turned. 'True. Yes, that I remember. I mind when you were ill – when you first came – and the lad wouldn't leave the door.'

'He's changed so.'

'Ah, Sally my love,' Bron's voice was quiet, affectionate,

half amused, 'it isn't just the lad that's changed, mind – now is it?'

Sally, her eyes on the diamond pattern of the scrubbed tiled floor shook her head. 'I suppose not.'

Bron looked at her. 'A demon he was when you left to marry,' she said quietly.

Sally's head came up sharply. 'But Bron – what was I supposed to do? I couldn't take him with me.'

'Of course not. We all knew that. I'm just thinking that perhaps the lad himself didn't see it that way. You were all he had.'

'No! Not by that time – he had everyone here.'

'Not the same, *cariad*, not the same. It's not your fault, mind – it's not anyone's fault – but it seems to me our Toby's learned to do without anyone. What he wants he sets out to get for himself. An' I wouldn't want to be the one to stand in his way, either, for all he can be such a charmer.'

Sally sighed, hitched herself on to the kitchen table, one leg swinging. 'You may be right,' she half smiled, an edge of bitterness in it, '– and so may he. Perhaps to be free of other people is the best way to be.'

'Ah, now – you don't mean that –' Bron stopped. When she spoke again her musical Welsh voice had sharpened perceptibly. 'Well now, look what the cat's brought in. Slumming are we, Kate Buckley?'

Sally turned. Kate leaned in the doorway, smartly dressed in brown and beige, her small hat stylishly tilted, her matching parasol sloped against her shoulder in the manner of a soldier with a rifle. She laughed outright at Bron's waspish tone. 'You said it, not me. Hello there, Sal. How's tricks?'

'Pretty good. You?'

The handsome face sparkled with faintly malicious curiosity, 'Just fine. Been playing pirates?'

'What? Oh – this?' Sally touched the healing gash on her cheek, grinned a little. 'Old war wound.'

499

'Very becoming I'm sure.' Kate turned to Bron. 'Well, my Taffy friend – dust off your best bib and tucker – you're invited to a wedding –'

'Oh?'

'That's right.'

'Whose would that be, then?' Bron was repressive.

'Whose do you think? My very own. Two weeks on Saturday.'

'Oh?' Bron said again provocatively, and Sally hid a smile. 'Quick, isn't it?'

'All the style nowadays, didn't you know? Kiss the girls goodbye and back to the Front –'

'He's a soldier then?' For all her efforts Bron could not keep her curiosity in check, nor could she quite conceal the gleam of envy in her eyes.

Kate preened. 'A sergeant no less. In the Gloucesters. A lovely hunk of a man. A tram driver in civvy life. Ding, ding!' She pulled an imaginary bell cord, grinning.

'Congratulations,' Sally said.

'It's him you should congratulate,' Kate said pertly. 'He's marryin' a girl that's done well enough for herself I don't mind tellin' you – supervisor I am now, down Silvertown.'

'Ammunition?'

'That's right.' Kate shrugged, 'Bullets for the boys. An' long may it last, I say –'

'You're enjoying your war?' Sally could not quite keep the caustic edge from her voice.

Kate was ready for it; had perhaps, Sally thought later, actually provoked it. 'I should say. Anything wrong with that?'

Sally shook her head.

'Not as if I'm the only one,' Kate said and winked, very deliberately, at Bron. 'Eh, Bron? There's folk not a million mile from 'ere might say the same if they were honest as me.'

'That'll do,' Bron said sharply.

Sally glanced at her in surprise.

Kate, expression blandly innocent, smiled. 'I'm all for it meself. Nothin' wrong with enjoyin' yourself; it's po-faced hypocrisy that I can't stand. Well – better go – the bride-to-be's got a few more calls to make. The Bethany church, ten o'clock, two weeks on Saturday. Got that?'

Bron nodded, avoiding Sally's eyes, and with no goodbye turned back to the sink.

As Kate, with a last spiteful smile at Bron's sharply turned back, shut the door behind her, silence fell.

'What was she talking about?' Sally asked, her curiosity aroused as much by Bron's obvious and transparent discomfiture as by Kate's words.

'Oh, nothing much.' An iron saucepan clattered loudly in the sink. 'You know Kate. She's got a tongue that spreads poison the way a knife spreads butter, mind.'

Sally shook her head. 'Didn't sound too poisonous to me. But then I don't know what she was talking about –' She eyed Bron's back and waited.

Bron resisted temptation for a creditable moment longer, then turned, wiping her hands on her apron. Her good-natured face was solemn. 'They did cause some gossip, it can't be denied. But it was true I know that Doctor Ben asked him to cheer her up –'

'What are you talking about, Bron?'

'Why –' Bron hesitated for a second longer, 'Why Miss Charlotte and Mister Peter – when he was home, see? They – they saw a lot of each other – though natural it was, of course it was – it's just there was talk, see?'

'Talk?' The single, questioning word was flat.

'Well – you know what people are.' Bron was still wiping her hands absent-mindedly on her apron. 'Nasty minds they've got, most of them.'

Sally forced her voice to lightness. 'You're not saying that there's anything in this – talk?'

Bron's expression was becoming more and more worried. 'Why no – of course not – but –'

The silence was infinitesimal. 'But?'

'Well – it's the letters – one almost every day she gets from him, and one a day like a religion she writes back.' Bron's voice had dropped to a conspiratorial whisper. In her relief at finding someone, at last, to speak to of her worries the words tumbled over each other, 'I don't like to say it, truly I don't, Sal – but you can't help wondering, can you? I mean – she doesn't write to Doctor Ben like that – once a week it is, if he's lucky. And his letters – why they're read at the breakfast table for all to see. But –' she had joined Sally at the table, pulled out a chair and sat down, her work roughened hands folded before her, her honest face earnest, 'but not Mister Peter's – oh, no – they're read upstairs in that – that boo-dwar as she will call it! – and then packed away in ribbon, under all them nighties of hers, with his picture –' She stopped at the look on Sally's face, 'Well, I couldn't help it, see?' she said, indignant and defensive at once, 'I was tidying the room and – well – I just happened to find them – an' it isn't right, is it? I mean – his own brother –'

Sally was sucking her lower lip, her schooled face inscrutable. 'You really believe that Miss Charlotte – Doctor Ben's wife – is having – or had –' she hesitated, 'an affair – with Mister Peter?'

'I don't know, do I?' In her defensiveness Bron resorted to near temper. 'I'm only saying there's bin talk, and she does keep his letters and his picture in her drawer, and – you know what an airy-fairy creature she is – who's to know what goes on in that mind of hers?'

Sally, eyes distant, nodded.

'That bloody Kate,' Bron muttered. 'If she'd kept a still tongue I'd never have said.'

'Kate doesn't know about the letters?'

'*Diawch!* Of course not!' Bron looked hurt and scandalized at once, 'What do you take me for, Sally Smith?'

'I'm sorry.'

Bron stood up. 'Mountains out of molehills. There's probably nothing in it.' She cast a sudden anxious glance at Sally, 'You'll say nothing?'

Sally forced a reassuring smile. 'Of course not, Bron. Not a word. As you say – there's probably nothing in it –'

'Right –' Bron smiled, relieved, 'Now, a cup of tea for you?'

Three days later Sally left to go back to France. She found it harder, this time, to leave Philippa, who at nearly four years old and so much like her father in looks and temperament seemed suddenly much the most precious thing in the world. The weather had turned miserable; cold and wet, the sea a sullen grey that merged with the chill horizon. As they neared the French coast the distant echoes of war grew louder; she had forgotten, almost, that sound of incessant bombardment. The train journey to Amiens was drearily slow, the compartment, which she shared with a group of politely curious young officers, as cold as an ice-box.

She did not immediately contact Ben. She had known from the start that she could not repeat Bron's gossip; but for the moment, fresh as it was in her mind, she was not sure she could trust herself. Much as she longed to see him, it seemed better, for the moment, to stay away.

It was two days after her return, with rain and mist and already freezing temperatures making life in the trenches all but unbearable, that he came to her. She was astonished to see him; by mutual consent he had kept away from her billet except for the most innocent of contact.

One look at his face told her the news was bad.

503

'What is it? Ben — what's happened?'

He slumped into a chair wearily, lowered his head to his hands. 'It's Peter,' he said baldly. 'A sodding sniper got him. They don't think he'll live.'

Chapter Eighteen

I

Peter Patten's war was over. He first suspected it when he saw the look in his sergeant's eyes in those first strange and deadly clear moments after the bullet had smashed into his back; knew it with clarity in some small, still part of his soul as later he lay in a daze of pain and morphia in the comparative quiet of the Casualty Clearing Station. What he did not know until very much later was how very close to death he had come.

Once or twice, after they told him, gently and with a firmness that left no room for hope, that he could never expect to walk again, he wished they had not saved him.

The months that followed were harrowing – months spent in hospitals first in France, then in London, whilst his comrades in France fought on through one of the bitterest winters in living memory. Men shivered and cursed and froze in the trenches, died of exposure and of influenza, fought across ground where the corpses of their friends – and of their enemies – sprawled, preserved in the gaunt rictus of death, trapped in the frozen mud. The cold was searing; it was a winter of ice and snow and brutally low temperatures. It was as if the elements themselves had turned against the men who struggled to break the ghastly stalemate that held Europe in its death grip. As Peter hovered between life and death the Battle of the Somme ended at last, hostilities stopped as much by the sheer impossibility of fighting through the appalling weather conditions as by the achievement of any clear objective by either side. In the middle of that terrible December, on the day that the monk Rasputin was murdered in Russia the fighting at Verdun, too, eased at last, both armies simply too exhausted and too weakened by casualties to continue.

Peter lay through those first months, apparently docile, a favourite with nurses and patients alike, his slight, bright good looks honed to beauty by the privations of illness, his courage and his easy good manners a fragile shell to protect himself and others from the bitterness growing within. He had been ready for death – though, in truth, he knew he had never truly believed in it – but this? A lifetime of paralysis, of dependency? He had never even contemplated such a thing and in the quiet moments of the long, pain-filled nights he railed at the flawed fate that had allowed it to happen. Death would have been infinitely preferable. Because it was his nature to smile, he smiled, and was commended for his valour; yet in his heart and in his soul the canker grew. He hated his useless legs with an inflexible hatred that would have astounded those who tended him each day, who saw only the gilded smiles, the warm, bright eyes, heard only the gallant banter: 'And how are we today, Major?' – 'Tres beans, Sister, thanks. Nearly got up to practise my golf swing in the night but thought I might disturb the others –'

He was not well enough to face the journey back to England until half-way through January. Ben came to see him the day before he was due to leave. Both Ben and Hannah had visited him as often as they could; but not even for them had he been able to lower his obstinate, flippant guard. Perhaps especially not for them.

'Back to Blighty, then?' Ben said, settling his huge frame gingerly on the flimsy chair the smiling nurse had provided.

'Looks like it. Hospital in London, I gather – don't know which one.'

'Barts,' Ben said, 'I just asked. You'll be well looked after there.'

Peter nodded.

'And you'll be within striking distance of home, too. Pa and Charlotte and Ralph will be able to come to see you –'

Peter's smile was brilliant. 'That'll be jolly, won't it?' Charlotte. Lovely, childlike, vulnerable Charlotte, whom he had held and comforted as she had cried in terror. Charlotte who – he knew – had loved him; had loved the Peter Patten he had been before a sniper's bullet had split his spine – Charlotte, who so much needed to be protected and cared for. What good would a cripple be to Charlotte? He looked at the brother to whom she belonged and smiled until his face ached. 'Let's hope the weather's a bit better in London.'

'I gather not. Worst winter since the eighteen eighties, or so they're saying.' Ben dug into his pocket and brought out a couple of packets of cigarettes. 'Here – present for you.'

'Thanks.'

'Hannah sends her love.'

He nodded.

Ben held out a hand. 'Good luck, old lad. Take care of yourself.' In his rugged face was a sorrow that it was beyond words to express. Ben it had been who had finally had to convince him that there was no hope.

'Yes, I will.' For one moment the gleaming smile died and a bleak glint showed in the blue eyes. 'Or at least, I dare say, the rest of the world will.'

They shook hands in a suddenly unnerved silence, both perilously aware of the other's emotion. Then with a quick lift of the hand Ben was gone.

Peter watched him stride away on the long, strong legs that carried him with such unthinking sureness and speed. He sat for a long time, very still, his face remote.

Then he closed his eyes and with an enormous effort of will relaxed upon his pillows.

Charlotte.

He did not want to see her; assured himself that in his present state she would not want to see him. Illness, he knew, frightened and disturbed her — a cripple surely must be abhorrent, whether she could bring herself to admit it or no, and he trusted that she would leave it as long as possible before facing him.

She came the day after he arrived in London; his first visitor. And with a shock he realized, in the moment she sat beside him and took his hand, in the moment she did not respond to his quick, practised, lying smile, that she knew. She was pale and thinner than he remembered, her fair beauty more delicate; and as she looked at him in that first, long moment of silence he saw, with a stab of something close to fear, that she understood with the perception of love precisely how he felt; she was not to be fooled the way others had been fooled.

He could not bear it.

He had nursed his hatred, nursed his hurt until the hiding of it had beome essential to him — a game to play deadly seriously — the only thing to make it worth while opening his eyes each morning. He could not bear what he saw in her eyes.

The silence was a long one. She leaned to him and her lips brushed his cheek very softly. When she sat back her eyes were brilliant with tears she would not allow to fall, but her voice when she spoke was controlled. 'Peter, darling. You're home at last. I've been out of my mind with worry.'

The habitual, brilliant smile flickered with brittle ease, totally at odds with the look in his eyes. Her hand was still in his, childishly small, very soft; his own skin too had lost its masculine, trench-toughened roughness over the past months of inactivity, and the soft, rhythmic stroking of her fingers upon his was silk upon silk. He tried gently to disentangle his hand from hers. Her fingers tightened very slightly, and she would not let him go. She had amazed herself in coming. She had thought – had been afraid – that the beauty of him, the bright courage, the warmth of which she had dreamed for so long, might not have withstood an ordeal the horror of which she could only imagine. She had been terrified that her own weaknesses would betray her. But as she had entered the ward and seen, unobserved, the spare, fair face, the lift of the handsome head, she had realized with a shock of emotion and – yes, delight – that had all but stopped her heart that she had never seen anything as beautiful as this helpless, damaged man. She had loved him before; like him she had been more than aware of the possibility that the bullet that had crippled him might well have destroyed too the fragile web that had spun between them. But it had not. Here, at last, was her prince. Handsome, a hero – and defenceless. She had never in her life experienced anything like the wave of love that had overwhelmed her as she had taken his thin, fragile hand. No warrior now; no strong arm to threaten, defend, take what was his. Like a great, calm sea the love and the strength rose in her; she had seen with clarity the depths of his fear, the cutting blade of his bitterness – she and only she could help him; she knew it with a certainty that would not be denied. With enormous tenderness she lifted the tense hand she still held and laid it against her cheek.

Almost, he flinched from her, turning his head a little on the pillow, unwilling to look at her, unmanned by her nearness.

'Peter.'

He shook his head.

'Look at me.'

At first he would not. She let the moment stretch, waiting. At last, reluctantly, he turned his head.

'I know there's no hope of recovery — you won't walk again. But', she held his eyes steadily, willing him to listen, to understand, 'that doesn't mean that you'll never be happy again. Believe me. You have to believe me. Your life isn't over. It isn't. It's simply a new life beginning. And it will be a good life. I promise you.'

'Charlotte,' his voice was low, 'look at me! *Look at me!* What good am I?'

At the far end of the ward a bustling nurse pushing a trolley was briskly dismissing visitors. 'Doctor's on his way, off we go, please.'

'I won't listen to such nonsense. You hear me?' As the nurse advanced officiously, Charlotte released his hand and stood up. 'It's no good. I simply won't listen. You'll have to believe me in the end, because I won't let you do anything else —'

'Doctor's on his way, madam —'

'Yes, I'm going.' She leaned across and kissed Peter lightly on the forehead. Her perfumed hair brushed his brow. He clenched his hands upon the starched bedspread. She smiled and graceful as a bird in dove grey and white she left him, the eyes of the other men in the ward following her appreciatively. Peter watched her go, and for the first time since the bullet that had destroyed his hope of life had struck he felt the shaming burn of tears behind his eyes, the ache of them in his throat.

Make her stay away from me — sweet Christ! make her stay away! — I can't stand it —

'Morning, Major — Doctor's on his way — feeling better, are we?'

'Right as rain, Sister.' The blithe and graceless smile gleamed, 'What time are you off tonight? Fancy a night at the Savoy?'

She came almost every day, sometimes alone, sometimes escorted by the limping Ralph or by the frail, indomitable figure of his father, Doctor Will. No one questioned the propriety of her visits – what more natural than that a fond sister-in-law should visit a gravely wounded man? Sometimes she brought messages from Hannah or from Ben. They discussed the news of the war, which still showed no sign of a conclusive ending one way or another, and in March they discussed the events in Russia that seemed slowly but very surely to be leading to revolution and Russia's withdrawal from the war effort. They discussed the possibility of American intervention. In April they discussed Toby's leaving, a subaltern in the Buffs, and the rift that quite obviously had opened between the boy and Sally. In short they discussed everything but themselves. Since that first visit Charlotte had kept the tone of their conversations determinedly light, almost impersonal, though her smile and the light in her eyes each time she saw him, the brief, tantalizing kisses, the soft curl of her fingers about his were like another, wordless dialogue that danced about their prosaic conversation like music. Little by little he came to look forward to her visits as slowly, very slowly, he began, almost without realizing it, to accept her vision of himself and to realize that her love, far from being diminished, had developed from a childlike infatuation to an emotion much deeper and stronger. Of the future he did not – could not – think. It was enough that each day she came, always dressed and groomed with infinite care, her eyes always finding him with unerring accuracy wherever in the room he might be. As for Charlotte – she watched him grow stronger and less afraid each day, and laid the plans that one day would make him, and her, happy. Seeing sometimes that shadow in his eyes she knew the battle was not yet won; he had by no means come to terms with his terrible disability, with his dependency on other people – but when in early May 1917 his doctor announced him far enough along the road to recovery to be sent to a convalescent home in Surrey, she did not worry as she once would have done at the thought of his brooding alone, away from her, in strange surroundings.

'I shall come at least twice a week. More if I can manage it.' With already practised hands she tucked the blanket about his legs and adjusted the back of the wheelchair. 'I hate the thought of your being farther away, but it isn't so very far – and when I come I can stay longer. You'll be more comfortable there – Sister was telling me it's a perfectly lovely place – an old manor house with splendid grounds. We can go for walks –' she would not respond to the sudden, bleak quirk of a fair eyebrow, 'and it certainly couldn't be a better time of year. The woods will be full of bluebells, you lucky thing. Thank heaven that dreadful winter's over at last – I really thought I might die of cold once or twice – *and* you'll be out of the way of these beastly air raids – honestly, I thought once we'd got the best of the zepps they'd give up, but these awful little aeroplanes are worse if you ask me –'

He made one last effort to hold to his anger, his bitterness, his independence. 'Charlotte – it's no good! There's nothing for me – you know it! I'm chained to this bloody contraption for life –' he took a breath, holding her eyes with his, brilliant, long-lashed, intense, 'a half-man. No man at all.' His knuckles whitened upon the arm of the chair as if he would rip it from beneath him and fling it to a corner. 'Useless!'

She smiled calmly and with a conviction that simply would not be swayed. No torture would have wrung from her the truth that over the past months had settled quietly and secretly into her soul. 'Nonsense. I won't listen to you. Go to Surrey. Eat your eggs and drink your milk. Do everything you're told. Build up your strength –'

'For what?' he interrupted her, his low voice blazing, '*For what?*'

She bent to him, took both his hands in hers. 'For the future.' And then, with a small, unfathomable smile, before she turned and left him, 'For me,' she said.

II

'I must say,' Fiona remarked casually, her long legs draped in the elegant falling folds of her dark riding habit, propped upon Sally's windowsill, 'your friend Eddie Browne is quite a dashing thing, isn't he?'

'What?' Sally lifted her head from her dour contemplation of the fire. Even at this time of year the vast, high-ceilinged room with its graceful, tall windows, once the drawing room of a stylish town house, then the much-abused headquarters of a Highland regiment and now the chill billet of Lady Marston's corps of drivers was ice cold. 'How the devil would you know? You've never met him.'

'Wrong. We — bumped into each other the other day.' The fractional hesitation was obvious and deliberate. Fiona slanted a narrow, pale glance across her shoulder and smiled beatifically.

As she had intended the words brought her Sally's sudden attention — which had been for at least the past half hour notably in other more private quarters. 'You — what?'

'Bumped into him. Well. Found him, I suppose is more accurate —'

Sally sat up, her expression an almost comical mixture of affront, indignation and laughter. 'Fiona MacAdam! If you think that just because —' She stopped.

'— you dragged me out from under a burning building —' Fiona continued in equably agreeable tones '— it gives me any right to interfere in your private life —'

'Exactly.'

'I'm nosy,' Fiona explained with a devastating smile.

'You're impossible.'

'Yes. That too, probably. Anyway — having heard the odd snippet from you and from Hannah about this young man I decided it was high time to make his acquaintance.'

'You what?'

'You said that once, Sal. Honestly – it can't be denied – breeding does out –'

'Oh, shut up.'

'You see what I mean? Hardly devastating repartee? Anyway –'

'You said that once,' Sally said.

'Anyway,' Fiona ignored her, 'knowing the young sergeant's name, rank and regiment – oh, and if you haven't seen him for the last ten minutes, he is still a sergeant –' she grinned at the involuntary answering twinkle in Sally's eye, 'I took it upon myself to have a word.'

Sally turned and looked at her, this time the brewing storm clouds of temper overpowering the easy give and take of friendship, 'you – what?'

Unimpressed, Fiona could not repress her laughter. 'Sally! I'll have to take you in hand! Are they the only two words you know?'

Sally was not to be so easily deflected. She stood up, walked to where Fiona lounged in the only comfortable chair in the room, perched herself on the windowsill directly in front of her. 'You – went to find – Eddie Browne?' she asked, her husky voice very emphatic. 'Might I ask why? Might I ask – how dare you?'

Fiona did not answer immediately. She studied with an odd, tender amusement the fierce face before her. 'Sally, my sweetheart,' she said, apparently irrelevantly, but suddenly with no affectation, no amusement in her voice, 'you haven't been yourself lately, have you?'

Sally held the pale eyes for a moment, then looked away. 'I'm tired.'

'So are we all.'

'What's that supposed to mean?' The words were truculent, the expression on the sharp-boned face perilous.

Fiona affected a sigh. Her eyes were very alert. 'What you're suffering, dear heart, is so obviously over and above the demands of duty, so very obviously –' she hesitated, half laughed, 'female – if I might use the words to a fighter for equality?' Her tone was light, the expression in her narrowed eyes attentive, 'I have to admit that I jumped to a conclusion. Two conclusions. One of which turned out to be wrong. The other I'm still certain is not. What I want to know is – if it isn't Sergeant Browne – and having spoken to him, much to my disappointment,' she grinned unrepentantly, 'and perhaps to his – I suspect it isn't – who is it?'

Sally's face closed like a shut door.

Fiona leaned forward, true, warm sympathy in her face. 'Sally – what is it? You seem –' hesitated, 'so very unhappy?'

There was a brief moment's fraught silence. The unexpected, open question – the unexpected sympathy – had caught Sally so off guard that the composure which, with practice, had become second nature, had deserted her. Tears stood in her eyes. She sat for a moment, rigid, upon the windowsill, and then with a loss of control that was as shocking as it was sudden she bowed her head into her hands and gave way to painful, all but silent weeping.

Fiona surveyed the shaking shoulders for a moment. Then quietly, knowing instinctively that the weeping girl was for the moment beyond banal words of comfort, she got up and went to the corner of the room where she knew from many previous visits the kettle and the gas ring were kept. A few minutes later, with the quiet, miserable tears abated and a sniffing, red-eyed Sally, abashed but in control once more, watching her with wary eyes, she deposited upon the small table a tray containing a pot of tea, a jug of milk and two dubiously clean cups.

Sally said nothing as, still in silence, Fiona poured a splash of milk into the cups and then the tea. 'This war's having a most devastating effect on me. It's making me positively middle class,' she said conversationally.

Sally accepted her tea with muttered thanks.

515

Fiona took hers back to the chair, sniffed it, tasted it, lifted her eyes to her friend.

'I don't know what to do,' Sally said.

'Try starting from the beginning.'

Sally ducked her head, sipped her tea, blinking.

'I'm a good listener,' Fiona offered.

'I can't.'

Fiona shrugged, lifted her cup again.

'It – it isn't just me.'

'It rarely is.'

In the ensuing silence they drank their tea. Sally, the tears having started after so long, was having trouble in staunching them.

'For heaven's sake, Sal,' Fiona said at last intently, 'cross my heart, wish to die, spit in any bugger's eye – I won't tell, whatever the deadly secret is. But what in God's name's wrong?'

'Ben Patten,' Sally said abruptly.

Fiona stared at her. 'Ben Patten? Doctor Ben Patten? Hannah's brother?'

Sally nodded, already regretting the impulse that had made her speak. But yet there was relief too. His name lay on her tongue for almost every waking hour, and so rarely could she speak it.

Fiona sat for a very long moment in silence. Then she let out a long, sighing breath. Her expression was very concerned indeed. 'Well. You've certainly kept that quiet,' she said at last quietly. 'How long?'

Sally's sudden laughter was almost a sob. 'How long? How do I know? A year? From the moment I saw him? Ask me how badly.'

'How badly?'

Sally pulled a wry face. 'Bad.'

Fiona heaved a long, slow breath. 'Why don't you tell me – right from the beginning? – I'm no one's favourite nanny, God knows, but you know what they say about a troubled shared?'

516

Sally grinned, half-heartedly. 'Right from the beginning, you say? You've got all night?'

Fiona considered. 'Well – there's a baby captain of the Scots who thinks he might be on to a good thing this evening, but it never hurts to keep them on their toes. Yes. And all tomorrow if you want it.' She set her teacup aside.

Sally sat for a very long time, hunched against the light of the window. Behind her the setting sun dipped, scarlet in a forget-me-not sky. The light upon her face, Fiona slouched in the armchair, the pale eyes alert and affectionate. 'Tell you what –' she moved lazily, picked up the bag that lay beside her chair, 'forget my lousy tea. It so happens that I'd filched a little something as a sundowner.' She reached into her bag, brought out a bottle. 'Genuine Latour. Not easy to come by, old thing. Got a couple of glasses? Not that it matters, but it does make things a little more civilized.'

Sally fetched glasses and a battered corkscrew. Fiona, with some ceremony, broached the bottle and poured the rich wine. Then she sat on the floor, gestured Sally to the chair. 'Right,' she said, with an iron smile, 'get on with it.'

The bottle was emptied within the hour. Sally surveyed her half-empty glass. 'And then – last night – we had this row. My fault, really. I get so tired of –' She stopped.

'Of his tender conscience?' Fiona asked shrewdly.

'Yes. And – more than that –' Sally made a small, sharp gesture with her free hand, '– with his absolute conviction that he's *right* all the time – that he knows what's best for everyone – he's so damned certain about what's right and what's wrong.'

Fiona laughed a little softly. 'Adam was probably the same. It's what drove Eve to try the apple.'

'Charlotte didn't want to marry him in the first place. It's been a total disaster from the first moment. He knows it. But he won't admit it. He'd never hurt her. He thinks of everyone but himself.'

'Oh really?' Fiona's voice held the faintest, caustic edge of sarcasm. 'And have you told him about this – rumour? The interesting gossip you picked up about the distant, reluctant wife and the interesting brother?'

'Oh, of course not! How could I? Especially now –'

'Oh, sweetheart, how truly and despairingly working class of you.'

'Fee, it isn't funny!'

Fiona drained the last of her wine. 'I know it isn't.'

'And you've got entirely the wrong impression. You don't know him as I do, Fiona – I love him. Stupid it may be, but I can't help it! I don't care where it's leading. I don't care if he's tied to someone else. I just wish that sometimes – sometimes –' Her voice trailed off. Fiona watched her. 'That sometimes he'd be a little more –'

'Human?' Fiona offered cheerfully.

Sally made a very rude noise.

Fiona gracefully came up on her knees, leaned one elbow upon the arm of Sally's chair, looking up at her intently. 'Thank you for telling me,' she said very soberly, 'for telling me it all.'

Sally grinned lopsidedly. 'You mean you're still talking to me? Hardly fit company for an "Honourable" am I?'

'Better than you know.' Fiona, never serious for two moments strung together, made a bony fist with her hand, bounced it on Sally's knee, 'Half the blue-blood bores I know don't have any better background.'

'You do know that I'd rather you didn't – spread it about?' It was only barely a question.

Fiona spread exaggerated, laughing hands. 'Who would I tell? Who do I speak to? The question is – what are you going to do?'

Sally looked through the window at the dying sun. The night before, after an argument that had started from nothing and had finished in tears and exhaustion, they had made love as violently as that first time, with the guns of the evening barrage booming about them like the knell of doom. 'I don't know. It's all so odd, isn't it? The war, I mean – everything's changing – nothing's permanent – it's so hard to see anything clearly.' She dropped her face into her hands for a moment, rubbing her eyes. 'It's as if we're all different people than we were.'

'I suppose we are.'

Sally shook her head. 'Not Ben. Ben's the same. He'll always be the same. Oh God – I truly can't see where it's going to end. Sometimes I get so tired of it – the secrecy, the hole-in-the-corner nastiness of it all – I just want to stand up and shout it out: I love another woman's husband. He loves me. So what? Other times – I just want to run away.'

'I heard a rumour', Fiona said carefully, 'that Sir Brian was thinking of offering him a research post after the war.'

Sally's head jerked up, her brows drawn together.

'He hasn't told you?'

'No.' The word was brusque. 'Where did you hear that?'

'Hannah mentioned it the other day. Sally – if it's true – and I wouldn't be surprised – then any breath of scandal –' She stopped.

Sally was sitting very still, her eyes distant.

'He won't leave his wife, Sally.' Fiona laid a sympathetic hand upon her arm. 'You know it. Sir Brian Bix-Arnold is a stuffed shirt of the oldest and direst order. The slightest sign of anything so devastatingly improper as a love affair –' She made a movement of a finger across her throat. 'And as for divorce! You might as well talk of murder! Ben would be out before his feet had touched the floor. You know it.'

'Yes.'

'This appointment could be the beginning of a truly brilliant career. Sir Brian has taken Doctor Ben Patten under his wing – his influence is enormous – and he's the best man in a field that Ben, I gather, feels quite passionate about – that he's already spent a lot of time on. His work on gas gangrene, with Sir Brian has made him quite a name –'

'I know. I know!'

'He won't give it up, Sally,' Fiona went on inexorably. 'Whatever he says, he won't give it up.'

Sally leaned back in the chair. The sun had gone, the shadows gathered in the corners of the lofty room. The fire had died, and the air was chill. 'I know,' she said again.

Fiona sat back on her heels, picked up the empty wine bottle, surveyed it a little ruefully then stood it on the windowsill. Then she turned back to the still figure in the chair, her head cocked a little to one side, her small, tentative smile encouraging, faintly teasing. 'Are you sure you couldn't manage to fall for the entertaining Sergeant Browne, bless his subversive little soul? So far as I can make out there's no fragile Mrs Browne to complicate matters.'

Despite herself, and as Fiona had intended, Sally had to laugh. 'Yes, I'm quite sure. And honestly, Fee, you've got hold of the wrong end of the stick entirely. If I did fall for him he'd almost certainly run a mile!'

Fiona laughed at that. 'You may be right.'

'I most certainly am. So you can stop matchmaking. God almighty – another emotional involvement's all I need just now!'

'Ah well,' Fiona stood up, brushed her long skirts, 'it was worth a try.' The mischief died as she looked down at the shadowed face, 'You aren't sorry you told me?'

'No. You were right. It does help a bit – to have someone to talk to.'

'Even if she can't come up with an answer?'

Sally's smile was bleak. 'There is no answer, Fiona.' She shook her head, a quick, almost exasperated movement, 'There is – no – bloody – answer.'

*

The Southdown Convalescent Home nestled into softly rolling countryside a mile or so from the village of Beestone in Surrey, a brick-built manor house in eight acres of parkland. Each time that Charlotte stepped from the train on to the tiny platform of the little country halt she lifted her head and breathed the soft air with pleasure. The walk to the home was through narrow lanes, the hedgerows alive with birds and threaded beautifully with every kind of wild flower. Low, wooded hills lifted to the summer sky, gentle and green and as undisturbedly peaceful as time itself. She never hurried; there was no need. Peter would be waiting – looking for her. His face would light at her coming, like a candle lit before a shrine. His hand would reach for hers. And the golden, helpless beauty of him would fill her with that astounding, enchanting lift of love and strength, of pure, invulnerable certainty that was his gift to her. She had never been so utterly happy; had never, she knew, looked so utterly lovely. And her plans were laid, very surely.

'I think', she said, strolling in gentle June sunshine, the wheels of his chair crunching upon the gravelled path, 'that we should live in the country. The air would do you so much more good. Think how pleasant it would be – French windows into a pretty garden, perhaps a little stream –'

He glanced round at her, smiling, happy to join in the game. They often did it – spoke of things that would not – could not – be, as if they were possible. 'Bit different from the old Bear.'

'Oh, yes.' Her answering smile was gentle, secret, 'Very different from that.' They had reached the top of a low ridge. Below them a small ornamental lake edged with willows glimmered like quicksilver in the sun. 'Would you like to stop here, or shall we go on down to the lake?'

'Can you manage that far?'

She laughed softly. 'Silly boy. I can manage much further than that.' With easy competence she manoeuvred the chair down the slightly sloping path, then found a flat patch of grass and turned the chair so that he should have the best view. 'There.' She checked the brake, tucked the blanket around his legs then arranged herself very decoratively at his feet, her skirts spread about her like the petals of a flower, her lifted face flower-like too, the skin flawless, the blue eyes wide and bright.

He looked at her helplessly, enmeshed in her shining beauty, in the delicate almost virginal feminity of her.

She saw it, and she smiled. Then she turned a little, leaning against the chair, her knees drawn up in front of her, hands linked loosely around them. 'I think Ralph's going to ask Hannah to marry him at last.'

The silence lasted long enough for her to slant a small glance across her shoulder at him. He was looking at her with such a funny, astonished expression that she giggled like a child. 'Oh, come on – Ralph's adored Hannah ever since we were children together.'

'Well, I know that. But – well, I suppose I just never thought he'd get round to it. Whatever possessed him?'

'I did.' The words were light. Charlotte had picked a small pile of daisies and was threading them into a chain. 'I had a sisterly chat with him. Faint heart never won fair lady and all that. I mean – distant adoration's all very well, but it's a bit impractical, isn't it?'

'Do you think she'll accept him?' Peter was watching her with a fond mixture of amusement and surprise.

A small, indefinable expression flickered across the pretty face. 'I hope so. She'll be a fool if she doesn't.' It was no part of Charlotte's plan to consider any such nonsense. She held up the chain, shaking it out. 'Did you know that Ralph actually tried to get himself killed? You know – the business of the medal and all that? He told me. He swears he wasn't being brave at all; he was trying to get himself shot. Ironic, isn't it?'

Peter was silent.

'He thinks Hannah knows. Or at the very least suspects.' She added a couple more flowers to the chain, draped it across her silk-clad knees. 'He's writing to her. Today. Of course – if they marry –' she hesitated, threw a swift glance at his face, 'it would be perfect, wouldn't it? They're both so good with the children. So dedicated. So – when we go to live in the country – they can run the Bear.'

Not looking at him, she rose very gracefully. His eyes followed her movements, faintly, questioningly puzzled. She leaned to him, lifted slim arms to drape the chain of flowers about his neck. 'Because we are going to live in the country, Peter, aren't we? Just you and me – with a garden, and a stream – happily ever after.' She did not draw away from him but leaned closer, watching him. She saw his lips part a little, saw the sudden hurt, the depth of longing in his eyes. And the moment before her lips met his in a long and gentle kiss, she smiled.

When she drew away they were both trembling. Peter's face clenched suddenly in a grimace of anger and frustration. 'Charlotte!'

She laid a cool hand against his lips, her other hand moving caressingly in his thick, unruly hair. 'Don't say anything, my love. Just think about it. Think about you and me in a little cottage somewhere. Think about me taking care of you, loving you, for ever and ever. Think about summer days like this – winter evenings around the fire – No!' She felt his involuntary movement and gently tangled her fingers in his hair, tugging at it. 'Don't say anything.' She bent to him again, kissed him again, and this time his hand crept up and cupped her head, holding her to him. She drew away at last, dropping a feather-light kiss on his nose, his forehead.

He shook his head uncertainly. 'You aren't serious?'

She watched him, sudden, provocative mischief dancing in her eyes. Then she laughed, reaching for the handbrake, swinging the chair around, 'Of course not. It's a game, isn't it? A game we like to play?'

He craned his head to look at her. His skin was golden with sunshine, the fair hair bleached to gold.

She smiled down at him.

'Yes,' he said after a moment, a little less than certainly, 'of course. That's all. A game we like to play.'

III

In the late autumn of 1917, in the month that saw the final convulsions of the Bolshevik Revolution which took Russia out of the war, and the devastation of two war-weary armies in the battle for a tiny village too appropriately named Passchendaele, Ben Patten snatched a short leave. The previous months had seen success for Allied arms at the Messines Ridge, and signs of a slow but sure advantage gained in Flanders, until the weather had again taken a hand and bogged down both attackers and defenders in a quicksand of mud that sucked horse, man and machine into its gruesome maw with indiscriminate relish. Earlier in the year there had been near revolt in the battered, blood-drained French regiments who had fought so gallantly and for so long along the Aisne. Europe was war-weary, yet still the nightmare showed no sign of ending.

The night before Ben left for England Sally lay curled against him in the narrow bed that saw all of their lovemaking, in his quarters in the château at Amiens.

'Are you looking forward to it?'

'Going home?' He moved a little, restlessly. 'I don't know. Funny, isn't it? In a way it's all you think of – going home – yet when it happens –'

'Mm.' It was a common problem. Men were known, now, actually to refuse leave, or to stay in France rather than to leave their mates and face loved ones who had so little idea of what life in the front line was like that they might have been strangers.

Sally shifted a little, rolling away from him. 'They're bombing London again – badly from the look of the papers.'

He had lit a cigarette. The smoke spiralled into the chill dusk of the room. 'Yes. Since the bad raids in July the pressure seems to have been fairly steady. It's funny –' He trailed off.

'What is?'

'Charlotte. I'd have thought she would have been terrified – remember how she was about the zepps? But – she seems to be taking it in her stride.'

'Not much else she can do, is there?' Sally's voice, despite herself and as always when Charlotte's name came up, was brusque.

The small silence was not easy. 'Sally?' Ben said.

'Mm?'

'I've been offered a post. After the war. With Sir Brian. Research.'

'Yes,' she said. 'I know.'

The silence this time was deafening.

He stubbed out his cigarette, turned to her, leaning on one elbow, massive above her. 'You – know?'

'Yes. I heard the rumour months ago.'

'Where from?'

'From someone who'd heard it from someone who'd heard it from someone. Come on, Ben – you know how word gets about.'

'You didn't say anything.'

This time she allowed the silence to develop to truly difficult proportions before saying, 'Neither did you.'

'I – wasn't sure if I would take it. There didn't seem much point in saying anything until I'd made up my mind.'

'And now you have.'

He rolled on to his back, his eyes on the ceiling. 'It would be utter stupidity to refuse such an offer.'

'Yes.'

She turned back to him, her hand moving in the thick curled hair that covered his chest. 'You'll tell Charlotte?'

'Yes. Of course.'

'She'll be pleased, I expect.' Her voice was dry, 'I daresay she could quite fancy herself as Lady Patten.'

His arm tightened about her, crushing her to him. 'Sally – Sally!'

'Stop it. We agreed. Now is now, and next is next. The war isn't over yet. We could all be dead by tomorrow.'

'Hannah said you were up at the Front again last week – dodging bullets was the way she put it. You didn't tell me?'

Within his arms she shrugged.

'Oh, Sally, be careful.'

'I always am. Be careful yourself. Don't get run over by a tram back in dear old Blighty.'

'I won't.'

They lay in quiet for a moment. Then, 'This job,' Sally said, 'it would mean a lot to you, wouldn't it?'

'Yes. The chance really to do something. To work with the best minds – the best facilities –'

'Jolly handy, Hannah and Ralph deciding to tie the knot at last.'

'The Bear, you mean? Yes.'

'So. You'll move out? Move –' he felt rather than saw the small, wry smile, 'up west?'

'Sally –'

'All right, all right.' She turned suddenly, sliding on top of him. Outside, unnoticed, the evening barrage had begun. The window rattled. 'Well, given that you're off tomorrow, Ben Patten, you might at least make your goodbye something I can remember while you're away?'

'A research post?' Charlotte, pretty as a picture in green

and white, her teacup precisely balanced upon her lap, smiled with the polite interest she would afford an affable stranger, 'Is that good?'

Ben was standing with his back to the fire, the height and breadth of him dominating the room, his own teacup lost in his big hand. 'It's very good indeed. An honour, in fact. Sir Brian is a remarkable man. I admire him enormously. He's brilliant in research and he has influence. I'd be a fool to turn down such a chance.'

Charlotte's expression had not changed, there was nothing in the pleasant smile, the bright, serene eyes to indicate the sudden sharpening of her interest. 'What – exactly – would it mean?'

'We'd be based in London, and in Oxford –'

'And –' Charlotte had lowered her eyes and was tinkering delicately with the slender silver spoon that lay in her saucer. 'The Bear? What of your work here?'

He shrugged a little. 'That would have to go, I'm afraid – but with Hannah and Ralph here to carry on, and Pa too whilst he wants to, I won't be too badly missed. Anyway – who knows? – with this kind of opportunity I might find myself in the position where someone actually listens to me – I can do more good under those circumstances in a year than I've managed in a decade fighting a bunch of bureaucratic idiots who don't know typhus from a cold in the head.'

Charlotte nodded slowly, very thoughtfully. 'I see.'

'So – you wouldn't mind?'

His wife lifted her handsome head, the innocent eyes wide. 'Mind? Why ever should I mind? Why Ben –' there was the slightest, acid edge beneath the pretty laughter that brought a faint flush to his face, 'you don't mean you're actually *asking* me? Of course I don't mind. Of course you must take it. I think it's all rather –' she drew the word out in capricious amusement, '– splendid. Oh, yes, of course you must take it. How very exciting.'

Ben drained his cup, set it on the mantelshelf. 'I'm glad you're pleased. Now – you're sure you won't come to see Peter with me?'

'Oh, no. I don't think so. The poor man sees quite enough of me I assure you. I'm sure he'd rather see you alone. Besides, he'll be home very soon – we're converting the dining room as a bed-sitting room for him, did you know? It will give him the independence he needs, but still enable us to care for him.'

'Yes. Pa told me. He told me, too, how hard you've worked to help Peter. I wanted to thank you.'

Very precisely Charlotte placed the cup she held upon a small table. 'Don't be silly, Ben. No thanks are needed. Anyone would have done the same. Off you go. You'll miss your train.'

'How did Peter seem?' Will Patten, frail, indomitable, the old eyes still windows into a soul that, despite all, found much to amuse it, tamped down the tobacco into his pipe and settled before the fire.

Ben sat in the chair opposite, elbows on knees, nursing a precious brandy. 'Quieter than I remember him – but that's not surprising, of course. I thought he looked remarkably well. He seems to have come to terms with his paralysis extraordinarily quickly. I must say, I wondered how he'd be once the first shock wore off – so many of them simply', he gestured with the glass, his face sombre, 'give up.'

'You can hardly blame them.'

'No.'

'And the war? Is it true we're on the offensive at last, or is it just flag-waving propaganda?'

'No. It's true. There's a feeling that it can't last much longer. Oh – there's a long road ahead, but – well, it has to end sooner or later, doesn't it? Or there'll be nothing left.'

'And – you think there's a chance we'll get there after all?'

'More than a chance, yes. Though – who knows – Fritz may have a few surprises for us yet.'

They smoked in companionable silence for a moment. Then, 'Good news about the research post,' Will said gruffly. 'I remember old Bix-Arnold. We were at Oxford together. Good man. Bumptious. Narrow-minded. Opinionated. But good. You're doing the right thing.'

Ben hid a smile, finished his drink, stubbed out his cigarette. 'I'm lucky to get the chance.'

'Nonsense, m'boy. He's lucky to get you. Though from what I remember of old BA, wild horses wouldn't drag it from him.'

Ben grinned openly at that, stood and stretched. 'I'll turn in, if you don't mind.'

The old man nodded peaceably. Ben stood for a long moment looking down at him, affection warm on his square face. Then he touched the narrow shoulder.

'Goodnight, Pa.'

'Night, lad.'

A small light burned beside the bed in the pretty, feminine bedroom that he was sharing with his wife, his own room having long since been allotted its quota of refugees. Charlotte, her fair hair loose about her shoulders, the graceful folds of a rose-pink nightdress with high, frilled neck enveloping her slim body, was sitting up in bed, propped against a pile of pillows, a book upon her lap.

She glanced up as he entered, smiled coolly.

He had been home for three days and three nights and in that time they had not once made love.

Very precisely he began to remove his clothes, folding them neatly, stowing them in drawers and wardrobes, incongruous amongst pale and perfumed silks and satins.

'I want to talk to you', Charlotte said, closing her book, a finger keeping her page, 'about Rachel.'

'Oh?' He shook out his cravat, folded it carefully.

'I think she should go away to school. And soon.'

He stopped. Turned, staring at her in surprise. She outfaced the look without a tremor. 'Go away to school?' Ben asked.

'Yes. She's becoming impossible. And the influence of that dreadful school you all insist she attends is as much to blame as anything. Just because you live in a stable, Ben, it doesn't mean you have to be a horse. I won't have a daughter of mine growing up a gutter urchin.' She lifted her chin and regarded him levelly, her mouth set in a straight, sure line, daring him to challenge her.

Ben said nothing for a moment. He turned back to the mirror, started to unbutton his shirt. His first sight of Rachel had been something of a shock. The child was truly beautiful; not with the fragile prettiness of her mother, but with a strong and brilliant beauty that was stormily matched by an intemperate and volatile disposition. Only he, Charlotte and Sally knew the inadmissible roots of the child's looks and nature. Yet within moments of being with her, her thin arms thrown vice-like about his neck, the music of her excitement bubbling about him, he had been totally enchanted with her once again. 'Oh, Papa, Papa! I'm so pleased to see you! Darling Papa! How long can you stay? Will you come with me to the park? Have you seen Flippy? She's grown so much! And Pippa's had puppies – do please come and see them. Oh, and Papa! I had a letter from Toby, a letter just for me! He's been promoted – he's a – oh I don't know – a something else now. Isn't he clever?' She had gabbled and laughed, interrupting herself, kissing him, swinging about his neck, her eyes alight with love and laughter.

'You really think she needs to go away?'

'Yes.' The word was flat. 'She's running wild. The home isn't what it was, Ben – there are too many children and not enough help – not enough discipline. I don't want the child growing up an undisciplined hooligan.'

– And you do want her where you don't have to see her every day. To see the black hair and blue eyes, the enchanting, goblin smile, to see the obstinate courage of her when once more she faces your dislike and disapproval – his doubts were all in his face as he turned to look at her.

She returned his look without turning a hair, without a flicker in the cool, steady eyes. 'I've found a school,' she said composedly. 'It's in Suffolk. Near Bury St Edmunds. It's a lovely old house in very nice grounds. It's run by two sisters, very well qualified. I was there last week and I was most impressed. The girls I met were beautifully mannered, the school curriculum seemed to me to be very well planned.'

'You seem to have got it all worked out?'

'Yes. There wasn't much else I could do in the circumstances, do you think? I mean – you can hardly want me to run to you with such trivial household decisions whilst you're so very occupied in your work in France.' Her tone was faultless, yet he glanced sharply at her, detecting the irony in the words.

'And Rachel? How does she feel?'

Charlotte made an infinitely small gesture of distaste. 'Oh, how do you think? I told you – the child is totally undisciplined – she threw herself about and screamed like a wildcat. What would you expect? If the day has come when a ten-year-old child can impose her own wishes upon parents who are only doing what's best for her then the world has changed indeed.'

There was a silence that was broken only by the rustle of Ben's clothing.

'It's arranged then?' Charlotte asked.

Ben, in his dressing gown, turned. She had tilted her head to look at him, the lamp behind her gilding her hair, limning her delicate features in light, leaving her wide eyes in shadow. Her white hands, soft and smooth, were folded upon the book. He could see the rise and fall of her breasts beneath the silk of her nightgown. He cleared his throat.

'Ben? It's arranged?'

'Yes. If that's what you want.' The sudden thudding of his heart, the stirring of his body was totally uncontrollable. In the abrupt silence he saw her face change almost imperceptibly, her body stiff and still beneath his eyes.

Her hands, as she marked her place in her book, closed it, laid it upon the bedside table, trembled a little. 'Good. I'll go ahead and make the arrangements.' Not all her efforts could keep the tension from her voice. She turned from him, sliding down under the covers, her back to him, her shoulder hunched almost to her ear.

He let the dressing gown slide from his shoulders, stood naked above her. She would not turn her head. 'Charlotte,' he said.

'I'm very tired, Ben.'

'You're my wife, damn it!' His voice was very low. As he reached for the bedclothes she turned on her back, staring up at him, rigid with dislike. With disgust.

He was beyond control. Beneath the nightdress her body was smooth and cool, her skin soft and delicate as silk. As his bulk, thrusting, fell upon her he knew he hurt her – in truth at that moment he wanted to hurt her, to produce some warmth of reaction, some fire to rise to his, even, if necessary, in hatred. She lay inert beneath him, lifeless as rag, cold as charity. As his climax came she opened her eyes and watched him, unblinking. When he had done she withdrew from him fastidiously, slipped silently from the bed and left the room. He rolled on to his stomach, face buried in the pillow. He heard the water running in the bathroom next door, heard the bedroom door open again, heard the opening of a drawer and the smooth rustle of silk as she changed her nightdress. He rolled on to his back, watching her, as she came back to the bed. She did not look at him. As if she were alone she smoothed the sheet, plumped the pillows, slid back into bed, settled herself with her back to him and turned out the lamp.

He lay in the dark and the deafening silence for a very long time, listening for guns and thinking of Sally.

Chapter Nineteen

I

The Russians were out; the Americans – fresh, vigorous, eager to show their mettle – were in; and with them came a new wave of optimism. Through a gruelling winter and into the spring of 1918, which had seen the launch of a desperate and costly German offensive designed to break the backs of the Allied armies before the incoming American troops could make a significant difference to the balance of arms, the fighting had continued sporadically and viciously along the length of the Western Front. Now, with summer approaching and more and more units arriving from the United States, the German offensive had failed and it was becoming obvious that the race against time was lost. The American troops – irresistibly friendly, keen as mustard to get into the fight and above all well fed, well equipped and well paid – were regarded with a mixture of mostly good-natured resentment, equally good-natured amusement and rarely expressed heartfelt thankfulness by the war-weary troops who watched them march into the shattered villages of France and Flanders, swinging, fresh and confident, down the patched, unevenly cobbled streets, bringing new blood and new hope to the battle.

Eddie, sitting with Sally in the window of their favourite *estaminet*, lifted an ironic glass to the column of troops that marched, singing, towards the station. 'Here's to the Yanks, God bless 'em. With a bit of luck we'll all be home by Christmas.'

Sally smiled, acknowledged his words with a lift of her own glass.

'Poor young sods. They've no more idea what they've got coming than babies.'

'They'll learn, I guess.' Sally was watching with pensive eyes a young girl who was serving at the tables, plump and pretty, her long brown hair hanging almost to her waist, eyes bright with laughter as she parried the advances of the hopeful young soldiers she was serving, obviously revelling in the attention she was being paid.

Eddie's eyes followed hers, then quizzically he looked back at her.

Sally laughed wryly at the unspoken question. 'I was just thinking', she said not altogether lightly, 'how very ancient I feel sometimes.' She lifted a hand, absently rubbed at a grease-stained finger.

He chuckled, but his eyes were sharp. 'Don't be daft, lass. You don't look a day over forty.'

She pulled a face, stuck her tongue out at him, sipped her drink. The marching boots crashed rhythmically outside the window.

Eddie rested a chin on his knuckle, watching her. 'What'll you do? After the war, I mean, when you go home?'

She studied the dirty finger as if it had suddenly become the most absorbing thing in the world. Then, shrugging a little and without looking at him she said, 'I don't know. I don't actually have what you might call a home. I could go back to Bruges – but I don't know what's happened to Philippe's parents – and anyway, without Philippe –' She trailed off, a faint flinch of pain in her eyes. Nothing that had happened since had erased the agony of that loss. 'There's Philippa, of course – I must make some kind of home for her.'

'You won't go back to your friends at the Bear?'

She shook her head. 'No.'

He waited for a moment, watching her closed face,

waiting for her to elaborate. When it became obvious that she would not, he reached for his packet of cigarettes, offered her one. 'Why not?'

She shook her head. A flicker of irritation at his persistence brought her eyes to his. 'I just won't. It isn't what I want to do. That's all.'

'Fair enough.' He lit his cigarette, watched the drifting smoke. 'Anyway – things have changed, haven't they? Happen folk like your Pattens have had their day.'

She frowned a little. 'What do you mean?'

He shrugged. 'Seems to me we've had our bellyful of do-gooders. Time we took a hand ourselves. Take them on at their own game. We need a Socialist Government, working folk in Parliament. That's the way to get welfare for our people, education for our children, decent homes, a living wage. That's the way to get rid of the parasites, to ensure the working people of the country – the poor buggers who've been fighting this war – get a fair crack of the whip.'

The narrow, green-flecked eyes watched him affectionately. 'The way to build Jerusalem?' Sally prompted softly.

'Happen so. Why not? The first thing that'll happen after this little lot is an election; and if I don't miss my guess it'll be an election that at least some women'll vote in – have you thought of that?'

She nodded. 'Hannah was talking about it the other day. If the Government keeps its promises – it certainly looks as if the war's done for us what none of our own efforts could. Crazy, isn't it?'

He lifted a shoulder. 'It's a bloody good job it's done something. Anyway –' he leaned forward on his elbows, his dark face lit with enthusiasm, 'think about it.' He grinned his quick, abrasive grin. 'Remember what they used to say about women voters? That they'd vote the way their husbands or their priests told them? That a woman voter would be a Conservative voter?'

'I certainly do.'

'Right – so what we're going to need is women active in Labour politics to persuade them to use their own judgement. Want a job?'

She stared at him, then laughed a little. 'Are you joking?'

'Never been more serious in my life. You'd probably have to work for nothing – be a bloody uphill struggle too at first; the most we can hope for is to form an Opposition this time –'

'You're serious?' She was looking at him incredulously, 'You really believe that the Labour Party will get enough seats to form an Opposition?'

'Never believed anything more. It's got to happen, Sal. The world's changed. They can't keep us down any longer. You fought for the vote; you've as good as got it. You aren't going to give up now, are you?'

'I – hadn't thought about it.'

'Well –' he leaned back in his chair, pushed his cap to a jaunty angle upon his dark head, 'think about it now. The prospective candidate for Barnsley North can do with all the help he can get.'

She shook her head, gently. 'I don't know, Eddie. If you're serious –'

'I'm serious.'

'I don't know. There's Philippa to think about –'

His eyes had narrowed a little. With a sudden movement he straightened in the chair, leaned towards her, his voice very quiet. 'And not just Philippa, eh?'

It was impossible, under the acute, dark gaze, to prevent the rise of blood to her face. 'What do you mean?'

'You know what I mean, lass. I mean the fella, whoever he is, that's been leading you such a dance over these past months.' He did not stop as she opened her mouth to deny it. 'Time and again I've meant to offer to push his face in for you – still will, if you like. Just tell me his name – I'll straighten him out. Happen someone should –'

'Eddie!'

'Don't deny it, lass. I've known you too long.' He laid a brotherly hand upon hers, his smile dying. 'Is he worth it, Sal? Seems a right shame to me, a girl like you – mooning over a lad you can't have – I assume that's the trouble?'

She nodded wordlessly.

He offered a cigarette, and this time she took it, as much to give herself space to recover her composure as for any other reason. As he lit it for her, she looked at him through the smoke. 'How did you know?'

'Don't be daft – sticks out a mile, doesn't it, when a mate gets moody? And when your blue-blooded friend came snooping around with her clever questions – I put two and two together and came up with a nifty four. She thought it was me; I knew it wasn't. So – it was someone else. You quite sure you don't want me to duff him up for you?' His smile was heinously cheerful.

She could not resist laughter. 'Oh, Eddie! – You surely don't want to lose all your stripes in one fell swoop at this stage of the game?'

'Ah.' He blew a stream of smoke into the air. 'Like that, eh? A gentleman of some influence?'

'You could say so. And that's all I'm going to say.' Her voice was firm. 'It isn't your business, Eddie, any more than it's Fiona's. I'm a grown-up girl and I'm perfectly capable of sorting out my own troubles.'

He grinned brief acknowledgement of that. Then he sobered. 'It's a mug's game Sal, take it from me. The war won't go on for ever. Then he'll go back to his wife. They always do.'

'I know.'

He watched her for a long, quiet moment, then shrugged. 'You're right. It's none of my business. Just remember; it's a big world out there, and there's a fair bit on offer.'

She grinned slyly, 'Including an unpaid job with you?'

He shrugged, gracelessly returning her smile. 'It was worth a try. Hey — I don't suppose your Fiona what's-her-name'd be interested? There's a cat to put among the pigeons if ever I saw one!'

Sally drained her glass, stood up, bent to drop an affectionate kiss on his cheek. 'Why not try her? I wouldn't put anything past Fee. Now — I have to go — see you soon.'

She left him sitting at the table, an expression of deep thought on his face.

Hannah's decision to accept Ralph's proposal had not been an impulsive one. She had carried the letter around with her for a week, confiding in no one, before she had penned her answer. But once taken, she had had no doubt that the decision was right. In a way it had been surprisingly easy; they knew each other so very well — and if it promised to be a union based more upon friendship than on passion, then who knew but the bond might be stronger for that? Only one condition she had attached to her acceptance; she would not marry until the war was over. 'I want no uniforms at my wedding, my dear, and no sound of guns,' she had written, 'I want us to marry as I want us to live; in peace.'

A simple ambition, she thought sometimes, wryly, as she held the hand of a boy who cried for his mother as he died or responded to the cheerful greeting of a man whose eyes were burned out and deadened by gas, but still painfully difficult to achieve.

'When *will* they give up at last?' she asked Sally tiredly, her skirts kilted about her knees, her aching feet in a bowl of soothingly cool water. 'They say the Germans have lost a million men — a *million*! — since the spring. And it's only August! They surely can't keep sustaining such losses? They're falling back everywhere — we pushed their line back eight miles here on the Somme just a couple of days ago – why won't they stop it? Men are still being killed by the thousand – for what? They can't win.'

'Hard for them to accept that, I suppose.' Sally tossed her a towel. 'Whoever loses this war is going to have to face the charge of squandering millions of men's lives for nothing. Not easy to face, that.'

'And meanwhile men are still dying.' Hannah dried her feet, pulled on her stockings. Her billet – a small bell tent that she shared with another Sister – was chaotic, the belongings which had followed her through four years of warfare packed up once again in boxes and bags, ready for yet another move.

Sally glanced around. 'Where are you off to, do you know?'

'No. We're following the advance. They've moved so far forward that we're doing no good back here.'

Sally grinned. 'Reminds me of the latest story – some Americans were sent up the line a week ago to relieve an Aussie unit –'

'And?' Hannah cocked a slightly wary brow.

'They haven't caught up with them yet.'

Hannah laughed. Sally perched herself on the edge of the narrow bed. 'It really is finishing, isn't it? At last?'

'It certainly looks like it. The only question seems to be how long?'

'And then – peace. Funny thought. I've almost forgotten what it's like.'

'So have a lot of other people.' Hannah folded the towel, looked vaguely about her for somewhere to put it.

'And you and Ralph will marry and live happily ever after.'

'I hope so.'

Impulsively Sally stood and put an arm about her friend's shoulders. 'Of course you will. And you both deserve it. I'm so glad for you.'

Hannah smiled into the strong-boned face. 'And you? What will you do?'

The arm dropped from her shoulders, Sally turned away, half-shrugging. 'I don't know. I'll find something. I have Flippy to think about.'

'Will you come back to the Bear?'

Sally hesitated for a moment before gently shaking her head. 'No. No, Hannah, I don't think so.'

Hannah did not argue. 'You'll always have a home there, you know that, don't you?'

'Yes, I know.' Suddenly Sally ached to tell her, ached to have done with the pretence, the lies. I love your brother. He loves me. He's locked in a marriage that's been a misery from the start. I can't come back to the Bear because I can't stand to see him every day – to be so close, and not to touch him, not to share with him the everyday things that people take so much for granted. She smiled brightly. 'Did you hear about Toby? He's a full lieutenant. Quite the young gentleman.'

Hannah nodded. 'Ralph told me in his last letter. Apparently Toby's thinking of studying law after the war? Ralph's sure he stands a good chance of getting in – especially with his war record.'

'Nineteen – if that –' Sally said very quietly, 'and a war hero. Funny thought, isn't it? I wonder how they'll cope, these lads, when they get home?'

'Don't worry about Toby,' Hannah said drily. 'He'll cope.'

Sally's sudden laughter was sharp. 'That's true.'

'Well –' Hannah had emptied the bowl and tucked it into a box, 'that looks about it. Coming over to Mess? Lunch is billed as something as a celebration before we leave. And I don't know when I'll get to see you again.'

Sally tucked an arm in hers. 'Don't worry – you won't lose me as easily as that. Let me know where you are – I'm sure someone will want *something* taken there!'

The August sun was hot, beating down from a clear sky, turning the trodden earth of the compound to dust. Hannah tilted her face, savouring the warmth. 'I just hope that whatever is going to happen happens before the winter comes again,' she said soberly. 'Just give me a roof over my head when it rains and a fire to sit by and I swear I'll never complain again.'

Hannah's wish was not entirely granted; it was November before pen was put to paper in the forest of Compiègne and the guns fell to silence. In the three preceding months the fight was as fierce as ever; young men died still, wastefully and terribly, with the prospect of peace hovering tantalizingly close. And, as if the suffering had not been enough, a new scourge appeared, killing friend and foe, decimating armies and civilian populations alike. Influenza. Throughout a debilitated Europe the disease raged, felling the old and the young with an indifferent and indiscriminate hand.

But, at least, the war was over.

And, just a month before it had been ended, the Representation of the People Act had enfranchised eight and a half million British women.

'So – you're off home to get started on making a country fit for heroes?' Sally cocked a not too derisive brow at Eddie, who slouched grinning opposite her.

'Something like that.' He reached for the wine bottle, refilled both their glasses. 'You see before you the official Labour candidate for Barnsley North. So – early release and off I go. God – isn't it bloody quiet?'

Sally nodded. The almost unearthly silence that had fallen two days before as the guns all along the line had ceased their thunder was strangely unnerving. She knew herself not to be the only one who had found difficulty in sleeping in the quiet night.

'You decided what you're going to do yet?'

She shook her head, turning the glass in her hand, watching the light that glinted jewel-like in the blood red depths of the liquid. Watching her he was suddenly aware

542

of a brighter gleam in her eyes, a slight trembling of the firm mouth.

'Sal? Something up?'

It was a long time before she lifted her head. When she did the tears stood clearly in her eyes. 'I heard from Philippe's sister. She's been back to Bruges.'

'And?' he asked, very gently.

'They're dead. Both of them. Anselm at the start of the war. And Alice –' she swallowed, 'Alice a month ago. Flu. Oh, Eddie – it's so unfair! – To suffer it all and then to die like that.'

He nodded, the dark eyes sympathetic.

'I had thought – that perhaps –' she trailed off, ducked her head again. 'Alice was the closest thing I had to a mother – it would have been somewhere to go.' She had been surprised herself at how badly Annette's sad news had hit her. She dashed her hand across her eyes and took a quick mouthful of wine.

'You've no family?'

She looked at him in something close to surprise. So well had they come to know each other that she forgot that he knew nothing of her true background. 'No.' She hesitated a moment before adding, 'Not that I know of, anyway.'

They drank their wine in a silence that held nothing of awkwardness, everything of warmth and friendship. Eddie refilled the glasses, clicked his fingers at the waiter to bring another bottle.

'Are you trying to get us both drunk?'

He grinned. 'I could think of worse ways to spend our last evening together.'

'Our last –?' she stopped, surprised at the small twist of pain the words had startled in her. 'Why yes – I suppose it will be.'

'You'll miss the rissoles even if you don't miss me.'

She laughed at that. Always he could make her laugh. The bleak wave of sadness had receded a little; they had all lived with death for too long now not to be able to face loss when it came.

'Once upon a time,' Eddie said, leaning back in characteristic pose, holding his glass to the light and studying it with apparent absorption, '– a very *very* long time ago – I came across this girl. Leaning against a posh car, she was, in a street in London –'

Sally smiled, wrinkled her nose.

'"Aha!" I thought – "One of them snooty upper-class London pieces as fancy themselves in trousers, eh?"' He had, obviously deliberately, broadened his accent.

Sally giggled. The wine sang in her tired head.

'So – not being backward in coming forward, like – I accosted her –'

'What happened?'

He leaned forward conspiratorially, pointing a finger. 'I got my come uppance, that's what. Sharp as a needle she was – and about as upper crust as I am meself. Funny thing –' He twirled his glass idly in his fingers, his eyes upon it.

'What?'

His glance flicked to her face and away. She saw curiosity in the bright depths. 'D'you know I don't know a damn' thing more about the lass now than I did then?'

Sally flushed a little. 'Oh – I don't know –'

'I know she's a gaol bird. I know she's got a temper on her when she's roused that'd do well in a wildcat. I know she's got political leanings, and a tongue in her head. I know she's a widow who's been –' he caught the glimpse of danger in Sally's eyes quickly enough to prevent the next words, acknowledged it with his most graceless grin, 'well – you know. I know she worked in an orphanage before the war.' His suddenly sharp glance caught her. 'What I don't know is how she got there.'

She leaned her chin on her hands, looking at him. 'You know what curiosity did to the cat, don't you?'

'I'm a lot tougher than that.' He tilted the bottle, refilled her glass.

'You really want to know? It's no great story.'

'You tell me yours,' Eddie filled his own glass and toasted her, 'and I'll tell you mine. How's that? We shouldn't part knowing nothing about each other. Now should we?'

'All right then. If you really want to know –'

She was amazed at how easily it came, how the memories flooded back as she talked. Josie. Toby. The soup kitchen. The tenement block with its squalor, its dangers, its easy camaraderie. Those first days at the Bear; her debt to the Pattens. She did not tell him the full reason why they had first taken her in – that after all was someone else's secret, not her own – and she did not tell him of Ben and the complex, difficult, impassioned relationship that had developed between them, for that too was a secret not hers to tell; but all else she spoke of, and found herself smiling often. The exploits with Hannah – meeting Philippe – the magic of their love, the horror that war had made of it –

Eddie sat and listened, dark face intent, watching her face with brilliant eyes.

'So that was how I came to be leaning on Colonel Foster's Talbot in a London street when this cheeky lad accosted me –'

'And bought you a cup of tea.'

She laughed.

'Which has led on to many a bottle of wine –'

'And many a rissole,' she added.

'Great oaks from little acorns grow,' he intoned solemnly.

The wine bottle was all but empty.

'You said you'd tell me yours,' she pointed out.

'So I did.' He lifted a finger. A waiter appeared at his side. Eddie lifted the bottle. '*Encore, s'il vous plaît.*'

'Eddie – neither of us will walk a straight line out of here!'

'So who cares? Straight lines are for tomorrow. Now – where to begin?'

*

He saw her to her billet at three o'clock in the morning, in rain that teemed into the darkened streets, poured from roofs and from gutters, ran in the cobbled roads. Oddly, despite the wine she had drunk, Sally felt absolutely clear-headed; very aware of the friendship that had engendered this evening of confidences and laughter, aware too that, as Eddie had pointed out, this would be the last such evening they were likely to share. Such farewells were taking place, she supposed, up and down the long line of the Front – people who had shared danger, privation, the desperate intimacy of fear, parting to go back to a life that had been the subject of so many dreams, so many longings that now, attainable, seemed all but unreal. They walked in companionable silence, arms linked. She had liked the story he had told – of an able and enterprising lad born into an able and enterprising working-class family that stood none of his nonsense but knew his worth and encouraged him to make the most of himself. Self educated, self reliant, self confident – Eddie Browne would take the world by the scruff of its neck and shake it until success fell from it to his feet, she had no doubt of that. Neither had she any doubt of his ability to achieve his ambition of becoming, sooner or later, one of the first of a generation of Socialist MPs. In that connection she had, gently but firmly, once more refused the offer of a job; a suggestion that had been promptly and shamelessly offered when she had admitted that, upon the death of Philippe's parents, she found herself in the – for her – quite extraordinary position of being financially independent.

'Well. Here we are.' They had stopped walking. She turned to look at him. Water dripped from the peak of his cap, darkened the shoulders of his greatcoat. A single light from a near-by window slanted across the wet cobblestones. A child cried plaintively.

They looked at each other for an odd, sad moment in silence. 'I can't believe it's over,' she said very quietly.

'Oh, it's over all right.'

She nodded. 'When are you off?'

'Tomorrow – next day – some time soon, anyway.'

'So – I won't see you again?'

'No.' He made a fist of his hand and grazed her chin gently with the knuckles. 'Good luck, pal. Keep in touch?'

'I will.' How many such promises were being made? How many would be kept?

He grinned, turned to leave.

'Eddie!' She took two quick steps after him, lifted her face, kissed him very hard. 'There.' There was the slightest wobble in her voice. 'Something to remember me by.'

'Oh, I won't forget you, lass,' he said very quietly. 'And what's more I don't think you'll forget me.'

The moment held them very still, very close, the rain running from his hat, teeming down her lifted face. Then he turned and strode away. And though she stood to watch him until he turned the corner, he did not look back.

II

Hannah and Ralph were married early in the new year of 1919, a month after the General Election, which had seen a Conservative-dominated Government returned firmly to power; but, with fifty-nine seats, the Labour Party were, as Eddie had predicted, the largest single group in opposition. By the time of the wedding both Sally and Hannah had been back in England for nearly a month. Ben too, thanks to string-pulling by the influential Sir Brian, was home in time for the celebrations, but only just.

Sally, firmly resisting all blandishments, had refused to return to the Bear, but had taken rooms in a respectable street not too far away. With her had gone Philippa, Marie-Clare and little Louise. Toby was still in France.

547

The wedding, at Hannah's insistence, was a small one, held in the chapel around the corner from the Bear, the only guests family, Sally, who served her as Matron of Honour, and – to Sally's delight – Fiona MacAdam, elegant and sardonic as ever, down from her family's country home in the north where, she assured Sally, 'I'm leading the most gruesome life possible, my dear – just nothing to do from morn till night but talk to the butler and arrange a few flowers. I never thought I'd actually miss bandages and hypodermics!'

Hannah wore a suit of heavy cream lace over satin, the folds of the skirt falling to between calf and ankle length, her short thick hair shining beneath a wide-brimmed rose-trimmed hat.

'You look absolutely lovely.' Sally, herself resplendent in glowing green that complemented her pale skin and green-flecked eyes and showed a very neat turn of ankle, fussed about Hannah in the chapel porch like a mother hen, handing her at last the prayer book with its flower-decked ribbon that she was to carry with her to the altar.

The ceremony was short and very simple; the look on Ralph's face as he kissed his bride, for whom he had waited so long and patiently, brought an unexpected lump to Sally's throat.

The reception was held – the Bear still being full to overflowing with unplaced refugees – in a large upstairs room at the Queen Victoria public house in the Commercial Road. Charlotte, delicate as an angel in sugar pink and white, supervised with competent authority the conveying of her crippled brother-in-law up the steep stairs and his settling into a comfortable chair. Champagne was served; and Sally, relieved at last of her matronly duties, found herself in company with Philippa and Rachel, the latter having been allowed home from school for the weekend especially for the occasion.

'So – school isn't so bad after all?' Sally asked smiling, breaking into the child's monologue about netball and hockey and school plays and a friend called Patricia. 'You weren't keen to go in the first place, as I remember it?'

Rachel grinned engagingly, the brilliant eyes shining. 'Oh it's topping! Patricia says it's probably the very nicest school in England and I think she's right. The two Miss Beatties are super and we've got this absolute love of a PT mistress – she's quite stunningly pretty.' She giggled a little. 'Patricia says that at least half the girls are in love with her!'

Sally allowed her gaze to drift around the gathering. Ben stood with Ralph, glass in hand, deep in conversation. Charlotte, on the other side of the room, gestured for a waiter to refill Peter's champagne glass. Fiona, talking to Doctor Will, caught her eye and winked. Sally grinned back.

'Oh, for goodness' sake!' her daughter said, suddenly and very ill-manneredly to her cousin, 'Can't you talk about anything but this silly Patricia?'

'Philippa!' Sally, her wandering attention brought sharply back, stared at her usually easy-going offspring in amazement. 'Don't talk to Rachel like that – it's very rude!'

Rachel laughed. 'It's all right. She's still a baby. She doesn't understand.'

'I am not! And I jolly well do!' Poor Philippa was pink with anger. 'You've talked about that horrible old school and your horrible old Patricia ever since you came home!'

'There's not a lot else to talk about, is there?' Rachel's tone was disparaging.

'Flip! Rachel! Now stop it, the pair of you.'

'Why don't you be a very sensible pair of girls,' a coolly amused voice said from behind her, 'and sneak yourselves a glass of champagne each? And don't speak a single word to each other until you've drunk it. I think you'll find it will improve relationships no end.'

'Fiona!' Sally could not help but laugh. 'You're outrageous! Girls – you're to do no such –'

But Rachel, eyes gleaming with mischief, had already caught Philippa's hand. 'Come on, Flip.' She flashed a brilliant smile at Fiona, 'Let's be good girls for a change and do as we're told –'

Sally watched them go, turned to Fiona grinning. 'Honestly, Fiona!'

Fiona shrugged elegantly. 'I thought it a very good idea. And quite obviously so did they. Anyway – I wanted two minutes to talk to you – when are you coming to see me?'

'Soon.'

'How soon?'

'I – don't know. But I will come. I promise. I'm only just getting settled into my new home.'

A small waitress replenished their glasses. Fiona sipped hers appreciatively. 'I saw a friend of yours the other day.'

'Oh?'

'One Edward Browne, ex-sergeant. He came to ask me for a donation to Labour Party funds.'

Sally choked on a mouthful of wine. Fiona thumped her back helpfully. 'He didn't!'

'Oh yes he did.'

'How is he?' Sally had not admitted even to herself just how disappointed she had been that Eddie had not answered the two letters she had sent to the address he had given her when he left France. She had not tried again.

'He's fine. He didn't win the seat, but he did well enough to augur well for next time. Meanwhile he's secretary or some such thing of the Yorkshire Labour Party – and my home, as you know, is in Yorkshire –'

'And – he came –' Sally was still coughing a little, 'to ask you – You! – for a donation?'

'That's right. And to offer me a job.'

'Unpaid, of course.'

Fiona grinned. 'Of course.'

'He's got the cheek of the devil, that one.'

'He's got more than that.' Fiona lifted immaculately plucked brows. 'Actually I was quite tempted.'

Something in her tone made Sally look at her very sharply. 'By the opportunity to donate to Labour Party funds? By the job? Or –' she paused, growing, disbelieving laughter in her eyes, 'by Eddie?'

Fiona shrugged.

'Ladies and gentlemen – if you would take your seats at the table?'

'Fiona?'

Fiona turned away, the flash of a provocative smile gleaming over her shoulder, 'Duty calls. I do believe that I'm sitting with that lovely old man – Doctor Will, everyone seems to call him. What a charmer –'

It was ten in the evening before the last of the revelry was through. The bride and groom had been seen on their way to the station and a honeymoon trip to Devon after the reception, and family and friends alike had repaired to the Bear for light refreshments and more champagne. Both Sally and Fiona had left early – Sally on the excuse of little Philippa's bedtime, Fiona talking vaguely of another engagement that evening, though Ben suspected that their evening would be spent together, and that Sally's eagerness to be away had had more to do with him than with her lively daughter's supposed fatigue. He had been home for three days, and they had had no time together. Their last meeting had been in France, the night before Sally had left, a long night during which neither had wanted to sleep for fear of wasting precious moments, a night during which neither of them could bring themselves to speak the words that both knew would have to be spoken. So she had left without saying goodbye; and now they met, unbearably, in public, smiling and exchanging casual greetings, avoiding each other's eyes. He stretched his long legs to the fire, sighing. In the chair opposite his father's head nodded.

'Pa? Time for bed, I think?'

Doctor Will's head jerked up. 'What? What's that? Oh. Yes. Been a long day.'

Ben stood and stretched, helped his father to his feet. 'Do you need any help upstairs?'

A little touchily the older man grunted. 'Help? Why should I need help?'

'Just wondered.' Ben hid a small smile. Frail the old man might look – frail, indeed, he might be – but his spirit was unchanged.

'Where's Charlotte?'

'She's helping Bron to settle Peter in.' The faintest shadow of a frown flickered across Ben's face. In the three days he had been home he had hardly seen Charlotte, nor had an opportunity to speak to her. Her devotion to his crippled brother was, it seemed, absolute. She had taken on the role of nurse – almost of mother. And how could he, Ben, object to that? 'I'll turn in, I think.' He laid a hand upon his father's shoulder. 'I'll see you in the morning.'

He trod quietly through the sleeping house. At the door next to the one that led into the room he shared with Charlotte he stopped for a moment, listening.

'Papa?' The little girl's voice was a whisper, 'Is that you?'

Smiling he slipped through the door. By the glimmering light of the nightlight that stood on the side table he saw Rachel's eyes, wide and still gleaming with excitement. 'I can't sleep.' She wriggled over to give him room to sit beside her, 'I've tried and I've tried, but I just can't.'

He ruffled her hair gently. 'Stop trying. Then it'll happen.'

She nodded very unsleepily, the tangle of her hair night-dark upon the pillow. He looked at her, at the heartbreaking beauty of her, at the trust in her eyes. 'You're happy, poppet? At the school?'

'Oh, yes, Papa! I truly am! It was so funny – I was so frightened – I didn't want to go at all – and then –' her smile shone in the dim candle flame. 'Well, then it was all right. Patricia says she thinks I'll be form captain next year – she's junior house captain, you know – she'll probably be head girl in a couple of years.'

'So – you wouldn't want to come back home? To leave?'

'Oh, no!' The child sat bolt upright. 'Oh, please, Papa – no! I won't have to, will I?'

He shook his head, pressed her gently back on to the pillow. 'No, no. I just wanted to make certain. I've got a new job.'

'Yes, I know. Mama told me. You're helping Sir Brian Bix-Arnold, aren't you? Patricia was frightfully impressed!'

He laughed a little. 'She was? Well – I just wanted to make sure that you were absolutely happy – that, now the war's over, you wouldn't rather come back home?'

She shook her head on the pillow. 'No, thank you,' she said very firmly.

'Fine.' He bent to kiss her. 'Now – close your eyes and count to two hundred and fifty. I bet you'll be asleep before two shakes of a lamb's tail! Good night, my little love.'

'Good night, Papa.'

Charlotte's pink and white room was empty, the fire flickering in the grate, a lamp lit by the bed, the covers turned down. As always as he entered he felt an intruder; too big, too clumsy – too male – for the exquisitely feminine room. He stood for a moment in the middle of the floor, quite still, his big head thown back, broad shoulders flexing. Seeing Sally had unsettled him; in the months they had been apart he had almost persuaded himself to believe that their parting was for the best. The sight of her today, the sound of the husky voice, the ready laughter, had twisted in his soul like a knife. But – for her own good as well as his own – he must leave her alone. The new post with Sir Brian was God sent; a chance to do something truly worthwhile. It would, too, give Charlotte the life style that she had for so long hankered after;

perhaps it wasn't too late for them? She had looked perfectly lovely today –

He loosened his cravat, shook the heavy coat from his shoulders; turned as the door opened quietly.

'Ben?' Charlotte stood silhouetted in the doorway, looking as fresh and as pretty as she had twelve hours earlier. Her fair hair was swept up, revealing the delicate line of neck and throat, the small, well-shaped ears, emphasizing the striking bones of her face, rather more prominent than in her extreme youth, but no less lovely for that. 'I'm glad you're still up.'

She came into the room, closed the door with a small, sharp click behind her. 'I want to talk to you.'

Ben started to undo the buttons of his dress shirt. 'Is it important? It's getting late – won't it wait till morning?' The bed lay between them, the sheets turned down, crisp and inviting. Her small, firm breasts swelled visibly beneath the fine material of her gown.

'Yes, it's important. And no, it won't wait.' She brushed past him, her perfume drifting into the room with her. On the far side of the room, as far from him as she could get, she turned, her chin up, her hands folded composedly before her.

For the first time Ben sensed the well-disguised, finely strung tension that held her. His hands dropped to his side and the smile left his face. 'Charlotte? What is it? What's wrong?'

There was a long moment of silence. He saw the breath she took to steady herself, saw the fingers that had been loosely laced before her tangle and clench, though the composed and almost expressionless face did not change, and when she spoke her voice too was cool and steady. 'I think you'll agree, Ben, that our marriage – if it can be called so – has been something of a miserable failure?'

He stood as if struck, watching her.

She waited for a moment, and as he did not reply spoke smoothly on, a speech she had rehearsed over and over.

'That being the case I'm sure that you'll have no great objections to what I am about to suggest.' Her glance flicked across his face. 'I no longer wish to live with you as man and wife. I'm willing to do the minimum to keep up appearances, if you should wish it, but I want you to know and to understand that as far as I am concerned for all practical and –' a tremor of distaste twitched at the corners of her mouth, '– physical purposes – this marriage, which has always been a sham, is over.' She stopped again and waited, her eyes sharp and wary upon his face.

Ben had drunk a fair amount of champagne in the course of the day; suddenly he was aware of it. His brain seemed incapable of thought. He spoke very carefully. 'What – exactly – do you mean?'

Impatience sharpened her voice. 'I mean precisely what I say. Our marriage is no marriage – I'm simply being honest about it and saying I no longer care to support the fiction. You have your new post with Sir Brian – you'll be moving between London and Oxford, it will be a perfectly acceptable and reasonable thing for you to have an establishment of your own somewhere. I intend to move into the country –' she hesitated for one last moment before adding, very clearly, 'with Peter.'

The words shook him from his shocked stillness. He took a quick, almost involuntary step towards her. 'You – what?'

Still absolutely composed she stood her ground. 'I'm going to live with Peter in the country. Surrey, I thought, or Kent perhaps. It's perfectly obvious that he shouldn't stay here – the country will be much better for him in every way. I'll find a bungalow – it will have to be a bungalow, of course – somewhere where no one knows us.'

'Are you trying to tell me', Ben's voice was very quiet, threaded thinly with anger and with disbelief, 'that you're leaving me – for *Peter*?'

'Yes.' The word was simple, sharp and absolutely firm.

'You can't do that.'

'Oh, but I can. I'm going to.'

'You can't!' His head was clearing a little, though astonished anger seethed. He stabbed a finger at her. 'You can't!' he repeated. 'You of all people? You'd never survive the scandal!'

'There won't be any scandal.' She was completely self possessed. 'I've already told you – I'll do whatever is required to keep up the minimum of appearances. But I won't live with you –'

'And you expect me – simply – to agree to this?' His voice was rising despite himself.

'I wouldn't expect you to do anything simply.' Her voice was caustic. 'But yes, I hope you'll agree. When you've thought about it.' This time it was she who stepped forward, face lifted to him fiercely. 'Think about it now, Ben – who would be most harmed by a scandal? You're thinking of divorce? You won't divorce me! Think of it! Think of the publicity– "wife leaves war hero doctor for crippled brother"! – How would Sir Brian like that?'

He caught her arm, held her, his face very close to hers. 'Oh no.' His voice was harsh 'You've miscalculated, Charlotte. You think I'd let that stop me from divorcing you if you go through with this?'

She neither flinched nor moved in his grip. She had in the past months lived this interview a dozen times, had countered in her head his every move. 'Perhaps. Perhaps not. So – I have something else for you to think of. What of Rachel? Take me into the divorce court and I swear I'll make sure that every last miserable fact about our marriage will come out – including the reason why you married me.'

'No!'

'Yes!' Her voice was rising to match his. 'This whole damned mess started with that child – you should have let me get rid of her when I wanted to! God above, she isn't even *yours*!' She wrenched her arm free, stood glaring at him. 'And I wish to Christ she weren't mine! Don't you realize that I can never look at her without seeing him? The gipsy pig that beat me and raped me and sired her? Oh, no, Ben – don't think I wouldn't tell – she means nothing to me. When we part she goes with you. Keep her at school – do what you like – but keep her from me.'

He stared at her in appalled silence.

Her voice went on inexorably, 'If you want her – and everyone else – all those important new friends of hers at that school she thinks is so fine – to know she's a gipsy bastard conceived in rape – fight me. And –' she lifted her head, watched him for a moment before adding softly, 'if you want your precious Sally Smith to lose the good name she's somehow acquired even if she's never been entitled to it – then drag me through the courts, Ben. Try it. I'll see her pilloried. A lot of good that'll do her and that daughter of hers –'

He froze. 'Sally? What has Sally to do with it?'

She threw a hand up in an impatient gesture. 'Oh, Ben! Don't play the innocent with me! I know! I know about you and Sally Smith. I can give you dates and times –'

He was shaking, fighting off an anger so deep that he feared only violence could ease it. He stepped back from her, hands clenched by his sides.

'I had you watched. A very reliable and rather dirty little man with a penchant for posing as a war correspondent. It was an offchance – but it came up with pure gold, didn't it Ben?' Apparently unafraid, she stepped to him, forcing him to look at her, 'How dare you?' she asked softly. 'How dare you condemn my love for Peter – that's clean, and pure – when you've been wallowing in *filth* with that woman? And then – you'd come to me –' A spasm of disgust crossed her lovely, even features. She shuddered. There was a moment's stark silence. Then 'I wish you luck of her,' she said. 'What you do or who you do it with is nothing to do with me any more. I'm going

557

away with Peter. We're going to the country – somewhere where no one knows us. We're going to be a respected and respectable couple; a war hero and his devoted wife. I intend to be a pillar of the community. I'll take tea with the vicar and sell home-made cakes at the village fête. I'm going to get Peter away from this squalid place if it's the last thing I do. He – we – are going to live somewhere that's clean. Somewhere where people stop to pass the time of day. Somewhere where he can see the sky, and the trees, where he has a garden to take an interest in, where I can look after him – make him happy – and you're going to let us. You're going to do nothing to stop us.'

'He won't do it.' Ben's voice was suddenly certain. 'Peter won't do it. You're my wife.'

'Peter will do it. I can assure you he will. Ask him yourself. He needs me, Ben. More than he's ever needed anyone in his whole life. I love him. I can make him happy. When he wanted to die I showed him the reasons for living. Oh, yes. He'll do it.'

'The family –'

'I don't care about the family. What have they ever done for me? It's Peter I want. And I'll have him. Nothing will stop me.'

'Including your own daughter's good name?'

'Including that.'

'You're mad.'

'I've never been saner.'

He turned from her then, crashing a huge fist into the bedpost, not feeling the pain of the blow.

'I've worked it out very, very carefully, Ben,' she said quietly from behind him. 'There's nothing you can do. Nothing that won't bring your own world crashing about your head. And about Rachel's. It's up to you. I don't want a divorce. I don't want the broadsheets with my name and face all over them; I don't want the expense, and I don't want the notoriety. But – if you insist – I'll do everything I've said. I'll ruin you, and Rachel, and Sally Smith. And at the end of it I'll still have Peter. What will you have, Ben?'

'Peter won't do it,' Ben said. 'He won't do it.'

'Ask him,' she said.

'I will.' He turned his head to her, looking for a sign of weakness, of uncertainty, and finding none. 'I bloody will!' Blindly he turned to the door, threw it open; in time to see a face white as paper within its ebony frame of hair, the shining sapphire eyes blank with shock as the child backed away from him, turned, fled into the room next door.

'Rachel! Oh, Christ! Rachel!'

He followed her into the room. She had flung herself upon the bed, her head buried in the pillows, her shoulders shaking. 'Go away!'

'Rachel – please, darling – listen to me –'

'Go away! *Go away!*'

He did not know how much she had heard, could only guess from her reaction that she had heard it all. He gathered her into his arms, held the tense, resistant, shaking frame, cursing Charlotte, cursing his own self-absorption that had forgotten that he had left the child, wide awake in this room with only an ancient, thin wall between her and her mother's raised voice. 'Rachel, my love –'

She pulled away from him with a violence that appalled him. '*Go away!* I won't listen! I won't!' She crouched amongst the tumbled bedclothes like a small animal brought to bay.

He straightened the bed, soothing her, trying to control the shaking of his hands, to calm his voice to gentleness.

She turned from him, in her clenched arms a battered bear she had dredged from the rumpled depths of the bed. 'Go away.'

'Rachel!' He reached a hand to her shoulder, drew it back sharply as she shrank from him. 'Rachel, listen to me – please, darling – it'll be all right. I promise it will.

No one will hurt you. I won't let anyone hurt you. You know how I love you – how I've always loved you?'

The child did not respond.

He stood up. Much as he hated to leave her, she was in no condition to listen to him now. 'We'll talk tomorrow,' he said. 'Please, darling, try to sleep.'

She neither moved nor answered.

He turned and walked to the door. As he turned to close it she shot upright in the bed, the bear clutched to her breast. 'It's true, isn't it? The horrible things she said about me – they're all true, aren't they?'

He stood in helpless silence.

'Don't let her do it,' she said. 'Please! *Please!* Don't let her tell people! I couldn't bear it!'

For a moment he could not speak. Then, 'Don't worry, my poor little love. Rest. Try to sleep. We'll talk in the morning.'

He shut the door with infinite care.

Peter's door stood a little ajar, as if awaiting a visit. Lamplight fell softly across the hall. Ben did not knock. He pushed the door, stepped across the threshold, confronted his crippled brother.

Peter sat in bed, a magazine haphazardly open on his lap. Smoke from his cigarette coiled about the room; not the first, from the haze that hung in the lamplight. As he lifted his thin face to the opened door he meticulously stubbed out the cigarette, closed the magazine. Looked at Ben with eyes that were wretched in a face that was set and blank with determination.

Ben closed the door behind him without turning, his eyes never leaving his younger brother's face.

'You've spoken to Charlotte,' Peter said, his voice very low.

'I'd say rather', Ben said drily, and wondered at his own composure, 'that she'd spoken to me.'

The blue eyes, avoiding his, drifted down to the counterpane. Long, thin, almost effeminate fingers picked at the loose threads. Beneath the bedclothes the outline of the useless legs was clear.

'She tells me you've made some –' Ben hesitated. In face of his brother's helplessness it was maddeningly difficult to hold to his fury, '– rather unorthodox plans?'

For a very long time Peter sat, head bowed, hands picking at the fabric of the counterpane. Then he lifted his head. The wrenching pain was still in his face, but his voice was firm. 'I need her, Ben. You don't know how much. I'm sorry. I'm truly sorry. If I had thought that you loved her – that she loved you –' He stopped. The silence was heavy with tension. 'I'd have done anything – anything – I'd have died before I'd have taken her from you. But –' In the quiet the unspoken words hung between them – you have so much. I have nothing. Nothing, now, but Charlotte.

The lamp gleamed upon the tense, unhappy face that was so used to laughter. Shockingly it shone upon the tears that glimmered upon cheekbones planed sharp with suffering.

'Jesus Christ.' The words were very low, all but toneless. Ben turned and left the room. Walked the few steps to the parlour, where the fire still glowed in the hearth, and the glasses of celebration stood empty about the room. On a table near the hearth, lit by the last light of the coals, a bottle stood, half empty. He picked it up, tilted it. The neck clattered unsteadily against his teeth. The champagne was warm, too sweet. He put the bottle back upon the table, sank to the floor in front of the embers of the fire, his back propped against the armchair in which his father usually sat, his legs drawn up in front of him, arms wrapped about them, his head bowed to his knees.

Loud in the quiet, the mantel clock struck eleven.

III

In the long silence that followed the unimpassioned telling of the difficult tale Sally, very carefully, poured the tea.

'So.' Settled neatly upon a chair she displayed a fair imitation of composure. 'What are you going to do?'

Ben accepted his tea with a minimum of interest and set it on the table beside him. He looked as if he had not slept in days. 'There's nothing I can do.'

'You aren't going to fight her?'

'I can't. She's right in what she said. She has Rachel, and you as hostage –'

'Forget me. I can take care of myself if anyone can. But Rachel? You really think Charlotte would carry out that threat?'

'Yes. I do.'

'And –?'

'The child's life would be ruined. You know it. There'd be no way to keep it quiet.'

Sally sipped her tea. The pleasant rooms – a sitting room, dining room, three bedrooms and a kitchen – that she had rented were very peaceful. Maire-Clare, with one look at their visitor's face, had taken the children, with commendable lack of fuss, to the park. 'And you?'

'Me?'

'What would happen if you divorced her – if it all came out?'

He shrugged.

'You don't care?'

He lifted a drawn face. 'You know I care.'

Having forced it from him she could hardly complain. 'And us?' she asked very quietly.

'She tells me –' he could not, Sally noticed, in his bitterness bring himself to speak his wife's name, 'that

providing we are circumspect she has no objection to our
– liaison – continuing –'

'That's very good of her.' Sally was waspish.

'But –'

'But only – very – circumspectly?'

'Yes.'

'No,' Sally said.

'Sally –'

She shook her head. 'No,' she said again. 'Ben – listen
to me. Are you going to let her do this? Are you really
going to let her use the fear of scandal against you? I
don't blame her for leaving you –' even in her pent-up
state she almost laughed at the flicker of shock in his
eyes. 'Oh, for God's sake, man – just because I love you
isn't to say that I don't see why she doesn't! She's right!
It was always a disaster! Surely you know that? Surely
you can see why she wants Peter?'

He turned from her, his face grim.

She looked at him, amazed. 'Ben. You don't understand, do you? She's leaving you for – for a cripple. And
that hurts? You don't see that that's *why* she wants
him?'

The eyes he turned to her were narrowed.

'Ben – in Peter she has everything she needs in a man.
Can't you see that? And I don't begrudge her it. Good
luck to her. What I do begrudge her is her hold over us.
Over you.'

'Rachel –'

'Yes. Rachel. That's the sticking point. But – Ben – she
already knows. Sooner or later she's going to have to face
it. Why bring her up to live a lie? A scandal now will
hurt her; but it won't kill her. With your support – and
mine –' the last words held the trace of defiance, '– we
could see her through it – it isn't right – it isn't bloody
right! – for her to think that the world would despise her
for something that isn't her fault!'

'She asked me – begged me –'

'Well of course she did! The poor little devil's twelve years old! She's found herself a bolt hole in a world that's not been kind up till now; of course she's frightened to lose it! But it isn't the only one! We could show her that. God Almighty, Ben, if I can live with it –' She stopped, biting her lip.

'That isn't the same.'

The sudden gulf that yawned between them was terrifying.

'It isn't right,' Sally said obstinately, edging round the precipice. 'If Charlotte wants to do what she wants to do – well and good. Let her take the consequences.'

'It isn't only Charlotte who would take the consequences.'

Sally set down her teacup, stood up, walked to the window, stood for a long time looking into the tiny walled garden, which was shadowed by a leafless walnut tree. 'How well she knows you,' she said.

The quality of the silence very subtly changed. Hostility sang in the air between them.

Sally turned. 'Be honest, Ben. Is it Rachel? Is it me? Or is it Sir Brian Bix-Arnold? Will you go along with this – charade – to keep your precious research post?'

He did not reply.

'Do you even know?' she asked softly.

The face he turned to her was all but expressionless.

She walked back to the chair opposite him, sat down, leaned to him. 'I won't do it, Ben. I've been through three years of deception, of squalid, hole and corner love. For nothing. Over and again I swore to myself that I'd stop. But I was never strong enough. Now it's up to you. Let Charlotte go. She can hurt nothing but your pride. If you divorce her I'll marry you – or if you don't I'll live with you. But openly, Ben. I won't – I can't – spend my life and my love skulking in corners. If you give in now she'll hold us to ransom for ever! Stand up to her. Stand up to the world. If you're good enough for the job, make your Sir

Brian take you, willy-nilly. If Rachel, bless her, has to face up to the fact that you aren't her father, help her to do it now – don't let her think that it has to be swept under the carpet in order for the world to accept her!' Passion blazed in the slanted eyes, the always husky voice was hoarse with feeling.

Ben leaned forward, his elbows on his knees, his eyes fixed on some distant point beyond the worn carpet at his feet.

'You won't, will you?' Sally's voice was suddenly very quiet. 'You'll let her do it to us.'

He lifted an anguished face. 'Sally – you're right. About Rachel. About you. If it were just that –'

'But it isn't. Is it?'

'No.'

'This job. The research post –'

'I can't turn it down. I can't lose it. We're so close to a breakthrough. It means so much –'

Sally's face had changed. The anger was gone, an odd, tired sympathy had taken its place. 'You've worked so very hard –' she said, suddenly, almost reluctantly.

He leaned forward, his eyes intense, 'Sally – everyone thinks they've fought the war to end wars. They haven't. It will go on. One way or another, it will go on. The killing will start again; the wounding, the disease that follows it. I've had to watch so many die – your own friend Josie, remember? – helpless to save them once the poison had taken them. Now I have the chance – money, equipment, the chance to use the experience I gained in that filthy war! I can't let it go. I *can't*!'

She slipped to her knees in front of him, laid her hand upon his. 'I know. I know.'

'I can't let anything jeopardize that. I may not be able to do anything – but supposing I can? How can I give up the chance?'

'You can't. I know you can't.' She released his hand, sat back on her heels. 'It's no good, is it?'

He shook his head.

'It's bad enough what Charlotte's doing to you, without me hiding around every corner waiting to be caught by a prying eye –'

'Yes.'

'And that's what you came to tell me?'

'I suppose so. Yes. Though I hadn't realized it.' His voice was very tired.

She turned to sit against his legs, gazing into the dying fire. 'Perhaps it's as well. We've known since France, haven't we?'

'Yes.' His hand rested gently upon the mass of her hair. She leaned to him. It was a very long time before either of them spoke.

'I ought to go,' he said.

She lifted her face. Very very gently he bent and kissed her. From outside the door came the sound of light, happy voices. 'Flippy, do wait – you'll break your neck dashing about like that.'

Sally scrambled to her feet, dashing a hand across her face. He stood, caught her to him, crushing her, then let her go as the door in the hall opened. 'Shoes off, now – you're so very muddy –' Marie-Clare's voice sang out.

'Goodbye, Sally.'

She said nothing. She heard his voice in the hall, bidding goodbye to Marie-Clare and the children. Then, as they erupted into the room, exclaiming at the darkness, she heard her own voice, bright and cheerful as if it belonged to someone else. 'Well, where on earth have you three been? We thought we'd lost you. Doctor Ben couldn't stay – but never mind – there's muffins in the kitchen for tea –'

Epilogue

The summer of 1919; a world at peace, though many found it hard to believe. In Germany, in January, the National Socialist Party had been formed. In April the League of Nations was founded, a slender thread of hope for future years.

For Sally it had been a busy winter and a busier spring as she helped Hannah and Ralph with the resettlement and repatriation of their refugees. The bleak months had passed, lightened by friendship and by the companionship of her daughter, and of Marie-Clare – who had announced her firm intention of staying in England with Sally – and little Louise. She saw nothing at all of Ben, apart from the briefest and most unavoidable social contact. The move had gone ahead: Ben now had an apartment in Oxford; Charlotte, with Peter, had moved into a tiny village not far from Maidstone in Kent. If the family found the arrangement a strange one, after a word from Ben ranks were closed and no one spoke of it. Only Bron expressed any opinion to Sally.

'Funny way to carry on, if you ask me – anyone'd think it was Mr Peter she was married to – but there, the poor man needs someone to look after him, I suppose – and with Doctor Ben busy all the time –' She had slid a small, questioning look at Sally, obviously hoping for an enlightening comment. Sally had said nothing. Bron had shrugged, accepting defeat philosophically, 'Blessed shame, mind, about poor Mr Peter – and what he'd have done without Miss Charlotte I really don't know

– there aren't many as would take on a crippled brother-in-law.'

'No. There aren't.'

'Pass the salt, would you? These potatoes are next to tasteless!'

Gradually, and with relief, the Bear settled back to normal life. With Ben gone Sally once more spent her time helping Hannah, who was in the throes of reorganizing her milk depot, her midwives, her health visitors. She visited Bolton Terrace just once, but could not bring herself to go back; she could not blame Bill Dickson for his inability to welcome her. She spent a lot of time with the children, Philippa and Louise, and as spring turned to summer the hurt she nursed so secretly very slowly began to heal. The time came when she no longer woke every day with the feeling of loss heavy on her heart; and a restlessness began to stir. The world beckoned. As the budding leaves of the walnut tree tentatively opened to the sunshine, Sally too began to lift her head and look about her; began to think of the future.

The letter that brought a sudden sparkle of laughter to her eyes, and an impulsive decision to her heart came in June. Still holding it she ran into the garden, where Marie-Clare was pushing Louise on a swing they had fixed in the tree.

'Marie-Clare! Would you pack a few things for yourself and the children? We're going on a trip.'

'Oh, where, Mama? Where are we going?' Philippa, who had been impatiently awaiting her turn on the swing, flew to her, and hung excitedly on to her hand. 'Where are we going?'

'To Aunty Fiona's. For a little holiday.'

'Where's that?'

'It's in the country. In a place called Yorkshire.'

'Will we go on a train? Will we?'

'We most certainly will. And we'll stay in a beautiful big house. With servants. What do you think of that?'

Philippa's big eyes grew bigger.

'Now – come on – help Marie-Clare to pack. I'm going to the post office to send a telegram.'

'So – here you are at last.' Fiona slipped an affectionate arm through Sally's as they strolled in the garden of Fiona's family home. The building behind them, sleepy as a dozing cat in golden June sunshine, was huge, a rambling, pleasant maze of a house to which Fiona's parents had welcomed their visitors warmly. 'And about time too.'

'I'm sorry. I know I should have come before. But – there were things –' Sally's voice trailed off. 'Your letter just seemed to come at the right time. So – yes – here we are –'

The formal rose-trellised and fountained garden ended in a ha-ha spanned by a plank bridge. In the meadow beyond, Philippa, Louise and Marie-Clare ran hand in hand, laughing, knee deep – in Louise's case waist deep – in buttercups. A little summerhouse looked out across fields and a river to the picturesque lift of hills beyond. Fiona sat on the bench, her eyes upon Sally, who stood leaning in the open doorway watching the children. 'So. The – problem you had,' Fiona asked gently, 'it's sorted itself out?'

Sally bent her face to the perfumed petals of a rose she had picked in the garden, and nodded.

'Are you going to tell me how?'

Sally hesitated for a moment. 'It's over. That's all.'

'Dare I say – good?'

Sally smiled. 'You dare.'

'Good. Then – good!'

Sally turned, leaning against the door, her head tilted to the slanting rays of the sun.

'Hannah's refugees are all settled?' Fiona asked.

'Yes. Most have gone home – some wanted to stay.

Hannah's sorted them all out the way only Hannah could. She really doesn't need me any more.'

'And – she's happy?'

'With Ralph, you mean?' Sally turned her head as the shouts of the children rose above the sound of bird song. Sunlight gilded her face and hair. 'Oh, yes. They're perfectly suited. He loves her dearly.'

'Lucky old Hannah,' Fiona said drily. 'And – Toby?'

The rose twirled gently in Sally's fingers. 'He's fine. He's going to university. To study law. He's going to be very, very rich and very, very famous, so he tells me.' Pensively she laid the flower to her mouth. 'He probably will be, too.' Another buried pain, the rift with Toby, a small, sore spot she tried not to probe. 'I hope so.' She strolled to the bench, perched herself beside Fiona, pulling a crumpled envelope from the pocket of her flowered cotton skirt. 'And now, Fiona MacAdam – are you going to tell me what this is all about?'

Fiona leaned back, stretching long legs, uncaringly elegant. 'I've taken up with a bunch of fallen women.'

Sally waited smiling, watching her.

Fiona slanted a laughing glance. 'And jolly good fun they are, too. To say nothing of their kids.'

Sally made a great show of patience.

'Eddie,' Fiona said, as if the single word explained all.

'Eddie,' Sally repeated, 'Eddie Browne introduced you to a bunch of fallen women?'

'That's right.' She leaned forward, elbows on knees, a lock of hair falling across her broad, white forehead, shadowing eyes that were bright with enthusiasm. 'Eddie, as you know, didn't make it to the Mother of Parliaments. Not this time, anyway. So while he's waiting for the call he's set about the locals –'

Sally grinned, 'Physically?'

'All but. He's on the Council. He's wangled his way on to every committee in existence and a few that weren't until he got there.'

'Another one building Jerusalem?' Sally's voice was wry.

'In his own way, I suppose, yes.'

'With a bunch of fallen women carrying his coat?'

Fiona was suddenly serious. 'Sally – give him his due – he's doing a lot of good. Shaking up the Establishment. He's a breath of fresh air –'

Sally laughed. 'He's that all right.'

'Will you listen? Do you know how many girls – young women – have been left ruined by the war? Can you imagine how many fatherless children there are? How many daughters have been turned from the door, into the street to starve, because on the last night – or the first night – of their soldier lover's leave they could not bear to let him go without loving him? Do you know how many were lied to? How many were widowed before a ring was ever put on their finger? And do you know the plight of these girls now – a child at their skirts, no family, no job, no money? No roof over their heads?' In her enthusiasm Fiona had failed to notice the quite open gleam of amusement in her friend's eyes. She stopped suddenly, warily, at the undisguised twitch of Sally's lips. There was a moment's silence before her explosion of laughter. 'Oh, good Lord – hark at me! Teaching my grandmother to suck eggs!'

'Teaching the one who invented eggs to suck eggs more like.'

Fiona sobered, nodded. 'These girls need help, Sally. No one knows better than you. Practical help. A roof over their heads, someone to help them care for their children so that they can earn a living.'

'And this is what Eddie's got you involved in?'

'That's right. Organizing. Fund raising – we need to buy decent places for the women to live in – employ people – oh, there's so much to do.'

Sally nodded thoughtfully.

Fiona turned and caught her hands in a strong, warm

grip. 'Please – come and join us, Sally. We – I – need you – it's difficult for me, you see – they aren't my people, they distrust me sometimes – you can't blame them.' The words held no resentment.

Above the field where the children played a lark sang, shrilly and sweetly, climbing high into the summer air. The children's voices lifted, laughing. Sally's thoughts slipped for a moment to the memory of a small girl abandoned to the London streets by a mother who had been unable to face the bitter fight for survival; a child who sometimes now seemed so remote, so very far removed, that it was difficult to remember the depths of her fears, the wretchedness of that precarious existence.

'Sally? You will come? You will join us?'

'Course I will. You knew I would.'

Fiona jumped up, drawing Sally after her, slipping an arm about her waist. 'Bless you! Now, listen – there's a meeting tomorrow, over in Bradford – Eddie's set it up for us.' She grinned at the lift of Sally's head. 'Oh, yes – he knew you'd come, too. Anyway, the problem is this; we're meeting some opposition from the diehards in the local community – well, we would, wouldn't we?'

They strolled into the sunshine, Fiona still talking excitedly.

In the buttercup field beyond the ha-ha Philippa, catching sight of her mother, waved energetically before diving, with more vigour than elegance, back into the golden sea of flowers in pursuit of the shrieking Louise.

Sally stood for a moment, watching them. Fiona, smiling, fell to friendly silence.

Above them the lark soared, singing.